Courtesan

ALSO BY DIANE HAEGER

The Ruby Ring

My Dearest Cecelia

The Secret Wife of King George IV

Beyond the Glen

Pieces of April

Angel Bride

The Return

Courtesan

A NOVEL

DIANE HAEGER

THREE RIVERS PRESS • NEW YORK

Library of Congress Cataloging-in-Publication Data
Haeger, Diane.
Courtesan : a novel / Diane Haeger. — 1st Three Rivers Press ed.
1. Poitiers, Diane de, Duchess of Valentinois, 1499–1566—Fiction.
2. Henry II, King of France, 1519–1559 — Fiction.   3. France—History—
Henry II, 1547–1559 — Fiction.   4. Courtesans—Fiction.   I. Title.
PS3558.A32125C68 2006
813′.54—dc22   2005029966

ISBN-10: 1-4000-5174-6
ISBN-13: 978-1-4000-5174-8

Printed in the United States of America

Design by Lauren Dong

10 9 8 7 6 5 4 3 2 1

First Three Rivers Press Edition

To my mother, Meg

and

to my husband, Ken

for their unwavering love and support. And for believing from the

first that this was a story I was meant to tell.

Book One
1533

A Court without ladies is a garden without flowers.

—King François I

1

IN DAWN'S SEMIDARKNESS, she stood ankle deep and motionless at the river's edge, her tall silhouette blending with
the bare white elms which braided through the cloudless winter
sky over Beaumont-sur-Sarthe.

The pungent aroma of wood smoke from village chimneys
mixed with damp earth and laced the air near the shore as she
plunged naked into the icy water. She felt the chill, sharp like
needles, as it quickly turned her skin to gooseflesh, but to Diane,
discipline was sacred. Defiantly, she moved deeper into the rapid
current. She finally came to the surface, water dripping from her
hair and face, and her alabaster skin glimmering with the sheen of
early morning light on water. A flock of geese flew in precision
above her, but made no sound. In this state of meditative peace,
she bathed alone until the thoughts returned and her mind began
once again, to echo the fear.

It is too late . . . You cannot turn back now . . . You have come too far . . .

Since she always bathed at dawn, Diane reached the inn just as
the royal coachmen were loading the first of her brocade-covered
trunks back onto the King's coach. Six of His Majesty's best Spanish stallions swayed as two of the guards attached them to a tooled
silver harness. At least four of the animals were required to pull
the awkward lumbering vehicle. Diane grimaced at the prospect
of another long ride in it. The price of the King's hospitality, she
reminded herself, and looked away. Before her in the cobblestone
courtyard, two mongrel dogs fought over a scrap of meat. They
had garnered all of the attention from the velvet-tuniced coachmen so that she could return unnoticed from the river. She said a
silent prayer and slipped past them.

Clothed only in a thin cambric dressing gown, she slid through the paneled door. The musty smell of dried wine on scarred oak tables dizzied her, but she crept steadily toward the staircase. In the candlelit shadows she heard laughter, then the faint sound of whispers. A man's voice; then a woman's. She passed quickly, not wanting to hear them. Not today. When she finally reached the welcome privacy of her room, she closed the door and leaned against it to catch her breath. She let the wet dressing gown fall to the floor around muddied feet and ran her hands through the full masses of wet blond hair. As she sank onto the tousled bed covers, she sighed. *Is it really too late to turn back?*

The King's driver had misjudged the distance and his error had forced them, in the dark of night, to surrender to the only room and the only inn left for miles. In the center of the small room was a large soot-smudged fireplace with a chipped stone hearth. Next to it was a bed hung with tattered blue tapestried bedcurtains. Hewn beams and a spray of cobwebs decorated the walls. From the single latched window came a ribbon of daylight and the shouts of an old woman as she kicked the two dogs in the courtyard below.

The fire sputtered and crackled. It was nearly out. Diane felt the chill again but this time it passed through her as Charlotte padded into the room, carrying a large speckled-blue pitcher full of water. She found her mistress staring hypnotically into the last glowing embers of the fire, her skin nearly blue with the cold.

"Pray God, Madame! You're close to freezing!" she declared in a heavy peasant voice. She slapped the pitcher onto an old oak bureau then, in a brisk maternal sweep, covered Diane with the remaining heap of bedcovers. "Swimming in that river is madness, Madame. If you don't freeze, you're sure to die of the pox!"

There was a long silence between them as Charlotte gathered up the fine Dutch linen undergarments from a trunk at the foot of the bed. Diane watched her, the complex network of wrinkles on Charlotte's full face now highlighted in the gray light from the window. Her kind face was a comfort this morning.

Another servant entered the room in soundless velvet slippers, carrying in one hand a large silver jewelry casket; in the other, a freshly starched headdress. "I have spoken to His Majesty's coachman, Madame," said Hélène, in a wispy childlike voice. "He expects we shall reach Court by midday."

Diane nodded but said nothing.

"Have you decided what you shall wear when you are introduced once again to His Majesty?" Charlotte asked. "If I might suggest, the moiré silk, or the velvet are both splendid." Confident that her suggestion would be heeded, she did not wait for a reply. She padded with heavy labored steps, back to one of the trunks that lay open, beneath the small latched window. This trunk, like the others already on the coach, was lined with an assortment of silks, furs, petticoats and headdresses.

"It must be perfect. Simple. Solemn. I can afford no mistake in this." She paused a moment, and brushed her slender fingers across her slim white throat. "Prepare the velvet with the white lace collar."

Wrapped in the bedcovers, Diane moved silently to the hearth and a small petit-point hassock. Hélène opened the jewelry case and arranged a selection of necklaces and rings. Charlotte laid the chosen gown across the bed near the stockings and underskirt. She smoothed out each article with her short rough hands as Hélène moved to the fire to add a few sticks of kindling. A blaze quickly took hold and gold flames licked the walls of the tiny room. The elements of their mistress's costume now in place, Charlotte took up the pearl-handled comb from the table by the bed. With firm, even strokes, she began to untangle the partially drying tendrils of Diane's thick blond hair.

When it was nearly dry, she stood. She could put it off no longer. She must dress. It was an elaborate ritual of camouflage Diane detested. First her breasts were tightly bound. Then her hips were flattened. She was covered next in a long-sleeved blue shift; then a heavy leather corset. A bell-shaped canvas underskirt followed white jersey hose, and finally, her gown. It was simple black velvet with a low square neckline. Across it, Charlotte hung a heavy rope of pearls. The long cuffs, trumpet shaped, were turned back. Their lining was marten fur. She would change into the more formal gown later, after they had been received at Court. *His Court.*

The dressing of her hair followed. The silky blond waves that fell uncurled down her back were pulled sharply away from her face, pinned and then hidden beneath a black silk bonnet. Slowly, the tall, sensual animal who had come up out of the river was transformed into the picture of nobility. She stood still as the folds in her veil were straightened. Her gown was brushed. Gown, headdress and slippers; they all must be perfect. But no cosmetics . . . never any cosmetics.

When the dressing ritual was complete, Charlotte stepped back and studied Diane as though she were a painting. She held the point of her chin between two fingers, her heavy brows fused in a frown. "If you are not certain about this, Madame, we can just as easily send word to His Majesty that you have fallen ill on your journey. It would be simple enough to tell him that we were required to return home."

The tender concern of the old woman calmed the edges of her own dark fear. She looked at her maid, the hulking body, the skin hanging in aging ruffles from her neck, and her eyes, deep and sincere. Diane smiled.

"It will be all right, Charlotte. Five years is a long time. You shall see. With everything that goes on at Court, people should scarcely remember."

She spoke with conviction, but her words masked a fear greater than she could admit, even to herself. Five years. Who would recall? Five years since the scandal which had rocked the Court and sent her and her husband, Louis, back to Anet to wait out his last days in informal exile. Now Louis was dead and the King had invited her to return.

HIS MAJESTY'S COACH swayed and plunged as the royal guard led the way toward Blois. Inside, Diane and her servants were battered about the dark, stale-smelling cabin. Charlotte, with her red-gray curls beneath a crimson hood, dozed on Hélène's shoulder. Diane looked across at them, relieved that she had a few moments to herself. Her head fell back against the red damask cushion as she looked out across the winter landscape of Touraine. The forest was dotted with bare elm trees and patches of melting snow. Across the plowed colorless fields were thatched houses and occasionally a small country church.

Dizzied by the sight and by the fear, she took a small mirror from her velvet handbag and raised it to her face. Gently she rubbed her hand across her cheek. The image that met her was not that of a great beauty. Her nose was too long and her eyes were too deeply set. But her skin was clear and she had a serene elegance, which had always caused people to notice her. Life had been kind. She was certain she did not look anywhere near thirty-one. Her body was still firm and strong and she needed no cosmetics with which to mask herself. She was convinced that daily cold baths held one of the many secrets of youth. In a society where water carried plagues and many were bathed only at birth, after childbirth, and after death, there were few who understood her love of so dangerous a ritual. Yet in spite of the gossip and the stern objections of everyone who knew, Diane continued to bathe every day.

She took a breath and closed her eyes. The sharp clop of hooves on the cobbled road beat to the steady rhythm of her heart. She had made her decision to return to Court. She would face her past . . . she must. So much had changed in these last six months. So much was changing. After a moment, she twirled the wedding ring on her finger. Then, without a thought, she took it from one hand and put it onto the next. It was time to start living again.

THE KING OF FRANCE stood surefooted, preening at the stately reflection which stared back at him from the long amethyst-framed wardrobe mirror. His straight chestnut hair fell smoothly over each ear, framing sleepy amber eyes and a long prominent nose. His thin lips turned upward, satyrlike, above a neatly clipped beard. He lightly touched it. Pleased with himself, he let out a ribald laugh so that a row of straight white teeth showed. Again he looked into the mirror. Behind his own image he could see the collection of courtiers. The categories and titles seemed endless; ambassadors, almoners, doctors, surgeons, apothecaries, barbers, grooms, stewards, pages and valets. All counted themselves among the fortunate who held a place on his payroll. They hovered around him expectantly, in their silks, brocades, their jeweled toques and their fashionable leather doublets. Their skin was perfumed with the exotic scents of ambergris and sandalwood. It blended with the scent from the fireplace and wall sconces, from which fragrant juniper burned.

These ambitious nobles whispered to one another as they strolled casually around the sumptuous apartments whose furnishings were priceless. The floors were inlaid tile of bright blue, orange and gold. They were blanketed in places with hand-tied rugs from ancient Babylon. The rugs were covered with dozing black hunting dogs. The vast limestone walls were warmed by tapestries in pale blue and rose, sewn with gold, depicting the exploits of the gods.

The King's *lever,* the official rising ceremony, was a complex affair. It took place in this manner each morning under the scrutiny of a select few who were given the honor of watching him rise and dress. At the first hint of sunrise, the heavily carved bedchamber doors were cast open. A string of ambitious nobles and gentlemen servants filtered in and formed a ring at the base of his bed.

Across the room, a glowing orange fire blazed. The massive stone mantel above was decorated like all of the others in the palace. It bore the King's crest: the salamander amid the flames with the motto NUTRISCO ET EXTINGUO (I feed on it and extinguish it) wrapped around a golden crown.

Amid this splendor, the King's courtiers volleyed for the first audience or the closest seat to His Royal Majesty. Each one of them was so taken up by his own cause that they were oblivious to the King. Aware of their preoccupation and bored by it, François proceeded impetuously to urinate into the cavernous hollow of the fireplace. The yellow stream extinguished the flames and sent billows of gray smoke wafting across the room. As he turned to face his audience, he shook his head at their averted eyes. He had hoped this morning to rattle just one of them.

Jean de La Barre, First-Gentleman-of-the-Chamber, cleared his throat and came forward as though nothing out of the ordinary had occurred. He held two morning costumes. One, fashioned in the Italian style, was made of emerald green velvet and encrusted with jewels. The other, styled by a French designer, was claret satin with fur at the collar and wrists. François waved approval as Barre held each one forward in turn. After a moment of indecision, he looked toward a sharp-faced, silver-haired courtier, who stood near the stone hearth.

"Well, Montmorency, how do you think We shall fair in the green this morning?"

"Excellent, of course, Your Majesty," the Grand Master judiciously flattered. "You honor the color by the wearing of it."

"That is to say then . . ." the King began to smile, "that I do no justice to the red?"

"Your Majesty shines gloriously in all colors. Alas, it should prove an insurmountable task to decide which costume should be benefited more by the wearing."

François' grin widened and his sleepy eyes twinkled with delight. Perhaps there would be some fun this morning, after all.

He fingered the green doublet and puffed trunk hose that Barre held for him. As he did, the echo of footsteps grew outside his bedchamber. The King looked toward the door and the costume fell to the floor. Like the preceding mound of red satin which the King had discarded, this one was quickly scooped up by a gentleman-of-the-chamber. It was then whisked back to the royal wardrobe in a motion as smooth as a finely orchestrated dance. Then the door opened and a tall, elegantly dressed man burst in. He was Principal Tutor to the royal children.

"Your Majesty!" he panted, struggling to catch his breath. He lowered his plumed toque as he neared the Sovereign. François turned slowly. "I am afraid to report, Sire, that it is Prince Henri again."

"Will that boy give me no peace?!" he bellowed and flung himself onto an ornately carved settee. Two of the hounds raised their heads, growled, then fell back to sleep.

"Oh, very well, Saint-André. What has he done now?" the King groaned. His eyes were closed and the rest of his long face was pinched.

"I am told that Monsieur La Croix wished the Prince to recite his Latin in the company of his sisters, the Princesses Marguerite and Madeleine. Well, Sire, he quite plainly refused, and when Monsieur La Croix raised his voice, His Highness picked up the poor man, carried him downstairs and tossed him, fully clothed, into the well!"

The other courtiers muffled snickers as the King lay his head against the back of the settee. This was not the first time the King's second son had sought publicly to embarrass his father.

"And the condition of La Croix?"

"If Your Majesty shall pardon my candor, it took four of your best guards to retrieve him. I regret to inform you that he has asked to be relieved of his duty."

François opened his eyes and picked up a large jeweled wine decanter from a stand near the settee. Tilting his head back, he began to drink at such a pace that the crimson colored liquid dripped down his beard and fell in little drops onto his bare chest. In a sweeping motion, he rubbed the wine with his hand and tossed the heavy silver decanter onto the carpet. "So be it. Bochetel," he said, leaning over to one of his Secretaries of Finance. "See that Monsier La Croix is compensated for his trouble."

After the secretary had made note of the King's command, Saint-André advanced further. "Shall there be a flogging for His Highness, then?" he cautiously asked.

"No! No flogging. The boy has endured enough of that sort of thing in Spain."

Saint-André's expression grew more tentative. He lowered his head. "Will there be punishment then for my son, in His Highness's stead?"

The King studied the tutor. He brought his finger to his chin until the moment of recollection. "Ah yes, your son is that tall fellow always in Henri's company."

"Yes, Your Majesty. My son Jacques is companion to the Prince, and as such, it is he who customarily takes His Highness's punishment."

"So he is. Well, this time it is not so simple a task. Until We decide on a proper course of action, you are to inform the Prince that he shall be sent ahead to Fontainebleau. A fortnight alone with the Queen should be sufficient penance for any crime."

"Very well, Your Majesty."

"So, my son is fond of yours, is he?"

"I am told that he is, Your Majesty."

"Then the Prince shall not have your son's company on his journey."

"As Your Majesty wishes. Will there be anything further?"

"No, Saint-André. I suspect that is quite enough for one day."

When the tutor had gone, Barre returned. He went back to preparing the King's wardrobe as though the exchange had not occurred. The others present shuffled around the room or engaged in private whispers to mask the fact that they had heard everything. François only shook his head, propped his chin in his long hand, and slumped farther down in the settee.

"Oh, Monty, what in the name of God am I to do?"

The Grand Master moved forward with his hands clasped firmly behind his back.

"I tell you, that boy means to have me pay for his blasted incarceration for the rest of my life!" the King moaned. "And yet I cannot undo, God forgive me, what either of my sons endured at the hands of the bloody Emperor! I had no choice . . . You know I had no choice. It was either my sons, or me!" He sprung forward and paced the length of his bedchamber. His strides were long and his sable-trimmed dressing robe streamed back like the wings of a great crimson bird.

Anne de Montmorency was brusk, sober and ambitious. He was one of three men who held the most influence over the King. They had all been with him since before his accession to the throne eighteen years ago. It was Montmorency, however, who held a place in the King's heart upon which no other courtier seemed likely to encroach. Monty (as the King called him to avoid the embarrassment of his feminine name) had fought beside him in the wars, shared the same games and the same whores. For his fidelity, he had been rewarded with the most powerful post in the French Court.

"I know that Your Majesty has not agreed in the past upon this score, but I still say that your son requires less restrictive companionship."

"Oh, nonsense. You've always been too soft on the boy, Monty. Your judgment is tainted."

"Most humbly, Your Majesty, it would do him far more good than the imperious sort of governors he has thus encountered since his return from his Spanish prison."

"And why would that be?" he asked, beginning to show his irritation.

"If I may hazard a guess, I should imagine His Highness sees tutors such as Monsieur La Croix as a further extension of his captors. A boy his age is bound to rebel."

"Well, I still say that lenience is not the answer! Not for insolence!"

"But perhaps Your Majesty would find it the answer to adolescence."

"Great Zeus, Monty! Why must you always disagree with me? It doesn't look at all good," the King moaned.

"If I may remind Your Majesty, you have remarked to me many times that my unfeigned opinion is of value here."

"Oh, so it is," he acquiesced, as he looked around the room at his more laudatory collection of advisors. "But We really must disagree with you in this. If you recall, We have tried that approach at your urging with Monsieur Renault. Surely you have not forgotten him. The old fool deserted Us within a month's time, despite his reputation for managing boys far more difficult than Henri. No. There must be another way to bring him around."

Another intrusion at the bedchamber door distracted the King.

One of the guards gripped the iron handle, but before he could open it, François was chiding him.

"Well go on! Open it, you fool! Go on! Ah, it appears I shall have no peace at my *lever* this morning, as it is!"

A young chambermaid, costumed in an aubergine velvet gown, slipped past the guards and hurried into the chamber. Her head was lowered and the rest of her face was hidden by a veil and hood.

"Well, what is it?" François gestured impatiently. As he stood before her with his hands at his hips, his dressing gown flew open again. The girl gasped and surrendered her face to her hands. Seeing her embarrassment, the King looked down. Until that moment he had not been aware that beneath his open dressing gown, he was completely bare. Amused, he strode casually toward her and closed the robe.

"Well then, that was a sight now, was it not? You may consider that a . . . *royal vision* if you like! Hah!" he chuckled, as pleased with his sense of humor as he was with himself.

The pages, gentlemen-of-the-chamber and guards followed the King's lead and laughed among themselves. The young girl could not compete with the King's bawdy humor or the laughter of so great a throng of men. She began to cry into her hands. Suddenly her innocence pleased him.

"Well now, *chérie,* it cannot have been that awful, can it?" he joked, and the guard behind her winked in return to the King. "All right then, come, come. What was it that brought you here to my bedchamber at such an hour?"

She could scarcely raise her head much less manage a reply.

"Out with it, girl," snorted the corpulent Chancellor Duprat, another of the King's powerful aides, as he moved closer. "His Majesty has not got all day!"

"I . . . I have come to claim the Comtesse de Sancerre's things."

"Oh, was that her name?" the King muttered, brushing a casual hand across his face so that only Montmorency, Duprat and a few others nearest to him could hear.

"Come here, *chérie,*" the King finally said.

As the girl advanced, he took her hand as if to shake it. Then, without a blink of his eye, pulled her hand down onto his bare penis. A look of sheer terror overcame her shy face, and she struggled with an involuntary spasm to free herself.

"What is the matter, Mademoiselle? Surely you know what an honor it is to hold the *royal jewels!*" he said, tilting his head back with a throaty laugh. The wise courtiers once again followed suit, watching skillfully to laugh only so long as their King.

"Very well, *ma petite.* There you go. Now, off with you!" he said, pointing to the mass of deep blue silk spread out on the floor near his bed. The girl, who by now had managed to collect herself, bowed discreetly and filled her arms with the opulent cloth. She then backed out of the chamber with careful steps through a filter of laughter.

After she had gone, the King turned to Montmorency. "Who was that?" he asked with an impetuous grin.

"Really, Your Majesty, I must object," he replied, knowing from experience why the King had asked. "She is just thirteen and only this month returned from the convent. We really have been all through this sort of thing, have we not?" he asked with as much of a discouraging tone as his position would allow. François scowled back at him.

"Your Majesty might recall that it was precisely these kinds of ladies, I shall grant you of slightly less noble breeding, but these types nonetheless, who led you into trouble the last time."

Trouble for the King meant the French disease, syphilis, so named because it was believed to have originated in France and then spread to various other European countries during wartime. The King had fallen victim to it several years before, and after a series of brutal treatments, now cast a wary eye at the prospect of its return.

"I think Your Majesty would agree that we have managed to keep you amused with a rather steady stream of . . . well, more certain types of ladies, those whose backgrounds we can more thoroughly investigate."

"Like the Comtesse de Sancerre?"

"Precisely. Then of course there is always your *favourite,* your Mademoiselle d'Heilly."

"Yes, yes." He wrapped his arm around the Grand Master and strolled back toward his mirror. The courtiers and dignitaries followed them like yearling geese. "But it is the variety that amuses me, Monty."

Jean de La Barre, having heard the exchange, took this cue to move forward. "Sire, I feel I must tell you that as it is, Mademoiselle d'Heilly is very angry after your . . . selection for last evening. It would appear that she expected to be invited to your bedchamber."

"Well, I am King, and she is only my whore!" he bellowed, raising a small vase of Venetian glass from the nightstand and tossing it toward the fire in a self-indulgent show of superiority. The vase hit the wall above the mantel and splinters of glass sprayed the room. After a moment, he recanted. "Oh, perhaps you are right. After these many years, she has come to expect certain things. Very well them, Barre. Have the jeweler fashion something for her. Emeralds are her favorite. Have it delivered to her apartments with a note professing my undying love and humble apology for my . . . indiscretion. The Court poet, that one she so enjoys, can create something endearing, do you not suppose?"

"Most certainly, Sire."

"All right then, see to it at once. And on your way, pay a visit to my companion of last night. Duchesse . . . no, no, Comtesse of . . . of whatever. Invite her to dine with Us. Tell her I shall come to her apartments at noontide. Oh, and Barre . . . since they tell me she is married . . . do see that she is alone."

AFTER HIS *LEVER,* the toilette and dressing ritual complete, the King spent time alone on his silver prie-dieu in his private chamber for prayer. Then he advanced to his outer apartments to read his dispatches. He would also converse with his most intimate advisors, collectively called the *conseil des affaires.* He did not attend to the formal business of the Court until late morning, after having heard Mass in the royal chapel. Only then, properly attired and disposed, did the King of France receive those who had business with him.

"Well, what have we on the agenda today, Duprat?" the King asked. Antoine Duprat, an obese, odorous man with blue fluid eyes and pale fleshy cheeks, looked up with surprise and then began to riffle through a collection of papers for the list of the King's appointments.

Duprat was His Majesty's Chancellor, Chief Secretary, and the second of three in most favor at the Court of France. He was a ruthless little man who in his time had killed and ruined lives without benefit of contemplation. Now the years and the haunting echo of death taunted him and he spent his days far more absorbed by gluttony than in either corruption or hygiene.

He sat beside François at the head of a long table in one of the drawing rooms. On the King's right, sat Grand Master Montmorency and the Cardinals de Tournon and Lorraine. Philippe Chabot, Admiral of France, and the final member of the King's triumvirate, had garnered the other end of the oblong-shaped table. He sat there, arms folded, his full lips set in a perpetual sneer.

As the *conseil des affaires* began, a man dashed out from beneath one of the large wall tapestries at the far end of the room. He headed directly for the King.

"My most humble pardon, Your Majesty, but I do crave a word with you on this matter of the Pope's niece. I really can wait no longer. His Holiness, Pope Clement, anxiously awaits your reply."

The small dark-haired Italian man spoke quickly and in a French tongue thickly laced with the sound of his native language. Montmorency and the others turned around in their chairs. The man advanced still nearer to the King. Chabot, who was closest in proximity to him at the end of the table, bolted from his chair. He drew a long pearl-handled dagger from the scabbard at his waist and held it beneath the man's chin. The royal guards rushed behind him and drew their rapiers. Montmorency rose and advanced toward the end of the table, but his gait was slower, more deliberate.

"Monsieur," he began without looking at the Ambassador. "How long is it that you have been in residence here at Court?"

"It is now six months time, my lord."

"Six months? Well, certainly that would seem sufficient time for you to have noted that His Majesty hears no business until after Mass."

The Ambassador looked over at the King for confirmation, but François said nothing. The Italian Ambassador, who was also the Duke of Albany, lowered his head again. He took a deep breath and advanced further toward the King. The unexpected movement caused five chamber guards to raise their rapiers, and with them, to bar the little Italian man from advancing farther. Through the maze of steel he spoke.

"I do beg Your Majesty's most humble pardon, but I have been patiently awaiting an audience with you for several days. His Holiness the Pope grows more angry with me by the day for the delays and I . . ."

"Silence!" The King at last voiced a thunderous command, his large amber eyes reduced to slits. The active room of courtiers fell silent. All eyes turned upon the Ambassador.

"If you persist in forcing the matter without allowing Us time to consider the proposition, you must then relate to His Holiness that the answer is, 'no.' Never shall my son, the Crown Prince of France, be made to marry a commoner, even if she has had the good fortune of having been born the Pope's niece!"

The King stood as the last words left his mouth. The guards advanced from a nod given by the Grand Master and they escorted the grumbling Ambassador from the drawing room.

The Treaty of Madrid had bound France with Spain and taken away France's claim to Milan. Now, after seven years, peace was losing its appeal for the French Monarch. Each day he grew restless for territorial superiority over the Holy Roman Emperor, Charles V. There was something to be said for an Italian alliance, should he choose to forsake the treaty with Spain. Lately he had given it more than passing consideration. Such a marriage as the Pope proposed, through the Duke of Albany, would certainly secure his superiority over the equally ambitious Emperor. It would possibly even see Milan returned to him. Since his childhood he had been taught to think of Milan as his own. His great-grandmother, Valentina Visconti, had been the daughter of the Duke of Milan. It was his birthright. Milan belonged to France. Undaunted by his past acquisition and loss of that great city, and no matter what the treaty prohibited, François meant to have it once again under the French Crown.

But it was not only territory that the French King craved. It was the world of Italian art and architecture that the key of Milan would open up to him. Leonardo da Vinci had answered the call, but he had arrived in France so aged that he had contributed little more to French history than having died there. Still there was Michelangelo, Raphaël and Cellini to be courted. Such cultural greats as these had all rejected his entreaties to come to France. If however, he could win the return of Milan, he might one day count them among his own national treasures. With their help, he dreamed that he would create the most magnificent palaces on earth. He would have in his personal collection works of art praised by all. If he could achieve this, the masters would no longer share their great gifts with Italy or Spain or even with England. Their work would all be for him; for France.

"Perhaps Your Majesty should reconsider," Chabot suggested cautiously once the Ambassador had gone. "A Medici marriage would bring to France a very strategic and much needed alliance with Italy."

Philippe Chabot, a small and impish looking man, was as cold as he was ruthless. Unlike Montmorency, he had not won his place in the triumvirate; he had taken it.

"The dowry alone, quite likely, could finance your next campaign . . . provided of course, that there is to be a next campaign." When he saw by the King's expression that he had not completely abandoned the idea, Chabot continued. "And we must not forget that he is offering Pisa and Livorno in the bargain."

"But marry the Dauphin off to a merchant's daughter? Make a commoner the next Queen? For the love of God, there is not enough money in all of Italy for a concession like that!" the King declared. Then he remembered Milan. The desire for it made him soften. "We shall give the matter over to further consideration. In the meantime, send the good Duke of Albany back to His Holiness with Our complete refusal. . . . Then let Us see just what else they may propose."

The serve was a good one and Claude d'Annebault, though considerably smaller and less physically agile than the King, returned the serve with force. His Majesty scrambled for the return.

"All right, Claude! Show Us what you've got between those legs of yours!" the King called out to his opponent. He whacked the small leather ball into the air with the force of his racket and it sailed across the string net.

The gaming court in winter for *jeu de paume* was a large indoor hall several yards from the main chateau. Inside was a long row of wooden benches. When the King played, they were always brimming with courtiers and heavily perfumed ladies to cheer him on. Both the King and his opponent wore tan puffed trunk hose over silk stockings. Their shirts were loose fitting and made of muslin. Montmorency stood on the sidelines beside Chabot, Barre and Duprat. Chabot took great pains to cheer the King with more animation than his rival, Anne de Montmorency.

"Bravo, Your Majesty!"

"Good return, Your Majesty!"

Both men looked bitterly at the other as the words flowed simultaneously from their mouths. Admiral Chabot flashed an insipid smile and took a step forward, away from the Grand Master. The two men despised one another and nothing was spared between them in their quest for the King's favor.

They watched the King's studied volley. Perspiration dripped from his forehead as he poised an arm overhead and prepared to return a serve. The movements of his tall, forceful body were at once strong and graceful. He was in the prime of his life and everyone who watched him play could see it. Yet, when his opponent missed the game point, it appeared to everyone that he had done so intentionally. The opponent, Marshal Claude d'Annebault, also among the King's inner elite, hopped across the net and bowed before the Sovereign.

"Good match, *mon vieux!*" declared the King. "But see to it that you practice a bit more before We sport with you again!" He playfully cuffed the Marshal's head as he turned to leave the court.

"Splendid game today, Your Majesty," Montmorency flattered. As he walked on the right of the King, Chabot, as always, was on His Majesty's left. Jean de La Barre and Chancellor Duprat trailed behind them.

"Claude was too easy with Us in this game, Monty. He could easily have claimed victory in the final set. I suspect he fears truly to challenge the King."

"Your Majesty is much too modest. You are playing better than ever."

"So I am, indeed," he agreed, and slapped the Grand Master on the back.

François smiled his same devilish, thin-lipped smile as a wealth of ambassadors, courtiers and nobles surrounded him to congratulate him on his victory. Across the court, he caught among the ladies, the willing eye of the woman with whom he had spent the previous night. *The Comtesse of something-or-other,* he thought. She stood out easily amid the other ladies with whom she pretended to converse. She was striking, though he had remembered her as more slightly built. And she had looked younger than she now appeared, layered in her eggshell blue silk and her smart French hood. When she saw that she had caught his eye, she smiled and slowly lowered her head. The King returned the nod.

Two young pages, both of noble families, stood before him. One had been given the honor of holding a large silver bowl while the King splashed water onto his face to cool himself. The other, François de Guise, the newest page to the King, offered him an embroidered towel. His Majesty liked the boy, and so chose to honor him with his thanks. Guise blushed.

"Barre!" the King shouted.

The First Gentleman hurried toward the Sovereign through the sea of brocade gowns and ermine capes.

"Did you see that Mademoiselle d'Heilly received her trinket?" the King inquired, though careful to exhibit only minimal interest as he gazed once again in the direction of the noble woman with whom he had spent the previous night. Again she smiled. Again he nodded. His afternoon diversion had been arranged. One of the pages took away the silver bowl. Young Monsieur de Guise, who had offered him the towel, now advanced with a jeweled, almond-colored velvet cape. He lay it gently across the King's shoulders.

"Most assuredly, Sire," Barre replied. "I am told by her senior-most attendant that she squealed with delight as the jeweler bore it to her on a velvet pillow."

"And the note, Barre. What of the note?"

"As you commanded, Sire, he inscribed a sweet lilting verse professing your undying affection and most sincere apology."

"My love, Barre! My undying love! Anne will not let me off so easily with this one of last night. The lady was devastatingly beautiful and Mademoiselle d'Heilly becomes very jealous if they are, any of them, nearly so beautiful as she. What was her name again?"

"The Comtesse de Sancerre, Sire."

"There you see, Monty? My taste is not always for servants and whores. We suspect, however, that she was 'arranged' for Us."

"The Comte and Comtesse de Sancerre are the invited guests of Chancellor Duprat, Sire. Certainly Your Majesty's charms enticed the lady beyond that."

"Yes, indeed," he agreed. "We still do rather well with the ladies, do We not?"

"Your Majesty's charms are unrivaled."

He smiled and then beckoned with his long arm the return of his new page, François de Guise.

"Come closer." He motioned to the boy whose face was beset by deep black eyes and a tousle of russet hair. The stalk-thin boy, all arms and skinny legs, was here in a place of such honor as a favor to the Cardinal de Lorraine, the boy's uncle. It was the cleric's great fortune also to be counted among the King's closest friends. He shielded the boy with his arm so their discourse would not be overheard, much as he had done earlier that morning with Barre. "We have a little job for you to do," he said, walking Guise away from the others. "Late this afternoon, after my appointments are concluded, you are to bring to my bedchamber that young maid I met earlier this morning. I believe her to be in the employ of the Comtesse de Sancerre."

"But Sire . . ."

The King ignored his objection. When he looked back his amber eyes glittered with resolve. "And if she is unwilling, you are to pay her . . . whatever it takes. Do you get my meaning?"

His dark eyes widened over a large hawkish nose and a long exaggerated chin. "But, Sire, Grand Master Montmorency, to whom I report, gave me the strictest order about—"

"Boy," the King cut him off. "Your family is much loved at this Court, and with that in your favor, your ambitions will take you as far as you please. But you must learn one rule above all others. You must never circumvent the wishes of Your King for those of his subordinates. Do we understand one another?"

"Indeed, Your Majesty."

"Splendid. I am so glad."

"I shall arrange it at once."

"And François, my boy, I needn't remind you that you are to say nothing of this to the voice of my conscience over there," he added, indicating Montmorency.

HER SERVANTS WOKE to the sound of the coach wheels on courtyard gravel. They stretched, straightened their gowns and headdresses, and waited silently for the door to open. A string of pages waited, dressed in blue doublets and puffed trunk hose with red velvet slashes and bright red hose.

The first person Diane saw as she stepped from the cabin was the Grand Master, Anne de Montmorency. Graciously, but with a little too much affectation, he strode before the line of servants and extended his own hand to help her down.

"Welcome back, Madame La Sénéchale," he said in a rough, sober voice from behind the neatly pointed silver beard. His steel blue eyes were cast upon her, yet looked through her, as though she were not there.

"Le Sénéchal was my husband, Monsieur Montmorency. I think it will be much simpler from now on if people were to address me by my birthright, simply as Madame de Poitiers," she replied in Montmorency's same tone of formality. Then she waited as the two women of her household were helped to the ground.

Montmorency bristled but extended his arm to her anyway as they passed through an arched doorway into the chateau. There was an immediate and instinctive dislike set about between them at that moment. It was one which both of them, for civility's sake, tried to disregard.

"The King, of course, shall want to know," he began again as they walked, "if the transportation that he extended to you was pleasing." The deepening of his antagonistic tone made it clear that her comfort was no concern of his. His inquiry was nothing more than a matter of protocol.

"Quite pleasing, Monsieur," she lied as they entered the hallway of the chateau's new wing. An elegantly dressed young woman waited in the shadow of a carved oak staircase. When she saw Diane, she lowered her head.

"This is Mademoiselle Doucet," Montmorency said without looking at either the young woman or at Diane. "She will be your attendant during your stay."

The young woman lifted her head and looked at Diane. Her face was plain and her hair was a dull ash-colored blond, but she was wrapped in enough silk and fur to have been mistaken for one of the King's daughters.

"Monsieur, as you can see, I have brought my own ladies. They are all I shall need to attend me."

Montmorency screwed his angry face tighter and leered at Charlotte and Hélène. Both of the women were clothed in rich fabric but nothing near the style or fashion of the young woman's gown.

"Due respect to you . . . Madame . . . de Poitiers," he said, putting the emphasis on her family name. "But His Majesty has graciously appointed you Mademoiselle Doucet. As you undoubtedly can see, she is entirely more well suited for the . . . demands of life at Court."

"You may thank His Majesty for me, Monsieur, but explain that I prefer the company of my own attendants."

"You will find that independence to such a fault is rarely seen as flattering by our most benevolent King, Madame."

"Nor, if I recall correctly, is impudence . . . Monsieur de Montmorency."

His eyes locked with hers. Neither moved. Then he broke the deadlock with a courteous bow. "Will you at least permit one of my men to show you to your accommodations then?"

"But of course, Monsieur."

A tall blond guard came forward and bowed. Diane and her ladies then followed the young man down the hall toward a stairway, leaving the Grand Master alone and scowling.

The mahogany stairway, shaped like a twisted vine, led to a long, narrow gallery capped by a high vaulted ceiling. They followed the page down a smaller shadowy hallway ablaze with thick tallow candles in mounted braziers. Diane swept down the damp hall disguising her fears of uncertainty with a purposeful gait as Hélène and Charlotte followed behind her.

"I shall get through this," she whispered to herself. "I must get through this."

After an hour had passed, she received word from the King. As Hélène and Charlotte began to stuff the two armoires with their mistress's gowns and nightclothes, she was informed that His Majesty had been made aware of her arrival. He was most anxious to see her. As soon as she was rested and properly attired, he instructed her to send word through one of her ladies and he would give her an immediate audience.

She shuddered as Charlotte unlaced the travel-worn black

damask mourning gown in which she had journeyed and Hélène silently draped her in the modest black gown which she had chosen for her meeting with the King. Diane had forgotten the feeling one had when faced with the magnificence and the enormity of Court. It was that same feeling now which crept up her spine like a warm, slow death. *I cannot leave now,* she thought again. *I have come this far. Now, I must face him.*

*F*OLLOWING THE KING'S VICTORY at *jeu de paume,* he adjourned to the audience chamber where he would hear anyone who had business with the Crown. Both the destitute and the nobility could attend these more public hearings called "pleadings of the door." The name of the ceremony was given due to the proximity from which most of the subjects (unless they otherwise found favor with the King), were forced to speak.

Montmorency advanced past a large wall of windows. Against the heavy leaded panes, fresh flakes of snow fell like feathers from an open pillow slip. On a dais carpeted with crimson velvet at the far end of the vast hall, was the King's throne. It was covered by a canopy of blue silk peppered with small gold fleurs-de-lys. The King sat there in a doublet of gold satin beaded with lapis, rubies and jade. Through the slashings of the shirt sleeves (the fashionable practice of inflicting vertical cuts along the fabric to expose the color and textures underneath), was another shirt of red. It matched to perfection the feathered toque which tilted to just the right angle over his neatly bearded smile. François, who was fascinated by Italian fashions, had his tailors copy for him that country's most current styles.

Near the King, a cortège of his intimates joked to help him progress through the tedium of the day's ritual. A silver cord in the center of the room marked the place through which no man, except those few intimates, might pass. The large vaulted doors at the end of the room were pressed full of those few who would attempt it.

As Grand Master in charge of the King's household, it was his duty to inform His Majesty that among those who had business with the Court and were ready to be received was the Grand Sénéchale de Normandie, Diane de Poitiers.

"She shall be first," he replied and tossed a devilish look at the courtiers around him.

Although he tried to concentrate on the next few names proposed to him, François' mind wandered. It wandered to romance. It wandered to lust. It wandered to the memory of Diane. He felt a rush of excitement akin to a child, at the anticipation of seeing her again. He remembered her well. He would be willing to wager that she had not changed. There was something timeless about her. Hers was not a raw, savage beauty, nor even a particularly seductive one. Her beauty was due to elegance. At times he remembered her appearing almost regal. She was a strong-looking woman. He remembered that too because it was an unusual attribute for a woman of her breeding. He thought of the long, firm limbs . . . the fine thin neck. He had heard rumors that she bathed naked in cold river water to preserve her youth. He shifted in his seat impatiently.

His first wife, Queen Claude, had enjoyed her company enough to have conferred upon her the honor of Lady-in-Waiting, whenever she was at Court. Diane and her husband, Louis, had been regular fixtures in royal society; before Claude's premature death; before his own imprisonment in Spain. Before he had been forced to take his enemy's sister, Eleanora, as his second wife. But all of that was a lifetime ago. So much had changed. *Diane* . . . He rolled her name around in his mind. Elegant Diane, enigmatic . . . strong. He loved the challenge of it. Yes, he was anxious to see her. Once again, things were beginning to look interesting.

🙟

"MADAME DE BRÉZÉ, La Grande Sénéchale de Normandie. His Highness, King François I." The scribe called out the introduction in a high stiletto voice.

As the King looked up, Diane de Poitiers strolled across the floor, costumed in an austere black velvet gown with a high lace collar. Her blond hair was gathered into a net under a black cap from which one small pearl glistened.

"Your Majesty," she said, curtsied, and then rose up to look directly at him.

François was breathless. He wondered how he could have forgotten the details of her; the long line of her nose, her slim, pink lips and the cool, graceful bearing of a Dorian statue. She drew men unintentionally; the King of France was no exception. He stood on the dais, descended the three stairs and held out his arms to her.

"Ah, yes. At last you have arrived! Come. You may embrace Us."

Diane advanced cautiously and surrendered to his arms as they closed tightly around her. She winced as she felt his huge hands fondle her buttocks through the folds of black velvet, as if it were the most natural thing in the world for him to do.

"How good it is to see you again, *ma chère Madame*. You have been sorely missed by this Court. How long has it been?"

"Five years, Your Majesty."

"Impossible! Oh, could it be? I fear, though I can scarcely believe that it was, before the Queen's death?"

"My deepest sympathies."

"It was a great loss," he said with appropriate remorse. "But now she is with God. And on that same sorrowful note, We were equally saddened to hear of the death of Our dear Louis. He was a friend and a humble servant of the Court. We shall mourn his death with you for a very long time."

"I thank you," she replied, lowering her eyes with her own competitive look of regret. This time when she looked up at him, she did not release him from the gaze of those shimmering blue eyes. They were almost hypnotic, and he sought to break the spell that he felt by summoning a steward and taking another sip of spiced wine.

Although she no longer wore the azure blue gown that had been so vivid in his memory, her mourning black seemed strangely more appropriate. The color against her alabaster skin was stark and dramatic. She was nothing at all like any of the women after whom he had spent his life lusting. She did not flirt, nor did she tease. To his total amazement, she wore none of the compulsory cosmetics or perfumes indispensable to a woman of breeding at her age. Yet, despite the fact that the flower of her extreme youth had passed, he knew that she would not have benefited by such contrivances had she used them.

"Well, now. Shall we really give them all something to gossip about?" he whispered with a cruel smile, as he leaned toward her.

Diane's confident expression faded. "Must we?" she whispered, but he did not reply.

"I cannot say, however," he began again in a louder more commanding voice, "that I honor your father's passing in the same way that I honor the death of your husband. I understand from the jailers at the Conciergerie that he died peacefully. Surely there is some solace for you in that."

So it had begun. The topic was inevitable, though she had not expected the need to face it so early upon her return. She had dreaded this event for days. It had nearly prevented her from returning to Court at all, and now he was making sport of it. Yet, perhaps the way he was speaking would put an end to the gossip, once and for all. Better to face rumor directly from the King, she considered, than behind both of their backs. She faced him, summoned a stoic expression and prepared to speak as loudly as he had.

"Though I loved him, Your Majesty, it is no secret to anyone that my father was a disgrace to his family and to his country in those last years. It is not easy for me to speak of him other than to say that his sins would have been forever borne by his children and our children after that, were it not for the gracious lenience of our great King."

"Your dear Louis informed Us, not long before his own death, that your father was not of sound mind during those years; that he died not knowing his own name or yours. We are a most Christian King, and We do feel sympathy for that."

"Here he goes again," Duprat mumbled to Guise, the inexperienced page who stood enthralled beside him.

"It was not difficult to see the embarrassment that his illness brought to a family so great as yours," the King continued. "We found the knowledge of that, and your father's incarceration, to have been punishment enough. His sentence of death seemed no longer to have been necessary . . . so I overturned it. It was as simple as that."

"Ha!" whispered Montmorency to the Cardinal de Tournon. "If he feels compelled to expound like this, then why does he not tell all of those groveling hordes at the door why he really pardoned her father?!"

The dimly lit hall which had been filled with pleas and shouts toward the King before Diane's entrance, had now been rendered completely silent by this uncommon exchange. Everyone knew the story of how His Majesty had suddenly pardoned Jean de Poitiers as he stood on the hanging platform, convicted of treason.

"Well!" exclaimed the King with a good-natured smile. "We would say that is quite enough of that dreary business! Now that we understand one another, we shall speak of it no more!" Then he leaned toward her and cupped his hand around his mouth. "That should keep all of the gossip mongers going for a while," he whispered, and sat back straight in his throne. "So then, Madame, if you are amply restored from your journey, you would do Us a great honor if you would consent to dine with Us this evening. We are giving a banquet to honor Chancellor Duprat. Surrounding him with beautiful women will be the best gift that We could give him."

"I should be honored, Your Majesty."

"Splendid! I should also like very much for you to meet my Anne."

The thought of the King's mistress calmed her, even when he reached out and took both of her hands in his own.

"Ah, *chérie*," he began with what sounded dangerously like sentiment. "Things have changed a great deal for you and I since you were last here. You, losing your dear Louis, and I, my Queen; my Claude . . ." But, as they began a slow cadence toward the door which was still bursting with courtiers, he added, "I am so convinced that you and my little Anne shall get along famously. We can scarcely wait for you to meet."

"I should like nothing better, Your Majesty."

The King set a slow pace in the direction of the door, enjoying the curious audience he had for this exchange. He slid his arm around her waist again. Diane tensed but continued her steps. The long ermine cape, which the King wore tossed across his shoulders, fell to the floor. At the same moment that Diane felt the fur brush against her, the King once again slid his arm down from her waist to the rise of her buttocks. He managed the movement so casually, his face belying no change of expression, that she wondered if he had realized at all what he had done. The tension returned and blossomed into a shiver, but she continued to work her way toward the door as though, through the yards of white petticoats and black velvet, she had not realized his hand was there.

"Do I recall correctly, Madame, that you enjoyed the classics?" he asked, as they passed beyond the silver cord.

"Your Majesty has an excellent memory. Books have always been for me the sustenance of life."

"How very unfortunate for our dear Louis," he quipped. Diane smiled once again, though this time she strained a little more to do it. "Join me in the library tomorrow after vespers, then. I have a recent acquisition that you will no doubt enjoy seeing."

As he took her hand in his own and raised it to his lips, they exchanged a glance. When she saw that he was smiling rakishly, Diane quickly lowered her head.

"Until tonight, then," he murmured to her as though speaking to a secret lover. Just as quickly, she turned and vanished into the odd assortment of citizens who still crowded around the door.

The English Ambassador, who had been privy to the subtleties of their exchange by standing nearest the silver cord, turned to see his aide staring longingly at the closed door through which she exited.

"Well, John, what do you think?"

"Splendid creature," he replied, still unable to alter his gaze, as though his longing alone could draw her back into the room.

The English Ambassador studied his young protégé and then added, "There is something about her, John. Mark my words, if she is not the King's mistress already, she soon will be!"

> Since it was certain, he gave himself willingly to her as if he were entirely hers. They united themselves to one another with promises of love. They embraced each other and kissed each other as if they were two doves.

Diane read by forming the words silently across her lips and imagining the young knight burned into the pages. She shivered beneath the thick, woolen wrap which lay draped across the large, canopied oak bed as she prepared to rest. Over and over she had read *Le Roman de la rose,* trying harder each time to fix his image in her mind. Dark curled hair. Skin shaded from pale amber to burnished gold over well-defined muscles; all the things she had longed for and been denied. Her mind raced to the image of a young hard body of a knight whose muscles had grown more firm by the duels he fought. Duels for love. For honor. Did such a man exist beyond the pages of her mind? She took in a breath and then sighed. Her eyelids were heavy with sleep but her heart and body were eager and seeking. She cursed the fate that had seen her married for eighteen years to someone she did not love.

She had come to care for Louis, but it had not begun that way. At the age of fourteen she had pleaded with her aunt not to force the union. He was thirty years her senior; an ugly man with a hump in his back. He lived in an old castle so far out in the country that she feared she would never see another soul except the villagers of Anet. But to society, it was an exceptionally good match and so her pleas had fallen on deaf ears. Time passed, and after her adolescent tears had ceased she had learned how to be a wife. She bore him two daughters and when he died she had a huge monument erected to him in Rouen. But he had never made her feel passion. The knight who lay tucked between the pages of her worn blue volume of *Le Roman de la rose* was as close as she could ever expect to come to someone she could adore. She had spent eighteen years married to Louis. Her youth was gone. Now she had only her dreams.

Or so she believed.

3

MONTMORENCY! Grand Master Montmorency! Present yourself at once!"

The shrill, insistent tone belonged to the King's mistress, Anne d'Heilly. Her voice resonated like the sound of a bell through the vaulted stone hallways as she plunged into each closed chamber door in the east wing. Followed by her collection of puzzled attendants, she shrieked the Grand Master's name again and again so that the walls nearly bowed with the piercing sound.

"I know he is here! I know it! Where else could he be? Not at chapel . . . his apartments . . . Fit to run the entire Court, is he? Ha! We shall see about that! Montmorency!"

Yards of emerald green taffeta flowed behind her as the train of her gown swept across the tiled floor. Her headdress hid a mane of soft chestnut hair, nearly the exact color of the King's. The headdress had been designed in Venice to accentuate her eyes and delicate bone structure. On her face, she wore a thin layer of *ceruse,* an opaque face powder made of white lead. Her lips were kept crimson and her cheeks bright with an ocher-based shade called China Red.

In the beginning, she had worn the cosmetics to appear older to the King. Now that she was twenty-six, she worried continually about savoring the vestiges of her youth. She daubed herself liberally with the romantic scent of violets; currently the most fashionable fragrance, and on a gold chain which swung from her waist, she carried a pomander so the scent the King most enjoyed would continually surround her. It also served to diffuse the odor of the others at Court who, like herself, washed little through the long months of winter. She dressed regularly in shades of green and preferred silk to brocade for the feel of it next to her skin. The King had once told her that green was *her* color as it set off the loveliness of her emerald green eyes. When he was feeling enamored or repentant, as he had that morning, it was usually emeralds that he bestowed upon her.

As she continued marching down the hall, opening one after another of the heavy carved doors, her fury increased. Then as she cast another open, she froze and the screeching stopped. A captain of the guard was rutting with a servant girl against the far wall of the empty chamber. Torn from his pleasure by the disgruntled murmurs of Anne's ladies behind him, the Captain turned with a start. His eyes were glazed and his honey-colored face was glistening with sweat. Seeing the royal *favourite* at the head of the circle of women, he hung his head. The young girl gasped and then dashed into the wardrobe.

"How dare you?" Anne growled as she collected herself and marched toward him. "You are in the King's employ, Captain. His Majesty pays your wages to work, not to fornicate with the help like a stud with a brood mare!"

The young man continued to hang his head as Louise d'Heilly, Anne's sister and principal attendant, hustled the other ladies from the room.

"You risk a great deal, Christian," she whispered when they were alone. "Where is your superior, Grand Master Montmorency?"

For a moment he did not reply; only stared at her with a seductive smile. The look which passed between them was not one which passes among strangers; nor even between master and servant.

"I know only, Mademoiselle, that he is not with me," the dashing young Christian de Nancay said as he continued to meet her gaze.

"Well, once you rid yourself of that smug expression, I suggest you locate him and tell him that I have need of him. If you do not do as I say, rest assured I shall see you back where I found you, with the rest of your sorry lot!"

As she spoke sharp and undaunted, her tiny nose flared. It excited him, but he knew his place . . . for the moment. She was right, it had been through her influence alone that he had a place at Court. He was not titled nor nobly born. His gift in life, like hers, was his beauty and his ability to use it.

"As you wish, Mademoiselle," the young man complied, tossing his head back with a smile no longer of insolence, but now of confidence. As he smiled, he began to rehook the codpiece of his puffed trunk hose. The pace at which he did it took on a seduction all of its own.

"I shall be in my apartments when you find the cretin," she added, her voice less brittle as she turned quickly, not wanting to acknowledge his smile.

Once she had left him, the only sound was her elegantly slippered feet as they echoed on the icy marble floors of the south wing at Chateau Blois. "Mademoiselle de Colliers," she said to another of her servants. "Do you know the name of that whore who was with the Captain just now?"

"I believe that she is one of the downstairs kitchen maids under Clothilde Renard, Mademoiselle."

"You are to inform Madame Renard immediately that I wish the little trollop relieved of her duties, and out of this house by tonight."

"As Mademoiselle wishes."

Anne sighed as she entered her own lavish apartments. It was like a sanctuary and, for the moment, it was a comfort to be there alone. François' behavior with the Comtesse de Sancerre had been an embarrassment to her and she wanted nothing to do with his usual excuse making today, even if it meant more jewels.

The rooms themselves were soothing to her. The walls were

hung with green brocade, reflecting the King's preference. At the center of the bedchamber was a large mahogany bed covered in emerald green tapestry. On the night table beside it, was a small enamel of herself that the King had commissioned. In the large sitting room was a collection of green tapestried couches and delicately carved chairs. All of them were placed on large Italian carpets. There were tables inlaid with marble and tortoise. They were covered with silver bowls, candlesticks and flagons of wine. Over the mantel of the massive fireplace was an imposing painting of her lover, the King of France. It served always to remind her of her place and the reason that, when he desired it, she willingly gave herself to him.

Louise d'Heilly loosened her sister's headdress and took it into the dressing room as Anne fluffed her own matted hair. This time she would not give him the benefit of her raging jealousy. There were a hundred ways to get the better of the King of France without his knowing it. She saw to it that they were even. François had his indiscretions.

She most certainly had hers.

"WHERE IS SHE?" Montmorency asked one of her ladies who had met him at the door.

The young woman pointed into the large vaulted sitting room and then disappeared behind a curtain. Montmorency found Anne d'Heilly sprawled in silhouette on an embroidered daybed beneath a huge paned window. He gazed around the room as long as he could, since seeing her lovely little face would inspire in him an anger that he felt unable to deal with today. He loathed that face; those perfect features. She was so rude . . . so cruel . . . so alluring.

Anne did not reply nor even acknowledge him for several minutes, though she had heard his heavy steps across her tiled floor. She hated him. He hated her. They loved to taunt one another, given half a chance. It was a game, like everything else at Court. But this was not his day. He had drunk too much and slept too little last night, and he was in a foul mood; not at all prepared to spar with the King's whore.

"Mademoiselle beckoned me while I was having my breakfast, and I do not like being beckoned. What is it you want?"

His voice was like splintered glass, but she did not respond. Instead she lay her head back and tore a large bit of flesh from a pomegranate. Pink juice dripped onto her cheek and the slow movement was almost seductive. Satisfied with the impression she had made, she sat up and wiped her face. At the sight of her, the blood rose from a small vein in his neck and wrapped crimson red like a band around his forehead. Anne d'Heilly saw it, and smiled.

"I haven't all day, Mademoiselle d'Heilly. What is it you wish?"

"Monsieur is a servant of the King, and would do well to remember his place."

"Surely Mademoiselle forgets that she is not the King."

"Perhaps more important to remember, Monsieur, is that there is no one else quite so close to the King as I."

Point. She was close to winning again, and he had not wanted to play at all. She did speak the truth, however, and it would be most unwise to push her now. He knew from experience that in the end, a courtesan always held greater influence with this King than even his closest friends. He had been reminded of his place, and skillfully. Finally, Montmorency bowed to her.

"Then I am at your service, Mademoiselle."

"Ah, good. So you are. Yes, well then . . . you may tell me if it is true."

"I am afraid that, once again, Mademoiselle, you have me at a disadvantage."

"I want to know about that woman . . . the Sénéchale."

Montmorency bit his lower lip until he felt it begin to bleed. She could have asked any one of her servants for such innocuous gossip. This was too much! It was an insult and they both knew it.

"You certainly could have asked Nançay if that is all the information you desire! He knows all that I know of such matters, and it is certainly his company that you prefer."

Montmorency pushed the line. Her affair with the young Captain, Christian de Nançay, was no secret on the back stairs of Court. Their eyes locked in a combative stare.

"The Captain is useless refuse. Chancellor Duprat is a glutton, and Admiral Chabot requires payment that I am not inclined today to give. Like the others, you too serve the King. So, you see, you are what is left to me. Not desirable, but practical just the same. I have heard the gossip, and I must know if she . . . if that woman, has had the courage to return in full view of this Court, and if she has, what precisely she expects to accomplish!"

"How is it that you expect me to know?"

"You are His Majesty's keeper, are you not?! Since you do make it your business to know the King's business, what better informant might I ask than the one who is most highly paid?"

"My wish is to serve you, dear lady," he lied, knowing that he was outmatched today. "I shall tell you all that I know."

Her angry face softened.

"That would be Madame de Brézé, about whom you inquire. Though now that she is widowed she prefers to be addressed simply as Madame de Poitiers. As to her present locale, she has indeed returned to this Court, which has been, I might add, at the request of His Majesty the King."

As he spoke, he sauntered toward a table near the fire, then fingered a large apple in a silver bowl in the table's center. "The lady has taken up residence in the east wing and was summoned some time ago to a private audience with our Sovereign. Beyond that, I am afraid I can tell you nothing."

There was a long pause.

"Those who have seen her say that she is very elegant . . . very sophisticated. I can trust only a man's opinion in this," she said in a voice barely above a whisper.

Ah, so when all of the sparring was done, that was the real reason he had been summoned. He was the only one at Court who despised her enough to tell her the truth about another woman!

"I would agree with your sources, Mademoiselle."

"So then. Would you also say that she is more beautiful than I?"

"Not actually," he said, contemplating carefully and turning the apple around in his hand. He took a bite. The question had surprised him. Beauty . . . Now there was the chink in her armor! Perhaps he hadn't lost, at that. He forged ahead.

"No, no. Not more beautiful at all. She has . . . rather a sort of, how shall I say . . . a regal sort of countenance. She reminds one of the King's beloved late Queen: her Majesty Claude."

Anne's face flushed. Game point. He had done it. She was young and beautiful enough to compete with any other woman except the memory of François' dead wife! She turned from his view. Montmorency may have won this round but she refused to give him the satisfaction of knowing it. Seizing the victory, the Grand Master bit into the apple again and then stared at her, his bright eyes glinting in the afternoon light.

"Will there be anything else, Mademoiselle d'Heilly? My breakfast awaits."

Anne struggled in vain to retain her composure. When she did not reply, he bowed, linking his hands loosely behind him.

"Ah well, if not, then I shall say adieu." As he turned to leave, he placed the partially eaten apple back down on the table near the fruit bowl, then looked up one last time, his lips smiling with a cruel confidence.

"Heathen!" she muttered from behind clenched teeth as he slid quickly out the door and down the long winding hall. "You, my dear Montmorency, may have had this laugh on me, but you may bet that it is I who shall be your final undoing!"

When he had gone, she gazed back up at the shimmering painted image of the King that hung over the mantel. He had been painted in a magnificent black velvet cloak sleeved in sable. He was mounted on a black mare, caparisoned in silver fringe. Colorful sparks from the fire cracked and popped beneath it. The painting recalled for her an earlier time, when nothing and no one had come between them; when she had had more confidence than jewels.

Though the years had strengthened her position with the King, they had also weakened his desire for her. There had been many tears and many affairs; some noble, like this new threat; some common street whores or kitchen maids. François' appetite was endless and she had finally come to accept with a weary acquiescence the fact that he never slept alone. But then neither did she. He was a man of unbridled passion and no matter what fascination her beauty held for him, she was only one woman. She knew that she could never be enough for him, so she protected her heart by sharing her body.

"Find Christian," she snapped, her voice thin and implacable. Mademoiselle de Colliers curtsied. "And inform my sister that you and your ladies may have the rest of the afternoon to yourself, once he arrives."

"Will you be attending Monsieur Duprat's party this evening, then?"

"Oh yes, of course. I shall need you all to help me dress. But wait until near eight before you return."

Anne rose and walked slowly toward the mirror that hung near the fire. She pinched her smooth cheeks to fill them with their own natural blush. She would not be made a fool of by any man, not even the King of France. Casually, she tugged at the stiff décolletage of her sweeping emerald gown. The movement defined the cleft between her firm breasts. She placed her hands around her tiny waist, as if to insure that she still had her figure. She did. Reassured of her beauty, she smiled. The knock at the door brought an even larger smile.

Christian de Nançay entered slowly, and closed the door. He leaned against a heavy carved pillar and gazed at her with a piercing sensuality. Their scene that morning before the other servants had not angered her so much as it had excited her. There was danger in their liaison and for her, danger and passion were inextricably mixed. He moved forward and stood before her, blond curls framing his angular face and the burst of young manhood evident beneath his codpiece. They both knew why he was there. It was not the first time.

Anne walked slowly toward him and put her hands to his chest as they gazed at one another. "You have been very bad," she whispered. "I would have thought that after last night—"

The young Captain did not answer but kissed her, prying open her mouth with his own. His force urged her on. She would not regret this, no matter what the cost.

"She means nothing to me," he finally whispered into her ear as he licked and nuzzled the lobe. "I cannot have you nearly often enough. It was nothing more to me than a physical need; like eating . . . sleeping . . . it was not at all like this . . ."

Anne smiled and slowly began to unfasten his doublet. She wanted him in spite of his indiscretion with the pathetic little maid; perhaps because of it. As she began to lose herself in the strength of his arms, she became aware of a sound; a collection of footsteps; then a low rumbling of voices. It was the King and his entourage. She could hear François' laugh and the dull monotonous drone of the Cardinal de Lorraine. Her heart quickened and she struggled to free herself from Christian's grip. To be found out would be her ruin. He never came to her in the afternoons any longer. Perhaps he knew. Perhaps Montmorency had seen. Told.

"Holy Virgin! It is the King! Quickly, Christian, you must hide! In the fireplace, hide there! You cannot be seen leaving now, it is too late. Go quickly, please!"

Reluctantly, the amorous Captain stole into the cavernous hearth. The glowing orange embers were nearly extinguished. He stepped beside them and hid in the side wall amid the cinders. He held his breath. At the very moment when he had hidden himself away, her chamber door swung around and hit the wall behind it with a great thud. Anne now too held her breath, though the pace of her heart quickened.

"Gentlemen, I shall meet you in the gallery shortly. Until then I do not wish to be disturbed."

Anne heard the King as he slammed the large vaulted outer door to her apartments. The rest of the footsteps continued down the corridor and the Cardinal's drone faded. Anne looked up nervously to see a smile, not anger on her royal lover's face. She breathed an inaudible sigh of relief and went to his waiting arms.

François had intended to spend the afternoon with the Comtesse de Sancerre, but her husband's greed had got the better of him. The Comte had chosen the opportunity to barter his wife.

When the King arrived the Comtesse was not alone as she had been instructed. The Comte de Sancerre was there with his wife. It had been no secret that the King's previous *favourite,* Françoise de Foix, had also been married and that the liaison that had lasted several years had given considerable wealth to the husband as well as the wife. But financial arrangements had been the furthest thing from the King's mind, and he did not enjoy surprises.

He had looked at the woman trying to recall what it was that he had found so appealing about her the night before. The light of day was cruelly honest. It revealed a hard face with cracks where the thick white ceruse had dried and broken like a plaster casting. He had felt a shiver and suddenly missed his little Anne. So he excused himself, leaving the Sancerres arguing wildly as he walked down the hall.

Now François pawed Anne furiously. "Just lift your skirts, *mon ange,* just the skirts this time," he whispered. Without further words between them, she lay face down on the smooth, green bedcover. The King raised her heavy skirts from behind. It was time for her to earn her place.

Christian de Nançay smiled as he stood motionless within the corner of the massive white stone fireplace watching His Majesty have his way with Mademoiselle d'Heilly. Then, to his surprise, his own breath quickened at the sight of so supercilious a lady bent over the bed, her small white bottom thrust in the air and a ribbon of white lace edging the small of her back. A tangle of her chestnut hair met the lace. Moved to act by his own heightened lust, the wise Captain chose instead to bide his time in awkward silence. There would be enough for him later. Of that he was certain.

It did not take long for the King to satisfy himself. When it was over, he sat on the edge of the bed and wiped his brow with the back of his large hand. He paid little mind to the sweat-soaked shirt or the sour odor of perspiration that clung to his chest. Anne lay motionless on her side, looking up at him as he panted. Her heavy green gown was wrinkled and wet. All she could think of was Christian, who she was certain had watched the entire episode.

After a moment, François looked over at her with a smile,

slapped her thigh affectionately, and walked casually toward the fireplace. Anne held her breath. She was ruined. He had seen Christian. They would both be punished. Perhaps killed.

"François!" she cried out instinctively and leapt to her feet. "What are you doing, *mon amour*?"

She tried not to let him hear the terror in her voice, but she was not successful. The King turned from the entrance to the fireplace and looked at her quizzically.

"I've got to piss," he said with a smile and aimed himself into the large cavernous receptacle that stood as tall as he.

She longed to cry out and to thrust forth the chamber pot, but she knew that he liked to do as he pleased when the urge occurred. Billowing clouds of gray smoke from the near-dead embers filled the fireplace. Anne put her hand to her mouth so she would not scream. The King looked at her as he laced his codpiece and straightened his doublet.

"Ah! much better . . . What is it, *ma chère*? You look terribly strange."

She could not speak. Her throat was dry. Anne could only manage to shake her head. François chucked her under the chin and shook his own head.

"I must go. Montmorency has me meeting with the English Ambassador in half an hour. You understand."

She shook her head again.

"Then be a good girl and give me a kiss to send me off. You know how I detest sparring with Monty. He is so good at it."

When he had gone, Anne raced back into the bedchamber. Nançay emerged from the fireplace covered with ash that had turned his blond hair and his shirt powder gray. One of his soft doeskin slippers was wet and he smelled of urine. He coughed and tried to brush away the soot. She raced toward him.

"Christian, no! Not on the carpets. They'll be ruined!"

He turned to her, his face burning with anger.

"Now, now, do not be cross. It doesn't become you. It is just that you look so . . ."

Before she could finish her sentence, he grabbed her arms and drew her toward him. The soot on his face and clothes mingled with her own cosmetics and left a gray-sooted print on her cheeks. He kissed her with a vengeance, intending to take something at that very moment for his troubles. She struggled but was no match for him. As he forced her down onto the carpet, she freed her lips and bit his tongue hard. He screamed in pain and a streak of blood ran from the corner of his mouth. Instantly he released her and put his hands to his face, moaning like a wounded animal.

"Bitch!" he screamed, trying to insult her but the bloodied tongue purged forth from his mouth made the word unintelligible.

Anne sprang to her feet with a look of disgust. She wiped violently at her gown to rid it of the soot. "You disgust me, you filthy helot! Now get out of here before I call the King back!"

Christian limped from the chamber still holding his mouth. He had fallen victim to the one threat that mattered. She must not inform the King of their affair. He could do anything he pleased at Court, as long as he was careful. But if the King were to discover it, his career and his life would be over. No woman, not even Anne d'Heilly, was worth that.

When he was gone, she smiled like a lazy cat, her green eyes shimmering. That would teach him. He would be sorry he had forced himself on her. He would apologize and she would forgive him. He was too worthy a lover not to. But first he must wonder for a while. She may have to give herself to the King at his every whim, but that did not mean that she was there for the taking by the rest of the world. That was a lesson the amorous young Captain would not now soon forget.

DOWN THE LONG HALLWAY glittering gold with torchlight, Diane ran. She had gotten lost in *Le Roman de la rose* and she had fallen asleep. Now she was late for the King's banquet. She had not planned to make so conspicuous an entrance on her first evening back at Court. Like it or not, however, it appeared she was about to.

She clutched her full black silk gown abut the knees, hiked it up and, abandoning all decorum, scurried past the statuesque hall guards motionless in blue and red livery. As she neared the grand hall, the faint sound of laughter and music deepened. Her heart quickened. *Perhaps I can steal in behind someone and find a seat,* she considered. But there was only one main entrance to the large, sunken hall.

As she peered in from behind a heavy velvet curtain, she could see that the room was a sea of people, all laughing, talking and moving about. The King's guests wore velvets and satins in brilliant hues. There were men parading in multicolored brocades and silks. From the top of the stairs the reds and blues, yellows and bright greens blended in a prismatic kaleidoscope of color.

The guests milled around three long tables that were set together to form a great U-shape that lined the room. The tables were covered with white sheets of damask and great silver candelabras. The aroma of incense and perfume mingled with the smell of roasting mutton, veal and of wine. An abundance of candles and torches burned brightly on the walls as on the tables, and their flames bathed the room in a smoky orange hue.

"Madame de Poitiers!"

The scribe announced her name as he plucked her from behind the velvet curtain in the doorway. Fortune was not on her side.

She entered the massive banquet room through a grand staircase. It led down two flights, half of them to the side and ending squarely in the center of the room. In her simple black gown she was completely set off amid the opulence of Court.

The walls and pillars of the room were fashioned of cold white stone. From above, it felt like a giant chasm waiting to engulf her. The King's ambassadors, courtiers and servants pivoted as they gazed upward at the doorway. The lute player stopped playing. The laughter ceased. That one moment seemed to her like an eternity. Her heart was the only sound she could hear in the momentary, deafening silence.

The King was seated in a throne across the room at the head dining table. Diane loomed above him. Having himself enjoyed the privilege on these state occasions of being the last to enter, François was awestruck at the power that her entrance now commanded. She was stunning in black silk, her slim white neck rising from it. Around her neck was draped a strand of simple white pearls. François gasped at her beauty. As she began tentatively to descend the stairs, he rose and came from behind the long dining table, meeting her as she reached the last step. Diane curtsied and he took her hand in his own as they began to walk together into the room. the conversation around them and music recommenced.

"Your Majesty, please forgive me. I am late when your invitation was so specific."

"Not at all, *ma chère,* Madame. You have had a long journey. Tonight your tardiness is easily overlooked."

"I am afraid that Your Majesty is too kind."

"Tomorrow, of course, would be another matter," he added with a self-important grin.

She bowed her head as the King's dogs circled around her, sniffing hungrily for a piece of meat that lay near her on the cold stone floor.

"*Mes amis!* You remember Louis' wife, Diane de Poitiers. Treat her as you would treat Your King. She has been too long away from Our Court."

Diane glanced up and found the silent eyes of Anne de Montmorency not far from the King. François had not addressed her as the Sénéchale, nor had the scribe. She had asked it of the Grand Master in passing, and despite the dislike she knew he felt, he had seen to it. Montmorency was thorough; not trustworthy, but thorough. She gave him a decorous nod of thanks. He extended one back and then turned from her to begin speaking with Chancellor Duprat.

Her arm still tightly bound by the King's grasp, she found herself being led into the throngs of smiling, ingratiating courtiers who clambered to meet her. There was no hope of retreating. The grand hall was warm from the press of bodies, the smoking candles and the two blazing hearths.

Diane began to feel ill. She had not eaten all day and the faint smell of body odor that she had detected from the King when they met earlier had now matured into a pungent smell. The strong, musky perfume in which he was bathed did not mask it; rather it fused the two odors into a vile stench. Trying with difficulty not to choke, she lost herself in introductions to the remote and imposing Cardinal de Lorraine and the small, hawk-faced Admiral Chabot, who stood beside him.

"It is very rude of Your Majesty not to introduce me."

The voice which came from behind, masked by the shifting sea of people, was shrill and brittle. Diane turned with the King. Before them stood a fragile looking young woman with long chestnut curls spilling out from an emerald-studded turban. Her eyes were bright green and were set off by the jewels on her gown and in her headdress. Her small body was made even smaller by the tightly corseted gown.

"Forgive me, *mon amour,*" the King said, turning fully around with an expression of surprise. "Diane de Poitiers, may I present Anne d'Heilly."

At last. His Anne. She was young, and yes . . . every bit as pretty as they had said. Diane smiled almost too graciously at such great fortune. She had clearly worried for nothing.

"I am honored, Mademoiselle," Diane said as she nodded to the King's *favourite.* The young woman's suspicion was masked by a calculated smile.

"Charmed," she replied to veil her instinctive sense of rivalry for anyone whose beauty paralleled her own. Then she linked her arm boldly with the King's. As she did, she thrust forth her heavily jeweled hand, glittering with more emeralds, diamonds and gold than Diane had ever seen on any one person.

"His Majesty and I wish to welcome you, and hope your brief stay with us shall be a pleasant one." The words were studied; spoken from her mouth, not her heart. Almost before the King could nod in agreement, she added, "Now come along, *chéri.* You have been absolutely ignoring the Cardinal de Tournon, and you know how petulant he becomes when he is left to his own devices."

In one of those brief, yet fateful encounters where nothing of substance is said, yet everything of importance is conveyed, Diane had met the King's official mistress.

As he was whisked away by Anne d'Heilly, the other courtiers who had surrounded Diane began to disband. She searched desperately for a familiar face, and finally she found it. In one corner of the room beside a marble pillar, was His Highness François II, Dauphin of France. He stood huddled with the Comtesse de Sancerre, with whom his father had spent the previous night.

The eldest son of the King of France was tall and his face was striking for so young a man. He had dark straight hair and a prominent patrician nose that rendered unmistakable the resemblance to his father. He wore a toque, trunk hose and doublet of mulberry velvet with snow white slashing. His sleeves were covered with rubies and sapphires.

His eyes had been roving searchingly about the room, only half concentrating on the much older woman who desperately sought his attentions. Those same eyes grew bright now with the recognition of Diane. He smiled. She nodded a smile in his direction. She pretended not to watch, but out of the corner of her eye she could see the young Prince whisper something in the woman's ear and then begin to make his way toward her.

"Madame Diane!" he called out.

The other courtiers around her bowed as he neared them and opened his arms to her. Upon closer inspection, she could see youth and manhood joined on his face. Beneath small, clever eyes, he sported a neat, dusty beard amid the faint remembrance of adolescent pimples. Despite them, he was still a strikingly attractive young man. Like his father, he had the stately bearing of a King. Also like his father, he used it to his advantage. He had changed a great deal in five years. Time in the Spanish prison with his younger brother Henri appeared to have somehow strangely enriched his spirit, not broken it.

"His Majesty said that you would be returning to Court, but I had no idea it would be so soon! I am so glad that you had the courage to do it. Oh, do give us another hug! How is Françoise?" he inquired of her elder daughter.

"She's growing into quite a young lady since the two of you played in the orchards behind Anet." Diane smiled.

"Ah yes, hide-and-seek for hours," he said in a voice thick and richly urbane. Then he began to laugh. "Mischief would hardly be the same without the little minx! Oh, I would so love to see her. Where is she now?"

"She is in the convent Filles-Dieu with her younger sister, Louise. I am pleased to say that they are both doing splendidly. And look at you! Your Highness has grown up as well. You are not the fair little boy who used to hide from the Queen behind my skirts."

Montmorency's fleshy wife, Madeleine, strained to hear their conversation.

"And your brothers?" she asked. "My Louise will certainly want to know about Henri and Charles."

The Dauphin battled a disdainful smirk and a sarcastic tone. "I am afraid little brother Henri has been woefully bad, Madame. Father has sent him on to Fontainebleau to seek his punishment by spending time with our Spanish Queen. But there is Charles. See over there, by the fires." He pointed.

Diane turned to see a chubby, flour-faced boy sitting on the hearth, stroking one of the hounds.

"Perhaps you would graciously consent to give him a turn. I am afraid he is too uncertain of himself to dance with any of the younger girls. But I know he would most definitely dance with you."

His words, cast-off and thoughtless, startled her like a sudden shaft of lightning. She looked at the future King, so slim, young and exquisite before her. His youth, like his brother's was a sharp reminder of her own age, and the time she had wasted.

AFTER BEING COAXED by the Dauphin to dance with young Prince Charles, Diane was breathless. They danced two Galliards, a long and strenuous dance full of strenuous kicks and hops designed for the most athletic. Diane then took refuge at one of the long tables. The room was bursting with music and laughter. She finally breathed a sigh of relief and began to bask in her own precious, if momentary, anonymity. As she sat with a goblet of wine, she watched a popular new form of the Galliard called the Volté, and waited for her breathing to return to normal.

Anne d'Heilly was more beautiful and much younger than she had imagined, she thought as she watched her dance with the English Ambassador. Diane was certain that they would never be friends, but she also felt happily absurd about her former suspicions. The King was just an unbearable flirt. He loved women. He always had. Of course, he had only been taking the liberty to which Kings grow accustomed. It had meant nothing more.

As she bit into a moist hunk of veal, Diane realized that she was ravenous. The table before her was covered with a virtual orgy of food. Meat pies were piled high on silver dishes; tureens were spilling with stew. There were capons and roasted partridge, giant plates of hare and venison, cakes made of pine nuts, sweet cup custards and marzipan. Every dish was set out for the guests on silver serving dishes; each one ornately appointed and turned. Servants, dressed in the same familiar blue and crimson uniforms, kept wine flowing from giant ceramic urns that they lugged about the room.

She swallowed the last bit of her meal with a sip of wine and leaned back in the high-backed crimson tapestried chair. When the meal was complete, each guest was presented with his own silver ewer of Damascus rose water and a fine embroidered linen napkin with which to wash. When the napkins were unfolded, each guest found imprisoned inside a little bird, all of which, for the further enjoyment of the guests, began to hop around on the table and peck at the plates and dishes.

At the same time, another new dance step was being shown to the King. He watched intently from his seat the *Branle des torches,* so named because as the steps progressed, the dancers passed torches between themselves. The rest of the room watched as the King studied the steps to the echoed sound of the trumpet, clarion, viols and lute. The courtiers were careful not to applaud or to condemn the step until the King had done so. He looked regal dressed in a doublet of red silk, the collar of which was braided in gold. His toque was brown velvet, plumed with one large white ostrich feather.

"He will not like it, you know."

The voice of the man next to her came echoing out of his large silver chalice. Diane, who had not until that moment noticed him, turned to see who had addressed her.

"I beg your pardon?"

"The dance step, I mean. I have been watching His Majesty for a long time now. I have studied him at all of these affairs and I wager it will be too intricate for his liking," he said as he tossed out a coin, which clinked as it hit his dinner plate.

He was a thin graceful man, costumed in a doublet of indigo velvet, the slashings of which showed a yellow shirt of linen and lace. His hair was light and curled around his forehead. It matched the vague, dusty beard which came to a point at the end of his chin. He could have been handsome had it not been for the lack of a rugged quality which Diane had always found appealing.

"Watch," he said, directing her gaze back to the King's table.

Before the King, a young page now twirled and hopped to the lute player's tune, his torch leaving a streaming trail of light as he moved it. Just as the boy bowed at the dance's completion, the King stood.

"Bravo, my boy! Come everyone, young Guise, the Cardinal's nephew, has given us a new step to try! Lute player, the music!"

"One would hope, Monsieur, that you know your women better than your King," she quipped, pulling the coin to her own plate and turning back to him.

"Most assuredly." He smiled. "Allow me to introduce myself. I am Jacques de Montgommery, Captain of His Majesty's Scots Guard."

"And I am—"

"Oh, I know who you are. I am most honored to meet you, Madame La Sénéchale."

"Ah, I see that my reputation precedes me."

"I have heard only the most favorable things."

"Then you have undoubtedly heard that I prefer to go by the name to which I was born, not by the title that was given to me when I married."

He jutted out his lower lip and shrugged his shoulder as if, with his movements, to say, *whatever you like*. "And what might that name be?" he added as he picked a stray piece of meat from his red and yellow balloon sleeve.

"Diane. Diane de Poitiers."

"Diane." He rolled the name around on his tongue as though he were tasting it. "Lovely name."

"Quite common really," she replied, trying to negate his flattery.

"Ah, but the novelty is with she who bears it."

"You flatter me, Monsieur."

"I should consider myself fortunate to do so, Madame."

"Do you manage to be so charming with everyone?" she asked, finding it difficult not to be just a little taken in by him.

"Only when I see something worth the effort. Ah, they are beginning the next Galliard. Please . . . you must dance with me."

Standing beside him, she now saw what a tall lean man he was. He smiled a confident, effortless smile and he danced as gracefully as he spoke.

"The color becomes you," he said, gazing down at her gown.

"It is black, Monsieur. A mourning costume. My husband has died only six months ago."

"Still, Madame, with every color of the rainbow exhibited here tonight, these women look like peacocks while you are like a beautiful black swan."

"Monsieur, you must agree not to flatter me so. It is not proper."

As though he had not heard her, Montgommery clutched her wrist and whirled her around to the tune played by the quartet. It was only after the dance was over, and he had bowed his thanks to her, that he answered her remonstrations. "Ah, Madame, I know that you have been away a long time, but you may as well learn early on how things have changed here. The moralist cuts a poor figure in King François' Court."

Diane looked at him strangely, but he was no longer looking at her. She turned around to see what had averted his gaze. It was the King who was standing across the room, near Admiral Chabot.

Although the Admiral was talking intensely to him, His Majesty appeared lost to the words, staring instead across the room at Diane. Anne d'Heilly, who was still clutching the King's arm, watched His Majesty watch Diane. The forced smile which the *favourite* had worn earlier in the evening now faded as she nodded, pretending to be listening to the Admiral, but all the while, never breaking her gaze from Diane.

Montgommery, standing across the room from the King, could see the scene from its full perspective. His smile became a sneer as he fingered his yellow moustache.

"Well, well, well," he muttered so only she could hear. "It appears that things are just beginning to get interesting around here."

BY THE TIME DIANE slid between her heavy damask bedcovers, it was nearly dawn. Her feet ached from dancing and her head was spinning from the wine.

There had been, in all, five interludes to the meal. Each time the lute player sounded a tune, the table was stripped of the meal. In place of the food, the tables became a stage and five different kinds of entertainment were enacted. There was a mystery play during which the guests were encouraged to guess the ending for the prize of a lock of His Majesty's hair. Afterward, the food was returned and dancing recommenced. Another hour passed and the food was again cleared away. Four acrobats, dressed in multicolored costumes, leapt upon the tables to further entertain the guests. By the early hours of the morning, a young singer, whom the King had coaxed into asylum from Venice, took the stage.

After the banquet Diane had gone a little reluctantly on the arm of Montgommery to the King's private apartments. There, with a select group of the King's closest friends, she watched and drank more wine as His Majesty and the Cardinal de Lorraine discussed Plato's *Dialogues*.

As dawn washed the horizon with a blurred pink sunrise, Jacques de Montgommery offered to escort Diane back to her apartments. Once there, faced with her half-open chamber door and the flood of morning light from her windows, he had wasted no time in conveying his intentions.

"I should like to share your bed," he whispered. His words fell off into the folds of her gown as he swayed from the wine.

"Monsieur, you insult me!" She pushed him away and poised her hand to slap his face. As she raised her arm, he caught it; the strength of his conviction returned.

"You still have not figured it out have you, my pretty one? Do you think any of those people in the King's apartment tonight have gone to bed alone? Even the good Cardinal is at this very moment likely burrowing beneath his bedcovers with one of Mademoiselle d'Heilly's willing ladies. It is simply how things are, and you are far better off if you learn to accept it."

"Stop! I will not hear this!"

He still had a firm grip on her arm and she struggled to free herself. "Do not play the virgin with me! Everyone knows you bedded the King, and with your husband's blessing; all to barter for your father's life!"

There. He had said it; said what everyone had thought. Said what all the others in their little groups had mumbled when they saw the King take her out to do a Pavane. She had felt their stares. She knew their envy. She had waited until her husband had died, secured with his estates, and then, as brazen as a common strumpet, had strolled back into Court to finish what they had begun. There was no point in denying the accusation. Montgommery was drunk. He would probably not remember having said it in the morning anyway. Diane simply stared at him a moment longer, watching him sway back and forth. Her silence drew more frustration from him, but then, before he could act on it, she turned away.

"I am going to bed. Alone! Good night, Monsieur!"

He grabbed her arm again and pulled her forcefully back to face him. "Very well, then. Go off to your cold empty bed! But for all of your righteousness, you shall soon be just like all the rest of us. It is part of the plan. Eat, drink and be merry, says our good King. I simply thought you might as well initiate yourself sooner than later."

"Well, clearly, Captain Montgommery, you thought wrong!"

And so the scene between them had gone. Diane had left him standing bleary-eyed at her doorstep. She had heard him rustling about for some time in the hallway before he finally went away.

"Who was that, Madame?" Charlotte asked as she rubbed a thick finger across her cheek and met her at the door.

"It was no one, Charlotte. No one. Go back to bed."

This definitely was not the refined Court she had known with Louis, she thought, as she rubbed her red and swollen feet against the edge of her bed. But so far, the unpredictability intrigued her. It was a side of courtly life that she had not been permitted to see before. There was so much about life in general that she had not been permitted to see. She would need to use great caution here, but for the time being, Diane had decided to stay.

THE KING PULLED his head slowly from the pillow as Anne slept motionless in his arms. He was restless. Bedding the ambitious Comtesse de Sancerre the night before, with Anne in her apartments just down the hall, had done little to stave off the wanderlust that grew to nearly violent proportions within him.

Anne had known where he was and what he was doing and yet she had said nothing. It had spoiled the fun of being bad. Now, all that he felt as he lay in her arms was the dull ache of being unfulfilled. But since women were not the real problem, neither were they the answer. The real issue was power. François wanted Italy.

He would never forget his disastrous defeat at Pavia . . . the price he had paid. He had been forced to marry the Emperor's ugly sister. It had been part of the bargain for peace, and for the safe return to France of his sons. François burned to make the Emperor pay for their imprisonment; François burned again for war. He could not help it. He could not deny it. The desire coursed through his blood; through his body; searing him; taunting him. If he could just gain Italy then he, not the Emperor Charles, would dominate the Christian world. It would be a fair trade for what he and his family had been forced to endure.

He tossed fitfully in his bed as his mind raced, his body wet with perspiration. Opening his eyes, he stared up at the painting by Andrea del Sarto called *Caritas* that graced a wall near his bed. Never in his life had he seen art as beautiful or as moving as he had in Italy. He wanted it. He needed it. He would find a way to have it at any cost; any cost but that of the life of the Dauphin. Nothing would be worth selling the joy of his life, his eldest son, to marriage with a merchant's daughter. It seemed that there were times when the only thing in his life he had done right was to sire that boy.

But in trying to gain the return of Milan, there was something else to consider: the delicate balance between England and France. There was not only the Emperor, but there was Henry VIII. François detested his English counterpart, finding him unprincipled and uncivilized. But he knew that, at the very least, a broad-based civility between them was essential. The presence of the Pope in Rome did little to balance out this powerful triangle. Despite his forbidding presence, the Pontiff had not been a real threat or a support to any side. It was in reality a weak papacy. Clement VII blew with the winds. Now, as subtle as a spring breeze, the winds were changing. In François' mind a stormy offensive was brewing against the Emperor. At this point Henry VIII held all of the cards, and the sly fox knew it.

If Henry sided with the Emperor against François, there would be no hope of France taking Italy. There would be no hope of his ever gaining back what he had lost. Unless of course, to get what he desired, the King of France gave the Pope what he desired in return. A French bridegroom for his niece. Perhaps then the pontiff would find the courage to stand with France against the Emperor, after all.

As Anne slept, François rose and looked back at her. She did not stir. She was not troubled by any of this, and she had no idea how it troubled him. As long as she was rich and adored, he thought, she was happy. The tile floor was cold beneath his bare feet and he shivered in the alcove near his bed. After another moment, he rapped on the door for one of his gentlemen-of-the-chamber to stoke the fire which, in the early hours of morning, had begun to sputter.

Henry VIII or Pope Clement. Those were the choices if he meant to regain Milan from the Emperor. And yet, surrendering his eldest son, his heir, to a degrading political marriage . . . in that there was no choice at all.

"No," he whispered. "I cannot. I must not. The English Ambassador will suggest a course to ally with Henry VIII. I will meet with him tomorrow. There will be another way. There must!"

François crawled back beneath the covers and pressed himself against Anne's warm flesh. The heat from her body warmed his own cold skin. It aroused him even more than his thoughts had done. He ran his rough fingers across each of her breasts. The contours of her small body excited him. Thank God for his little tart. In her arms he could stave off all of this madness, if only for a while. He reached up and, as she slept, stroked the fine alabaster flesh around her neck. What a good tumble she still was, when he was so inclined to have her. It always amazed him, even now, how ready and willing she was to secure her position by any means he desired. She knew how to please him. Like all successful courtesans, she had made his pleasure her life's work.

He touched her cheek and her eyes opened. She was beguiling, always knowing when he wanted her; always making him pay for her favors in one way or another. So beautiful and so cruel. He craved the contradiction. It was still early, he thought. As the servant stoked the fire to a fitful blaze, he drew the bedcurtains. There was still time before his *lever* began to avail himself, at least once more, of his little Anne's very potent charms.

"PLEASE, MADAME, PERMIT me to speak!" Jacques de Montgommery called out.

Diane continued down the pillared open gallery that faced the enclosed garden. She was holding open her book of verse as though she were concentrating on some particular passage. She looked down, but still could hear the sound of Montgommery's footsteps on the stone as he advanced behind her.

"Please, I ask only for a moment. Then I shall go away, if that is still what you desire."

Diane slowed and turned around. He looked ill. His skin was pasty and he had not changed his clothes from the night before. His doublet was gone and his yellow shirt was crumpled and stained.

"You look dreadful," she said.

"I suppose that is part of the penance for my behavior last evening. It is no match for the way my head feels."

Diane closed her book and drew a little nearer. As she did, the smell of wine and vomit caught her and she stepped back, placing her hand to her mouth. Montgommery saw her and stepped back a pace himself.

"Ah, yes. I am sorry about that. I wanted to see you the first moment I could. To apologize. I behaved horribly. I had no right. You certainly had not encouraged my advances."

"We barely know one another, Captain. How would you have had time to know whether I would be encouraging or not?"

Feeling his legs about to give way beneath him, Montgommery leaned on one of the large stone pillars. The touch of it was cold. He lay his head against it to try to dull the throbbing. He felt as though he would be sick again, but first he must settle this. He took a deep breath so that he might continue.

"From the moment I first saw you, Madame, I knew that you were someone I should be privileged to know . . . and know, I mean, only in the most proper sense of the word."

The wine he had drunk, and which had turned on him, seemed to have tamed his ardor. She felt safe in allowing him to continue.

"You are an extraordinary woman, Madame; quite different from anyone I have ever met; certainly quite different from anyone at Court. I should be proud to call you my friend . . . if that is all you would desire of me."

Diane looked at the pathetic dirty mess of a man who now was surrendering his pride to her. In place of her anger there was compassion. "And I have your word as a gentleman that there will be no more midnight seductions outside my apartment doors?"

"I am most certainly, Madame, a gentleman of honor. Although, I grant you, you have very little cause at the present to believe me. No, there will be no more events like last evening; what of it I am able to recall. Unless of course, it is you who wills it."

He grimaced and then smiled.

"Well, I would like to have a friend here, and it just might as well be you. You were right about one thing, I have been gone a long time. Things are so different from how I remember them." She drew in a deep breath and crossed her arms as though trying to decide. "Very well, then. But we shall speak no more of last night." Having decided, she smiled. His easy charm had made it simple to forgive him, and difficult not to like him.

"Then we are friends?" he asked, drawing near her again.

Overwhelmed again by the odor, she took a reflexive step backward and raised her hand as though to stop his advance.

"Friends," she repeated. Her smile broadened and warmed the soft contours of her thin face. "Now you, *mon ami,* are in need of a bath and some rest."

Jacques de Montgommery stood in the gallery as she strolled down the corridor away from him. He watched until he could no longer see her shadow cast against the stone wall and he knew that she was gone. Despite the pain which throbbed in his head and the churning in his stomach, he managed to smile. He had done it. She was not so formidable as she looked at first.

She believed he had drunk too much and had spoken foolishly. He had been drinking, but he remembered vividly every word he had said. He remembered the touch of her skin as he tried to draw her near, and the strange, freshly washed scent of her body. She obviously did not think he recalled his accusation about her and the King.

It had been a foolish thing to say if he were to gain her trust . . . even though it was true. It must be. Why else would the King of France, at the very last moment, mysteriously have pardoned her father when he had been sentenced to die for high treason? Clearly, she had sold her body; and in return, her father's life had been spared. That was quite a power she must wield over His Majesty. Such knowledge would certainly increase his own influence, should he manage to bed her, now that the King clearly wanted her back.

The King must have grown tired of his little bitch. Why else would Diane have been summoned from the comfort and security of her dead husband's wooded estate after five years? And why, more curiously, had she come alone if that was not precisely what she had expected? Perhaps he could bed her and then bribe her. If they were to have an affair, she would be vulnerable to him. After what she had already endured, she would do anything to keep herself from future scandal. His head whirled with the possibilities. Yes, bedding her would be sweet, and he meant to become very rich in the bargain!

DIANE WENT ON with a light heart to her appointment with the King. Anne d'Heilly's youth and beauty had given her a confidence behind which to hide her fears, and at least now she had one ally at Court in Jacques de Montgommery.

"So you are not only beautiful but punctual as well," François said with a wry smile, as he and a collection of courtiers and guards came into the library.

Diane curtsied. His Majesty then instructed his entourage, who had hoped to be included in this intriguing encounter, to leave them alone. Diane moved to protest but thought better of it. She held her breath as he closed the doors on his disgruntled friends. Silence followed. The royal library was a shadowy, musty-smelling room, paneled and shelved in dark oak. Leather-bound books lined the walls. In the center of the room between the shelves were three long carved oak tables, each with large candled lamps for reading. A small intricately carved chest had been placed on the table nearest the door.

The King advanced and opened it. Inside were several volumes that he took out and set aside as though searching for just the right one. Diane stood silently beside him gazing around the vast, tomb-like chamber. The frescoed ceilings were edged in gold. Masterpieces ran the length of the walls. She recognized the one in the place of prominence. It was Anne d'Heilly, painted as Danaë by Primaticcio.

"Ah ha! I have found it!" the King exclaimed finally and thrust forth a large claret leather-bound volume, delicately tooled in gold. Dusting off the cover with a brush of the back of his hand, he then handed it to Diane. It was a rare copy of Oppian's *The Chase,* in the original Greek. As she slowly turned the pages, edged with gold leaf, her heart raced.

"Where did you find such a thing?" she asked, barely able to speak.

"I am the King of France, *ma chère,*" he replied as if nothing else need be said.

Diane fingered the pages of vellum; a fine lambskin cloth. Each of them bore one of four hundred miniatures, brilliantly illuminated in shimmering shades of red, blue and gold.

"It is exquisite."

"Beauty seeks beauty. Consider it a gift," he replied. Their eyes met. The King covered the hand that held the book with his own hand. As she had the day before, Diane pretended not to notice his advance.

"Oh but, Your Majesty, it is so rare. I could not possibly—"

"Please take it. It would give me great pleasure. After all, you are quite correct. It is rare, and that would make the refusal of such a gift all the more insulting."

As Diane closed the book and looked up, her eyes shimmering with excitement, the King again met her gaze. Slowly then, he withdrew his hand from hers. "I am the fortunate beneficiary of many precious manuscripts such as these," he added in a softer voice. "There will be others . . . if you become interested."

It was not clear whether he was referring to the books, or to himself as the point of interest, and Diane was certain, as she gazed into his liquid amber eyes, that the ambiguity had been intentional.

LATER THAT AFTERNOON, Diane, Charlotte and Hélène took the longest path back to her apartments after vespers. The sun still shot its muted shades across the horizon, but now there were clouds, as though there might be rain. Diane had wanted to show her servants some of the detail of the chateau she remembered.

Blois was a castle rich in history. It had been built in the thirteenth century by the counts of Châtillon. It was here that Joan of Arc had stopped to have her soldiers take Holy Communion. King François' first wife, Claude, had been raised here. When he became King, he had enriched it in the Italian manner, for his love of her. Then she died, and he seldom liked to come here anymore.

The three women strolled across the open courtyard, laughing and chatting, heading toward the distinctive exterior staircase which was, in itself, a work of art. This architectural and artistic innovation was the talk of France, and Diane was anxious for them to see it.

The staircase was a spiral-shaped incline, and at each landing there was an area that looked down on the common below. But they were not only stairwells. From them, courtiers and nobles had often stood, as from a balcony, for jousts and plays set down in the courtyard.

As they rose to the steps of the third level, they could hear the sound of laughter coming toward them from the hidden landing above. Then a woman's voice, shrill and chatty. It was Anne d'Heilly. Diane remembered the voice, and the hostile eyes that had gazed at her from across the room the night before. But it was too late, though she had considered it, to turn the other direction and avoid her. Just as the thought passed across her mind, Anne d'Heilly turned the corner onto the landing where she stood with her two ladies.

She stepped down in a full gown of green brocade edged in gold. The collar and the cuffs of her sleeves were faced with sable. Her head was adorned by a hood edged in gold. She was followed by a train of courtiers and attendants all laughing with the same wicked laugh as she.

"Madame La Sénéchale, what great fortune!" she said, smiling her acid smile, and laughing with her friends, having addressed her with the title she well knew Diane did not wish to be addressed. "We were just speaking of you."

A chill raced from Diane's spine and blossomed on her face as she gazed into the contemptuous green eyes. The courtiers behind her engaged in a collective muffled snicker.

"Monsieur Sourdis here was just telling us something that he had discovered in his work for the King. A fact little known, I am sure, and one that I found truly fascinating."

Diane and Anne studied one another like two prowling cats as Anne played at civility. "Did you know, Madame, that on the very day that you were being married, I was being born?" Anne d'Heilly smiled with satisfaction and glanced around again as she said it. "Can you imagine such a coincidence? It truly surprised me, since you certainly do not look to be so much older than I."

Diane looked around her at the sea of vengeful faces all hoping to humiliate her; all in the name of their mistress's insecurity. She considered her words carefully, but there was no choice but to say them; not if she hoped to survive here.

"Then, Monsieur Sourdis," she began, looking over at Anne's accomplice. "I am afraid you are mistaken. His Majesty's valet had mentioned to me only last night at supper that Mademoiselle is twenty-six. That would make her five at the time of my wedding."

She forced the tone of her voice to remain stable, even though her throat had gone completely dry and her legs were in danger of giving way. She then turned her head toward Mademoiselle d'Heilly with as much confidence as she could enlist and added, "It was a natural error in calculation."

"I am certain. A simple mistake."

Their eyes remained locked in a sustained combative stare. After a moment, Anne lifted her skirts as if to proceed down the stairs. Before descending, however, she turned and looked again at Diane. Her green eyes shimmered with the same hostility they had from the moment of their first introduction.

"Well. It is apparent that I have underestimated you, Madame. Age has only sharpened your mind. I would not have expected that. It is comforting to know what I may anticipate when I am older."

Diane stood a moment on the landing trying to catch her breath after Anne d'Heilly and her entourage had passed by.

Charlotte, who had gripped Hélène and held her in the corner of the landing, still pinched her arm to prevent her from speaking out against the attack. Diane looked over the stone balustrade and down onto the courtyard. Her cheeks still burned. She watched them laughing and whispering as they went through the garden and into another wing of the chateau.

The King's mistress had implied volumes more than she had said. Never had Diane expected such hostility by returning to Court. *Such unbelievable . . . such petty childishness!* In all of the time she had attended the former Queen, she had always been welcomed. She had made friends with both the former Queen and the King's former *favourite*. But things were very different now. Everyone seemed to want to remind her of that. Anne d'Heilly obviously mistook her presence here as a threat to her own security with the King.

If only she knew that I detest his wandering eye and his indiscriminate appetite. What a mockery he makes of love! If only I could tell her how a man like that sickens me and would never share my bed. Never! But of course, she could tell Anne d'Heilly nothing. To calm the royal *favourite*'s fears, Diane would need to risk insulting the King, and it was not worth that. At least not yet.

ANNE D'HEILLY SMILED like a cream-filled cat as she lounged on a spray of red and green silk pillows spread about the floor near the fire. The rooms of her apartment were filled with the same group of people who had attended her earlier that morning on the grand staircase. A young boy played a tune on the lute as a gentle mist appeared outside and the bright morning skies darkened for rain.

"Very well, Monsieur Vouté, read us another!" she commanded as she took a sip of spiced Madeira wine from a large silver jewel-encrusted chalice.

Jean Vouté was a Court-appointed poet but was considered by everyone to be her personal jongleur; for he had made his way at Court by writing verses exclusively to flatter and please the King's young mistress. He had done his job well, but not by flattery alone. The slim little man, with squinted eyes and a pointed chin, possessed the uncanny ability to surmise the situation with the skill of a politician, and then never failed to act upon it.

Vouté stood and faced Anne as well as Philippe Chabot beside the roaring fireplace. He bowed cordially to the one on whose grace he depended. She nodded back.

"If it please you, Mademoiselle, I have composed a little trifle for your enjoyment. It is a poem about a woman. One well past her prime . . ." He looked around the room and nodded as he spoke. "I call it 'The Wrinkled One.'"

A smile broadened slowly across Anne d'Heilly's little cherry mouth. "Please continue."

He read the words slowly, punctuating each line with his own distinctive flair. As he read, each face in the salon, one by one, broadened. Their smiles were evil, brought on by thoughts of an impetuous act that is about to be undertaken against another. When he had finished reading the verse, the King's mistress clapped her hands together in wild adulation, her mouth open in a wide laughing smile.

"Oh, bravo, Monsieur Vouté! Simply brilliant!" she squealed. "I think this is a work to be shared!"

"My thought exactly," Chabot concurred. "If you will permit me, I have taken the liberty of having it written down for the enjoyment of . . . others."

As he said the word "others," their eyes met. So did their mirrored grins. "Splendid idea, Philippe. I am certain there will be someone on whom these words will have a particular significance. Perhaps if you were to make several copies available, the appropriate people would be certain to have an opportunity of reading it."

The message was clear to both Chabot and Jean Vouté, who stood nearby. Then Anne reached down to her chest and removed a large diamond and ruby brooch from her gown. "You have done well, Jean. Take this for your trouble."

"My most humble thanks, Mademoiselle," Vouté said, and bowed dramatically with a sweeping hand before him. He took the brooch in his long reedlike fingers and then pressed it to his lips. "I shall treasure it always."

"All right, enough of this. All of you, out, out, out!" Her countenance changed quickly and she cast her guests from her chamber like troublesome pets. "I would like to rest a while before I take supper." The crowd of lounging courtiers disappeared quickly and without incident. All but Philippe Chabot.

WHEN THE DOOR to her chamber had closed and the last person had gone, the Admiral drew near to her. Gently he brushed up behind her, the velvet of his doublet against the silk of her gown. She grimaced as he grazed her neck with his wet lips.

"Oh, Philippe, please! Do stop that. I am simply not in the mood."

"But when will you be in the mood, *mon amour*? You have made me wait such a long time for the return of your favor."

Anne turned toward him and began to run her small nimble fingers beneath the acorn-colored doublet, and then across his shirt. "You know the King is here today. It is impossible."

He embraced her with the timid persistence of an eager child and again grazed her neck with his lips. "Oh but I want you so," he moaned.

Anne lifted his head from her neck and kissed him. Her tongue outlined the curves of his lips and then entered his mouth. He moaned and, as he did, Anne dropped to her knees before him and began to lower his stockings. The moan became a long gasp with the progress of her touch. As she lowered his trunk hose over his buttocks, his penis sprang forth and her kisses turned to gentle, rhythmic licking.

"Oh, do not stop . . ." he begged with breathless whispers, but after a moment she looked up into his eyes with cold conviction and rose to her feet.

"Now that is only a taste, *mon cher,* of what is in store for you," she declared as she straightened her skirts. "But to get what you want, my dear Philippe, you must first help me get what I want."

"Oh, yes . . . anything!" he murmured, his face strained with the pain of unfulfilled passion.

"Good. Then bring me a plan to rid us of that woman, and I shall gladly finish what I have started."

RETURNING FROM morning prayer, Diane could hear Hélène's laughter and Charlotte's throaty chortle as she neared her apartments. Their happy sounds flooded the entry to her apartments as she opened the door.

"Oh, mistress, you must read this!" Hélène giggled as she ran toward her, and thrust forth a sheet of rolled parchment. Diane took it in her own hands and unrolled it. Her face filled with the blood of anger as she read the words.

"Where did you get this?"

"It was on the doorstep when we returned from our meal in the kitchens," said Charlotte.

Hélène and Charlotte looked at one another, then both looked back at Diane. "There was another just like it on your writing table," Hélène added. Before she could finish her sentence, she felt the sharp pinch of Charlotte's thick fingers on the skin of her forearm pressing her to silence once again.

"We thought it would please you, Madame, to read something with a bit of humor to it," said Charlotte. "If we have acted inappropriately, I take full responsibility."

Both women hung their heads like great broken stalks as Diane looked back at the parchment to read the rest of the verse.

"This is her doing," she muttered as she read the words. "She means to insult me by these verses."

"You, Madame?" Hélène asked, her softly knitted eyebrows closing in a frown. "Why, that simply cannot be. It is called 'The Wrinkled One.' It is about someone old and ugly, which, if you will permit me, certainly does not describe you."

"It is an epigram, Hélène; a dramatization of the facts for effect."

"I cannot believe anyone would stoop so low," Charlotte declared, and yet remembering as she did, Mademoiselle d'Heilly's hostility on the spiral staircase two days before.

Diane walked into the sitting room of her apartment, her serene confidence gone. She fell into one of the tall, cushioned chairs and washed a hand across her eyes. "No. It is a message for me from her. There can be no doubt about that. She fears I wish to steal the King and she is fighting viciously with all that she has."

DIANE FELT AS if she had been granted a reprieve. After their encounter in the library, affairs of state had taken the King and several of his advisors to his palace, Chambord, leaving the rest of his entourage at Blois. In his absence, His Majesty had left word that he wished his guests to carry on as they pleased.

Knowing no one at Court but Jacques de Montgommery made socializing difficult, so Diane contented herself throughout much of the day by reading, sprawled across the heavy poster bed. Books were a passion that she had acquired long ago. They had helped her stave off the lonely and isolated hours married to an older man in the prison of his country castle. Books truly had been for her, as she had told the mocking King, the sustenance of her life. The growing resentment toward her from Anne d'Heilly became more evident each day and Diane was, in fact, quite happy to stay tucked safely inside her apartments, poring over the wonderful volume that she had been given by the King. She had grown accustomed to idleness and solitude early in her life.

By their fifth day at Court, conditions outside the old stone palace had turned abysmal. The gray skies mirrored the gray brown slush on the ground. Then on the sixth day, as an explosion of rain tore through the winter sky, a tall uniformed boy from the King's guard delivered Diane a written message which changed everything. It was from Anne d'Heilly:

> *Please join me for an evening of entertainment. My private apartments. Tonight at eight.*
>
> *Anne d'Heilly*

Beneath the invitation was another message obviously written in a different hand, for the strokes were more forceful. *I do so look forward to learning more about you,* were the words scrawled in bold black ink. Diane's heart was racing. It was a ruse. It must be. Anne had made her feelings quite clear on the staircase landing earlier in the week. Once again, however, Diane was trapped by protocol. If she was to refuse the invitation, it would be an insult to what was ostensibly a grand gesture of friendship. If she accepted, there was no telling to what evils she would be subjected.

"Madame, perhaps we could say that you are ill and unable to attend," Charlotte suggested as she sat before an embroidery stand. Hélène sat near her on the windowseat, unwinding a spool of yellow string for the piece on which they were working.

"No, Charlotte. If something is in store for me, she will only postpone the invitation. I cannot run away from her, unless I choose to leave Court altogether."

"You are very brave, Madame."

"No, Hélène, she simply leaves me no alternative . . . and she knows it."

Hélène cast the spool of string on the floor and bolted from her seat, sending the embroidery stand tumbling to the floor.

"She is not fit to take supper in the same room with such a lady as you, Madame. Even if she is the King's mistress!"

"I commend your loyalty, Hélène, but it is precisely because she is the King's mistress that I must go." Diane walked slowly to the door and then turned around. "But first, I am going to chapel," she said. "To try to find some strength to face what undoubtedly lies ahead."

4

𝒲ELL, GENTLEMEN?"

The King waited until the carved oak doors to the council chamber at Chambord were closed. Then he turned back toward the long, narrow table. The English Ambassador to France had just seen himself out, having delivered his recommendations for improvement in relations between the two countries.

"Well then, what do you think?" he asked.

François stood, his hands on his hips, facing his three senior advisors, all of whom were still seated at the long council table. Montmorency looked down at a stack of papers which he was shuffling. He was visibly perplexed by the delicate situation that had been left for them to decide. Philippe Chabot shifted in his seat and propped his chin in his palm. He tried to avoid the King's gaze. François loomed at the head of the table and surveyed their blank faces.

"It is an unusual suggestion," Duprat finally said, his heavy face worked into a frown. The King gripped the back of his own large chair and leaned forward. The air was filled with tension. It had been a long day in a dark, damp hall and they were all weary. "You do know what he was really suggesting beneath that polite exterior of extended vagaries, do you not?" asked the King.

Duprat and Montmorency exchanged a glance as they watched the King's anger build.

"He suggests that We plead Our good brother's case before the Pope!" He slammed the large tapestried chair into the parquet floor to punctuate his claim. "*Mon Dieu!* That is what he wants for the promise of his support against the Emperor!"

"The Ambassador requests only another hearing of King Henry's case, Your Majesty. He believes your support could have great influence in Rome," Chabot cautiously defended.

"He requests an annulment, Admiral!" the King raged, "and he wants France to support it so that he can marry that whore of his, Anne Boleyn! How can he even ask such a thing as annulment when the Queen already has a daughter by him?" Chabot lowered his head. "Gentlemen, my friends . . . we are a Catholic nation. Henry VIII requests that all the world turn their heads while he commits a mortal sin, and he wants our support in doing so; can you not see that?"

"Well . . . I suppose by a stretch of one's imagination, it could be seen, as the English Ambassador paints it, as a case of incest, which King Henry is trying to put right by divorce. After all, Your Majesty, he did marry his brother's wife."

"His brother's widow," Chabot corrected.

"Monty, *mon vieux,* what say you of this?" the King asked as he sat back down among his aides.

"I say it is preferable to the marriage of your son to the Pope's niece . . . Your Majesty."

François ran his jeweled fingers through his thick chestnut hair and then sat down. In this world alliances were everything. England or Italy. Spain or even Turkey. He closed his eyes. "Perhaps We should leave no stone unturned in this expedition of Ours. Very well. We shall put the matter over to further consideration. We shall have an answer to give to both King Henry and to the Pope by the time We return to Blois."

ANNE D'HEILLY'S APARTMENTS were lit with the bronze glow from brightly burning wall sconces and the reflection of the flames from the large carved fireplace. The air was filled with the gentle scent of rosewater and dried hibiscus leaves that were set about the rooms in large silver urns.

In the far corner warming his hands before the fire, was François de Guise, the Cardinal's young nephew and the King's newest page. He was chatting in low tones with one of Anne d'Heilly's attendants, a striking raven-haired girl names Caroline d'Estillac.

On the other side of the room, Admiral Chabot leaned against a rich paneled wall beside Jacques de Saint-André, the son of the tutor to the absent Prince Henri. Even though the Admiral looked like he was listening to Saint-André, he could not take his eyes from Anne. He watched her flit about the room checking the wine and the silver trays filled with tiny meat pastries. He also saw when she landed on the lap of Christian de Nançay, Captain of the King's Guard.

Philippe's narrow eyes narrowed still further as he watched, with kindling jealousy, Anne whisper seductively in the young man's ear. He understood her attentions toward the King, but her open flirtations with a minor military officer was offensive. The

Admiral glared at the Captain hoping to convey his anger, but Nançay looked in the other direction.

Jacques de Saint-André, the young man who stood beside Chabot, was tall and slim, with an angular jaw, pronounced cheekbones, and smoky sensitive eyes. His cropped blond hair seemed naturally to brush itself in a direction away from his face on which he had only recently grown a neat pointed beard. Costumed in a white satin doublet, puffed sleeves, gold brocade trunk hose and a plumed toque to match, he leaned casually against the casement of a long window. As Chabot fumed, Saint-André surveyed the ensemble of courtiers who slowly gathered in the various rooms of Mademoiselle d'Heilly's apartments.

"This is quite an ensemble," he quipped, and took a sip of burgundy from a silver chalice. "To what do we owe the pleasure of this mysterious event?"

Still unable to break his gaze from Anne, Philippe replied from the side of his mouth. "To incredibly good fortune, my boy. And if all goes as planned this evening, the pleasure will definitely be mine."

"Where is His Majesty, the King this evening?"

"Gone to Chambord with Grand Master Montmorency, to receive the English ambassador."

"What a shame," Saint-André said smugly, "that he will not be here for the . . . festivities."

He took another sip of wine and glanced around the room. That would be the extent of his inquiry. He intended to mind his own business, knowing that it was decidedly safer that way. But one thing was remarkable and highly suspect for a group of Anne d'Heilly's usually eclectic friends. All of her guests were suspiciously young. So far, all except for Admiral Chabot.

As Diane neared the wing which housed the apartments of Anne d'Heilly, she could hear noise and laughter much as she had her first night at Court. But this time, unlike the last, she was not late. Her invitation had been clear. Eight o'clock, and it was just that now. Her stomach tightened. *Perhaps I should have feigned illness,* she reconsidered.

"Madame Diane! How good of you to come," Anne d'Heilly called out and swept across the room toward her. "We were not certain you were coming. It was getting so late."

Though her instinct was to refute the lie, Diane bit her tongue. She would do her best not to give Anne the argument she obviously desired.

"Please, make yourself comfortable. Try to mingle and meet some of the others. I do not believe you know anyone here; a difficult task, but not insurmountable," she said before disappearing into a collection of her elegant guests.

Diane took a goblet of hot spiced wine from one of the stewards and drank it quickly. At the very moment that she lowered the empty cup from her lips, Jacques de Montgommery drew near her from behind a group of ladies.

"How wonderful to see you again," he said with a bow, and then taking her hand in his own, kissed it politely.

"You look much improved since we last met," she replied with a crooked smile.

"And you look magnificent as ever," he returned, and tipped his plumed toque to her.

"What a rogue you are, Captain. Always so quick to flatter."

"Not so much a rogue as I would like, I am afraid, since my manner results in nothing more than your avoidance of me."

"Not at all, Monsieur," she laughed nervously, and tried her best to sound sincere. "I have just been feeling a little under the weather myself these last few days." It was easier to lie than to tell him that, in truth, she had been reluctant to make herself visible since the incident on the staircase with the King's mistress.

"Well, now that you are well again, you must agree to go riding with me once we have arrived at Fontainebleau. Mind you, I shall not take 'no' for an answer this time, and I do promise to be ever the gentleman." He smiled and touched the tip of his beard.

"Fontainebleau?"

"Why, yes, of course. The King is to return tomorrow from business at Chambord, and the entourage will leave shortly after for his palace near Paris."

"But we . . . I have been here little more than a week."

Montgommery laughed out loud and took a long swill of wine. "Silly girl. If you mean to find a place to settle, this Court is not the place for you! His Majesty loves nothing better these days than to uproot us all and take us packing from chateau to chateau. Apparently he finds excitement in the moving. After having been here the better part of two years now, I personally find it nothing more than tedious. On such trips the lot of us, those who do not share his bed or his favor, that is, are reduced to scrambling for inns or farmhouses at which to spend the night whenever he deems that he is weary. It is a bit like the game of musical chairs; hundreds of courtiers, servants and guards, all scrambling at the same time for only a few dozen beds. The great bulk of us know only too well the sound of chattering teeth or the feel of sod under our blankets for having to make our bed in any field we can find."

Montgommery took another sip of wine. "But then we all do what we have to do, to stay in His Majesty's good graces, do we not?"

"Well, you could be right, Monsieur. Perhaps this Court is no longer a place for me." She glanced around the room. "So many things have changed, and I feel positively ridiculous here. There is not another single person in this apartment anywhere near my age."

"Oh, Madame, surely you are mistaken. The Admiral is at least that!" He caught the slight in his words as he said them, but delivered them so quickly that he was at a loss to stop their expression. "Or older!" he added feebly.

Montgommery by her side, Diane tried to mingle but all the while she waited like a hen for slaughter. Anne d'Heilly might wear a mask of civility, but her eyes, those piercing emerald eyes, gave away her true intent.

"Oh, they are going to do the Passepied! Madame, dance with me!" Jacques pleaded.

Before she had a chance to object, they were gliding together toward the area of the room that had been set aside for dancing. It was opposite the hearth, where the large Turkish carpets had been rolled back. As she danced, Diane could not stop her thoughts from drifting back to the anonymous poetry that had mysteriously made its way into her apartments the day before. She was certain that it was the work of the King's mistress. Before long, however, she was caught up in the complex steps of the latest dance and even began to enjoy it.

"Oh, I have had enough, Jacques!" She laughed and broke from him.

She walked toward a table filled with silver trays of small sweet pies and candied fruits. Beside them, a steward stood clad in red and blue livery, holding a tray of silver wine goblets. Diane took one and handed it to Jacques, then took another for herself.

As she began to breathe easier, she wiped her brow with the back of her hand and noticed her companion's attention begin to wane. His eyes looked beyond her. After another moment of his fading attention, Diane turned around and found the subject by whom Jacques was now so openly riveted. It was Anne d'Heilly's attendant, Caroline d'Estillac. The very stylishly dressed young woman had been commanding attention from a bevy of other courtiers for the better part of the evening. At the moment, she was speaking with the King's new young page, François de Guise, but it was clear that she was caught up in Jacques de Montgommery's flirtatious glances.

"Nice looking pair, do you not think?" Diane grinned as she looked back at Jacques.

"Oh, she would never couple with a boy like—"

Before he finished his sentence, he caught a glimpse of the smile broadening on Diane's smooth pink lips. The surprise of her observation returned his attention completely to her.

"Well, are you not full of surprises!" he declared. "Not only are you rich, beautiful and principled, but you are sharp as a pin."

"I take it, Captain, by your open flirtation that the young lady has not, shall we say, set her principles quite so highly as I have."

"Dear lady, there is no one in all of France to whom I would rather give my heart so much as to you. But, as I told you, this is a very different Court than the one that you saw through the rose-colored glass of the Grand Sénéchal de Normandie."

"But then, your heart really has nothing to do with your interest in her, does it, Captain?"

He laughed an easy laugh and reached out to touch her cheek. "You really are quite an exceptional woman, Madame de Poitiers. I shall very much look forward to our ride together at Fontainebleau, but not nearly so anxiously as I shall attend the loosening of your principles."

AT THE EVENING'S BANQUET, Diane sat at Montgommery's right. Caroline d'Estillac sat on his left. Late into the evening Diane had turned and inadvertently seen the two of them holding hands and intertwining their legs shamelessly. Her back turned to them again, Diane could only hear the muted strains of the mating ritual. It sickened her. Jacques took love from the highest bidder, Diane thought. At this moment she had nothing to bid, so he had turned elsewhere.

The sting of rejection dizzied her as she continued to sip her Bordeaux and pick at the moist flakes of pheasant meat which she had shoved to the edge of her plate. After a moment, she took a handful of her supper and cast it to the floor beside her where two hunting hounds lay in wait.

"Oh, splendid, Vouté is going to play!" Jacques declared, sliding his arm down from Caroline's shoulder, and planting it on her thigh.

Diane turned her attention to the center of the room. A small man with stringy black hair came forward. He took a chair that had been placed in the center of the dining tables. Everyone applauded as he positioned the lute on his lap and brushed away the strands of hair which fell limply into his eyes. Diane leaned back and took a lingering sip of wine. The evening is nearly over, she thought. It would not be long now before she would be safely tucked in bed.

The lute player had a strange nasal voice, not at all pleasing, but the others seemed so enraptured by his words that Diane tried vainly to focus on him. The little man sang flowery lyrics about love and devotion, peppering each phrase with a myriad of double entendres. After each song, he was applauded wildly, which necessitated his launching into another even more wicked verse. Diane leaned back in her chair trying to block out the view of the unscrupulous attendant who now was fondling Jacques de Montgommery beneath the table cover.

"Sing your newest verse!" a woman's voice implored, and the shrill tone of it jolted Diane from a state of comfort, back to a harsh reality. It was the voice of Anne d'Heilly beckoning another song. Diane's heart began to race again as she caught a glimpse of the fiery emerald eyes.

"THE WRINKLED ONE"
This is the tale of an old and toothless coquette,
Nothing is lacking . . .

The poet chuckled as he sang, and a sea of muffled laughter filled the room. There were sideways glances toward Diane.

Wrinkles,
white hair,
falling teeth,
A state of alarming decrepitude.
But she is one who will never obtain
the lover she desires, no matter what she does,
for painted bait, catches no game!

Diane's skin turned to gooseflesh. Now it was completely clear. The poetry left in her room. The guest list tonight of adolescents. She sat completely still, unable to move. As Vouté sang his cryptic verse, Diane turned her gaze slowly, hypnotically toward the fire. There, Anne d'Heilly raised a small glass goblet in salute to Diane and smiled her Cheshire-cat grin.

Nearly everyone saw the exchange between the two women so, by custom, their gazes were now forced upon Diane. She was not the champion but the challenger, and it would be up to her to respond. To Diane, the echo of their pregnant whispers and their wry snickers was deafening.

My God, I am not a woman of the world after all, I am only a helpless child!
I am cub to her lioness. I am completely defenseless against her wrath. She rules

this Court. The look on the faces of everyone here shows me that. They want her to win. They want me to lose. She is the champion! Yet I cannot leave here. I cannot, God help me, risk insulting the King!

Once Vouté had finished singing the final lines, he stood to take a long lingering bow toward Anne d'Heilly. Then he turned to face Diane, removed his toque and, with it, took one last, long sustained bow.

She wanted to choke. She wanted to die. Her face was hot with the flush of embarrassment. Her throat was dry. She turned to Jacques to rescue her; to take her away from these rooms. What she saw was the last thing she would have expected. Jacques de Montgommery was laughing as loudly as all the rest.

"Traitor," she muttered as the blood drained from her face.

She felt ill and could feel the dinner that she had just eaten rising in her throat. But she could not leave. She was frozen in her seat. Racing from the room as she longed to do would be tantamount to an admission of defeat. It would be admitting to everyone that Anne d'Heilly's elaborate plan had worked.

"Just laugh it off," Jacques whispered to her from the side of his mouth, as he clapped his applause for Vouté. "Next month she will find someone else on whom to prey."

"I will not be sick . . . I will not be sick." Over and over she whispered it to herself like a litany as the sour taste seeped from her throat up into the sides of her mouth.

After what seemed an eternity, Admiral Chabot called for a brisk Galliard to be commenced while Jean Vouté received his congratulations from the hostess. As the various couples who wished to dance shuffled their way to the dancing area, Diane was able to slip undetected between them. She staggered out the side chamber door into the fresh evening air.

SHE VOMITED IN the snow behind a thick of evergreens outside the corridor behind Anne d'Heilly's apartments. Diane was weak and could barely stand as she leaned back against the cold trunk of an elm.

"Are you all right, Madame?"

She heard a man's voice behind her. She did not recognize it, and in that there was some comfort. She took a small silk handkerchief from a pocket in her gown and wiped her mouth, then the sweat from her brow.

"Mademoiselle d'Heilly is far more cruel than she is beautiful," the young man continued. He moved toward her from the shadows near the apartments from which she had just come. "No wonder Henri despises her."

"Henri?" she asked as she looked up at him and then blew her nose.

"Oh, forgive me, Madame. I have forgotten my manners again. I speak of His Highness, Prince Henri, His Majesty's second son. My father is his tutor and I, his companion. Well at least when it pleases the King, I am. Jacques d'Albon de Saint-André, at your service," he said and bowed to her. Diane looked at him closely, studying his firmly sculpted chin, the cropped blond hair and the sensitive eyes.

"Oh, yes, I remember you. You were talking to the pretty red-headed girl near the fireplace earlier in the evening; Captain Montgommery's girl."

"Everyone is Montgommery's girl at one time or another."

"Oh, surely you exaggerate," she said, taking his arm and letting him lead her to a cold stone bench nearby.

"I wish that were true. But it is all part of the game."

His words reminded her of what Jacques had told her on her first night back. But now the last thing Diane wished to speak about, or even think about, was Jacques de Montgommery. He was now her enemy, as was nearly everyone else at Court. Then the image of Prince Henri returned to her mind. It had been years since she had seen him.

"Little Henri. Such a dear boy," she said, changing the subject after a moment with a retrospective sigh. "I have not seen him since before . . . well, since before . . . his time in Spain. How is he?"

"If you will pardon me for saying so, hardly the little boy it appears that you recall, Madame. Life has been difficult for His

Highness. I do what I can but if you ask me, he never did quite recover from those years in that dreadful Spanish prison."

"But he was such a happy child."

"That may well be true, Madame, but there is barely a trace now of that happy child whom you recall. He is a young man just barely out of boyhood; and a very angry young man at that. He seems to resist everyone and everything just for the sheer pleasure of it. But please, you will keep that between us. He would never forgive me for saying so."

There was a pause between them as Diane leaned back against the ivy-covered wall behind the bench and took a breath. Then it occurred to her.

"If you are companion to His Highness, then why are you not with him at Fontainebleau?"

"I have said too much already. But then, perhaps the risk is worth it. You have a kind face, Madame. My father has always said, you may see the true nature of a person's heart through the window of his eyes."

Diane smiled, having heard the same thing and having had it ring true on more than one occasion.

"The King forbade me to go with him, as His Highness's punishment."

"Punishment?! Why, he is practically a grown man! What could he have done to deserve punishment by the King?"

"Madame, I take my life in my hands for saying so, for the King forbids anyone to speak of it. But in his anger, the Prince tossed one of his tutors into the well for making him recite Latin."

A smile broadened on her face and Diane began to chuckle. Perhaps it was the way he described it. Perhaps it was the image of a small dotty man being dragged, legs dangling, screaming Latin profanities. Whatever it was, the thought of this young Prince in the sea of such viciousness and amid so many games began to warm her heart.

THE CANDLES IN THEIR sconces sputtered and the fire dwindled to a small red glow in Anne d'Heilly's apartments. Still at the dining table where they had spent the evening, Jacques de Montgommery sat tangled in the arms of Caroline d'Estillac. He was kissing her face and neck as she fondled him beneath the table covers. François de Guise, the King's newest page, lay passed out beneath a window. A full tankard of wine in his hand tipped small droplets of red liquid onto his doublet as his chest rose and fell.

Pinned against a door frame, Anne d'Heilly looked hungrily into Captain de Nançay's powerful blue eyes and whispered breathless seductions to him. The sound of another man's voice intruded upon them.

"All right then. Vouté has helped me fill my part of the bargain. Are you now ready to fill yours?"

It was Chabot who whispered anxiously behind Anne. Her face flushed, and without turning around she said in a low tone, "If you will excuse me, Captain, I have business to which I must attend. But I shall return." She followed the Admiral a few paces and then softened her look of irritation. "I always pay my debts, Philippe. I will meet you in your chamber at half past midnight. Do not expect me to stay. Do not even ask. I shall be quick with you but it will be well worth your efforts."

"It always is, *mon amour,*" he muttered through foul breath and then stole quickly from the room.

"What was that about?" Christian asked when she returned.

"Just business, my pet. Nothing for you to worry about."

"Well, are you ready to quit this party for the evening? I was hoping to take advantage of the King's absence. That is of course, if it pleases you," he added, humility now consuming him; a result of their earlier exchange.

"There is nothing I would like better, believe me. But first I have a small debt to settle. I will be no longer than is absolute necessary, of that you may be certain. You may wait here for me, but if anyone comes . . ."

"I know where to hide," he said. They smiled at one another, the past anger having been forgotten.

"Oh, I do adore you," he muttered.

"Of course you do, *chéri,*" she replied, kissing him on the cheek, and then hurried alone to the Admiral's apartments.

*T*HE ROYAL UPHOLSTERERS had left Blois several days early. Their destination was Orléans, a town in which the King and his entrouage were likely to sojourn on their way to Fontainebleau.

It was not easy to tolerate the descending of the King's massive entourage on their small towns and villages, so that even the craftsmen were given soldiers to accompany them should a town unwisely refuse or impede their passage. They were, except for large towns like Orléans, meager villages with high taxation and little profit. At best they were managing a living on the land. They knew what the presence of the upholsterers foretold.

When His Majesty later descended upon one of them, it was in the company of hundreds of hungry, raucous, lusty courtiers, soldiers, clergy, ambassadors and servants. Most of his companions, like the King, were oblivious to anything but their own enjoyment. It often took months to recover the livestock and remedy the damage that the royal party left behind. Entire stables were killed for dinner, gardens ruined and houses plundered.

Once the King's journey had begun, the roads running across Touraine were clogged with the steady stream of courtiers. Strong stallions heavily laden with His Majesty's *nécessités* and with his best friends groped their way, inch by steady inch, ambling through the forests and along the streams. Leading the train were the King and his *petite bande.* His little band was a group of the most well-placed and beautiful ladies at Court. Anne d'Heilly and the King's two daughters, Marguerite and Madeleine, reigned over several of the other noble wives and daughters on whose company the King insisted.

The silk-covered horses and the carts balked and slipped beneath the weight of articles that the King required to make the journey pleasant. Tents with bright blue and gold fleurs-de-lys were fastened down with velvet-covered sacks of chaff, which would become beds for the royal entourage who would not be blessed with an inn or a barn. There were carts loaded with casks of wine to be distributed as good will among the townspeople on whom they would descend. Sharing their wine, to the King's mind, made the gorging and pilfering on the towns somewhat easier to reconcile.

Then there were the chests. Hundreds of chests all covered in brocade or tooled in Spanish leather and stuffed onto the wheeled carts. Many contained Mademoiselle d'Heilly's gowns, the newest from Paris and Venice, and her personal effects: gold-framed mirrors, silver hairbrushes and dozens of gold flagons of perfume. Others held His Majesty's personal china, glassware, artwork and furniture stuffed in heavily packed hay. François loved to keep his beautiful things with him all the time, so down came the paintings; da Vinci, Raphäel, del Sarto, and the Flemish tapestries, the table covers, the silver and the gold. Down it all came as they set off, bound homeward. Bound for Fontainebleau.

DIANE SAT HIGH on her horse's gold and black leather saddle amid mounds of black silk. She was draped in a brown marten fur cape whose soft tips whispered at the base of her black tapestried hood. Her elegant copper-colored horse cantered through the mire and splashed dollops of mud up onto the edge of her gown.

François rode beneath the drapes of his royal litter several horses ahead of Diane. Closed off from the elements, he was oblivious to the cold winter wind that whipped across the faces and into the costumes of all who had the ambition and the constitution to follow him.

Fanned out across the miles like a river made of brown and gold fur, the rest of the Court trod slowly behind their King. As they rode through the cold windswept valley, they were serenaded by the sounds of trumpets and lutes, and they told stories to help pass the time.

When they reached the forest, Diane had fallen back a few paces and could see Montgommery directly before her. As he rode, he conversed with Caroline d'Estillac and Madeleine de Montmorency, the Grand Master's wife. Though he laughed and gossiped with both women, it was clear that his attention was directed openly toward Caroline.

Diane watched his easy smile. She heard his musical laugh. *To even imagine an attraction to him!* she thought, her pride having suffered more than she would admit. As she watched him, she did not notice the four horses that rode up from behind to surround her, and slid into the same easy cadence as her own steady mount. Jacques de Saint-André, the young man who had been kind to her in Anne d'Heilly's garden, smiled and tipped his purple velvet toque.

"I was not certain you would be going on to Fontainebleau after what happened last evening," he said.

"Nor was I," she replied, matching him with her own warm smile. "But then, I never have been one to give up without at least a bit of a fight."

"I might have known it by the look of you; and I, for one, am glad of it," he said, then turned his head forward to the string of horses that they followed. "It was becoming awfully dull before you came around." His words were simple and he had a kind face. She liked that, and she liked him. Then she turned to the other young men who had ridden up with him.

"I pray you have not brought me more of Mademoiselle d'Heilly's *allies* with whom to deal," she smiled.

The young men looked at one another and then laughed, having all been present at the festivities that final evening at Blois. "No, Madame, I assure you, these three are Prince Henri's very best friends. Madame de Poitiers, may I present François de Guise, nephew of the Cardinal de Lorraine. He has been newly appointed as a page in the King's chamber," said Saint-André. Guise extended his gloved hand to her.

"I am a friend to all possible, and an enemy only when necessary," he judiciously replied.

She studied his gaunt face, hollow eyes and hooked nose and was put quickly at ease.

"This is Charles de Brissac," Saint-André continued. "His parents are both tutors to the royal children. He has known His Highness for many years."

"Madame," said the coarse-featured young man as he smiled.

"And I believe you already know Antoine de Bourbon."

This final young man was tall and husky, with honey-colored hair and wide violet eyes. She looked over at this young member of the prominent house of Bourbon, feeling a surge of empathy for him. His family had never quite recovered from the treason committed by Charles de Bourbon, the same act in which her father had been implicated.

"Antoine," she nodded.

"Would you object if we rode with you a while?" Saint-André asked.

"I should be glad for the agreeable company." She smiled. Then, after a moment, she looked back at Montgommery who continued ahead of them beside Caroline d'Estillac. Diane craned her neck as she watched him lean over to whisper something in the young lady's ear.

"Be careful of that one," urged Brissac, as he too looked ahead at Montgommery. "He will break your heart and a thousand others before he is through."

"That sounds rather harsh," she remarked, and tightened her grip on the reigns.

"I think not," agreed Saint-André. "But whatever you may think of him now, I can promise you this. He shall try in every way to court you because you are a fine lady and because you have a great deal to offer someone like him. But all the while he shall be bedding her, or someone else like her, because only they can give him the something more that he craves, almost as much as money or position."

"That is obscene!" she scoffed.

"Obscene perhaps, but true," Guise chimed.

Diane looked at him. The fur from his collar fluttered near his mouth, soft like snowflakes, as he spoke. "You know, they are now saying that he has made Mademoiselle d'Estillac pregnant, though she scarcely shows evidence of it."

"And I dare say she will not show it if he has his will," predicted Bourbon.

Diane rode between the four young men in silence for the next few miles. Their banter had sent her reeling. They sounded like fish wives. Jacques de Montgommery had been the first man she had even considered courting since her husband's death. That thought had been a mistake. Now she felt utterly foolish. He was charming, educated and very disarming. She had been taken in by that. But like a house of cards, he had come tumbling down at the first sign of trouble from Anne d'Heilly. It had not taken their gossip to show her that. How could she ever care for someone who could not find the courage to defend her; someone who had no honor?

Montgommery and Caroline still cantered several horses ahead of Diane and her new acquaintances. They were all watching when he grasped the bridle of Caroline's mare. All the while, talking and laughing, he casually led their horses in the direction of a thicket of lichen-covered trees to the side of the road. Saint-André looked at Diane and then tilted his head and his gaze toward the duo as a manner of pointing.

"So predictable," François de Guise said, and shook his head.

"At least, Madame," said Charles de Brissac, "if you continue on with him, you must not say that you were not warned."

AFTER THE ARRIVAL of the Court at Fontainebleau, the King was called upon once again to face the situation between himself and the Emperor Charles. François needed Milan. He wanted it so badly that he could taste it. He wanted vengeance on the man who took so much pleasure in surpassing him.

He had not forgotten the way Charles had won the coveted seat of Emperor against him. François had paid 300,000 gold florins in his campaign to win the title. Charles had paid over 800,000; and Charles had won. That had begun the rivalry. Taking his two sons hostage had escalated the rivalry to hatred. But François was avoiding a direct attack on Milan, even though 30,000 royal French troops lay in wait at the country's borders ready to advance. This was chess and one wrong move could spell another Pavia. Another disaster. Another defeat.

He scratched his beard and leaned back in the large oak chair at the head of the table. The other chairs in the large vaulted library were filled with the King's advisors, among whom were the Cardinals de Tournon and Lorraine, and Claude d'Annebault. But most integral to the session was the King's triumvirate: Admiral Philippe Chabot, Grand Master Anne de Montmorency and Chancellor Antoine Duprat.

"What are the chances we can bring Milan under Our Crown if we invade now?" the King asked.

"Limited, Your Majesty, without a solid alliance," Montmorency confessed. "And I am afraid that an English alliance against the Emperor, though most preferable, is no longer an option."

"King Henry feels that he no longer needs an intermediary with the Pope, as he has proceeded with his marriage to Anne Boleyn without his divorce from the Queen," explained Annebault. "His hasty move is probably because she is so very obviously pregnant, and he is hoping for a son this time."

François slammed his fist onto the table. The force of the blow sent the papers before him up and then feathering back down in a scattered array on the table.

"It is a perfect time to take a look at Your Majesty's other options," offered Duprat. "The Pope has sent the Duke of Albany back with a counterproposal to the marriage between the Dauphin and his niece, Catherine de Medici. He now includes Reggio and Moderna. It is a very generous proposal. There were also substantial hints in the offer that His Holiness would support you in your bid for Milan if such a marriage were to take place."

"With those strongholds under the French Crown, our chances of victory in Milan are much improved," noted Chabot.

"Never!" François bellowed. "He wants the Dauphin, and he shall never have him! Not my son!"

"There is always the Sultan, Your Majesty," ventured Duprat.

"The county would be in an uproar if we sided with an infidel!" gasped the Cardinal de Tournon.

Montmorency expelled a long breath then looked at the King. "Respectfully, Your Majesty, an ally is an ally. Suleiman rules the entire Mediterranean sea. His power matches the Emperor in every respect."

"The Sultan is willing to stand with you," Duprat agreed. "He has pointed out, through his Ambassador, that the Emperor is most vulnerable in Italy at the moment, after his sobering experience in Germany. He believes that between the two of you, victory would be absolute."

"But an infidel, man! Good god, what are you asking me to do? We are a Christian people!"

There was a long silence. All eyes rested on the King.

"And yet," he finally conceded, "this is not the time to stand on ceremony. We are running out of options if we mean to have Milan again."

"There is one possibility which has not yet been considered," Chabot interjected. "Perhaps Your Majesty would be well served to consider a variation on the Pope's proposal if you do not wish to side with Suleiman."

"What sort of possibility?"

"Your Majesty has a second son. Prince Henri is also of appropriate age and would make an equally handsome bargaining chit for Italy."

"That is preposterous!" Montmorency growled. "He has been through too much!"

"Henri?" The King said his name as he looked up in amazement. "But he is so sullen; a veritable delinquent."

"Be that as it may, Your Majesty, he is still a Prince of France; from the same house of Valois as the Dauphin. Is that not really what is of foremost importance to his Holiness the Pope?"

François scratched his beard as he considered it. "Henri," he pondered, and then lost himself in the image of his second son. "What a delight he was to his mother; but oh, what a plague he has been on me. I fear he shall never forgive me for sending him to prison in my place."

"Then perhaps Your Majesty should consider the possibility that marriage would settle him, give him direction."

"Your Majesty, please!" Montmorency sprung to his feet, growling like a bear. "Surely you could not consider such a disastrous thing for His Highness in his tenuous state! He is so fragile!"

"Grand Master Montmorency, I shall thank you to remember that I may do as I please! It is I who am King! Besides, I think Henri is not fragile so much as he is insolent. I thank God every day of my life that he is not my first son; not the Dauphin."

Philippe Chabot let a smile pass across his lips for only Montmorency to see, but the Grand Master would not be put off.

"Your Majesty, if Suleiman does come back with the necessary support against the Emperor, you shall be able to conquer Italy and you shall have surrendered your son for nothing!"

"Oh, do shut up!" Chabot snapped.

François sat expressionless, toying with his rings. He studied the face of each of his advisors. Both had their points. If he chose to side with Suleiman, it would be the first real offensive since the disastrous defeat at Pavia. So many lives had been lost. Such a price had been paid. By the power of God Almighty, he alone had been made King. It was up to him to make the final decision and to live with the consequences. But Montmorency was right. Like it or not, Henri too was his son and the boy was troubled. He would ask him to sacrifice no more for France. At least not for the moment.

"And to think," he whispered, slowly stroking his beard. "Sweet Milan; it was mine once." He held up his hand to the others. "I had it right here . . . right here in the palm of my hand."

"So Your Majesty will again," said Duprat. "One way or another. And when that day comes, then there shall be no limit to the glory of France."

OVER THE TOP OF THE garden hedge, Prince Henri had a perfect shot at his brother. Like a cat in wait, he perched silently, scarcely breathing, for the precise moment in which to strike. Metallic black eyes glimmered in the sunlight beneath thick waves of ebony-colored hair. Charles, his full-faced younger brother, stood beside him peering through a break in the hedges.

"Henri, stop it. I don't want to watch anymore," the boy whined.

"Then be gone with you, you whiny little toad, before I decide to beat you senseless. Go on!"

After his brother had gone, Henri returned his gaze to the other side of the hedge where the tall, thin Dauphin, the very mirror of the King, groped and pressed himself tightly against the raised gown of Marie, the daughter of the Comtesse de Sancerre.

"Please, Your Highness, it is not proper," she moaned as he skillfully raised her skirts still higher, his other hand pressing deeply into the cleavage between her two breasts.

"But I will it, and I am to be King!" he muttered as he plied her neck with moist, ardent kisses. "Besides, no one is to know. Just let me do it a little," he persisted as she weakly tried to free herself from his large groping hands.

Henri raised himself over the hedge, observing his brothers' curious bestial behavior. He had seen the stud in the stables last spring as he had persisted in mounting the King's prize mare, but this human encounter was foreign to him. Even more, it was repugnant.

He could not believe that people could actually enjoy committing such an uncivilized act. It was an odd thing to watch, all the skin and sweat, and Henri found himself taken from his own mission. He watched as his brother coaxed the young girl into submission between the boxwood hedges.

"Splat!" The stone reeled from the sling shot, pelting the Dauphin on his bare, rising buttocks.

François shook his head, and without needing to identify the offender, yelled, "Great Zeus, Henri, I shall get you!"

He faltered as he raised his puffed-velvet trunk hose, and then charged through the bushes after his younger brother. Henri was faster. He ran like the wind between the neatly cropped hedges and through the maze of tall yews and rose bushes. Only a stray bramble impeded Henri's speed, and he finally tumbled to the ground. The two brothers wrestled in the dirt. Henri's fierce anger

overcame his older brother's agility. Henri pulled François' arm
behind his back and screwed it tightly. Both boys were panting
hard from the run.

"Petty little bastard! No wonder Father despises you," the
Dauphin muttered, trying to catch his breath. Henri twisted the
arm tighter and his brother wailed with pain.

"Does not!"

"Does too!"

"Take it back, François!"

"I will not!"

Henri forced his brother onto the ground and pushed his face
into the loose dirt. "All right!" he screamed. "I take it back. But
wait until Father hears what you've done to me. Spying on me like
some seething little lecher, and then flogging me to boot!"

Henri freed his grip on François, who wallowed face down in
the dirt. "You don't really want to do that, now do you, brother
dear? After all, then I should be forced to confess on whom you
were pouncing when I spied you! The King should be most un-
settled to know it, since he has been doing the very same thing
himself to the same little whore!"

Henri loosened his grip on the Dauphin's arm.

"You wouldn't!" François cried. Tears spilled onto his dirty
face as Henri grabbed the limp arm and screwed it tighter once
again. "All right, I won't tell him!"

"Then we understand one another, do we?"

The Dauphin shook his head in agreement and, upon being
released, made his way back to his feet, brushing furiously at his
dusty garments. "What I understand is that I despise you as much
as Father does!" François continued to brush at his dirty stockings.
"I will tell you what else I understand. I understand that you are
going to punish all of us for the rest of your days for what happened in Spain!" He stood erect now and positioned himself in
defense. "Well, little brother, it seems that you have forgotten that
I was in that spartan prison with you! I faced the same harshness,
the beatings, and the same putrid odors; I remember it all as well
as you. I, however, have managed to face our obligations as any

true man of honor would have, and you do not see me whining on and on about the past, or torturing Father for it!"

"He left us alone there for four years!" Henri cried out. "My God, François, I was six years old! I could not even speak our own language by the time we were allowed to come home! How can you forgive him when he returned to the safety of France and let his own sons bear the burden in exchange?"

"The King was needed here. We endured what was necessary for him and for France," the older boy stoically replied.

"But how can you be so passive when the mere mention of it incites in me such violence I could likely kill him if he were here! We spent an eternity in that dark, awful smelling place, and God, how I hate him for it!" Henri's nostrils flared and his eyes welled with tears as he seethed the bitter words.

"I suppose that is what separates the two of us, little brother. Two sons of a great King. One is to be the next ruler of France and the other is destined for a life of banal obscurity. You see, Henri, I have had the grace to forgive His Majesty for what circumstances forced him to do. You are not a child anymore. It is time you tried to grow up and forgive him as well."

"Never!" Henri seethed. "I shall never forgive him! Never!"

"Poor little bastard," the Dauphin sighed, shaking his head.

HENRI WALKED SLOWLY toward the palace, taking a different path than his brother had. He did not want to see anyone. It hurt too much, and his mind was still too full. The anger, the bitterness, and the pain were all jumbled together and impossible to separate. He wandered alone through the formal gardens, past the white iron gazebo, and past countless stone benches, until he knew by the scent of fresh basil and thyme that he was near the kitchen gardens.

The kitchens were a sanctuary; so full of earthy smells and all teeming with life. He liked to go there sometimes and just wander among the staff. He could share a mug of wine or a cup of mint tea and a joke with one of the stewards. They were a curiosity to him with their rough hands and their honest faces. He knew that they were not comfortable with him there. He was, after all, a royal Prince and they were his servants. But Henri thought of it as a place to take refuge from the world; a world away from the excesses and hypocrisy of his father's licentious Court.

He felt himself smile, and then quickened his step. The aroma of freshly baking bread came to him first, then the rich aroma of roasting pheasant. Capon. Partridge. But it was the cake made of pine nuts and marzipan, his favorite, which sent him bolting through the open doors.

As he entered the pantry, he could see the servants gathered around the large stone ovens. They all stood beneath great collections of dead birds that were suspended by the feet from the rafters in preparation for the meal. The walls and low-beamed ceiling were brown and thick with grease. Ropes of onion and garlic hung near the door. Henri pushed aside the servant blocking his view, to see a lifeless bloody mass emerge from the loins of the dog around which the kitchen help had crowded. He was mesmerized by the sight.

"It is so helpless," he whispered, looking at the wet, pink puppy, its eyes still sealed.

"Just nature taking its course, Your Highness," said an old woman named Clothilde, who knelt before the dogs.

"Why is the mother not tending to him like the others?"

"She may not, Your Highness."

"What will become of him?"

Clothilde reflected a moment and wiped her flat nose with a dirty hand before uttering her reply. She rubbed her hand slowly over her chin and mumbled, "Well . . . if she doesn't open the sack soon, the pup'll surely die . . . But then she's got five others to keep her busy."

"No!" he shouted. The kitchen maids, the cooks and stewards looked at him from their crouched positions around the bitch. He had startled himself with his own reaction. "What I mean to say is, is there not something we can do?" The cooks and servants all looked at one another with various expressions of surprise. Clothilde rubbed her nose again.

"We could cut it loose. But then it's likely that the *maman* won't have a thing to do with it."

"Cut it!"

"Your Highness, it needs mother's milk. It'd be cruel to give it life just to have nature snatch it away." There was a note of tenderness in her voice as she rubbed the back of her hand on her long soiled apron, which long ago had been white.

"Please! You must do what you can," he pleaded in a quiet whisper. The old woman, who was hardened by too much work and too many babies herself, was touched by his naiveté. She let a gentle smile pass across her coarse full lips.

"Roland, bring me a knife."

"Oh, Clothilde—"

"Just do it!" she ordered, and the hulking servant washed in perspiration, rose to his feet. He looked at her one last time and then proceeded with a groping movement into the bowels of the hot kitchens.

Henri knelt by the dog who now tended to all but one of her newborn pups, biting at their sacs and licking up the blood. Knife in hand, Clothilde lumbered with a huffing sound, and knelt beside Henri. As graceful and as careful as the artists upstairs, she raised the pup and began to cut the thick casing around him. The mother dog raised her head and let out an impotent growl. Finally, freed from its amniotic prison, the little wet pup squirmed and squealed. As she had predicted, the mother dog ignored it.

"What would make her choose one of them over the others?" Henri asked.

"Some are just bad seeds, Your Highness. Only God knows why. We'll feed it sheep's milk and pray for the best."

He looked at the mother dog who lay several feet away licking and nursing her five other offspring. The orphan, whose eyes were still sealed, squirmed and squealed so helplessly that Henri felt compelled to pick him up. The animal, which fit into the palm of his hand, instinctively began searching for its mother's nipple. Henri drew the little mass of wet fur near to himself, then cradled it with the awe and wonder with which one holds a baby for the first time.

Henri had never loved anyone except his mother, whose quickly fading image consisted now of barely more than a few random memories. The sound of her laugh. The smell of her hair, freshly washed with camomile. Yes, he remembered her hair, but he could no longer remember her face, her touch or her love. *What will become of my poor Henri?* she had asked as she lay dying in her bed at Blois. She knew his father had no use for the boy then, nor would he ever. He was too consumed with his heir, the Dauphin; his François.

Since there were no extra crates or rags that were not needed in the running of the enormous kitchens, Henri looked around to improvise a bed for his little charge. He took a large wooden bowl from one of the cooks and set it at the opposite side of the raging kitchen fire. Then he began to remove his doublet and lined the bowl with his costly yellow silk shirt. Clothilde and Roland looked at one another but neither uttered a sound. Henri replaced the doublet on his bare back like a vest. The pronounced muscles of his arm swelled through the sleeveless jeweled vest, more in the manner of a laboring servant's body than the son of a King.

After the pup had fallen asleep, he was placed near the fire at a distance from the other newborn dogs. Henri looked around the large basement kitchens now that the little creature had been secured, and he sighed. He felt his stomach grumble. All of this and his fight with the Dauphin, and now he was famished.

As Clothilde began to cut a warm cake and Roland went to fetch the sweet wine, Henri sat down on one of the long oak benches at a trestle table in the rear of the low-ceilinged kitchen. He ran his fingers through his hair and watched an old man with no teeth on the opposite side of the bench, rubbing laboriously at a large tarnished-silver urn. Another man sat a few feet away. He and a small barefoot boy plucked feathers from the carcass of a pigeon which the man held between his knees.

"He is a nice enough boy, do you not think?" Clothilde

whispered to Roland as she lay three neat slices of cake on a chipped ceramic plate.

"For the son of a King, yes, I suspect he is."

"Such a nice smile . . . but such terribly sad eyes."

"THERE YOU ARE, you bastard!"

Henri yelled at Jacques de Saint-André and then charged toward him in the middle of the formal parterre. "Where have you been? The pox on you for hiding from me!"

"Oh, no games with me, Your Highness, not today. *Jésu!* I should flog you myself, instead of saving it for my father to do! The real question is, where have *you* been? You know, he has gone again to the King about you. God save you, will you never learn?"

"Learn to obey our Sovereign King? Let the devil take me first!" he said, and then spat on the ground. "Now come on, old friend, do not be cross. Why not play me a game of *jeu de paume* instead?"

"I am not in the mood, Your Highness. You really put me in a very unenviable position with my father over this, you know. He is angry and yet I must defend you."

"Then do not defend me to him! I have told you that before, and I mean it. Despite what you all seem to think, you, dear friend, are not my keeper; and neither is your father. I swore when we returned from Spain that no man would ever do that to me again. Not even the King!"

They walked silently down between two neatly clipped rows of conical shaped yews to the edge of the lake. Two ducks cut a path across the undulating surface of the water and a chilly evening breeze began to stir around them.

Jacques was a patient and a gentle young man. The seven years difference in their ages had fostered in him those qualities. It had also made him the single one of Henri's friends capable of understanding the torment and the rage. Just for a moment today, before he had seen Henri's face, the dark eyes smoldering with their misery and their loneliness, he had forgotten.

He stood silently, watching Henri systematically remove his

shoes, trunkhose and doublet, leaving nothing on but thin silk stockings, then step slowly into the icy spring water. It was still cold. Water carried plagues. This was dangerous. It too, like the frequent disappearances, was an open act of hostility. More than a swim, it was an act of aggression against everything that was decorous and proper behavior for the son of a King. Jacques knew that for now this was Henri's only defense against his wounded youth . . . against a man who openly despised him. He sighed a bitter sigh of pity and, full of compassion, obliged the boy by steadying himself and following him into the water.

"Jacques, I want you to tell me something. Honestly. Have you ever . . ." Henri's voice was uncertain. He paused a moment. "Have you ever *had* a girl?"

Jacques watched the ducks turn in the water and go back the way they had come. Then he looked at Henri, stiff as a statue and gazed back at the main house. "Once. The cook's daughter at my father's manor. But if you ever tell him, I'll swear you made it up!" he defensively added, and then asked, "And Your Highness?"

Henri turned around and looked at Jacques who had managed to come into the lake so far as his knees. He stood, his arms wrapped around his chest, his cheeks and nose red with cold. Henri, who was up to the point of his thighs and completely oblivious to the cold, smiled at how humorous he looked. The sight made him relax. "No," he confessed. "But I did see the Dauphin this morning. He was doing it with one of the King's new whores down behind the stables."

"No!" Jacques laughed. "And you watched? Henri, you devil!"

"It was strange. Ugly. In fact, degrading." He began to wade back up to the point where Jacques was standing. His face, beneath dark curls, was intense. "What is it like? I mean, what does it feel like, to do it?"

"Great Zeus! Everything should feel as splendid. I would likely kill for another chance at it. Hopefully one day when I meet the right girl, all I shall have to do is ask. Lord, how I envy you! All the beautiful young girls at this Court and you have only to choose a willing partner to assist you."

"I hate them."

"You do not mean that."

"All of them so puffed and painted. All smiling and squealing, and smelling of all sorts of potions. I cannot bear the thought of doing *that* with one of those little creatures. The thought of it turns my stomach."

"Well! You certainly are not your father's son!" He laughed again, but this time, nearly as soon as the words had left his mouth, he froze. His skin went ashen. "Oh, forgive me, Henri . . . sir . . . Your Highness. I had no place. Please, forgive me."

"It is all right, Jacques, but if being his son means rolling around with some whore like a barnyard animal, then I would just as soon be the son of a bitch!" He walked past Saint-André and back up onto the grassy shore. After a moment he sat down amid the long spindly blades and began to dry himself with his elegant trunk hose.

"Jacques?"

"Your Highness?"

"How did you know what to do? When you did it, I mean."

"Oh, you should not worry yourself about that. It comes as naturally to us as it does to those animals. You shall see. By my life, you shall see."

No. Not Henri. He would see no such thing. He would not forge around on sweaty female flesh, whining and pleading for the pleasure. He did not intend ever to be that vulnerable. After all, they were really all like Anne d'Heilly. Different hair. Different eyes, perhaps. But inside they were all the same. They gave their bodies as payment for their jewels, their furs and their manors in the country. In return, they took men's souls. He had been a victim of everything else in his life; he would not now fall victim to anyone so closely resembling his father's prized mare.

By the time they rounded the corner of the formal courtyard, it was dark. The two friends crept silently through the entrance to the east wing, which housed the royal apartments.

Undaunted by the lateness of the hour, Henri's groom bowed to the two boys, and then led the Prince into his dressing area where a silver basin of warm scented water awaited. Two other servants stripped off his doublet and his stockings, still moist from the lake. Jacques de Saint-André sat down on a small stool as Henri allowed the page to wash his chest and back.

"Then I take it you are going to attend?" Jacques asked as Henri was then rubbed with a light musk oil.

"Attend what?"

"I was certain that you knew. The King is having a gathering in his private apartments after supper and has invited Father and me. Father of course is ecstatic to have finally been asked, even though the word is that the King again wants to discuss Machiavelli. It is bound to be embarrassing if Father attempts to outshine the King with regard to *The Prince*. They say His Majesty reads nothing else so much as he reads Machiavelli."

"Ah, another opportunity for the old bastard to show how much he knows. How I despise those evenings. Sorry, old friend, but a lesson in Latin from your father would be a more welcome diversion."

"Well, if you will not come for the King or me, at least come for the show."

"Show?"

"Mademoiselle d'Heilly and Madame de Poitiers. It went on the entire time we were at Blois."

There was a long pause before Henri finally said, "Yes, I had heard she was back at Court."

"Indeed she is, and I shall tell you, it is like watching two cats. Or rather, a cat and mouse. It is most entertaining, if a little cruel on the part of Mademoiselle d'Heilly. Madame de Poitiers is not particularly bloodthirsty but she is quite beautiful, which makes it worth the sport."

"Then she has not changed."

"So you do know her."

"I shouldn't flatter myself. She let me wear her colors in my first tournament, some years ago."

"How grand," Jacques smiled and tilted his head back with a dreamy-eyed expression.

"On the contrary. I am certain that she does not even recall it. I was not eleven years old at the time, and yet I fancied myself in love with her."

"How did you get the courage to ask for her colors when you were so young? I could only bring myself to ask my mother for hers at my first tournament."

Henri shrugged his shoulders as the valet covered him with a red velvet robe. "I don't know. She just had such a kind face. I saw her across the field. You must not laugh . . . but it was as if there was no one else there. I thought she was smiling at me, so I rode up before her dais and she gave me her scarf. I hardly had to ask. Her husband, an old man with a hump in his back and these volumes of white hair, was beside her. He only laughed at me, but she just said, 'Ride well, kind sir. May God ride with you.' Imagine that. 'Kind sir.' I was ten years old!"

"Well, she does remember you."

Henri looked up, unable to hide his surprise. "How do you know that?"

"Your name was mentioned one night at Blois. She remembers you quite fondly, as a matter of fact. So, now that you know, will you not come to your father's apartments tonight and keep me company? She is certain to be there and at the very least, it may well put a smile on that sorry face of yours."

"I cannot, Jacques. The King would take it as a sign that I had forgiven him in some small way. No, *mon ami*. I would rather die than give him that."

IT WAS PALE PINK; nearly dawn. Like the night they had met, Diane once again, if somewhat reluctantly, permitted Jacques de Montgommery to escort her from the evening's debate back to her apartments. They strolled from the royal apartments in the east wing and out across the garden toward her own apartments in the west wing. Morning dew glistened on the shrubbery and the sun was just beginning to come up between the trees behind the lake.

"Perhaps you could tell me, Captain, if your intentions toward me are legitimate, as you say, why is it then that you did not defend me?"

Diane posed the question and her words tore into the seductive mood which the unconscionable Montgommery had subtly tried to cultivate between them the entire evening. He stopped only after they had passed back into the chateau, and then leaned against one of the marble pillars that lined the corridor. She stood before him and watched in the candlelight as a crooked smile broadened across the feminine, alabaster features of his face.

"I am a gentleman of honor, Madame. But I am not a fool."

Diane spun around in anger as soon as he had said it, and marched quickly down the corridor away from him. He surprised even himself by following her.

"Now that is not to say that if you were to become my wife—"

This time it was Diane who stopped. She barred his words in mid-sentence with her own. "Your wife? Sir, you are walking in your sleep! That is, without a doubt, the most fantastic dream that I have ever heard."

"Perhaps. But those widow's weeds of yours will grow tiresome soon enough. Think on it, Madame. After all, you know that I do mean to court you."

He was being pompous again. The confident tone, which was meant to seduce her, only irritated her more. She no longer cared why he had not defended her. She shook her head, and began wailing again.

"If you are a man of honor, as you say, then you are a man of your word and you promised there would be no more talk of that, if we were to remain friends."

"So I did," he conceded. "It is just so important to me that you know my position on this. Soon you will need to become more . . . realistic, shall we say. This is a Court for the young. Just look around you. You are a widow who, though the petals are sweet, has passed the bloom of youth. Not that I believe it, mind you, but that of course is what others will soon be saying, if you continue on here unmarried or unattached."

"Of course." She mocked her agreement with a forced smile. "And so being the gentleman that you are, you mean to rescue me from my impending dotage?"

"I will not have you make light of me, Madame. My position here as Captain of the Scots Guard is secure. I am well thought of. I can offer you a place by my side that will allow you to remain at Court long after the King tires of his impotent flirtations with you."

"And just exactly how do you know he shall tire of me?" she asked, her hands now placed pointedly on her hips. "Perhaps I shall become his mistress."

"No. Not you!" he said with confidence. "His Majesty is not your style. I should venture that you like a man all to yourself, which of course, you can never have with the King of France."

"You are very sure of yourself, my dear Jacques. But you would be better served to be mindful of your tongue. You are not so young and desirable to look upon yourself that this manner of talk shall always be tolerated."

By the time the conversation had concluded, they were at the head of the long dark corridor, still untouched by the early morning sun. Her apartments were before them. Montgommery paused and took a torch from the wall to light the empty pathway. He then handed it to Diane. She looked at the cold darkness through which she would pass, and then back at him.

"Since you appear so able to exist here alone," he said, "you certainly can have no need of an escort any further. So, I shall here bid you good night. I ask only that you consider what I have said."

Diane took the torch from Montgommery and proceeded to her apartments without looking back.

BEFORE DAWN, HENRI rushed back to the kitchens. Clothilde, Roland and the rest of the kitchen staff were already dashing about the dark aromatic chateau cellars, preparing breads, roasts and pies while the rest of the Court slept. Henri came down the long staircase which ended in one of the small kitchen anterooms used for storing grains.

He looked across the maze of other rooms to the place near the fire. To the left, near a cord of freshly cut wood, lay the tan-and-white-spotted dog wound around her pups, who were already nursing and pushing one another away from the bulging nipples. Across the hearth, alone in his makeshift bed, the wooden bowl and elegant shirt, was the little abandoned pup.

Henri neared and stood over the bitch and her brood of squealing newborns. He felt his anger rise. The contented mother lifted her head from the cushion and gazed up at him with a look of defiance. Or so he thought. Henri moved away from her and knelt beside the single puppy, cushioned by his shirt, at the other end of the fire. Its tiny chest heaved as he slept. Clothilde lumbered past him with a large pot of hot soup, the steam rising around the features of her heavy face. She shook her head.

"He don't look good, Your Highness. Won't eat a thing from the tip of the rag."

Henri looked down again at the little animal who bore no resemblance at all yet to a dog, as he let out a tiny squeal, as though from some terrible dream. As he did, his small body began to tremble. Henri stroked the little animal with a single finger as its helpless whimper touched off in him a chill of sadness that came from his very soul.

"So alone," he whispered, "so all alone."

Clanging pots. Shouting. The scent of fresh morning pies and roasting meats. The walls dark and thickened with grease. Servants rushing about. All of them were symbols of the continuation of life. He looked back down at the animal and fluffed the shirt beneath him, hoping to provide him with more warmth.

"Best not get too attached to the little mongrel," Roland urged as he passed beside the fire, his own heavy arms full of wood. "Clothilde doesn't expect him to last the day." Roland's face was gentle, his words were honest. He put the wood down and put a large, coarse hand in comfort to the Prince's shoulder. "I'm sorry, Your Highness. It's just nature's way."

Henri could say nothing in reply. He could not bear to stay in the stifling, aromatic kitchen another moment. He felt the perspiration dripping beneath his shirt, his heart racing with a familiar panic. He felt as though he was in prison again, and he must escape. In a long-legged stride, he dashed back up the stone staircase that led to the east hall.

DIANE STROLLED ALONE down the Grand Gallery. She had been to vespers and then for a stroll in the smaller and less formal of the royal gardens. They had just begun to show the first colorful signs of spring. Even the constant irritation by the King's mistress could not dissuade her from pleasure in that.

The day was warm, and more snow was melting. As she now walked, her black damask gown caught the sunlight and warmed her skin through the rich fabric. It was soothing, and with each pace she became more entranced by the intricate stucco figurines poised around the paintings that lined the walls above her. She was unaware of anyone else in the path.

"They say she is a witch. How else could she maintain her youth at her age?" The voice was shrill and haunting. "I say she is the goddess Diana come down to earth as evil Hecate. Perhaps she means to cast a spell on the King!"

A retinue of courtiers chuckled and whispered to one another as they looked over at Diane and watched her jolted back from the meditative state. Of all the barbs that had been hurled her way over the past weeks, this was the most heinous. To have one's character defamed or one's loyalties questioned was a tolerable nuisance to retain a place at Court, but to be accused of witchcraft meant a certain trial and perhaps even public execution. This animosity had reached serious proportions.

"Are you referring to me?" Diane called to the voices in the darkened corridor. Anne d'Heilly stepped forward, her face alive with a vicious smile.

"Madame Diane, what a surprise." She looked around at her

companions who shook their heads in agreement. "My friends here and I were just discussing the origin of your puzzling youth. For one who is no longer young, you still manage to maintain the appearance of it. It is most remarkable."

"What is it that you really mean to say, Mademoiselle?" she asked with a pointed tone.

Anne looked around at the others once again with the mock expression of surprise. "Why Madame, you wound me. I simply desire to know what potion you use. I thought I might find it useful when I am your age."

"The potion is cold water!"

"I think it is not the water so much as what you do to it," returned Anne. "An incantation perhaps?"

"If she is truly a witch, I, for one, should relish an opportunity to be bewitched by her," came a voice from the shadows.

Anne d'Heilly stopped in mid-sentence and let her eyes trail away from Diane. All eyes followed hers and turned to face the darkened corridor from which the voice had come. As he stepped forward, Prince Henri bowed to Diane and removed his toque in a sweeping motion. As he rose, his ink black eyes were still upon her. His hair in color matched his eyes, and fell in sensual curls around his face. It was the sweet face of a boy; but beneath it was the powerful and well-defined body of a man.

"How good to see you again, Madame Diane," he said and then turned toward Anne. "Mademoiselle d'Heilly, if you have any serious proof of witchcraft, I am certain the King would be grateful to know it. Witchcraft is, after all, a sin against God . . . but do remember," he admonished, "what a heavy price one can pay for gossip of the like. It is often turned on the accuser rather than the accused."

Anne d'Heilly stood motionless, nostrils flared. The blood which had flushed into her face mirrored the color of the Prince's shirt. "Pay heed how you speak to me, boy! You are not in so well with the King these days."

"And are you so certain that you are?"

He had struck just the right chord. Without benefit of further argument, she turned on her heels and strutted down the hall, her entourage following obediently behind her.

Diane's lips parted in a smile of amazement. Under the strain of the moment she did not know whether to laugh or to cry. "How can I ever thank you . . . Your Highness?"

He lowered his eyes, and then, fighting for words, he said, "Walk with me in the garden?"

SHE HAD FORGOTTEN the strong features of his face and the impish grin when he smiled. Those things about him had not changed. But now he was nearly a man. Thick neck. Broad shoulders. Legs already begun to muscle from excessive exercise. Still he was so young . . .

She looked at his eyes. Black and bottomless. Despite the smile which rested beneath them now, there was an angry, tortured fierceness in their depths; an anger edged by loneliness that he did not hide so well as he might have thought. There was no trace at all of the charming little boy who had worn her scarf in his first tournament all those years ago.

Henri led Diane into the King's private garden before she said a word. There, she took a deep breath and put her hand to her chest. "I really cannot thank Your Highness enough," she repeated.

"It was my pleasure to get the better of her. And please, I do insist that you call me Henri."

"Oh, I could not possibly. It would not be proper."

"Would you feel better if I commanded you?" he asked with a smile and then blushed for having said it as they strolled amid the new spring greenery, the dormant rose bushes, and little pockets of unmelted snow.

"If it is any consolation, Madame, my father's mistress finds great pleasure in being rude to everyone who cannot serve her in some way."

"Well, I thank you, Your Highness, Henri . . . but in this case I think it is much more than that between us." She hesitated to go on, having wanted very much to put the past behind her. But she felt a strange camaraderie with this lonesome boy; one which craved honesty between them.

"I fear that she has decided to believe the rumors concerning my father's pardon and my relationship to the King."

Like everyone else, Henri had heard the stories; but he had loved her as a boy in a way that would allow no stain to mar her. Looking at her now, he still could not bring himself to alter that opinion.

Diane's father, Jean de Poitiers, had held an honored position at Court. It was in fact this position which had paved the way for Diane's marriage to the highly placed Jacques de Brézé, Grand Sénéchal de Normandie. But during the battle of Pavia, Poitiers had conspired with the King's traitorous Constable, Charles de Bourbon, the King's most powerful and trusted aide.

Their aim had been to unseat the King and turn France over to the bloodthirsty Emperor Charles V, whose intention it was to take France under the Spanish Crown. To protect his own position and his good name, Diane's husband had been the one to reveal the plot of her father. The offense was high treason, punishable by execution. But, at the very moment that his head was to be severed from his body, a mysterious pardon arrived that had been personally sent down from His Majesty.

Diane's father was not to be beheaded after all; but rather, by the good grace of His Majesty the King of France, Jean de Poitiers would spend the rest of his life in prison. The story at Court, and in all the noble houses of France, was that his young nubile daughter, Diane, had paid with her body the debt he owed to France.

"If you told me it was not true, I would believe you," Henri said quietly, a childlike innocence borne out on his handsome face.

"They say I bedded your father. Why else would he have pardoned a traitor?"

"Clemency is the privilege of the King. Doubtless your husband served His Majesty well."

The two strolled on among the mazed paths of hedges in spite of a mild spring mist which began to fall when the sun hid behind the clouds.

"You know," she said, eager to change the subject, "I really cannot believe how much you have changed since I have been away from Court."

"Not really so much."

"Indeed. It is only your eyes which tell me that you are even the same person."

"And yet you have changed scarcely at all since Saint Germain-en-Laye."

"Ah, yes. Your first tourney."

"You granted me your colors."

"I remember. You wore them with honor."

They stopped as they came to the place where the King's garden ended and the kitchen gardens began. He had not been aware until he smelled the familiar aroma of basil and thyme that they had come so far. He had not meant to bring her here, to his secret place. She was the first woman with whom he had let down his guard.

Despite his father's example, and perhaps because of it, Henri had cut himself off from all substantive contact with women. He had meant what he had said to Jacques. He despised their perfumes and their games. More exactly, he feared them. Diane's manner was different. Subtle. Effortless. It awakened within him the same childhood attraction that he had felt for her all those years before.

"Oh, Your Highness!" Clothilde called out as she hobbled toward him from the open kitchen doors. "The tarts are ready; just come from the oven. I've got your favorites . . ." It was not until then that she saw that the Prince was with a woman. "Oh, your humble pardon, please!" She bowed repeatedly in Henri's direction, then toward Diane.

"Please do not apologize. Diane de Poitiers, may I present Clothilde Renard, the finest pastry cook in all of France."

When he spoke, his voice gained a new confidence. The servant blushed and averted her gaze in the manner of a young girl.

"It is a pleasure, Madame Renard," Diane said as she extended her hand. Clothilde wiped the grease from her hands on her dirty apron which rode beneath her sagging breasts. She took Diane's hand reluctantly in her own and squeezed it.

"I would be honored, Madame, if you would sample one of my tarts," she said nervously. "I am told that the Banbury are the tastiest." Clothilde looked at the Prince and then back at the woman. She saw a spark of something between them but she was not at all certain what. Without waiting for a reply, she began to bow, then step backward, heading steadily in the direction of the open kitchen doors.

"That would be very nice, Clothilde," Diane called out as she disappeared through the double oak doors. She looked back at Henri. "What a lovely woman."

"The best. Perhaps it will sound strange, but I believe that she is my touch with reality. If it were not for Clothilde, I sometimes think I would not likely be here at all," he replied, still gazing at the door, a smile lingering on his face.

Now, for the first time, there was a silence between them. Also for the first time, Henri began to feel awkward. "Well, I . . . perhaps I shall see you more often now that you have returned to Court."

"I would like that," she smiled. "It would be nice to finally have a real friend here."

THE KING OF FRANCE was a man tormented.

He wanted the return of Milan. He wanted all of Italy under the French Crown, and the longing he continued to feel grew stronger, more consuming, every day. Italy was an ambition that would not rest.

He sat in the tall carved chair near his bed and watched Marie de Sancerre sleep. For a while she helped to stave off the yearning, but she was only a child. Anne had not looked much older when he had first taken her to his bed; and this one had been almost as good. Or perhaps it was just that his own age made him savor this new conquest more than he might have in his youth.

The girl, the daughter of the Comte and Comtesse de Sancerre, stirred beneath the heavy tapestried bedcovers. François watched as she turned onto her back. The movement exposed tiny round breasts dotted with small pink nipples. *Ah, innocence!* She had it. He wanted to have his own again. This one had been worth keeping her irritatingly ambitious parents around.

But would she be worth losing Anne? Could he start over with her? Her innocence to give him strength? No. He did not want her as badly as he wanted back those early days of carefree abandon; before he had become King. That was what he *thought* when he looked into her wide violet eyes. What he *knew* was that she was younger than his youngest son.

What an old fool I am, he thought. She stretched again, opened her eyes and pushed her cascading yellow mane from her face. François bolted from the chair and dove back between the bedcovers with her.

"Tell me how it was? I must know," he urged.

"Sire?" she asked, wiping the sleep from her eyes.

"How was it between us this time? How, I mean, was I?" He encircled her head with his large hand and began to stroke her hair. "Do I . . . do I excite you yet, even in the least?" He tried not to sound as though he was pleading.

"To be truthful, Your Majesty, I am afraid there is still not much pleasure in it." She cast her eyes away. "I hope that I have not displeased you by my honesty."

"How old are you, *mon ange*?" he asked, then propped himself on his elbow beside her. He could see her hesitate before she replied.

"Nearly thirteen, Sire."

François gasped and rolled onto his back. "And your mother . . . your parents, do they know you are here with me?"

"Yes, Your Majesty, they do."

"What did they tell you, Marie?"

The girl returned his gaze and then sighed as though her reply was a great struggle. "They told me to give you whatever you desired and to ask nothing in return."

"Guard! Guard!"

An army of guards rushed into the bedchamber, their rapiers drawn. "Captain, take this child back to her parents and inform them that they will be required to leave Court before the sun has set. I cannot stand the thought a moment more!"

The little girl screamed, terror stricken, as she was plucked naked from the King's bed. "No! No! Please! They will kill me!"

François watched her thrashing limbs. Great God, a child of thirteen! He turned from her as the guard covered her mouth with his hand to stifle her screams.

"Let her at least have a gown, for Lord's sake!" he ordered and covered his own face with his hands to avoid further sight of the pleading girl.

Chabot and Montmorency both sprinted down the hall and into the King's bedchamber in just enough time to see the child being dragged, kicking and screaming, out of sight.

"What is it, Your Majesty?" the Grand Master panted.

François' sigh was heavy. "Oh, nothing a dose of reality has not cured."

$\mathcal{H}$ENRI HAD DECIDED to attend the ball that his father was giving that evening. It had not been an easy decision since he had not attended any of the functions in over two years. But there was the thought, the possibility, of once again seeing Diane de Poitiers. For a moment, Henri let his anger pass.

"What will Your Highness wear?"

"What?" Henri turned to the sound of his valet's voice.

"To the banquet, Your Highness. What will you wear? I shall need to prepare it. I thought perhaps you might select from the maroon satin doublet with the topaz and pearls or perhaps the teal blue. If I may say, both are exceptionally smart on you."

"Choose whatever you like."

Henri stood still as his valet draped a white muslin riding shirt around his back and then pulled each arm in through the sleeves. As he began to cover the shirt with a brown leather doublet, another servant was dispatched to answer a knock at the door. Henri turned to see the face of Roland, his cap in his large hands and his head lowered.

"I am sorry to come to you like this, Your Highness. I know it's not proper, but Clothilde has sent me."

At the grave look on Roland's face, Henri pushed past his valet and cast the doublet onto the floor. "What is it? Is she ill?"

"No. I am afraid it's the pup. He's dead, Your Highness. Just gave up, not an hour ago."

Before Roland could utter the last few words, Henri raced out of the room past him and down the long corridor toward the kitchens. His leather soles pounded against the tiled floors as he broke into a run. Roland hobbled behind him but, having been born with an uneven leg, he was no match for the furious speed of the Prince.

Henri fought back tears as he ran down the long staircase, and through the Grand Gallery then past the library and past the tapestry maker's shop. He ran down the dark winding stone kitchen stairs two at a time so that he lost his balance and tripped at the bottom. Clothilde sat by the fire and looked up when he came in. The other servants stopped what they were doing and bowed to Henri.

"Where is he?"

Clothilde looked toward the little makeshift bed he had made and then motioned for him to advance. After a moment, he knelt and stroked the pup's tiny face with the back of his finger. The skin was still warm.

"We will bury him for Your Highness," Clothilde said.

"No! . . . I will do it!"

With trembling hands, Henri lifted the rich yellow shirt with the dead animal wound inside. Clothilde and Roland followed grim-faced out into the garden behind the kitchens.

"At least let Roland dig the grave."

After it was done, Roland stood aside as Henri lowered the silk shirt into the hole. "Oh, Your Highness, not the shirt as well. It is such a fine thing," Clothilde whispered.

"Leave it with him! It was the only thing he had in this wretched world."

Honoring his wishes, Roland and Clothilde stood by as Henri himself shoveled the last heap of dirt. Then when he asked, they left him alone, a silhouette in pink sun, standing over the small makeshift grave.

BY THE TIME his friends had coaxed Henri out of his apartments and they walked the chateau's labyrinth of corridors, the vast banquet hall was already filled to capacity. It bowed with the sound of raucous chattering courtiers and the noxious scent of mingling perfumes. Ambergris, Tibetan musk, and damascene rosewater; all of it fought the rancorous odor of unwashed flesh and soiled garments too fragile to clean. Music and laughter were everywhere.

Flanked by Brissac and Bourbon, Henri took a goblet of wine from a steward's tray and swiftly emptied it. After their reunion, he and Madame de Poitiers had arranged to play a game of *jeu de paume*. Although they had spent much of the following afternoon on the courts, now, only one day past, the prospect of seeing her again made his heart race with fear.

"Henri!" Jacques de Saint-André came up behind the Prince and slapped him across the back as the collection of noble young men rallied around one another. "So good to see you here! What a surprise!"

"With any luck, the King shall not have occasion to say the same," he replied, motioning across the room toward his father and then emptying the second cup of wine. "Let's get a drink, shall we?"

Jacques smiled and put a hand on Henri's shoulder. "So, are you going to tell me what brought you out, or must I spend all night guessing the reason."

"I simply felt like it, that is all. Must there be a reason?"

Jacques' smile fell. "No, Your Highness, no reason at all."

François de Guise and Charles de Brissac joined them. "What a surprise, Your Highness," Guise said a little too loudly. "It is good to see you here!"

Brissac surveyed the crowd. "It is a lovely party."

"Another of the King's pretentious displays," Henri grumbled.

His four friends exchanged a glance as the Prince headed for the large double doors that led outside.

"I need some air," Henri said. "I cannot breathe."

INSIDE THE BALLROOM the music and laughter had reached a crescendo as the King danced the Passepied with Montmorency's wife. The Grand Master himself sat at the King's long table watching them and fingering the ends of his silver mustache. Then, the sound of discordant chatter began to rise up near him from the darkened alcove that surrounded the entrance. The shrill sound of a woman's voice grew steadily louder. Soon it surpassed the music. Montmorency finally turned around and saw the Comtesse de Sancerre, followed several paces behind by her husband, who was dragging their sobbing daughter, Marie, by the shoulder. All three were trying to get past the guards who stood sentry at the door inside the alcove.

"You must let me see the King! You must! There has been some mistake. I demand to see the King!" shouted the Comtesse.

Montmorency, part of whose function was the smooth maintenance of the King's household, leapt from his seat to intercede. He instructed the guards to pull the three uninvited guests back behind the marble pillar.

"What seems to be the trouble?" he asked, looking at the Comtesse and then at the guards.

"Not you!" she shouted again. "I demand to see the King!"

"Well, as you can see, Madame," he said, pointing toward the dance floor with a jeweled finger, "His Majesty is engaged at present. Perhaps, if you made an appointment with his secretary—"

"An appointment? Ha! His Majesty has banished us! It is not bad enough that he sullies our good name, and that he has had his way with me and with our daughter, but now that she is made pregnant by him, he sends us packing!"

"Surely, Madame, there is a better time for this. At present the King is entertaining."

"Indeed! I know all about his entertaining, Monsieur! You have only to look upon our daughter for the effects of that!"

People had begun to stare. Heads were turning in the direction of the dark alcove and a hush had fallen over much of the crowd as they tried to make out the rest of the bits and pieces of what was being said. Finally the King too was drawn to the tumult. He excused himself from the dance and moved toward the alcove.

"How could Your Majesty?" the Comtesse shouted at the King and motioned to her young daughter, who sobbed into her hands.

"Take them to the library at once," the King commanded in a controlled voice and then nudged Montmorency along with him into the hall amid the hushed whispers of the crowd.

"Well, it looks like the old boy hasn't lost his touch," Chabot whispered to Anne d'Heilly from their table.

"Oh, do shut up, will you, Philippe? Do you ever know when you have said enough?"

The Admiral tipped his head to the side and then stuffed his mouth with the breast meat from another pheasant, allowing a ribbon of grease to dribble down his chin. She turned away from him in disgust and looked back to the now empty corridor through which Montmorency, the King, the Comte de Sancerre and his family had passed. At that moment Anne d'Heilly could not decide if she was more angry or curious.

FRANÇOIS CLOSED THE double doors and put his hands on his hips. Three sword-bearing guards stood behind the trio who were now seated in a row on one of the King's settees. Marie de Sancerre, who had not given up her tears, sobbed continually into her small hands.

"Very well, then. Out with it. How do you know the girl carries my child?"

"How dare you?" the Comtesse began to rage again. "Marie is a good and honest girl. She gave herself to no one but her King!"

François looked down at her. "Is this true, child?" he asked with a tender note of concern.

When she did not reply, her father nudged her and she looked up with a face that was swollen and wet. "No, Your Majesty," she whispered.

The room fell to a hush.

"What? Who the devil else? Who?" her mother raged, and hit her about the face and neck so that she was not able to reply.

"Answer your parents!" the King commanded.

They waited.

"The Dauphin, Your Majesty."

The King paced the length of the book-lined room. The Comte and Comtesse were silent. They waited for his response. The guards stood at attention behind the carved-oak settee which held the trio. Montmorency stood near the door, knowing better than to speak out now.

"Bring the Dauphin, at once," François ordered.

The minutes before the boy came into the library were filled with the strain of silence, the far-off sound of the music and the King's angry scowl. François II finally entered the vaulted book-lined repository with the guard who had sought him. His arm was draped around a short dark-haired girl; they were laughing, and a flagon of wine was dangling from his hand.

"Get rid of her," the King commanded in a seething monotone.

"What is it, Father?"

The younger François looked at the sullen group before him. He looked at Marie de Sancerre who was still sobbing. He saw her father's rage. The blood left his face. His heart stopped.

"Father, I . . . it is not what you think . . ."

"Now, now, my boy . . ." He stifled his son's confession and thrust a goblet of wine in his hand. "Ah, there is nothing like two men bedding the same whore to turn back the hands of time! My son, my own dear son . . . I feel like a boy again myself. Monty, do you recall that time in Italy before the wars; that tall willowy maiden . . . what was her name?"

"So then you are not angry with me?"

The King's angry face softened. He put his arm around his son as though they were the only two in the room. "One of us has made her pregnant, boy. The child will need to be provided for."

The Dauphin's mouth fell open and he gazed over at the young girl he too had bedded.

"I will make you a bargain, my son. If you will agree to tell my Anne that it is your doing, then I shall overlook the duplicity of the entire affair. We shall tally it up to an enormous adventure, as Monty and I did all those years ago."

"Gladly, Father!" The Dauphin smiled. The relief was evident on his long thin face.

"Cruel bastard! You sound as though she were a piece of meat!" the Comtesse muttered. The guard hit the back of her head with his hand just enough to sting.

"Be mindful of how you address your Sovereign Lord," he warned in a firm baritone.

"Oh, Your Majesty, please!" the girl pleaded and dropped to her knees. "I want to be with you! Do not make me go! I love you!"

"Quiet, Marie," her father urged.

"Love, you say? Foolish girl," he scoffed. "What do you know of love? You loved me so much that you bedded us both! Did your mother give you instruction in that as well?" Tears spilled down her cheeks. She could say nothing in defense of herself. "Love, hah! Such a foolish word, and how like a child to use it at a time like this! I am a King. You are a child. I had you and now I shall pay for the pleasure."

The Comtesse de Sancerre stood and straightened the bodice of her gown, preparing to confront the King. "Your Majesty, there is another solution that would bring harmony to all concerned." The King would not look at her so she proceeded without invitation. "My daughter is well educated. She is the correct age, and of course, of the appropriate station to become the Dauphine. My husband and I propose that the boy marry her and give a name to the child."

The King began to chuckle before he turned around. After a moment the sound blossomed into a raucous fit of laughter. The

Dauphin and the guards smiled as the King began to grip his sides and double over. Montmorency stood silently by the King, his face expressionless.

"Are you mad, woman? He is to be King! I'll not have him married to a whore who gives herself to the highest bidder! Ha! Who would sire the future Kings of France when she tired of my son? The stable boy? The cook? The Captain of the Guard here, perhaps?"

The Comte and Comtesse de Sancerre exchanged a defeated glance. All three stood and prepared to leave the library. "I assume, Your Majesty, that you are prepared to make good on your responsibility to pay for the privilege of defiling our daughter?"

The King's nostrils flared and his face flushed crimson at the tone she had dared to use with him. *God, what a mistake it had been to look twice at her,* he thought.

"If she were not carrying a child of royal blood, I would throw the whole lot of you into the conciergerie and let you rot there for plotting against me as you have! You played me for a fool, and I shall not have that in my house!"

"Father, please," François urged and put his own arm on the King's shoulder.

The King took a deep breath and, after a moment, his voice returned to its even pace. "The girl will be sent to the convent Murate to bear the child. After it is born, it shall be returned to Court to be raised with the others. I shall grant a small stipend for the girl to use as a dowry. There will be nothing more."

"But Your Majesty must be reasonable," the Comte de Sancerre cautiously objected. "Who will want her once word of this is out?"

It was only now, that the course of the indiscretion was defined, that Montmorency stepped forward. As he did, the King and Dauphin turned away.

"Perhaps you should have considered the risk more thoroughly before letting your daughter whore for you. The King has made you an equitable offer. I would advise you to accept the terms."

The King looked back over his shoulder and then, with no further thought, as he and the Dauphin walked together toward the door, he added, "Handle the details, will you, Montmorency? My son and I have a banquet to attend."

THE NIGHT AIR had gotten cold.

As Henri leaned against the ivy-covered railing before him, he inhaled deeply. His nostrils burned with the brisk rush of air. He could see the figures of a man and a woman coming forward from the gazebo. They were laughing and she was clutching his arm. Henri gasped as the moonlight illuminated their faces and he could finally see that the woman was Diane. The man with whom she strolled was the promiscuous Scots Captain, Jacques de Montgommery.

The moonlight caught the folds of Diane's black silk gown, which was set off with gold lace. Her blond hair was gathered away from her face into a net shimmering with the same gold. Henri felt his legs falter. Then, to his surprise, she noticed him.

"Well, there you are!" she cried out and waved to him as he leaned against the terrace balustrade. "I have been looking for Your Highness!"

She marched up the staircase to the terrace leaving Montgommery several paces behind. She was smiling and her cheeks and the tip of her nose were pink from the night air. "Thank you, Jacques, for your arm. Save me a dance later, perhaps?" she asked with a smile. Montgommery scowled at Henri, who appeared to have captured Diane's attention. He stormed off without further word.

"I wanted to congratulate you on your victory yesterday," she said when they were alone.

"You could have won. You play very well."

"Now you are the one who is being kind."

"Not when it comes to sports. In that, I mean what I say. You played an excellent game."

"Very well, then. I thank you," she replied. It took no more than a moment for both of them to realize that Henri was now quite unashamedly staring at her. She became uneasy under his adolescent gaze.

"You look truly magnificent," he managed to mutter, as he took her hand and gently kissed it the way he had seen the other men at Court do. The smile left her face as he held her soft white hand to his lips. As soon as she could, Diane pulled away and began to rub her hands together as though they had gotten cold.

"It really is a splendid party, do you not think?"

"For one of the King's gatherings, I suppose it is."

"Well. Why, don't we go back in? You know, Henri, I would very much like to dance if you should ask me."

The moment that followed was so long and awkward that she was almost sorry she had proposed it. He peered in through the glass doors, as though he were looking for someone.

"I do not dance," he finally said, still not looking at her.

"Oh, nonsense. Everyone dances."

After a moment, he looked in her direction once again. His expression had grown distant; his posture formal. "To be more precise, Madame, I do not dance well," he said. "It was by the King's request some years ago that I not attempt it publicly for the embarrassment it caused him."

Diane did not know what to say. The mood between them had so quickly shifted from familiarity to tension that now she too felt awkward. She looked over at him, but once again, found him looking away from her and back into the ballroom. She was certain that he must have caught the eye of some young girl, just as Montgommery repeatedly did when they were together. That duplicitous behavior among courtiers that at first had enraged her, now had almost begun to seem almost commonplace. Detaining the Prince out here like this, much less thinking that he might be interested in a dance with her, was nothing but foolish.

"It is getting chilly. Perhaps we should go inside," she suggested.

"Yes, I think that would be wise."

Henri turned without acknowledging her and began to walk toward the door. At the same moment when they reached the entrance, Anne d'Heilly stepped out of the same door on the arm of

Admiral Chabot. They were close enough that their stiff skirts brushed together and forced the new rivals to pause.

"Why, good evening, Henri dear," Anne said with a Cheshire-cat grin. "Why, and who have we here? Yes, of course. It is the widow in black. Have you taken to defending her everywhere now, or just in dark corridors and on moonlit balconies?" She waited for Chabot to hide a laugh behind his hand before she continued. "Most unwise, unless of course, you mean for people to talk."

Her words were harsh. Henri turned to Diane who stood behind him. He was surprised and yet strengthened by a sense of desperation in her eyes before she lowered them.

"How dreadful, Mademoiselle d'Heilly, that you can find no one your own age with whom to occupy yourself. The children are playing up in the nursery. Perhaps you would be more comfortable with them. At least they are less likely to contest your cruel taunting."

"Listen, little Prince, you cannot speak to me like that and get away with it," she seethed, but Henri refused the bait.

"Go on now. Be a good girl. I can see Madame here is growing as weary of your games as I."

As he spoke the last words, he clutched Diane's hand firmly in his own. Then, brushing Anne aside as though she were a servant, he led Diane through the open door, back into the safe throngs of clamorous guests.

"Well, it would appear that you have made a habit of rescuing me from the wrath of Mademoiselle d'Heilly," Diane whispered, as they moved back into the ballroom.

"Nothing should bring me greater pleasure, Madame. But I confess, I think you do quite well on your own."

"Oh, not so well as you might think." She smiled.

Henri squeezed her hand to guide her as they wound through a maze of dancers, now doing the Branle, a lively country dance full of strenuous swings and lifts. The dancers tried to bring them into the steps but Henri pushed past them. The odor in the ballroom was acrid. A blue-gray haze had made it suffocatingly heavy.

The thick air was in sharp contrast to the crisp and quiet of the garden.

"From what I have seen of this Court since I have been back, there is bound to be gossip, now that you have twice so publicly gone against her on my behalf."

"Madame, I have been talked about for a long time now. I venture very little of it, in the form of flattery."

Diane looked over at him, her face glowing brilliant with sincerity. "That is difficult to believe, since there are really so many nice things that one could say about you."

She watched a hard-edged expression return to his face. He looked away. "I must tell you, Madame, that I am not at all accustomed to flattery."

Diane stopped when they reached the archway that led out into the new Grand Gallery. The music was not nearly so loud there and the odors not so thick. She turned in front of him so that he was made to face her. "Then perhaps I have overstepped my bounds."

"It is only that I am not worthy of your trust, Madame," he replied in a soft, vulnerable voice.

"Why would you say such a thing?"

"They say I am difficult. The King says so himself; quite publicly, in fact. He hastens to add that he often wishes, for both of our sakes, that I had not been born at all."

"Well, I do not think you are difficult in the least. Besides, I do not care what *they* say, even if the *they* to which you refer includes the King of France. You have certainly been a friend to me, and for that I am eternally grateful," she declared and then quickly leaned over to kiss his cheek.

She smiled. Henri could not. After a moment, when the awkward silence between them seemed destined to return, she looked across at the dancers. But Diane knew that he was watching her.

His mother, Queen Claude, had been Henri's last contact with any sort of affection. Not since he was a very little boy had anyone treated him with the least modicum of tenderness. Since then he had closed himself off to it. No one understood his pain or the betrayal he felt. No one took the time.

There was Montmorency who had tried to be a father figure, believing that Henri had no real father in the King. But, though he cared deeply for the Grand Master, in Henri's eyes, Monty had one fatal flaw—he loved power above all else. His heart ached for more than the ambitious Grand Master felt free to give.

Slowly, out of Henri's desperate need, grew a powerful resentment of everyone and everything around him; his way of reconciling the pain. The loss. Through this turmoil, Diane de Poitiers had emerged. To him, she was all grace and kindness; what the world should be. But more than that, she had displayed a vulnerability which, until now, had been completely foreign to him. It drew him to her in an inexplicable way, in spite of his fear. No one in his life had ever needed him. Here, now, he had come upon this lady who was virtually helpless against the mysterious hostility of his father's powerful mistress. He could be Perseus to her Andromeda. He might finally have a purpose. Very few people would risk Anne d'Heilly's disfavor by defending a newcomer. Very few, except of course, the King's malcontent son.

THE NEXT WEEKS that passed brought a change in Henri, the cause of which to everyone but himself was thought to be quite mysterious. Each day he swayed more naturally toward the humor and easiness of Diane's companionship. Slowly, he began to blossom under her kindness.

After their initial reunion at Fontainebleau, the awkwardness that he had felt in her presence vanished. In its place, a sensitive and caring young man had begun to emerge. She too had welcomed their friendship, anxious to find some little enjoyment in her stay at the French Court.

Two days after the King's party, the Court had moved again. This time the Court was installed at the royal palace of Saint Germain-en-Laye near Paris. There, Henri and Diane took long walks in the King's gardens and rode for endless hours in the deep evergreen forests surrounding the chateau.

Henri, who resented all things intellectual as a symbol of his father's arrogance, now began to discuss Petrarch with her. He read Machiavelli, which he had always avoided simply because his father favored it. He even read *Le Roman de la rose* again because she had mentioned that she especially liked it. Each day after vespers, since their arrival at Saint Germain-en-Laye, they challenged one another to a heated game of *jeu de paume* on the back courts of the chateau.

"Oh, the deuce! I missed it!" Henri cried, pealing with laughter, as the heavy leather ball sailed past his racket and into the thick of grass behind him. The midday sun was cooled by a sweet spring breeze that blew gently across the outdoor court. On the sidelines, Hélène sat busying herself with a white needlepoint rose while Charlotte dozed and intermittently batted at a particularly persistent fly.

"Oh, come now, Your Highness can do better than that!" laughed Jacques de Saint-André as he paced the length of the court as referee.

"Whose side are you on? I have to beat him at least once!" shouted Diane as she batted another ball over the net. Then, as Henri returned the volley, Diane moved a little too close to the left and was struck in the forehead by the heavy sailing ball. Under the impact, she lost her footing and went tumbling to the ground.

"Diane!" Henri cried, dashing over the net toward her. Jacques and Hélène followed. Henri knelt by her side and supported her in his arms. "Oh, Diane! Diane . . . say something, please! Are you all right?"

"Jacques, please, get some water!" Hélène urged.

Jacques sprang to his feet to find one of the royal guards who were positioned discretely around the courts.

"Madame, it is Hélène. Can you hear me?"

Diane tried to clear her head by blinking. When she opened her eyes, she found herself looking into Henri's gentle but frightened face. "Yes, I am fine," she said a little weakly, as she tried to sit up.

Jacques came running back followed by two of the King's guards; one of whom was carrying a small pail of water.

"Stop all this fuss now. I am fine. It was really very clumsy of me." She smiled at Henri whose face was still filled with fear. "Truly," she added for his benefit. "Now, if you would just help me up, please. We were not finished with the game."

"Oh, but we are!" Henri insisted. "Jacques, help me lead her over to that bench." The two young men took her beneath each arm and helped her from the court.

As Henri hailed his guards to assist them, he happened to meet Charlotte's reproving gaze as she sat in her chair on the sidelines. Although she sat erect with concern, she had not moved during the incident, and now it was apparent that neither had she taken her judgmental eyes from Henri. He knew, as they looked at one another, that the years had made her wise. He also knew that she had seen far more from him toward Diane than just tender concern.

DIANE AWOKE IN steamy darkness.

Her windows had been closed and the room was still from the lack of fresh flowing air. She raised herself onto her elbows and lit a candle beside her bed. There were no sounds from Charlotte or Hélène moving around in the outer room, so she resolved to be quiet herself in hopes of gaining a few moments' peace. She swung her feet around to the side of the bed and again touched her head where a smaller, more firm and painful knot had developed. She smiled, remembering Henri's concern for her.

"Difficult boy, indeed," she muttered to herself, until her thoughts were interrupted by the sight of a green satin-covered box that had been placed on a small round table near the window. The box was square and tied with white lace ribbons. She lit another candle and carried it toward the table.

Turning the box upside down, she could see there was no note. Her heart quickened, as she thought of her previous gift from the King. She had hoped in the past few weeks that his interest in her had faded. She took a deep breath before she gained the courage to pull off the ribbons.

Inside, on a bed of red satin, was a small silver medallion with the Latin inscription VICTORY on the surface. Diane smiled again as she pulled the military medal from the box. It was round and etched with the image of one soldier bending over the limp body of another on what appeared to be a battlefield.

"Ah, there you are," said Hélène as Diane stood in the arch of her bedchamber door.

"Did you sleep well? I see you found the gift," Charlotte said, looking up from a game of cards the two women were playing at a small oak table near the fireplace.

"Who delivered it?"

"One of the royal guards, Madame, though he would not say for whom he bore it."

"Did he say nothing, then?"

"Only that he was told you would understand once you opened it."

"Was it from the King?" Hélène asked anxiously.

Charlotte swatted her. "That will be enough!"

"It is all right, Hélène. Would you please see to the black velvet gown with the white lace bodice for this evening," Diane instructed, and then stretched her arms up over her head and began to yawn. It was dark, but much cooler in the sitting room than her own bedchamber had been, and she quickly began to feel more alert.

"But, Madame," Charlotte objected after Hélène had gone back into the bedchamber. "You cannot possibly dine in the King's company with a knot on your head like that. There is bound to be gossip; how a lady could sustain such a blow in polite society."

". . . and Hélène, ready the velvet turban as well," she added, over Charlotte's head. "That should hide my battle scar!"

AMID A LOW ROLLING FOG, an entourage of the King's favorite courtiers gathered the next morning for the hunt. Outfitted in fur and leather to stave off the early-morning chill, the riders sat astride their elegantly draped horses and bantered among themselves as they waited for the King. Diane's black stallion lowered his head to feed on the mossy grass at the base of a sapling just as Jacques de Montgommery rode up beside her. They watched together as a groom came out from the stables and helped Prince Henri onto his tooled-leather saddle.

"Well, well, well. Look at that, will you. The peevish Prince is about to grace us with his presence," Montgommery muttered to Diane from the side of his mouth, smiling all the while.

"You had best watch your manners. He is the King's son," Diane returned. The firmness in her voice made him bristle as they both looked back over at the young Prince. She had been unable to thank him for the medal, as he had not gone to the King's dinner the night before. She had hoped to thank him now. Henri nodded to her but then, to her surprise, he led his horse in the opposite direction, joining Guise, Saint-André and Brissac.

"Well, it would seem that your little protector has forgotten his own manners this morning," Montgommery continued to harp. "Let us just hope that the King's mistress does not show up for the hunt. Then you would really have no one to save you!"

"Jacques, why must you be so malicious? I am really very bored with how small you sound." She punctuated her words by pulling the reins of her horse so that the animal turned away from Montgommery's mount. After a moment, he nudged at his horse and followed her.

"Oh, come now," he smiled. "I only meant—"

"I do not have the slightest care what you meant. You are very rude."

"I don't know what gets into me sometimes. Things were going so splendidly between us. I am sorry I spoiled it. Forgive me?"

Diane looked into his eyes. "Where is Mademoiselle d'Estillac?" she asked, changing the subject. "Perhaps you should try your pretty words on her."

His countenance changed with her clipped tone and he shifted in his saddle. "Why would you expect me to know?" he snapped. "I am not her keeper!"

"But you are her lover! Tell me, Jacques, is it true that while you attempt to conquer me, she carries your child?" Diane asked angrily.

He opened his mouth as if to reply. Then, thinking better of it, he shook his head and cantered his horse over near Grand Master Montmorency, who was speaking to the King's daughter, Marguerite.

"Well," she whispered to herself. "I see that I have my answer."

THE KING WAS THE LAST to take his mount and join the group of riders. Despite the magnificent green hunting costume, he looked more worn and tired than anyone had seen him. There were dark circles beneath his eyes and his skin was ashen. Diane had heard the rumor which had been circulating among the courtiers that the King was once again contemplating war against the Emperor. It was said he could think of nothing else. She made the sign of the cross as she considered the prospect.

As he sat on his horse surrounded by his friends, the Master-of-the-Hunt brought forth to the King a map detailing the area where a burrow of wild boars were thought to nest. The hunt was led by the pack of yelping dogs, followed by the thundering hooves of the courtier's horses, as they rode furiously toward the burrow. Dashing across the mountainous countryside, the King took the lead easily, passing his companions. Then Henri surprised the group by coming from behind to take the lead.

The two horses sprinted neck to neck. White clouds of early morning air puffed from their nostrils. The King turned his head with a start, surprised to see Henri pacing him so easily. He dug his spurs into the animal's flanks to make him gallop harder. Diane saw the rivalry manifest itself from several lengths behind. When the King and Henri's horses neared a grassy clearing, both father and son tumbled to the ground in a grappling display of anger and passion.

The King rolled onto Henri trying to pin back his arms but was downed by Henri's knee as he thrust it into the King's face. Dust and leaves puffed up around them. Limbs flew. Both of their chests heaved with fury. Henri stood up, only to be felled once again by a long spindly branch to the back of the knees. Again they grappled as the stunned riders looked on. Montmorency took a step forward but the Dauphin reached out a hand to stop him.

"This is between father and son," he cautioned.

"Why, you little bastard!" raged the King, as he struggled to his feet beneath his son's bold defiant stare. "So you think you can whip a King, do you? All right, little man, since that is what you appear to have become, then I will challenge you to a man's game! A joust, full armor, six days hence in Paris!"

The crowd of courtiers continued in stunned silence. No one dared move until the King willed it. Finally he was on his feet and brushing the dust and leaves from his tooled-leather riding doublet.

"Brother, do not take him for a fool! You know how good he is," the Dauphin urged, as Henri swaggered toward his horse. "Ask for his forgiveness, before it is too late!"

"Never!" seethed the second son, as he slowly lifted himself back onto his stallion.

"Then, brother, you are an even bigger fool than I thought. You deserve his wrath!"

BY MIDMORNING, the King had cornered the boar and had slain him with a wide stroke of his ivory-plated sword. The other riders had dismounted to stretch their legs and share a toast to the victory. Henri brushed dust from his stockings as Jacques de Saint-André stretched his arms over his head. François de Guise came up beside them and took a pewter goblet of wine from one of the stewards.

"Is that not Diane de Poitiers over there, speaking with Montmorency's wife? I did not know she liked the hunt," Guise remarked with a smile.

Henri looked across the field at her. She stood beside Madeleine de Montmorency and the Princess Marguerite, laughing, and holding a goblet of wine with both of her hands.

"I hear that she takes exercise just like a man; and to look at her I believe it. The woman plays *jeu de paume,* and she even swims in the winter; if you can imagine it! Perhaps she thinks she is her namesake, Diana, goddess of the hunt."

Henri whipped around and shot Guise an evil glare. His body tensed as though he were preparing to strike. Saint-André, the eldest among them, intervened.

"I am certain he meant no harm, Your Highness."

"I only meant that she is rather an extraordinary woman . . . not a bad one," he stammered and then looked helplessly toward Saint-André.

When it was clear to him that he would not be able to please the Prince, Guise thought better of continuing, and resolved to finish his wine. Saint-André, who had watched the entire episode, had thought at first that he too might attempt a bit of good-natured needling about Henri's being so defensive. Something told him not to. They both stood silently and watched him walk off alone into the woods.

Two wild boars were roasting on spits and large platters of partridge, pear pastries and sugared almonds were brought forth and presented to the hungry riders. They drank a sweet liquor made from wild cherries called maraschino. Diane waited until the meal was nearly ready knowing that the anticipation of the King's hungry companions would serve to mask her disappearance.

At first she wandered toward the horses as though she were just strolling, and then when she felt she might pass safely undetected, she darted behind one of the sleek, glossy animals and into the woods in the direction that Henri had gone. She found him crouched beside a small pond, near a collection of moss-covered boulders, skipping stones into the water.

"They are serving dinner," she cautiously said. "Are you not hungry?"

"Did you know a stone will skip four times before it drowns?"

Diane found it an odd choice of words but considering the somber mood of the entire afternoon and the humiliation he had endured in front of the others, she resolved to make no point of it. "I have not seen you since my rather ungraceful fall on the gaming courts the other day."

Henri skipped another stone across the water. "And how is your head?" he asked, not turning to face her.

"Much better, thank you." She drew closer and crouched down beside him. "May I try one?"

Their eyes met for only a moment before she took the small stone from his hand and tossed it across the pond. It skipped twice and then sank.

"I feel like that—like I am drowning sometimes. This life of mine is like one huge ocean waiting to just swallow me up," Henri said softly. "You know that the King has challenged me to a joust."

"Will you accept the challenge?"

"I suppose I must, mustn't I?" he asked and finally turned to look at her.

In his young eyes she once again saw the anger and the loneliness she had seen that first afternoon when he had rescued her from Anne d'Heilly. She had not noticed it in him since that day. "I wanted to thank you for the beautiful medallion. It was just what I needed to make me smile. It seems I do so little of that lately."

"I am glad you liked it. It belonged to Bayard," he finally said in a softer voice. "He was a noble and great knight in the early wars with the King."

"Yes, of course. He is already a legend. Will His Majesty not be angry that you have given such a priceless thing to me?"

"It belonged to me!" he snapped, and then waited a moment, trying to quell his anger. "It was a gift to me from my mother. Bayard had given it to her. I wanted you to have it. After all," he added, "you have certainly earned it."

The conversation between them was disjointed. Uneasy. Diane persevered, trying to adapt to the rhythm of his thoughts. He was troubled. She knew it. He was not behaving like the boy she had come to know over the last weeks. Having seen the exchange between him and the King today, she now understood why. Something about their relationship touched off in Henri a profound rage. The King perpetuated the boy's penchant toward violence. She was now certain how he had earned his reputation as *difficult*.

"I wonder if you would meet me behind the kitchens later

today," she asked. "I have something I would like to show you. It is with Clothilde."

"Then you have been to see her?"

"Why, yes. Several times," she smiled. "She was right. Her Banbury tarts are the best I have ever tasted."

He stood and wiped his muddy hands on his puffed trunk hose. The intensity was gone from his dark, bottomless eyes and he managed a weak smile.

"When shall we meet?"

"How about at three, just outside the kitchens?"

She smiled and turned around to head back to the camp before anyone noticed that she and the Prince were gone together.

TWO LITTLE BLACK PUPPIES tumbled beneath their own legs as they scampered toward Henri. He stopped on the path and stared down as the little animals panted and scratched at his stockings. He bent down to stroke the frisky head of one. At that same moment, he looked up at Diane who was standing before him.

"Clothilde told me what happened to the puppy," she said.

Henri continued to stroke the little black animal's furry head as the other scratched and yelped to be picked up. They were awkward, lumbering little pups with coal-black eyes, large paws and fur that stuck straight up from their heads and tails.

"Their mother was one of the King's best hunting dogs," she explained. "Unfortunately, as you can see, their father was somewhat less distinguished. The Gentleman-of-the-Hounds was about to put them down when I convinced him to surrender them both to me."

As Henri continued to stroke the one and look into its big, sparkling eyes, the other pup leapt into his arms and began licking his face.

"Do you like her?" Diane asked.

"She is wonderful!"

"Oh, I am so glad. I so wanted her to please you." She caught the way it sounded and lowered her eyes for a moment. "What I mean to say is, after all, I owe you so much. The other at your feet is a male."

Diane clasped her hands together in front of her gown, thrilled that, if even for a moment, she appeared to have made him happy. Henri scooped up the other puppy and now held them both, one in each arm. They were active, happy little dogs; both wiggled under his grasp and licked his face. Henri laughed at the surprise of it. He could not remember anyone ever giving him anything just for the pleasure of it.

Still carrying the squirming puppies, he lunged forward toward Diane, meaning to kiss her cheek. But then, as his lips met with her warm skin, he was unable to tear himself away. He parted slowly from her, both of their smiles weakening. Their faces were close to one another, both still and motionless. They looked at one another. Almost at once, Diane's face began to flush. Her lips parted.

"So, what will you name them?" she asked in a whisper, nearly choking on the words.

"I do not know . . . no, I do know!" he paused, as the puppies continued to yelp and lick his face. "Since she is such a naughty little thing, I think her name should mean the same. I will name her Friponne. And he, poor little devil, who is crushed by his sister's persistence, will be Friper."

"Diane . . . Diane, are you here? . . . Diane!"

It was Jacques de Montgommery. From the distance of his voice, she realized he must be in the King's parterre. But each time he called out, the voice grew stronger. She had forgotten, in her excitement over giving Henri the dogs, that she had agreed to meet him there. Now she was late.

"I must go," she said.

"Is the Captain courting you?" he pointedly asked as the puppies began to squirm in his arms.

"Diane!" Again, it was Montgommery's voice.

"Such a thing would be inappropriate. I am still in mourning. I can be courted by no one yet."

The tension in Henri's face fell away. He smiled again. "Well then, I suppose you had better go. Thank you again for the dogs," he said, beginning once again to smile.

IT WAS GRATITUDE. Simple appreciation.

Or so Diane told herself as she walked away from the kitchens in the direction of Jacques' voice. He had only kissed her cheek, merely brushed it. He was a boy who had loved the gift and had become overwhelmed. Young men were wont to do such things. She forced her mind away from the thoughts and the direction in which they were proceeding. She forced her mind from the image of Henri.

"How was your game?" she asked with a wave, spying Jacques sitting on a sculptured stone bench beneath the shade of an elm. Behind it, a stone wall covered in ivy lent privacy to the spot.

"I played well, but lost. The Dauphin is a devil on the court. Besides, thoughts of you drive me to distraction when we are apart. I wish you had watched me play."

"I told you I had an appointment," she replied, ignoring his flattery.

They walked along in silence for some time through the mazes of emerald hedgerows. He tried to hold her hand and when she would not let him, he finally grabbed it and forced her to stop.

"She is with child," he whispered. "But she has gone to Toul to have it dealt with."

Diane felt the blood drain from her face. He could not have meant it. "Dealt with?" she said with an expression of such horror that even he was moved. He took both of her hands in his own and held them up.

"She means nothing to me," he said. "I knew her before I met you. It really is none of your concern, but since I mean to court you formally when your mourning is complete, I wanted there to be no deceptions between us."

"What do you mean, dealt with?" she repeated, her mouth gone dry.

"There is an old woman in Toul who helps young girls out of . . . awkward situations," he explained, still holding her hands. Diane tore them from his grasp and buried her face in her palms.

"Oh, it is too awful to hear!"

"She means nothing to me, I tell you! None of them do! You must believe me!"

"Saint-André tried to warn me about you weeks ago, but I would not listen. Jacques, please," she began to plead. "You must do what is right and honorable. Marry her and give your child a name. At least then I can still face you with some sense of honor."

"Madame, I know it is a shock, but listen to reason. She does not desire to marry me nor do I desire to marry her. She has been betrothed since her birth to a man from her village. What happened between us was nothing more than a trifle that went too far afield. Now it is all being handled."

"Handled? Dealt with? The words sicken me! How can the act of love mean so little to you?"

"Love? Oh, Madame, open your eyes! You said yourself that night at Blois that love had no bearing on any of it between Mademoiselle d'Estillac and myself. Well, you were right. Diane, *mon amour* . . ." He clutched her shoulders in his long thin fingers, and began to shake her. "This is the Court of France! It is not some fairy tale place from the recesses of your mind! Your husband had you hidden away for so long that you know scarcely more than a girl about the ways of the world!"

"Be that as it may, I will not be a party to it, Jacques. It is too dreadful even to consider. God gave that child life. You have no right to take it away simply because it does not fit into your master plan!"

"Fine!" he yelled. He had finally lost his temper. "You need know nothing further! I wanted to be honest so that the courtship that is to commence between us is pure. I have seen to that."

"You speak as if I have agreed to it already."

"It is only a matter of time between us. You know that as well as I. You shall not receive so generous an offer from any of the others here, that I can promise you! Now that you are a widow there is little left for you. There will be many who will want you for their mistress, to be sure, because you still have your beauty and the King's ear, but what can you offer for which some-one would marry? Your youth and your child-bearing years are gone. What real use are you, but to me? Marrying me is the only way."

He was cold and calculating. He smiled when he spoke as though they were deciding social engagements instead of lives. He appeared to feel nothing for the other two lives he was about to destroy, caring only for the promotion of his own. Diane pulled herself from his grasp in complete devastation and ran from him as if she were running from Evil itself.

DIANE RAN THE ENTIRE length of the gardens. She thought that if she could run fast enough, then perhaps she could outrun the heinous truth forced on her by Montgommery. The ugliness of Court was trying to swallow her. The ugliness of this world now far outweighed its brilliance. Still her legs could not carry her nearly fast enough to escape it.

As she ran into the chateau and down the long, empty corri-dor, her thoughts returned to Henri. *Dear, sweet Henri. So noble. So in-nocent. Was I ever so pure?* As she neared the gallery which housed the chapel, she was overwhelmed by the desire to see him again. He would help her outrun the evil. She must make sense of this some-how. With someone. Unable to think of anything but that, she ran all the way to the royal wing of the Chateau Saint Germain-en-Laye.

The guards doubled in numbers as she entered the east wing. Lined along the stairs to the hallway, they were armed and clad in blue and crimson doublets, emblazoned with the King's crest. She passed them and raced up a small flight of stairs. She could hear laughter echoing amid the silence, and was drawn to it. It was Henri's voice.

"Your move," she could hear Jacques de Saint-André say, as she neared Henri's apartment. Then there was a moment of silence.

"Ah you bastard, you've won again!" he said with a laugh. Henri looked up through the open door to see Diane barred from entry by the crossed rapiers of two guards. He sprang to his feet from behind the chess board and charged toward the door.

"It is all right," he admonished. "Return to your posts."

Henri was alarmed by the distress in her eyes. He saw the heaving of her chest. He could tell she had been running.

"Please leave us, Jacques," he asked, never looking away from Diane.

When Jacques had gone out of the room and closed the door behind him, Diane fell into Henri's arms. He encircled her awkwardly. Never having held a woman, and feeling uncertain about what to do with his arms, he moved them aimlessly up and down her back. At the very same moment, when some deep instinct would have him clutch her closer to him, he was barely able to touch her. Despite his discomfort, she seemed to melt naturally into the contours of his body.

As they stood alone together in the silence, his own heart quickened with the thought of her breasts pressed against his chest. The warmth of her body. The softness of her arms on his neck. After a moment, she pulled away and shook her head as though someone had just awakened her.

"Forgive me. I do not know what came over me. Please, forgive me . . . I just saw you standing there and I—"

"Please do not apologize, Madame. What is it? What on earth could have troubled you so? Was it Mademoiselle d'Heilly again?"

"No. Nothing like that. I do not know, exactly. I just . . . oh, it is too awkward to speak of."

Diane turned from the sight of his puzzled expression and walked toward the oriel window. Frippone padded over to Henri's feet and began to yelp. He scooped her up into his arms in an attempt to quiet her.

"Please, Madame, what is it? We are alone. You may speak freely."

"I had some distressing news just now," she said, gazing out onto the courtyard, trying vainly to steady herself. "Something ugly and dark . . . and I . . . well, I think of you as my friend here. I have no others. Not really. Something led me here to you. I do not know, for comfort, I suppose." After a few moments when Henri made no reply, she was forced to turn back and face him. "Now I have embarrassed you. Oh, I am so sorry."

Henri put the squirming dog down onto the floor, and she scampered back to her place by the fire beside her brother. "On the contrary, Madame," he whispered. "You have given me a great gift by coming here. It is a rare thing to be needed by someone else. I have never been fortunate enough to know such a sensation before now."

The energy between them was charged. She moved back across the room toward him, as though not under her own power. She stood facing him again; facing the endless eyes. The dark, heavy brows. The black spirals of hair near his face. That face . . . the key, and yet . . . inaccessible. Impenetrable. So full of pain and suffering. Full of a latent . . . a dark power. She could hear nothing but his breathing, the warmth of it so close to her face. Like her own, it quickened. It was difficult for either of them to look away; or want to.

"Please, sit down. I shall have Jacques bring us some tea with mint and camomile. My mother drank it when she was upset."

"No, Henri, I cannot stay."

All at once she was exceedingly awkward; herself, adolescent. The reality of what she had done fell upon her. She should not have come. It had been improper.

"I do thank you for the offer, but your kindness has been medicine enough," Diane finally said, wishing not to confuse him more than she knew she already had. She moved toward him and touched his chin lightly with her fingertips. "Most of all, thank you for not thinking me completely mad for coming here."

"I could never think that of you," he whispered as she turned to leave.

"Please apologize to Jacques for me, for having interrupted your game."

"I won anyway," he said and then he added, "Will you still want to play *jeu de paume* tomorrow?"

"Yes, of course. I will give you a chance to win back the medallion."

"That is for you to keep, Madame . . . no matter who wins."

Jacques came through the open door and passed Diane. They nodded to one another. Diane said nothing. Then she was gone. Jacques looked back at Henri. He was still standing in the middle of the room watching the empty doorway; his lips slightly parted, eyes dark and intense.

"Great God! You are falling in love with her!"

Henri turned away, knowing his face had betrayed him. Jacques advanced and put his hand on Henri's shoulder.

"Do not be a fool, man! She is old enough to be your mother. You are just a boy to her."

"Silence! Do you hear me, silence!"

"Forgive me, Your Highness, but you know it is your best interest I have at heart. I could not bear to see you hurt like that."

The energy had not left the room with Diane. Both of them felt it.

"I know, Jacques," he conceded, after a moment. "But you do not know her as I do. She is so vulnerable and alone. She is not like anyone else here in this miserable place. She needs me."

"And when she has had you and tossed you aside for Jacques de Montgommery, where will you be?"

"What are you talking about?"

"How could you not know? He certainly has made no secret of his interest in her. I heard that when her mourning is over they will announce their courtship. The gossip is that he has already proposed marriage."

"Impossible. She would have told me."

"Be careful of that illusion, *mon ami*. Women never tell you everything. It is part of their great allure."

Henri sat back down at the game table, his mind racing from

images of Diane to his own deep fear. He began lining up the chess pieces on the board with a veneer of indifference.

"Well, are we playing chess or not?" he said piquantly when Jacques continued to stare at him.

"Of course. As Your Highness wishes."

DIANE HASTENED DOWN the hall and out of the royal wing. She prayed that no one had seen her.

"How could I have been so careless?" she muttered to herself with her head discreetly bowed. "Think of the scandal, you fool! Coming out of the Prince's private apartments in the broad light of day! What on earth were you thinking? Oh, I am such a fool for even wanting to believe that they were wrong about Jacques. But I am an even bigger fool for allowing such a vulnerable and tormented young man to console me. I will not . . . I cannot afford to make that mistake again, or it may well be my last!"

And then, as she began again to run in her elegant velvet slippers across the tiled floor, she did not know how or why, but a line came to her from some strange, dark place inside her. It was a line which at first she did not recognize as from the pages of *Le Roman de la rose*.

> He did not know if she were a lie, or the truth. He drew back,
> not knowing what to do; he dared not draw near her for fear.
> Fear of being enchanted.

*Y*OUR MAJESTY, we have another response from Rome," declared Chancellor Duprat. "The Pope has received your rejection of terms for the marriage. He has continued to sweeten the deal now by adding Parma as well. With these strongholds, you shall have Italy once again in the palm of your hand!"

"And I would sooner surrender it forever than see the Dauphin married to a merchant's daughter, no matter what riches they offer! All of you know my position."

"But Your Majesty, I beg you to reconsider," Admiral Chabot interceded in the dim council chamber. "In addition to the property, she comes dowered with a great sum of money, and if we play the game well, there is now a hint that the Pope may actually add the Duchy of Milan to sanction the match! There is rumor already that he is trying to obtain it as a wedding gift!"

"So, you would recommend for Us, for all of France, a commoner, and a foreign one at that, as future Queen?"

"Sire," said the Cardinal de Lorraine. "Think of the thorn in the side of the Emperor that this marriage would become. As we speak, he recommends one of his own to marry the girl so that he may further his own ambitions. We would take that away from him."

François whipped around to face the Cardinal. "Not the Dauphin. She is beneath him."

"Your Majesty, it is far more serious than that to which the Cardinal alludes," said Duprat. "I have it on good authority from my men in Rome that the Pope is, at this very moment, also negotiating the marriage of his niece with the Duke of Milan, Francesco Sforza, should His Holiness find his negotiations with you unsatisfactory. You know as well as I that Sforza is the Emperor's puppet. If that union is agreed to, where will that leave Milan when you mean to claim it?"

"What of my proposal of another son, if not the Dauphin?" Admiral Chabot cautiously forged.

"Oh, not that again!" Montmorency sighed and put his hand to his head.

"A second son of France is better than no son at all," Duprat agreed.

There were rumbles of agreement with the declaration.

"Gentlemen, please!" Montmorency bolted from his seat, leaned forward and balanced his knuckles on the table before him. "You must all listen to reason! You cannot subject that boy to such a thing. He is not prepared for an institution the magnitude of marriage. He lived four years of his life behind iron bars. We all see every day what scars he bears from that. I know him, and I tell you he is not ready!"

François' mind whirled with the prospect of the continually sweetened deal which the Pope had proposed. He still felt the conflict between the desire to succeed against the Emperor and his belief that Henri had suffered enough already by his hand. But the facts were clear. As the second son of France, Henri's marriage was simply not so important as the Dauphin's. He could be sacrificed.

It was not as if Catherine de Medici was completely without her connections. Though orphaned since birth, her father had been Lorenzo de Medici, Duke of Urbino. Her mother, Madeleine de La Tour D'Auvergne, was French, descended from the sainted King Louis XI. The child was descended from Cosimo de Medici, one of the most distinguished figures in Italian history. Like it or not, Chabot was right. The match could be a brilliant way of getting back a foothold in Italy.

"Very well, then," he finally said. "We shall give it over to a vote by secret ballot."

Each council member took a piece of parchment and quill from the inkwells before them. Having sealed their responses, they then tossed them toward the center of the table.

"Scribe!" the King called. "Read the results aloud."

Each man watched the others as they were read. Montmorency held his breath.

"Six for the marriage, and one against."

"Well, I certainly find no objection, so long as His Holiness is willing to help us recover Milan." He looked at each of his advisors. "Very well. So, then it is settled. Duprat, you may dispatch the Ambassador for Italy with our revised proposal for the marriage between his niece and Our second son. For that union, We demand the cities of Pisa, Livorno, Reggio and Modena. Also, of course, a substantial dowry, perhaps 600,000 ecus would be appropriate for the son of a King. In return for his niece's hand, We will give to the Prince and his bride 80,000 ecus of his maternal inheritance, the Duchy of Orléans, with a guaranteed annuity of 50,000 ecus a year, and the chateau of Gien for their personal use. Now, let us see what His Holiness shall say to that!"

HENRI DETESTED THE PROSPECT of being among the guests for supper in the King's private apartments, but he was obsessed with seeing Diane again. He felt he must discover the truth about the relationship between she and Jacques de Montgommery before it was too late.

Saint-André was right. At least to a point. Henri's feelings for her were changing in ways he did not like; changing in ways he did not understand. He found himself thinking of nothing but her, thinking about her hair, trying to remember the shades of it; trying to remember her skin, the fresh, earthy scent of it; how it had felt to hold her in his arms. He had even thought of himself like his brother, with her . . . inside of her. But that had been too much. That was something which he still could not understand. There was only one thing about his relationship with Diane de Poitiers which Henri knew to be so without question, without desire or need to understand it. He wanted to be with her.

"Rumor has it that His Majesty is once again readying the country for war," said François de Guise. "They say he is making some mysterious bargain with the Pope to do so."

"I, for one, would be glad of it," Henri replied dryly as he sipped maraschino amid the trio of Brissac, Guise and Saint-André. All of them but Henri, in costly costumes and jewels, searched the room for the young painted demoiselles who filtered in through the open doors and circled casually around them. Guise stuffed his mouth with an entire sugared plum from one of the fruit baskets on the table behind them, and then looked around.

"Would you go to war if we did?" Brissac asked Henri.

"Gladly! Anything to be rid of the nauseating sight of our good King."

Saint-André laughed at Henri's cryptic tone, but he stopped short when he saw the King enter from his adjoining chamber near them. Anne d'Heilly was on his arm. Emeralds dripped like green fire from her ears and she wore a rope of pearls around her neck.

"Great Zeus, she is gorgeous!" Guise whispered as he set the pit of his plum on the table near the fruit bowl.

"She is a whore!" Henri snapped.

Guise shrugged his shoulders and lifted his wine goblet. Brissac seemed not to notice or care about the Prince's foul mood. He was far too interested in captivating the attention of the sensuous-faced brunette across the room, who had just smiled back at him.

"What is bothering you?" asked Saint-André. But before Henri could respond, the Prince's wise friend had his answer. Diane de Poitiers entered the King's apartments beside Madeleine de Montmorency and Henri's face came to life.

"So, that is why you braved the King's supper. I should have known. Is it not enough to know that she means to marry Montgommery?"

"I told you, I do not believe you! But, if it is true, I want to hear it from her."

Henri lunged forward as though he were about to go to her. Saint-André grabbed his arm to stop him. "Your Highness, I bid you, do not make a fool of yourself!"

Henri shook free of his grasp with a vengeance and whirled around, his eyes lit with anger. "I am afraid it is too late for that."

"No . . . it can never be too late."

"Look, Jacques, be my friend or be on your way! I need no more enemies in this dreadful place!"

Henri headed off in Diane's direction without waiting for a reply. He brushed past Montmorency and did not speak to his brother, the Dauphin. He walked so briskly through the crowd of guests that he did not see the King behind the Cardinal de Lorraine. He stood near a long, covered table blocking the path. There was no way for Henri to gracefully avoid the Sovereign.

"Well, if it is not my son, the little man! Look, everyone, it is Henri. Tell me, boy, to what do we owe this rare pleasure? No one better to insult this evening?" The King flicked his hand with a casual smile and then began to chuckle. "Did you all know we are set to joust together in Paris next week? Yes, the little Prince thinks he is ready to be a man." The others laughed, following the King's lead. François slapped his son on the back when he saw him stiffen. "Oh, come now, boy, learn to take a ribbing. You never could, you know. So intense. Morose, actually. Why can you not be more like your brother?"

The Dauphin smiled from the King's side. "Yes, Henri, why is it that you are not more like me?"

"Perhaps it is the company he keeps," said Anne d'Heilly, with her savage smile.

Henri looked at her, completely unable to see the beauty in her that the others saw. For him it was masked by too much evil.

"Let me pass," he said. "The air in here is foul as death!"

FROM BEHIND THE HEDGE, Henri could see them silhouetted in the moonlight beneath a wooden arbor. They were facing one another. Montgommery was talking. Diane was not. It almost looked as if he were pleading. His hands were clasped on her arms, above her elbows. He was clutching her tightly. Shaking her. Then she turned from him.

"I think she is crying."

Henri turned with a start. Saint-André crouched behind him, peering with him through the foliage. "No. She would never cry. Not for the likes of him . . . and for that matter, what in the devil are you doing here?"

"Ah, perhaps you are right, not for him. But whatever they are saying, it cannot be pleasant."

"It does not look like a courtship to me," Henri said with a crooked smile. "And you . . . you still have not told me what you are doing here."

"I came to apologize for what I said earlier. You are the best friend I have here and, above all, I would like to believe that I am your friend, as well." Henri's lips lengthened into a smile. "Just take care with her. All right?"

"That is the woman I am going to marry, Jacques. I only just realized it myself. So you see, it would be impossible for me to take care, as you say. I will do anything to have her."

Henri leapt over the low hedge behind which they had been hiding and strolled out across the lawn toward the gazebo. They still did not see him. As he drew near, he could hear them arguing. With the distance between them and the sound of the crickets, he could only make out a few words. It was Diane who said, "How dare you . . ." and Montgommery who kept insisting that she listen to reason. Henri wanted desperately to stand behind the protection of the large birch tree before him and listen to their exchange, but he sensed more keenly, just from her tone and the few fragmented words, that she needed his help.

"Madame, what are you doing so far from the party?" he asked as he strode up beside them, trying his best to make it look as if it were a coincidence. For a moment he was obscured in the shadows, and Montgommery searched the darkness to see who was speaking. As he squinted and strained, Henri strolled out of the moonlight shadows dressed in an elegant gray velvet doublet with royal blue slashings. He tipped his toque to the Scots Captain.

"Good evening, Montgommery. You know, I believe the King was calling for you earlier. Something about a woman who was looking for you. I do not recall her name precisely . . . I believe, perhaps, it was . . . Estillac? Caroline, was it? Anyway, His Majesty seemed rather intent on locating you. Perhaps you should be getting back."

Montgommery could not help himself. He leered at the Prince. "As Your Highness wishes," he said as he bowed. Then he looked back at Diane. "This affair is not settled between us; not nearly settled!" he said, and then left the gazebo without debate.

Almost before he started across the lawn, Diane began to laugh. She raised her hand to her mouth to stifle the sound. "Oh, your timing is something! I am afraid you are not going to be very popular with the Captain, in the future. And how can I ever thank you for that?!"

Her laugh was sweet. It was a rich sound which came from her heart. Henri knew instantly that, unlike the others who fawned around the King, she did not laugh for effect.

"I was not certain you would wish to thank me if you had agreed to court him," he finally said.

First the laughter stopped. Then her smile faded. "Your Highness—"

"Henri," he corrected her.

"Very well. Henri, I have told you that it would not be proper for me to court anyone at present. I am afraid the Captain sometimes forgets his manners. There is nothing more to it."

Her tone had been almost scolding. It was harsh and yet edged, he thought, with a hint of some kind of fear. She had not spoken to him like that before. Feeling as though he had said too much, Henri looked away, yet he knew that he could not stop now. She must know. He must tell her. He must show her how he felt. He gathered the strength to turn his gaze upon her once again.

"You look magnificent tonight. The black color against your fair skin . . . your hair . . ."

He took her hand in his own and gently kissed it; then held it near his lips, as he had seen his father and his brother do so many times. He only hoped it was proper. He felt as if his heart would crash through his ribs or stop altogether. His stomach was knotted. His lips were dry. But after he had touched her hand to his lips, he could not find the strength to surrender it.

He looked down at her. The bodice of her gown was black silk crested with white lace. Across her breastbone was a string of pearls. They drew his eyes downward. Down to her breasts; the same breasts he thought of in the night sometimes. The easy smile had left her face. Without a single word between them, he knew she felt the power of his eyes; knew she felt the intensity as he continued to hold her hand. That touch was their connection. The skin of her hand was soft; smooth like velvet. Like nothing he had ever known . . . or would know again. He would never . . . could never be here again. Not exactly like this. With her.

Now, he was only mildly aware of a strange force growing inside of him. A force pulling him toward her. Closer. Easing the fear. Replacing it with a warm, almost numbing sensation. He saw her lips, long and slender. Pink. The color of a musk rose. Slightly parted and moist. Slowly, he moved toward her and then pressed his firm lips against hers in an awkward yet powerful adolescent kiss.

"Henri," she gasped, putting her fingers to her lips. "You mustn't ever do that again."

"But why? I thought that you cared for me."

"Your Highness must not think of me in that way. If I have given you any reason to believe there was anything more than friendship between us, I am very, very sorry."

"But you must know how I feel about you before that bastard Montgommery sweeps you away."

"I believe that you care for me, Henri, as I care for you. But when one is young, feelings of friendship can often be mistaken for different and even deeper emotions."

"But, I love you, and I have reason to believe that you feel the same!" He blurted out the words and then stood before her with his lips parted, his eager face flushed.

Diane felt her mind begin to whirl. She leaned back against the gazebo to steady herself. "You have no reason," she calmly replied and then took his hand. "Henri, you must listen to me. You are the son of a King. I am a widow with two daughters who are nearly your age. I was young once myself. I know what you are feeling, but you must believe me, it is not love."

As Diane struggled to convince him, she could see from the corner of her eye the shadow of a man coming down the lawn toward the gazebo with a large retinue around him. She moved away from Henri to a place behind a thick tangle of ivy, hoping to see who it was. As he passed beneath the light of the moon, Diane could see to her horror that it was the King.

Her heart began to race and she was choked with fear. Their presence alone together here could be very damaging to them both. But how could she convince a headstrong boy like Henri, who thrived on being the bane of the King, that for both of their sakes he must hide? She had no idea what she might say to convince him. She must say something. Anything. But as she turned back, prepared even to plead with him, she found herself alone. Just as the King and his courtiers came upon her, she turned around in time to see the shadow of a young man heading alone into the protective thickness of the forest.

THE COURT MOVED TO PARIS from Saint Germain-en-Laye the following morning. The King's favorites, his *petite bande,* his confidants and his aides, rode with him in a train of royal barges down the teeming river that flowed into the Seine. The others would follow on horseback.

Henri had done his best to avoid Diane before they departed. He did not attend vespers in the chapel when he knew that she would be there, nor did he show up for their game of *jeu de paume.* When he found that she would be going by the King's barge, he resolved to take his horse. Jacques did not ask him about the meeting in the gazebo but he knew it had not gone well. The flicker of light that Diane de Poitiers had illuminated in the eyes of the young Prince had once again dimmed.

Diane herself was consumed by the entire incident and berated herself for having encouraged it. *It is my fault. I should have seen it coming. I should have seen the signs of it. If only I had not gone to his room that afternoon. I was too familiar. It was wrong of me. Dear Mother Mary, help me now,* she silently prayed and clutched her small leather prayer book to her breast. *I am just so alone. So lonely. He is young. Strong . . .*

She thought of his body as he had stood there before her in the moonlight. She had watched his eyes narrow as he had held her hand; felt the gentle touch of his fingers. He did not love her in some chaste way. He had wanted her. She knew that. It was not difficult to see in one so young. Her knees grew weak at the thought of him. A shiver ran through her. She could feel her nipples tense against the velvet bodice of her gown; feel a deep, disturbing surge.

"Madame?"

"What? Oh . . ."

Jacques de Saint-André had sat down beside her on the tented royal barge but she had not noticed. They rode in the second barge behind the King as soft music from the lute player drifted back to them on the wings of a gentle breeze.

"Why are you not with the Prince?" she asked, gazing out at the trees and the thatched roof cottages that lined the shore.

"He asked me to go on ahead. He wanted to ride alone."

She looked at him for a moment, as she had never before. He had a kind, sensitive face. Gentle eyes. Henri trusted him. She trusted him.

"Oh, Jacques," she whispered. "It seems as if I have made a terrible mess of things."

"He cares deeply for you, Madame."

"He fancies himself in love."

"I suspected as much. You are the first person that he has valued, besides Montmorency, who showed him the least bit of favor."

"I knew it must be something like that. Oh, Jacques, what am I to do? He is such a kind and gentle young man. I have no wish to cause him any more hurt than this life has given him already."

There was a long silence between them. Jacques gazed out across the river. A cool spring breeze lashed across his face and rippled his blond hair.

"I suppose then, Madame, you must be very certain about what you do want to do before you act upon it."

She clutched his arm and took in a deep breath. "Oh, you are both so wonderful and so very young. The very notion of such a thing is impossible."

"Yes, Madame. I would agree with you for myself, but Henri is different. Spain aged him in a way that you or I will never completely understand. He seemed to lose any remaining vestige of his youth there. Since then, he has always seemed old, you know; well beyond his years."

Jacques shifted in his seat and adjusted his toque, which the breeze had pushed back on his head. "Yet in the past month I have seen him smile and laugh as though he were a child again."

"And you think it is because of me?"

"All I am saying, Madame, is that I believe you wield an enormous amount of influence over His Highness just now. More than you know. As his friend, I would ask you, please, to consider the knowledge of that well before you act."

Diane gazed back out as the barge swayed and moved its way into the city of Paris. She could see the Cathedral de Notre Dame in the distance with its two beautiful high pillars rising up toward the cloudless sky. As they neared the city, the royal barges converged into the city's canals.

These congested waterways were steadily swollen to capacity with the tangle of barges and fishing boats. The Seine was a major artery for supplies and travel. It was also a pestilent sewer, teaming with the odor of refuse. Diane smiled in disbelief at the beauty that was Fontainebleau forty miles away, as she covered her mouth to the vile stench that filled the air of the city.

Jacques' words haunted her so that she barely noticed the filthy streets, used as a dumping ground for the town's refuse. Holes and blue-black puddles of grease were stepped over, as the entourage made their way from the landing up the rue Saint-Honoré toward Les Tournelles.

She did not see the thatched roof dwellings or the timber front mansions flowing out of the twisted dirty streets. She missed the sight of the beggars and the dirty faced children who were kept back by the pointed rapiers of the King's guard. The shops full of silks, velvet, books and pictures. The hollering of fish mongers. Weavers. Butchers. The sight of all of them were lost to her.

Be certain, Jacques had said.

Certain of what? Was he suggesting that she was falling in love with a boy half her age? It was too absurd to consider. He was a handsome and sensitive young man who one day soon would meet and marry a beautiful and dowered young woman. They would laugh together about his infatuation one day. Yes, years from now, she and Henri would share a private joke about their stolen kiss in the gazebo. *I am too old. I have children. I have a past. I am a widow. It is impossible.*

*T*HE DAYS OF SPRING at the Court of France were strung together by an endless series of banquets, hunting parties and poetry readings in the gardens. For Diane, things had finally begun to develop a rhythm. Even the constant uprooting and the endless ceremonial journeys were beginning to seem commonplace.

Since the Sancerre trio's ouster from Court and Anne d'Heilly's return to her place as undisputed *favourite,* the vicious poetry that had regularly begun to find its way beneath Diane's door had ceased. Anne no longer used the regular gatherings as occasion to slight her. Diane had also managed to rekindle old friendships with the Grand Master's wife and the King's two daughters, Madeleine and Marguerite. For the most part, she would have considered herself quite content had it not been for one element: the breach with Henri.

Diane had tried to get word to him through Jacques as soon as they had arrived in Paris. She had proposed a neutral game of *jeu de paume* in an attempt to ease the tensions between them. She had only hoped to discourage his advances; she had not wanted to lose his friendship. Much to her surprise, however, a polite refusal to her invitation was returned through his valet. The very civil explanation to her was that His Highness was kept quite busy of late, training for his upcoming joust with the King. Diane knew the real reason for the turn of events between them and she felt responsible.

I have hurt him, she thought. *But what other choice did I have?*

"HÉLÈNE! CHARLOTTE! Where are you with my gown!" Diane called. "I shall be late for the King's ball!"

Diane was not herself. She had been nervous, and the tension had caused her to lose her temper several times that day. Tomorrow the King would fight his son. They would joust. France had a passion for the sport. It brought out all of Paris, who celebrated wildly in the taverns, inns and brothels of the city, before and after such a match.

Tomorrow the stands would be filled with music and courtiers. Beautifully painted women would spill forth from the stands, waving the scarf of their colors at the victor whom they had chosen. Banners would fly and trumpets would herald the arrival of the final athletes of the day: King François and Prince Henri.

Part of the thrill of the joust to a gentleman of honor was the danger. It was a perilous sport, and one opponent was as likely to be felled as the next. In times past it had been more dangerous but after several serious injuries and deaths, modifications to the sport had been made. Each man would be dressed in full armor. Rather than riding directly at one another, the arena, called "the lists," was divided by a long wooden panel. Each man rode toward the other on opposite sides of a low barrier. It was also no longer the intent to fell one's opponent; the purpose was to break a lance against the opponent's shielded body.

Diane looked out of her open casement window at Les Tournelles onto the courtyard below. There she could see the lists being constructed. As the afternoon sun dimmed, the men carried large sheets of wood which were then bolted together to form the divider. Diane thought of Henri. He was young and strong. His well-developed body could survive the rigors of a joust with the King. But accidents had happened. It was dangerous.

Her mind wandered back to their kiss and the cool taste of his lips pressed against hers.

"Stop it!" she cried out. "Hélène! Charlotte!"

The two women came into the room together. Hélène's arms were full with a long black gown. Charlotte held the black velvet slippers and the jewelry casket, neither of them having apparently heard her cry.

"Are they really going to fight?"

"Yes, Hélène, they are," Diane replied, turning back from the window.

"Imagine giving a ball to celebrate a battle with your own son! Joust indeed! If you ask me, it is all-out war. He hates the boy and all of France knows it," Charlotte muttered to herself as she set the jewelry casket on the bed then handed Hélène a pearl and ruby brooch.

"No, not that one," Diane said. "Tonight I shall wear the crescent."

The two servants looked at one another again.

"The talisman?"

"Yes, Charlotte, the talisman. You do not approve?"

"Well, Madame, since you ask, it is just that you have so many more, well, so many more stunning pieces than that old bit of ivory."

"That *old bit of ivory,* as you call it, was given to me many years ago as a good luck charm," Diane reminded her.

She looked down at the pendant, perfectly shaped as a crescent moon which hung from a thin chain of solid gold. She remembered with the clarity of yesterday, the day she had received it. The woman was old, her hair gray and matted. *I know not who you are,* she had said, moments after Diane had plucked her from the river, *but I would have drowned. I owe you my life.* When she told the old woman that her name was Diane, her gray-blue eyes had blinked with astonishment. Then, she had reached under her gown, pulled a pendant from her neck and thrust it into Diane's hand. *I was told long ago,* she began again with a quivering voice, *that one day, there would be someone to whom I should give this. When the time came I would have no doubt who that was. Now, I am certain. You see,* she said, pointing to the shape of the ivory. *A moon. Symbol of Diana, goddess of the moon. It is your symbol. Please take it. It has brought me luck. Now, it shall do the same for you. One day when it is time for you to pass it along, you also shall know it.*

"Yes, tonight I shall wear the crescent," she declared and then turned around.

Her servants both backed away as Diane took one final look at herself in the mirror. What she saw caused her to draw nearer to her image. There were two tiny lines beside each of her eyes. She touched them.

"Ah, well. The first signs of it," she sighed. "Tonight I shall be glad that the ball is a masked affair."

"Madame, you are beautiful!" said Hélène.

Diane turned and kissed her whimsically on the cheek. "And you are a faithful servant."

Finally, Charlotte hooked the black velvet mask over her eyes and beneath Diane's headdress. When the costume was complete, she turned back around toward them and smiled, hoping that there was still some modicum of truth in her young maid's declaration.

SHE SAW HENRI before he saw her.

He was standing alone by one of the long open windows through which Diane could see the glowing crescent shape of the moon. Henri was the only one in the room who did not wear a mask and yet that did not particularly surprise her. He stood against the window, looking from side to side and swilling a large gold chalice of wine. She was so struck by the image that, for several moments while she was sheltered by a swell of guests, she hid herself and watched him. She had not known, until that moment, how completely alone someone could actually be in a room filled with so many people.

"Not very sporting of Your Highness to come without a mask," she finally said, trying her best to sound casual.

"I do not like games," he replied without looking when she came up beside him.

"Then why did you come at all?"

"Only because the King threatened to send me back to Fontainebleau for another month alone with the Queen and her Spaniards, if I did not comply."

"Oh, Henri, I am sorry."

"Do not be. By now I have grown accustomed to it. People are like puppets to him, and he is the grand puppeteer. He says 'do this . . .' so we do. 'Do that,' and so we do . . . we always do. Not bad once you know the rules," he said sardonically, and finished the rest of his wine.

It was more awkward than it had ever been between them. He still had not looked at her, yet there was a kind of anger in his voice that told her he had closed himself off to her. Nothing she said could make him react. He set his empty goblet on the tray of a passing servant and took a full one. He did not seek to continue their exchange. Then, when there was nothing else she could say, Diane unfastened the crescent-shaped ivory pendant from around her neck and held it out to him.

"So then. Tomorrow you joust."

"Tomorrow the King exhibits publicly his disdain of me."

"Well, I should very much like for you to have this with you. I was told by an old woman once that it is a talisman of sorts; that it brings good luck to whomever shall wear it."

Henri took the pendant and looked for the first time into Diane's masked eyes. "It is crescent shaped, just as the moon is tonight."

Diane nodded, surprised that he had noticed.

"It is very beautiful."

"Yes it is. It is also very special to me."

"It is the shape of a crescent, and you are Diana . . . like the goddess of the moon. This is your symbol. Are you certain you want to give it to me?"

"Very certain."

"Then I shall fight for your honor tomorrow with this pendant beneath my armor," he declared in an uneasy and faltering voice, more like the one she had heard beneath the gazebo when he had said he loved her. With an overwhelming instinct of fear, she turned from him. He could see that he had made her uneasy.

". . . Just as I did in my first tourney when you gave me your scarf. Remember?" he added. Diane continued to look away. "Madame, I meant nothing more by it. You have made your feelings clear. But please, let me ride for you. You know that I have no one else."

Her heart swelled beneath her elegant black damask gown. She smiled and then turned to face him again. What could she say? Now she was being foolish. She had offered peace between them by giving him this talisman. He had done nothing more than agree to take it; and she desperately wanted their friendship.

"Very well, then. It would be a great honor, Your Highness, if you should ride for me tomorrow."

Just as Diane had agreed, the King and Grand Master Montmorency came up beside them. Diane turned, then curtsied to His Majesty.

"Why, Henri," said the King in mock surprise. "Your presence here tonight surprises me."

"I was not aware of a choice in the matter," Henri sniped.

"I believe that I made your choices quite clear. And Madame, what a pleasure it is to see you here as well. Where have you been keeping yourself these past few days? Do not tell me that this foolish boy is the only one fortunate enough to have enjoyed your company."

"Madame de Poitiers was only being polite, Your Majesty. She was inquiring of me the reason for our match tomorrow."

"And what did you tell her?"

"I was forced to confess to her that intense dislike and a great desire to inflict pain between the opponents were the only motivations I knew. Now, if you all will excuse me . . ."

Montmorency lowered his head, anticipating the King's reaction. Diane and the King watched him fade into the crowd.

"Blasted boy! Damn! How sorry I am to have given seed to him! Madame, I assure you, you are wasting your time on the ungrateful wretch!"

"I have found no problem with him, Your Majesty. Prince Henri is always very proper with me."

"Then perhaps we should all take lessons from you, for if you speak the truth, you know a very powerful secret!"

"Madame, Prince Henri is, well to be plain . . . he is disturbed," explained the Grand Master. "His Majesty believes that the years in Spain fostered in him a kind of illness of the mind that we are thus far at a loss to cure."

"I see. Well I am sorry then if I have overstepped my bounds."

"It is not your fault," said the King. "You could not have known. And if he is, as you say, proper with you, then perhaps there is some small ray of hope; for you would be the first. Ah! They are doing the Passepied. My favorite! Do come dance with me, Madame. Help me forget all this trifling."

Diane's instinct had been to go after Henri, but by now he was hopelessly lost amid the panoply of courtiers and dignitaries. François was tugging at her hand, bidding her to join him. She must dance with him. One did not reject such an offer.

"Rumor has it, Your Majesty, that we will soon be at war again," Diane remarked. François turned from her and bowed in time to the music.

"Tell me, Madame, have you ever been to Italy?"

"I'm afraid I have not had the pleasure."

They turned again and circled past other partners. When they were reunited, they again bowed and joined hands.

"It is the most beautiful land in the world, with riches that you can scarcely imagine. There are cathedrals, sculptures and art to overwhelm. Come, I will show you what I mean," he suddenly declared, and pulled her from the dancing area. The rest of the guests came to a halt as the King led Diane de Poitiers by the hand, out of the ballroom.

Henri surged forth protectively from his place by the open window. Jacques held him from advancing. "Where is he taking her?"

"Steady yourself, Your Highness. She is a grown woman."

"But she is no match for these people! She must give way to the King and his whore or be thought disobedient! I know how he works, and I shall not let her become one of his conquests!"

His anger had won. It turned his face crimson with rage and forced his lips into a sharp, thin line.

"You cannot protect her forever."

"And why not, if she will let me?"

Across the room, Anne d'Heilly and Admiral Chabot rose from their seats and advanced in the direction that Henri had gone. The Dauphin and the young Prince Charles followed after them, both laughing and kicking one another mischievously from behind.

"I am going with them," Henri declared. Jacques pulled harder at his arm, nearly tearing the fine red silk sleeve.

"Your Highness, do not, I bid you!" He cleared his throat. "What if she had chosen to go with him?"

"Never! I shall never believe it!" he declared and broke free of Jacques' grasp, pushed over a chair in his path and darted toward the door after them.

THERE WERE NO AIDES nor any servants when they reached the King's private apartments. Even the guards whose post was inside the chamber doors had vanished. François had dismissed them all; dismissed them so that he might show her his private collection of art. Diane walked in slowly, several paces behind the Sovereign. On the wall to the right of the roaring fireplace, lighted by glowing wall sconces, were two dark oil paintings. Diane stood close, pretending to study them.

"They are quite beautiful, Your Majesty."

"Please, *ma chère,* when we are alone, I would much prefer it if you would find it in your heart to call me François."

Diane's heart began to race. Desperately needing to change the subject, she moved closer toward one of the paintings. "There is great depth in this work," she said.

"Not nearly so much as in my favorite. Come, let me show

you," he offered and extended his arm toward what she could clearly see was the door to his bedchamber. Diane shrank back, but the King held out his hand. "Come, please."

"La Gioconda," he proudly announced. Then he turned to gaze, himself, on the illusive face in the painting before them.

Diane gazed at the wall on which a relatively small, gold-framed painting hung from a velvet cord. It was the picture of a woman; serene and mysterious, her long dark hair parted in the middle and framing an expression one could not quite call a smile. Diane thought it a curious study of an odd-looking girl.

"It is magnificent," she lied.

"She and her husband had been friends of Leonardo, or so he told me before he died. Her name was Madonna Elisabetta Gioconda. She was called Mona Lisa. Is that not the most beautiful name?" As he spoke, François began to finger the delicate white lace at the base of Diane's neck as naturally as if it were on his own garment. "I saw it hanging in Clos Lucé, the home I had given him near Amboise when he came to live in France . . ." He leaned over and grazed her neck with his lips. They were moist. Warm. Wanting. He was not thinking of Leonardo da Vinci, nor of Mona Lisa. Nor was he thinking of his dear little Anne. His lips traveled up Diane's bare neck and to the lobe of her ear. His voice grew low and husky as he continued to speak in between kisses, and little bites at her skin. "It is one of my favorites . . ."

Her heart raced. She did not dare offend him but she would not bed with him.

"Please, Your Majesty. It is too soon for me," she whispered as his hand groped from her neck down to the tender pink skin of her bosom. Lost in his own passion and trying to work her slowly toward his large canopied bed, François continued to surround her with his lips and arms.

"Your Majesty, our Louis is only dead ten months! I still grieve for him!" She had added the word *our* as a way of defining her husband in hopes of kindling his decency and arresting his ardor. The ploy worked. As though she had slapped him squarely across the jaw, he broke away from her in a reflex action. His eyes were now wide and alert though his face was still filled with the flush of passion. Diane watched his heaving chest. She could hear his breathing as a long silent look passed between them.

"Please forgive me. I was insensitive."

"On the contrary, Your Majesty is most indulgent. That is why I was certain you would understand." Diane lowered her head, wanting to appear humbled by his attraction to her.

François wanted to believe her. He did not want to believe that she would reject him so boldly. After a moment, he made his choice. He took her chin in his large warm hand and held it.

"I can also be a patient man, *chérie,* when there is something so lovely and exciting as you for whom to wait." His words made her shudder but she was able to manage a weak smile. "In exchange for my patience, I should like to be the first to know when you feel your mourning is through."

Diane wondered how often he had said that; how often he had called himself a patient man and held a woman's chin so delicately, to keep her from looking for a means of escape. She wondered how many times it had worked. Just as the King set free her chin, Anne d'Heilly cast open the chamber door. She strode in, followed by Philippe Chabot and the Dauphin. Prince Charles lurked behind them.

"Ah well, so there you are, *mon amour*! We have been looking everywhere for you and here you are entertaining again. And so soon after your little indiscretion with the Comte de Sancerre's daughter?" she asked, pouncing onto his bed, her voice full of sarcasm.

"Madame Diane asked to see my paintings. She has seen them and now she is leaving," he defended and then turned toward the entourage at the door. "What the devil are the rest of you doing here?" he raged at the sight of Admiral Chabot, two of his sons and three guards. Chabot bowed humbly and exited the wide chamber door just as Henri entered. Henri had heard the King declare from a hallway away that it was Diane's idea to come there, not his own.

"François, take your brother back to the party," the King ordered the Dauphin and Prince Charles. He did not see Henri, who slid behind one of the huge wall tapestries near the door. The other two boys whispered like children at their father's dilemma, and then left the room.

"So now tell me, are the paintings all that he has shown you, Madame La Sénéchale?" Anne asked, her voice full of anger. "I certainly do hope so for your sake. You know my darling François is an incurable tease. He fancies himself enamored of every woman he meets. At least until he beds with them."

"Anne, that is enough!"

"Nonsense, *mon amour*. It is important for Madame to make an informed decision about with whom she will bed. Now, you do have a diversionary penchant for the more mature ladies here at Court. That is well known. No doubt she was witness to your indiscretion with the Comtesse de Sancerre herself; or was that before you arrived, Madame? It is just so hard to keep them all straight!"

Diane watched the anger rise on the King's face, but she said nothing to defend herself. She said nothing because she knew that Anne d'Heilly would have liked nothing better than to turn this incident into a great cat fight.

"Oh, come now, *mon cher,* you must admit it. While maturity does seem to grasp your attention a bit sooner than the rest, of late, those possessing it never do seem to be able to retain it. Witness the child's mother, the poor Comtesse de Sancerre, and before that—"

"Anne! You go too far!" François bellowed.

"I think I shall say goodnight, Your Majesty," Diane whispered and without waiting for his leave, rushed from the King's bedchamber.

LARGE BLUE BANNERS sewn with royal golden fleurs-de-lys and images of the salamander flapped in the gentle spring breeze around the courtyard of Les Tournelles. Courtiers and peasants filtered together into the shaded wooden stands which looked down onto the tournament field. A balustrade with access from the palace had been prepared for the King's family and guests.

Diane took her place in the royal box between Grand Master Montmorency and the King's young son, Charles. Charlotte and Hélène sat behind her. Anne d'Heilly, dressed in royal blue silk, her gown and cap encrusted with jewels, chatted with two of her attendants and sat comfortably beside Admiral Chabot.

The joust between the King and his son would be the day's crescendo. It would be preceded by several others to pique the interest of the crowds. Among the early riders, the Dauphin François would ride against his friend, Guy Jarnac. Antoine de Bourbon would ride against Charles de Brissac.

The fanfare from the trumpets sounded, marking the parade of contestants who were about to make their entrance. A cool breeze mixed the dust and sent it swirling through the arena. Beneath the stands, shabbily dressed peddlers scalped tickets and made bets for the victors, while pickpockets worked the crowds. The throngs of people pressed tightly into the stands roared with excitement as the opponents pranced in, each astride a dazzlingly appointed horse. The field glittered with polished armor and the brightly colored peacock feathers that poised atop each helmet. The combatants waved toward the stands with gauntleted hands, and the furious applause increased.

The King and the Dauphin were first to enter. They strode in on opposite sides of the wooden guard. Both of their horses were decked in blankets of royal blue and gold with brilliantly colored gems lining the reins. Henri, who entered the field next beside Saint-André, did not wave at his introduction. The noise fell to a dull roar of murmurs and whispers at the sight of him. Amid all the colors and pageantry, Prince Henri rode a white horse draped with a blanket of black velvet with white silk piping. The large plume which rose from his helmet was black. Diane gazed down onto the field at the private tribute intended for her.

"How odd," Diane heard Anne d'Heilly mutter to the Admiral from a few seats away. "To wear mourning colors in a joust. It is as if someone is going to die. Does the boy have no sense at all?"

"Perhaps, *chérie,* it is because today the King will send that sorry son of his back to his Maker."

The two tittered evilly between themselves and looked back down onto the field. *I pray for your immortal soul,* thought Diane as she discreetly made the sign of the cross for Anne's benefit.

The day was long and the sun grew more intense with each joust. The Dauphin won his match with his friend, Guy Jarnac. The crowd had cheered this dashing young Prince as he neared the stands in his black tweed under-armor garments, a purple velvet cloak tossed casually over his shoulders. He had come to watch the other matches. He sat regally between Montmorency and Diane and called with a wave for his gentleman to bring him some wine.

By the time the King and Prince Henri entered the courtyard again, the sun was a fiery orange ball which had begun to descend behind the arena. Both men rode as the others before them, toward the royal stands, their silver visors raised. Diane's heart quickened as she was once again faced with the evidence of Henri's infatuation. She smiled at him and placed her hand to her chest where the pendant had been. He nodded his head as far as his armor would permit, and then, pulling his jeweled reins, led his horse off the field toward the judges who would check his armor and lance.

The King waved to his Anne and she stood to blow him a kiss. The crowd cheered their public display of affection. There was no love lost among the people of France for François' political liaison with Eleanora, the enemy's sister.

"Well, imagine that," whispered the Dauphin as he downed the first and called for another cup of wine. "It would appear that little brother Henri is quite taken with you," he remarked, leaning toward Diane, his body washed in the sour smell of sweat and horseflesh.

"That is absurd, Your Highness," she scoffed and pushed back a strand of hair that had come loose from her cap.

"I think not, Madame," he began to snicker. "He wears your mourning colors on the field, does he not?"

"Surely if it is anything at all, it is a coincidence."

Montmorency said nothing but the words rang through him like a shot. Could the boy be falling in love with her? A woman twice his own age. A woman of such a questionable past. No! It was unthinkable. Unacceptable. That was *his* boy. Henri was like one of his own sons. She was dangerous. He hadn't liked her the day she came to Court, and he did not like her any more now. He must put an end to it. It was that simple. Just as soon as the tourney was over, he would see to it. Perhaps he should get Henri away from Court for a while, and away from such temptation . . .

LANCES SPLINTERED and chips of wood flew into the stands, as the King and his son rode repeatedly at one another. Henri clutched his thighs tightly to his horse as his father broke his third lance against the scorching armor. The crowd cheered wildly for their King. By the time the sun had begun to set, the King had broken three lances to Henri's four. Each rider rode with a vengeance, and to the crowd's disappointment, neither managed to fell the other.

Inside the prison of his tightly fitting armor, Henri's body was bathed in sweat from the afternoon sun. Beads of perspiration dripped from his brow into his eyes so that he could barely see through the slitted silver visor. *I despise you,* he thought as he looked ahead at his opponent. His father. His King. *Nothing would give me greater pleasure than to fell you. Right now, here in front of your chamberlains, your ambassadors, your subjects and your whore. And I could do it. How easy it would be. I felt you falter when I last struck a blow on the last lance. I saw you sway and grab for the pommel. Oh, how I despise you!*

"What is wrong with the King?" Chabot whispered to Anne. "His pauses are long and he seems to falter. Perhaps we should send the physician to the field."

"Keep quiet," Anne hushed. "He is King. He shall win. It is nearly over anyway."

As expected by nearly all who had wagered, the King was given the match in spite of the tie. They had broken four lances each. Someone in the crowd behind Diane remarked that Prince Henri had missed the last lance by such a wide margin that it appeared he had missed it intentionally. "Superior performance," the judges said as the King and Prince paraded, visors up, before them to hear the decision. The crowds poured onto the dusty field and gathered around the contestants. The throngs of peasants who tried to near the King were held back by a queue of royal guards. Due to the weight of the armor, the King and Prince were helped down from the horses with the aid of several gentlemen-of-the-guard. The King's horse was then taken back into the stables as he, the Dauphin and Prince Charles were led back to the chateau surrounded by a collection of supporters.

"Shall we go, Madame, and join the others?" Charlotte finally asked, uncomfortable from the long hours they had spent on the bare wooden benches.

"You go on ahead," Diane replied. "I should like to sit here a little while longer."

Charlotte looked back to the place on the field that held her mistress's attention. Prince Henri stood there alone, still in full armor. His helmet was in his hand, and he was stroking the black nose of his snow white horse. Then she looked back at Diane.

You do not think I know, but I do, she thought. *I see it in your eyes every time you look at him. Every time he looks at you. Dear girl, he is but a boy . . . God help you both for what you are about to do.*

"MIGHT I HAVE A WORD with Your Majesty?"

Montmorency deftly maneuvered a place beside the King, Anne d'Heilly, and their entourage as they strode toward the entrance to the chateau on a flagstone path. *I must protect the boy,* he thought. *Not only from those self-seeking opportunists who would marry him so carelessly to a commoner, but now too from a middle-aged harridan.*

"What is it, Monty?" the King beamed, fresh from his victory, his wet arm draped around Anne d'Heilly's elegant beaded gown.

"It concerns the Prince Henri, Sire."

"Oh, really, Montmorency! Can this not wait?" Anne snarled and reached over protectively to brush a wet strand of hair from the King's brow.

"Anne is right, *mon ami*. I have just defeated the boy; taught him a lesson. Can I not revel in it a while longer before you bring me news of more trouble?"

"But Your Majesty, it is of the utmost importance," he persisted.

"Very well then. The rest of you go on ahead. I shall only be a moment."

He waited until those who had circled around him had gone in through the carved stone entrance before he turned back to the Grand Master. "Very well then, Monty, what is it?"

"Your Majesty is aware that the boy and I are close."

"Yes. Yes." He waved. "What of it?"

"Well, I find it is most distressing to report, Your Majesty, but I have been witness to a return of his sour temperament of late."

"You tell me nothing that I have not seen myself. Yet, it was only a couple of weeks ago, back at Fontainebleau, when his tutors reported to me that he had much improved."

"Indeed, Your Majesty. He was much changed, until the other day."

"And what do you speculate has been the catalyst?"

"Perhaps this is no more than a phase. You know how common it is in young people to volley between ecstasy and despair. At any rate, I should like to propose a holiday for the Prince, with your permission of course; get him away from Court for a while. A change of climate would certainly divert his attentions from whatever, or whomever, appears to be troubling him."

The King lowered his brows until he was frowning. Then he began to smile. "Are you suggesting, my dear Montmorency, that the boy has found himself a tart?"

"That I cannot say, Sire. But if it is a young girl who is the cause of his malaise, then the change of scene should all but cure it. If you also find it necessary to make a marriage between him and the Pope's niece, this obstacle, whatever it is, can only stand in the way."

The King appeared to be considering the matter. He put his hand up to his neat triangular beard and began to stroke it. "Perhaps it would be in order," he said, and then thought a moment longer. "So be it. We will send the Prince and his companions to . . . to Cauterets!"

"A brilliant idea, Your Majesty. I know you shall not regret this. There is nothing like a mineral spring to ease the pangs of adolescence. I shall organize it at once."

"You do that, Montmorency. And bring me a list of suitable companions who might accompany him. Yes, perfect," he said, and then added with a sneer, "But in the meantime, I shall be the one to select his chaperone, and old friend, you have given me a splendid idea! I believe that I have just the candidate."

"I WOULD LIKE TO SPEAK with you about my son, Prince Henri," the King began as he offered Diane a seat in the long, cold hall called the council chamber.

The vaulted room was paneled in rich wood and furnished only with the long council table, twelve chairs around it, a cabinet by the window and a tapestry near the fireplace. François was seated at the other end of the table between Philippe Chabot and Anne de Montmorency, a sea of empty chairs away.

"I understand from the Admiral here that you were very modest in our conversation last evening," the King began. "He tells me that the boy seems to have taken quite a fancy to you. No doubt it is a maternal sort of attachment, he was so young when his mother died. No one since the Queen seems to have been able to do what you have accomplished in a matter of weeks," he said, and then snapped his fingers. One of the liveried servants, who stood silently by the door, advanced and filled his silver goblet with wine.

"He actually seemed to be coming around until recently, something near to being civilized, or so We are told," he continued. Diane shifted in her seat. "Montmorency here seems to think there is a woman involved." She began to feel faint. Her mouth was dry. "On the Grand Master's sage counsel, and in an attempt to revive the boy's most recent heightened spirits, We have arranged a holiday for him at Cauterets. Do you know the place?"

Diane cleared her parched throat. "Cauterets, yes. Mineral baths in the Pyrénées, is it not?"

"Precisely. Well, *ma chère,* We shall come straight to the point."

He beckoned for another glass of wine and motioned that one was to be poured for her as well. Diane was grateful for anything to wet her throat. She was not certain she would be able to speak again if he asked her anything else.

"We would consider it a great service to your country if you, along with your attendants of course, would agree to attend the Prince on his holiday, as chaperone. We shall be sending his companions Saint-André, Brissac, Guise and Bourbon along with his staff. We have thought perhaps you, as well, might benefit from a change of scene." He leaned forward. "Time to consider and reflect," he added, punctuating his remark with a sly grin.

Diane's eyes widened and she turned from the King so that he was unable to see her flush. Montmorency bit his lip wanting to burst forth his objection. This was not at all what he had intended.

"We are aware," the King continued, "that the prospect of escorting a group of young people, no matter how lovely the destination, is not particularly enticing in and of itself; which is why I am prepared to offer you an inducement."

Diane looked back toward the King to see his lips turned in an uneasy smile. "Your Majesty," her voice cracked. "Such a thing is hardly necessary in my service of the Crown."

"We are certain that it is not. Just the same, Madame, We would feel better about the entire affair if you would accept a small token for your troubles." He stood, then strode over to the oak cabinet set between two of the long windows. He took a small book from inside. "We recently had to take a small chateau on the Cher river called Chenonceaux into Our possession for unpaid debts to the Crown. This was among its possessions."

He handed it to Diane. She fingered the delicate pages of the tiny prayer book beneath the inlaid leather binding. "It is yours if you will do Us this one small favor."

"It is a travesty that I should come to have such a personal and intimate article," she murmured as she contemplated the intricate scrollwork of inlaid gold. "The owner must miss it very much."

"I am certain that Monsieur Bohier would not think so at all, since surrendering it along with his other belongings saved him from complete ruin, or a far worse fate," Chabot snapped in a harsh nasal tone.

She wanted to object. She wanted to tell His Majesty that it was she from whom his son should escape. But she could not risk it. If she attempted to confess the truth now, an accusation would surely fall back on her from this surly Admiral who now sat picking food from his teeth with his fingers.

Montmorency wanted to object as well. He fought his own urge to stand and silence the King, explaining that there had been a great mistake. But he could not. He had no proof of his suspicions against her, only a raging feeling inside himself that their friendship, if it was allowed to continue, would somehow harm the Prince.

"Very well, Your Majesty," Diane recanted. "I shall prepare my things at once."

"Splendid," he grinned. "You leave by morning's light."

TO THE NOBLES it was called "taking the cure" at Cauterets. For many years it had been the site of healing for the infirm and aged, with eleven sulphur springs bursting forth from the rich earth. It was also an exclusive mountain resort for the aristocracy set in an idyllic mountain village with the snowy peaks of Vignemale in the background.

At the mention of the excursion by Montmorency, Prince Henri had sprung back to life like one of the King's painted jesters. The trip was long and arduous; up steep inclines and around sharp bends into the sheer cliffs of the Pyrénées mountains. But the weather favored them, and a light spring breeze urged them onward. To pass the time they sang songs and took turns reading from *The Canterbury Tales,* the medieval English story about an unlikely troop who travel together on a pilgrimage of their own.

After they had reached the inn, Henri lay sprawled on the embroidered counterpane on his bed. His arms cradled his head as he stared up at the ceiling. The room was rustic with low black wooded beams that Jacques, being the tallest, had to duck beneath as he moved about.

"How many here know who we are?" Henri asked and kicked off a shoe onto the floor. "Well, I suppose the proprietor and his wife, since one of the King's men made the arrangements."

"Can you stop the word from spreading?"

"I do not understand, Your Highness."

"It is quite simple. I wish to be anonymous here."

"That would seem most unwise, Your Highness. For security's sake."

"It is so beautiful. So pure. I feel so alive; as though I have never lived before," he said, and bolted from the bed toward the window which opened onto a sloping meadow and snow-capped mountains in the distance. "Just look at that!" Henri cried, beckoning his friend toward the window. Both of them looked down onto the meadow below. Like the one through which they had just come, it too was blanketed with green clover and bright red poppies, all swaying rhythmically in the breeze. In its midst, a shepherd boy, followed by his flock of sheep, called out softly for a lost kid. Henri leaned against the wooden casement of the window trying to catch his breath.

"I want to be like that, Jacques." He pointed back out the window. "No worries. No cares. If only for a little while." He looked up from the window and his sad eyes persuaded even his most stalwart friend.

"I shall see what I can do."

"I have not had an official portrait done in years. I know no one will recognize me if I have your help. See the guards as well.

Tell them to wear their own attire. No uniforms," Henri called out as Saint-André headed for the door. "Oh, and have Guise tell the others as well. It will be like an adventure!"

THE HEAVY COPPER dinner bell sounded just as Henri and his companion were descending the narrow, spiral stone steps toward the small dining room. The cool breath of dusk blew in through two open windows which looked onto the stone courtyard. The breeze blew the thin gauze curtains and caused the candles in their wall sconces to sputter.

The common rooms of the inn were not unlike the Prince's room. The beamed ceilings were low and dark and there were only a few candles to light them. Copper pots and ladles hung from the open beams and clanged together gently in the breeze. The inn was not elegant. It was musty and rather old, but the people came for the springs, not for the accommodations. It was thought to be very smart among the privileged class to come to Cauterets, and while there, to live a novel spartan existence. It was all the rage to purge one's body of the excesses of nobility in the pure mountain air before returning to the comforts of their opulent lives.

Diane was already sitting on one of the long wooden benches between Hélène and François de Guise when Jacques and Henri came down the stairs. Everyone looked up casually, but it was Diane who blinked hard at the sight of the young Prince in coarse wool pants long around his calves, and a shepherd's surcoat with a long black hood hanging down between his shoulders. His dark eyes sparkled as he came into the room.

"I hope we are not late. I am famished," he said as a short, stout woman with a red cotton bonnet lumbered past him with a steaming iron pot of soup. The other guests looked up from their conversations at the communal table but paid little attention to his entrance. Henri glanced around the room and, feeling that he had been sufficiently disguised, smiled.

Around the courtly entourage was an oddly matched set of guests. There was the white-haired judge from Lyon who rarely spoke but instead, when he desired something, repeatedly tapped his cane on the wood floor. There was a newly married couple from Rouen, a banker and his wife from Paris, and the village priest who regularly took his meals at the inn.

"It is so lovely here!" Henri exclaimed with a hearty smile. "I can scarcely wait for the baths!"

He sat down on the bench across from Diane and broke off a large hunk of bread from a crusty loaf in the center of the table. The same stout woman returned from the kitchens, clanging dishes and whistling to herself as she set the assortment of food on the bare wooden tables.

"Where did Your Highness get those awful garments?" Brissac muttered, his hand hiding his mouth to disguise the shock of the sight.

"I paid the shepherd for them," he whispered, "and I shall thank you all to remember my name is Henri, simply Henri, or you shall spoil all my fun."

The old woman then set a large steaming tureen in the center of the table and slammed down a large clay jug of malmsey.

"*À votre santé!*" she wheezed and everyone nodded to her as the old judge from Lyon leaned in and greedily filled his bowl first.

"So nice to have new faces among us. From where do you people hail?" asked the priest, Père Olivier, as he took his turn and scooped up a spoonful of the stew. Everyone exchanged a quick glance, all of them afraid to speak contrary to the wishes of the Prince.

"From Paris," Diane calmly replied and then took a sip of wine.

"So have you all come for the baths, or are you here to see the travesty?"

"What do you mean?" Henri asked as he took a bite.

"My little church in the village that those blasphemous swine got their hands on."

He brushed a piece of bread around in the stew and when it was soaked, he tossed it to the large dog beneath his feet.

"People have been coming from all parts to see it; some others from Paris not long ago. Natural curiosity, I suppose. Never thought God would allow it to happen to His house. Sacrilege is what I call it. Ought to burn it to the ground instead of keeping it as it is, in shambles. There's just the shell left now. Some of the people want to rebuild . . . But . . . I don't know."

Diane's face faded to ashen. Her smile was gone. "Someone burned a house of God?"

"Burned it down to nothing. We saw it yesterday," the young bride chimed in and then stifled her comment upon seeing Diane's grave expression. She coughed nervously and raised her goblet.

"Not just any someone, Madame. The Lutherans did it," the priest explained. "They've been only too glad to claim responsibility."

"But why? I know they take issue with the papacy but what on earth does that have to do with a house of the Lord up here in the mountains?!"

"They left placards afterward saying, THIS HOUSE STANDS FOR WHAT A FEW MEN BELIEVE. They broke a stained-glass window that was nearly two hundred years old. The sacred altar was scavenged. There were sheep feeding from it like a trough, when I finally found it at a little place in the valley."

"And why do you not report such criminals to the King?" asked Jacques as he leaned over his steaming earthen bowl.

"The King, you say?" he asked with a disdainful chuckle. "God bless His Majesty, but the poor bastard's no better than the rest of them. His own sister's one of their worst! You know she leads a whole colony of them from her palace in Navarre!"

"But there must be something that can be done!" Diane interjected.

"I am afraid not, dear lady. Yes, I am out of a parish, to be sure, but I am never out of my faith. I hold vespers each day in the meadow across from the remains of our church, and I hear confessions in the village in a room behind the butcher's house. It is not what I would have wanted but it was God's will and for now we make do."

"I would like to see it tomorrow," Henri said, as he pushed the spoon around his bowl.

"Oh, but why?" Jacques asked, leaning in toward the Prince.

"It is bound to be disheartening, and there is very little you can do."

"I simply want to see it."

"I shall go with you," Diane announced, her voice low and resolute.

After the last of the stew had been consumed and the remaining bread thrown down for the dogs, the young bridegroom, who said his name was Michel, pulled a reed pipe from the pocket of his doublet, and began to play. His young bride, with corn-colored hair and a quiet, oval face, gazed at him adoringly. Everyone else sat back on the benches to listen. He played a hypnotic piece that tangled with the soft breeze that blew through the open windows.

Only when it was safe and the others were relaxed did Henri's eyes begin to wander toward Diane. He gazed at her hair and watched the way the light played off the loosely braided strands. He watched her eyes, sparkling blue, focused intently on the young musician. He swallowed hard as he marked with his own eyes the contours of her breasts behind the tightly fitted bodice of her black satin gown. God, she was beautiful, he thought, longing for tomorrow.

THE NEXT MORNING, Henri held Diane's hand as they made their way through the clover, down the steep incline of the meadow. They walked into the valley, then onto the cobbled streets at the entrance to the village. The lane on which they found themselves seemed like a continuation of the fields. There were flame-lit poppies, irises and bright yellow primroses inextricably braided into the gardens and window boxes of each tiny thatched house.

The town was crested by enormous, gentle green trees that rustled and tossed stray leaves onto the stones. There were other dashes of color on the narrow twisted village lane. A purple drape before a window, a young woman's yellow kerchief; and everywhere, the intoxicating scent of flowers. They had walked only a short distance through the village when Diane gripped Henri's hand and came to a halt.

"Dear God," she uttered, staring straight ahead, forcing Henri's eyes to follow hers. There, at the end of the lane before them, were the charred remains of the church that Père Olivier had described.

They slowly advanced with neither of them breaking their gaze. They looked in silent horror at the blackened frame, like a grotesque skeleton; the carved archway that once held the doors, the soot-covered stone belfry, and the tumbled tombstones which lay beside it.

"Are you certain that you want to go on?" Henri whispered, overcome himself by the enormity of the destruction. She nodded and they continued to advance, their hands linked.

They walked slowly over the charred ruins that were once pews, communion rails and crumbled walls. Diane genuflected and made the sign of the cross in the direction of the place where the altar had once stood. As she did, she saw beside her shoe in the ashes the imprint of a small crucifix. Like everything else around them it had been reduced to ashes so that only the outline remained.

"God, forgive them," she uttered, "for they know not what they do."

Diane and Henri faced one another for a long moment where words have no place. As they stood wide eyed, gazing around at a manner of devastation foreign to them both, Henri saw, through the fallen timbers, a dirty-faced man hauling beams from the ashes. Henri charged at him, his eyes filled with rage. Both men sailed into a billowing pile of soot as rotted boards came crashing down around them.

"I ought to kill you myself!" Henri raged and landed a blow to his jaw. The stranger moaned and sank beneath Henri's firm grip. He did not struggle.

"Please, Henri, let him go!" Diane screamed as she ran after him.

"Dirty, rotten bastard!"

Diane strained and pulled at Henri's meager shirt. "Please, Henri! Listen to me! This is no way to settle it!"

Finally he heard her. The Prince, still dressed as a shepherd, stepped back and brushed off his hands that had become black-ened in the fray. "Of course not. You are right," he muttered, his breath quickened by the tangle. The man staggered to his feet, blood dripping from the side of his mouth. He faced Henri. "Are you responsible for what has become of this great house of God?"

The man wiped his face with the back of his dirty sleeve and left a streak of blood across his cheek. "No. But I mean to say that I am glad it happened."

The stranger with the matted black hair and the defiant eyes spat into the ashes. Henri grabbed him by the shirt once again.

"Where is your respect, man? Can you not see where you are?" he seethed.

The man's face was hard. This time he did not flinch, but flicked Henri's fists from his soiled shirt, as one would rid oneself of a bothersome pest. Again their eyes met. "It does not look like much of any place at all; at least, not now." His lips stretched into a sarcastic smile.

"I could have you hanged for your insolence!" the Prince bel-lowed and again aimed his fist at the stranger's face.

"Henri, be still!" Diane urged, and pulled his poised arm back behind him. The man was urged on by Diane's cautionary words.

"This church and the priests in it had everything up here; warmth, food . . . even women! Yeah, how do you like that? Now they are just like the rest of us. Ha! And I am glad they were fi-nally made to pay," he said, licking his lips.

The two men exchanged another combative stare before the stranger bent down to pick up his small pile of partially charred wood. "At least now I can heat my stew and my cottage for a night or two."

After he had gotten what he had come for, the man stalked off down the lane and disappeared into an alley between two buildings.

"Why did you stop me?" Henri raged and swung his head around toward Diane. The blood of anger had flushed his face and a small vein in his neck pulsed with fury.

"He is nothing but a scavenger. It would have come to no

good. Besides, you know the King does not see it as the threat it truly is. The reformist movement that his sister the Queen of Navarre so embraces is a pastime; like poetry or *jeu de paume*. He entertains heretical debate as a way to clear the palate for the evening meal."

Henri felt the press of a hand on his shoulder. He whipped around, prepared again to strike. Diane turned around too.

"Père Olivier!" she exclaimed, faced with the gentle eyes of the cleric they had first met at supper.

"Mademoiselle is correct, you know. It will do no good. The people here see it as a sign of the times."

"But there must be something that can be done. Surely such violence is not the answer."

"The people are hungry and tired; too much taxation and too many wars. They are swayed by a movement that, to have them renounce the true faith, promises them everything they lack. To many of my overburdened flock, prayer was their greatest consolation in these difficult times. Now they have lost even that at the hands of those reformers, the Lutherans."

"I had no idea that they are against God," Henri gasped.

"Can you look at what they have done here and think otherwise, my son?"

Diane took her small black-velvet purse from the folds of her skirt and emptied the silver coins and a strand of pearls into the hands of the village priest. She closed her own hand around his.

"Oh no, my child, I cannot take this."

"You must. It is important that you rebuild God's house. You must rebuild! If you do not, they will have won!"

Her urgings brought a slow smile to his kind face. "This will go a long way toward our work. May the Lord bless you for your kindness." He deigned and made the sign of the cross before her.

A CART COVERED over by a plank of wood served as the altar. A pewter mug was used as the chalice for the rite of Communion. The gathering was a meager collection of assorted faithful. Many of the village young who embraced the new ideas were absent. So too were the poor; those who were promised a better life by renouncing the hypocrisy of the Church. Those who did attend were the sick and the elderly. There were also a few wealthy patrons from one of the several inns down the hill.

Despite the devastation they had seen that morning, Henri felt he had been blessed with a new and powerful insight. He knelt through the Mass, his fist closed tightly around a small, gold crucifix, a gift from his mother. His mind was whirling with conflict. His heart was bursting with a clash of feelings.

He had grown up hearing about the Protestant Reformation. The French Court was known throughout Europe to be sympathetic to its followers. The King himself often introduced it into the discussion circles, and it seemed somehow to be woven into all civilized conversations. His Aunt Marguerite, the famous Queen of Navarre who rebelled against dogma, was inspired by it. It was a philosophical issue aimed at the wealthy and well educated; or so he had always been made to believe.

In the years since his return from Spain, Henri had never been allowed to hear the other side. Now, as he knelt there in the meadow beside Diane in the soft valley of clover, his knee resting near the folds of her voluminous black silk gown, he felt changed. The alteration in him had been profound. At the same time, he believed he had never been happier and more full of hope for the future than he was at that moment. Surrounded by the purity and beauty of life, exposed to its dark side, Henri knew that this one incident, this moment in time, would somehow change his life forever.

Père Olivier approached them after the service and thanked them as he had the others, most of whom now made their way back into the village. After kissing Diane's hand, he leaned in with a smile broader than they had seen before.

"I haven't much way to repay your kindness but there is a tavern close by if you would consent to share a humble tankard of ale." He whispered the words but his eyes danced with the delight of a child, which made them both laugh.

"We should be pleased to join you," Henri smiled.

The tavern was a little stone building at the end of a dark and crooked alley. It was not the kind of place either of them had ever been, or likely would be again. It became an adventure. Henri winked at Diane as they ducked to pass through the low beamed door into the small crowded cellar. The priest led the way through the press of people, to a small wooden table near the back of the room.

Once inside, they were completely enveloped by the shouts, the laughter and the earthy aroma of the coarse villagers. Père Olivier raised his hand toward the proprietor, a robust man with little hair and the veined face of a drinker, who stood behind a long oak bar. Almost before he could lower his hand, three tall pewter tankards of ale were tossed down before them, each sloshing waves of white foam onto the table. Diane laughed out loud at the novelty then raised her tankard.

"À Dieu!" she declared.

"À Dieu!" they echoed and clanked their tankards together.

As Diane lowered hers to the table, Henri laughed at the small arc of foam that had crested around the top of her mouth. The priest chimed in with a chuckle as Henri reached up to brush it away. But as his fingers met with the smooth skin of her chin, and lingered there, Diane's easy smile fell away. She lowered her eyes and took a handkerchief from her velvet purse. Père Olivier leaned back in his chair, watching them, and then took another sip of ale.

"So then, are you to be married? Is that why you've come away from Paris? Oh, no need to blush on my account. Your simple costume may fool the others, my boy, but I know nobility when I see it. You'd not be the first gentleman to want to enjoy the simpler life while he's here. Your parents disapprove? Perhaps it was hers. Difference in your ages, I'd wager."

Diane was startled by his words and let her mouth drop open before she again raised her handkerchief to cover it. She looked over at Henri but said nothing.

"No, that is not why we are here at all!" he snapped and shifted forward in his seat. "Why would you ask such a thing?"

Père Olivier looked with wise eyes, first at Henri, and then over at Diane whose head was still lowered.

"Oh, now I have offended you, my friends. Please, my humble pardon. It is simply that I have married so many in my work that I am afraid at times conjecture is difficult to avoid. You may say you are not to be married, but rarely in my many years of service to God have I seen such devotion in the eyes as I do with the two of you." He took another sip of ale. "I always watch the eyes to predict a happy union. The eyes do not deceive."

Diane coughed nervously into her silk handkerchief.

"Well you are mistaken. Sorely mistaken! Madame is a friend; my chaperone here. Nothing more."

"As you wish, but if you should change your mind; if things should change between you, I mean, I should be honored to be the one to join you in marriage," he said as he shrugged his shoulders and downed the last of his ale.

Despite his conciliatory words, it was clear that Père Olivier did not believe Henri. Diane knew that the young cleric had the entire story of who they really were formulated in his mind. Whatever he thought, the outcome was still the same. He saw something. It frightened her to be that transparent. She looked away, wanting to spring from the table and leave them both sitting there. She wanted to go back to Anet where it was safe; where her life was certain.

She looked around the room with anxious eyes. Then, across the room near the door she saw a woman. A collection of men hovered around her at a small wooden table. Diane had not noticed until just then that it was a corner of the room immersed in a strange, dark silence. She was an old woman with frizzled white hair worn long around her shoulders. The men watched in silence as she studied another man's hand.

"Who is that?" she asked.

Père Olivier turned around. "Ah, yes, old Odile." He smiled. "The fortune-teller. They say she can tell you everything about yourself just by studying your hand. She sees your past. She also claims to know the future!" he said with half a laugh.

"Is such a thing not blasphemous?" Diane cautiously asked.

"Oh, she means no harm. It is entertainment, pure and simple.

If I believed it was more than that, I certainly could not condone it. I can call her over if you would like to be entertained."

"No!" Henri snapped. "I know what is in my future, and I do not need an old woman to confirm it!"

"Could you call her over for me, Father?"

Henri turned to Diane. She was looking up at the priest. Her face was grazed by the sunlight from the small box window near their table. Père Olivier stood, brushed off his robes and moved through the crowded tavern toward the woman he had called Odile.

"Madame, you cannot be serious!" Henri whispered. "What if she gives us away? It will ruin everything!"

"I think you give her too much credit, Henri. She is an old woman, probably trying to make enough money for food and a couple of tankards of ale. What can be the harm in seeing that she has just that for tonight?"

Henri was able to carry his objection further when the cleric returned to the table with the woman by his side. When they drew near enough, Diane saw that she was not really as old as she had at first appeared. Her eyes were bright, a shade of green, and her face was nearly free from lines and the spots of age. But the hair, frizzled and completely white, gave her the sage appearance that Diane was certain she had purposely sought.

Odile sat down and drank from one of the half-full tankards that had been sitting on the table before it was offered. She brushed the foam away from her lips with the back of her sleeve, and then motioned for Diane to surrender her hand.

"Hmmm . . . a long life," she said, in a dark liquid voice. "And children. Three."

"I have only two."

"I see three," the old woman firmly replied.

She looked at Diane to punctuate the confidence of her words. As she traced the long, thin palm with her fingers, her green eyes began to narrow. "This is most extraordinary," she said and then paused a moment, going back over the same line on Diane's hand. "I see power. Such power. Oh, it is such a strong image!"

"All right, that is enough!" said Henri. "That is nonsense, and you are frightening her!"

"I speak only the truth," said Odile, looking directly into Henri's eyes. "Have you anything to fear from that?"

"But there must be some mistake," Diane said, breaking the intensity between the Prince and the fortune-teller. "I am anything but powerful."

"Oh, but you are, *ma chérie*. It is all right here before me; before you! Your future holds for you great strength; the power to lead; to change."

Henri shuddered. If this woman was right, there was only one way that Diane could garner that kind of influence. But how could it be? It was not possible. The image of Diane with the King clouded Henri's ability to reason. Each time he imagined them together it tore a little more at his heart. His breath quickened and he was flooded with fear. There could be no worse fate than that. To have her in the bed of the King of France would, for him, be far worse than death.

"Do you see anything else?" Diane cautiously asked, clenching her other fist beneath the table.

"Ah, yes. There is something. A matter of the heart. I see that it is intertwined with the power. As though the source of the power . . . is the love."

"And what in Heaven's name do you mean by that?" Henri snapped again, forcing himself from his thoughts.

"It means, my dear young man, that this woman before us, though I know not how, will one day rule a great many." She cleared her throat and then looked back at Diane with the same luminescent green eyes. "I do not understand it myself, my dear girl, I can only tell you what I see. But yes, one day you shall have more power than you can imagine . . . and it will come to you through your power over one who adores you."

A week of simplicity at Cauterets was like a lifetime compared to the mire and deceit of the French Court. The altitude tended to make one a little dizzy at first so that caution in all activities was recommended and encouraged by the keeper of the inn.

They began each day in the warm sulphur springs. Then each night after supper, Charles played his lute while Michel played the pipe, and everyone danced around the tables in the dining room. They laughed, sang songs together, and fast became friends. Even the mayor from Lyon gave way his propriety. He danced with the innkeeper's wife, and confessed that his name was Jean.

Diane and Henri attended vespers each afternoon at Père Olivier's church in the meadow. Afterward they stole away with him for a tankard of ale at the little stone tavern. They heard more from him about the reformers and their clandestine activities in both France and Spain. They talked about philosophy and art, history and theology, but after that first meeting in the tavern, the village priest chose to honor their secrecy and never asked them again to reveal their true identities.

"Go on, lad, dance with her!" urged the old innkeeper who served soup for the guests. François de Guise was flinging a puffing, wheezing Charlotte about the room on his arm, and Jacques was dancing with Hélène.

"Go on!" the innkeeper urged again. She smacked Henri on the back and winked at Diane.

"I am afraid I do not know how," he finally conceded and shifted in his seat.

"Oh, go on, laddy boy! I'm sure she'll teach ya. Will ya not, deary?" she prodded at Diane with a gapped-tooth smile. Michel whistled a rousing tune on his pipe and the rest of the guests laughed and clapped their hands to the time of the music. Their happiness was infectious.

"Will you dance with me, then?" asked Diane in a voice just above a whisper.

He wanted to reject the idea but he could not for, in an instant, he found his hand tightly wound in hers as she led him just outside the open door and into the courtyard. Their movements were slow and studied, and were not to the rhythm of the music inside; but gently and carefully she gave him the patience with which to learn to dance.

After a while in the evening breeze, his uncertain expression passed to a studied smile as he continued to peer down at his feet and twirl around to her lead.

"Well, imagine it," he chuckled. "I am dancing!"

"That you are." She smiled back at him. At that moment, under the shimmering light of the moon and the scratching music of the crickets, they looked into one another's eyes. There, each of them uncovered something new. But it was Diane who made the greatest discovery. It was as if she had never really noticed his eyes until then. Until that day, that very moment in the freedom of Cauterets, his had been sad, lonely eyes. Now, there in the cool glow of the moonlit sky, they were strong eyes; passionate and questioning. He gazed at her until she blushed like a girl, and he made her dance with him again and again. They did not speak. There was no need. There was only the sound of music and laughter and the rustle of her skirts as they swept over the cobblestones.

THE NEXT DAY they took a shorter route back from the village after vespers, winding their way through a deep green clover meadow. It was a steeper grade down which they needed to pass to return to the inn, but the poppies were much more lush and the view of the valley had beckoned them since their first day in Cauterets. Diane ran down the hill ahead of Henri, her black silk gown flowing behind her with the breeze.

"Oh, how I wish I were a boy! To always be free like this!" she laughed, running with her arms outstretched.

Diane ran down the incline laughing and skipping. The fresh air blew through her thick blond hair and pulled it away from her face so that she did not see the large stone beneath her feet. She tripped suddenly and went reeling, head first, into the masses of rich meadow grass and red poppies.

Henri ran after her, shouting her name, but as he neared he could still hear her laughter as she lay in a pile of her rumpled skirts. Henri knelt beside her and grabbed her hands. His face was full of anger. He was prepared to shout out that she had needlessly alarmed him, but before he could, he met once again with her eyes; those same fragile blue eyes into which he gazed the night before.

They looked at one another as her chest lightly heaved from her running. Slowly, a breath at a time, each drew nearer the other. There amid the rustling trees, the poppies and clover, Henri pressed his lips to her cheek and then slowly moved them over to meet hers.

"You mustn't," she whispered, but this time she did not struggle against him as he pressed her soft rose petal lips more firmly on his own; breathless and urgent. She was powerless against him; his youth; his urgent virile body. *I must be mad,* she thought, as her mind whirled. *I know that I am!*

Diane grew weak beneath the weight of his straining body as a primal instinct drove him to press her back beneath him into the soft clover. Kissing her. Touching her. Unsure and yet powerful. She opened her mouth to him, guiding his tongue over her own. It was warm. Like liquid fire . . . and she was weak. She wanted just to lie beneath him here, alone, and give in to what she knew he thought was love. They were alone. He was young and he would recover from his first experience. *Oh, it has been so long . . . so very long.*

She felt the firmness of his hand on her thigh; his lips trailing a path on her neck. The press of his body against her own. Then she became mildly aware of a distant sound. Thundering. Pounding. Hooves of a horse digging into the loose earth. Growing louder. Diane sat up, looking around in a panic. She shook back the strands of hair that had fallen into her face, and quickly straightened the bodice of her gown. It was François de Guise. Henri moaned and moved away from her.

"What the devil do you want?" Henri shouted when Guise was near enough to hear him. He rose and walked over to his friend who stopped his horse near them on the hill.

"I beg Your Highness's pardon, but a messenger has just come from the King. He says we are to return to Court at once. He asked that I give you this." He extended a letter with the King's seal and added as he did, "The messenger also relayed that it is of the utmost urgency."

"What is the news? Has something happened?"

"Perhaps the letter . . ."

Henri snatched the parchment from Guise. "Damn him!" he growled. "Even with this distance between us, he still manages to plague my life!"

DIANE LAY ALONE on her bed in her black silk shift and blue jersey stockings, trying to rest before supper. But she could not sleep. The depths of what she had just felt frightened her. She had broken the boundaries of decorum.

I am too old for romance with a boy. She closed her mind to the mere possibility of it. *It can go no further. I was right to think that he is infatuated.* She grimaced and shook her head. *There can be nothing but danger and heartbreak in it for us both. He does not need a lover so much as a mother. The King said so himself.*

Try as she might to push the thoughts from her mind, they crept back in. Silent thoughts. Deadly thoughts. To have a young lover, a boy to teach, to mold into the perfect lover. The image of his hard body pressed against her own in that field brought her from the state of dull, dazed half-slumber to a tortured awakening.

She bolted from her bed wet with perspiration. Beads of sweat dripped from the top of her lip. Her heart raced. She was lying to Henri and lying to herself. There was nothing maternal about her feelings for him, nor did he want that from her. She poured water into the white porcelain basin at the foot of the bed and splashed it onto her face over and over until the upper portion of her shift was soaked.

No matter how much like a man he looked, no matter what feelings he had managed to awaken in her, he was still a boy. The son of the King. That was a dangerous combination for a widow by whom the King himself was tempted. If she wanted to keep her place at Court, she must not lose His Majesty's favor; that was a balance every courtier walked. But her thoughts were not so self-ish as they were realistic. What would be left to her if she fell from grace and was sent back to exile in the cold, lonely domicile of Anet?

She shivered as the cool breeze washed through the window across her wet skin. She was already in disfavor with Anne d'Heilly. That state of affairs alone could spell her ruin if it continued. Were it not for the King's amorous intent and their mutual love of the arts, she was certain she would already have been sent home.

Diane rubbed her hands up and down the gooseflesh that had formed on her arms. God help her, in spite of it all, she wanted to feel his touch again. She wanted him, once again, to kiss her. She wanted him. He wanted her. Neither of them were betrothed or married. It seemed so simple. He was a young man eager to give his love. She was a lonely widow desperate to receive it. What real harm could there be in helping him reach the confidence of manhood which, in the face of the King, seemed so intent on eluding him?

He trusted her completely. She wanted to trust him. They were *compagnons d'armes* in a war that seemed, though in different ways, directed only at the two of them. They were both inexperienced and uneasy against all the intrigue and ugliness of the French Court. For all her money, her connections and her noble birth, Diane was not so worldly as she might have been. She had been hidden away. Sheltered. This return to Court had been difficult. Henri had made the path easier. He had made her depend on him. It lessened the differences between them. And though she would not realize it for some time, the bond between them, which even death would not sever, had already begun to form.

"WE UNDERSTAND, Monsieur Henry, that you leave by the morrow," Michel said as he bit into a piece of bread at the dining-room table where all of the guests had gathered. "My wife and I have become quite fond of all of you and of this place. Rarely have I had such a welcoming audience for my playing. You shall be missed."

His wife nodded in agreement.

"Not so fond as I have become of this place. It is painful for me as well, to part from it," Henri replied and once again tried to engage Diane in a glance.

The other guests as well had come to share Michel's fondness for the mysterious group who said they were from Paris. They asked questions and drank continuous toasts to prosperity and to the happiness of their new friends. Between the dialogues and the embraces, Henri struggled to find a way to request a private moment with Diane. Though she avoided his gaze, he could not help staring at her. She drew him like a magnet. He traced her long thin nose with his eyes; the nose that gave way to those lips. *Those lips that I have kissed,* he thought. *Now, by the indifference she is showing me, she would have me believe that it never happened.* He grew more rigid in his seat as Michel moved near the dancing area with his flute. He would play the music for a last dance for the group who, as the mayor had muttered, would probably never be together again. Jacques took Hélène's hand and the mayor led Michel's bride in a dance.

"Dance with me?" Diane whispered.

In his surprise, Henri found himself unable to object. He let her lead him outside into the courtyard where he had first learned. As they moved alone through the steps in the shadows of the moonlight, she finally met his gaze. He drew near enough to her to feel her breath.

"I have had such a wonderful time here," she whispered. "This place is magical to me. It is as if here, all time around us has stopped. I wanted you to know how special this has been."

Henri tried to smile but he was tortured by her nearness. He wanted to claim her as his own; hold her in his arms and kiss her as he had done that afternoon. But he dared not. When the music ended, she curtsied to him as part of the dance and slipped a small piece of parchment into his palm before she returned to the open dining hall.

The men shook hands. The women embraced and said their tearful adieus. Michel's wife promised to write and perhaps to visit Henri's fictional address on the rue des Étuvres, when they were next in Paris. It was only after most of the guests had retired, and Diane had bid an early good night, that Henri glanced down at the folded slip of paper. His heart raced as he read the words which, by now, he knew well.

Before I stirred from that place where I should wish forever to remain, I plucked with great delight, the flower from the leaves of the rosebush, and thus I had at last, my rose.

It was the last line from *Le Roman de la rose*.

THE JOURNEY BACK to Court was arduous, with sloping hills and twisted roads. But this alternate route, charted for them by the King's guides, would be more expedient and the urgency of their return required it.

Charlotte had fallen ill near Targes and Hélène and Diane were forced to attend her closely. As the ride on horseback would have proven too strenuous, a sedan chair, draped with heavy tapestry to block the wind, was hastily constructed for her.

They traveled down through the villages of Agen and Cahors, surrounded by bare, wild hills. Past Brivé and Limoges. The final night of their long journey home was spent in Chateauroux on the banks of the river. Henri and his friends were welcomed by the mayor of the town and would stay the night at his manor. Diane and her attendants stayed at the home of Monsieur Dutel, the town's wealthiest merchant. It would be their last night together before returning to Court and Henri desperately wanted things more clarified between them.

Throughout their journey home, Diane avoided being alone with him. They had not shared a private word since their final morning in the baths at Cauterets. He had gone there after receiving her poetry, expecting a change in her. A change in him. But she was indifferent. They sat together in the warm, effervescent sulfur water speaking about Père Olivier and what they might further do to help him rebuild the church. Their conversation was cordial; at times, even happy. But for all the smiles and the plans, she had made no mention of their kiss in the meadow the day before. In his overwhelming confusion, neither had he. Now was his final opportunity to establish things between them.

Diane descended the stairs just as Hélène showed him inside. She stood midway between the top and the bottom of the carved mahogany staircase as Hélène looked up at her. Henri's eyes followed. He gasped at the sight of her. Diane had not expected to receive visitors and she was not properly dressed. Her thick blond hair was loose and hung long over her shoulders and she wore a loose fitting dressing gown of embroidered white silk.

"Please leave us," she said to Hélène, and descended the rest of the stairs with a silver hairbrush still in her hand. Henri waited to speak until they were alone.

"I think you look more beautiful than I have ever seen you," he whispered and moved closer to her. Then he stopped. He could see in her eyes that something had changed. "I have missed you," he added with an awkward cracking voice.

Diane steadied herself against his troubled expression by turning to sit on a small oak and pourpoint couch near the fire. After a moment, she took a deep breath and then looked up, beckoning Henri with her hand.

"Are you all right?" he asked when he was sitting beside her, their faces lit by the copper-colored flames.

"No. I am not well at all. Henri, what happened between us that afternoon was very special to me. You must know that . . ."

He reached over and put his hand on top of hers as she spoke, but her body grew more rigid with his touch. It made him pull away.

"However," she continued, steeling herself to him. "It cannot . . . it must never happen again."

"But I do not understand. What has happened? Have I done something foolish to displease you without even knowing? Because if I have—"

"No, of course not. You could never displease me. Your friendship has brought such joy to my life, you shall never know." She paused and turned away. "It is just that I am so afraid."

"Of me?"

"Of this! Of what is happening between us. What happened in those beautiful mountains; what surely would have happened had we stayed, would be viewed by others at Court as scandalous; as something absurd, even grotesque! You must know that."

"Damn them all! I do not care what any of them say!"

"But I do! I must. Henri, please be reasonable," she said calmly. "You must understand, until now, my life has been so ordered; so predictable. Now, with you, all of it has become so tangled and confused."

"How strange that sounds to me when, for the first time in my life, I have found a bit of harmony with you. You know, once upon a time not so very long ago, I thought this could never happen to me. I was sure of it. I ran from everything and everyone. But when I met you, from the first moment, everything changed."

"Please do not be angry with me," she whispered, brushing a hand across his cheek. "I just need some time. Surely that is not so difficult to understand."

"I could deny you nothing. I think you know that. Just say that no matter what, you will always remain my friend. If I have that to hold on to . . ."

She put her finger to his lips to silence him, and said, "Then it is promised."

CHARLOTTE DID NOT SURVIVE her illness. She was buried quietly in the town of Chateauroux on a hill washed with gray tombstones. Hélène and Diane stood motionless over her grave, watching with unflinching eyes as three nameless, faceless men lowered the unornamented box into the ground. Finally the gap-toothed grave digger carelessly heaped the last mound of rich soil onto the box, and the townspeople looked on through the wrought-iron bars, whispering and pointing fingers at the mysterious collection of mourners.

When it was done, they rode in solemn procession back into the deep emerald green forest, toward the chateau Villers-Cotterêts. Henri and Diane cantered high on their horses beside one another, still dressed in black, under the royal canopy with the blue and gold fleurs-de-lys. As they wound their way through the forest, with the chateau in sight, the sun had already descended. They had seen the lights from the chateau for miles through the sparsely populated village and the surrounding forest.

"Jacques, take Mademoiselle Gallet to Madame's apartments," Henri instructed as the group dismounted in the chateau courtyard.

The King's grooms advanced to lead away the horses as Saint-André walked toward the chateau with Hélène. Amid the commotion of lowering trunks and congregating servants, Henri managed to grip Diane's hand. He pulled her forcefully away from the courtyard and down a stone path lined with beech trees, to a place behind the stables. There in the moonlight, surrounded by the brisk night air, they held one another in silence. After a moment, Henri pulled his arms from around her and cupped her face in his firm hands.

"I feel as if we have lived a lifetime with each other," he whispered. "And no matter what happens now that we have returned, we will face it together."

His youthful idealism touched her, and she almost believed it. Diane smiled and turned her head to kiss one of the hands that rested on her cheek. "I think you are the best friend that I have ever had," she whispered.

"I know that you are the best friend I shall ever have."

They embraced again with the determination of companions who carried with each of them a deep impenetrable secret. Then Henri waited silently while she shielded her face with her cloak, stole back up toward the courtyard and into the doors of the chateau. He stayed alone in the dark for several minutes trying to collect himself. Facing his family would be difficult. So much had changed. But she had promised, and he trusted her.

DIANE STROLLED ALONE down by the river's edge to meet Jacques de Montgommery as she had promised him she would do. She had come early to be alone and to collect her thoughts. It was some time amid the shadows from the trees before she realized that she was smiling. She could not recall ever having been this happy. Although she had tried to deny it to herself and to Henri, she cared deeply for him. He was young, but he was also mature and handsome. As though plucked from the pages of a medieval romance, Prince Henri was like her shining knight. Just when she had given up ever finding happiness, he had galloped into her life and saved her. She strolled in the warm summer breeze and found her mind ambling back to thoughts of their afternoon together in the hills around Cauterets. She remembered his youth. His strength. His passion. Again she smiled, feeling herself blush at her most private thoughts.

"There you are!" Jacques declared with a smile as he advanced quickly toward her, late for their meeting. He took her hands in his own, and kissed each of them.

"Welcome back! Oh, I have so missed that pretty face of yours. How dull it has been here without you."

Diane smiled back at him, retrieved her hands and clasped them behind her. They began to stroll together on the dirt path bordered by stones, beneath the ordered chestnut trees.

"I was so pleased that you agreed to meet privately with me like this," he said.

"Well, are we not friends?"

"Yes, of course. It is just that you were so angry with me before you left. I was not certain you would ever want to see me again."

"Well, that seems such a long time ago, and now I feel inclined to forgive you. A great deal has happened."

"As it has at Court. In fact, as we speak the King is meeting with his *conseil des affaires* and Prince Henri in private session."

Diane stiffened at the mention of Henri's name. "Do you know what they are meeting about?"

"Why, yes, of course. I have just come from my post in the King's chamber. But I am not certain that I should be sharing His Majesty's private affairs, even with you."

Diane turned to him. Her smooth lips turned up in a sensual smile. "If I let you kiss me, will you tell me then?"

"I will tell you anything if I may kiss you!"

"Here, on the cheek," she pointed as demurely as a young girl.

Jacques leaned toward her and took her chin in one of his long slim hands. He drew near her a little at a time, attempting to savor the moment he had been given. When he was close enough to whisper to her, he said, "This news is certainly worth more than your cheek. Please do give me a taste of your sweet lips. You will know the news before anyone, even Mademoiselle d'Heilly."

"The cheek, Jacques," she insisted. He kissed the spot on her cheek near her ear, and then grazed her skin with his warm tongue. Diane was startled by his advance, and jumped back.

"You see just how good it might be with us?"

"All right, Jacques, enough teasing. Now it is your turn. What do you know of the business between the King and Prince Henri?"

"I should have known. It is always back to that dreadful boy," he declared with irritation, his eyes cast upward. Then he looked back at her with a pointed stare.

"What is it between the two of you?"

"Answer me, Jacques. What do you know?"

"All right, all right," he said. He found a large stone between the trees, sat down, and then looked up at her. "Well, it seems that, for some time now, there have been secret negotiations taking place between the King and the Pope in Rome. His Holiness has a niece whom he means to marry off; and he has been bartering her with every power in the Christian world. It would seem that due to her relations, the little girl holds the key to Italy, and apparently the old goat has been holding out for the best match he can make."

"And what has that to do with the Prince and the *conseil des affaires*?"

"It would seem, my lovely, that our good King has won. Prince Henri is to marry her."

". . . There is some mistake," she whispered.

"I was standing right there when the Chancellor read the King's reply. There is no mistake."

Diane clutched herself at the waist and exhaled as though she had been pelted in the stomach. Without turning around, she leaned against the tree behind her for support. She was sick. The bile rose from her belly into her throat with a swift force. She fought it.

"I must go," she said in a faint tone and turned. He grasped her arm and stopped her. "Let me go, Jacques!"

"What in the devil is going on between you and that boy?" he charged. She threw her head up toward him. His eyes met with hers. She was near tears. Seeing the ashen pallor that had overtaken her, he had his answer.

"You stupid fool! I should have seen it coming. Why, by the look on your face I will bet he has even bedded you already, hasn't he? Oh, what a fool you made of me with your feigned virtue and chaste kisses, when all the while you have been sharing your favors with that pathetic child!"

"Leave it alone, Jacques. You do not understand," she whispered and twisted her arm until she was free of his grasp.

"You are right about one thing. I do not understand how you could choose a boy when you have a man bowing at your feet! I am the one you should be sharing your favors with, not him!"

Diane did not hear his last few words as she ran down the footpath as fast as her legs could carry her. She must get away. She must. From Jacques. From Court. From everything. She ran through the gardens, past the other courtiers, without a care to what they might think. She needed to find the safety of her own apartments inside the chateau. She was going to be ill.

"I WILL NOT MARRY HER!"

"Do not be insolent with me, you little bastard!" the King raged.

"I will not marry her, I tell you! I want to choose my own wife!"

The King and his son stood squarely opposing one another;

both with hands on their hips. They were so close that Henri could feel his father's warm breath and see his chest heave with anger through the heavily jeweled doublet.

"You are the son of a King, boy. Your will is not your own!" The son, who had grown the height of the father, said nothing in return and the King grew weak beneath the intensity of the confrontation. "Oh, why can you not be more like your brother and obey your Sovereign King?"

"Because, sir, my *brother* would not be pawned off to a merchant's daughter for the sake of a little land and gold!"

"Pay heed how you address the King," Montmorency cautioned from behind the young Prince, but his words were as good as whispered in the wind.

Across the room, the King was snorting wildly and stalking up and down with his hands still firmly on his hips. Then, in his rekindled rage, he turned over a table, and the silver goblets and decanter on top were sent clanging onto the bare tiled floor. The Dauphin, Chabot and Montmorency remained silent. Sensing complications, the Duke of Albany, who had negotiated the marriage for the Pope, interceded with Henri.

"Your Highness must listen to reason. A marriage is really such a small thing. Do with your heart what you will but you must consider the consequences on all of France if you refuse. Truly, sharing your title with the Pope's niece is in all of our best interests."

"All of *our* best interests?" Henri repeated with a mocking laugh. "Ha! You mean to say all of *your* best interests, do you not? I am not Dauphin! I shall not be King! It is in *my* interest to marry a woman that I love!"

"Well, that is simply not how it is for any of us!"

The King spit the words with fury as he raced back to face his son. "I have done my duty to this country willingly, and married who was chosen, as have all the others who came before us. Marrying for love is for servants and peasants, not for a Valois Prince! Get a mistress for that, boy!" And then he paused. A wry sneer broke across his angry face. "Or perhaps, little man, you already have."

The truth in his father's words disarmed the younger opponent, and he searched the room frantically for some show of support. There was none. Not even from Montmorency. The King, quickly assessing the change in Henri, sneered more broadly.

"Perhaps Madame de Poitiers has consented to rid you of more than your smugness!" he proposed with an evil laugh. This tactic of the King's changed everything and Henri steadied himself against his own oncoming rage. If news of their liaison were out, he could no longer protect her. Chabot advanced to the side of the Ambassador, looking dangerously like reinforcement.

"Respectfully, Your Highness, I am afraid that the issue is no longer open for debate. The agreement has already been signed."

"Signed? Signed by whom?"

"Why, by the King and His Holiness Pope Clement, of course."

The room was still. Ice cold. After a moment to catch his breath, Henri laughed again.

"And I suppose you have chosen the day, time and place for the deed without consulting me, as well!"

Looking around at the lowered heads, his angry smile turned to disbelief at the firmness and exactitude with which his life was being irrevocably molded. He was trapped. The matrimonial prison to which he was being sentenced was far worse than any Spanish incarceration he had known as a boy. It was an impossible circle. If he married the Pope's niece, he lost all hope of a future with the woman he loved. If he asked permission to marry Diane instead, it would mean her certain banishment from Court—or even a worse fate, if His Majesty willed it.

"And if I refuse?" he finally asked.

"Then you shall be bound, gagged and carried to the altar!" raged the King. "But, by God Almighty, you shall marry the Italian!"

Diane knelt in the shadowy oratory before a statue of the Virgin Mary. She was so deep in prayer that she was startled by the touch of a hand on her shoulder. Seeing that it was Saint-André, she made the sign of the cross, stood and walked together with him back out into the corridor.

"Madame, I am sorry to disturb you here, and I would not have come if it were not necessary . . ."

"What is it, Jacques?"

"It is the Prince, Madame. He returned to his apartments a short time ago. To be plain with you, Madame, he returned very drunk. He will take no food and will speak to no one. He only insists on being left alone in the center of the floor of the bedchamber with a jug of wine and some odd-looking crescent-shaped pendant that he refuses to surrender. I am worried about him, considering the events of the day. I know that it is asking a great deal, but it seems you are the only one he will speak with anymore. If you would go to him while the banquet is on," he proposed, "I can see that you pass undetected into the royal wing."

"Take me to him, Jacques."

Diane and Jacques could hear the odd noises as they approached Henri's apartments in the east wing of the Chateau Villers-Cotterêts. There were the warbled strains of someone singing, along with the crashing of silver as it hit the bare floor. When they came to the door, Diane stopped.

"Are you certain you would not like me to come with you? He has a violent nature when he drinks too much."

"Thank you, Jacques. You are a good friend, but he will not harm me."

"I will be just outside if you need me," he said and touched her shoulder.

The room was dark, except for the silver glow from the moon through the long, open casement windows. There was no fire. There were no candles burning in their sconces. There was only a misty breeze through the windows which chilled the large, drafty rooms, and sent the wall tapestry near the window rippling on its heavy iron pole. Henri sat just as Jacques had described it, on the floor, his arms wrapped around his knees. Beside him was a large jug of wine he had brought from the kitchens. He held her ivory pendant close to his chest. Her heart ached at the sight of him; so defeated. She closed the heavy door behind herself and the round iron handle clanged against it.

"You there! Out! I do not wish to be disturbed!"

Before he could finish his sentence, he saw that it was Diane. She came beside him and stood looking down at him; at the crescent pendant which he held. After a moment, she could see the sparkle of tears in his dark eyes. Diane sat down beside him on the cold tile floor and he fell naturally into her arms. They held one another silently; she with one arm around his shoulders and the other stroking his thick, dark curls.

She could feel the pain. The helplessness. She raised a hand to his face. At first it was just a touch; no more than a comforting hand brushed across the turn of his jaw. Compassion. The touch became a caress. He turned his head and kissed her hand. The warm feel of his skin was dizzying to her. The whisper of his breath so near to her own. Then, with their two bodies pressed closely together, it became something more. Diane could feel herself once again, as she had in Cauterets, begin slowly to sink into the deep forbidden abyss which nearness to him brought. But this time, there was no fear. There were no other thoughts. There was nothing else but the nearness of him.

"I wanted it to be you," he whispered.

"I know . . ."

Henri looked up at her. His eyes were filled with angry tears. Her own blue eyes were tinged with sadness. He moved closer to her. His lips, at first, only brushed hers. Then they met in a soft, gentle kiss, barely touching. He pulled away and looked once again into her eyes. Like a mirror to his own soul, he saw forever there. His life. His future. Everything was in her eyes. There was nothing else. No one. As though by a force, a primal instinct deep within him, he moved his own solid arms around her and kissed her again. This time the press of his mouth against hers was more powerful. She opened her lips to him, and he felt a surge of dark pleasure. A small sigh came from the moist hollow of her throat and he felt it echo through his entire body. A deep and powerful ache coursed through him. It was a longing he had never known before this moment. By instinct alone, Henri moved his hand behind her neck, still kissing her. Now it was she who sank willingly into his arms.

He stood first, then helped her to her feet. Once again he was awkward. Unsure. The faint sound of the music from the King's banquet echoed around them as they faced one another in the shadow of the moonlight. It highlighted her face as she turned away.

"Do not go," he whispered, and then squeezed her hand. "Please."

She followed him to the large canopied oak bed with the rose damask bedcurtains. He lay down first and looked up at her, not certain of what to do. After a moment she motioned to the back of her gown. With trembling hands, he moved toward her and unfastened the tiny pearl buttons on the back of the black silk. His fingers grazed the warm skin of her bare back and he could feel his own heart pounding.

When she was free of her garments, Diane turned slowly to face him. The moon shimmered through the window near the bed onto her ivory skin. He was riveted to the sight of her small white breasts with their tawny nipples hardened by the cold of the drafty room. He had not known until that moment what to expect when he saw her. Nothing could have prepared him for the beauty of her body. The broad shoulders. The gently sculpted curves of her hips, and the small patch of blond hair between her legs.

It was awkward. He tried not to look at her, but for Henri, women's bodies had only been images in paintings, and in his mind. Until now. She sensed it. As if she knew his thoughts, she took one of his hands and drew it down onto the soft fullness of her breast. He gasped at the touch of her. Her breast felt like imported silk. Overwhelmed by a force completely foreign to him, Henri hurriedly pushed her back down onto the tapestried bedcover and began to kiss her neck. Then her breasts. First one, and then the other.

She began to unhook his shirt, then she watched him remove it. Next his trunk hose and stockings. Diane had never seen such a firm, strong body as his. But his movements were awkward. Hurried. So, slowly, patiently, she began to guide him. She took his hand and raised it to her lips. She kissed the soft fleshy inside of each palm and then ran her tongue along the length of each finger, pushing one and then the other, lightly between her lips. Then they lay back together. When she finally drew his hand down, it was to guide him. Just a small movement of her hips, and like some kind of velvet dream, he was inside of her; closer to her than he had ever been to anyone.

To Henri, it was not only a joining of their bodies, but a bonding of their two souls. It was what he had wanted. What he had craved. He wrapped his legs around hers, and groaned as the movement drew him deeper inside of her. He closed his eyes and moved his fingers across her neck and breasts with the delicate touch of one who is blind. Somehow she made him feel as though he had done this before. He was not ashamed. As he moved with the flow of her beneath him, he felt his own straining body begin to pulse. He felt his blood course, and begin to converge; to race downward. Down. Down. He was drawn like a spiral. He felt himself on the edge of a warm, dark pool into which he must plunge. Each thrust pulling him down to the warm, dark center of infinity.

When it was over, in no more than a few short moments, he rolled onto his side, tears spilling down his cheeks. Diane reached up and kissed them away as they clung to one another in the cool, misty darkness.

DIANE RODE BEHIND MONTGOMMERY, her powerful black stallion following his, through the dark, shadowy forest around Villers-Cotterêts. It was the first week of September; a month since the announcement of Henri's marriage, and the heat of summer was stifling. As they rode, fingers of warm sunlight peeked through the thick trees and cast shadows on the moss-

covered tree trunks, giving some little bit of relief from the searing heat. When they reached a small clearing, covered over with
long reeds of new summer grass, Diane slid from her horse into
his arms. When he tried, she let Jacques kiss her. After a moment,
he broke away from her lips and smiled.

"That is so much better than kissing your cheek." He smiled
and kissed her again more forcefully. Diane fought herself from
pulling away from him. The feel of his thin, rough lips against her
own sickened her.

"*Je t'adore . . . Je t'aime . . .*" he whispered into her hair. "Please reconsider and say that you will marry me. There is surely no reason
now to refuse me."

"Dear Jacques, despite your overwhelming pomposity, you are
really rather sweet," she said, as he clutched both hands around
her waist, smiling at her praise. Diane looked into the long face
and hollow eyes; the thin angular cheeks, more like a woman's.
She could feel his lanky frame pressed against her gown; feel the
bones, washed over with thin flesh. There were no well-defined
muscles. No firm arms to embrace her.

"But I do not love you the way you want me to, or the way you
deserve."

"So it is love, is it? Well, *ma chère,* those things come in time.
More importantly to our future happiness, I believe that I now
know that the Prince was nothing more than a dalliance." He
pushed away a small blond curl which had blown into his eye and
continued.

"Shall I tell you how it happened between you? Oh, do let me.
Let me see . . . you were lonely, yes, very lonely, and in his youthful ardor, the poor melancholy Prince took advantage of your
weakness. Yes, it was just like that, wasn't it? But, not to worry.
You will recover after he is fully married, and I want to be there
when you do. I, my love, am a real man, and I will make you forget
that you ever knew him."

His tone was playful, as though he was composing a trifle
about someone else. He was having fun with her. He was making

light of Henri's feelings. And of her own. Then he pulled her even more closely to him so that she would know his straining ardor; feel the swell beneath his codpiece.

She detested his condescension, the insufferable drone of his voice. Her body filled with revulsion as he kissed her, but she did not pull away. Jacques de Montgommery was the key to her sanity. He was the only path to safety from her feelings for Henri. Feelings she knew now that, if she let them, could easily destroy them both.

Despite the intensity of what had passed between them that night, she had left his apartments without looking back. There was the reality of his impending marriage. Anything between them now, with so important a political liaison in the balance, would be a dangerous game. Diane believed she risked everything by harboring even the slightest romantic feeling for Henri. Her indifference to him was a matter of survival; a measure to save them both.

When her official period of mourning ended, she had agreed to be courted by Jacques de Montgommery. It was a loathsome alternative. She did not love him. She never would. But she did not have the luxury of time; time to wait, alone and vulnerable, until someone else might show an interest in her. Seventeen years as the wife of the aging hunchback Sénéchal de Normandie had made her a realist. She knew that no matter what became of the marriage now proposed between Henri and the Pope's niece, she would never be considered a suitable alternative for the son of the King so many years her junior. She also knew in her heart that, no matter what she felt for him, she had not been born to be a courtesan.

"Say you will marry me," Montgommery droned.

"But, how can you still want me, knowing how I feel?"

"Well . . . as any other husband would be, at first I shall be angry, of course. But, when you come to me, pleading on your knees, I shall look into those enchanting blue eyes of yours and be bound to forgive you." He tossed his hand into the air with a twist and added, "He shall marry his Italian, and we shall go on with our secure and very comfortable life."

"You certainly have thought it through."

"I have thought of nothing else since that first night we met."
He leaned in and kissed her again but she pulled away when he
tried to part her lips with his tongue. She stifled the shiver that
ran up her back and blossomed through the rest of her like a violent clap of thunder.

"Oh, please, say you will . . . please!"

"I need more time, Jacques. You must be patient with me. I
shall give you your answer as soon as I have one myself."

His eyes narrowed and his thin lips tightened. "You might as
well agree. There really is no use waiting for the boy. He shall have
to marry the Italian."

His words were sharp. She moved to rebuke him, but before
she could object, he drew her close to his chest and whispered
again in her ear. "Oh I just know you will say yes. And I will make
you such a splendid husband . . . You will see."

AFTER HER RIDE in the woods, the afternoon was busy for Diane.
Soon the royal entourage would depart for the wedding in Marseilles and there was a great deal to be done. Her wardrobe must
be coordinated, jewelry selected; new headdresses to be fitted. Her
mourning period had come to an official close and her limited
wardrobe now necessitated changes. Though she continued to
prefer the stark contrast of black and white which she had worn as
a widow, she now had more liberty with the colors, fabrics and designs.

She sat in the window seat which looked down over a large
forest of trees. There was a selection of sketches for new gowns
spread out on her lap. Attire was the most costly aspect of any stay
at Court. For Diane, it was no exception. Everyone in attendance
of the King was expected by His Majesty to wear only the finest
fabrics and the most costly jewels, so that they might bear a more
natural place beside him. No expense was ever to be spared if one
hoped to keep company in the King's circle. Gowns and doublets
were sewn of velvet and silk. They were lined with the rarest furs.
Otter. Marten. Ermine. Sable. There were marble beads, gold and

silver rings, bracelets and chains. There were jewels: rubies, diamonds, emeralds and garnets. A courtier could easily find himself in financial ruin for overstaying his time at the Court of France.

Diane looked down at the sketch before her. A gown of black and white satin with a gold-embroidered yoke for the betrothal dinner. She cast it aside and looked at another. Black velvet with a collar of speckled lynx and puffed sleeves. This gown was for the gala celebration for the Pope's arrival in France. She tossed the sketches aside with all of the others and lay her head back against the window. The first thing she saw when she closed her eyes was an image of Henri.

A spasm of pain coursed through her. She saw his sad face and the dark soulful eyes. She could almost feel his touch. The firmness of his bare body pressed against hers. She shook her head to make the images disappear. She had started toward his apartments more times than she could count over the past month. Several times in the darkness of early morning she had even made it as far as the royal wing. But always she stopped herself, knowing in her heart that she was doing what was best. At least what was best for Henri.

"Are you quite ready, Mademoiselle?"

Diane heard the words as though from a distance. She opened her eyes. Jacques de Saint-André sat across from Hélène, who was contemplating a particularly good hand of cards. Diane watched her toss down a card and then look up at him with a faint smile. As she did, the heavy wooden door out in the main sitting room slammed shut. Hélène excused herself to see who it was.

"And just when I was finally about to win," he grumbled and then cast a good-natured smile over at Diane. A moment later, Grand Master Montmorency pushed past Hélène and stormed into the room, his blue velvet cape swirling around him. Diane looked up from her sketches.

"Madame, if you would be so kind, I have come to have a private word with you."

Diane came to her feet and walked toward the door without

giving him the benefit of a direct regard. "I do not believe we have anything to say to one another, Monsieur, that cannot be said in passing."

He looked over at Hélène and then cast his eyes for a moment longer on Saint-André. "Madame, please. My business concerns Prince Henri, and I haven't much time. I leave for Marseilles tonight to begin preparations for the wedding."

Diane swallowed hard and took a breath to steady herself. "Leave us, please," she finally said.

Jacques and Hélène withdrew and closed the door.

When they were alone, Montmorency tossed his cape onto the back of a chair at the gaming table and sat down. "Please, Madame," he said, indicating with his hand his desire that she should sit across from him. After a moment's contemplation, she did, and looked intensely into his eyes.

"Will you offer me some wine before we speak?" he asked, fingering the hand of cards on the table before him.

"I haven't any wine here and, as you can see, I have sent my attendant away, so there is no one to serve you. Now please, say what you have come to say and be quick about it." She returned her eyes to his and waited for him to speak.

"Very well then. I know we did not begin on the very best footing, Madame, but to be plain about the whole thing, I like you. Yes, indeed I do. You are bold and direct, and so shall I be."

"Have you ever been otherwise?"

He looked back at her and forged ahead. "The boy is miserable, Madame, and for all he has been asked to endure in his short life, it pains me to see him this way. He will not eat, he sleeps only so much as he must, and he refuses all company, preferring instead to stay alone in his apartment gazing into the fire."

"Well, I am sorry to hear it, Monsieur, but what has this to do with me?"

All at once they were staring at one another. She knew that he knew. She challenged him openly. A battle of wills. Their words were chosen. Exact.

"I think, Madame, that his happiness has everything to do with you, and I am prepared to give you one thousand ecus to have you give the boy what it is he craves."

"And what exactly might that be, Monsieur?" she asked, leaning back in her chair, her hands folded gracefully on the table.

"Why, whatever it is that you had been giving him up until recently, of course."

"One thousand ecus. That is a great deal of money, Monsieur Montmorency. I wonder if His Highness knows what kind of a 'friend' he has in you; one who would go to such lengths to retain me for him."

"The Prince knows nothing of my coming here, and would be most angry if he did."

"I should imagine."

"Madame, it is a generous offer that I make to you; but there is of course a stipulation, should you decide to accept my proposal."

"Of course."

"For the sum I named, you would see that he is kept happy, but you would also agree not to further impede, by any means in which you currently appear to be engaged, the King's plans to marry his son to the Pope's niece."

There was a long and uncomfortable silence between them. Diane studied the chiseled face of a warrior who seldom lost. "So that is what this is about," she finally said in a controlled tone, and at the same time thrust back her chair so that it toppled over behind her. She stood looming above the Grand Master.

"Since we are being plain with each other, Monsieur Montmorency, now I shall take my turn. No one is more aware of His Highness's obligations to the Crown than I, and I assure you, I have done nothing to dissuade him from that course. No matter what has or has not passed between the Prince and myself, be very clear about one thing, sir. Neither I nor my favors are for sale to you, or to anyone else!"

"Madame, please," he pleaded, and rose to meet her. His hands, like hers, were balanced on the table between them. "You must listen

to reason. I care for the boy like a son. He has had so little pleasure in his life."

"And so you would buy me for him like a prize mare?"

Montmorency cleared his throat with his hand to his mouth.
"Madame, you have twisted my words, and with them their intent. I may be many things, but I am not a fool. It is very clear to
me what he feels for you, and what he thinks you feel for him. Be
sure of one thing, Madame, as you weigh this. His Majesty means
for this marriage to take place. You have no hope of ever marrying
him yourself, and your encouragement of that fantasy can only
bring the boy unhappiness. Please, Madame, I implore you. If
you care for him, even in the slightest way, then all would be
served by this arrangement. Your estate shall be made more secure, France will have its tie to Italy, and the Prince shall be happy
once again."

Diane paced back and forth behind the fallen chair. She knew
whatever she said next would affect the rest of her life. It was not
enough that she had resolved not to see Henri alone until after his
wedding. She knew now that he still harbored hope. She had once
made the Prince a promise of her friendship, and with the idealism of youth he expected her to keep it. For her, that alliance now
was the most dangerous thing in the world. She had no choice.
She looked back up at Montmorency. When she spoke, it was with
disarming resolution.

"I will not take your money, Monsieur . . . but neither will I
stand in the King's way. I will continue to refuse to see the Prince
privately. After he has married, I pray God that the infatuation he
now feels will pass."

"May the Lord bless you, Madame. You are doing the best for
all concerned."

"But for that assurance, Monsieur, it is I who have a condition."

"You have only to name it."

"You must get word to the Prince before you depart for Marseilles this evening that the Captain of the King's Scots Guard,
Monsieur de Montgommery, has proposed marriage and that I

have accepted. You must tell him that he has no reason to delay his wedding."

Diane moved toward the window and looked out onto the grounds and an emerald hedge clipped into the shape of a huge diamond. It was over. It must be over. "Now please leave me, Monsieur."

"Thank you, Madame. I know you shall not regret this."

Montmorency fumbled at the card table and then, tossing the blue velvet cape across his shoulders, headed directly for the door. As he put his hand on the heavy iron handle, he turned back around to her.

"I was away from Court a great deal when you were here with your husband. Tell me, did you not know the Queen, his mother, quite well?"

"I did."

A faint smile passed across his thin lips. "Ah, well then. Of course, that explains it. You see, Madame, you mustn't blame yourself for this awkward state of affairs. His Highness is very young and impressionable. The death of his mother at so young and tender an age left him, I believe, quite vulnerable to the attentions of a mature woman; one so close in age to the former Queen. I went through it myself, many years ago, of course. For me it was my governess; wonderful old woman. I swore one day I would marry her. Can you imagine it? Fortunately for us both, she had the good sense to turn me down. She died the year my first son was born, but my memories of her shall always be fond. So you see, you may rest assured that in time those emotions, along with all of the other vestiges of a man's impetuous youth, shall be relegated to a few bewildering memories. One day he will thank you for it. You shall see."

As he slammed the heavy wooden door behind himself, the iron handle clanged against it. The sound was like cannon fire in her mind. The feeling in her heart was as black as death.

IANE FALTERED as she stepped from the last royal barge onto the hard Provençal soil of Avignon, seventy-five miles from Marseilles. The sun was hot. It intensified the colors. The azure blue water. The mix of beige, russet and mauve coloring the hills. The bleached bone white of the rocks. An extraordinary palate.

They arrived in the south by barge a day later than they had anticipated, owing to the turn of the tide down the Rhône. Diane had found a seat for herself and for Hélène on the last barge in the queue, some four barges behind Henri. She had wanted to be as far from him as she could be. She must attend the wedding. To avoid it now would be to invite gossip. But she had decided after the ceremony to return for a while to Anet. It had been six months since she had seen her daughters. She needed time with them. Time alone. Time to reflect and to mend.

She faltered again as she climbed the steep, limestone incline. She did not adjust as quickly as she had expected to the shift from water to land. Hélène clutched her about the arms to steady her.

"Madame, are you all right?" she whispered, as Diane regained her footing and pushed onward up the rocky hill to the waiting assembly of horses that would take them on to Marseilles.

"It is my legs. What I really need is to walk a while to steady them."

Hélène's round eyes narrowed with concern. She watched Diane glance back down at the string of royal barges, still thick with courtiers and massive luggage chests. Though there was a steady stream of servants who were transporting the cargo up the hill, it would be some time before the caravan would be ready to depart. The area at the top of the hill was shaded by a grove of cypress trees, and Diane found herself longing for the freedom of a moment's solitude.

"Then I shall attend you, Madame."

"No. I appreciate your concern, but I need a few moments to myself."

After she had reassured her maid, Diane ambled slowly down the path of tall grass and cypress trees which lined the road. When the voices and the grunting noises from the men who hauled the heavily laden chests had begun to fade behind her, she took a deep breath. This trip had been far more difficult than she had expected, but soon Henri would be married and she would return to Anet to see her daughters.

As she walked, she breathed deep the warm Provençal air, filled with the fragrance of spices and lavender. It had been a long while, she thought, since she had noticed anything so beautiful; it had been since Cauterets. She quickly forced the thought from her mind and replaced it once again with thoughts of her two daughters. It would be a comfort to see them. She needed the reality of family just now.

"You must be careful not to go too far; it would be only too easy to find yourself lost out here."

Startled by the sound of a man's voice, Diane jumped back onto the heels of her leather slippers and turned around. Brissac, Saint-André, Bourbon and Henri were coming toward her across a field of lavender. It was Jacques who had spoken, and who advanced toward her now. Henri hung back with Brissac and Bourbon and peered up into the sky as though he did not see her.

"Thank you, Monsieur. I shall be careful."

She tried not to do it but after a moment her will escaped her. She looked over at Henri. He was still several feet away from her, beneath the shade of a tall cypress tree. He stood there in emerald-green satin; the plume in his velvet toque and the large white tassel from which his dagger was slung at his side were gold. She had not realized until she looked at him just then, how great a sacrifice she was about to make for France. She looked back at Jacques, and her eyes asked the question she could not.

"Talk to him, Madame. Please," he whispered. He then motioned to Bourbon and Brissac with a wave of his yellow, balloon sleeve and they began to walk back toward the moored barges, leaving Diane alone with a great distance between her and Henri.

Finally, he looked down and his dark, brooding eyes met hers. His brows were raised; lips parted, as though he were waiting for her to speak. In his eyes, she saw the return of the same pained fierceness by which she had been so struck on the day they had met. A songbird chirped in the tree above them, masking the deafening silence.

This was the first moment that they had been alone together since that night in his chamber nearly two months before. Now, standing there looking at him, she wanted to abandon everything she had promised God and everything she had promised herself. She bit her own tongue to stop herself from blurting out what she longed to say; what she knew he longed to hear. As the silence between them grew more heavy, the sadness in his eyes changed to fury. After what seemed an eternity with nothing more than a penetrating look between them, he turned away from her and began to head down the road after the shadowy figures of his friends.

"Henri, wait!"

Moved to stop by the sound of her voice, he stood motionless in the road, his back to her. The bottom of his green satin doublet rippled around his thighs from the warm summer breeze. Slowly he turned and looked at her once again.

"I wanted . . ." she faltered. "I wanted to wish you the best tomorrow, when you meet her. I wanted to tell you . . . be happy."

His lips pressed tightly together at the sound of her words, and his thick brows lowered over glittering black eyes. He waited. Then, when it was clear that she had nothing more to say to him, he turned swiftly and ran down the dirt road away from her.

THE NEXT MORNING, Henri stood alone on the veranda of the Pope's sumptuous villa with a sweeping view of the ocean. He could prolong it no further. The wedding festivities began tomorrow, and today he must meet his bride. Now he and the rest of the royal family had been summoned for the formal introduction.

Henri had made no further attempt to contact Diane. He understood now that there would be no point.

This will be the end of me, he thought. *I will meet the Pope's niece and then tomorrow the marriage will be performed, and that will be the end of my life.* Lost in the bitter taste of his third goblet of wine, he did not hear the Pope finally make his entrance back inside the villa.

Pope Clement VII was attired in a long, starched white gown. His white beard met the point of his gold, jewel-encrusted pectoral cross. His fingers were covered with jeweled rings. He made his way down the sweeping stone staircase and into the salon followed by two Cardinals in long red cassocks and birettas.

"Finally," the King smiled as he took the Pope's hands.

"Yes, finally," echoed the Pontiff, with a faint smile over his taciturn face and yellow jowls. "Have you brought the boy?" he asked, moving directly to the purpose of the reception.

Just at that moment, he began a violent fit of coughing. He lifted a hand to his mouth as two of the green-clad pages brought one of the heavily carved chairs for him. François looked around and caught sight of Henri who was still standing alone on the veranda. He motioned for Montmorency to retrieve him. The room fell silent except for the coughing. After a moment, Henri came forth through the flapping crimson drapes. The Pope, his yellow face now flushed red, extended his jeweled hand to the Prince. Henri kissed his ring and then looked up. The two men studied one another as François tentatively looked on. The King cleared his throat. Montmorency stood behind Henri, a hand placed gently on his black silk shirt. Two gulls screeched as they flew past the open window.

"Indeed . . . you shall do nicely for my little Caterina," he mumbled in Italian.

After another moment of inspecting Henri as though he were one of the King's chamberlains, the Pope snapped his fingers above his head in the direction of a woman who stood behind him in the doorway. Henri thought that he could not possibly have seen her. He must instinctively have known she would be there. She was a plain woman. Her nose was large and hooked and her heavy brows fused together over her eyes. She wore a huge round, blue turban set back on her head, and a long-bodiced gown with puffed sleeves and a huge full skirt. It was the highest of fashion in Italy. Anne d'Heilly merely winced at what she considered to be hopelessly common.

"That is not—" Henri managed to gasp as he looked in the woman's direction. The Pope chuckled and ran his fingers the length of his white beard.

"Oh, goodness no, dear boy. That is Maria Salviati, Caterina's aunt." The laughing made him begin to choke once again and he reached for a silver chalice beside him on a tray. After he had taken a sip he added, "She is a good woman, a Medici herself." The Pope looked up at the dark-haired woman. "All right, Maria," he said in Italian. "It is time to bring her." The Pope rose to his feet and turned so that he, Henri, the Dauphin and the King stood in a semicircle facing the open double doors. Once again everyone in the room fell silent. François dabbed at the hair around his ears, insuring it was in place. The Pope coughed into a handkerchief. Henri wished he had taken just one more goblet of wine.

After a few moments, a small, frail-looking girl with dark bulging eyes came around the corner and through the doorway. She too had thick lips and a large nose. Her features were bold and her skin was sallow. She was so unassuming that when she turned the corner beside her aunt, Henri thought her to be another attendant and he continued to look on at the empty doorway. But then the Pope stood.

"Ah, now this is my little Caterina!" he exclaimed upon seeing her. When he extended his arms, she drew forward, kissed his cheek and then lowered her head shyly. Henri closed his eyes.

"Merciful heaven," muttered Anne d'Heilly beneath her breath. The Pope took his niece's hand and led her forward, toward the King. She looked up from beneath a coronet of dark braids in which was nestled one ornamental ruby at the center of her forehead. From larger than average ears, pendant earrings of pearl and ruby glittered. Her gown was gold and white, with voluminous puffed sleeves and full skirts that overpowered her.

"She looks like a well-dressed mouse," the Dauphin snickered to Admiral Chabot also beneath his breath.

"Merciful heaven," repeated Anne d'Heilly.

"May I present my niece, Caterina Maria de Medici," said the Pope, as he led her toward the King.

François was aware that he towered over the young girl, and so he sought to reassure her with his smile. Feeling sufficiently superior, he extended his hand. But instead of taking his in return, she went down onto her knees in the gold and white gown and then dropped completely onto her chest, prostrating herself on the bare marble floor. As she kissed the King's slippered feet, he looked around the room with a startled grin.

"Oh, my merciful heaven!" Anne said, raising a hand to her lips, doing her best to muffle a snicker. The King tossed her a sharp stare and she released her hand quickly, back down to her side.

Montmorency glanced at Henri. His lips were pursed tightly and his eyes were open now, but cast upward. Henri looked as though he were going to be ill. Catherine remained prostrate on the floor before the King. No one said a word. After a moment he bent down and clutched her arm, drawing her onto her knees.

"Here, here, *ma chère,* let me help you."

"You will forgive her," said the Pope. "She has spent most of her life in the convent. She has not had the attention to protocol that I would have wished for her."

"On the contrary. We are most humbled by this reverent and charming display."

She was still on her knees when she spoke. "It is my great honor, Your Majesty, that I am in your presence. It is, however, a dream far greater than I could have imagined, that I am to become your daughter."

Her voice was deep for her young age; almost husky, and her French was awkward. But both had a certain charm that captured the King.

"And her Latin is far better than her French," the Pope interjected to excuse the poorly constructed phrase.

"Do not worry," said the King, as he drew her up to her feet and chucked her gently beneath the chin. "She will learn soon enough." Still clutching her tiny hand in his own, the King led her to his left. "*Chérie,* this is my son, the Dauphin. One day he will be King. I should like the two of you to become friends."

"It would be an honor," she repeated and curtsied fully.

The Dauphin smiled and then nodded. "The King led her further to his left.

"And this . . ." said the Pope. "This will be your husband. Henri, may I present my dear niece, Caterina Maria de Medici."

Henri looked at the Pope who beamed at her as if she were his own child. He then looked at the rakish grin splashed across his brother's face and at Montmorency's studied gaze. Once again she curtsied. He searched in vain for something pleasant to say, but as he looked into her bulging, watery eyes his mind went blank.

"Perhaps we could all use a bit of wine now," suggested Montmorency as he put a comforting hand, once again, on Henri's shoulder. Henri looked away from the Medici girl and helplessly back toward the King.

"Splendid idea," said His Majesty.

One of the Papal guards, who held a long jeweled halberd, ushered the group from the grand salon into a cavernous dining hall. But Henri could not move. He watched the Pope kiss Catherine and take her arm as they walked from the room. His heart sank. As Montmorency turned to join the others, Henri gripped his shoulder.

"Please, Monty . . . *mon vieux,*" he whispered urgently. "I beg you, find me a way out of this!"

Montmorency turned and faced the pained expression that he had seen so often on Henri's face. "I am sorry, my son, there is nothing more that I can do."

"*In nomine Patris, et Filii et Spiritus Sancti . . .*"

Great fingers of light through the massive stained-glass windows washed the nave of the cathedral with muted colors as Henri and Catherine prepared to take their final vows. Diane daubed the perspiration from her brow with a blue silk handkerchief as she watched the tiny girl in the magnificent gown of white and gold brocade. The gown was accented with the jeweled portion of her dowry for France. Her waist was belted in gold with eight large balas rubies set off by a diamond in the center. At her throat she wore a string of eighty pearls and a pendant set with large diamonds, emeralds and rubies. Her short fingers were covered with rubies, diamonds and gold.

Diane gazed through the glitter at the plain little face; the dark eyebrows and the large nose. A pang of regret rose from her heart. She tried to quiet it. She felt a trickle of sweat between her breasts beneath the layers of heavy damask. Then she shivered. It would soon be over. She had only to bear a few more moments. She steadied herself with a hand on the back of the pew before her as Henri and Catherine turned, and knelt on two silver prie-dieux at the altar.

The Pope gave the nuptial benediction himself, bestowing greater solemnity to the event. He blessed the golden ring and held it up to the Lord. Diane made herself watch as Henri slipped it onto the girl's finger. The Pope was then helped to one side, owing to his ill health. But he beamed broadly through his long beard as the Cardinal de Tournon said the final portion of the Mass. He then raised his hand to make the sign of the cross and announced that by God's holy ordinance, Henri de Valois and Catherine de Medici were man and wife.

THE KING AND THE POPE walked arm in arm, and whispered to one another as they led the new couple and a collection of drunken courtiers up the sweeping stone staircase. There was no choice left to either the bride or the groom; the two elders were anxious to see the union consummated and now led the pathway to that ultimate end. Behind them came Queen Eleanora, François' Spanish wife; the Dauphin, Montmorency, Admiral Chabot and the Cardinal de Lorraine as though it were a party. The air was thick from so many bodies pressed so closely together in the stairwell, and Henri felt as if he would choke. But his thoughts were arrested when the entire procession came to a halt at his apartment doors.

As he stopped, Henri was forced to face the King. François planted his arms firmly on Henri's shoulders. It was a sign between gentlemen signaling that the other must now engage in his duty, no matter how distasteful. He swiftly pulled his son to him and kissed each cheek. He then took Catherine's trembling hand in his own, raised it to his lips, and kissed it.

"Madame La Duchesse," he began, "tonight you become a permanent part of this house, and nothing shall please Us more than when you are fat with Our first grandchild!"

The crowd, who had long since abandoned decorum, peeled with laughter and whistles. The King and the Pope exchanged a sideways grin. Clement patted the King's back. Henri glared at the two men who had conspired to ruin his life, and he watched as Clement kissed his niece. He then made the sign of the cross before them.

"Now, my children," he said in slurred French, "to your jousting!"

Glad to be free of the callous Court, Henri took Catherine's small, moist hand and led her into his apartments. There, the Cardinal de Lorraine blessed the nuptial couch as Ippolito de Medici swung a smoking censer past the bedcurtains, filling the room with hallowed incense. Beside the bed, Catherine's attendants waited to undress her.

"Go with your ladies," he instructed. "I shall join you shortly."

"As you wish," she replied and followed her aunt and her cousin into the dressing room.

When they had gone, Henri turned to his boyhood friend with frantic eyes. "Brissac, please, has there been any word or any message from Madame de Poitiers? Anything at all?"

"I am sorry, Your Highness. I inquired as you requested and I was told that she left the banquet shortly after your departure. I am bound by honesty to tell you that she left with Jacques de Montgommery."

"Damn her!"

Henri took a deep breath and blew it out, as though trying to recover from a blow.

"So be it. Help me out of this thing, will you. If it is jousting they want then, by God, it is jousting they shall have!"

CLEMENT, A PACE BEHIND François, lumbered back down the long staircase toward the sound of the music and laughter in the large grand salon. The festivities were still active despite the presence of the first blush of sun that had begun to ascend through the long casement windows. When the King entered the hall he grabbed a spilled silver goblet from one of the long tables and banged it against the wall to gain attention. The noise ceased. The musicians stopped playing.

"We are most pleased to announce," he began, in a deep, ceremonial tone, "that we have gone together to ensure the consummation of the marriage between Our new daughter and the son of France."

"And we have come back to report," the Pope continued for him, "that the Duc and Duchesse d'Orléans jousted valiantly!"

Shouts and cheers of laughter rose from the throngs of remaining drunken nobles who sat sprawled among the lavish furnishings. Pope Clement raised an empty chalice that he too had taken from the table.

"May Almighty God bless them both now, and may my niece be with child before I take my leave from France!"

In a corner, Diane sat alone sipping a cordial, trying in vain to numb herself. She had left Jacques at the door to his apartments. She had said she would be only a moment, promising to return to him. But she had wanted to hear it; needed to hear that it was really done between them.

Diane had returned to the banquet hall, not expecting the news to pierce her the way that it had. She let the pain pass through her, and then managed to smile. She had served her purpose well. She had helped a shy young Prince into manhood; readied him for a wife. Someday he would take her aside and thank her for having known when to walk away. He had said he loved her, but what could he know of love when he was so filled with the aimless ardor of adolescence? It would have been easy to confuse the two. Her only regret, now that it was over between them, was that for a moment, she too had allowed herself to forget how to distinguish between love and desire.

THE MORNING DEW on the leaded windowpane blew across Henri's cheek with a gust of the salty ocean breeze. His eyes opened and he was with Diane. He could feel the warmth of her body next to his. He moved to touch her. Then he remembered. Outside, the sound of horses, their hooves on cobbled stones, the shouts of the stable masters woke him from dazed half slumber. Next to him, Catherine slept bundled in a small heap beneath the layers of white muslin, so that all he could see was the gold tassel and the top of her white nightcap. He grimaced when the image of what he had done with her returned to him.

Last night he had been beyond anger. Beyond pain. The wine he had drunk had seen to that. He had taken it out on this girl whom he had seen only twice in his life, and to whom now, he was forever bound. All of the weeks of confusion and defeat had reached a violent crescendo in her small, chaste body. He was certain that he had hurt her. He had not been gentle, as if he could force the memory and the pain of Diane further back in his mind, with each violent jabbing thrust. When it was over, he had rolled away, and turned a deaf ear to her sobbing. He hadn't the strength to deal with her anguish, as well as his own.

The sounds outside drew Henri out of bed. He moved to a small window and turned the brass handle. It opened onto the courtyard. Two horses, yet without riders, were saddled and packed. A group of guards mounted on royal stallions waited nearby in the early morning mist. Henri shook his head trying desperately to ward off the effects of the wine that he had drunk. As he gazed out of the opened window he finally saw Hélène, Diane's maid, emerge from the villa in a traveling cloak and hood. After another moment, Diane followed.

Henri put a hand to his forehead and brushed back a dark curl.

She was leaving Court without even saying good-bye. Once again he felt utterly helpless. All of his life he had been helpless; a puppet.

"He says, raise your leg, little puppet," he whispered. "And so I do . . . I always do . . ."

He was first a marionette for his father, and now for his country. This marriage to the little Florentine girl, which he had just irrevocably consummated with a degrading performance for his father and the Pope, was the most dramatic example of his position. For reasons to which he was not privileged, he had been married to a merchant's daughter and told nothing more than that he must do it for France.

More than pain now, he felt bitter rage. It was rage at a system that he was not permitted to understand, and yet that had the power to keep him from the only happiness he had ever known. He watched in silence as Diane, dressed in a black velvet gown, cloak and hood, was helped onto her horse by one of the equerries. Henri extended his hand past the glass, and with his finger traced the outline of her body, as she took the leather reins and stroked the horse's dark mane. Then, following the lead of the King's guard, she clicked her heels, and followed the guides out of Marseilles, and out of Henri's life.

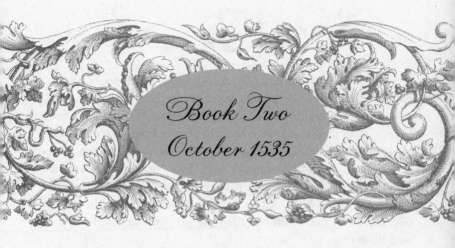

Book Two
October 1535

Thus are pretty rosebuds carried by the wind as well as flowers full blown,
and children snatched away are mourned a hundred times more than
the old who die.

— BRANTÔME

$\mathscr{A}$NNE D'HEILLY BURST through the open doors to the King's council chamber and entered the inner sanctum without bothering to knock. Her shoes, the latest style from Venice, with small cork soles and covered in blue velvet, echoed beneath the matching blue gown, as she swept across the tiled floor toward the long mahogany table. It was the *conseil privé;* the larger gathering of nobles on matters of state, and so the room was packed full of the King's advisors. Everyone was there but Chancellor Duprat, who had died the previous year following a long illness.

The King's private chamber at Saint Germain-en-Laye was vast, with high arched ceilings, newly frescoed in pastel shades. On the walls were large, gold-scalloped wall sconces and long mirrors between a series of small paned windows. Golden light poured through them, across the room on one side, leaving the other side in the shadows. Seeing Anne, the King rose from the carved high-back chair at the head of the table.

"What is it, *mon amour?*" he asked.

The other men of the council thrust back their chairs and stood in deference to the woman now elevated to Duchesse d'Etampes. The King had recently arranged for the marriage of his *favourite* to a noble but impoverished courtier. He then gave them the Duchy of Etampes as a way of bestowing greater power and respect upon the woman who continued to share his life.

"It is that blasted husband you've given me!" she screeched. "He wants more money to keep quiet. Always more money! He has sent word that he cannot live on the stipend you pay him."

A smile broke across François' face, curling his mustache upward, as if to say, *is that all?* He came out from behind the table and took her hand.

"Well, gentlemen, as you can see, Our attentions are required elsewhere. The matter that we were discussing has been concluded, has it not?"

Chabot cleared his throat. Antoine du Bourg, the new Chancellor of France, sat back down and began to collect his papers. Anne de Montmorency was the only one who dared to raise his head in the direction of the King.

"Then we are to proceed?" he asked.

"Yes. Increase the troops to forty thousand but hold them as they are until after Christmas. Also, I wish word be sent to my sons at the camp that they are to be at Amboise for the holiday. It is time I see them again."

"Are we at war then?" asked Anne in a careless sing-song tone as she rolled a large gold and ruby ring on her middle finger.

François chucked her beneath the chin with a single finger like a naughty child, and slipped his arm about her tightly corseted waist. "That is nothing for you to worry your pretty head about, *mon amour.* Come, we shall speak of your new husband and see what it will take to quiet him."

"Your Majesty! Your Majesty!" Triboulet came rushing in through the open door in his wildly colored costume. "There is a band of reformers posting signs all around the village below us!"

The King turned his head and stared down at his jester, annoyed by the interruption. "What do you mean, they are posting signs?"

"Against the Church, Your Majesty. Condemning the hypocrisy and the greed of the Catholic Church! I've just come from town. I've seen them myself! There is a huge band of them and they are angry!"

François looked around at his collection of unmoving advisors, his eyes narrowing with anger. "Well! What are you all just sitting there for? Is this why I pay all of you, to sit and do nothing?"

"But Your Majesty said just last week, in the presence of the Queen of Navarre, that free expression was to be tolerated in France!"

"Free expression, not heresy, Monsieur du Bourg, was espoused in the presence of Our sister! Now do something! Do something at once!"

The King's inconsistent religious policies were only one sign of his discontent. The year after his son's marriage in Marseilles had been a difficult one for him. The second year marked a further series of disappointments. One by one, his carefully laid plans were falling down around him. The Pope had waited in France following the marriage of Henri and Catherine, in the hope of seeing his niece with child. François too had prayed for signs of conception, which would have solidified this misalliance; a union, highly unpopular with the Court and the French people. Finally, Pope Clement had returned to Rome without the news he sought. Within ten months of the marriage, he was dead. All of François' hopes of the Italian provinces that he had been promised died with the Pontiff. No Genoa, no Pisa, and no Milan.

The new Pope, who had taken the name of Paul III, refused to honor the secret contract between the two men, terming it "clandestine." He believed that it was not in Italy's best interest to support such claims. The final blow to the King had come when the papacy ordered the return of the jeweled portion of Catherine's dowry. The jewels were not Clement's personal possessions, it was argued, but rather articles of the Holy See, and therefore had not been his to give.

The King of France had surrendered his pride and his son with that marriage, in the hope of regaining Milan. In return, he had gained an exceedingly unpopular daughter-in-law, who after nearly two years, still was not pregnant.

Exercising great determination, he had managed to look forward, nursing his wounds in hopes of a second powerful marital alliance. Philippe Chabot had just returned from England where he had proposed to Henry VIII a marriage between that King's eldest daughter, Mary, with François' third son, Charles. But that too had proved to be a phantom goal. Henry VIII would agree to such a match, now that he was married to Anne Boleyn and he had declared his daughter, Mary, by his previous Queen, a bastard on one condition. His requirement for such a marriage was that both the bride and groom agree to renounce all claim to the English throne. They must also acknowledge Anne Boleyn's future children as the only rightful heirs.

When François found the conditions unsuitable, he issued a counterproposal suggesting Charles as the bridegroom of Boleyn's infant daughter, Elizabeth. But that did not fair better. Henry VIII would agree to that proposal only if François would persuade the new Pope to lift his excommunication.

In the silence, the Chancellor rose to his feet and called Christian de Nançay, Captain of the Guard. The two men exchanged words. The Captain then took two of the other guards and rushed from the King's council chamber to handle the disturbance outside. Once they had gone, François put his face in his hands. Anne poised her hands on her hips.

"What are you going to do about that husband you've given me?" she whined.

François lowered his head as he stormed toward the door. "Oh, leave me alone, will you! I must think!"

After a moment of unbearable silence, Anne pointed her chin in the air, turned on her heels and went out into the corridor after him.

"Well, that is that," Chabot sighed once the King and his mistress were gone. "It is to be war then."

"There is really no other choice," Bourg agreed. "With the new Pope in Rome so disagreeable, everything has changed."

The Cardinal de Lorraine shook his head. "A war is the only way His Majesty will ever get back Milan now."

There was a rumbling of voices from several of the other men at the table who echoed the sentiments of the Admiral. Montmorency was not among them.

"Such conjecture is vastly premature, Chabot," the Grand Master huffed. "And you serve no purpose by second-guessing the will of the King."

"If his foreign policy is as tenuous as his stand on religion," Bourg shook his head, "then may the good Lord help us all!"

Montmorency searched each of their faces. Such fierce competition among them and yet all of it masked by Machiavellian civility. They really were so pitiful. After a moment, he gathered up his papers, stood, and looked back across the council table.

"Seems such a shame that it has all come apart like this," he said with a sneer.

Chabot rolled his eyes. "What are you talking about?"

"Only that so strategic a bargaining chit as His Majesty's second son should be wasted upon a merchant's daughter . . . and a barren one at that." Montmorency strode across the room and then turned back around once he had reached the door. "His Majesty is bound to be furious when he remembers who it was that encouraged such a travesty. And you certainly cannot say you were not warned."

DIANE SAT NEAR the fire but her eyes were directed at the window where fresh drops of rain fell gently past the long sheet of glass. Jacques de Montgommery sat at a small table at the other end of the room. He was playing chess with Françoise, Diane's eldest daughter. Hélène sat in a third seat watching as Montgommery lost.

"Maman! Maman!" Louise, Diane's younger daughter, ran into the room and nearly tripped over a hassock by the door. "Hélène has had news from Court! May I read it? Oh, please may I?"

Diane looked up as though she had been brought back from a deep sleep. Louise, who was nearly thirteen, bounced into the room and twirled about with the letter in her hand. Hélène stiffened. When Louise did not surrender the letter, Diane stood and walked toward her daughter.

"Now, now. Give that to Hélène. Letters are a private matter," Diane reproached.

The girl looked up at her mother and began to giggle. Louise was her willful child. She was the mirror image of Louis. She had his dark, thick rings of hair and her coal-black eyes were framed by thick straight brows. She also had his temperament. After a moment, Diane grew stern so that Louise reluctantly surrendered the letter to her mother's maid.

"Oh, do read it aloud. Please!" Louise whined. She fell onto the floor and propped her elbows on Hélène's knees.

"Do get up, you spoiled thing!" her sister scolded, but Louise stayed put beneath the game table and did not move her arms from Hélène's lap. Everyone was silent as she read the single page of parchment to herself. Diane sat down in a smaller red velvet chair near the table and put an affectionate hand on Montgommery's shoulder.

"News from Monsieur de Saint-André?" she asked. Jacques took her hand from his shoulder and kissed it.

"Yes, Madame."

"He is well?"

"Yes, though he says he has lost weight at the camp. He explains it by saying that the food is no more enticing than the company." She smiled as she read the line.

"And the Prince," Diane continued. "Is he also well?"

"He does not say, Madame. Only that he will be accompanying His Highness home from camp. They have been called home to Amboise by His Majesty for Christmas."

Hélène folded the letter and placed it on the table.

"Does he have other news?" Diane dared to venture further.

"He does ask when we shall be returning to Court."

To this Jacques turned around in his chair. He lifted a hand and ran his long fingers gracefully through his smooth, pointed beard.

"Well, my dear, it is a good question," he said. "Will you return? You know I must myself return to service before the tenth, and it would be so splendid if we could go together."

Diane stood and walked back toward one of the windows which ran the entire length from the parqueted floor to the vaulted ceiling. She ran her hand along the frame.

"I wonder if it will ever stop raining. Everything is so gray this time of year."

Jacques strode toward her and encircled her with his arms.

"What do you say, *ma chère?*" he pushed. "Will you return with me? It is time for you to get back for more than just one of your brief visits anyway."

Diane turned and saw Hélène perched pensively on the edge of her chair. Her daughters were both gazing up at her expectantly, knowing the honor that it would be for the entire family.

"I do not want to leave them at Christmas."

"Oh, nonsense. They are nearly grown women. Besides, they will be going back to the convent after the New Year and you will be left alone in this big, ugly old place."

Diane gazed around the large room. The paint on the ceiling was cracked. The tapestries were shredded. The roof leaked and even with the fires fully stoked, it was a dark and drafty old keep. She thought of Court and the comforts there in winter. She thought of her own splendidly decorated apartments; the parties and the banquets. It had been over a year since she had any occasion to wear anything formal. She had chosen not even to have any new headdresses or gowns made since last season. In the two years since Henri's wedding, she had returned to Court only once. It had been last summer when she knew, through Jacques de Montgommery, that Henri was safely away at military camp.

She had gone to Fontainebleau for only two weeks to attend a celebration of His Majesty's birthday. The invitation had been personally written by the King. The image of François, and the memory of his persistent overtures, shot through her mind. It wound around to memories of Anne d'Heilly and her vicious taunting. The images terminated with the memory of Henri. The kiss they had shared in Cauterets. The forbidden night. The wedding in Marseilles. The pain she had caused. The disappointment. The sadness.

"Oh, please . . ." Montgommery cajoled, drawing her out of her reflections. "It would be so good to have you near me."

Diane gazed into the reassuring depths of his eyes and the long soft face of the man she did not love. She had been so weak the last time. So afraid. She had been like a servant while Anne d'Heilly had been like her master. The King's *favourite* had been in complete control. It could not be that way this time if she returned. But had she changed enough to bear it? That was impossible to know, unless she returned . . . with Montgommery.

"Well, Hélène, are you ready to return?"

"Oh yes, Madame. Most ready . . . if you are, that is."

"I suppose it is time." She took a deep breath and then smiled. "So be it. We shall leave with the Captain."

Hélène could not contain her smile.

"Then, if you will excuse me. There will be much packing to do."

Diane nodded her approval and then walked over to a carved writing table near the fire, drawing out a quill and a fresh sheet of parchment.

"*Maman,* Père Augustin is here," announced Louise, who had seen him through the window. She scurried to her mother's writing desk. "Will you be coming to Mass?"

"Yes of course, dear. You and Françoise go along with Jacques. I shall join you in a few minutes."

When they had all gone, she dipped the long golden-tipped quill into the ink well. The pen hovered over the blank parchment for several moments before she lowered it and scrawled the first words of a note to the King of France. She had not yet decided exactly how to say that, with his good grace, she was finally prepared to return.

MONTGOMMERY STOOD BEFORE the others did and, after receiving the blessing, walked out under the eaves of the private Brézé chapel. He rubbed a long hand over his chest and stretched his other arm over his head, arching his back like a cat. When Diane came out beside him, Jacques pulled her by the waist and kissed her.

"Please! We have just come from Mass!" she admonished him and wiped away the wetness from his kiss.

Diane walked out into the muddy courtyard between the chapel and the chateau. She had come to regret her decision to return to Court already. It had been peaceful in this protective estate. It had been safe. The pain had finally dulled, and now was nearly gone. The order to her life had returned and she was not at all certain that she desired to change that.

"We shall need new paint in the spring. And that roof over the ballroom leaks," Diane said as she studied the facade, a light rain still falling.

"Oh, why do you not just sell the place, *ma chère*? It is such an old sleeping giant. Certainly it is nowhere near its former glory." Jacques crossed his arms over his chest and gazed up at the main building. "Having been owned by the Grand Sénéchal de Normandie, and with the ample woods surrounding it, I am certain we could still net a fair price."

Diane stopped in the center of the courtyard. She lowered the velvet wrap from her head. A light rain fell on her cap and her cheeks. She brushed it away and turned to Jacques.

"This is Louis' ancestral home. It is my children's birthright. How can you ask that of me?"

"Because it is cold and archaic and once we are married I shall refuse to spend another night in it!"

Jacques had a way of being direct and then smiling afterward to lessen the severity of what he had said. Diane looked into the hollow green eyes above the smile. *I wonder what I ever found attractive about him,* she thought. *How did I let it get this far?*

"I had no idea you detested it so much here."

"Well, shall we say, I simply prefer the comforts of Court to the more rustic life you have here at Anet."

Jacques followed her down a small staircase, past a lion's head statue poised on a stone pedestal. She stopped a moment and looked up into a collection of trees.

"They will be so beautiful in the spring, all of them green and rustling, full of new life. Birds will sing from all of these branches. And the geese will bathe and flutter in that pond. Louis taught our daughters to ride out there, past the gardens." She looked up at him. "I cannot sell it."

Jacques encircled her with his long arms and kissed her again. "You are so beautiful when you are determined," he said and then pressed his mouth upon hers. His tongue swept inside. He clung to her with a vengeance until her urge to pull away was stronger. "Oh, when will you let me have you again? You know how I ache for you!"

"Must you bring that up again? We were having such a lovely day."

"What is it then? Am I not good enough for you now that we are returning to Court? Perhaps you think that you shall have another chance with the King?"

"Jacques, please, don't be petulant. It is really very unbecoming."

She tried to turn away but he grabbed her gloved wrist, twisting it so that she was forced to turn back toward him. "That is not what you said in Marseilles! You liked my hot blood then!"

She detested his childish, angry outbursts, but he spoke the truth. Even now, nearly two years later, she could not bear to hear it. That night after all the wedding festivities had finally wound to a close; after Henri had married Catherine and she herself had drunk far too much wine, she had nursed her wounded pride by finally letting Jacques share her bed. Now the shadowy memory of that single intimate encounter with him made her blood run cold. Then, she had accepted it as her only way out of the quagmire of confusion in which she had felt herself drowning. She was a woman. He was a man. She had needed a man then. Not a boy. Or so she had convinced herself long enough to allow it to happen.

When he wrote and asked, six months later, if she would receive him on his holiday, she agreed. She needed a new life. At the time it had seemed right to include him. When he came to Anet, Diane had been determined to love him. Her daughters, alone and fatherless, were charmed by his pristine manner and glamorous tales of courtly life. He returned many times after that, and finally in spite of the lie she had told Montmorency, Diane truly did accept his proposal.

But her love did not grow. She began to feel trapped. She made excuses and threw up roadblocks to the marriage to which she had previously agreed. Now she found herself caring for him less each day. She thanked God she had been given the foresight not to marry him yet. One loveless marriage was enough for any one lifetime. Returning to Court now was the only way for her to rectify her mistake with Jacques and for both of them to get on with their lives.

"Well, answer me! Ha! So that is it! Perhaps it is not the King you want, but rather the King's son! You are not going to start things up with that boy again, are you?"

"Jacques, let go of my hand."

She did not break her gaze from his. Her words had been slow and punctuated. He recanted. Diane rubbed her wrist with her other hand as she looked at him.

"I am simply not ready to give you that part of myself," she whispered. "I am sorry. I need more time."

"By the time you are ready, Madame, the point shall be mute, for I fear I shall be too old to bed anyone!"

A smile broke across her face and she reached up to brush a finger across the soft skin of his cheek. "You really are a dear, dear man when you choose to be. But more often than not, Captain, you are thoroughly impossible."

Jacques took her hand from his cheek and kissed it. His voice changed to a sincere and pleading tone from its former harshness. "Let us set a date then. Just give me a date, whenever you choose, and I shall be a happy man."

"I cannot think about it now. But after the new year. Please, Jacques, just let us wait until then."

16

THE DAUPHIN SAT ON THE FLOOR of Anne d'Heilly's salon early on Christmas Eve with his knees drawn up near his chest. He was half swallowed by a sea of bright blue, gold and green overstuffed silk pillows. On his legs, he balanced a dark wooden lute. Next to him, in a blue embroidered gown and raven hair, sat Agnese Pachecho, his mistress.

François was now eighteen, and this Spanish honor maiden to Queen Eleanora was his first officially acknowledged paramour. Surrounding the lovers were the younger members of the King's *petite bande* of ladies. Folded out around them like petals on a rose, were their ladies-in-waiting. Beside them in the hearth, the yule log blazed as the Dauphin strummed at the lute halfheartedly and chatted with the people around him. Gentlemen and courtiers lingered around the edges of the room decorated with holly and ivy, conversing in small collections as they sipped wine from their expensive Venetian crystal goblets.

Near the fire, the King sat with Anne d'Heilly as she stroked the tiny pet marmoset on her lap that he had given her for her birthday. The King nodded to his son and he then began to sing.

> *I waited, waited for the Lord,*
> *he bent down to me and heard my cry.*
> *He brought me up out of the muddy pit, out of the mire . . .*

Diane grew rigid at the sound of the Psalm sung so rollickingly by the Dauphin. *Sacrilege!* she thought, and discreetly made the sign of the cross. She had been back little more than a week, but it was a decidedly different Court than the one she had left two years before. She had heard the gossip that the King was suffering from some sort of malady brought about by too many mistresses. Also in her absence, Anne d'Heilly had been married and thereby elevated to the exalted title of Duchesse d'Etampes. But the most striking change at Court was the strengthening air of tolerance for the "new religion."

At every dinner and ball, in every group of courtiers who gathered, the endless topic was the Reformation. Although he refused to make a public stance either way, it was the King himself who had personally approved the translation of the Psalms into secular verse. Now, not only were they being sung blasphemously by his own son here in the palace, but in every other fashionable salon in France.

Diane slid behind the large circle of courtiers and onto the terrace. The crisp winter air rushed at her. The laughter and the music dimmed. She took a deep breath and then looked up at the stars. The sky was clear enough to see the constellations. After a moment, her eyes drifted down to the shadow of a young man who sat a few feet from her on one of the stone benches. He seemed as unconcerned by the cold as she. His back was turned to her but she recognized him at once. There was no mistaking the outline of his shoulders, the tufts of thick, dark hair.

"Hello, Henri."

He stood and turned around. They were separated by the white stone bench. He had not expected this, and the sight of her disarmed him. He wanted to smile but in the next moment the pain returned. He turned away from her, trying in vain to gaze up at the stars. His head was filled with a hundred things to say, and nothing at all. She walked around the bench and stood beside him. For a moment, she looked up at the sky with him.

"You have changed a great deal," she said.

"I did not think you would be here, or I would not have come."

She put a hand to his shoulder to make him face her.

"Dear Henri . . . are you so angry with me still, that you cannot bear the sight of me?"

"You know that is impossible," he said, finally shifting his eyes to her.

His voice had deepened, and his face had matured. There were more angles; more definition to the chin and jaw. There was the hint of a beard that had been shaved away. Any remnants of a child's softer features were gone. For a moment they stood breathless at the sight of one another.

"How are you?" she finally asked through a tentative smile.

"As well as I am supposed to be after what was taken from me; and what was forced in its place."

"And your wife, is she well?" she asked, ignoring the sting of his remark.

"I would not know. I have only seen her twice since Marseilles."

Again there was silence between them. Through it, a charged energy began to grow. The turbulence inside her swelled. She fought it. It was a battle that would have had her saying what she longed to. After a moment, she lost.

"I have missed you, Henri, and our talks . . . and *jeu de paume,* well of course, that certainly is not the same. I have never found anyone so willing to defeat me as you were."

"And I have missed you a thousand times more than you could ever know." He turned toward her unexpectedly; the veneer of anger fallen away, and behind it, the open and sensitive youth who she knew could break her heart if she let him. He raised his hand to touch her cheek. "How I have missed you, and dreamed of you. I have longed for you, when I thought I could never long for anyone . . ."

"Henri, please," she said, turning from his touch.

"Did you really think your leaving me would change that?"

Diane sighed. She had known one day she would face this, but seeing him was far more difficult than she could have imagined. She had not been prepared. He moved behind her and spoke with the breathy intensity of a lover.

"I know you said that things would change; that I would change, but I love you still. No matter what you want for me, or whom you wish me to be with, there can be no one else but you."

"Please . . . do not do this."

Laughter from the doorway and the emerging of more guests broke the strain between them. Diane moved casually to the corner of the terrace and sat down on another of the stone benches. She was weak. Henri sat beside her. After taking a moment to collect herself she said, "You know I prayed for you. I truly expected to see you and your wife getting on much better, perhaps giving His Majesty the grandchild he desires."

"Do not mock me, Madame! You know full well that she is nothing more than a tie to Italy for the King! I did not want her then, and I do not want her now!"

Before he could say another word, his brother, François,

appeared in the doorway and came toward them. He was accompanied by three young girls, none of whom were his mistress, and all of whom clung to his sleeves, whispering to one another with drunken laughter.

"Why, Madame Diane! Welcome back!" the Dauphin said with a taunting smile and extended his hand. "And dear brother, Henri, I might have known I'd find you trailing after her the moment she returned." Diane stood and curtsied to the future King. "You have been sorely missed," he added. "How long has it been, Madame?"

"Almost two years," Henri replied for her in a sharp tone, before Diane could speak for herself.

"Well yes, so it has. I believe it would have been the occasion of Prince Henri's wedding, after which you left so abruptly. That would be, well, let me see, it is November . . . why, it would be two years last month! How strange of you to recall it so readily, brother dear."

His tone was sarcastic, his motive cruel. Henri could not imagine hating him any more than he did at that moment.

"I was called away on business," she explained.

"Indeed." The Dauphin arched an eyebrow, and looked at each of them as though they were harboring some great secret.

"Well, if you will both excuse me," Diane asked after a painfully long silence, and curtsied once again to the Dauphin.

"Madame, wait!" Henri called out, but before he could get beyond his brother, she had gone back into the crowded drawing room.

Henri stared contemptuously at his brother. "Move aside!"

"Really, Henri. Is it not time to let go of your nursemaid and find a real mistress? That is, if you do not like the wife Father bought for you."

"Move aside, I said, or I shall knock you into that garden without a second thought!"

By the time he found her, the discussion circle had ceased and the royal ensemble was playing a ceremonial Pavane in honor of the King who had changed to a new and more extravagantly jeweled costume he wished to display. He had snatched Diane as his partner the moment she had returned from the garden. The rest of the Court watched respectfully as the two danced alone in solemn procession.

Henri stood beside a huge wall tapestry. While the others marveled at the footwork of the King, Henri only watched Diane. He watched her pass through the simple steps, her brilliant blue eyes following the King's lead. The dance called for the King to walk behind his partner then lead her by the hand a few gliding steps. Next, each of them bowed to one another to the beat of the drum. After the dance was complete, other couples began to make their way onto the small dance area. At the same moment, Henri rushed up beside her.

"Please do not deny me. We must talk. I leave the day after to-morrow once again for the camps!"

The next dance began. As custom dictated, the formal Pavane was followed by the much lighter Tourdion. The others began to line up around them. Henri and Diane had no choice but to begin dancing with them. Most of the courtiers were drunk and were staggering and laughing as they whirled past one another. No one noticed or cared about the intensity between the young prince and the older Madame de Poitiers. First the ladies danced facing the gentlemen. Then the ladies paused while the men danced. Diane reluctantly took Henri's hand and, as the dance warranted, let him draw her near.

"I know that you care for me, I can see it in your eyes, even if you will not tell me," he implored beneath his breath.

Across the room, Anne d'Heilly had come up beside the Dauphin and the three girls. "Well, well, well. Will you look at that," she whispered. "Little Prince Henri is dancing, and rather well. I wonder where he finally learned."

"Why, of that too I am certain. He learned in Cauterets," François glibly replied.

HENRI TRIED TO keep time to the music as the dance drew near its conclusion. "You are everything to me. Why can you not see that?"

"Henri, please, you must stop this! What happened is in the past. Now we must let go of it," she implored while rendering a smile for the King, who stood on the sidelines.

"I have waited two years for this moment and after tomorrow I will be gone again . . . I cannot leave things like this!"

The music ended. The gentlemen bowed to the ladies. Henri bowed to Diane. As a crowd of guests surrounded her, she made her way quickly from the floor before the music began again. Henri followed. She was quicker. She stole past the crowds and past the posted guards. She ran down the small private flight of stairs away from the chamber. She ran down a long hallway, dimly lit by the golden glow of sputtering candles. Henri caught her just below the sweeping stone staircase. The charged emotion rendered him oblivious to the others who walked past them chatting and saying good night. He grabbed her arm and twisted it so that she would face him. He could hear the delicate seam on her silk sleeve tear beneath his force. Their eyes met. Both of their chests were heaving from the run. Diane's face was flushed.

"You may be able to run away from me, Madame, but you cannot keep yourself from the truth!"

"What truth? There is no truth!"

"But there is . . . and in your heart you know it! Despite our ages, despite everyone and everything that is against us, I loved you the first moment I saw you!" he seethed, in a low tone, just beneath his breath. "I love you still! No matter what you try to make me believe, that will not change. If you remember nothing else, remember what I told you two years ago. I have in this life only one heart to give, Madame, and long ago it was given to you!"

DIANE CLOSED THE DOOR and leaned against it. She was glad that he was going. Glad that the temptation would be gone. Her knees were weak. She tried to breathe more deeply but it did not help her heart's pounding. The control she had felt when she returned to Court had now completely abandoned her.

"Madame, are you all right?" Hélène asked as she shuffled half asleep toward Diane. "You look flushed. You are not ill, are you?"

She put a comforting arm around Diane and led her away from the still-open door toward her bedchamber. The coverlet was turned back and the pillows had been freshly plumped. Her copy of *Le Roman de la rose* was on the night table.

"There now, let me help you out of those things. Oh, you really do look as if you are ill. What on earth has happened?"

"I am fine. It has just been a long night. I need to sleep."

Diane stood bracing herself against the bedpost as Hélène unfastened the small pearl buttons which girdled her into her satin-edged ball gown. Her mind wandered as her eyelids grew heavy and began to close. She was tired. So tired. But tomorrow was Christmas. It would be better tomorrow. She sat on the edge of the bed and watched passively as Hélène pulled off her shoes and her white stockings.

"Thank you," she said after a moment. "I can manage the rest."

"Madame, perhaps it is not my place. Charlotte would have scolded me for even asking, but you have seen him, haven't you?"

Diane peered up at her through the thin haze of her own confusion. She did not need to reply.

"If you would like to talk—"

"No . . . no thank you, Hélène. I really can manage it."

"Well, if you are certain there is nothing further I can do for you, then I shall bid you good night."

But Diane could not sleep. Rest was beyond her. As she lay beneath her covers, her heart pounded until she thought it might burst through her chest. She was still in the Dauphin's apartments, Henri before her. She could see him; feel the intensity between them. His hand on hers as they danced had been like a powerful narcotic; numbing her; ruling her. Beneath his grasp she became totally helpless. The power in that touch even now beckoned her back to something so forbidden that if she allowed it, she knew that Henri, and his dreams, could quite easily destroy her.

THE KING HAD MOVED his Court again after the Christmas holidays. On the first of February they had come to Blois to celebrate Candlemas. There his Majesty acknowledged the inevitability of war. The Duke of Milan had died unexpectedly, leaving the sought-after city without an heir. It was providence, his aides convinced him. The good Lord meant for him to have it back after all. The Emperor, however, would not give it up without a fight.

François' two eldest sons had returned to the troops long before the ringing in of the New Year, and the King was left at Court to be swallowed up by obligations, and to sulk about the dwindling state of his alliances. He now entertained only the slightest hope of a Franco-English accord with Henry VIII that would have solidified his position against the Emperor. He sighed out loud when he thought of it. It had been many years since he had known such complete frustration.

A reply to the marriage he had proposed between his third son, Charles, and Henry VIII's infant daughter, Elizabeth, had been postponed indefinitely by the English Monarch. François' ambassadors had returned from England with rumors that the child's mother, Anne Boleyn, had lost the affections of the King. Boleyn, it was said, had promised the King a male heir as the impetus for him to divorce his first wife. Her inability to produce what she had assured, along with her demanding and impossible temperament, had now sent His Majesty into the arms of yet another woman. This one apparently was one of the Queen's own ladies-in-waiting, a young girl named Jane Seymour.

It was further rumored that King Henry was once again seeking counsel for a second divorce. If that should occur, as it had with the previous Queen, their daughter, like the Princess Mary before her, would also be declared a bastard. If Elizabeth's legitimacy were called into question, a marriage between her and Charles would be pointless. The only hope in this dwindling race for allies was King James of Scotland. Though a lesser power than Henry VIII, he had become an ally worth cultivating when so few were to be had. Now widowed, the Scottish Monarch was said to be searching for a wife. The King of France had seized the opportunity by offering him a French bride. While he waited for a reply, he decided to go to Chenonceaux.

BY THE TIME they had made their way north through the Loire Valley and the forest of Amboise, the harshness of winter had faded. In its place was the fragile beauty of spring. Everything was fresh. There were a dozen different shades of green; vibrant red, yellow, and violet. François had wanted to escape. He had begun to feel as if life, his life, had been personified and, as a great foe, was now seizing on his weakness and finally catching up with him. His health too had been failing, and his only thought was of escape. He chose as his sanctuary a new royal acquisition, a small chateau along the edge of the river Cher, called Chenonceaux.

His military concerns entrusted now to Admiral Chabot, as each mile passed, François felt the enemy inside himself begin to fade. On the road once again, he began to laugh. Anne d'Heilly held the King's hand as their horses slowly ambled along the banks of the river, and she watched as the grave expression that he had so often donned of late, slowly faded away.

When the King took the lute from his jester, the rest of the band sang the words to *La Guerre,* a song composed for him by Jannequin to mark his victory over the Emperor Charles in 1515. It was the kind of song he needed to sing just now, and no one could begrudge him that.

The first view of the castle was a magnificent one. The gravel path that led from the main road to the chateau was guarded by two stone lions at the end of a long, arched column of plane trees. The riders paused, taking in the vista that burst forth majestically before them. The small chateau was made of stone, painted a pale yellow, with pointed and gabled roofs and lovely, large stained-glass windows. It stood directly out on the water and was accessed by a drawbridge. To the right, separate from the chateau, was a small turret, a guard house. After the overwhelming elegance of Fontainebleau and the massive opulence of Chambord, this little manor was charming and unique, even at a distance.

"My, how beautiful," uttered Catherine in her broken French. Diane smiled and took in a deep breath. The others led their horses toward the stables, where several young grooms stood waiting to help the King's party from their mounts.

"There is quite a history here," boasted the King with an arm extended. "On this very site was once a Roman villa. That building over there," he said, pointing to the isolated turret, "was part of it."

"Imagine it," said Catherine, like a wide-eyed child whom everyone hears and yet to whom no one really listens.

The central vestibule was low and intimate with a vaulted ceiling. An innovative triangulated and ribbed design, it was a work of art in itself. There was a long table filled with freshly cut spring flowers along one wall, placed there in anticipation of His Majesty's arrival. A large painting of the *Three Graces* occupied the other. When everyone gathered inside the doors, the King began to inspect his recent acquisition. The rest of the group followed, whispering among themselves. The first room to the left was the guard room, decorated and warmed with huge tapestries. The King and his entourage then passed through the Gothic chapel that hung out over the river. The gallery, the main drawing room with its magnificent ceiling and the entire chateau seemed to shimmer as the light from the water played into the colorful windows of stained glass. The King's smile broadened as his tour of the lower level was complete.

"Well. What do you think of my home?"

"It is magnificent, Your Majesty," said Christian de Nançay.

"Splendid, Father," said Princess Madeleine.

"Truly lovely, Your Majesty," echoed Jacques de Montgommery.

"It is terribly small," observed Anne d'Heilly with a scowl, a look that crinkled her nose and wrinkled her forehead.

"Yes, of course. That is the charm of it," replied the King, as he winked at Diane, who tried to stand inconspicuously behind the King's *favourite*.

ANNE D'HEILLY SAT BEFORE her mirror contemplating the prospect of another evening; another dinner with the King's insufferable little band. More decadence. More indulgence. It had all been orchestrated long ago. There were no surprises. And she was tired. She would have given it all up just to be loved. That thought surprised her. François loved her in his own way, but it was not the real love she needed more strongly each day. She had always been a showpiece for him; the grand prize of his manhood. He had certainly been her prize. She had played the game and won the King of France. But she was not without her own faults in this game of indulgence. She had enough infidelities herself to force her to silence. It had all become so predictable. The coming together. The seduction. The gifts. The apologies. The betrayal. The hurt. Other mistresses. Other lovers. The breaking apart. Only to come back together again. And so it had gone. On and on. And on.

"I must act now. There will be no better time to pave the way for my revenge," she muttered venomously to herself, hardened by the thought of her own bleak existence.

She had taken the first step in her final revenge against Diane de Poitiers by asking that Montgommery be brought to her. Her heart, thought Anne. Therein lies the key.

Now, she sat at her toilette table letting her sister, Louise, remove her headdress. She gazed at her reflection in the mirror as the mass of chestnut locks tumbled onto the shoulders of her white silk dressing gown. She touched a soft strand near her face and smiled. Revenge was sweet. She could tolerate the mindless chambermaids with whom he dallied but it was Diane de Poitiers who continued to be the real threat. She was the only one with enough power and style to unseat her any time she chose. And after all, why had she returned to Court yet again if she did not mean once again to attempt to steal the King?

If she would ever lose her royal lover to another, it would be to a woman like that. She felt able to compete with the Sénéchale's beauty; even her intelligence, now that she was Duchesse d'Etampes. But Diane had one advantage no gift from the King could ever match. The blood coursing through her veins was not noble. Her heritage had not been bought. She had chosen not to heed Anne d'Heilly's earlier warning to leave the French Court. For that sin above all others, noble blood or not, Diane de Poitiers was now about to pay, and dearly.

"Answer the door," she commanded her maid when she finally heard the knock.

Jacques de Montgommery entered the chamber and stopped only a few feet from the door. He was dressed in a brown doublet edged in gold. His cape, trimmed in ermine, was clasped near his throat with a gold buckle. His stockings were the color of honey; the color of his hair.

"Why, Captain, you must forgive me. I had completely forgotten I had called for you," she said with a feigned note of sincerity. After no more than a moment standing at her toilette table, her eyes fixed on him, she turned and walked toward the large, heavily draped bed in the other corner of the room near the fire. The silk dressing gown fluttered around her ankles as she moved.

"I was just about to settle in for a rest," she said, excusing her revealing attire. "But, do come in now that you are here. I will send for some nice mint tea."

Montgommery stepped cautiously into the heavily scented chamber. He had been summoned to her apartments before but always when the King was present; and always when she was fully clothed.

"That will be all, Mademoiselle de Colliers," she said. The servant bowed her head and left the room. Now they were alone.

"You need not bother about the tea on my account," he said, removing his tilted toque and awkwardly clutching it at his waist.

Anne smiled at him, showing her perfectly straight white teeth. He was attractive in his own way, she thought. Yet she was at a loss to define how he had his choice of the ladies at Court, as Philippe Chabot had said. He was tall and thin with thick blond hair. His delicate features were covered by only a wisp of a beard and neatly trimmed mustache. She found his genteel mannerisms not at all to her liking. But that was not the point of it.

"Ah, well then, we will dispense with the tea. Perhaps you would prefer something stronger?"

Without waiting for a reply, she advanced to a small table in the center of the room. It was oval shaped and ornately carved, covered with a rectangular piece of tapestry that touched the tiled floor at each end. On top were several glass decanters on a silver tray. "I have claret, of course, but the anise wine is far stronger."

She took a goblet in her hand and looked at him. Montgommery shuffled a few tentative steps closer to her, his toque still clutched in both hands. He did not like being alone in the *favourite*'s apartments. If the King were to see him there, and she in her underclothes, his future would be ruined.

"Please sit down."

Anne motioned him toward a velvet-cushioned armchair near the fire, then she sat beside him in a matching chair. They sipped their wine but did not speak. She made no move to begin a conversation nor to explain why she had summoned him. As the moments passed and he sipped the strong anise wine, he began to forget about the King, and about Diane. He had never been this close to Anne. She was splendid. Such delicate small bones; such fine small features. His eyes drifted down to her rosebud mouth. As she lowered the small crystal goblet, a drop of the amber-colored liquid glittered there. Half dazed, he looked away. Behind her was the open bed; the bedcurtains half drawn, the pillows and counterpane already rumpled.

"It is a lovely chateau . . . do you not think?" he said at last, and swallowed hard.

"No, I do not think so at all. I think that it is hideously small and I am frightfully bored."

Her lower lip turned down into a pout and Jacques was mesmerized by the sensuality of her face. He could not tear his eyes from her lips; so wet and full. So forbidden. Anne watched his eyes grow hungry as she licked each lip; first the top, then the bottom . . . slowly, seductively. She leaned forward, pushing her full breasts through the lace edge of the dressing gown. He let his eyes stray from her mouth, down over her figure. She could see the hunger in him. Ah, yes, this revenge would be sweet. So sweet. Just as she moved to stand, the door to her chamber flew open and the King's guard, Christian de Nançay, strutted in.

"Well, there you are! I have been looking everywhere for you, man!" he said, advancing toward his fellow guard, Montgommery, who, thinking it was the King, had sprung to his feet the moment the door had opened. Anne stood beside him only partially dressed. Nançay glared at Montgommery. At Anne. Then at the tossed bedcovers behind them. He saw the half hidden flush of desire on both their faces.

"The King has returned and I am certain, Captain, that he shall have need of you as I am just off of my duty. After all, that is why you've come along to Chenonceaux, is it not, to attend His Majesty?"

"You had better leave. But I have enjoyed this time with you immensely," Anne said in the same bewitching tone with which she had begun to seduce him. "And later, if you would like, we can continue . . . where we left off."

Nançay lunged at her when Montgommery had gone.

"So, did you bed him?"

"When will you learn that what I do does not concern you?"

"Does not concern me? How can you say such a thing when you know I am mad about you?"

"Oh, how you disgust me when you snivel, Christian," she said in a throaty growl, then sat down on her bed. "I take whom I want, when I want, and that pleading of yours does nothing to endear yourself to me."

"Then you were with him! Oh, *Jésu*! will it never cease? First you test me with the Admiral and now with my fellow guard! Why, in the name of God, when I adore you and you can have me?"

"I can also have the King of France and that has not stopped me! As for you, His Majesty was not in need of another guard here at all, was he? You made that up so that you could come bounding in here to spy on me!"

She slid beneath the bedcovers and lay back on the pillows. After a moment, she looked up. There was utter distraction in Christian de Nançay's handsome young face.

"If it helps, *mon cher,* I will tell you that I did not bed with him. *Yet.* All that we had shared before you charged in here was some anise wine."

The Captain knelt beside her bed. He tried to take her hand but she refused to give it. "Everyone knows that you despise her, but must you do this? Must you really go through with something so drastic just to spite Madame Diane?"

"It is the only way I can truly have my revenge on her and it is an opportunity I shall not miss! Besides," she said, beginning to smile, "I had never noticed what a truly attractive man Montgommery is. Now, do be a dear and let me get some rest. I shall not want to miss a moment of this evening after all."

COMPARED WITH THE splendor exhibited at the more magnificent chateaux, supper at Chenonceaux each evening was a simple affair. There were no elaborate plays or costumed servers; no masked dances or ceremonial Pavane entrances. There were only sounds of the lute and harp played together by a boy and girl from the village.

To entertain the guests, the melodious strains of their instruments mingled with the throaty call of the frogs up from the river. The sounds and the simplicity made Diane think of Cauterets. The open windows and the fresh breeze reminded her of the inn. They reminded her of Henri. But that was another world. Another time. She closed her mind to it and looked around the table at the King's other guests.

Across the table, between Anne and François de Guise, sat a strikingly attractive boy with blond curled hair who, despite his youth, wore the cassock of an archbishop. He had the same long nose as Guise and the same lanky build, but his eyes were less brooding and his features were less pronounced. There was no mistaking the fact that they were brothers. He laughed easily at something Anne said, then leaned back in his chair, fingering his chin, too adolescent to be bearded.

"That is Charles de Guise. He is Archbishop de Rheims," whispered the Princess Madeleine, with an awkward half smile when she noticed Diane looking at him. "It is one of the most important Church offices in France."

"He is terribly young to be an archbishop."

"His uncle is the Cardinal de Lorraine," she replied, as though no further explanation would be required.

Diane nodded toward the Princess but said nothing further. Instead, she sipped from a globlet of red wine and watched as the *petite bande* hung on his every word and laughed a little too boldly at his humor. She watched Anne d'Heilly lower her chin and flutter her eyes as he spoke. She watched Catherine de Medici, in her satin puffs and velvet ruffles, lean awkwardly toward him, not knowing quite how to flirt.

As the evening progressed, she listened to him speak of literature, architecture and of philosophy with the confidence and ease of a much older man. Princess Marguerite, beside her, compared him in giddy whispers to Mercury, the god of eloquence. *He has managed to charm everyone here,* she thought. *He shall go as far as he chooses at the Court of France.* It would be many years and a great deal of maneuvering between them before Diane would realize just how right her instinct had been.

AFTER THE MEAL HAD been cleared, the King rose to leave, but bid his guests to stay and enjoy themselves. He announced as his excuse for retiring, to a new and waiting chambermaid, that the hunt the next day would commence at an early hour. Once the King had gone, the rest of the guests returned their attention to the table, contentedly sipping their brandy and listening to the young Charles de Guise's discourse on the writings of Plato.

As the night progressed, the candles flickered in their pools of melted wax, and the embers of the fire glowed a pale orange. Each hour's passing saw another guest retire. As the sun began its pale pink ascent, Diane found herself alone at the dining table with the Archbishop. She sat fingering an empty goblet and listening with singular fascination as he spoke about his favorite subject, the wisdom and elegance of the early Greeks. His large brown eyes lit up and the thoughts flowed from his tongue with the perception and verve of a master. Finally, neither of them could ignore the rising sun through the same open window from which they had seen the stars. As the early morning mist turned slowly to a gentle spring rain, she finally felt tired.

"I have so enjoyed this," said Diane after a yawn. "But I must have a few hours sleep so that I shall be fresh today for the King's hunt."

Charles de Guise smiled. He looked as fresh and rested as if he had just risen from a nap.

"I do thank you for indulging me for as long as you have. It is a rare thing to find a woman who will truly listen to talk of the great masters."

"Well then, I shall say good night," she said as she stood.

He stood beside her. "I shall be honored to escort you to your room, if, of course, you shall permit me."

As they climbed the dimly lit staircase, a steward went behind them, snuffing out the remaining candles with a long, silver wand. The smell of burning wax trailed them and mingled with the crisp scent of early morning rain. The sound of voices and laughter came from the room next to hers. She was tired. For a moment she thought it sounded like the King. Then she remembered. Jacques had been given the room next to hers. She stopped in front of the long, closed wooden door. Charles de Guise stood beside her. Again there was laughter. Then the voice of a woman.

"Madame, it really is not proper," he whispered with a curious smile as she pressed her ear to the door.

The laughter inside was followed by soft little noises. Sexual noises. Again the man's voice. Diane put her hand to the round iron handle.

"I really must object if you mean to open it," he said.

Diane turned to him, her face pale and her lips parted.

"It is my fiancé's chamber, Your Excellency."

"All the more reason, Madame, not to look."

Diane turned back toward the door, ignoring the remonstrations, and slowly turned the handle. She pushed open one side of the heavy double doors as Charles de Guise made the sign of the cross.

"God help us," he murmured as he peered in behind her.

They were stopped by the sight of two naked bodies pressed together on top of the bed, each writhing with the rhythm of the other. Diane stood motionless. The man was Jacques. She stood unable to tear her eyes away as he worked himself furiously on top of the woman. Her legs were wrapped tightly around his buttocks as it rose and fell. After a moment, the woman turned her head toward the door. Diane let out a small, impotent cry when she saw that it was Anne d'Heilly.

Not her. Not Anne! Her knees began to give way beneath her. She thought she would faint. Charles de Guise clutched Diane at the shoulders just as Jacques looked up.

"Diane! Oh, dear Lord, no!"

He shouted her name and tore himself from Anne's body. He stumbled onto his knees and then bolted naked from the bed, continuing to cry out her name in long, pleading breaths. He ran through the door after her, trailing the rumpled bedcover behind him and trying to cover himself with it as he ran. Anne simply laid there shamelessly, on the stark linen sheet of Montgommery's bed, smiling her cat smile. Slowly she ran her fingers down the glistening milky white flesh of her breasts and then turned toward the door, where Charles de Guise still stood, looking at her.

IT HAD RAINED while she slept. Soft rain; gentle rain; cleansing the air of the foul rancor of deceit. Diane lifted a hand to her eyes and brushed the back of her knuckles into them to wipe away the little crusts of sleep. She sat up. The rain had stopped. The air was crisp. A faint gold ray of sun came through her window. It had been the sun across her cheek that had roused her. Drops that had landed on the roof now fell onto the casing around her window and then down past the glass. Drip. Drip. It was quiet except for that sound. Finally quiet.

She had not admitted Jacques to her room to explain himself this time, though he had pounded relentlessly on her door throughout the early hours of morning. She had finally fallen asleep with a velvet bed pillow wrapped around her ears to drown the sound of his pleading. Always his pleading. She hated that. Not long after it had begun, Hélène had urged him from the other side of the door to retire, trying to warn him that he risked waking the King, but he would hear none of it. He was moaning like some half-crazed animal, sometimes yelling, and then in turn there was that awful pleading to be heard echoing down the dark corridor.

All Diane wanted now was to blot out the world and its cruelty. Just when she thought that perhaps she had begun to rise above the deceit and the ugliness, once again she found herself drawn down into the dark and seamy mire. She had not changed. Nothing had changed. It was still the same scandalous Court and she was still the same vulnerable woman.

THE KING LED HIS CORTEGE of ladies, courtiers and groomsmen through the deep forest away from the chateau. Jacques de Montgommery was noticeably absent from them, but no one inquired of Diane as to where he might be. Chenonceaux was a small chateau. His pleading strains outside her door had been missed, it seemed, by only His Majesty and the chambermaid with whom he had spent the night in the servants' quarters, in the attic.

The King's sorrel-colored stallion was draped with a jeweled blanket of red and gold and was weighted down by jewels around the trim and along the bridle. His doublet of gold silk matched the blanket on which he rode. He was content. He had a beautiful mistress, a pious Queen, and a string of lusty young girls to content him. As he tore through the forest, trailed by the thundering hooves of the other mounted horses, he laughed and tossed back a joke to his groomsmen. The country air put him at peace. He was miles from the war, the Reformation and the problems that plagued his realm.

After a stag had been scouted, the King was called to approve it by the size of the prints left behind in the meadow grass. He then ordered the groomsmen to go ahead and corner the animal, and ordered that the dinner tent be pitched in an open meadow. It was a giant tent, round in shape and of fabric striped in light blue and gold and peaked at the center. One by one, the priceless Turkish carpets were lain to cover the damp ground and the paintings were hung by cords from the frame of the tent. The china and silver was then brought from large wicker baskets and set out on the carved-oak dining table.

Diane was among the last riders to arrive at the camp. As she neared the area where the other horses were tied to a moss-covered tree she felt another hand on her bridle. There was no one around but Anne d'Heilly.

"Madame de Poitiers, have you not neglected to pay your respects to me this morning? You know that as Duchesse d'Etampes, I am now your superior."

"I have no respect to pay you . . . Madame," she said and turned away from Anne's icy emerald glare. "Now, kindly let go of my horse."

"How does it feel, Madame?" Anne badgered, refusing to surrender the bridle.

"I have no idea what you are referring to."

"How does it feel to have the man you love stolen away from you?"

"So that is why you did it? Because you thought I wanted the King?"

"Why else?" she asked, the cold fierceness of a deliberate act defining her face.

Diane was about to say, in a reflexive response, that she did not want the King and that she never had. She was about to tell her she could have Jacques de Montgommery too, for all that he had meant to her. The first words had even formed on her lips. Then she thought better of it. Anne had humiliated her. She had tried to wound her much more deeply than that, but it had failed.

Now, sitting before her, each of them still on their horses, she looked at that smug little face, the little rosebud lips and the arched brows; she could not bring herself to put her rival's unfounded fears to rest. At least not yet. There had really been no indication that it would make a difference if she did. Anne d'Heilly believed so strongly in some vague competition between them that it had required an act this drastic. It was not likely that any reassurances she could give now would change a thing. Diane looked at her again.

"Madame de Brosse," she began in a low controlled tone, calling her by the name of the man she had married, in an attempt to deliver her own direct slight. "You have the world at your feet, and if your disdain of me was the only reason for surrendering your body to a servant of the King, who himself has no more morals than one of the hunting hounds, then I pity you. I truly pity you!"

The two women glared at one another; the fire between them was at a flash point. Neither would give way to the other.

"I want you away from Court," Anne seethed.

"I am an invited guest of the King."

"But you are not welcomed by his *favourite*."

"And, if I choose to stay?"

"If you do not retire to your estate of your own accord, then your existence among us shall take a decided turn for the worse. That, I do promise you!"

In that strange, singular moment between Anne's reply and her own, Diane thought of Henri. She suddenly wished that he would come out from behind one of the large evergreen trees around them and put this viper appropriately in her place, as he had done for her so many times. He was the only one who could do it. But Henri was not here, and there was no one but herself to fight the battles that had come so routinely to plague her.

"I could go to the King," Diane ventured.

"He loves me. He will never take your word over mine."

Anne's stare was fierce and contemptuous. Diane, who had begun to learn something from this competition between them, met it completely. Therefore she could not see the wild wolf, whose hungry, yellow eyes peered out from the wild brush behind her. Though she did not see it, her horse smelled the danger. Suddenly, he bolted. In a powerful leap, he reared up onto his hind legs, braying his own fear with a highly pitched whinny. Diane tightly gripped the reins, unaware of the danger behind her, but she could not steady him. In that same moment, Anne looked behind Diane and saw the ragged gray wolf coiled to attack.

"Wolf! Dear God, it is a wolf! Run! Run!"

Anne's terror-stricken screams warned the others. She turned the bridle of her own horse away from Diane and the imminent attack, and galloped for shelter behind a thick cluster of trees. Catherine and Marie de Guise, the Cardinal's niece, scattered behind bushes as the wolf sprung from his place and leaped at Diane's chestnut-colored mare. In his frenzy, his sharp molars pierced her calf. One deep, growling bite. She recoiled at the searing pain.

The Princess Madeleine began to cry as she watched the scene in horror. Diane continued to wrestle with the fearful horse who was now being attacked by the savage animal. Madeleine's sister, Marguerite, grabbed her arm and dragged her into the shelter of the woods behind the others. Diane was left alone.

Again the horse reared and then whinnied in pain as the savage wolf gouged with his teeth, again and again into the animal's hind leg. As he reared up again, this time erect, the force was too great, and Diane was thrown to the ground, hitting her head on a large boulder. She groped in the dirt, trying to inch herself away from the attack site, but she could not move.

The King and two of his guards, who had heard the screams, dashed back toward the clearing just as Diane had fallen to the ground. When he saw the wolf, His Majesty motioned to his men and then circled around behind the seething animal with a poised crossbow. The others watched from the safety of the trees and bushes. The guards distracted the animal so that François de Guise and his brother could go to Diane, who now lay unconscious in the wild grass. Just as the wolf prepared to leap onto Diane's limp body, the King shot a single golden-tipped arrow. The savage animal faltered, then swayed, and finally collapsed onto the ground with a whimper, and was dead.

*T*HE KING HAD SENT a diamond and emerald brooch. The young Archbishop de Rheims had sent her a book of architectural style, based on the work of the Roman master, Marcus Vitruvius Pollio. Her room was lined with white roses picked by François de Guise. They had saved her life. Fortune had been on her side. For her ordeal with the raging wolf she had sustained relatively few injuries. A bruised arm and a bump on the back of the head were impairments that would mend. The puncture on her leg, however, would not be so quick to leave her. The King's physician, after a thorough inspection, had insisted upon complete bed rest for the wound to properly mend. So, for the two weeks following the King's hunting party, she had limited herself to a quiet game of cards with Hélène at her bedside and supper in her room.

Now, Diane thought she would go mad. One more hand of cards or another game of chess and she was sure to lose her mind. She sat propped in the bed, draped in her nightclothes and surrounded by a sea of velvet cushions. The King's physician had forbid her even to dress until further notice. Bed rest indeed! She had not been impaired a day in her life. Even with the births of both of her daughters, she had been in bed no more than a few days. If only she could swim, the fresh water would certainly heal her wounds far better than these foul smelling plasters and potions he insisted on using. *Oh, to feel the sun and the air, the gentle breeze from the river . . .* She looked up. The windows were all neatly latched; that was also by order of the royal physician, Pierre de Bourges. There was no air and it was stifling. She looked over at the clock in the corner. It continued to tick. That same monotonous tick. Tick, tick, tick.

A knock at the door brought Hélène to her feet. She closed the book and placed it on the table beside the small carved chair. Jacques de Montgommery entered slowly, as the door was opened. His long face was drawn and the soft feminine features had become more harsh and shadowed. He was dressed austerely in a costume of plain gray wool. There were no jewels or the customary medallions draped from his doublet. Diane had not seen him since that night. She sat up in the bed to a nearly rigid posture. Jacques saw the change and stopped at the foot of the bed. He removed the gray plumed toque and held it in both hands as a symbol of humility; just as he had done when he had gone to see Anne d'Heilly that first afternoon.

"I am sorry, Madame. He would not wait to be introduced," Hélène softly said.

Diane looked at him. His face pleaded with her, though his lips did not. She was glad he did not beg this time. She knew she could not bear to hear it.

"It is all right, Hélène. You may leave us, but leave the door open and remain just outside. The Captain will not be long."

Hélène looked at her mistress and then at the estranged suitor. "As you wish," she said reluctantly, and left them alone.

The moment she was gone, tears filled his eyes and he lunged forward to the side of Diane's bed. As he dropped to his knees, he put his head in his hands and began to sob. Diane recoiled at the performance.

"Stop it! Stop it this instant, do you hear?" she whispered through clinched teeth.

After a moment, he lifted his head and wiped the back of his hand across his wet eyes.

"It is only that I love you so."

"Love? Now there is a laugh! I would be an even bigger fool than the two of you put together if I continued to believe that."

"You have every right to be angry, but you must listen—"

"There is nothing to hear, Jacques. What was between us is over."

"But, *mon amour,* you cannot mean it. You are angry with me. I understand that. But I know that with time, that shall pass."

"It is over between us, do you hear? There is nothing left!" she said, in a more determined voice. Her eyes met his, squarely. To her surprise, his own tired eyes sharpened into angry slits at the sound of her words, and he rose back to his feet. After no more than a moment, any sign of the repentant suitor who had entered her room vanished. In his place was a fierce and raging man.

"You will not humiliate me like that! You are mine; you accepted me and I will never let you go!"

"Do you dare to speak to me of humiliation, Monsieur, after what occurred in that room just next to mine?" Her eyes were filled with fire, and the rage in her heart made her quiver as she spoke. "It is over between us and if you ever, ever try to see me again, I will go straight to the King! I swear it!"

Their eyes were locked. She meant it and he knew after what he had done she would do it for less.

"The King! The King comes!"

Hélène burst back through the door just ahead of the royal guard. There was still an intensity between them but Diane fought to take her eyes from Jacques, with the nearing sound of soldiers' heavy footsteps. After the first appearance of the royal guards who flanked her door, the King swirled around the corner in a red velvet cape which was cut to his knees and lined with sable. Anne d'Heilly walked a pace behind him in her revealing emerald ball gown. Her new perfume preceded her and within moments, the closed room was filled with the overpowering aroma of Tibetan musk.

"I hope Your Majesty will forgive me for not rising," Diane said.

François advanced to her bed with a smile and took her hand. His fingers were covered with chunks of rubies, emerald and gold.

"Only if you will forgive me for not coming sooner to see you. But I trust you did receive the brooch in my stead?"

"Oh, yes indeed, and it is far too extravagant."

"I would agree with that," murmured Anne from the foot of the bed.

"Nevertheless, I shall wear it with great honor," Diane said, finishing her sentence, and then glancing at the Duchesse d'Etampes with her own newly kindled hauteur. The King ignored them both and snapped his fingers over his head.

"Nothing is too good for one of our own," he said as he beckoned François de Guise to bring the tall velvet-covered chair from beside the window.

"But, Your Majesty, it is you who risked your life to save mine. It is I who owe you a debt of gratitude."

"I would have done the same for any of my band. So tell me, how are you getting along? You have my personal physician tending to you. Is he seeing to your care?"

"Quite well, Your Majesty. You were most generous to extend his service. He feels I shall make a full recovery."

The King shifted in the chair. "Yes, well . . . to the matter at hand, Madame. The royal physician has informed me that you will require several additional days in which to convalesce. Regrettably, however, I find that I am required back at Fontainebleau for strategic talks with my commanders."

Diane looked past the drawn bedcurtains at Anne's triumphant smile. "France's victory is of the utmost importance. Your Majesty must return at once."

François shifted again and scratched his beard. "Indeed it seems I must. But I insist that you take all the time you need. It is lovely here," he said, looking around the room, "and a perfect place for you to recover. We shall leave the royal physician at your disposal, and your girl there as well," he said, glancing with disinterest at Hélène, who stood near the door.

"That is most gracious of you, Sire."

The King looked up at Jacques, who still stood at the head of Diane's bed. "And since I desire for you to be well protected while you are away from Court, I certainly can spare Montgommery here and a few of his men for the few additional days," he said with a charitable smile.

Diane did not move her head but shifted her eyes toward Anne as the King spoke. She would have given anything, God help her, at that moment to tell the King about the entire vile affair. But even with Anne's unrelenting cruelty, Diane still could not manage to entertain the notion of revenge.

"I thank Your Majesty for your concern, but I think it would be best if the Captain returned with the rest of you. I am certain to be fine here in this lovely place. Besides, he will be of far better service to his country if he attends his King right now, and not me."

François looked at the Scots Captain and then back at Diane with animated surprise, but his look was ineffective. Neither betrayed the other. "Well then, as you wish," he replied with a flick of his jeweled wrist as he stood up beside her bed. "Then, when you are well, we shall look forward to your speedy return to us. Will we not, *mon amour*?"

"Oh yes indeed," said Anne. "We shall count the days."

THE NEXT MORNING Diane watched from her window as the King and his cortege mounted their brightly draped horses and set out for Fontainebleau. As they rode down the long tree-lined causeway which led into the forest, Chenonceaux was transformed, once again, into the quiet chateau that it must have been before the King and his friends had descended upon it. At least now she was alone with her thoughts. Since the incident with Montgommery, Diane had craved the peace of solitude to mend her wounded pride. At last she had found it.

After another week, she began with short walks around the chateau, and by the month's end, with permission of the royal physician, she was taking strolls with Hélène in the garden. After much disapproval, Bourges reluctantly agreed to let her swim once again in the river.

"I have been in that room of mine for so long I had forgotten how beautiful the sunlight could be," she exclaimed with a smile, a walking stick in one hand and her other arm wrapped in Hélène's. They strolled slowly out past the formal parterre to the point of the forest. A crisp breeze blew from the river and a collection of leaves whirled past them.

"These days have not been easy for you, Madame," Hélène said cautiously.

"God tests us in curious ways."

"Those among us whom he tests the most are often the strongest."

Diane squeezed her maid's hand. "What a friend you are to me, Hélène. You cannot imagine how much it has meant."

"You are very kind, Madame, but such feelings take little effort for you. I am always, before all other things, at your service."

As they strolled past the aviary, back through the ornamental boxed hedges which overlooked the river, Diane noticed the figure of a man coming toward them from the chateau. With the sun in her eyes, however, she could not make out his identity. As he neared, she could see that it was the King's physician. Just beyond him in the gravel-covered courtyard, a royal guard stood at attention beside his horse. Bourges was waving a letter. By the time he reached them, he was so winded that he simply thrust the document at her without speaking. Hélène looked at her mistress as she cracked the red wax seal. They both knew at once who it was from. Diane read the words slowly and deliberately:

My dear Madame,

I beg you to send me news of your health so that I may act accordingly. For if you continue to be ill, I should not wish to fail to come to see you and be of what service I may. The truth is that I cannot live long without seeing you. I am not afraid to risk the loss of my father's favor in order to be with you. Honor me, I pray you, by granting my deep desire to serve you. I assure you I shall know little peace of mind until my courier returns, bringing news of your health. I beg you therefore, to send me a true word.

Your most humble servant,
Henri

"Madame?"

Diane folded the letter and looked up at Hélène, her face expressionless and white as chalk. She could not reply. Her mind was racing too fast to speak.

Bourges stood with his hands behind his long cape. "The royal messenger waits for a reply, Madame," he said impatiently.

She turned her back to them both and walked a few steps. She gazed out at the swiftly flowing river beyond the chateau and tried to steady herself. *Dear God, can it be that he still loves me? After everything; the harsh words, my denial, and all of the insurmountable odds, he can still find it in his heart to care for me?* Diane felt that she had never in her life experienced the pure love of the kind Henri was offering. So many people had promised so much, and they had all betrayed her. Louis had not loved her. He had married her because her status was beneficial to him. Then there was Jacques. Her dreams of an honorable gentleman, as in *Le Roman de la rose,* had been dashed long ago by the reality of her ordered life. She was becoming cold. Hardened. She was a realist. For two years she had turned her back on the first person who had truly made her happy, in the name of that reality. What would become of her, she wondered, if she were to go on this way?

"Madame, the royal guard . . ." Pierre de Bourges began again.

Diane turned on her heels and put her hands to the sides of her black velvet headdress. "Please! I cannot think! I need time to think!"

Hélène intervened with the physician. "Perhaps it would be best if the guard were taken to the kitchens for a meal and some wine. I shall come when Madame has a reply to give you."

Diane turned around only after she could hear Bourges's heavy feet as he stomped through the garden back toward the chateau. She had heard Hélène, but it was as though she had listened to her from a distance. All of her thoughts were of Henri. The intensity of his brooding eyes; his dark waves of hair . . . the kindness of his soul. Oh yes, God save her, she wanted him as much as he wanted her. She had, from nearly that first moment almost two years ago when he had stepped out of the darkness at Fontainebleau. She had never admitted it to a single human being—not even to herself; until now.

Hélène stood beside her. Dutifully. Silently. She watched her mistress's pinched face slowly soften. She watched a faint smile pass over the slim lips and then fade away before she turned away.

"God help me, I have tried to forget him," she whispered.

Hélène advanced and put her hand on Diane's shoulder, just barely touching it.

"Oh, Hélène, I am so wretched . . ."

"No, Madame, you mustn't say such a thing! You are kind and generous. It is easy to see why he loves you. It is no more difficult to see why you love him."

"But he is married!"

"You loved one another long before that."

"Then you do not think me awful? Oh, he is so young. He has a wife. Such a thing would be a sin!"

Diane turned to Hélène with pleading blue eyes. Her gold hair shimmered in the light from the sun. Hélène took in a breath to give her strength.

"Once, a long time ago . . . I loved someone." There was a pause; a painful break in her voice. "But I cast it away, choosing to listen to others instead of to the words of my own heart . . . Madame, that has been, and will remain, the most profound regret of my life."

The two women looked at one another. It was the first time either had shared their greatest secrets. Now between them, there was no class; no distinction by which they were divided. They were just women with love and pain and loss. Diane took in a breath, one that almost made her heart stop. Then she uttered the words which would soon come to change not only her life, but the entire history of France.

"Very well, then. You may go and tell the messenger that I have a reply. He is to tell His Highness that I have recovered from my wounds . . ." Again a breath. ". . . and that if it is still his desire, I gladly await his arrival."

ENRI'S ELEGANT WHITE MARE cantered ahead of six guardsmen. He rode down the causeway, shaded by the arch of plane trees, to where the two stone lions loomed at the entrance to Chenonceaux. As he neared them, he stopped. Henri leaned on the pommel of his saddle and gazed out at the chateau before him. She was there, just ahead of him, and she had asked him to come. Finally, she wanted him. Yes, finally.

He was disheveled and fatigued from the two-day ride, but he did not care. He had stopped only long enough to eat and to take a few hours rest. He had left camp the moment her message had arrived.

When the royal guards came up beside him, Henri nudged his horse onward into a gallop and headed toward the large stables beside the chateau. As he stepped from his mare, he clutched Diane's note in his leather-gloved hand to give him courage, and walked on toward the two carved entrance doors. The King's physician came out and headed toward him.

"Your Highness," he said with a short polite bow.

"How is she? Is she all right?"

Bourges, a sour-looking man with an even more ill-tempered disposition when it did not suit him, studied the young Prince with one eyebrow raised. He was lovesick. That was obvious. He cursed the thought of so sinful a union, but replied.

"Her wounds are healing properly, Your Highness. If she continues to use the dressing I prescribe, there will be only a slight scar."

One of Henri's guardsmen took his horse as they walked on toward the open door to the chateau.

"Please show me to her chamber."

The doctor stiffened. His two bushy black brows arched in a marked look of contempt. *Imagine it,* he thought. *That woman and the King's son. He is but a boy! She no doubt wants only one thing from the likes of him.* But he managed to keep his sentiments to himself. Bourges walked on silently beside the Prince. Three of the guards who had ridden with Henri followed the two men into the house. When they all came to the top of the stairs, the doctor pointed toward the closed chamber door directly before them. Two of the guards scanned the halls as they always did when accompanying the Prince. The other positioned himself before the closed door and drew his sword by which to stand guard.

"Open it."

"Should we not knock first, Your Highness?" Bourges objected.

Henri shot him a look that required no further question.

Diane and Hélène were sitting at a small tapestry loom by the open window when the doctor opened the door. The breeze from the river rippled the edge of the fabric and the edges of their gowns. Diane looked up with surprise at Henri who stood in the arch of the doorway, a rapier at his belt. His shoes were caked with dried mud and his dark hair was windblown. He bowed to her. After a moment, she gently set down the needle and rose.

"Please leave us," she said.

Even when the door was closed and they were completely alone, neither one moved toward the other. It had been so long. Henri wanted to rush at her, but he could not move. He could only stand there, looking at her; her beautiful milk-white skin in the jet-black gown; her long pale throat rising out of the low, square bodice laced with a heavy gold chain. Finally, Diane moved toward him.

"I was afraid you had died," he whispered.

She extended her long fingers toward him and cupped her hand beside his cheek. They both knew what his coming meant. He raised his own hand to hers and kissed it.

"If anything had happened to you, I could not bear it."

Diane drew nearer as he whispered to her. She tenderly kissed his cheek just above the line of his jaw. The feel of her soft lips against his flesh unleashed a long dormant passion between them. It overtook his gentleness, and he enveloped her in his solid arms.

As Henri drowned her in a myriad of passionate kisses, he pulled at her headdress. Her gold mane of hair tumbled down around her, and he buried his face in its sweet softness. Wanting her so badly, he rushed at her a little too quickly at first, but tenderly, she guided him. She could feel his hands tremble as she led his fingers to the hooks in back of her gown. The rich velvet fell from her and dropped to the floor beneath them. When she was bare to him, he saw the wound on her leg. He dropped to his knees and reached out to gently touch it with his fingertips.

"Dear God," he whispered, then lightly kissed the healing wound, breathless.

After a moment, she pulled him back up. He pressed her against the post of the bed, kissing her throat, her face, then her lips once again. "Oh, please . . ." Diane whispered as she trembled beneath his passion. Her legs were weak but she worked to free him from his chest plate, doublet, then his trunk hose. She gasped, as she finally drew his shirt over the sculpted muscles of his arms and saw how his body had changed. When he too was bare, he pressed himself against the warm flesh of her breasts. Her nipples were hard and pointed. Her mouth, moist and open to him.

"Oh, tell me we shall never be apart like that again . . ." he whispered into the sweet softness of her hair.

"No . . . we never shall."

He moaned at the feel of them pressed together as he forcefully covered her lips once again. They fell together onto the floor, with the velvet and satin of her gown and petticoats to cushion them. In his ecstasy, he felt her hands gently touching him; caressing, guiding him inside of her.

With her, it was as if it was the first time. All else was forgotten. That one forced time with Catherine had been a performance of state. To him, it had been a bestial groping. Like the horses in the field. Like his brother behind the hedgerow. He had not forsaken his love of Diane by that. Now, as they moved together on the floor, every curve of her body molded to his, and he was bathed once again in love. There was nothing else but the feel of her beneath him, the gentle arching of her back as he entered her, and the feel of her warm tongue deep inside his mouth. He felt her cool thin legs wrapped around his buttocks, binding them together as he thrust rhythmically inside of her. The mystery of that secret place; the warm, moist folds beneath the golden patch of hair; the deep musky smell of her skin and the touch of it, drove him deeper into his own passion.

"*Tu es si belle . . .*" he whispered. "*Je t'adore . . . Comme je t'adore . . .*"

Their movements were no longer fluid, but frenzied. He lost all control, and the primal feel of it excited her. Shafts of sensation began to run down from her stomach to her legs, bursting like bolts of lightning, as he drove himself deeper, deeper, inside of her. Pushing. Straining. He moved his powerful body on top of hers with a motion as forceful and violent as an ocean storm; waves surging forward, crashing, pulling back. She was blinded. She began to feel herself spiraling down, as though toward the end of some long dark tunnel. There was nothing but the darkness, and a ray of hot, white light at the end, then, a violent shudder as they moved toward one unity . . . one desperate peak.

THE FIRST RAYS OF SUN burst through the stained-glass window and washed their two blended bodies in hues of deep red and blue. They had not moved nor parted from one another. They had made love again later, on top of her bed, and it had been completely different. Almost as though they had been two different people. Henri had been slower. More patient. Diane had been free. More full of abandon. Again she had felt herself in the same dark tunnel, saw the end, the light, reached for it, and felt the indescribable burst of pleasure. Then, when they were both exhausted, they had fallen asleep just as they had made love; joined, as if one flesh.

Diane felt the wonderful throbbing between her legs as she stretched beneath the bedcovers. She looked down at herself transformed by the colors from the window as she lay with him. She ran a finger against the deep curved line of his chest. The skin was smooth and bare of hair, his body more firm, his buttocks small and round, his shoulders more broad than that first time, two years before. His breathing now was slow and rhythmic as he slept. He was the most beautiful man she had ever seen, there, next to her like that. She had taken him inside herself, taken all of him; all of the rage and all of the pain with which he had loved her for the past two years. Now that she had finally given in to it, she could not recall a time that she had felt so complete. Here, now, she had no regrets. No doubts. For the first time in her life, she had followed her heart. She had given in to what she now knew was her destiny. After a moment, as though he could feel her gazing at him, he opened his eyes.

"Am I dreaming?" he asked in a whisper, his dark eyes still clouded with sleep.

"Ah, you must touch me and see."

"I am afraid to move; afraid that I shall really wake and that you shall be gone."

She leaned over to kiss him and as she did, he pulled her on top of him.

"Thank God," he said with a sleepy smile. He kissed her again. His mouth was warm and demanding, and she felt herself sink into it. But after a moment in his arms, she broke away. She pulled herself from the bed and stood before him.

"You are not leaving . . ."

"Then come with me!" She stood before him completely bare, free and unashamed in her nakedness. As he gazed at her body, he was in awe of it.

"Where are you going?"

"To the river."

"But it is barely dawn!"

"That is the best time. Come!"

She pulled him toward her and coaxed him out of the bed. He laughed at her playfulness, a side of her he had never seen. She found his shirt and silk stockings and her robe, and the two lovers crept silently down the stairs and outside into the crisp spring morning.

It was just past dawn and the ground was covered with crystal drops of dew. There was no sound. They ran down to the water's edge holding hands as a heavy white mist rose from the river. Henri watched her cast off the robe and, oblivious to the icy water, plunge in. After a moment, he doffed his own garments and followed her. Henri was surprised how the rush of cold water invigorated him. He swam toward her and encircled her with his arms. After a moment, sylphlike, she laughed and broke free, diving away from him beneath the frigid, rushing currents. He swam after her and as they caught their breath in the shallow water near the shore, Henri pressed himself against her and kissed the cold skin of her breasts. Then her neck. He wanted her again. He knew he would always want her like this. Free and natural.

After another moment with her arms around him, he picked her up and carried her beneath a thick collection of willow trees on the sloping banks. There, he lay her beneath him, and they made love once again in the wet sand, where it touched the river's edge.

HE WOKE FIRST. His stirring woke her. It was sunset. They were still wrapped in one another, legs entwined, arms around one another. Diane opened her eyes as Henri pulled away, but she did not move. The candle beside her head sputtered in a pool of liquid wax. She watched as he rose and blew it out. The crimson color from the last rays of sun came through the window and then melted into gold as he tossed a fresh log on the fire.

She smiled with an infinite sense of contentment, as she watched him walk to the basin at the end of the room. She thought the movement of his firmly muscled body almost elegant. Henri filled the basin with water from the silver ewer beside it, and brought a cloth and the basin back to their bed. He climbed back onto the bed beside her, onto his knees, and twisted the cloth through the water. Without speaking, he moved the wet towel around her breasts, washing clean her flesh, so heavily laced with the scent of his own. She lay still as the cloth moved down the area of her stomach and thighs; past the cap of her knee, down to her toes.

"Do you know," Henri whispered and closed his eyes, "that I know every curve and every part of your body?"

"Hmm," she said with a calm smile as the cloth moved up again toward her breasts.

"I committed it all to memory when we were apart. For instance, if I move down here," he said, dropping the cloth to her navel, "there is a small indentation just down from here."

Diane's smile broadened. "And here, a little patch of hair, fine as a baby's."

She watched his strong fingers weave their way gently along her body with surprising deftness. She shivered, and the gooseflesh rose up. When he opened his eyes, he saw that she was aroused. It made him want her yet again. He pressed her head back into the pillows and moved onto her. Again they kissed, tender at first, then more desirous. He wound his arms around her back, taking her into his powerful grip.

"You know that I worship you. You, *m'amie* are my world," he said, whispering the ancient phrase that meant "my love."

"And you are mine."

"What will you tell Montgommery?"

"There is nothing between us any longer. I need tell him nothing," she said with a little half smile.

"Then you do not mean to marry him?"

She gazed up at him and ran her fingers through the tufts of his coarse dark hair. "How could I ever . . . now?" she softly asked, and then lay her head on his chest.

"Oh, how I envied and hated that man! I wanted to kill him for touching you when I could not. You are the only thing that has ever mattered to me; the only thing, and it was like watching a part of myself being torn away." He lifted her chin from his chest, so that she would look at him. "I told you this long ago, and it is still true. I am a man with but one heart to give, and it has been given to you. You must take great care with the knowledge of that."

She raised a finger to his lips. "Please," she whispered. "Do not make promises that would not be possible to keep."

"I know what I feel."

"You are young, *chéri,* and life is long. We have each other now, here, in this place. Do not try to promise me forever."

Henri pulled himself from her and rose onto his knees. He took her hands in his own. For the first time in his life, he sat bared to another person and yet it was as natural as if he had done it a thousand times before.

"I prayed for the day when you would want me, though it seemed an eternity. And then, through the grace of God, finally you were given to me. Without you I am nothing; I am only empty and alone. Madame . . . *m'amie,* I am your humble servant for as long as you will consent to have me."

Diane looked into his eyes, which were no longer deep and brooding, but filled with the sensitivity she had seen in Cauterets. They blazed with the fire of new passion. Diane felt mute. He was a Prince; Duc d'Orléans, kneeling and humbled before her. It was not just, as she had led herself to believe, an adolescent infatuation. For the first time, she realized the magnitude of his passion for her. It was also now, gazing into those eyes, that she finally felt secure enough to give her own heart to him in return. As though he knew it, or could sense the change in her, he leaned toward her, still clutching her hands.

"I love you," he said, as he parted her lips with his own and then kissed her. After a moment he added, "I love you with everything I have, and with all that I am."

"And with all of my heart . . . I love you."

Tears welled in his eyes and masked his surprise as he brought her to his chest and kissed her. For two years he had longed to hear her say it; imagined her saying it to him. But somehow, when it happened, it still caught him by surprise. He could not remember another human being ever telling him that he was loved. Not even his mother. Diane de Poitiers changed all of that pain, all of that loss, with the uttering of three simple words. With her in his arms like this, the shackles that had bound his life with hate and misery were now cast off as easily as silk from fresh skin. He was not a prince with her, he was just a man. A man in love. She had done more for him than she could ever know, and he would fight for the rest of his life to make her happy.

ONE DAY PASSED into two, and three became four that they were alone together in their walled garden of Chenonceaux. The rest of the world and its complications lay beyond. They spent their days riding beside one another in the woods and along the river banks. They picnicked across the river where the trees were lush and gave more shade beneath which to make love.

Like children, they scratched one another's names into the bark of a tree. They talked for endless hours about their dreams and their hopes. They planned their future, oblivious to the realities of his responsibilities. They did not speak of the King, or of Catherine, whose images they could scarcely recall.

They found that they loved all of the same things: riding, *jeu de paume*, swimming, reading to one another. With each day, the bond they had sanctioned in the special chateau on the water deepened. He taught her how to play chess, a game she had never quite mastered. In their chamber at night, they would curl up on a thick tapestry beside the fire, with a marble board between them, and covered only in loose dressing gowns and bedding, they would play. She learned quickly under his tutelage and fast became a worthy opponent.

"You know, *m'amie,* this will not be easy for you," he said one evening as he watched her. She was contemplating her next move, and her face was lit by the golden hues from the fire. "People are bound to think that you have corrupted me with your worldly ways, and that you have stolen my heart from my wife."

"Well, haven't I?" she said, capturing his bishop. He waited for her to look up at him. After a moment she did.

"Madame, that which is not possessed by one, can never be stolen by another. My soul belonged to you long before she ever set foot in France."

Diane smiled and leaned across the board to kiss him. "But you know that this must remain a private matter between us, *chéri.*"

The corners of his mouth turned down into a pout. After a moment, he recanted. "Of course you are right. For now, at least. I shall not muddy the waters for either of us, just yet. But one day it will all come out, and then I shall want to show you off to every petty, envious courtier at François' Court. Then it will be said that weak-willed, melancholy little Henri is not so dim, for he has won the greatest prize of all!"

Diane reached over and touched his cheek. "But until that time, we must be very, very cautious. If His Majesty were to catch wind of it, I would be most expeditiously ousted from Court, and from you."

"I would kill him myself, if he were ever to lay a hand on you!" Henri snapped, as the image of his father, long forgotten, filled him with the old rage of his boyhood. In his anger, he reached out to her as though she were a tonic, and she willingly gave in to him. He pulled her dressing gown away and kissed her bare breasts until he could feel the nipples harden beneath his lips. He looked down at her smile, and then buried his face in the curved area between them. He pushed the chess board aside; the carved wooden pieces clattered as they fell against the marble board.

Henri held her in the powerful way a man holds a woman, and he kissed her with all of the masculine passion she could have hoped to feel; yet in his soul were the unfulfilled needs of a boy lain bare to her. She lay beneath him on the cold tile floor, surrounded by her robes and bedding, feeling his passion, and yet sensing an even deeper side of him beginning to surface. It was like the rebirth of a child who had died long ago; a rebirth for which she alone was responsible.

But his was not the only resurrection. Diane had denied her own passion for so many fallow years, that finally giving in to it was like a wellspring. The change in their relationship had meant new life for them both. She no longer cared about the difference in age between them, that he was married, or that one day he would leave her. For now she felt certain that he loved her; and that was enough. She looked over at him and wondered what it was. What was this odd, almost divine force that had propelled them so relentlessly toward one another? Deep within herself, almost to her core, she had loved him; first as a mother loves a son, now as a woman loves a man. To deny it, as she had done, was to refute her own existence. Loving meant life, new life for them both.

HENRI HAD BEEN with Diane for eight days when he was forced to leave Chenonceaux. He had to return to the military camp where his brother, the Dauphin, and Grand Master Montmorency awaited him. She stood in the round alcove adjoining her bedchamber and watched him dress. First, the white silk undergarments; the stockings, then the padded trunk hose. She watched them slide over the sculpted muscles of his calves and thighs. He did not look at her. He could not. Leaving her was too painful.

Henri slid the red silk shirt over his bare back. She watched the broad muscles contract and expand as he clasped it and then covered it with a dark blue doublet embroidered with the King's crest. He sat in a high-backed leather chair to put on his shoes. After a moment, he let them fall to the floor. He leaned back and looked up at her. Diane came to him without a word and slipped onto his lap. She clasped her arms around his neck and gently kissed each of his cheeks and they sat silently together in the chair, holding one another. Every moment was precious. They both knew there was no way of knowing what lay ahead. After a moment, he began to run his fingers over the line of her arm, recapturing her softness.

"Oh, how I wish we could just seize this moment and keep things as they are right now," he sighed as they looked out the open window onto the river.

"But you know we cannot," she whispered and lay her head on his shoulder. "We both must leave this place."

"Yes; back to the real world, with all of its ugliness and deceit."

"Nothing will ever be the same again."

"Nothing is constant in this world of ours, but my love for you."

"And mine for you," she added.

Diane followed the reluctant Prince down the stone stairway and into the grand foyer. It was early and the walls still radiated the night's chill. As they reached the bottom of the stairs, Henri was halted by the sight that lay before him. The foyer was lined with the King's guards. Each man stood at attention with his sword drawn and his blue-plumed toque at a right angle tilt. They lined the path to the opened double doors. As Henri descended the last stair, each guardsman, in turn, reverently bowed. It was the same motion they performed in the presence of the King. Henri stopped and looked at them. His heart began to race.

"What is the meaning of this? I am not the King! Why are you here?"

When they did not reply, he charged ahead to the opened doors and out into the gravel-covered courtyard. Diane followed. Hélène flanked the door beside the royal physician. Both of their heads hung solemnly. Diane looked at her maid as she passed by, but Hélène said nothing. As she turned back to Henri, Diane saw him falter, then she looked ahead at what he had seen. Assembled before him was an army of the King's guard on horseback. The dark horse in front bore the King's red, blue and gold banner sewn with the image of the salamander. Another horse that stood beside it bore a banner in black, the banner of mourning. Fifty more men stood in uniform in the circular area just outside the door. When Henri came out of the chateau they bowed ceremoniously, just as the others had done.

He looked back at Diane who stood in the arch to the doorway with the same expression of surprise. She feared the worst. The King must have discovered them, but she said nothing; she only waited. As Henri turned back around, he saw his old friend, Jacques de Saint-André, come out from the legion of guards and advance toward him. As he neared Henri, he bowed as reverently as the others had done.

"What in the devil is the meaning of all of this, Jacques?"

Diane advanced and stood beside Henri. Saint-André acknowledged her with a vacant nod and then looked back at the Prince. His face was drawn. He had not shaven and his garments were caked with dust and mud. It was clear that he had ridden hard from the camps.

"I regret, Your Highness, what I must tell you, but I do beseech you to be brave."

"Is it the King?"

"It is your brother, the Dauphin. He is dead."

"Dead? That is not possible. I was just with him."

"He died two days past, Your Highness, at Tournon, where he waited for your father to join him."

"I do not believe . . . I will not believe . . ."

"I regret that I saw it with my own eyes. The King suspects poisoning. The question of who, I am afraid, remains a mystery."

Henri felt himself pass into a daze. Though they had not been close since they were children, François was still his older brother; the brother by which he had tried to measure himself, and by which he had always failed. Diane reached around to steady him as he faltered.

"I am so sorry, Henri," whispered Saint-André in the voice of a friend as he lowered his head like the others.

Henri looked up again into the courtyard lined with royal guards, all lowered in bows to him. He looked again at Saint-André and then at Diane. Now, even she curtsied.

"Madame, please! Do not bow before me!"

Diane lifted her head just so that Henri could hear her, but continued her reverence in the fashion of the others.

"We show our respect because you are Dauphin now. Through the fate of so grievous a tragedy, *mon amour,* it is you now who shall next be King of France."

THE WINDOWS OF LES TOURNELLES in Paris were draped with great strips of black silk to block out the sun. They also muffled the sound of prayers from the Mass for the Dead, chanted by the townspeople who held vigil below. A black banner stretched across the gate to the chateau where twenty years before, the boy they now mourned had been given life. His body was finally borne on a bier back to the Cathedral de Saint-Denis, where he was to be entombed with his mother.

The King was a man inconsolable. In the place of the robust Monarch who had left Chenonceaux, now only the shell of a man remained. He shuffled around the dark halls aimlessly, muttering to himself and shaking his head. He spoke to no one, save for a few words, and took only enough food to keep himself alive.

The death of his eldest son had aged the hedonistic King the way no other bloodshed or tragedy could have done. In his grief, he longed for retaliation. Within a week of his son's entombment, formal charges were brought against Count Sebastian Montecuculi, the Dauphin's private secretary, who had come to France in the entourage of Catherine de Medici.

Montecuculi had several points against him, which made the charges of murder that much more viable in a Court crying for revenge. He was Italian, which not only tied him to Catherine, but to a possible greater conspiracy instigated by the Emperor Charles. He had also been the unfortunate one, when it was requested, to have given the Dauphin the cup of water, by which it was believed that he had died. But most strongly against him, a book on poisons had been found among his belongings.

He was tortured mercilessly until he confessed to the crime. Though once the torture ceased, he continually tried to recant his admission, the King was convinced he was guilty. He refused to discuss with his courtiers other possible suspects of which there were many. Instead, he set out with single-minded ferocity to see the Count executed for the crime. His sentence, so that the King might once again know peace of mind, was to be tied to four horses and torn to pieces.

IT WAS AGREED by them both that Diane should stay on at Chenonceaux a few days longer while Henri returned to Paris. He had wanted to pay his last respects to his brother who was being interred in the Cathedral de Saint-Denis, just outside the city. He desperately wanted Diane to accompany him but both were afraid of the suspicion that such a bold move was certain to arouse.

The Grand Master, now Lieutenant-General of the French army, was at the camp on the Rhône where he had taken command of the troops against the Emperor. After his brief stop in Paris, Henri then joined his friend Montmorency in Avignon.

In the evenings, as he sat idle, the new Dauphin wrote to Diane. A profound loneliness and despair marked the tone of his letters. By the time she rejoined the King's Court, now moved out to Fontainebleau, the communiqués had became desperate. They were long, impassioned letters begging her to write to him, pleading with her to profess her love to him, just as he continually did to her.

But she could not. A letter was a record. It need only fall into the hands of one disgruntled or ambitious courtier to spell her complete ruin and the possibility of their permanent separation. She could not take that risk. Not yet. Still the letters came, sometimes three a day by personal courier.

> M'amie,
>
> I do beseech you kindly to respond. Give me please just a sign that I have not so quickly lost favor with you. I promise an exchange of but one word from you would give me the strength to continue until we are reunited. You are always my life and my love. I commend myself to your good graces.
>
> Your humble
> servant,
> H

Diane tossed the letter into the fire in the privacy of her bedchamber and watched it surrender to the bright blue flames. When it curled into a black ball of ashes and fell into bits around the burning log, she rose and walked back into her receiving room. The Dauphin's personal messenger stood at attention near the door, his hands behind his back and his head held high at attention. Hélène sat by the window and looked up the moment Diane returned to the room.

"Will there be a reply, Madame?" asked the guard in a proper monotone.

"No, Monsieur. No reply."

IN THE INTERVENING WEEKS, the marriage plans for Diane's eldest daughter, Françoise, to Robert de La Marck progressed and she was required to return home to Anet to complete the contract. But even from her own home she did not feel safe in returning the Dauphin's ardent letters.

> Ma Bien-aimée,
>
> I fear the worst. It will soon be Christmas; four month's since you swore your love to me, and yet I receive not a single word from you. I

know that you are not ill, for the messenger who returns to me says that you appear fit and well. He, however, says further that you give him no instructions with which to return. I promise you that if I were to perish in the flames of hell, it could be no worse a fate than the pain of your indifference.

Diane folded the letter neatly in the same two places in which it had been received. Then, as she had done with all the others, she surrendered the royal parchment to the flames of her chamber fire and waited there until it had turned to ashes. She came out of the door moments later, and before he had an opportunity to ask, she said, "No, Monsieur, there will be no reply."

Hélène waited for the messenger to leave before she rose from her chair by the window and rushed up behind Diane.

"Madame, please forgive me, but that is the third letter in two days. His Highness must be desperate for word from you."

"I cannot risk it, Hélène," she whispered. "A letter might fall into the hands of the King's men. If that were to happen, I would be ruined. No. There is no one here who can be trusted." Diane looked into the deep, expressive eyes of her maid and at the simple fawnlike beauty of a woman who had become her friend. "What am I to do?"

"Perhaps you could send him just a sign; something to put his mind at rest while he is so far away."

"But would that be wise? We both risk so much."

"I think, Madame, it would be far less wise not to reply. His Highness shall be plagued with worry."

Diane thought back to one of Henri's first impassioned letters which now lay in ashes at the bottom the hearth. He had asked for *one word.* He wanted only a sign of their love to assure him, but what could she possibly risk? Diane walked to her writing desk. She pulled out a small sheet of parchment and said a prayer to the Virgin Mother to help her find the inspiration to allay her lover's fear. She sat down and gazed at the blank page. Hélène hovered near her, trying not to look. Diane dipped the long quill into the silver inkwell and put the wetted tip to paper. She drew an H to begin.

It lay there alone on the page; alone as he was; away with an entire army of French troops, and yet, with no one. Here was she at Anet, with her family and Hélène, and yet equally as alone.

When she imagined them together, the idea came to her. She would not give him a word at all, but a cypher. She crumpled up the piece of parchment and took another from the shelf on top of the writing desk. Slowly she drew a D. Beside it, she intertwined with it another D, only she reversed it. She connected the two letters, forming the letter H. It was what he craved; a sign of their union. D and H interlaced, to symbolize their love. He would understand. She blew lightly at the paper to help the ink dry and then folded it. Hélène sealed the wax over the opening as Diane looked up.

"What is between the Prince and myself," she began in a somber tone, "is a sin against God. Yet you do not judge me."

"Madame, I believe the greatest sin against God is to be false. If one is not true to one's self, then it is impossible to be true to God. I bear you no ill will for following your heart."

*S*INCE YOUR MAJESTY HAS ASKED ME, I shall be direct. It is my opinion that the Dauphin should divorce her."

"Divorce?" the King scoffed. "Impossible! I shall leave those unsavory matters to the house of England, at which my good brother Henry has become so proficient. No. Divorce shall not happen in the house of France."

It was the first of April, seven months since the Dauphin's death. Although the spring had put his consumption to rest, François' mood was still a melancholy one. The Cardinal de Lorraine, the ambitious head of the house of Guise, strolled slowly beside the King as they wound their way through the new formal parterre. The Cardinal pretended to appreciate the precision of the beauty around him, having been undaunted by the King's response to his calculated suggestion. After all, the idea was a new one. There was time. If his plan was to be accepted, it must be executed perfectly. He could not push. It must seem like the King's own idea. There was no margin for error when the honor of his entire family was at risk. He paced himself. He took a breath.

"The fact remains, Your Majesty, that it has been four years and yet the Dauphine has not produced a child. Now that Prince Henri is Dauphin, France is without an heir. As you know of course, that is an exceedingly dangerous state of affairs."

The King did not respond, but Guise knew that he had made his point. They continued to stroll. The Cardinal managed a sideways glance once he was certain the King could not see him. François stopped to admire an emerald yew clipped like a cone, but despite His Majesty's attempt to disguise it, the Cardinal could see the consternation on the King's face.

After a moment he said, "But We have taken Catherine on as if she were Our own daughter. How could such a thing even be considered?"

"Your Majesty need not concern yourself with the details of such a move. You need only say that you agree for it to be dealt with."

They walked the length of the garden, toward the pavilion. He was once again silent, careful not to overplay his hand. Jean de Guise, the Cardinal de Lorraine, was an artful man, not so handsome as he was wise. A tall, stately looking man with white hair and a neat pointed beard now gone partially yellow, he had been in service to the King most of his life. He was systematic, clinical and exceedingly ambitious; qualities that had not only secured him a high ecclesiastical position, but had also seen him named *compagnon de coeur* to the French Monarch. Being the King's confidant was a power base which, at the moment, with Montmorency in the south and Chabot also away from court, he reveled in sharing with no one.

But nothing at this Court was ever fixed, and he knew it. Looking toward the future, he had secured good positions for both of his nephews. One was Archbishop de Rheims; the other had recently been elevated from a royal page to one of the elite personal guardsmen to the King. Now the Cardinal knew he must seize this opportunity for his niece, Marie, the eldest of his brother's children, as though there would never be another.

"Have you someone in mind to replace the Dauphine?" the King finally asked as he looked up at the sky.

Guise waited a moment, reflective, then answered. "It is but a thought, Your Majesty, but perhaps His Highness would fare better this time with a French bride, someone with whom he has more in common."

"Indeed." The King looked at him, his lips pressed into one long, thin line.

"The Comte de Saint-Pol has a daughter. Her name has been proposed."

"Hmm."

"There is also Marie, daughter of the Duc de Vendôme."

"And?" asked the King, still appearing to study a white puff of clouds.

"Of course Your Majesty knows that the Duchesse de Longueville is now widowed."

"Ah, yes. Your own niece, Marie."

They were interrupted by two guardsmen escorting a messenger. "Word, Your Majesty, from the Lieutenant-General," he announced in a formal voice, and handed over a sealed slip of parchment to the King. François opened it. The Cardinal stood silently beside him as he read the communiqué.

"Monty has decided now to take on the Imperial city of Hesdin in the north," the King sighed. "He says that it is weakly garrisoned and may mean a stronger hold against the Emperor when we sweep back into Italy."

"But the men, Your Majesty, the lives. We have lost so many already. Is it not too great a risk?"

"When I made Montmorency lieutenant-general I did so giving him free rein. And we have come this far. If it means I may get Milan back one day, I must support him. I only pray God Monty is certain of what he is doing."

The Cardinal de Lorraine was not sorry that the subject had

been changed. He had still managed to propose his niece. It was what he had hoped to do. Plant the seed. And for now that would be enough. "If Milan is what Your Majesty desires," he said wisely, "then it is what I shall pray for also."

M'amie,
I write you this from camp near Therouenne. So many days and nights I have gone without the light of your smile or the tenderness of your words. Your sign to me alone is what gives me strength.

Diane folded the letter and pressed it into the bodice of her gown. She could not find the strength to finish reading it. She just made it to the edge of her bed before she collapsed on top of the covers. She had tried to ignore it, but with each day the pain increased. It had started with mild nausea; then blood coming from her private parts. Her flux, she had thought. The pain subsided, only to have it resume a few days later. Her breasts were swollen and sore and she found it more difficult each day to keep down the slightest bit of food.

"Madame, please, let me call the doctor," Hélène pleaded as she rushed toward her. "His Highness would never forgive me if you were ill and I did not—"

"No!" Diane gripped her belly and rolled onto her back on the bed, taking in deep breaths to try and stop the pain. After a moment she recanted. "Please forgive me," she said and pushed herself up onto the pillows. Hélène pulled the covers up around her. Diane was shivering and yet her skin was moist and warm. There was a film across her blue eyes and dark circles beneath them.

"I know what is the matter . . ." she said weakly. "I have faced it twice before. I was told at Cauterets there would be a third. The prophesy has come true, Hélène. I am with child."

Hélène covered her mouth with both of her hands to hide her horror.

"I thought it was impossible now. My oldest daughter is to be married soon."

Hélène's hands fell away from her face. "Oh, Madame, what will you do?"

"What can I do? The Prince has his wife. I have known that all along. I suppose that this is to be my penance."

Diane lay her head back on the pillows. The child was kicking again; tiny little waves of movement against her belly. Dear God, what would Henri think? Her lean body swollen by this child; both of their lives changed forever. And what did she think of it herself? To be a mother again . . . now. And without benefit of a husband. It would create a great scandal. He was bound to be furious. It was likely to put an end to everything. She tried to console herself, wondering now how long it might have lasted with him even under the best of circumstances.

$\mathcal{A}$s the fighting continued, the Court remained the next month at Meudon: a chateau southwest of Paris, which was one of the three seats of the wealthy Guise family. At the end of 1536, much against his will, the King's young daughter, Madeleine, his favorite, became the bride of King James V of Scotland at a ceremony in Paris. He had wanted to bind their two countries with a marriage . . . a marriage with anyone but his "lily."

Consumptive all of her life and weak at the time of her wedding, she had to be carried down the aisle before Notre Dame in a litter. In Scotland six months later she died in her husband's arms. Once again the great strips of black fabric draped the windows of the King's chateaux. Once again the banquets ceased; the jousting stopped. There was no music and no laughter. Only a hollow echo marking her death.

Shortly afterward, the King lapsed into a severe state of consumption himself brought on by depression. He was unable to move on as he had planned, to join the Dauphin and Montmorency in Thérouanne as they launched their latest attack against the Emperor. The Cardinal de Lorraine could not have been more pleased at this positive turn of events for it gave him time to continue the implementation of his plan to see his niece Marie named new Dauphine in place of Catherine de Medici.

Throughout the long, hot summer days the King was plied with a tincture of cider and syrup of roses to quiet the coughing brought on by consumption. Absinthe and the extract of lime blossom was administered to help him sleep. Now swollen and defeated, he would speak to no one save for his confessor. *My greed has done this,* he told himself. *I put my need to have Italy above all else, and now I am paying in the most dear way that I can for that desire. My son is dead. The Dauphine is barren. Now, my Madeleine. I have lost my little girl; my pale little lily.* She had been the reminder of his own youth. His own lost innocence. His mortality. *Oh, to look upon those eyes again! I would give it all to have her here.* But nothing could push back the demon lover who had lured him with his own ambition; not the claret, not Anne, not the volumes of his own tears.

Finally late in September, a proposed armistice was brought to him in the hand of the Queen Dowager of Hungary. She acted, she said, on behalf of the Holy Roman Emperor. It was only a limited truce that was offered, applicable only to Picardy and Flanders, both in the north where the French had been successful. But François asked no questions. He signed it immediately, hoping to quell the anger and rage of a God who, it seemed, was bent on his destruction.

IN THE ENDLESS DAYS which Catherine de Medici had spent alone since her arrival in France, the realms of astrology and prophecy had begun to consume her. She too had heard the gossip that the King was considering her divorce and nothing but fantasy held any real hope. Thank the dear Lord for Ruggieri.

"If only Henri would get me with a child . . ." she moaned as she paced back and forth in velvet slippers.

The chamber her Italian mystic, Giuffrido Ruggieri, occupied was dark. The windows were draped with long, black sheets of silk. Hundreds of long, white tapers burned throughout the day and spilled their liquid wax onto the tables, onto sconces, and onto the mantel above the fireplace. The room glowed. The bureaus were peppered with amulets and talismans. On the table near the fire were dozens of jars filled with hysop, citronella and valerian. Other smaller earthen jars were not marked. There were ancient, tattered books on the subjects of the stars and alchemy scattered open on the bed and on the tiled floor.

"If only I could have a child, then I am certain he would accept me as his wife. Is there not something you can give me? Some potion?"

Ruggieri moved toward the cluttered table. "I can give you something, child, but if you do not bed with him, it shall be of no use."

Her eyes brightened and she bolted toward him from her chair. "Let me worry about that. Just tell me what I must do!"

Ruggieri's thin face was pale from the long hours he had spent in darkened chambers. His hair and beard were long and white. After contemplating the Dauphine's troubled face for a moment, he turned toward his table and began opening jars. Catherine neared but recoiled at the pungent aroma which wafted from them.

"What is it?"

"Sheep's urine," he replied and opened another vessel. The liquid inside was a gray-blue color and more foul-smelling than the first. He looked up at Catherine with a half smile, Before she could inquire further, he said, "It is best not to ask. If you mean to cure yourself you shall have to drink it." Then he lowered his head to his work. In the space of half an hour, he had mixed together an elixir of sheep's urine, rabbit's blood and mare's milk that had been widely constituted as a philtre; a potion thought by the ancient alchemists to arouse sexual passion. After she had drunk it, Ruggieri smiled. A bit of the mixture framed her lips. He daubed it with his sleeve.

"Your Prince returns from battle tonight, yes?"

"Yes," she replied.

"Then go to him, child. And with God's help and mine, you shall be filled with his child by morning's light."

THE WELCOMING DELEGATION for the Dauphin's troops began to emerge from the chateau at Meudon after the sun had set. The grounds and the courtyard were lit by a hundred flaming gold torches to illuminate the path of the approaching legion. Diane stood behind Catherine and Henri's sister, Marguerite. Marie de Guise, the Cardinal's niece, stood quietly beside her. After a moment, the echo of thundering hooves signaled their arrival, as another band of courtiers emerged from the long glass-paned doors of the south wing of the Cardinal's chateau. They had been waiting only moments when the first rider, carrying the large brilliant blue banner splashed with the emblem of the salamander, wound his way up the wooded path to the grand entrance. Another moment passed and the Dauphin's brightly draped horse thundered into the courtyard. Clustered around Henri, riding high on their mounts in a swirl of dust, were François de Guise, Jacques de Saint-André, Claude d'Annebault and Anne de Montmorency.

Henri had changed. Diane could see that from the first. His look was more wild. More fierce. His dark hair was long around his ears and he had grown a dark mustache and beard. But it was far more than his appearance. After he stepped from his horse, she could see that he walked with a more confident stride. His head was higher, his pace more commanding. Embroidered onto his doublet in silver thread she was shocked to see the interlaced D and H cypher.

He gave the bridle over to a groom. Jacques walked beside him and they were whispering something between themselves. Jacques had the same wild look as Henri. His light hair too had grown long, and was brushed away from his face and behind his ears. The other men dismounted after the Dauphin and his companion. Then they ambled collectively toward the chateau in their soiled uniforms and mud-splashed, soft leather shoes, laughing and slapping one another's backs. Catherine ran out to Henri in the dusty courtyard and wrapped her arms around his neck. His sister, Marguerite, followed behind her at a more delicate pace. Diane watched the exaggerated display of affection as Catherine kissed him on the lips, then on both cheeks. She stood silently for the moment and watched them embrace one another. When they turned, they walked toward the entry with their arms linked. Then Henri saw Diane. He broke away from Catherine instantly and advanced toward the others who still stood in a greeting line on the steps near the entrance.

"'Your Eminence," Henri said, lowering his head to the Cardinal de Lorraine. Then he moved to the left and embraced his Aunt, who was Queen of Navarre.

"Welcome home, Henri," she said. Again Catherine was at his side, clutching his sleeve.

He moved a few sideways steps and ran a hand nervously across his bearded face. It was the first time in weeks he had considered his appearance. He had not seen a mirror since he had left the camp. Marie de Guise, who stood next to Marguerite, curtsied next in his presence. Her uncle, the Cardinal, watched the performance, hoping for a promising exchange between them. He had spent enough on her gown to have paid the King's Captain a year's salary. But Henri moved on almost immediately after he had extended the requisite greeting. The next person in line was Diane de Poitiers.

"Madame," he said as he took her hand. The action of extending his hand forced Catherine to let go of his arm. But still she stood beside him, watching him. Watching them. Henri then put Diane's hand to his lips. "How is it, Madame, that you are more beautiful each time we see one another?"

Diane lowered her eyes. It was an awkward thing for him to have said. Not at all like something he would have said aloud before he had left. Afraid to draw further attention, she stepped back a pace and kept her eyes lowered. Catherine, who had missed none of the exchange, clutched greedily at him again and fought to stave off a jealous rage.

"The King has requested our immediate presence in his chamber as he is unwell enough to greet you here," said Catherine, more for Diane's benefit than for Henri's.

"Oh, no! Not tonight. All I want is a very hot bath and a large cup of claret. You may have your people tell His Majesty that he will have to wait until morning if he wishes to extend his audience to me."

CATHERINE'S PACE QUICKENED as she reached the corridor down which Henri had gone. The sun had begun to set and the last brilliant bit of orange burst through the panes of the long, leaded west windows. As she walked, she clutched the amulet. Around her neck, a small sack containing the ashes of a large frog. Around her waist she wore a belt woven of goat's hair. Like the philtre, these were charms from Ruggieri to induce pregnancy. She would stop at nothing to have Henri's child. Her advisors had suggested that now, when he was so newly returned to civilization he would be most vulnerable to sweet perfumes and soft words. If she had to beg him to bed her, she would. A child was her only hope of remaining his wife.

The echoed sound of footsteps before her caused her to stop. She had caught up with him and now he was near. He was also finally alone. She must go to his chamber but he must not know that, like a spy, she had followed him. Afraid that Henri would be angry, she ducked behind a massive tapestry and peered out from the corner. He stopped. Catherine clutched the amulet at her chest. She was not really spying on him. After all, he was her husband.

She watched him stop in the center of the corridor, accompanied only by his own shadow cast boldly against the wall beside her. He glanced around to see that he had not been followed. Then he rapped on one of the closed doors. Catherine held her breath. The tapestry behind which she had hidden was just a few steps away. After a moment, the door opened. Diane de Poitiers was on the other side, dressed in a white linen dressing gown. Catherine could see her breasts through the fabric. She bit her finger to keep from screaming. They kissed. She watched them. Lips touching. Hands tenderly at each other's faces. Then she drew him inside.

✺

FRIPPONE AND FRIPPER, the two hounds Diane had given him, lunged at Henri, both of them whimpering and barking.

"Oh, I have missed you!" he said, burying his face in her hair. He pressed his body against hers and covered her mouth with kisses. Then he stopped. His eyes moved to her face and then down to her belly. He looked at her again. His joyous expression faded to the blankness of a slate. He leaned back against the heavy door as though he had been struck. Then he looked at her again with one long expressionless stare. So he knew, thought Diane. He had felt it. And now there was silence between them. Deadly silence.

"Oh, Henri, please say something!"

"So . . ." he said, pulling himself from the wall. "Who is to be the father of it, then?"

Diane's smile faded to match his own blank expression. "Why, you of course," she replied with a nervous half laugh and then tilted her head to the side, waiting apprehensively for him to respond. She watched his eyes widen and his mouth fall open. "Yes!" she repeated when she could see his surprise. "Of course it is you!" She punctuated her words with a larger smile. "Henri, there has been no one else. There never could be. I thought it was impossible after all of these years but—"

"Mine?" he repeated, incredulously. "My child?" He clutched his forehead and leaned back against the door again; his lips parted.

"I am yours, *chéri* . . . as is the life within me."

Henri lunged for her. Taking her in his arms he twirled her around so that her legs and gown fanned out behind her.

"Mine? A child? Oh, I worship you! . . . oh!" he shrieked, and then put her down. All at once he began to pat her as though he had nearly toppled a precious vase. "Oh, forgive me! Great Zeus! Oh . . . have I hurt you?"

"I am fine," she laughed and clasped her arms around his neck once again. "I have borne two others, remember? I will not break."

"Oh, I want to give you the world! You have made me happier

than I had ever dreamed possible!" He took her hands and held them up. He kissed them both, then said, "You know I want to marry you and that the King wants nothing so much as a grandchild. Now I can go to him and confess everything! I have heard rumors, even in the field, that he means to see to my divorce because Catherine is barren. It all will be perfect!"

Henri laughed loudly, joyously, with his head back and his eyes sparkling in the firelight. Diane had never seen him so happy. But she knew before she spoke that his happiness would not last. Gently, she ran a hand along the side of his face and in a firm but gentle tone said, "Henri . . . that is impossible."

"But you are with child! His grandchild."

Her smile faded, and with it, her own gentleness. Her arms fell away from him and she walked toward the fireplace, turning her back to him.

"On what grounds would you ask for this divorce, then? On the grounds that the marriage was never consummated?"

Henri hung his head, stung again by her remark. After a moment, he lunged toward her. "But there must be a way. This child inside you changes everything!"

"It changes nothing. Kings do not marry their whores. You have gotten me with a bastard child. Nothing more."

"Damn! I will not hear that! It is not like that between us!" he raged and slammed his fist against the wall.

"Well, what then? What grounds? Perhaps her adultery? Do you have any reason to believe that Catherine has been unfaithful to your vows?" She waited a moment. "Of course not! She adores you; that is apparent to everyone."

"She may adore me, but I despise her!" he seethed and bashed his head into the same wall in a defeated gesture. After a moment, he turned around. She was still gazing at the fire, her hands down around her newly rounded belly. "I will go to her and I will confess that I have gotten you with child. I will plead that she divorce me on those same grounds of adultery."

"Henri, you cannot bargain with her. This child changes nothing. Do you not see that she wants you?"

"But she does not have me!" he seethed; his rage was out of control. "I am yours! I always have been and I always will be yours!" He lunged toward her, pulling her into his arms and clutching her so fiercely that she could barely breathe. "There must be a way!" He trembled. "There must!"

SO IT WAS TRUE. The hushed whispers, the snickers on the back stairs as she passed. They whispered that Henri had taken a lover. And so it was true, he had taken Madame Diane. Or was it she who had taken him? Damn her! Just when Catherine had been willing to believe that Henri's return might finally signal the beginning of their real life together, the reality reared up at her, turning her as cold as stone. Oh, she had suspected it, even expected it since the day they were married. It was not difficult to recall his eyes; pained, passionate eyes that never left the sight of Madame Diane the entire day of their wedding. And the helpless look of regret that she had mistaken for apprehension.

Infidelity. Broken promises. They had defined her life. She thought of the way the King paraded his latest fancy before Anne d'Heilly; the way he paraded Anne before the Queen. Her mind followed to the memory of her Uncle, Pope Clement. She hated his memory for forcing her into this marriage; this prison where she was merely tolerated, and loved by no one. She had been the Pope's bargaining chit, and she was the King's regret now. Merciless bastards, all! Her Florentine blood boiled. She thought of the only maxim which could give her comfort now. *Odiate et aspetate.* Hate and wait.

THE NEXT MORNING Henri went to the King's apartments in the company of Jacques de Saint-André. He had been told shortly after his arrival that His Majesty was again ill. Henri had been prepared to see his father as he had left him, weak and defeated. But when he was issued into the large apartment by one of the King's guards, he found him huddled in a large black leather chair by the fire, elegantly clothed in a doublet of white and gold, with a collar of ermine. He had a large silver three-stringed rebec poised beneath his chin on which he was trying, rather unsuccessfully, to master a tune. Anne d'Heilly was at his side. The rest of the chamber was swirling with activity.

As usual in the morning, the room was full of courtiers and servants. Henri saw the Cardinal de Lorraine, who sat in a large velvet chair on the other side of the chamber reading a Book of Hours. His nephew, François de Guise, in his new post as guard, stood sentry at the door. His other nephew, Charles, Archbishop de Rheims, was playing a game of cards with Princess Marguerite.

The King did not see his son enter the room. Henri stood back for a moment, watching him. Despite the sumptuous costuming, the gems, and the King's active appearance, he was struck by how old and tired a man his father had become. The bloat around his abdomen had become even more difficult to disguise. The chestnut hair was now heavily peppered with brittle gray strands receding from his forehead. The lines, once lightly drawn beside his eyes, were now deeply etched. It was whispered in the most discreet circles that the King was once again suffering from a venereal malady.

As Henri stood there, it was the image of the King's mortality that captivated him. François I, once robust and untouchable, had become frail. Henri had never acknowledged the notion of his father's death before. As quickly as he had the thought, he pushed it away.

"I was told that you were ill," he said, managing to be civil as he approached. François stopped playing and looked up.

"Not to worry. It is nothing serious. I am afraid, my little man, that you will have quite a wait before you will have leave to commission my effigy for Saint-Denis."

Henri groaned and moved nearer. "I did not come here to exchange insults with Your Majesty."

The King looked at him with a vague stare. "Then why have you come?"

Henri took in a deep breath. His spirits were far too high with news of his forthcoming child to let even the King of France engage him in this tireless contest of wills.

"It was Your Majesty who summoned me," he said, looming over the King.

Being in this room around all these mementos of a man he detested ignited old fires in Henri. He tried not to look, but the images were impossible to ignore. The volume of Machiavelli's *The Prince* was displayed proudly on a table near the door, so that everyone who entered the room would be forced to see it. Over the mantel was the painting of a woman that Leonardo da Vinci had given him. *La Gioconda.* He took the painting with him everywhere he went as the ultimate symbol of beauty. It made Henri think only of the night that he had followed Diane to his father's bed chamber, and Anne d'Heilly had caught them standing beneath it. He looked away. Beside the bed was a charcoal sketch of his mother, done before he was born. She had been beautiful then; so healthy and full of life. It was too difficult being here. He wanted to leave.

"There is this issue of your marriage to Catherine," the King began, and suddenly Henri was catapulted back to his own tumultuous present.

"To be plain with you, boy, as you well know, she has not produced an heir. Though from what I gather, without a stud in the stable even a brood mare cannot get with a colt."

"Say what you mean to say."

"What would you say to a divorce? Perhaps a new wife with whom you would be more inclined to consider the issue of heirs."

Henri softened. He could not help it. He was close. So close. He sat down in the chair across from the King and rested his chin in his hand. He tried to discern the possibility of a ruse by looking into his father's eyes. Was it safe to propose Diane? Had he the slightest hope of predicting the motivation behind a master of manipulation?

"Perhaps Your Majesty can tell me, why is this the first I have heard of it from you?" he asked, stroking his chin as his father often did.

The King took a breath. They were playing a game with one another. A tactical game. The King was an old master while Henri was an eager novice. Henri wore his impatience on his shirt sleeve. It was so easy, it almost was not any fun at all. François paced himself. He waited.

"Because, my boy, I had hoped for the matter to resolve itself. As you know, I have grown quite fond of your little Italian bride."

Henri stood again, unable to bear the intensity brewing between them. As he walked toward the window, he clenched his fists then released them. Just being near the King forced a dark rage to build inside him; a kind that began to lure him to dangerous and deadly thoughts. If this was difficult, proposing Diane would be impossible.

"And this new wife . . . have you someone in mind?" Henri cautiously asked.

The King looked up at his son. Yes indeed. He did have someone in mind. Someone young and far lovelier than the Sénéchal's widow! Someone who could answer the boy's new and obviously flourishing appetite. Someone who would put an expedient end to this scandalous liaison between them. All of her excuses; her demure refusals to him; to the King of France! In mourning, indeed! Lies, all lies! All the while wanting a boy instead of a man. What a mockery that woman had made of him. Now what a mockery she would make of his son . . . if he let her.

"Yes. As a matter of fact I do have a candidate. I would propose Marie de Guise," the King declared with a tentative expression. "Though I would be willing to entertain an alternate selection if there is one who has not yet been considered."

The King challenged the Prince . . . man against boy. Henri tried to hold himself in check. His heart raced. He must say it now . . . must propose her now. There was no choice. Now, he must speak. Now, before it was too late. Now!

"Well, Your Majesty knows that I am fond of Madame Diane."

He heard himself say the words, though he could scarcely believe he had managed them when everything in his body had told him to stay silent. Uttering her name had put him in a vulnerable position with his enemy. The King brushed a hand across his face to hide the victorious grin.

"Ah. So there we have it, do we?" The King grinned, showing his teeth. "And, what do you suppose would become of this country if every Prince who had a whore tried to take her for his Queen?"

Henri had never hated his father so much as he did at that moment. He hated him with a violence and a rage that he had never known. The rage was like a power with a life of its own. His eyes slimmed to tiny slits of fury. The King had baited him. All along it had been a trick.

"Bastard! You vile, cretinous bastard!" He lunged at his father, tossing an oak table between them, onto its end. Three of the guards, including François de Guise, rushed after him. Two drew rapiers barring Henri from the King. Guise held Henri's arms behind him so that he could not charge further. Henri's chest heaved with anger and he thrashed wildly trying to free himself. After several minutes, he stopped. He stood there with his arms behind his back leering at the King.

"I am all right," he said to Guise, beneath labored breath. François then loosened his grip. Henri looked at the King who was still grinning. "You are an old pathetic man . . . hardly worth the effort." Henri turned away from his father in disgust.

"Foolish boy! Do you really think she could ever care for you? Ha! You are a child! You are a means to an end with her. She has the Dauphin of France in her bed! She is using you to get what she can and when she has it—"

"Heartless bastard!" Henri whipped around and shot his father another hate-filled stare. "You could not possibly understand what is between us!"

"No? Wait and see if she does not make a fool of you! In the meanwhile, you will take the Duchesse de Longueville as your wife, or things will stay precisely as they are!"

Those were the King's final words. He then picked up the rebec and the bow as though he had not missed a note, and once again began to play. When he could sense that Henri had not moved, he glanced over at François de Guise.

"This meeting is over. Guise, see him out of here."

❧

THE CARDINAL DE LORRAINE sat on the opposite side of the salon, facing the King. When Henri had gone, he raised his head from the Book of Hours. He looked over at the King and twisted the tip of his neat white mustache. So, it was Diane de Poitiers who had so captivated the Dauphin. Who ever would have thought! He stifled a grin. My, my, that did change everything. Opportunity had taken a turn right before him and if he was wise, he would seize it. Slowly, he closed the book and placed it on a silver tray on the table beside his chair. As he rose and took the pectoral cross between his fingers, François cast the rebec at the fire and bolted to his feet.

"Damn him! Damn the boy!"

"He is young, Your Majesty. His head is easily turned. That too shall pass."

"They have made a mockery of me in my own Court! He cannot undo that!" François began to pace back and forth in the small area near the fireplace; quick, heavy steps. "But I . . . I will have the last laugh, in the manner of your Marie! I will give him a new wife, to be sure. But he will not get his whore!"

"If I may venture a thought," the Cardinal began carefully. "Having been witness myself to the depth of the Dauphin's conviction here today, it is my firm belief that a second marriage would only serve to complicate the situation that has developed."

François de Guise, from his post on the other side of the room, had heard the entire exchange. He turned his head sharply in the direction of the King as his uncle proceeded to undermine the foundation of the delicate plan that would see his sister, Marie, made Dauphine. He moved to speak but was stopped by the sight of his brother who, with one glance, rendered him still. They both waited and listened.

"So what would you have me do?" the King asked. "Sanction the trollop to marry my son after all?"

"On the contrary, Your Majesty. I would keep things precisely as they are. Give him time. She is a woman who has turned the head of a boy. It was not so long ago was it, my friend, for us to recall the artful and persuasive power of a mature courtesan?"

The King smiled a reminiscent smile. The Cardinal followed with his own chaste grin. As he smiled, the Cardinal de Lorraine could feel his nephews bristle from across the chasm of the vast salon. Charles pretended to play another round of cards with the King's daughter, Marguerite, yet the older and wiser Cardinal knew that nothing had been lost on either of his ambitious nephews. But this was not a game. This was the honor of the family. He paced himself, knowing his thoughts and his words must be exact. He inhaled deeply. He let it out. Yes, timing was everything.

"But, your Marie. What of the match for her?"

"Well, Your Majesty, we certainly must put matters of our kingdom over our own personal ambitions. It also occurs to me that we are missing the greater issue in all of this. Perhaps there needs to be a stronger persuasion toward an interaction between the Dauphin and Dauphine . . . for the duty of perpetuation's sake, of course. He certainly does not seem willing to fulfill his duties toward his wife without encouragement. That would seem to me a far more efficient means of getting an heir than that of re-placing a wife. After all, he does not have to love her. He must only bed her. If such a thing were possible; a limited interaction between husband and wife, then your son would have his para-mour, France would have its heir, and all would be satisfied."

"Oh, I do absolutely agree. Perhaps you know that she is not my favorite among us, but Madame Diane is a wise woman," grinned Anne d'Heilly, with a single knowing eyebrow raised. "I am confi-dent that once he goes to her and tells her that there is no way for them to marry, she shall encourage him in the proper direction."

"What makes you so certain?"

"Well, after all, when she realizes that the only alternative to the Dauphine is younger and more beautiful than she, there is little doubt that you shall have all of the assistance you require in getting an heir."

The King looked at his mistress and then back at the Cardinal. "Of course you are right. Both of you," he conceded. "All along I have been looking to unseat the poor unfortunate victim in this, when I should have gone to the source to rectify the problem."

His Majesty had once again begun to tire from the excitement. He was still not himself. His eyelids began to droop over sleepy eyes, and he slumped in the large velvet chair. Anne stood.

"Perhaps a rest would be in order, *mon amour?*"

"I do not need a rest! I am not a child," he scoffed.

"And if I join you?"

"Bribes! Always bribes, woman, to get what you want from me!"

"And such a lovely bribe it is," said the Cardinal with a democratic smile.

"DEAR LORD, UNCLE. Why the deuce did you do such a thing? With one word you have undone everything we have tried to do!"

The Cardinal de Lorraine walked along without shrinking from the accusation brought about by François, his eldest nephew. The three Guises walked in a line down the vaulted corridor that led away from the King's apartments. The Cardinal established their even pace as he fingered the gold cross that rested at the center of his very thin chest.

"Do you play chess, my boy?" he asked François.

"No."

"Well, perhaps you should learn."

"You can speak to me of games after all our work? You have ruined it; ruined everything, and just when Marie was so close."

"Nonsense. She was close only to alienating all of us. In chess you must look ahead, not just to the immediate move by which, at any given moment you are faced, but to your next move . . . and your next. His Majesty is ill, François. He will not live forever, and had you not allowed your ambition to rule your senses, you would recall that one day very soon, young Henri shall be King. Now, I ask both of you, can you truly imagine that we should propose our niece as an obstacle to the Dauphin; barring him further from the woman with whom at the moment he fancies himself madly in love? No, no, my boy! Diplomacy, like chess, is an art. No, the Guise shall render no barriers to that divorce!"

"But what about Marie? You as much as promised her this marriage."

"Ah, not to worry! She will make just as splendid a Queen for Scotland as she would have made for France, or have you forgotten that the Scottish King is once again in search of a wife? Ah yes, I see that you have. Remember, my boy, not just the immediate move, but the next and the next! Meanwhile, in this complex game, we shall begin casting our support discreetly toward the Dauphin. Only in rather minor ways at first, of course, so as not to upset the delicate balance between the old regime and the new. The goddess of the moon may well teach us all a few things about that."

This final comment made Charles, the second son of the house of Guise, the one who most closely understood his elder's ambitions, stop in the corridor and look up in utter surprise.

"What does mythology have to do with any of this?"

A sage smile passed across the Cardinal's face, his white beard glistening like snowflakes in the afternoon sun.

"You will remember, my boys, the goddess of the moon was Diana. You doubt me, I see. Never the matter, you will discover it for yourselves soon enough. Whatever you may believe now, listen well. There is a new moon rising, and when this Diana makes her ascent, and I fear it shall be soon, she will undoubtedly eclipse all with whom we now find favor. We must be very, very careful; very sure of ourselves. If we can accomplish these things, rest assured, as we have for a great many years, the mighty Guise shall remain favored by the highest house, no matter what the obstacles."

"But you told His Majesty that you believed the Dauphin's liaison with her to be a passing affair," said the elder nephew.

"I told His Majesty what he wanted to hear. Remember, my boys, for the sake of the family, first diplomacy. Always diplomacy."

IT WAS HOT and no one could recall it ever being so unbearable, even for August. The air was still, wet and unrelenting, and the flies were more numerous than the courtiers. Diane lay half naked on top of her bedcovers in a loose-fitting shift of white cambric cotton. There were two blue silk ties near her breasts. She touched one of them gently and lay her head back against the pillows.

"I cannot keep this child. How can I?"

She thought that she had whispered the words to herself, but with the sound of them, Hélène looked up from her place by the window, as though she had been roused from a nap. Diane smiled back at her. This had been an unbearably difficult pregnancy thus far, and now with the heat, she was not certain at all how she would manage the remaining three months.

She felt like a prisoner in her own body, just as she was a prisoner in the King's Court. As her feet continued to swell and her belly grew, she felt less certain of risking public ventures. It took far too much energy and effort to keep up the pretense, and if it should fail, not only she but Henri too would be ruined. Gradually, she began to turn down invitations to play cards with the Cardinal's niece, Marie de Guise, and she no longer attended even the King's weekly banquet.

It is an impossible situation. It is not safe for a child of ours in this world, in this climate that is so against Henri; so against the two of us. It will be a bastard and I . . . even worse. What is between us is called criminal by nearly everyone. How can a child ever rise above that? And how unfair of me to ask it to try.

All of her life Diane had been honored and respected. She had been born to a noble family; wife to a great man. Her blood was royal, owing to a connection her family claimed to Louis XI. Yet, since she had come to Court, she had fought daily to retain that respect, which thanks to Anne d'Heilly's mysterious disdain of her, little now survived. Her liaison with Henri, now widely known, threatened her standing further still. She had few friends at Court any longer . . . and many enemies. She knew that if she acknowledged this child, a child born of an adulterous affair with someone half her age, she would lose everything. She had seen it too many times to doubt it. She would be nothing more than a noble mistress . . . a courtesan.

But this child would face a worse fate than a loss of honor. He would be ridiculed. Maligned. The progeny of a scandal. Henri was not yet King. He did not have the power to protect his own child or his lover from that sort of scorn. Henri's pride over his impending fatherhood prevented her from discussing the matter further with him. Each time they were together, he was brimming with plans and ideas for his child's future. He said nearly every day that his greatest desire was to be a better father to his child than his own father had been to him. Diane had not been able to bring herself to destroy his happiness. Not yet. But she must consider it. Henri was required once again to return to the front. He would be at Court only a few days more. Plans must be made. Her future. The child's future . . . their child . . . She ran a hand across her swollen belly . . . yes it was *their* child, no matter what became of it.

There was a knock at the outer door. Diane looked over and nodded to Hélène as she covered herself with a sheet. Hélène rose from her chair by the open window to answer it. Henri stood before her in a formal pose, one hand at his side cupping the handle of his sword, the other thrust behind his erect back. After a moment, he passed her and came into the room.

"Leave us," he said.

When they were alone, he looked at Diane with distant, defeated eyes. "I cannot divorce her."

He tossed his cape onto the floor and began to pace the sitting room of her apartments. Diane came from her bed and saw the rage inside of him; the bitter frustration.

"He will have me marry Marie de Guise if I reject Catherine. It is all a game to him. Damn him! And you know I will have no other wife if it cannot be you!"

Once he had said the words, Diane turned from him, pushing down the weight of her own private disappointment. She walked toward the window that faced the garden. There was a long silence between them before she said anything. When she spoke it was without turning around.

"I want you to bed with your wife," she quietly said.

"I will not! That is an obscene suggestion when you know I can be with no one but you."

"You can, and you must."

Diane turned back around and leaned against the windowsill. Even across the room she could feel his surging power, the power he possessed over her. The firmly chiseled face. The muscled arms. It was difficult for her to look at him and not be weakened.

"How can you ask such a thing when I am sickened by the very thought?"

He moved swiftly toward her, wrapping her in his arms to assure her. She let him hold her for only a moment and then broke from his grasp. "But, I adore you, *M'amie*. I live for you . . . only for you!" he uttered with pleading clouded eyes.

She was resolute.

"You are Dauphin now," she said. "You have a responsibility to France to beget an heir."

"What of my responsibility to you?! To our child?"

"*Chéri,*" she said, reaching out to touch his bearded face. "Catherine is your wife. Pretending she does not exist will not rid you of your duty to her."

Henri did not listen. He clutched at her with an open, raw desire, as though forcing her now could somehow make the duty to that Italian stranger disappear. Catherine was the enemy, but it was Diane who felt his rage. When he kissed her, it was with rough thrusts, pushing his tongue inside her mouth, biting at her lips. She tried to pull away, but he clutched her more tightly, branding her mouth and neck with angry, tortured kisses. He was not gentle. His urgent passion had already overcome him. Bound by his arms, with his heart pounding against her tender breasts, her own desire began slowly to surge up. She surrendered, and molded to him. After a moment, he scooped her into his arms and carried her to the open bed. They fell together onto the white linen, joined by their arms and Henri's furious kisses. He raised her silky shift and tore away his stockings.

"It is so unfair . . ." he muttered, still kissing her. "I worship only you . . . only you! *Tu es ma vie, m'amie . . . toute ma vie . . .*" He kissed her throat and bit the soft fleshy skin of her breasts as he whispered the words and the despair into her soft shining hair.

"God help me, somehow, no matter what it takes, someday I shall make you my Queen!"

THEY LAY IN SILENCE on the rumpled sheets, the rest of the bedding tossed to the floor. The room was completely dark but a cool

breeze blew across their wet bodies from an open window near
the bed. The distant sounds of the banquet below washed across
them. They were naked now. Flesh against flesh. Henri was curled
up beside her, his thigh wrapped over hers, his head resting on her
breast, his hand tenderly stroking her round belly.

"I wonder what his name shall be . . ." he whispered. When
Diane did not reply, he looked up, thinking that perhaps she had
fallen asleep. She was perfectly still and staring up at the canopy
above them.

"Plans must be made," she said in a voice of resolution delivered just above a whisper.

"What sort of plans?"

"For the child."

"He . . . or she is our child," Henri smiled. "His future is secure."

Diane sat up and leaned against the carved oak headboard.
Henri reached up and took a long strand of her blond hair between his fingers but he could not make her smile.

"Henri . . . I will not be the mother of a bastard child. I could
not live with the guilt of what he would be forced to endure on my
account. This child was conceived in love. In that, he deserves more
than you and I can give him. He deserves respect. The way things
are here with you and the King . . . myself and the Duchesse
d'Etampes . . . he will never have that if the world is to know he is
our child."

Henri's smile faded. "What are you saying?"

"I am going home to Anet. When I return to Court, to you,
and I hope with all my heart that you will still want me . . . he can
have all of the titles and honors you wish to bestow upon him as
your son, but on this I will not bend; no one can ever know that he
is our child."

HENRI CHARGED HIS HORSE through the thick woods around
Fontainebleau, but he felt a million miles from the thundering
hooves and the churning dust beneath him.

The plan would need to be executed without flaw for it to succeed. As Henri sat in disbelief that night in Diane's darkened

bedchamber, she weaved for him the elements of an intricate deception. In the intervening months, she had successfully negotiated the marriage of her daughter, Françoise, to Robert de La Marck. Her presence now was required at Anet to supervise the details of that union. It would be a convenient explanation for her abrupt departure, one that would go unquestioned by the Court. Meanwhile, she proposed that Henri should confess to the King a battlefield liaison with a village peasant. The King was to be told that the girl was now pregnant by him. She reminded Henri that as offspring of the Dauphin of France, the King would insist the child be brought to Court and raised with the other royal children. He would also predictably insist that the child's mother be installed in a good convent to avoid further embarrassment to Catherine. This would remove from them the fictitious paramour. Tales of extramarital children, and the need to make adjustments for them, were not new at the Court of France.

"I wish there was another way," she had said, as he had listened in horror to the plan. "But I cannot allow this child . . . our child, to be born into this kind of danger. In England they are still calling Anne Boleyn's daughter 'the little bastard.' At least this way, without me . . . he, or she, will have half a chance at a respectable life."

There were responsibilities. There was honor. Despite his protestations to her that night in her chamber, Henri knew that she was right. He also know that he must have a child with Catherine. France was vulnerable without a legitimate heir. When he was not with Diane, near her . . . beside her, he could see the obligation; see his responsibilities. But he was obsessed with this woman who meant life to him.

He had agreed to her pleas only because he loved her, but even now the prospect haunted him. By her plan, the child could be near to them both at Court and legitimatized as a natural child of France. Natural children, as bastards were delicately called, were an incidental element of royal life. The King had several. Infidelity was an expected course of events among nobility where marriages most often represented political alliances, not matches of the heart.

As he wound through the meadow and past the village, pushing his horse ever harder, he thought how cruel, once again, fate had been to him; as though he were a joke; a toy whose life was to be bandied about for no other reason but for the mere enjoyment of a mighty god. To have given him this woman, the woman he adored. To have given him her love. Now, a child, and yet being made to promise never to acknowledge to another living soul that the child was not only his, but theirs! What purpose could there be in such a fate? Who could find pleasure in such cruel irony? How, in the name of God, could he find the strength to overcome it?

Henri pulled the braided reins and stopped near the river in a meadow thickly carpeted with green grass and bluebells, his chest heaving from the exertion. He tasted the salty tears on his lips; felt the heavy pain of futility. Then the rage began to fill him like Vesuvius and he sprung from his horse. He drew his dagger and began to pace back and forth as though stalking imaginary prey. In his rage his face went purple; his body rigid.

"Never! Do you hear?!" He tipped his head heavenward and howled, full of anguish. "Damn you! Damn you all! You may have forced me into this hell! You may force me to stay here! But I have survived with one last shred of dignity and, by God in his Heaven, I shall not bed her! That one thing you can never . . . never make me do!!"

Book Three
Autumn 1537

A Prince ought to have no other aim or thought, nor select anything else for study, than war and its rules and discipline; for this is the sole art that belongs to him who rules.

— MACHIAVELLI

23

THROUGH THE HOT SUMMER MONTHS, the relentless battle between the King and the Emperor flared again. Henri returned to his place beside Montmorency at the end of August while Diane went to Anet to await the birth of their child. She would send word to him, she had said, when it was time.

Summer turned to fall with no sign of an end to the siege. Despite his personal quest for peace, Montmorency pushed on in the name of the King, forcing his way along the Val di Susa. More towns fell. More death. More destruction. The garrison of Savigliano. Pinerolo and Turin. The King himself had followed behind with the rest of the army, against the ardent pleadings of his sister and his mistress. He had joined Montmorency for the taking of the Piedmont region, as far as Montferrat, the prize at the border between France and Italy. François had wanted to spare nothing for this assault as the brass ring of Milan, not far beyond, dangled glittering before him.

But the heavy financial burdens of war on the country, and his own failing health, dampened the King's spirit. By November he was tired again. He was not the same relentless war horse who had claimed Milan for France twenty-three years before.

So, as the burgundy-gold fall leaves blew aimlessly across the courtyard, François returned home to Fontainebleau. Home to his Anne. He was tired of the struggle. Of the deaths. Of the meaningless war that seemed to have no end and was leaching his country dry of its money, its patriotism, and its pride. As he returned this time, he had so little to show for all of the losses that ambition had cost him. The Dauphin, his François, was dead, His daughter, Madeleine, too. Provence lay in ruin from the siege, the royal coffers were nearly dry, and the troops were worn down. There was little chance now that he could ever regain Milan by force. For the first time in years, François began to consider more than an armistice; a legitimate truce with the Emperor. Much to his surprise, he was advised that the Emperor was equally receptive to such an accord. Montmorency was dispatched immediately to Leucate along with the Cardinal de Lorraine, to pursue the idea of peace.

"NEWS FROM ENGLAND, Your Majesty, " announced Guillaume Poyet, as he strode into the royal apartments waving a crumpled communiqué.

Poyet was the newly named Chancellor of France who had received his post through his connection with Montmorency upon the death of Antoine du Bourg, earlier that year.

"King Henry requests a selection of French brides be sent to him in England, Your Majesty, and his Ambassador suggests that the King would not be opposed if Marie de Guise were among the contenders."

François was sitting for a portrait in his private drawing room at Fontainebleau. Clouet, the official Court painter, daubed the canvas with short strokes and continued to admonish the Sovereign. If he continued to fidget, the lighting across his face was sure to be ruined. On the other side of the chamber, near a long casement window, the young Archbishop de Rheims studied a chess move against him just made by the King's third son, Charles.

François scoffed at the news. He thought of Henry VIII. Queen Jane Seymour had not been dead a month. Three wives and all of them gone. One divorced. One beheaded. The other dead in childbirth. A selection of brides from France indeed!

"Our good brother is a pig!" he snapped. "We do not send French women for the choosing; not even for a King! As to the Cardinal de Lorraine's niece, you may inform the English Ambassador that We have approved her marriage to Our Scottish brother, James."

François stood and began to cough from the exertion. A steward rushed in with a goblet of wine; another with a silver jeweled walking stick. The portrait sitting was over. Clouet said nothing but began packing up his brushes and oils as the King brushed past him.

The Archbishop ran a hand through his full blond hair and smiled the sharp Guise smile. He watched as the King's son moved a knight across the marble chessboard and pretended not to notice the exchange between the Sovereign and his Chancellor. So it had been decided . . . his sister a Queen! This was the first he had heard of a confirmation. He knew his uncle would be pleased. He must be told at once!

At the Cardinal Lorraine's private instructions before his departure to Narbonne to help negotiate peace, Marie's name was discreetly withdrawn from the list. She would not be a replacement for the Dauphine of France. Following the confrontation between the King and Henri, discussions of a divorce between he and Catherine were also discontinued.

A discreet period of time passed. In October, Marie had been formally proposed as a new bride for Scotland. Charles de Guise knew that King James was pleased with the choice of his sister. Their uncle's spies had intercepted a communiqué from the Scottish Monarch. He had welcomed her as replacement for the Princess Madeleine. François needed to maintain the new bond with Scotland. There would be no impediment to a wedding. Marie would be Queen of Scotland. Charles would one day become a cardinal, and his brother, François, the most ill appointed of the three, had gained the confidence of the future King. He had worked that like a true Guise! The house of Guise was, as their uncle had foretold, rising in the shadow of the goddess of the moon.

He moved a piece again across the chessboard. This time it was checkmate. Prince Charles scoffed at his opponent's victory and stood on the other side of the gaming table. First he stomped his foot, then turned his lip out in a childish pout. He leered at the Archbishop and then advanced toward the King. François slapped his son's back and they smiled at one another.

"Oh, enough of all this!" he declared. "Let us have a game of *jeu de paume*. Is the match set?"

"Yes, Father," answered Charles. "You know it is the Dauphin who has agreed to challenge me."

"Ah, so it is. He is awfully good, you know."

"But I am better. I can win, Father, I can!"

They embraced and then François smiled and held the boy at arm's length. "Of course you can. After all, I am unrivaled on the court, and you, Charles, are most definitely your father's son."

HENRI WAS IN PRISON.

The Court of France was his cell; the King, his captor. He had been back at Court little more than a week and yet the prison of his mind was far worse than any Spanish captivity that he could recall; and it was Diane de Poitiers who held the key. She would not see him; *could not* had been her words. *It is not safe,* she had said. *Until just before the child comes. Then I will send for you.*

Each day stretched on into eternity. Each night he met his own private hell. *How was she? How was their child?* He was taunted. Tortured by his own thoughts that something had gone wrong. *I must see her. I will go to her. No! I must wait. I will wait, if only because she has asked.*

Henri paced the length of the royal *jeu de paume* court waiting for his brother and his brother's entourage. The fence around the court slowly lined with courtiers, dignitaries and nobles who found entertainment in the personal rivalry between the two brothers. Henri disliked Charles. He found him arrogant and spoiled. Even though they were the King's two remaining sons, they had never become close. There was the three years between them. And Charles had always been spoiled. The last son; *l'enfant terrible.* Henri detested that; envied that. The rift between them had only increased after the Dauphin's death. Charles was now the King's favorite. This match was really nothing more than a public exhibition to display that preference. It would be an arena for the favored son to please the master. Charles had whined and begged Henri for days for such a challenge. After their father, they were the two best players at Court, Charles said; unbeatable, he said. Henri knew he could defeat his brother playing with his eyes closed.

But since he had been forced to return from the front with a truce in sight, Henri had been seized by an insurmountable melancholy, which in Diane's absence, only violent exercise could quell. Beating Charles in front of the King would serve to stave off the depth of his despair for a little while.

Jacques de Saint-André stood on the other side of the net with his hands on his hips. He had tried volleying the ball to Henri, to ready him for the match, but he continued to miss it. The Dauphin's mind was elsewhere. He paced the length of the court. His head was down and his brow was lowered into a scowl. Something was wrong. She was not with him, and yet he knew. There was a bond, not physical or even mental. Something higher. Mystical. When he was not with her, he knew things. He knew if she was ill, or sad. He felt it. If she was in trouble. He felt it. Henri. Diane. Since the day that they had met, he was at a loss to know where one ended and the other began.

"Your brother shall be here any moment. Please, you must concentrate."

"I cannot do this!" Henri announced, not looking at anyone and not certain if anyone had heard. When he tossed the racquet to the ground, whispers rose up among the crowd. Jacques jumped over the net and ran toward Henri.

"Your Highness cannot leave now. The match is set."

"I must go!"

"But what will everyone think if you forfeit now?"

"To hell with the match! Something is wrong. I know it!"

"Madame Diane?"

"I do not know. I only know that I must go to her, and quickly!"

DIANE JERKED VIOLENTLY and rolled onto her side beneath the bedcovers. Beads of sweat formed on her brow and above her lip. She tried to relax; tried to slow her breathing, to try and end the torturous pain pulsing through her body. She lay bracing herself against the next spasm, rigid with fear. Hélène sat beside her squeezing her hand.

"Madame, please, just another breath. Just one more." She held her own breath to help pace Diane. But something was wrong with

the child. Diane could feel it. It had not been like her other preg-
nancies, and this was not like the other births. This child would
surely die, or it was going to kill her first. She had known the risk
of having this child at her age. It had fought her from the very beginning. Almost as though it was struggling for dominance of her
body. The violent jabs. The sickness. The bleeding. He would not
come into this world easily. Her fevered mind played tricks on her.
It moved to the image of Queen Jane. She had been told only that
morning that King Henry in England had lost his wife to childbirth. She considered the irony. *Poor Queen Jane is dead,* she had heard
them whispering in the hall outside her door. *Died in childbirth.* She
was supposed to have been asleep. Was it a sign? England's Queen
had been half her age. The clock struck six. A deep, stabbing pain
shook her. She stifled her screams by clutching the bedcovers.

"Have you called for His Highness?" she gasped, forgetting that
she had asked the same question only moments ago; and an hour
before that.

"Yes, of course, Madame," Hélène patiently replied. She looked
up at the midwife who stood at the foot of the bed with her red,
wrinkled hands at her face. She was an old woman from the village
who had spent most of her life delivering babies; and even more
time burying them. She was worried, and she took no pains to
hide her concern. The labor was taking far too long. There was
little else she could do now but pace and pray.

THE CLOCK STRUCK TWELVE.

It was midnight and Diane was weak. The child had nearly
sucked the last ounce of strength from her body, and still it would
not come. She lay beneath the crimson and gold covers on her
bed, her face ashen; eyes rolling back in her head, almost to a
close. She muttered to herself, whimpered and then lay quiet for a
time, only to begin it all again when the pain returned. Pain and
cessation. It went on with the heartless drone of a pendulum. By
two, it was pain that ground and tore and left her sweat-drenched
and pleading for her own death.

Through it all, Hélène had not left her side. She mopped her brow with a cool cloth and in her other hand held a rosary as she whispered prayers.

"I cannot go on . . ."

Hélène was rocked from her prayers. "Oh no, Madame! You must not say that. You must!"

Diane's maid bolted from the stool beside the bed and squeezed her hand more firmly. The midwife advanced from the foot of the bed and tore back the heavy covers. She placed her hands onto Diane's swollen belly to feel the placement of the child. Hélène ran a clean cloth through the white ceramic basin on the stand near the bed. She looked back at the midwife who muttered to herself as she continued to move her hands.

"She is going to be all right . . . isn't she?"

The midwife placed the covers back over Diane and shook her head.

"If it doesn't come soon," she said, gnashing her teeth, "neither of them has a chance."

IT WAS JUST BEFORE DAWN when the echoed thunder of galloping hooves broke across the cobbled stones of the old keep at Anet. The white mare snorted pillows of air as Henri brought him to a halt before the main entrance. He left the horse unattended, and in the dull blue-gray of morning, ran into the main vestibule of the chateau. He raced up the circular stairs without taking a moment to assess where he was going. Past the main hall he ran, to a smaller arched corridor that he knew would lead to the bedchambers.

"Diane!" he called out as he ran, his cape fanning out behind him. He opened one door and then the next, shouting her name, "Diane! Diane!" The commotion brought Mademoiselle Terre Noire, Diane's housekeeper, from behind a closed chamber door, her arms loaded with bedding. She did not recognize Henri as the future King of France.

"Monsieur, I beg your pardon, but Madame is indisposed . . ." she said and protectively barred the door.

"Where is she?" he charged.

Before she could reply, he leapt at the woman, toppling her to her knees. Disarmed by his force, the woman managed only to point weakly with a crooked finger toward a large curved door behind her. Without knocking, he flung it open and burst inside. Dawn had not yet broken. The rest of the room before him was dark except for one corner that blazed burnt umber from the fire. At the sight of him, Hélène bolted from her chair beside the bed. She did not bow to him or acknowledge his true identity, because of the midwife who was still at the foot of the bed.

"Thank God you've come," she said, touching his arm. Her cheeks were pale, tear-stained. Her round eyes were bloodshot from lack of sleep. Henri looked over at Diane. She moaned as the midwife touched her.

"What is it? What is wrong?"

"It is the child. The midwife says it is turned the wrong way and she is not of a proper knowledge to take it from the belly."

Henri rushed toward the bed. "Can you not do something?"

"I am sorry, monsieur, but she is in God's hands now," the old woman replied.

"God's hands?" he repeated the words. He looked at the two helpless faces before him; one young, one old. Henri flung himself onto the bedside and took Diane's hand. He squeezed it to try and rouse her. She did not know he was there.

"Hélène, bring me a cool cloth!" he said and ran his hand across her forehead, brushing back the wet curls of hair from her face.

"I am sorry, *chéri*," she whispered, her eyes opened to a half dazed stare. She tried to smile. "I am sorry but . . . I can go no further."

"Of course you can!" he said, pushing a smile past his own worried expression. "You must! I will not go on without you." He pressed her hand to his chest. "We can do it! You know that together we can do anything!"

Diane closed her eyes again. She was tired. The dark circles beneath her eyes. The shallow cheeks. She was bathed in perspiration and her skin was white; the white of death. He forced the thought of her death from his mind. On the table next to the bed was Hélène's rosary. Blue-speckled beads. A silver crucifix. Henri took it in his other hand and closed his eyes.

So then I am to be punished. Punished for Catherine. Punished for not loving her. He shook his head. He had never been able to see Catherine for the sight of Diane. She was his obsession. She was the only thing in the world. *I cannot lose her. Without her I am nothing. I am lost. Yes, God, I will do anything. Anything!* In that moment it was clear what must be done. What he must do. He gripped the rosary tighter between his thumb and forefinger. *Let them live! God in Heaven, I beseech you, let them live and Catherine shall have me . . . and a child . . . I shall make her my wife in more than our names!*

In that moment when one promises anything to change the course of fate, Henri made his pact with God; a pact that he knew would change his life and Diane's forever.

As THE GRAY MUTED light of the winter morning filtered through the leaded panes of the east window, Diane delivered Henri's child. A daughter. Sobbing without shame as he took the screaming, bloody infant from the midwife, Henri wrapped her tiny body in a blanket and took her to his chest with trembling hands. Diane looked up at him with a weary smile and a half-dazed look of contentment. In the end, the child had come without the aid of a surgeon, and everyone, including the midwife, had been mystified.

Henri brought the child to his lips and kissed the soft down on the top of her head. Hélène wiped the tears from her own cheeks as she and Mademoiselle Terre Noire wrapped their arms around one another.

"Dear Lord, thank you," Hélène whispered.

They backed away from the bed and retired with the midwife to chairs near the fire. After a moment, Henri placed the baby girl onto Diane's bare breast. Almost instantly she ceased crying and opened her eyes. They were blue; the same deep blue as her mother's. Henri looked in awe at them as Diane placed the child to her nipple and let her nurse. Henri sat down on the edge of the bed.

"If I had lost you," he whispered, "my life would have been over. I just never thought I would come so close."

❦

THE CHILD WAS BLOND like her mother, with the same wide blue eyes. For the two weeks of Diane's convalescence, she was rarely out of her father's arms and they were rarely out of Diane's company. When Diane was strong enough, they began to take walks around the grounds. One morning, two days before they were to return to Court, they walked out across the vast lawn, quilted winter white, their gloved hands joined and their heavy leather shoes crunching in the thick layers of freshly fallen snow. In his other arm, Henri held his daughter, burrowed beneath the folds of his black velvet cape. Here at Anet, they were a family. There was nothing in the world Henri wanted more. There could never be another time again like this; time with just the three of them. He took in a deep breath and let the cold winter air sting his nostrils as he tossed back his head.

"Oh! It is beautiful here!" said Henri with a wide-mouthed smile. "So far from all of it; so far from all of them." He squeezed her hand tighter as they walked down the few steps that led to a courtyard. Past a frozen pond. Past a stone lion perched on a pedestal, forever posed just ready to roar as the snow fell around him. From the bottom step Henri spun around and kissed her nose, which was red with the cold. It made him smile.

"Ah! I feel so good here. And with you beside me, I am complete."

Henri's words made her think of Montgommery. Another winter. Another lifetime. She thought of relating how much he had detested Anet; wanted her to sell it. She was so glad Henri felt as she did. But as the words formed on her lips she thought better of telling him. For all of his growth and his maturity, he was still young. Still volatile. Montgommery brought back a time between she and Henri that she was not anxious to recall. It had meant pain and uncertainty for them both.

"Wherever I am, I think I shall always want to return here," she heard herself say instead.

"Then indeed you shall. It is your home. I have never known a place like this. A real home. All of the King's palaces are nothing

more than showpieces for the monarchy. But this . . ." He pulled
away from Diane and opened his arm to frame the scene. "This is
truly a home . . . and it is one that I shall be honored to share for
as long as you will have me."

They walked down along the frozen pond and Henri lifted the
blanket to peer in at his daughter. He ran a finger along her cheek
and covered her back over with the cape.

"She'll need a name, you know," he said.

"I had not thought about it."

"You know, there can only be one name."

She looked at him.

"Her name is . . . it must be, Diane."

"Henri, that would be impossible! The King will know—"

"The King will know only that I adore you. He can make of
that what he will, but he knows that we have long been friends. It
would be most natural for me to do it." She shifted her head from
side to side as though she were looking for someone. Her brows
arched with the look of hesitation. She took in a breath and then
looked back at him.

"I think we risk too much."

"Please . . . do this for me," he pressed. His dark eyes glistened
in the reflection of the snow. "If she can have nothing else of her
mother, then I want her to have this one connection with you.
Please."

ENCIRCLED BY AN ENTOURAGE of royal escorts and covered with
a canopy of magenta silk, Henri and Diane rode beside Hélène
and a wet nurse through Touraine. A cutting winter wind slashed
against them as they wound their way slowly up the private cobblestone road that led to Amboise.

Hélène held the swaddled infant in her arms, covered in a tapestried blanket. The child's head and body were wound tightly in
white cloth to help keep her warm. Beside her rode a wet nurse
from the village of Anet waiting to fulfill her duty, to feed the royal
child. She was brought along at this early stage to help perpetuate
the ruse that the child had no mother. A message had been dis-

patched to Court. A child, it was said, named Diane had been born. The issue of Henri, Dauphin of France and a Piedmontese peasant named Filippa Duca. The child had been conducted to the Chateau d'Anet where Madame Diane had graciously received the Dauphin and his entourage. She was now accompanying him on his return.

The small party was trailed by the Dauphin's personal infantry of guards who rode in precise military cadence. As the gates were opened and the entourage passed through them into the courtyard, the deception would officially begin with Montmorency. The Grand Master, now the celebrated Lieutenant-General, stood firm-footed in the Gothic arch of the doorway. He was flanked by François de Guise, Charles de Brissac and Jacques de Saint-André. The King had sent no one of his own entourage down to meet his son. But these bold slights no longer affected him. Henri had long ago grown accustomed to his father's indifference.

"Are you absolutely certain that this is what you want?"

He whispered the words to Diane as he brought his horse to a halt with a tightening of the reins.

"No, Henri, I shall never be certain. But to protect that precious life, I know of no other way."

Saint-André and Brissac smiled across the courtyard at them. Guise waved an eager hand out from beneath his cape. Montmorency, the more stoic, stood motionless in a long ermine vest and shirt of gold silk with his hand behind his back.

A wave of fear passed through Diane as she looked at him. Time had only served to sharpen his features. The full dark hair that was once only touched with gray had now been consumed by silver waves. His appearance was cold and hard, like steel. He was the great unmoving General.

Jacques and François took the small flight of steps two at a time and came out into the courtyard, but Montmorency maintained his place beside the door. Henri took Diane into his arms to help her down. He was gentle with her; tender well past the point of friendship. The exchange between them was not lost on Montmorency.

So it has begun again, he thought, looking out at them. *Scandalous!* It was not so much that he minded the boy taking a paramour; that was inevitable. It was simply the particular paramour of whom he disapproved. She was too beautiful, too ambitious and far too bright to really care for a morose young man like Henri. But what was worse, when Montmorency was so inclined to admit it to himself, he believed that she threatened his own standing with the Dauphin, a position that had taken him a lifetime to cultivate.

He looked at her again, standing in the courtyard, whispering something to Hélène, who was once again holding the child. He thought that Diane de Poitiers looked almost regal in her black velvet gown, the décolletage low and pressed flat against her breasts, her neck draped with elegant pearls. Imagine, a courtesan accompanying her lover with another woman's child! She was shameless! Would she stop at nothing to possess the Dauphin completely? Montmorency stifled an urge to throttle her to death. Instead, he pushed forth an uncomfortable smile and moved on down the three stone stairs into the courtyard with the others. Henri advanced toward Montmorency at a half-running pace.

"Welcome home, Your Highness," Montmorency offered, in an appropriately humble tone. The two old friends embraced. Henri held the General close to his chest and slapped his back affectionately.

"Oh, it is good to see you!" he said with a jubilant smile. He pulled Montmorency out at arm's length to look at him and the two men smiled at one another. After a moment, Henri turned toward Hélène, who stood behind him with the child.

"Monty, my friend, may I present to you my daughter," he asked, and offered up the tightly bound infant. Montmorency faltered. He had eleven children of his own; four sons and seven daughters, but still he was awkward with them. His function had always been to beget them, not to handle them. Nurturing made him uncomfortable. It was women's work. Masking his reluctance, Montmorency leaned over and pulled back the blanket from around the child's face, as one might peer at a delicate piece of art. He was met by a blond wave of hair and deep blue eyes. The smile began to form on his lean lips before he looked up. When he did, he found Diane standing back discreetly beside Hélène and Saint-André, but her face was full of tender concern.

"She is a beauty, Your Highness," he finally said to Henri, and then took the infant into his own arms with such swiftness that it made Diane flinch. He brought the baby to his lips and kissed her head. Again he looked up at Diane to see if it had affected her. "Do you not think she is beautiful, Madame?" he asked with half a smile.

"I think she is exquisite . . . General."

Between them it was always a contest. A subtle matching of wills. To Diane's dismay, it was never anything that Henri could see. Or wanted to see.

"And have you a name for the child?"

Henri smiled, his body straightened with pride as he put his hand to his chest.

"Her name is Diane. I have named her after my good friend . . . Madame Diane."

Montmorency's smile became a sneer before the words were fully spoken. "Such a grand tribute," he said. The sneer widened.

"It was at the Dauphin's insistence," said Diane.

"I am certain that it was . . . Madame." As he said the last word, his eyes met with hers. They were the cold evil eyes of knowing. Henri broke the tension by pushing Montmorency inside with a tender arm across his back.

"Come," he said with a smile of contentment that Montmorency had rarely seen. "The child needs to get inside out of the cold."

They walked through the double doors and down the first long corridor before either of them said another word. Diane dallied behind with Hélène and Jacques, intentionally distancing herself from them.

"So tell me, Monty, did you and the Cardinal de Lorraine bring news of a truce with your return to Court?"

"I am afraid that God has not, as yet, seen fit to grant it."

"What is at issue?"

"Your brother's marriage. The Emperor has agreed to offer his daughter as part of the deal, with Milan as a dowry."

"But that is exactly what the King has wanted."

"Yes, but now it has become a matter of semantics. It would seem that they cannot agree on when Milan shall be handed over to France in your brother's name. The Emperor offers three years."

"And the King does not agree?"

"Through the claim of his Grandmother, Valentina Visconti, as you know, His Majesty considers Milan his own. He does not feel he should be made to wait for what he believes is rightfully his. The Emperor knows what a point of contention it is for his rival. I suspect at the moment it is a war of wills between them."

"And so the King would lose it all to a detail so minor as time?"

"It is more than a minor detail to the King, Your Highness. It is his honor that is challenged. You must remember he has lost the dream of Italy once before to the same arrangement; by the terms of your own marriage."

"He also lost a son by those terms. But then that has never mattered much to him, except when the son was my elder brother, François."

They climbed a wide flight of stone stairs that curved into another hall. They reached the end of another endless tapestry-lined corridor. Diane's apartments were here. She wished they were anywhere but here now that she would be forced to leave her child for the first time with the suspicious General looking on. After an uncertain moment, Saint-André gently took the child from Hélène.

"I shall see her installed in the nursery, Your Highness," he said to the Dauphin. Henri nodded. Diane reached a tentative arm toward the child; then drew back. It was a reflex. She would learn. She must. For the good of the child. After a moment, Saint-André turned away and walked on down the corridor with the wet nurse and the baby. For Diane, as for Henri, after this moment things would never be the same. Now, there could be no turning back.

"AH! SO THEN, you find the courage to return once again!"

Anne d'Heilly said the words to herself. She smiled her Cheshire-cat smile and then lay back on the green velvet-covered daybed inside her apartments. Beside her, on a small inlaid table, lay a tooled-leather volume of Latin verse; the first element of her strategy. She reached over and ran her fingers along the smooth grain of leather.

"Dear Vouté, you are such a genius," she purred. "Oh, my dear, dear Madame, what a collection of surprises await your return!"

Diane de Poitiers had misjudged her competition. Returning here was an open act of defiance. Ah, but then she had been warned. Anne reeled with the poison of anger at the thought of her rival. The ever-present breeding. The haughty air. As though merely by the fact of her birth, she was entitled to anything she desired. She could not have the King by direct means, so now she was using his son to get to him. Opportunist! Calculating courtesan! *Well, my dear, not in my Court!*

Her sister Louise and her other attendants would soon be here to dress her. Anne pulled herself from the daybed and advanced to a carved armoire. Her nightdress whispered along the floor, and her heart beat wildly with excitement. She pulled back one of the ivory inlaid doors, and from a drawer she took a slip of paper. It was a document in the hand of the Chancellor of France; a *lettre de cachet,* an order under the King's private seal. She need only skim the words, which by now she knew by heart, for this was her ace.

"Royal Order . . . confiscate . . . Chateau d'Anet . . . property of the Crown . . ."

She tipped her head back and laughed a shrill biting laugh. Yes, it was all so perfect. She had only to wait. It would not be long now.

24

D AMN HER!" Diane raged as she tossed the order to the floor. "She has tricked me, insulted me and slandered my name. But in this she goes too far!"

It was just past dawn. Diane had returned to her apartments from her swim in the icy river below the chateau. The sky's colors came in through the window in a breeze of pale pink and orange. The muted light cast a shadow on Diane as she stood, hair dripping, clad in a black dressing gown. The message that had been left beneath her door now drifted across the floor on the wings of a breeze through the open window. Hélène bent down to pick it up. She glanced at it discreetly, catching only a few words. "Anet. Property of the Crown." She did not need to read more. Anne d'Heilly was trying to take away Diane's home.

"Can she do that, Madame?"

"It appears she is going to try." Diane paced the length of the large vaulted drawing room, wringing her hands.

"What are we to do?"

"We will fight her, of course. Her games are one thing, but Anet is my husband's heritage! My children's birthright! And I will not give it up easily to this hateful woman who seems so bent on revenge!"

There was a knock at the door. Diane gathered her composure by brushing a hand across her face. Hélène helped her slip on a robe. She took several deep breaths to steady herself.

"That will be the Dauphin," Diane said. "You must not breathe a word of this to him."

"But Madame, surely he can help."

"No! He has his own problems with the King and the Dauphine. This is my responsibility and I alone shall see to it. Please, my friend, not a word."

Hélène slipped through one door as Henri came in another. He cast down his rapier and gloves and rushed toward Diane. As he held her, she felt the crush of velvet; the pounding of his heart. He smelled of sweat and Italian musk. She knew, because she knew him as she knew herself. He had finally done it. And she was glad of it. Catherine was his wife. He needed to give her a child. It was not easy for her to think of him with Catherine in that way; her fleshy, aromatic body rolling beneath his, but it needed to be done, and yes . . . she was relieved.

"It is all right, *chéri*," she whispered. "Truly, it is."

"But if I should ever lose you because of her . . ."

"You shall lose me by your will alone; never any way but that."

"I shall never will it! So it will only be death that shall part us."

"Only death," she repeated, sinking further into his grasp.

Now she was glad of his obsession with her. And it had become an obsession. She was glad that someone had come to love and need her as much as he did. There was security here in his arms. For her own part, she loved him more than she dared admit to herself, especially to him. There were so many women eager to take her place in his heart, in his bed. And he was so very young that she could not risk telling him. She could not bear to be that vulnerable. But looking at him now, looking into his desperate eyes so full of need for her, she knew that he loved her.

After another moment, he pulled away and flung himself into a chair near the fire. Diane watched as he rested his elbow on the arm of the chair and covered his face with his hand.

"There is something more," he said. Diane knelt at his feet.

"Please tell me."

"In His Majesty's effort to punish me, presumably for you, he has cut my personal annuity by nearly two thirds. I've only just discovered it."

"Apparently they had surprises in store for us both," she whispered.

"He says he will no longer pay for a staff separate from that of the Dauphine. If I want separate accommodations, I am to find separate funds. God! It is not bad enough that he commands me to lie with her, now he is hoping to force me to live with her as well!"

"What do you want to do?"

"What I want is to be with you!"

"Then let me give you the amount of your annuity."

"That is out of the question! I could not take money from you."

"Then we shall call it a loan. Please, Henri, let me do this for you. For us. You have given me so much already; your love, your devotion, a friendship when everyone else was against me. Besides, Louis left me more than I shall ever need, and once you are King you can pay it back."

Henri pulled himself from the chair and knelt beside her. He took both of her hands in his own and raising them to his lips, kissed each of them in turn. Then he looked at her with eyes glowing with devotion.

"Your kindness and love is a gift to me; a gift from a God who I thought despised me, until you came into my life." He touched her cheek with his lips. "I shall never be able to repay you for all that you have given me . . . but I promise you, Diane, as God is my witness, once I am King, I shall spend the rest of my life trying to be worthy of you."

NO MATTER HOW he shifted in his seat, the King could not stop the vague ache which plagued his bloated and beleaguered body. The velvet cushion beneath him was soft; too soft, and it pressed through to the chair's oak frame beneath him, sending a shooting pain up his spine. He shifted again. A young page rushed in and slipped another cushion behind his back. Again the King shifted, this time to settle the cushion.

His council, now seated around him, had been arguing for the better part of an hour; yet he had heard only a few random words of their heated debate. While they discussed the movement toward peace with the Emperor, François found himself strangely plunged into recollections of the past; recollections of his mother. Oh, how he still missed her. If it had not been for her ambitions, he certainly would not have become King. He had depended on her completely. She had been the only real woman in his life. She had ruled him with the single-minded power of a lover. Now she was dead. So too were the Dauphin François, and Madeleine; his pale beautiful lily. *What would you say now, Mother . . . oh, I do so wonder. Would you still encourage me to keep up the fight? Is Milan worth what it has cost me? My son and my daughter . . . myself?*

Once, it had been his sole obsession. King of France. King of Italy. He had wanted to be Emperor. Charles V had stolen that dream from him by bribing the Pope with a larger sum. Stolen dreams. Dwindling fantasies. Now he wanted nothing more than to wall himself into the safety of his precious garden at Fontainebleau; to watch his roses bloom and to grow old beside his Anne. But while there was still a chance, the slightest hope . . .

He gazed across the table. They were all there. All of the key players in this petty game of greed and ambition. Deceptively humble Annebault. Cunning Chabot. The ingratiating Cardinal de Lorraine. The Cardinal de Tournon. Montmorency, now elevated further to Constable Montmorency. The King's mind wandered to the night before. The grand announcement naming his old friend Constable of France as a reward for his military victories. And then there was Montmorency's face, almost contemptuous, as he sat beside the Dauphin and Diane de Poitiers.

Already the King had begun to regret the decision. Monty's allegiance had been swayed. He had seen it. The entire Court had seen it. His favor was with the Dauphin now . . . with *that woman*. But it was too late. He had proposed him. Parliament had approved him. No, he would not change his mind. Not now. But he would be watching.

"What have we today, Monsieur Poyet?" the King suddenly asked the Chancellor. His tone was dry and it cut off all conversation of the military strategy, which at that moment was at the pinnacle of a heated debate quite likely to have turned violent. An echoed silence followed. Annebault gazed up at the tapestry near the door, studying it as though for the first time. Chabot shuffled a selection of papers. Montmorency poured himself a goblet of water as the Cardinal de Lorraine dipped his pen into the silver ink well. He made a note to himself as Bourg looked up at the King.

"Your docket is full, Sire. You are set to discuss the issue of trade with the Spanish Ambassador after you are finished here. You then have a portrait sitting with Monsieur Clouet in the throne room at three. Then Monsieur Bochetel, your Secretary of Finance, the Comte de Saint-Pol and Diane de Poitiers all wish private audiences with you."

The King's look of indifference was replaced by a queer, almost evil smile.

"Confirm the meeting with Bochetel. Tell Saint-Pol that I shall meet with him on the gaining court, and then send word to Diane de Poitiers that I am unable to give her audience today."

"But Your Majesty can fit them all in. You have an opening just after four, and I have already—"

"I am unavailable to Madame La Sénéchale, Antoine!"

The King's words were sharp. The Chancellor lowered his head, silently chiding himself for his indiscretion. The members of the King's council began to rise, talking among themselves. The meeting was over.

So now it is she who wants something from me, the King considered. *Imagine it. Now she would like me to be of some service to her. She has changed the rules of the game, but I refuse to play.* Hearing her name as Poyet had said it was strangely reminiscent of the last time she had been given an audience. It had been five years already, when it seemed like only yesterday. She had just returned to Court. She had been so eager then. So fresh. Just newly widowed. Diane de Poitiers had seemed to him, then, almost untouched by life's vulgarities, if such a thing were possible. Old Louis had kept her hidden and out of harm's way at his country estate.

God, how he had wanted to conquer her! Wanted to, then. But now, five long years had passed since she had paraded into his throne room at Blois in that black velvet mourning gown. Now, she was no longer so favored. She had rejected him and, instead, taken his young son to her bed. She had betrayed him, and he felt nothing for her . . . nothing except, perhaps, the glimmer of revenge.

DIANE WAS NOT SURPRISED to have been refused an audience with the King. He, like everyone else now, knew about her liaison with Henri and disapproved. But this matter of her home was far too grave to avoid confrontation simply because he did not choose to deal with her. She would go to his chapel. He would be forced to listen to her there. She would tell him what the Duchesse had done. He may be angry with both her and Henri, but Diane could not believe that he had known anything about his mistress's plan to steal her home. No matter what His Majesty thought of her relationship with his son, even he could not be that cruel. And after all, her husband, Louis, had been the King's friend. Le Grand Sénéchal de Normandie. Yes, of course His Majesty would see to it that she did not lose Anet . . . if she could find the courage to ask him.

WHEN HE WAS AT AMBOISE the King always took his morning prayer alone in the Chapel Saint-Hubert. He found solace there. It was in this exquisite chapel as a boy that François had heard Mass each day. It was an elegant stone oratory in flamboyant Gothic design with stained-glass windows shooting shafts of light past elegant gables. It was warmed in winter by the uncommon luxury of two stone fireplaces. He closed his eyes, made the sign of the cross and knelt upon the red velvet prie-dieu. Images of his own childhood in this place crossed his mind and calmed his raging discontent.

He saw an image of himself as a little boy, playing with his sister, Marguerite, behind the great bastions in the courtyard that loomed high over the Loire. Each day they had watched over the walls at life below, a common life of which they knew nothing. They watched the town and its people beyond the river, a waterway teeming with an endless procession of barges and ships. When he was ten, they had pretended to have a ship of their own. François was captain; Marguerite first mate. Each day they sailed off to some new and exotic port, he at the helm. Trees tied with silk scarves became their mast and sails. The bushes that blew around them were the waves. He was not a King then; just a boy, like any other boy. And happy.

Diane knelt beside him and made the sign of the cross. The King did not see her at first, but as she drew forth the edict, the rustling of the paper caught his eye. When he saw that it was she, he tried to stand. Diane put a gentle hand to his arm to stop him.

"How did you get past my guards?"

"I am not completely without my influence, Your Majesty. If you please, I ask only for a moment."

"I would not hear you yesterday. What makes you think simply because you bribe my guards that I shall hear you now?"

She shoved the parchment at him.

"Whatever Your Majesty thinks of me, for the sake of Louis' memory, you cannot agree that this is fair!"

The King's eyes were clouded. He squinted to read the words. After a moment, he tossed it onto the floor with a deliberate thrust.

"And just what would you have me do about it? Perhaps you think I should help you." His words were sudden and raw. They echoed in the empty stone chapel. "How fitting that you should come to me, and I to reject you! Or have you become so caught up in your sordid interlude that you have forgotten all about your promise to the King of France?!"

He lumbered to his feet with a low, huffing sound. "You said you were not ready. Do you not recall? You said that you needed time, when all the while you were lusting after a child! I believed you then. I will not be so foolish now. If you seek assistance, Madame, I suggest you ask your neophyte lover!"

The blood slowly drained from her face. It was much worse than she had thought. She stood slowly, straightened the folds of her skirt and leaned against the King's prie-dieu to steady herself. He saw her weakness and seized ruthlessly upon it.

"What?" he asked with a savage laugh. "You did not think I knew you were bedding my son? Madame, I have known about your dirty little affair from the first, and if he were not to be King, I would have taken great pleasure in doing away with you myself!"

He moved away from her, a step at a time, in the direction of the door. Diane was unable to move. When he reached the door, he paused and turned around to face her. Once again, he was in command.

"You have lied and prostituted yourself, Madame. You have used me to get to my son. All in the name of your own endless greed."

"Your Majesty, please! It was not like that at all."

"But, it was exactly like that!" he declared, his voice booming across the cold stone chapel, his long nose pinched white with rage. The fury rose in his eyes, kindling an anger that frightened her. She took a step back from him and lowered her head.

"You were a grand woman once, Madame. If you can imagine

it, I even admired you. But, I did not understand you. I did not know what it was that you truly wanted from me. I thought you were a lady. I was wrong. In the future if I want you, I shall offer to pay for your services like I do with any of the other courtesans who inflict themselves on this Court. Then we shall see how faithful you are to my son!"

The words fresh on his lips, the King left the chapel and slammed the carved-oak door behind him. The echoed sound, once again, shattered the chapel's calm. Tears streamed down her cheeks faster than she could wipe them away. She clutched herself around the waist as her body jerked in a fit of uncontrollable sobs.

"You are wrong . . . It is not like that," she muttered, and shook her head from side to side. "I am not like that . . . I am not a courtesan!"

*N*EGOTIATIONS TOWARD A TRUCE continued over the next two months. Pope Paul III lobbied tirelessly for peace. By May, as the spring began to warm the chill from the heavy stones at Saint Germain-en-Laye, he had arranged a meeting between the two powers to take place at the medieval port city of Aigues-Mortes. Queen Eleanora was called from her self-imposed exile to mediate the meeting between her husband and her brother, one a King, the other Emperor.

Montmorency encouraged negotiations while Chabot openly opposed them. Henri, now grudgingly accepted as Dauphin, be-came a factor in this latest bid for peace. He hoped, along with Montmorency, for a resolution of the war that had drained the coffers of the state, and the spirit of its people.

By every indication, the meeting was judged a success. Amid a great deal of pomp, ceremonial handshaking and gift giving on both sides, the meeting had produced an entente. There was to be an informal understanding based on three key points. First they would wage war against the Turkish Sultan, Suleiman. They would also combat heresy, which threatened Christianity in both of their countries. Finally, they agreed to break off relations with Henry VIII so that he could no longer be used as a weapon for either of them. But still, through all of the negotiations, nothing was said about Milan.

The prognosis for the King of France was even less hopeful than the prospect of a lasting treaty. Montmorency informed Henri by letter, in early September, that the King was ill once again. As it had in previous years, the return of autumn signaled the return of his malady. It manifested itself in an abscess of his lower parts. Whispers in the royal household was that the King had once again contracted the French disease. The royal physicians had cauterized the infection and prescribed a course of Chinese wood, allowing him to return home. He would be returning to Fontainebleau, not on horseback as he had gone, but now like an old man, in a litter.

"HAVE YOU HEARD what that bastard has done? Well, you simply cannot allow it! I will not let you!"

Anne d'Heilly strode through the arched doors and into the King's bedchamber just as the pale pink sun had begun to rise. Barre was startled by the sound of her voice and rose to his feet from a chair near the King's bed.

"Please, Madame, His Majesty is still asleep."

"Well then, wake him!"

She pushed past the First Gentleman-of-the-Bedchamber, and on toward the bed, around which the heavy gold and red bedcurtains were still drawn.

"François, you cannot allow this! That old war monger will bring us all to ruin if you do not act!"

As she raged, Anne tore back the bedcurtains and lunged toward the sleeping King. Blankets drawn back, the stench of his disease overwhelmed her. Not even the constantly burning juniper in the fire and the wall sconces could quell it. She brought her hand quickly to her mouth to stop the reflex action, the need to vomit. He opened his eyes. He lumbered to prop himself onto his elbows. He squinted, struggling to see who had disturbed him. His large eyes were still thick with a white crust, so that he was forced to rub them furiously to see her. Again he faltered as he tried to sit up. Sourdis, the First Valet, rushed to his side with pillows. A spray of gold velvet and green silk was fanned out behind him. He washed a hand across his face, still squinting from the new bright light of morning.

"What . . . what is it?" he muttered through the dry cracked corners of his mouth.

"If you can imagine it, Montmorency has taken it upon himself to warn the Emperor of an uprising among his own people. Then he has informed him, your most evil enemy, that he may use France as a shortcut to get to Flanders. He plans to do this to stave off a revolt that, if successful, could only bring you more power!"

François shook his head, hearing only half of what she had said, and comprehending far less. He had been confined to his sickbed since his return from Aigues-Mortes. The disease, always insidious, this time had been so fierce that it had attacked not only his body, but his mind. Since he was for a time not in complete control of his faculties, the King's advisors feared for the security of France. They had been forced to confer the direction of the country over to the second in command, Constable Montmorency.

He wiped more of the white crust from his eyes as the enormity of what she had said began to come clear to him. Anne sat on the corner of his bed trying to ignore the sour smell of his infection. The King had trusted his old friend, and news of this defiance spurred the old thunder. Anne saw it and seized it. She described Montmorency's plan in detail.

"*Mon amour,* there is an insurrectionist movement in the Imperial territory of Ghent, and not long ago a collection of their leaders came here hoping to ally with us against the Emperor. Well, not only did Montmorency warn the evil Emperor of the unrest, but he offered swift passage through our territory so that he could handle the matter!"

François struggled to sit up and strained to see his Anne in the glaring light of day. After a moment's consideration, he swung his bare legs to the side of the bed with a heavy sigh. His legs were long and thin with a network of purple veins now around his calves.

"Bring him to me," was all he said.

HATE.

It was not too strong a word for what Anne d'Heilly felt for the Constable. As she waited in the King's bedchamber for him to wake once again and to complete his *lever,* her mind was filled with the tainted image of Montmorency.

She had never liked him; even in the beginning. As the years passed, she had come to detest him with the same violent passion that most people reserve for love. It was her great desire to witness the Constable's downfall. To that end, she chiseled away at his standing with the King on a daily basis. Montmorency was too rude; too arrogant. He had never given her the respect to which, as the official *favourite* of the King of France, she was entitled. But the quality that she found most unforgivable in this contemptuous noble was his single-minded ambition. It had been the instrument of his ascension. Now, if she had her way with the King, it would become his downfall.

When he had been dressed by his staff, François came to her at the chair beside his bed, the same chair in which she had begun to spend a great deal of time nursing him through his illnesses. He walked slowly, straining with each step as valets supported him on each side.

As he stood before her, even in his most grand blue silk doublet slashed with gold, he still looked ill. The pervasive stench from his open, oozing lesions confirmed it. The features, once majestic, were now drawn over a ghostly pallor of gray. The eyes, once brilliant, were now shot with red and rimmed with dark circles. She despised him like this, because his malaise was a sign of his mortality. A sign of her own dwindling power. Anne was thankful that he no longer wanted to touch her. She watched him ease into a chair, heavily padded beneath brocade, and take a goblet of wine. As he drank it, the liquid dribbled down his beard and onto his blue silk shirt. When he made no attempt to wipe it away, another servant advanced with a cloth. The young man daubed at his chin until the King swatted at him like a persistent fly.

"How did you come by this information?" he asked. He looked at Anne as though there had been no break at all between her telling of the tale and his reply now.

"I make it my business to secure your interests, *mon amour.* It is my duty."

As the King slouched in his chair, a heavy silver tray was set before him. It was neatly covered with a white cloth and held small meat pies in various shapes, lark pâté, and a dish of candied plums. François sniffed at the display as though the rich aroma was as pestilent as the most foul odor.

"Take it away!" he snarled.

A steward removed the tray from the King's reach as quickly as it had been presented. A long line of gentlemen-of-the-chamber passed it from one hand to the next, and saw it secured back down to the royal kitchens without a sound.

Outfitted in a sumptuous ermine cape with a jeweled chain slashed across his chest, Montmorency paraded into the King's apartment almost a full hour after he had been summoned. His toque was red velvet and plumed with the feather of an ostrich. He looked at the King from beneath it with impatient eyes.

"Your Majesty wished to see me."

"Sit," commanded the King.

Anne d'Heilly leered at the Constable with a look that could almost have been construed as a sneer. After a moment, he acquiesced and poised himself on the edge of a small wooden stool that had been placed across from the King's own chair. François did not like anyone to have the advantage of looming over him.

"Tell me about your dealings with the Emperor."

Montmorency's eyes widened. "What specifically does Your Majesty wish to know?" His tone was direct, almost insolent.

"I wish to know, my dear Constable Montmorency, how you could see your way clear to betraying your King?"

Montmorency looked at Anne. She was still leering. He snapped his fingers for a goblet of wine to be brought. It was a movement that bought him enough time to collect not only his thoughts, but his words. When he had received the wine and taken a long sip, he set the goblet down and said, "Your Majesty has been unwell. It has been my duty, as Constable, to act in your stead. My actions in this case, as always, have been for the good and future glory of France." He stared directly at the King with steel-eyed conviction and then added, "I have done nothing, Sire, to betray either you, or my country."

"Pretty speech, but a faithful servant to the King does not give a free hand to his enemy!" Anne harped.

"If Your Majesty would consent to let me explain . . ."

"It is all very clear. You deceive the King to your own ends!"

This time, François shot her a disapproving glare, then turned his attention back to Montmorency. The Constable cleared his throat. He had a speech prepared.

"Sire, I believe we can achieve our objective through peaceful means. The objective of course is, and always has been, Milan. Certainly that cannot have changed. And, after our meeting in Aigues-Mortes, I was given to believe that you, most of all, had every hope of obtaining it. When the German princes came to me with the news, I felt that warning the Emperor about his own domestic unrest was a show of good faith. It was a strengthening of the new alliance that you and I sought together, not two months ago."

"But, Your Majesty forgets," Anne interrupted. "What about Henry VIII? He will be furious at such an alliance. He is bound to see it as a venture that will lead to war against him! And what of those princes in the Netherlands whom he has already alienated?"

"Silence!" the King bellowed. "Let Montmorency be heard."

"Well, Your Majesty, now with the marriage of your son, Charles, to the Emperor's daughter agreed upon, and Milan as the probable dowry, I believed that good will between our two sides could only serve to facilitate this process. I humbly pray that you will forgive me if I have overstepped my bounds, but I envisioned a great opportunity in this event. I did not only suggest that the

Emperor pass through our lands, apparently Madame has neglected to tell you the rest of my plan. I propose to Your Majesty that we actually host the Emperor on his passage through France; organize a number of banquets, fêtes, even jousting matches. This shall serve to enforce the good will of France and the mangnanimity of its grand, its most Sovereign King. But more importantly than that, with your great show of generosity, I feel certain the Emperor would be hard pressed to refuse you the alliance, the marriage or, most especially, the return of Milan! You would have everything that you desire without the shedding of another drop of blood."

When he had finished his speech, Montmorency leaned back in his chair. He had listened to the words coming from his own mouth, timed their delivery and watched the reaction on the face of the King. Pleased with their effect, he reached for his goblet and took another sip of wine. "And you would advise this means, rather than another offensive, to gain Milan?"

"Your Majesty, please forgive my candor, but we have taxed the people to capacity for this war. Many lives have been lost. No, I do not believe that we should attempt another campaign. Not now."

The King brushed his hand across his face at the point of his graying beard. He studied Montmorency for several moments.

"It is rather a good idea . . . hmm . . . an invitation to our Court! Such a thing would allow me to appear magnanimous, indeed!" he declared, and then with a smile added, "Chambord is nearly complete. We could step up construction and host him there. Now that would be splendid!"

"I have taken the liberty of extending the invitation to the Imperial Court already. In Your Majesty's name of course. Word has already been returned through the Imperial Ambassador that he is most receptive to the notion."

The King did not falter or pause after Montmorency had finished speaking. He simply cleared his throat and said, "I trust you, Monty, like a brother. I have always trusted you. Very well then, if it is your sound belief . . . then it shall be my belief as well. We shall entertain the Emperor in grand style here in France. Nothing but the best and most grand to impress him. And for our efforts I feel certain, as you do, that we shall finally come away with Milan!"

Anne lunged from her seat, snorting wildly her dissatisfaction at the way in which the King had been swayed. Montmorency stifled a triumphant smile by taking another sip of Bordeaux. The smile lasted only until the King spoke again.

"But I warn you, Monty," he added, "if you are wrong about this, about him, then there will be only yourself to blame. And mark my words, you shall not be happy with the penalty that you shall be made to pay for such a grievous error in judgment."

"The message, Your Majesty," he nodded reverently, "is understood."

OR TWO MONTHS AFTER the Emperor left France for the Netherlands, and into the autumn of 1540, François, full of faith, waited for a decision on the fate of Milan. Montmorency tried to reassure him that it had been promised, and therefore it would be delivered. But each day the King found more reasons to doubt that the Emperor meant to keep his word. Each day also gave him more reason to doubt his old friend, the Constable. The Emperor had, after all, managed to leave France without ever having discussed Milan. The two Monarchs had touched casually, between their banquets and balls, on the issue of the Turks, and on religion. Nothing more.

When in February there was still no word from the Imperial Court, he instructed the French Ambassador to put the question directly to the Emperor. The reply was firm. Charles V formally thanked his good brother, the King of France, for safe passage through French waters, but said he had never made any such exchange of Milan as payment for their use.

François was devastated. He felt he had been made a fool of

once again. The memories of the Pope Clement affair and the disastrous Medici marriage echoed back at him. In a rage, he dwelled on only one thing; that it had been Constable Montmorency who had encouraged him to try peaceful means first.

"Come in, Monty. Please, sit down," the King stammered. The loss of his uvula caused him to speak like a child. He knew it, and now he was uncomfortable speaking more than necessary.

Montmorency strode the few paces from the door of the King's private chamber to the throne near his bed. It was in an alcove painted in brilliant blue with glittering gold fleurs-de-lys. There was no music, as there usually was. There was no conversation and no servants. There was formality in place of the usual activity.

On the other side of the room, a fire blazed. Red and gold shafts of light flickered beneath the gold salamander crest. Beside the hearth, the two Cardinals, Tournon and Lorraine, stood, their red robes shimmering in the firelight. Claude d'Annebault stood beside them. The three men were silent, trying in vain to feign nonchalance.

Montmorency turned his head quickly away from them, but he knew that they were there; and why. His heart beat wildly against his chest and he found it difficult to catch his breath as his face flushed with a hot rush of blood. For the first time in his life he knew what it must feel like to walk the last steps to one's death. His confident gait had vanished. In his mind everything was still; perfectly still.

The King stood on the dais that held his throne and leaned heavily on a gold and jeweled walking stick. Like his courtiers, François did not look directly at his Constable. All at once, Montmorency felt an overwhelming urge to plead with the King; to remind him of their years of friendship; the battles they had fought together, the victories and confidences they had shared. He knew before he was moved to speak that it would be pointless. This was to be his demise. But then, he had been warned.

"If it please Your Majesty, I would rather stand." Montmorency's voice cracked as he forced the words past his dry throat. He heard the rustling of the Cardinal's tafetta robes.

"Very well. Then I too shall stand."

The King gripped the top of his cane, the golden head of a roaring lion, and took the two steps down from the dais. The sun began to move through the east windows as it rose. It cast a streak of blinding sunlight across the King's face. For that moment, Montmorency did not see the tears forming in the King's eyes.

He came slowly toward the Constable. It was a great effort for him to walk now, but when he reached him, François put his arm around Montmorency and led him to the same sun-filled window. Both men looked down. In the courtyard below, courtiers strolled; some laughing, as they made their way back from the *jeu de paume* courts. Others were heading toward the chapel with their prayer books in hand. The church bell tolled and a collection of birds fluttered down from the rooftop and past the windows. These were the sounds and the signs of life. They echoed now, like memories, through the hollow, foul-smelling rooms of a once-great King.

"How is Madame de Montmorency?" the King finally asked.

He still did not turn around. The Constable was caught off guard. *Pleasantries?* he thought. *Now I am to receive pleasantries before he plucks out my heart?*

"She is well, Your Majesty. Thank you."

He looked out of the window in the same direction as the King. He could no longer see. The silence between them created a kind of blindness. A white light. He knew everything that he had worked for, all of the sacrificing, the planning; all of it was over.

". . . Because I have not seen her for some time, you know, and . . ."

Now it was the King who stopped. He had run out of conversation. There was another awkward silence. It was more awkward than before because now he knew that the King was fighting for the words. ". . . and the children?" the King asked, almost victoriously, after another extended pause. "They are well?"

"All are well, thank you, Your Majesty."

He was mildly aware that he was beginning to sound irritated, but Montmorency could not seem to chase the tone from his voice. Nor could he rid his body of the rigid posture that he had now adopted. Feet spread; chest extended; hands clasped behind his back. The posture of a condemned man, he thought. His body had automatically gone into a position of defense. He could not change the experiences of thirty years; not even for the King. His body knew what lay ahead, and it, not he, had reacted.

Montmorency had seen trusted aides dismissed before. Most often the less tasteful work was done by underlings, ambassadors or courtiers, unless of course those being relieved of their duty meant anything at all to the King. Then there was the code to contend with, the chivalric code. Machiavelli's *Prince* reigned supreme over the King's life, ghostlike; always haunting him, urging him to be, at an costs, *un vrai gentilhomme.* Montmorency had watched the King's dismissals on more than one occasion. Flashes from those scenes now passed across his mind. There were always words of concern about family and about finances; a kind of hypocritical interest before the final, fatal blow.

"And do you have enough money . . . are you, comfortable?"

Montmorency looked at the King. The blood that had been pulsing in his face drained away and he went white as winter snow. His heart ceased, or so he thought. *Finances!* Now he was certain that it was the end. There had been a war and Anne d'Heilly had won. She had finally gotten what she wanted; what she had always sworn she would. She had finally destroyed him. And then, something came over him. Something he could not control.

"What is it, Your Majesty? François, my good friend, what have I done? I can see that I have displeased you . . ." He moved toward the King. Just a fraction of an inch, but it was too swift, too pleading. The King moved back. ". . . if I have disappointed you in some way. Please, just tell me and I am certain that I can—"

He caught himself. He was pleading. Before the King and the Cardinals, who he was sure had rejoiced in his demise, he was begging forgiveness. This despite the fact that he had sworn he would never grovel. The King wiped the tears with the back of his hand. That was it, thought Montmorency. Tears. He would have had a chance if the King had been angry. If he had been furious he would have known how to fight it, but this . . . All was lost! The

King looked at him squarely, taking in a deep breath before he spewed forth the last deathknell.

"Monty, my dearest . . . dearest friend." He put his hand on Montmorency's arm. It was a hand covered with purple age spots and blue veins. "It is not anything that you have done . . . nothing that you can change. You have been a worthy general . . . and God knows, you have been a good enough friend. In fact . . ." He began once again to stumble over his words; the effects of his disease returning. "I can find no fault with you but that, God help me . . . you do not love those whom I love."

So there, he had said it. The King was sobbing now between his words; unashamed, but he had said it, Anne d'Heilly had won. Montmorency was absolutely still. He turned and gazed out of the window again. The garden was empty. There were no courtiers. No movement. The King, he thought, was completely resigned. There was nothing left for which to argue; nothing left for which he could fight. By her wrath, he had been completely destroyed.

"I SIMPLY CANNOT BELIEVE IT. And to have left Court without even saying so much as adieu. Especially to me!" Henri groaned.

"It cannot have been easy for him, *chéri*. I am certain he will write to you and explain the entire matter once he reaches Chantilly."

Diane sat beside Henri on a blue brocade settee, both of them still in their riding clothes when François de Guise had come to them with the news of Montmorency's departure. He said he had received word from his uncle, the Cardinal, who had been in the King's chamber earlier that morning. He explained that the King had personally relieved Montmorency of his duty. The official reason had been something about the Constable's inability to contend with those whom the King loved. The real reason, everyone knew, was Montmorency's inability to secure Milan.

"But to use him as a scapegoat for the entire affair is too much!" Henri cried. "It was her! I know it was her doing! She has always despised him, and she waited for precisely this chance to ruin him. Oh, I can imagine how she harped on the King . . . how she

nagged and badgered until he acquiesced. The Emperor never had
any intention of giving up Milan and she knew it. But she still
managed to use it against Monty! So many years of service and
His Majesty could give no better reason to his Constable than he
did not love the same people the King loved?"

Henri slammed his fist into the carved-oak table that held the
empty wine decanter. Diane could see the anger building. She knew,
when he was like this, that she was powerless to stop the fury. It
must run its course. She said nothing as she watched him spring to
his feet.

"And I am Dauphin. Ha! Now that is humorous, do you not
think? Heir to the throne of France and yet I am a part of nothing
here! All just to spite me. He treats me as if I did not even exist! I
know nothing of the workings of his councils, their opinions . . .
even his rulings! To learn of this through gossip, like everyone
else . . . oh, it is too much!"

He was so infused with his own anger that he did not hear the
chamber door open. "Papa! Papa!" cried the little girl as she raced
toward Henri. A tall man in a crimson and gold doublet followed
her breathlessly into the room.

"Please forgive me, Your Highness. I could not stop her. She
said she had to see you."

Henri instantly softened as he scooped his daughter into his
arms. He held her to his chest, kissing away the two little tears
that streamed down her cheeks.

"It is all right, Monsieur Duval. My daughter has access to
these apartments or my own, at her will."

"Of course, Your Highness."

"Now, what is this all about?" he said, kissing the tip of her nose.

She was a beautiful child, nearly six now, with long full dark
hair which, when she was three, had turned the color of her father's. She wore it pulled away from her face at the top and covered by a small blue cap that matched her eyes; her mother's eyes.
It was fortunate, Diane had always thought, that as she grew, she
looked less and less like herself and more like Henri; more like a
Valois. She had the same long face. The same slender nose and the

same ruddy skin. She had a curious nature and a key to her father's heart. But it was the second key. The first key belonged to her mother, a mother whom she still did not know.

"Papa, is it true?"

"Is what true, *ma mignonne?*"

"That Uncle Montmorency is going away forever."

Henri hugged her to his chest and then set her down before him. He then knelt beside her. "Where did you hear such a thing?"

The child looked up innocently at her tutor, who stood behind her. Then she looked back at her father. Henri's thick, dark brows began to close over his eyes. His reassuring smile faded.

"The Duchesse d'Etampes was speaking to Monsieur Duval in the corridor this morning," the little girl continued. "They did not know I could hear them. I could not make out all of the words because they were whispering but she did say that there was no hope of Uncle Montmorency ever coming back."

What the child did not confess to her father was that she had heard other things too. She understood declarations of love from her tutor to the King's mistress, and close kissing sounds, like her father often made with Madame Diane when they were certain that she was asleep. She knew that it could not be proper. After all, the Duchesse belonged to His Majesty just the way Madame Diane belonged to Papa. She knew that the sounds could not have been anything but wrong. Henri pulled her closely to him and she sat on his knee. He forced a smile. Diane gazed down at them but made no attempt to intercede.

"Yes, *ma mignonne.* It is true that Uncle Montmorency is going away. Sometimes adults have things they must do. Commitments. You will understand all of that when you are older. But I will tell you a very big secret that you must promise to keep to yourself. Uncle Monty may have to leave us for now, but he will not be gone forever. That I promise you, my sweet one. No matter what anyone else says to you, no matter what else you may hear, you remember what your Papa told you. One day I shall bring Uncle Montmorency back no matter what it takes; and your Papa can make you that promise because one day I am going to be King!"

The child seemed content with her father's reassurance and began again to smile. Henri patted her bottom playfully and pushed her from his knee. "All right now, give Papa a big hug," he said. His daughter did so, obligingly, gripping his neck and kissing his cheek. Henri smiled. "And have you one for Madame Diane?"

The child beamed and scrambled onto the couch. She kissed both of Diane's cheeks and hugged her neck as she had hugged her father. Henri watched them and for a moment he felt a pull at his heart. Seeing them together always evoked in him a curious mixture of happiness and regret.

"Guise," he began again, "if you would please, take Mademoiselle back up to the nursery." Then he turned his head back down to her. The blue eyes sparkled up at him. She smiled a wide, innocent smile. "And Papa will come to see you tonight after you have finished your supper, all right?"

The child hung her head but she did not sulk. "What about Monsieur Duval," she asked. "Will he not attend me?"

"Oh, he will be along shortly. But first Papa needs to speak with him privately for a moment. Besides, if you ask him very nicely, I will wager that Uncle François will give you a horsy ride all the way back to the nursery!"

The child's eyes lit up, and all thought of concern for her tutor passed with the prospect of a ride on Guise's back.

"With pleasure, Your Highness. Mademoiselle, your mighty steed awaits," said François as he surrendered himself to all fours and helped the giggling child onto his back.

When they had gone, Henri advanced toward Duval. He cleared his throat. Diane knew the tone. It was the same one he always used when he considered someone or something a threat to his child. She lowered her head.

"I know, Monsieur Duval, that you are aware my daughter is not of legitimate issue." The inflection in his voice warranted a response. Duval obliged with a grave nod.

"And you are also aware that due to that fact, she is naturally at greater risk of exposure to harmful gossip and injurious words. This may well be due to the carelessness of others who do not regard my daughter with the same importance as do I." Henri moved so that he was no longer looking at the child's tutor. He was staring, instead, in the general direction of the window that led out into the central courtyard. "When I took you on as Principal Tutor to Mademoiselle Diane, I was certain that I had made myself completely clear on all of these points. Primarily, that she was to be spared, at all costs, the imparting of any kind of news that could conceivably cause her any harm or ill; any news at all."

As though his feelings of impotence and rage had been recharged by the sun that showered his face in the afternoon light, Henri turned around with a vengeance. "Monsieur, my daughter means the world to me. Surely you can understand that. Ah, I see from your eyes that you do. Then you must also understand that there is nothing I will not do to protect her. I do not care what you do or with whom you do it, on your own time. But, in this you have been careless; careless and stupid; characteristics I do not tolerate in the care of my hunting hounds, much less in the management of my only child. I am certain you can understand my position. I believe that I have no choice. You are to pack your bags and I expect you to vacate your apartments and be out of this chateau by nightfall."

When he heard the heavy studded door close and he knew that Duval had gone, Henri thought of the dreadful slight to Montmorency as he muttered venomously, "For myself and half of this Court . . . Your Majesty . . . believe me when I say that your imminent demise, no matter when it occurs, shall never be soon enough!"

Book Four
March 1547

Donec Totum Impleat Orbum

(Until it fills the whole world)

—Official motto of Henri II

27

CATHERINE IS AGAIN WITH CHILD."

Henri made the announcement to Diane in a low, calcu-lated tone, as he stood in the doorway of her apartments. He cast his gray doeskin gloves onto the floor and then slumped into a red and gold brocade chair near the fire. He looked pensively into the flames for several minutes without saying another word. His black hair glistened in the light and matched his velvet doublet. He crushed his toque between both hands and sighed.

Diane let an uneven smile pass across her lips. She looked up-ward in a silent prayer and then walked the few steps to his side. "Thanks be to God," she said.

Henri looked up at her, at first, like a guilty child. Then his dark, absorbing eyes began to sparkle. He reached over, took her hand, then squeezed it. They were the same words she always said when the Dauphine was pregnant. It had been six years since Montmorency had been banished from Court, and this had been the third time she had used them.

"Then you do not mind?"

This was the same thing he always said at precisely the same moment after he had informed her of Catherine's pregnancy. Diane gave a half laugh and then knelt at his feet.

"Mind? How can you even think such a thing.? You will be King. It is vital that you have heirs."

Henri lay his head back against the brocade of the chair and looked into the fire for another moment before he replied. Of course she understood. Diane had twice escorted him personally to the Dauphine's bedchamber.

"I bed her because I must," he said. "You have shown me that.

The images of those times I can wash away in the love of your arms." The guilty tone crept back into his voice. "But every time it happens, every time she gets with child, I feel as if it is firm proof that I have betrayed you. After all, I had the requisite son first, four years ago. The line is secure."

And by Diane's prodding, he finally did have a son. The boy had been christened François II at Fontainebleau two years after Montmorency was driven from Court in the scandal with the Emperor. As Catherine's mystic had curiously predicted, the child was born ten years, nearly to the day, after Henri had been forced into the political marriage with the Pope's niece. Two years after the birth of François, a girl was born. She was named Elizabeth. Henry VIII, who had just beheaded his fifth wife and taken a sixth, had softened his policy against France. He had agreed to act as godfather to the child.

Through tragedy, Henri's own political position, along with that of France, had become more well defined. His father could no longer deny to himself or anyone else that one day he would indeed be King. In the autumn of 1545, shortly after his daughter's birth, his younger brother, Charles, died of the plague. Out of the six royal children, only he and Marguerite now remained.

Henri rose and walked to the window. It was snowing again. He watched the shimmering flakes whisper past the glass. He liked winter mornings because everything was so clean. Snow meant purity and honesty to him. It also meant Diane's colors: black and white. To others, black was the symbol of mourning. To him it was the symbol of passion. The blinding lust that forever bound them. He wore nothing but those colors now, in tribute to her. White for purity, black for passion.

He was glad to be finally with her again. Here with her, in her apartments, he could be himself. It was his custom to return to her every morning after Mass, as he did now, and every evening at quarter past eight. If the events of the day kept them apart, they always knew that they would have these times. But in the evenings before he could relax with Diane, he would take the long walk up the winding stairs of Saint Germain-en-Laye to the third floor, to the children's wing. There, he would visit his son and his daughter, Elizabeth, until half past seven.

Oftentimes, if his schedule would permit him, he would even get down on the floor with them and play. It did not matter the game, he simply wanted time alone with his children; to be the father that he never had. Then, when they were safely tucked in bed by the string of nurses and governesses that the Crown employed, he would kiss them each good night, blow out their candles, and at exactly half past seven, he would walk next door to see his daughter, his Diane.

The little girl was accorded every privilege of the other royal children. She had her own suite of rooms in the nursery, and a bevy of royal governesses, tutors and guards to attend her. She was schooled in music and in dance. Madame Diane herself supervised her lessons in the classics. She played with her brother and sister, who adored her, and had the free run of their apartments. Henri forbid even the slightest preference to be shown for the Dauphine's children. Although his son would one day be King, Diane, his *mignonne,* would always be the most precious to his heart. He disliked himself for that. It was not fair. In his own childhood, he had never been special to anyone. So he swore that despite his preference for one, the others would never bear the burden of knowing it.

"The child is to be born some time in November," Henri said. "Catherine is only a few weeks along, but somehow she knows. She always knows." Then as an afterthought he looked up at her. Diane simply smiled the same supportive smile and took his hand.

"Shall we ride this afternoon then, or under the circumstances, would you prefer the time with Catherine?" she asked him without the slightest intonation of jealousy.

Without waiting for his response, she rose and walked slowly across the room to where two of her ladies' maids were pouring cold water into a huge, silver tub. This was the procedure on mornings when the Court was so large that she could not have found the privacy to swim in the lake or river. Hélène removed her cap while another servant began to unfasten her gown.

"Of course we shall ride!" he finally replied, and when he saw her same reassuring smile he added, "We shall see her together later, after supper. We can both inquire about her then."

One at a time, her buttons were undone beneath Henri's gaze. He drew near. The shafts of daylight and the fire's glow shadowed her body. Her skin was shaded pale amber as she stepped from the gown, shift and stockings and sank without hesitation up to her hips into the cold water. As she sat motionless, taking the water like a penance, Hélène scrubbed her back with soap and a rough cloth. This was a test of her discipline, she always said. Cold water every morning of her life.

"You may retire," Henri finally instructed her servants as he took a huge towel and held it open beside the tub.

Hélène lowered her head and then quickly ushered the two other ladies from the bedchamber. When the heavy studded door closed behind them, Henri encircled Diane and kissed each of her breasts. Her nipples hardened with his touch. The taste of her skin was clean. Sweet. He pressed himself against her as the need grew.

"You have the most perfect breasts in the world," he whispered. "Perfection . . . sheer perfection."

His fingers trailed down across her hips and slowly she let the towel fall to the floor as he took her in his arms toward the huge canopied bed. Her head fell onto his shoulder and she could feel the warmth of his breath on her neck as he pushed her gently . . . gently . . . into the cool folds of fresh white linen.

When they made love, they did so as they had from the first. Completely. Passionately. Their two bodies formed together as perfectly as if Michelangelo had fashioned them in an exquisite union of marble. The rhythm of one was always the response to a movement of the other. The sheets on the bed were strewn with fragrant rose petals. Their scent mixed with the aroma of leather, and of flesh. She let out a silent little cry as Henri trailed his tongue along the back of her neck.

"You are my life, Diane . . ." he whispered, as though a reassurance for the child that soon would be born. "You are everything!"

They lay perfectly still for several minutes, still pressed together. It was snowing harder now. As the wind rose up, bare branches slapped against the window panes near their bed. Diane heard only the crashing of his heart as he lay with her. It had been too swift for her; too raw to have given her pleasure. It took her longer now to climax than it had when she was younger; when they were new lovers. But there would be other times, slower and more patient for her. As the years passed, Henri's desire for her only increased. Perhaps it was because he had come to worship her with an almost mystifying depth. Perhaps, in part, it was because she had taken the time to learn what pleased him. She knew what his fantasies were, and she denied him none of them. Whatever the reason, the bond between Diane de Poitiers and the future King of France had become impenetrable. There was no one, and nothing that could separate them.

After another moment, Henri rolled over and lay beside her. Diane put her hand beneath her chin and then looked over at him.

"I wish we had another child. I wish we had a son," he said.

It was a comment that she knew had been brought on by Catherine's latest pregnancy.

"I am glad that we did not," she laughed, and he knew why she said it. He could not forget that their daughter's birth had nearly killed her. ". . . and besides, I much prefer attending to your children than bearing my own," she added with a little chuckle.

The way she said it made him laugh too. He let a rush of air pass through his lips, and then looked up at the carved-oak canopy above them. Though it was Catherine who now gave him what he longed to share with Diane, the Dauphine's maternity had done nothing to dislodge Diane's position in Henri's life, as his wife had hoped. Rather, it had been the means by which a solid and respectable niche was carved out for her in his entourage.

After the birth of Catherine's first child, Diane was named official governess. She closely supervised their education, their diet and their daily upbringing. By Henri's order, her decisions superseded anything that even Catherine might have desired for them. Henri knew that Diane alone was responsible for the children's conception. Had it not been for her prodding, and for turning him away at appropriate moments, he would never have been able to bring himself to bed his wife. The honor accorded her was deserved.

"They really are the most perfect breasts in the world."

"I think that perhaps you are just the slightest bit prejudicial in your opinion of my body."

"Nonsense! They are perfect, I tell you. Perfect!" he shouted playfully. "In fact, one day when I am King, I shall have glasses made from their shape and everyone shall drink from them! What do you think of that?!"

"I believe that you are mad!"

"Mad for you! But otherwise, completely, undeniably sane. And to that end, I am to be King one day, you know, and we cannot have the *true* Queen of France going around calling His Majesty touched in the head, now can we?" He pushed her back onto the bed and playfully pinned her arms over her head. "Because, do you know what we do with those who slander the good name of the King? We . . . tickle them until they are positively mad themselves!" He charged at her with all ten fingers until she recoiled with screams and giggles.

"No, no! Very well!" Diane pealed with laughter. "I give in!"

Henri looked down at her, his black eyes twinkling.

"Oh, yes," he smiled. "I do so like the sound of that."

A FAINT LIGHT came up through the small hole in the floor. Alone, in a chamber that smelled of oak polish and heavy Italian perfume, Catherine lay flat on the floor, her fleshy hands pressed into the floorboards. Here was the secret beneath her carpet. She muttered a silent prayer and then put her eye to the hole. Catherine's heart began to race. It always did when she gained the courage to watch. What an irony, she thought, that the King should have chosen for her a suite of rooms that lay directly above those of her husband's whore.

After a moment, she could see them together. Two bodies, one wrapped in the other. The woman's legs were long and slender;

muscled around the calves. They were the legs of Diane de Poitiers. He was on top of her and they were laughing. Henri. Her husband. Her life. They rolled together, never leaving her view, almost, it seemed, in defiance of her.

As it always did, Catherine's mind whirled with a myriad of such evil thoughts that she could scarcely keep from crying out. Still, she would watch them again and again, and she would learn. For Diane was only a mistress. She was a wife. One day, Henri would grow tired of the forbidden fruit, as all men eventually did, and then . . .

WHEN DIANE ENTERED the outer room of Catherine's apartments, later that afternoon, Henri was already there. It was snowing again and even with the massive fireplaces all heavily stoked, there was a bone-chilling draft. But Diane was much too anxious to have noticed it. Henri had said come at four, and it was just that now. When she heard him already in the Dauphine's drawing room, she knew he had arrived early. She took a breath to suppress a twinge of jealousy, an emotion she would never allow him to see.

The Italian page at the door took her cloak and then retired. She was alone. They had not heard her come in. The conversation continued beyond the arched entry. Diane gazed around the corner of a white stucco wall. They were sitting together in the next room, beside the fire. Catherine was laughing and she had just put her hand on Henri's arm. Diane watched with disdain her attempts at coquetry. She straightened her collar, straightened her skirt, and with determination prepared to enter the lion's den.

CATHERINE'S APARTMENTS on the second floor of Saint Germain-en-Laye were ominous. Everywhere was the scent of Italian musk and incense. Heavy velvet drapes hid the last remaining light from the windows throughout the large opulent rooms. For all the years Catherine had now spent in France, she still preferred the Italian designs. Her rooms were cluttered with heavy oak furniture, stained dark, and then painted in ornate designs.

There was a collection of cabinets, chests and a heavy credenza painted black. The walls were thick with Italian tapestries, most of them hunting scenes. A long table draped in crimson silk near the door was covered with silver trays of jams, confits and pastries; another was covered with a selection of wine decanters and goblets. Though her obsession with astrology and mysticism was widely known, hidden from view now were the ever-present astrolabe, the charts and potions; evidence of practices of which her husband strongly disapproved.

As she might have guessed, Catherine had seen to it that they were alone. The expression on her full face when she saw Diane revealed that she had not expected further company.

"Good afternoon, Your Highness," Diane said in a confident tone as she stood in the doorway. She watched Catherine's expression change even before she looked up. Henri sprang from his seat and came toward her.

"Is it four? Oh, goodness yes, already. Catherine has been harping on me for approval of some sketches; ideas for the chateau in Gien. I thought I should make good use of my time here and come a few minutes early."

As Henri drew nearer, he reached out for her but Diane resisted. She believed that outward expression of their affection in the presence of the Dauphine would be cruel. Henri took her hand anyway and led her to the conversation area near the fire where Catherine was still seated, heavy now after the births of two children. Diane sat in the third chair. It was small, covered in brown velvet, and sufficiently lower to the ground than the other two. Catherine loomed over her, the corners of her thick lips turned up in a little half smile as Diane sank slowly into it. Diane silently wondered how long it had taken her to conjure up this subtle slight. She took a deep breath to steady herself. The smell of musk was suffocating. *Only for Henri,* she thought.

"Your Highness, I wish to offer my personal congratulations on your forthcoming child. It certainly is a wonderful day for all of France."

Catherine only nodded. Henri watched them, Diane could feel it without looking. She knew he was searching for the least bit of disrespect paid to his mistress.

"Indeed it is," Catherine added at the last moment. "The physicians tell me that it shall be in late autumn."

"Ah, an autumn child. How fortunate not to face the summer heat for the birth. My daughter, Louise, was born in autumn and I found it much easier to bear than my first."

Diane realized that she was making polite conversation and she detested herself for it. But like everything else in her life, she did so without complaint, for the love of Henri. Even after all of the years, it had never ceased to trouble him that, by his love for Diane, every day of his life he committed the sin of adultery. Yet, he told her many times that an eternity in Hell would be far easier to face than life on earth without her. Reconciling his wife and his mistress, if only in his mind, somehow made it easier to live with his sin.

"So do you hope this time for a boy or a girl?" Diane asked, trying to keep her voice reasonably pleasing. Catherine looked down from her chair. She brushed a hand across her face. Her fat fingers were covered with gold and jeweled rings that sparkled with the movement.

"I care only, Madame, that my child is a legitimate heir." She paused a moment in the stiff silence of the room to which Henri seemed unaware. Then she added, "Now then, may I offer you a cup of wine?"

Catherine filled a small silver goblet from a decanter on the table beside her chair before Diane could reply and handed it to her with an ingratiating smile. As Diane raised the goblet to her lips, something made her stop; a force telling her no, she must not drink the wine. Then, as she held the goblet up before her, the blood drained from her face. She looked at Henri. His cup was different. It was crystal and studded with stones. She could see through it that his wine was not the same as hers. She looked up at Catherine who was still smiling at her. The hand that held the silver goblet began to tremble.

"What is it, Madame? Do you not care for the flavor?" Catherine asked.

Diane looked at her again. The heavily jowled face glistening with perspiration. The raven hair. The dark angry eyes. It was the first time she had ever considered the possibility that Catherine could hate her so much that she might actually want her poisoned.

Suddenly Diane needed to escape. The urge was overwhelming. She was suffocating; smothered by the sour smell of musk and incense, by Catherine's smile and by the very real threat to her life. It took no more than a moment for Henri, who was studying the interaction, to see that something was wrong.

"Madame? What is it?" he asked, coming to the edge of his chair.

Diane managed to set the goblet down without spilling it on the small carved table beside her. "It . . . it is nothing. I am just feeling a little tired. I hope that Your Highness will forgive me, but perhaps I should retire."

"I will go with you!" Henri declared, springing to his feet.

Catherine rose more slowly. She watched Henri leave her room trailing after his whore as a dog does his master. She was careful not to laugh before they had gone. The plan had definitely unnerved Madame Diane, there was no question of that. It had been a grand idea. She would have to thank her mystic, Ruggieri, with something special for this one. She chewed her thick painted lip as her mind filled with evil thoughts. Then she lowered her hand over her belly, feeling the life with which Henri had filled her.

THAT EVENING, Diane stood beside Henri near the copper glow of the fireplace hearth. They were dressed, as everyone had come to expect, in costumes of fine black velvet. The sleeves of her gown were edged in white fur. His shirt sleeves were slashed with white silk. They watched across the crowded ballroom as the King made his entrance into the banquet to celebrate the Ides of March. The trumpets blared. The tune began for a stately Pavane. Everyone bowed. But His Majesty no longer paraded through an entrance as he once so elegantly had done. Now he passed into a room with a low studied shuffle and leaned heavily on a jeweled walking stick.

His once majestic face was covered with a thin patina of per-spiration from the exertion. François' physical symptoms mir-rored his political decline. He was now weak and acquiescent; a shadow King, ruled by the powerful orb of his mistress, Anne d'Heilly, and her small collection of aides.

The past two years had been difficult for the King, and his body bore the scars. Wars with the Emperor. A new battle with England over Boulogne and Scotland. Both of these hostilities had exhausted the royal treasury. Equally ruinous to the image of François' reign was the domestic situation. Poverty from excessive taxation had increased. There was discord among the people. Fran-çois' religious indecision was now blamed for the permissive hereti-cal climate rampant in France. Like a pendulum, he had sought, in his later years, to right the wrongs of his early reign by pursuing Protestants with a vengeance. Books were publicly burned. The accused were hung in chains from the Pont Saint-Michel. Many were burned alive at stakes in the Place de Grève. Despite the ex-tremity of the measures, it was widely acknowledged by both sides that Protestantism was now out of control in France.

Diane felt an unexpected burst of sympathy as she looked at the ailing King. *One need not love him to pity such a humble end,* she thought. Then she turned away, and the moment passed. She could not af-ford to care for a man who had not lifted a finger in her defense for nearly fourteen years. She looked around the room. Tonight it was filled with her own allies. She must concentrate on them. Henri did. Indignant over still not being included in major decisions as Dauphin, he confined himself to this small faction of intimates. He felt safe among them, and so did Diane, even when con-fronted by the even smaller but vicious faction of the Duchesse d'Etampes.

Among the rising powerful about whom all of France now whispered, was Jacques de Saint-André. He stood chatting with Charles and François de Guise, who were also counted among the inner elite. Charles, Archbishop de Rheims, had just returned from Rome and had come back a far more handsome young man than when he left. He had matured, Diane thought, as she studied the smooth lines of his face and the soft waves of blond hair that rose to a heart-shaped peak above his brows.

She smiled when she recalled her first impression of Charles as a young man. How ill-fitted he had seemed to a life in the clergy. He was the epitome of what the Protestants ridiculed so viciously; he had recently admitted to having fathered a child. He had also brought back from Rome a more apparent ambition. He and his brother, François de Guise, had already garnered great power with the future King; enough to surpass her with very little effort if they so chose. For now they were her friends, but she must take great care with them, she thought.

On the other side of Henri stood two more of his trusted friends, Charles de Brissac and Antoine de Bourbon. This was indeed a night of celebration. Henri was here and her two daughters had been invited to Court. But for the daughter they secretly shared, her family was together.

Diane looked out across the crowded room. Against one long wall, sitting on a sculptured wooden bench beneath the window, was her daughter Françoise and her husband Robert. They were whispering and laughing together like children. Diane smiled. Robert de La Marck was a good man. She had made a good marriage for her eldest child. They had been fortunate; they had managed to find love in their match. But perhaps it was not so much luck as it was logic. Françoise was as wise as she was pretty. That someone like Robert de La Marck should have fallen in love with her did not surprise Diane in the least. Françoise was tall and thin and just turned twenty-eight. She was, she realized for the first time, nearly the same age as Henri. She shuddered at the thought, and turned her face back toward the Dauphin and his entourage. *I will not think of that,* she thought. *Not tonight.*

At the moment, she had far more important concerns. Though Françoise was married, her second daughter, Louise, was not. Good matches for her daughters not only secured their future, but her own. If she chose carefully, there would always be a place for her should she ever fall out of favor with Henri. It was not easy to think in such terms now with so much love between them, but she had grown wise in her years at Court. Preparation, she had learned, could one day quite well save her life.

"POISON? What do you mean poison?"

Henri gripped her elbow after she had whispered the words. She had not wanted to tell him what she had suspected earlier that day in the Dauphine's apartments. At least not here, and certainly not like this. But he had insisted. He was pestering her relentlessly. She had no choice. He detested it when she kept anything from him and he would be cross when he discovered it. He was bound to find out sooner or later.

Now that her suspicions were revealed, Henri's face was stricken. He had asked her again what had taken her so quickly from the Dauphine's apartments earlier that afternoon. Nothing could have prepared him for her reply. As he realized the implications of what she had said, his eyes narrowed.

"I will kill her! So help me God, I will kill her myself!" he raged through clenched teeth. His eyes darted around the room for sight of Catherine. The movement of his head was swift, his body tensed. Diane put a hand on his arm with considerable force. Then she too looked around, but with a casual smile, as though their conversation had been only of the lightest nature.

"Henri, please. It is nothing that she has done," she whispered, still smiling. "At least nothing of which I am aware. It was just simply a feeling that I had there in her apartments. She gave me a goblet different from both of yours. There was even a different wine. I know how much she detests me and, well, I could not help but . . ."

Henri could see that, though they tried not to stare, others around them were straining to hear the exchange. Finally, his anger at a flashpoint, he gripped her hand and pulled her through the crowded ballroom with such ferocity that it was whispered that the Dauphin and his mistress surely must be engaged in some heated discord. Once they were halfway through the crowded room, Ruggieri, the Italian mystic, turned to the Dauphine.

"Well, well well," he said with a wry smile. "What do you suppose that is all about?"

"With any luck, Monsieur Ruggieri, it is a lover's quarrel," Catherine replied coldly before she turned away.

MAKING HIS WAY through the crowded room was like wading through mud. The faster Henri tried to walk, the more entrenched he became. Hooped skirts of heavy velvet and brocade impeded his path, but he forged ahead, clutching Diane's hand until it began to throb. He pulled her out into the corridor, past the stone-faced guardsmen in their red and blue livery. A group of the King's guests, who had gathered there, stared and whispered as they passed. Henri did not notice. He dragged Diane behind him through the two long doors and out onto the grand horseshoe staircase. She nearly fell twice on a thin sheet of ice that had formed on the edge of each of the stairs. He was snorting wildly and she could see his breath in the cold evening air.

"Henri, please! You're hurting me!"

"You cannot say something like that to me, m'amie, and then expect me to sit blithely by, doing nothing in your defense!" he shouted as he took the stairs, not caring who heard them.

The night air was cold. There was frost on the lawns and tiny crystals dripped from leaves on the trees. There was no one else foolhardy enough to brave the weather, except two guards, who spoke to one another in low tones as they headed toward them at the base of the horseshoe staircase. Before they were near enough to identify their future King, and perhaps perpetuate the gossip, Henri pulled Diane into the small alcove beneath the massive stone stairs. By now she was shivering. Diane wrapped her arms around herself, and then closed her mouth so that her teeth would not chatter.

"Henri, please," she said after she had caught her breath. This time her words were soft. Controlled. She waited for him to really hear her before she finished her sentence. They were facing one another. He was angry. He had been, as he often was in matters that concerned her, blinded by his rage. "Yes, *chéri*," she continued. "I fear her wrath, but what might we do? I must live here if I am to be with you, and yet her faction of allies has grown. In that there will always be a threat."

"That is not acceptable! There can be no threat to you!"

He turned away from her, not wanting to be brought so quickly from his anger by the look in her eyes. "From now on, you shall have a bodyguard. I shall also be arranging an official food taster, just as the Emperor had when he was in France. There shall be someone to go before you in everything. There will be no risks. Do you hear me, no risks!"

"Henri, I cannot live like that, and it would be cruel to put another man in harm's way to protect me."

"Oh, rest assured, there will be no serious threat to your new servants. Once Catherine and her entourage discover that I have made these amendments, they will not, I am certain, be willing to risk any action against you that would so clearly lead back to them."

After he finished speaking, she could see his tense expression fade, his rigid body relax. His lips parted. She could feel his warm breath against her face. He pulled her closer.

"I am sorry if I was cross. It is only that I could not bear for anything to happen to you . . . you know that . . ." he whispered. "The thought of . . . well, you know that I will do anything, and I do mean anything, to protect you!" He kissed her gently, and then pressed his lips more firmly over hers.

After another moment, Diane no longer felt the cold.

WHEN THEY RETURNED to the grand ballroom, Henri took her hand and squeezed it. It was a small movement down by her side where, in the crush of velvet and silk, he knew it would go unseen. He meant it as a show of support, a movement that said that she need not be afraid. He was there with her. Now and always. Diane glanced quickly around the room before she advanced farther into it.

Antoine de Bourbon came up beside them and began asking Henri something about the stag hunt that was planned for the next morning. Diane nodded a greeting to Bourbon and then turned away. François de Guise had caught her attention. He was laughing garishly over near the windows. He was drawing attention to himself with the exaggerated laughter. His companion was a woman, though between the plumed toques and the ornate headdresses around them, Diane could not identify her. She could, however, clearly see Guise.

His costume was fashioned of a very expensive brocade. The color perfectly matched his waves of reddish gold hair and the triangular-shaped beard at the point of his chin. Monsieur de Guise, it seemed, was newly betrothed, and that fact had dramatically improved his disposition over the past few weeks. It was a match so advantageous that everyone had come to treat him with a respect almost akin to reverence. His powerful family would have accepted no less for the eldest son. It was clear that his time had come.

His younger brother, the Archbishop, who now garnered powerful influence throughout Europe, had arranged the match. Guise himself had told Diane that he was greatly pleased by his prospective bride. Diane, however, doubted that now. As she gazed across the room, she could finally see the girl by whom he was, at the moment, transfixed. It was her own younger and unmarried daughter, Louise.

Henri felt the change in her posture. He followed her eyes until he saw them. "Brissac," he said with a hand over his mouth to mask the words, "would you be good enough to retrieve Guise." He pointed across the room. "And find Saint-André as well. I wish for all of you to meet me in the west wing in half an hour. And you are to say nothing of it to anyone."

"WHAT DO YOU MEAN, you have nothing prepared?" Anne d'Heilly's eyes flashed with fury at the poet, Clement Marot.

"Well, Madame, I only thought—"

The man who had once been one of her most staunch allies now stammered out a weak reply. Along with Jean Vouté, Marot had composed many cruel verses to slight Diane de Poitiers. But that had been before she had begun her rise to power beside the Dauphin. When he tried to finish, she interrupted him.

"You thought?!" Her eyes were combative and their emerald-green irises brilliant as she repeated his words.

"Yes, I thought that, well, that perhaps now with the King so ill and all . . ." Again he stammered. "That, well . . . perhaps the timing was not as, shall we say, opportune, as it once was, to deliver the same insults to her."

"Was not as opportune?" Again she repeated after him, her indignation growing. "Monsieur Marot, I pay you, and handsomely I might add, to entertain me with poetry, not advice. If you feel that you can no longer rise to the vocation for which you were selected, perhaps you should consider taking your services elsewhere!"

This was not the first time, of late, that Anne d'Heilly had been forced to defer to the power of Diane de Poitiers. But she could not, for all of the signs, allow herself to acknowledge her diminishing influence. She looked back at Marot, his words ringing in her mind. She caught him looking cautiously around the room. She knew he was trying to avoid being seen in secretive conversation with the fading *favourite*. Many others had begun to desert her in the same fashion. It was slow at first, with several of them playing both sides of the fence. But there was less need for pretense among them now. They saw, as she did, the inevitable. Even her one staunch ally, Philippe Chabot, had had the unbearable lack of grace to die on her, leaving her alone, in favor with virtually no one but the slowly dying King.

"Monsieur Marot, you are a poor excuse for a poet," she seethed, casting her wounded eyes upon him. "And you are an even poorer excuse for a friend. I want you out of here!" Then, as she turned away from him, someone pushed her from behind so that the wine she held splashed onto her very expensive green velvet gown.

"You imbecile! Now see what you've done!" she cried, but as she turned around, the reality of her own demise finally flashed before her, and with a vengeance.

"Why, did I do that?" said Diane, as though she were surprised.

"Oh, I am so dreadfully sorry. Please, accept my humble apology." Diane looked down at the soiled beaded velvet gown that it had taken six months to create and an instant to ruin. She had not meant to do it, but when it was done, she found that she could not help herself; she gave in to a very uncharitable burst of joy. "It is just so terribly crowded in here," she continued, fighting a smile, "with everyone pushing and shoving. Oh, and your lovely gown, and now it is ruined. Velvet never dries the same, does it?"

Anne d'Heilly's painted face went white with rage. "You are a stupid woman, Madame! As stupid as you are clumsy," she declared suddenly and turned away from her. She knew better than to accuse the future King's mistress of having orchestrated the slight intentionally. She no longer possessed the kind of power necessary to support it.

Diane watched her leave. After Anne had escaped into the crowd, she turned back around to see Clement Marot standing alone, holding his sides, nearly doubled over with laughter.

"Oh, thank you! Thank you! A thousand times, thank you! I never thought I would see it in my lifetime, but it was well worth the price of admission!"

"And what might the price have been?" Diane asked of the poet who had so often and so publicly sought to humiliate her with his cruel verses.

"I have paid the greatest price, Madame. The loss of your favor," Marot finally replied and then punctuated his words with an expression so humble that she nearly believed him. Nearly. Marot had been the poet bold enough to have written only against Diane one New Year when all the rest of his poems to the King's *petite bande* had been compliments.

> *What do you wish, Diane fair*
> *What can I bring you?*
> *You did not have, so I am told,*
> *As much good fortune in the spring*
> *As you are having in the fall*

"Madame de Poitiers, if you please, I have been foolish and I believe my carelessness may well have hurt you. For that I am profoundly sorry."

"Yes, well, none of us can change the past, Monsieur Marot. What is done, is done."

"But then perhaps, if I am fortunate, what they say will hold true, that time heals all wounds."

"Platitudes from a poet?" Diane asked with half a laugh.

He cleared his throat. "I am afraid it is the best one can hope for from an unemployed dilettante on such an unexpected moment."

The trite way he said it made her laugh, despite her dislike of this man who had helped to define her painful early years at Court. Like so many others who had snubbed her, now he too was clambering after her, begging her forgiveness. Also like the others, he sought to carve out a place for himself in the new regime by clever flattery, not sincerity. But there would be no place for the likes of either Clement Marot or Jean Vouté in the new regime. That was one thing to which Diane personally would see.

"OH, *MAMAN,* isn't this a lovely party? His Majesty even spoke to me, though I scarcely think he knew who I was. He could not have known that I was your daughter, because he was actually quite polite to me," swooned Louise de Brézé.

Louise, the whimsical younger daughter of Diane de Poitiers and Louis de Brézé, had come to Court at the Dauphin's insistence. Not only might she pass the holiday together with her family, but he had also suggested to Diane that this would be a splendid opportunity to formally secure for her a suitable husband.

"He looks so different up close, *Maman;* so entirely different than I had imagined," she continued and then cupped her hand around her mouth. "So old!"

Diane wanted to tell her to be mindful of her tongue, but she knew that there was little use in it. Louise had been her willful child and she had become an even more willful young woman. Beautiful, impetuous and willful. To the men at Court, these qualities had translated into exciting, and Louise had no shortage of suitors. Diane had seen for herself that François de Guise would become another of them if she were not careful. She knew that the marriage would be a difficult one to settle because quite possibly her daughter would refuse unless the candidate was to her own liking.

". . . and then that very handsome Monsieur de Guise was telling me all about his family seat at Joinville. It sounds lovely, *Maman*," she continued chattering in Diane's ear. "He is one of His Highness's best friends, is he not? They say he has begun to develop great influence here. Oh, I am certain a place will be carved out for him in the new regime. Quite a large place, do you not think?"

"Louise, I want you to keep away from Monsieur de Guise. He is nearly married, and his betrothed is a wealthy young woman with whom you have no hope of competing. An interest in him now can only mean heartbreak."

Louise began to laugh. "Humorous, do you not think, *Maman*? You telling me about the dangers of a married man?" She had not meant to be quite so insolent. But when it was out, she could not take it back. Nor could she rid the look of pain in her mother's eyes. "Oh, *Maman*, forgive me. I had no right."

Diane looked at her daughter. The elegant veneer only chipped by the girl's thoughtlessness. "They have sounded the call to dinner. You had better find your sister and Robert, and join them," she said and turned from her daughter, back into the crowd.

What Louise de Brézé did not know, what no one knew, was that her mother had never learned to take the references to her relationship with the future King of France with the carefree aplomb that it required. Confidence was essential to survive the ridicule and silent whispers cast at a royal *favourite*. Anne d'Heilly had learned it. Françoise de Foix had learned it before her. Both women had taken what the position afforded them, and had held their heads high.

But for Diane, the reality of being a mistress was still too painful. Her one fatal flaw, the one that kept her so vulnerable, did not come from the ridicule of others; it came from inside herself. Diane de Poitiers was above all things a profoundly religious woman. This affair went against all that she believed. She had never made peace in her heart with the sin of adultery, that she committed every day by loving Henri.

No one can be this happy, she often thought, *and commit a sin as great as mine.* She knew that some day, somehow, she would be made to pay for turning her back on the Commandments. *He may still love me now, but it has been fourteen years. He is still young. Soon I shall be forty-five. He is but twenty-nine.* In the darkest, most secret place of her heart, she was afraid. She knew only too well that from even the best of dreams one must eventually wake.

"I SHOULD LIKE SOMEONE sent out there immediately to get the preliminary figures," said Henri. "I wish to change it all. Enhance everything. The structure, the gardens, and especially the interior. Then bring me the figures. I need a working knowledge of what we are up against."

While the banquet progressed downstairs, Henri and his friends had gathered, as he had requested, in a small room on the second floor of Fontainebleau. It was an anteroom beside the King's drawing room. Henri stood against one of the long casement windows, looking out onto the garden as he spoke. Saint-André, Guise, Brissac and Bourbon were collected around him.

"But Your Highness," Brissac cautiously objected, "what you ask would take a small fortune. I saw Anet myself with you last summer, and it, well . . . it is in quite a sorry state."

Henri turned around. His eyes were sharp. "I am aware of the state of things, Charles, but Anet is her home. It means a great deal to her to know that no matter what, there is security there."

"But money . . ." Saint-André stammered, broaching the indelicate subject of the Dauphin's funds. As Henri's chief companion, he knew better than anyone the state of his master's finances. Even though Henri had his own accounts, every year Catherine used the majority of it for her household expenses and in refurbishing their chateau at Gien. Meanwhile, the King had still refused to turn over more than a minimum annuity on which he could live, and after her initial offer, Henri had refused to take more money from Diane. Saint-André's objection was legitimate.

"Of course we will not proceed with the actual construction until after I am King. However, I doubt whether you will find much objection to postponed payment for a potential royal commission of that magnitude," Henri replied, his voice full of confidence. "I also want you to commission a few artists, new ones, and see that they are French. Tell them positively no Italian designs. That will be the mark of my father's reign, not mine. The theme, as you might have guessed, should be black and white, to honor her."

"This could take some time, Your Highness."

"I have no time, Brissac!" he snapped. "I want the sketches as soon as possible. They are to be a gift. I want all of you on this matter at once, do you understand? There has been a threat to Madame's life, veiled though it is, and I mean to do everything in my power to protect her, and to see that she is not further disturbed by this."

"Threats? Your Highness, we had no idea," gasped Antoine de Bourbon.

"I am certain that you did not, but I want . . . I need to know that I can count on all of you, whatever my reasons. After all, you will be the core of my council, once I am King. One day I will need to lean on you absolutely, and I must know that you shall not question my authority in such matters." After he said it, he smiled and added, "Saint-André, you are likely to find a post as Grand Master. Brissac, you are sure to become Lieutenant-General, and Bourbon, *mon ami,* my cousin Jeanne is nearly of age. I would not be at all surprised if you were made her husband and the next King of Navarre."

His friends began to smile. It was very important to Henri that they understand; that they like him. These were his friends; except for Diane, the only friends he had in the world. He would honor each of them, if only they remained loyal to him and to the true Dauphine of France. After a moment, when none of them spoke out again, Henri cleared his throat and adopted a more stern expression.

"Brissac," he began again. "I want you to contact Roland Chrétien. You shall find him currently employed in the kitchens. You are to tell him that I have need of a personal body guard for Madame. The job is his if he should desire it."

"But, Your Highness," Bourbon cautiously objected. "Certainly there are other more suitable candidates from His Majesty's Guard."

"And any of them could be bought off for less than the cost of that very elegant cape of yours, my friend! No. I trust Roland with my life, and with Madame's life. That can be the only criterion." He let that declaration stand alone for a moment. Then he added, "When you speak with him, you are also to inform Clothilde Renard, the pastry cook, that she has been invited to join my staff as chambermaid to Madame. She is to report to Hélène Gallet at dawn."

Both Roland and Clothilde had been kind to him when he was a boy. Long ago he had promised himself he would help them. He remembered the day when Clothilde had tried to spare the life of a dying puppy simply because she had known what it had meant to him. He had not forgotten a single cake that she had made just for him; nor the ale and the friendship he had shared with Roland. This would be a beginning, a way finally to repay their kindness.

Henri turned back around to face the window. The room was warm. A thick coat of steam had formed on the glass. Henri fingered it until he had fashioned their secret emblem; the interlaced D and H that had sustained him those long months that he was separated from Diane. Then he turned around once again to his friends.

"Guise, fetch a slip of paper and copy this. Tell all of the artistic candidates that it is to be incorporated into their proposed designs, wherever possible."

When it was copied, Henri ran the palm of his hand over the glass, destroying the image.

"Oh, and Guise, one last thing. I could not help noticing you earlier with Mademoiselle de Brézé. I think it only fair to warn you that if you so much as touch her so that she is unfit for marriage, I will kill you myself. Is that clear?" Without waiting for a reply he added, "Now, gentlemen, I believe we have a banquet to which we must return!"

"I SWEAR IT, YOUR MAJESTY! I heard it with my own ears, I did! Just now in the anteroom outside of your apartments. The Dauphin was quite plainly making a fool of Your Majesty! Even picking his cabinet! Messieurs Saint-André and Bourbon were there, Monsieur de Brissac and even Monsieur de Guise!"

"How do you know this, Brusquet?" the King asked.

"Oh, they didn't know I was there because I ducked into the hearth. I was lucky there wasn't a blaze in it on such a cold night as this!" the jester chuckled and rung his hands nervously. "I just couldn't stand to hear it, Your Majesty. I knew it was proper to come to you."

"And where are they now?" asked the King in a controlled voice, the tone of which was just above a whisper.

"Still there, I should imagine, lording over your cabinet positions as if you was already dead . . . if you will pardon me for saying so, Sire."

The little man with the orange hair was so busy trying to convince the King of what he saw as subterfuge that he did not see the anger building. The King turned full force on him, sprang to his feet and tossed his walking stick across the dining table. The room, which was filled with courtiers, musicians and servants, was rendered instantly silent.

"Call the guards!" François bellowed in a warbled, almost unintelligible voice. "It is time I teach that thankless little heathen the cost of impropriety!"

François' cane was brought to him, but his anger seemed to give him a new burst of strength so that he did not need it. As he advanced through the crowded banquet hall, the only sound to be heard was Brusquet's labored breath as he hobbled, trying unsuccessfully to keep up with the King.

"BASTARD! Greedy, greedy little bastard!" the King raged in guttural sounds, brought on by the loss of his uvula. In the heat of anger, his body did not know the same curse. He flew up the stairs, followed by an entourage of men. "You are not King yet . . . not yet, bloody little cur!"

The tails of his crimson cape billowed behind him and even his aides struggled to keep pace with him. His apartments were not far from the staircase he had taken. François did not wait for his guard. He cast open the double doors to the room where Brusquet had hidden.

"All right, where are you? Come out here and fight me like a man!"

In a rage, the King began to toss furniture around the room. First a small table went crashing to the parquet floor. Then a fifteenth-century secretary, a gift from the Sultan Suleiman. The two silver ink wells sprayed black liquid onto the floor as they tumbled. Two more chairs were tossed. As the second one crashed to the floor, a leg broke free. He picked it up and began swinging it around the room as though it were a bat. He smashed a window, the very window in which Henri had drawn the cypher. Out went glassware. A mirror. An English tapestry.

"How dare you?" the King raged, blood pulsing into his face with every word. "Come out and face me like a man!" He swung at another table with the wooden bat. A rare Chinese vase careened onto the floor, smashing into bits.

"Your Majesty, please!" the Cardinal de Tournon, who had followed him, cautiously admonished.

But the King did not hear him as he swung around. The Cardinal had the foresight to duck at precisely the moment when the table leg would have struck his head. François continued on his rampage with no regard for what he had already done to the room, or what he had nearly done to his councilor. He lunged toward the cavernous fireplace. Perspiration bled from his pores as he panted between the words.

"Hiding from me, are you, boy? Mock me and then hide? Spineless, gutless excuse for a son! Hide from me now if you will, but I will get you! I swear I will get you!" He swung the bat into the fireplace hollow. By now a collection of courtiers and guards had gathered in the doorway of the small antechamber. One of them nearest the front was Claude de Guise, the younger brother of François and Charles de Guise. He was new at Court but like his brothers, Claude had been bred to value ambition above all else. Seizing the opportunity with no more than a moment's consideration, he turned from the scene and ran all the way back to the banquet room, praying that he was not already too late, to be the first to warn the Dauphin.

HENRI LOOKED UP at Claude de Guise. He was a tall, bony-faced boy whom he had personally seen brought here as a favor to the two elder Guises. Henri held a strip of warm capon between his thumb and forefinger and was ready to eat it when Claude advanced behind him.

"Your Highness, please," the young boy muttered in a breathless whisper. "I've come to warn you. It is the King. He believes that you have betrayed him. Brusquet overheard you and went straight to His Majesty. I know because I saw him just now and he is in a rage; tore up the entire room in which you and my brother met earlier. Now he seeks to find you!"

"So then let him come," Henri said blithely. He took the piece of meat into his mouth and began to chew it slowly, defiantly. Then he casually looked around the room as if daring the King to find him. Catherine gasped and lowered her head so that she would not be moved to speak out of turn. Saint-André put a hand to his lips.

"Henri, please," Diane whispered, "do not begin your reign with such a mark to color it. His Majesty is an old man who sees himself as he was, not as he is. You could surely kill him with the anger between you."

There was a long pause in which everyone around him held his breath. Finally, Henri stood and tossed his napkin onto the table.

"If you will excuse me, Madame," he said to Catherine in a controlled voice. Then bowed to her and turned from the table.

"Your Highness cannot run from him!" said Bourbon, springing up beside Henri. "What will people say?"

"They will say, Monsieur de Bourbon, that a wise Prince shall make an even wiser King." Diane interceded quickly with a reproving look, and then followed Henri from the table.

Surrounded by his entourage of Saint-André, the two Guises, Brissac and Bourbon, Henri and Diane walked briskly down the shadowy corridor away from the banquet hall. Steadily, the sound of music and the mélange of voices faded. It was replaced by the rhythmic echo of their gathered footsteps on the elegant parquet floor.

"Well, where shall we go?" he asked Diane as they paused on the landing of a steep spiral staircase. "Surely the King will seek me out at my apartments as well as yours."

Diane thought a moment and then looked at Guise. "François, may His Highness and I have the use of your apartments for this evening?"

"But of course, Madame. Anything."

"Good," she replied with a smile and they continued on down the labyrinth of corridors that led from the opulent wing to Guise's more modest accommodations.

"Thank you, my friend," Henri said and cuffed him lightly as they gathered before the door. Diane looked at the younger brother, Claude, who had been the first to warn them.

"You have acted with honor toward His Highness and myself," she said. "I promise you your allegiance shall not be forgotten."

The others left, hoping not to attract attention, but Guise and his brother, Claude, remained. They waited until the Dauphin and his mistress had gone inside and they heard the click of the latch. Then, when he could contain it no longer, a sardonic smile broke across Guise's large-featured face and he embraced his younger brother.

"Good work, my boy. It is just like the game of chess," he muttered beneath his breath, repeating his uncle's words from long ago. "Not just one move, but the next, and the next . . ."

DIANE AND HENRI stood together in the shadow of an early morning sun behind the stables; he not wanting to go, but knowing that he must. His white stallion was saddled. His guards were mounted and waiting. A thin blue mist fell around them as they held one another. He would go to Saint Germain-en-Laye. His three children had been permanently installed there to keep them from the unsettling existence of the Court's constant travel. It would be natural for him to leave on the pretext of seeing them. This, they had decided, was the path to the least amount of rumor.

During the night they had passed in François de Guise's small apartments, they did not sleep. Diane had managed to convince Henri that it was in his best interest to leave until both his anger and the King's had subsided. No more than a few days, she had urged. He must take no chances now. Diane, however, would re-main at Fontainebleau. Her daughters and son-in-law were still there. It would be inappropriate to leave without them, and she had all but decided on a husband for Louise. On the twentieth of March her daughters would return to Anet and then, she prom-ised, she would join him.

"When it is safe for you to come, shall we meet at Chenon-ceaux?" he asked. "It has been much too long."

"I would like that," she replied and then let him kiss her. The mist fell more heavily, then became a light rain. Diane shivered beneath her cape and the fur from her collar fluttered up around her face. Henri ran a gloved finger across the line of her jaw, to push away the fur, then he pulled her tighter, closing his eyes.

"Great Zeus! This is difficult! You know I despise leaving you," he whispered.

"But it is the right thing to do."

"Yes, I believe that is true."

"Kiss her for me, will you?" she asked, not needing to name their daughter.

"I will," he said, and then he added, "Shall we bring her with us to Chenonceaux?" Diane could see his face light up even at the prospect. "Monsieur d'Humières tells me that she rides like a champion already, and there are such nice woods there. I know she would adore it."

"Well, we can scarcely bring one and not the others, if we do not wish to incite rivalry among them."

"Of course you are right. What would I do without you to keep me to my course?" he asked, laughing a vulnerable little laugh; one that only she would ever hear.

"Alas, I fear we shall never know the answer to that!"

"I love nothing more than to hear you say that," he replied, and then the smile passed. "Come to me soon, *m'amie*," he whispered. "You know that I shall be nothing until you are with me again."

"And I shall be nothing without you."

HE HAD BEEN both friend and bitter rival to François I. Now at the news of the death of Henry VIII, the French King wept. They had been contemporaries, both raised as warrior Kings. Both steeped in military tradition. They had done what they had done for the good of their countries. They were brothers. Henry in England, the Emperor Charles in Spain, and he in France. Forgotten now were the battles. The discord. Henry VIII's break with the Church. Against the wishes of his ecclesiastical advisors, François had a Mass said for him at Notre Dame in Paris.

The news had struck him profoundly, for he knew that it was an omen; a sign of his own mortality. All around him, people waited for him to die; waited for the new regime. In this purgatory between life and death, François found to his own surprise that he wanted desperately to live, if only for a little while longer. There was nothing like the prospect of death, he thought, to make one appreciate the precious, transitory spark that is life.

As a drowning man grasps for the last remaining straw when all else about him is water, François clung to the few remaining faithful who were left to him. Desperate for support, he wrote to his sister, Marguerite, and asked her to come to France. But like her brother, the Queen of Navarre was also ill and could not risk the trip in winter's bitter cold. The only one really left to him was his Anne, the woman he had loved and at times despised. So together with a small entourage as the month of March neared an end, they set out on a pilgrimage between the various royal estates, hoping to outrun death.

Disregarding the bitter cold and the pain that plagued him, François traveled from Fontainebleau to Les Tournelles, then to Compiègne, to Villers-Cotterêts and to Chateau Madrid. But it was at Anne d'Heilly's house in Limours that he realized the force which he had been trying to outrun was now about to kill him.

When he was told that Henri, his last surviving son and heir was at Saint Germain-en-Laye, he instructed his guards to take him there. He made it only so far as a nobleman's palace in Rambouillet before he collapsed. At the King's request, word was dispatched immediately to Saint Germain-en-Laye, but no reply came. The Dauphin and Madame de Poitiers had taken the children to Chenonceaux.

THE GLITTERING CHATEAU on the river Cher was beautiful in winter. When the gray sky was free of clouds, it was like a canvas onto which the delicate chateau was painted. Henri's daughter Diane, who had just turned nine two months before, said once that Chenonceaux was her favorite place on earth because her father and Diane always seemed to be so happy there. She liked Madame Diane's house at Anet almost as much, though it did not have the same beautiful gardens or the great willow trees that sloped down to the shore.

She liked another piece of imagery. She told her father that when she was riding and looked back through the thick of trees, the way the house seemed to rise out of the water and shimmer against it at sunset was like a crown on the head of a great sleeping giant. Even though it was winter, there were the most magical sunsets there. While Catherine admonished her for possessing an overly indulged imagination, Madame Diane would always laugh with her at the images. They would ride through the woods envisioning together what the great giant would look like if he should wake and come up out of the water. It would have been a perfect holiday for Henri, the children and Diane, if not for one disjointed element: the presence of Henri's wife.

Catherine had arrived at Saint Germain-en-Laye the day before they were to leave for Chenonceaux. She announced then that she had come to see her children. Henri could not refuse her that. Nor could he find the words to object the following morning when she readied her entourage and her trunks and said she meant to join them at the little chateau on the river.

One afternoon at Chenonceaux, when Diane had taken their daughter riding out into the forest, Catherine seized Henri's solitude as a moment for herself. She stood in the doorway to the main drawing room on the first floor, watching him. He was sitting beside Francesco Primaticcio, his father's Court painter, watching him put the finishing touches on an allegorical painting of Diane as Diana in the guise of the huntress. The house was quiet. There was only the sound of the wood crackling in the fire and the occasional creaking of floorboards on the landing above. There was a tranquillity here that Catherine liked. She had not felt it since she had left Italy, and to be given moments like this alone with her husband, she almost did not mind that she must share the house with his mistress. Catherine advanced slowly. He was facing the fire. His back was to her, and both men were staring at the haunting image on the canvas. It was definitely her husband's whore, draped in flowing gauze and surrounded by cherubs and hunting dogs.

"Lovely. Really, lovely," she said, managing to sound sincere.

Henri turned with a start and rose to his feet. "I did not hear you enter."

"I was just standing there a while, watching you, thinking how peaceful it is . . . how happy we are here."

Henri began to pitch from side to side as though any moment he might bolt from the room to get away from her. She had a way of making him feel as if they were both children again, facing one another for the first time in the Pope's house in Marseilles. The anger. The resentment was all there when he looked at her.

"Thank you," he said, turning toward Primaticcio. "That will be all for today." When the artist stood and began to pack his things, Henri turned back to his wife. "Would you like to sit down?"

Catherine did not reply, but delicately slid her large brown velvet-sheathed body into the leather chair. Then she looked up at him. A smile broke across her thick lips and she motioned with her eyes that he should take the chair that the artist had just left. There was a long silence between them and Henri wanted to say anything to break it. He sat down and, in the silence, looked at her. Her wide-eyed gaze was repugnant to him; so loving and expectant.

"So, how are you feeling?" he asked, struggling for the words that would be construed by his wife as pleasant.

"I feel wonderful, Henri. Never so grand as when I am filled with your child."

Henri shivered. He hated it when she spoke as though there were something more between them than duty. She was still smiling; those cool black eyes of hers sparkling with her triumph over Diane. She ran a hand across her belly without changing her gaze.

"You know, I can feel him already inside of me. I feel certain that God will see fit to deliver me of another son."

Henri smiled a weak smile and then sprang from his chair. He began to wring his hands as he walked toward the window, hoping that he would see Diane and their daughter nearing the chateau to rescue him from this. It seemed like hours that they had been gone. Catherine stood. He could feel her advancing toward him as he gazed out of the window. He heard the swish of her fat legs against her gown.

"This is nice, having a bit of time to ourselves like this . . . an opportunity to speak privately."

Henri spun around ready to defend his relationship with Diane before Catherine could even utter a criticism, but the look on her face was so pathetic that he decided against it.

"Yes, I suppose it is," he conceded. But when she began to move toward him, he left the window and sat down at a small gaming table across the room. Despite the sincerity of her overtures, he was being stalked by a very clever fox and he knew it. "Have you had an audience with the children yet today? Elizabeth is almost totally recovered from infection, and they tell me François did ask for you."

"I have not seen them," she replied without hesitation as she sat down beside him and picked up a deck of cards. "Shall we play?"

Henri was indifferent to Catherine's lack of maternal desire now. But once, after the birth of their daughter, Elizabeth, it had infuriated him. It seemed that she loved nothing so much as being pregnant, and yet once the children were born she wanted nothing to do with them.

Humières, the children's governor, often complained that, though she wrote to him inquiring of their progress, she rarely visited the royal nursery. She almost never wrote directly to her children. That first year after Elizabeth's birth, Henri had considered approaching her, but he had thought better of it. His motivation was, as it always had been, for the sake of Diane. As official governess, she had come to develop a warm and tender relationship with each of his three children. In turn, they adored her as though she, not Catherine, were their real mother.

Henri loved to watch her with them, poring over lessons or reading them stories. Her affection for them was as natural as if she had given birth to them all. When he saw that she was willing to accept his children as her own, he resolved to keep his silence; for in this, he was bound ever closer to Diane.

He looked up again across the gaming table. The fleshy face and bulging dark eyes were directed toward him as Catherine waited for his reply to her request. There was still no sign of Diane or their daughter. So grudgingly, as though it were a supreme sacrifice, he agreed to play one hand.

"You know, Henri, I do believe that I love it here better than anywhere else in the world. There is something nearly spiritual about this place; something that quiets the mind and fills the soul. Would you not agree?"

He dealt her hand and looked up with a vague, disinterested

stare. He finally nodded in reply, and looked back down at his own selection of cards. *God, where was Diane? Would she ever return?*

"If I give you a son, my lord, will you give me this place as a gift, once you are King?"

"What?" he muttered, hearing her clearly and yet, unable to believe what she had asked. He cast down his cards and looked up at her again.

"I want you to give me Chenonceaux."

Henri felt an awful churning in the pit of his stomach at the mere thought that this nearly sacred place should one day belong to her. When he looked at her again, he saw that fixed black-eyed stare and knew that she was demanding a reply. His mind went blank. How could he answer that? How could he tell her no as boldly as he felt it? That he had all along intended it for Diane; for the woman he loved. How could he tell her that he had known that this place had been meant for his mistress alone, since the very first night he had spent there in her arms?

"There really is no place on earth like it," Catherine continued, undaunted. "And there are so many things I could do here. As a beginning, what would you think if we extended it across the river, enclosed the bridge and created a grand ballroom where we could entertain our Court?"

"Are we to play cards here, or not?" he snapped. "And after all, what if it is not a son?"

"But if it is," she persisted, "if it is, it would be the perfect gift. Nothing could make me happier, after everything, well everything that has occurred between the three of us."

"A gift is something freely given, Catherine, not demanded."

She lowered her thick lower lip as a hint of an oncoming pout. The room fell silent once again; a long, interminable silence.

"Good God, Catherine! We shall see, all right? We shall see!"

HE COULD HEAR them as they gathered in the main vestibule. First Antoine's whispers and then the echo of Diane's laughter as he sat at the gaming table with Catherine.

"Papa! Papa!" Henri's daughter Diane ran into the room in her dark riding clothes and darted onto her father's lap, disregarding the fact that she was far too old to do so. "Papa, we had the most marvelous time, we truly did! Uncle Antoine let me ride a big horse, the black one with the long white tail. And Uncle François raced me through the meadow, but I won!"

Henri kissed his daughter and then looked up. François de Guise strode into the room and removed his riding gloves. Diane came in behind him, their faces flushed from the ride. He whispered something to her that made her laugh and Henri stifled a twinge of envy. Behind them were Antoine de Bourbon, Claude de Guise and Jacques de Saint-André. A whispered exchange followed between Guise and Saint-André as Hélène came in through one of the small side doors.

"Ah, so there you are, *ma fille!*" Hélène said with a gentle smile. "They've kept you out well past time for you to rest."

"But I do not wish to rest. I am not in the least tired, and I have so much to tell Papa."

Everyone but Catherine chuckled at the child's endearing protestations. The Dauphine stiffened in her chair and gently lay down her hand of cards. Her private moment with Henri was over. She glared jealously at the little girl. Only after her father insisted that Mademoiselle Gallet was right, and he promised to come and see her after supper, did she agree. Reluctantly she curtsied to the others and skipped down the hall, her small hand wrapped in Hélène's.

After she had gone, a young steward brought a tray of silver wine goblets and set them on a small oak table near the door. Another entered the room a few moments later, and lay down a tray of confits and small cakes.

"Oh, splendid! I am famished!" Antoine smiled, as he bolted from a chair that was fixed beneath a large allegorical tapestry. Claude de Guise, the youngest brother, joined them and the two men began to bicker over who would win the few candied plums arranged in the shape of a crescent, on the outer edge of the dish. Catherine took a goblet of wine from a silver tray.

"You know," she said, directing her comment to Henri, "it really is not wise to indulge the child so. It will only serve to make her terribly petulant."

Diane sat tenuously in one of the leather chairs across the room, removing herself from the instant tension between husband and wife. François de Guise handed Diane a goblet of wine and then stood beside her. Everyone in the room looked at Catherine, who regretted instantly what she had been forced by envy to say. She knew that the little girl, named after his mistress, was Henri's favorite child. That fact was no secret to anyone who had ever seen them together. Catherine fought frantically for something to say that would diffuse her objectionable remark.

"So then, you had a pleasant ride," she said. "The air appeared a bit too brisk for me."

To Catherine's great surprise, it was Diane de Poitiers who now rescued her. "It was lovely, Your Highness," she said. "The woods around here still have some green, and Mademoiselle Diane enjoyed it so much that I believe it made it that much more special for the rest of us."

Catherine looked around. Guise and Saint-André were nodding their agreement. "I understand just what you mean," she agreed. Then the look of gratitude vanished. "I was saying that very thing to my husband before your return. I was telling him that the peace around here feels nearly spiritual. It is a place to which I know I shall never tire of coming. In fact, I beat His Highness at cards just now, and got him to promise this chateau to me; a gift for the birth of our next child."

"I said I would consider it!" Henri charged with a thundering voice of disapproval. "*Jésu,* Catherine! will you never learn to keep quiet?"

Diane looked at Henri but said nothing. One of her many gifts that set her apart from the Dauphine, was having learned very early in life when to hold her tongue. She wondered, as she looked at him so full of pent-up rage, what Catherine might have done to extract such an agreement.

He was tense. His eyes were charged and glittering; his face was pinched and white. It was to have been a special holiday, but nothing had gone quite the way he had planned it since their arrival. The primary problem was that the chateau was small. Diane knew that Henri did not relish sharing such familiar accommodations with his wife and his mistress. This was, after all, their sacred place, and Henri had meant their return to be special. They had so little time away from the rest of the Court. Away from Catherine. It was Catherine, however, who had installed herself in the largest suite on the ground floor; who even in these cramped quarters was at all times surrounded by her train of Italians, her own foods, her suite of ladies, and her two pet lap dogs. She had managed to make her presence known and felt at nearly every hour of the day.

When a servant came to say that supper was now served, Catherine was the first to rise from her chair, wanting to escape the tension that she had created. But none of them ever made it into the dining hall. As they all began to walk toward the door, a messenger, visibly shaken and out of breath, came in from the corridor. He said he brought urgent news about the King.

"Your Highness, the King is gravely ill." The messenger removed his toque and stepped into the room as he made the announcement.

"Ah well, he has been ill many times before. I am certain that the old dog will recover once again."

"It is the abscess, Your Highness. It has spread. I am sorry to inform you that the royal physicians do not expect him to last till month's end."

The room of courtiers fell silent. Henri moved to speak. He wanted to say something else trite like, "The King be damned!" or "The devil take him!" . . . or that "Surely his whoring has gotten him into this!" He had begun to form the words on his lips. It was a reaction. Those kind of comments had defined their relationship for more years than he could recall. But what he found as he stood there among his friends, his wife and his mistress, now surprised him. After everything François had done to him, after every harsh word between them, Henri could say nothing. Love mixed inside him with what he thought was hate. It swelled up until he thought he would choke.

"He is installed at Rambouillet, Your Highness," said the messenger, "and he is . . . well, he is asking for you. He knew that you might not come. He asked me . . . this is difficult, Your Highness, he asked me to beg if necessary. 'A dying man's last wish,' he said to say." Then the messenger hung his head.

"Thank you, Captain," he said in a steady voice. Diane looked at him with concern, but she did not speak. The only sound in the room came from Catherine, whose fat jeweled fingers covered her face, as she sobbed into them.

Henri looked around the room. Such sad faces. Everyone was looking at him; all of them waiting for him to respond. When no appropriate words came, he handed the full silver wine goblet to Saint-André, and walked out through the arched doorway. He walked the length of the coved vestibule and went alone up the stone staircase to his bedchamber. When he knew that he was alone, he slammed the door and leaned against it. His eyes began to fill with tears, so he closed them. When he opened them again, he saw her. It was the image of his mother.

IT WAS QUITE PLAIN. Not a faded, willowy apparition at all. She wore a white gown, the front of which was braided with gold embroidery. Her head was covered with a soft white hood and flowing veil. It was a costume long outdated at the French Court but one he recalled vividly from his childhood. He saw the delicate face, the beautiful eyes, and he knew that it was her. Henri passed his hand over his eyes, but when he opened them again, the image was still there.

"Maman?" he whispered in disbelief. His hands and legs began to tremble as he moved a few careful steps closer. The image began to fade with his nearness. He knew then that he was to move no closer. He missed her desperately. He had loved her, and she had loved him. She was the only one, until Diane. Now, gazing at her image, the wound from her loss felt open and raw again. He stood completely still near the door, not wanting her to disappear, filled with every boyhood emotion he had ever felt for her. The talks beside the bed, the sensation of brushing her hair, the smell of it.

After a moment, he began to see what looked like sadness in her eyes. Two tiny glistening tears fell onto her cheeks. Then he knew why she had come. The moment that the realization came to him, the image began to fade. Slowly, steadily, like a dwindling fire . . . the image dulled, and then in an instant, expired. She was gone. But Henri was filled with her. He understood. It was the most extraordinary thing that had ever happened to him and he knew that it would change his life. She wanted him to forgive his father. She wanted him to let go of the past so that he could rule the future. She wanted him to be a great King. To forgive was the measure of that greatness. Then, as effortlessly as if she had asked him, he did.

THE ROOM WAS DARK AND MOIST, and choked with the smell of death. All around the small, rectangular bedchamber in the chateau Rambouillet, the last bastion of the King's faithful held vigil. Princess Marguerite, Annebault, Sourdis and Barre all stood at the periphery of the room, whispering prayers for his immortal soul.

Henri looked at his father motionless on the bed. He was draped with a heavy tapestried blanket of blue and gold. His head rested on a blue silk pillow. His face was white as wax and he looked as if he were already dead. Catherine walked behind Henri. She had not ceased her sobbing since the King's message had come to Chenonceaux, but Henri had long ago lost awareness of it.

Diane waited in the hall outside of the bedchamber with François de Guise and Jacques de Saint-André. Anne d'Heilly stood in a corner with no one but her sister, Louise, to comfort her. She was no longer permitted to see the King. Just as he was to receive extreme unction, he waved her away. "Do not let her see me dying," the King had said, and they obeyed him.

Henri moved cautiously toward the side of the enormous carved bed. The heavy crimson bedcurtains were drawn back and the room was thick with the smoke of incense. He was surrounded by clerics and his confessor. As Henri drew nearer, he could hear the shallow resonance of his father's labored breath. He had been this way, they said, for four days. Henri's sister, Marguerite, sat on a small stool beside the bed. She reached up and took his hand. Henri squeezed it and could feel her trembling. When he looked back down again, the King opened his eyes. Marguerite nodded to her brother and stood so that Henri might sit.

"So then, you've come," the King whispered, gasping between each breath. Henri nodded and took the King's spotted, blue-veined hand. It was cold. Henri squeezed it hard and then sat down in the room lit with glowing tallow candles. He said nothing about the visitation, which was the primary reason he had come to Rambouillet at all. He believed it to have been a personal message between his mother and himself. It was something to help him deal with what he knew was about to happen. He tried desperately to fight back the tears; tears that marked a lifetime of regret. The King saw it

"Don't, boy," he whispered. "I am the least in this world who is worthy of your tears . . ." Henri squeezed the King's cold hand again and looked up, still fighting his tears. He brushed the back of his arm across his face and looked back down into his father's dim eyes.

"God, how many mistakes I have made, and how much I have hurt you," said the King. "Perhaps it is death that makes one look back with such clarity on the errors of a life. Henri . . . my son . . . I must speak to you plainly. I have little time to do otherwise. I must speak to you about the Queen; not Eleanor, but my Claude, the true Queen."

The sound of his mother's name coursed through him. The King could not have known, Henri thought, about the apparition, and yet this was the first time since her death that they had spoken of her. It must be the illness. Death was clouding his mind with reflections. He let the King continue.

"She was the most beautiful woman I have ever known. Not in the same way as Anne, but in her soul. It was her soul that was beautiful. Eternal. I was just too young . . . too foolish to see it then. I did not see her beauty. I did not deserve her."

Henri longed to interrupt his confession, but a greater power urged him to silence. "You, my son, had the grave misfortune of being the very image of the Queen. You were her favorite, and each time I looked upon you I saw the injustices done to her mirrored back on me tenfold. That was unbearable. I blamed you for being like her. I blamed you for reminding me of my weakness." Tears now fell from his gray, tired eyes. "I will not ask you to forgive me, for I do not deserve it. I will ask you only, my son, to believe that for what I have done to you, for all of it, I am truly, humbly . . . sorry."

Henri could contain his sobs no longer. He cast himself onto his father's chest and clutched his neck. Two tears streamed down the gray waxen face of the dying King, as he began to stroke his son's dark curls of hair.

THEY HAD TWO DAYS TOGETHER as father and son. During that time, Henri did not leave his side. The words between them were tender and forgiving. They spoke of many things; of the future, of heresy in France, of leniency for Anne d'Heilly. The King also warned him about the ambitions of the Guises, and of Madame Diane. Together they heard Mass and took communion. The King blessed the son, and the son forgave the father for a lifetime of betrayal. They embraced. Then, at two o'clock on March 31, 1547, the King of France took a last shallow breath and whispered, *"In manus tuas, Domine, commendo spiritum meum,"* called out, *"Jésu"* . . . and closed his eyes for the last time.

29

I CANNOT DO THIS! I do not know how to be a King!"

Henri gazed out an oriel window at the palace in Rheims, where later that morning he was to be crowned. Rheims was steeped with the history of France. The souls of Clovis, Charles

VII and Joan of Arc echoed in the great hollow of the Cathedral. Beside its mighty oak doors a scaffold had been erected between two carved pillars. On the dais, draped with blue and gold fleurs-de-lys, were three seats covered in black velvet. One for the King's sister, Marguerite, one for the new Queen of France and the third for the officially acknowledged *favourite,* Diane de Poitiers. Henri turned back around and looked at her with a face drawn from worry and lack of sleep.

"I am not prepared. I do not know the first thing about what it takes to rule a country." He shook his head dejectedly and walked away from the window.

"*Chéri,* you need only know that you *are* King. Whatever you do, however you do it, that shall be the truest measure."

"But, where do I begin?"

"Begin by believing," she said with a confidence that was his sole source of strength. "Believe that you alone are King."

Since the death of François I, four months before, Henri had shielded himself from this day beneath the cloak of an official period of mourning. Tradition set it at ninety days.

Until now he had been safe. After today, his life and Diane's would be forever changed. Henri turned back around, his eyes full of fear. He drew nearer to her.

"You must help me. You must promise to help me, for I shall not be able to do it without you."

"Then I shall be there."

Her assurances calmed him and she stepped back to give his garments a final inspection. They were newly prepared ceremonial vestments. The old ones, which his father had worn thirty-two years before, had faded.

The tunic that he now wore was azure blue satin sewn with gold fleurs-de-lys. The sleeves were trimmed with crimson. In fabric and design they were exactly like the previous coronation vestments, in all but two bold details. On the front of the tunic, boldly embroidered in pearl-colored satin, was the intertwined D and H symbol that Diane had created for him. Beside it, there was fashioned a new emblem. Three crescent moons were worked together, each with its own meaning. One crescent symbolized the pendant which she had given him fourteen years before. That had become for him a symbol of fortune. Another crescent symbolized Diana, the goddess of the moon, and the last crescent was the heraldic mark of a second son. These alterations to the ceremonial vestments were a major break with tradition and they both knew it.

Diane ran her fingers along the satin symbols and then looked up at him. "Are you certain this is what you want to do? It is, after all, a very public declaration."

"I am certain of nothing more than I am of this," he replied. "And could it have been more, I swear to you, I would have done it."

And he had wished to do more to honor Diane and his love for her. She did not know that since his father's death, he had repeatedly requested an amendment to his coronation that would have included her participation in the actual ceremony. But he was told with great vehemence that centuries of tradition had not even permitted the participation of the Queen, much less a mistress in so important an event. So, when his father's coronation vestments were found to be in poor condition, Henri had taken the opportunity of declaring his allegiance to Diane in this more subtle way.

"It is time, Your Majesty," said Saint-André, coming up behind them.

Henri turned and waited as four pages advanced. Each was dressed in a doublet of black and white velvet, the same D and H emblem sewn onto the fabric. They draped the long gold and ermine cape around his shoulders and then Henri reached out and offered his arm to Diane. As they strode together down the corridor, she saw the newest measure of his love for the first time. There was a row of guards positioned on each side of the corridor. All of them stood at attention dressed in new livery. Gone was the red and blue of the old regime. Their shirts were now black with white satin slashes. Their stockings were white, and on the breast of each black doublet were the same interlaced D and H, and the three crescents shaped into a ring.

"Well, *m'amie,* are we ready then?" he asked as they strode arm in arm down the corridor.

"Never more." Diane smiled.

DIANE AND HENRI went first to the private chapel at the palace in Rheims after the first coronation banquet. There were to be many festivities tonight and over the succeeding days and he wanted to spend this first night alone with her. But first, in the chapel, on a crimson prie-dieu with Diane beside him, the new King privately prayed for God to help him be a good man and a good ruler. Only then could he proceed unencumbered to her apartments. There in his presence, she was undressed and bathed by Hélène and Clothilde. At his instruction, her eyes were then covered with a long silk blindfold. Then they were left alone. Still clothed himself in the ceremonial tunic that honored his love of her, Henri held her close to his chest and kissed her.

"May I look now?" she asked.

Henri smiled and led her with her arms outstretched, slowly toward the bed. "Very well then, you may look now."

As she tore the cloth from her eyes, the playful smile faded. There, behind the half closed bedcurtain, on a white silk pillow, lay the Crown Jewels. They were a glittering array of gold, diamonds, emeralds, rubies and pearls. There were eight pieces in all. Among them were two triangular brooches, both set with diamonds, and each with a pendant black pearl. There were two rubies and a large square-cut emerald which was mounted in gold.

"Oh, Henri . . ." she gasped, "but these are . . . Anne's jewels."

"They were Anne's. Now they are yours," he said simply. He reached out and, from the collection, took a long rope of pearls, rubies and diamonds. He slipped them onto her bare neck. It was a heavy piece with eleven diamonds cut in tables and points. "This one was my mother's. My father presented it to her before I was born. She wore it for her last official portrait."

Diane looked down at the string of jewels that lay glittering in the cleft between the rise of her bare breasts. She fingered them delicately as if she did not believe they were real. But they were.

She had seen this piece many times on Anne d'Heilly. She knew the history. Henri took nothing away from his country's heritage by the presentation of this gift to her. Although they were indeed part of the Crown Jewels, this collection was only part of a larger assemblage established by his father twenty years earlier. At that time, François had chosen to present part of the jewels to the Crown and to keep the others for his personal use. The portion that lay before Diane now was the King's private collection.

"But why?" she muttered.

Henri took her hands in his own and held them together. "Many years ago, I gave you my heart when it was all that I had to give. I promised you then that one day I would lay the world at your feet. These, *m'amie,*" he said, pointing to the jewels, "are only the beginning."

"But what of Anne? They were given to her by your father."

"Oh, I suspect she was only too glad to surrender them to Guise. He told me, when he returned from her estate, that she thought he had come to kill her. I spared her life, you know; I suppose returning these without objection is the least that she could do in return."

"But the charges against her, the treason, will they not stand?"

This time she could not help but ask. Since the King's death, evidence had been uncovered implicating the Duchesse d'Etampes in a plot against the King. A messenger had confessed to carrying secret letters from Anne to the Emperor during his trip through France. The letters were said to detail what she knew about French military tactics and strategic points of defense. Fortunately for security's sake, the plot had been uncovered quickly and all covert strategy altered. But the evidence of treason against Anne d'Heilly remained.

"I made a promise to His Majesty that I would be merciful with her," he said and then looked at Diane. "And so I have decided to keep my word." He waited for her to object. He expected it. Anne d'Heilly's treason was a scandal that now rocked the entire Court of France, and the decision to free her from prosecution already tormented him. She had done so much to Diane; all of the plotting. The malice. Vouté. Marot. But to his surprise, Diane did not object. She took in a deep breath and, after a moment, smiled.

"Then it is as Your Majesty wishes," she said simply.

"After all," he added, as if he were trying to convince himself. "The Duchesse d'Etampes is receiving her punishment from a much higher source. I am told that her husband has rejected her and she is in danger from the townspeople who dwell around her and know of her crimes. Fading into anonymity, along with fear for her life, shall be punishment enough. I have taken back the jewels and all but one of her houses. Montmorency always admired her accommodations best."

It was the first time his name had been mentioned between them in several months. Diane lowered her eyes.

"I want him back, m'amie. I should like you to go with me to Chantilly to persuade him to return."

"When?"

"I have sent a messenger already. We shall leave tomorrow to speak with him personally, if you approve."

She had always known that this turn of events was only a matter of time. Diane had been given six long years without the complication of Montmorency but she had known from the beginning that it would not last. When she looked into Henri's eyes she saw the need there. Montmorency had been forgotten by everyone but him.

As a young man, the stern Grand Master had impressed the young Prince like no one else. Henri had long admired his sober judgment and common sense as qualities that he himself lacked. He also envied Montmorency's staunch patriotism and his military achievements. Montmorency had been the father Henri had never had. He had an influence with which even she could not compete. For whatever their grievance in the past, Diane knew that Henri loved the old immovable Constable, and so now, must she too. Love. Yes, that would be the common thread, she thought; the one that would wash away the past and help them begin again; perhaps this time, as friends.

When he could see that she would not oppose him in his desire to see Montmorency returned, Henri pulled her to his chest and kissed her. Then he looked down at the jewels spread around her.

"Do they please you?"

"They are far too extravagant a gift."

"They are only meager symbols of what I feel, Diane, and I shall not stop until the love that I bear for you has filled the whole world . . . *Donec totum impleat orbum.*"

He repeated the words that were to become his official motto, for he meant them exactly. There could never be enough jewels, estates or extravagances to show her and the world the extent of his devotion. She alone had believed in him, understood him, and she alone had loved him from the beginning.

THE NEXT MORNING, they lay together amid the spray of glittering jewels. The bedcurtains were still drawn so that they were alone. By the light of a huge tallow candle, Henri showed her the preliminary sketches for Anet. The work which he had most admired was by a young French artist named Philibert de L'Orme. He told her as they looked at them that a goddess required a proper temple, and with the help of L'Orme, he intended to build her one.

"I love his ideas," he said as they pored over the details drawn on large sheets of parchment and strewn across their knees on the heavy tapestried bedcovers. "His love of classic designs, as opposed to the Italian style, are what first endeared him to me. Saint-André favors him as well." Then he pushed the sketch aside and leaned over to kiss the tip of her nose. "When it is complete, I want Anet to be a tribute to you and to what we share. One day when we are both gone, I would like people to look at it and know that he who was King for a time, lived his life in devotion only to her." He lay his head back on the pillows and smiled a smile of vision. "Yes, I wish a new age to begin with L'Orme. He shall open the door for so many other young French artists: Cousin, Marten, Goujon. They shall all help me put my mark on Fontainebleau, the Louvre, and most especially, on Chenonceaux."

Diane lay back beside him and they looked at one another. He touched the cleft between her breasts where the long string of jewels still lay. He ran his fingers slowly along the hard, geometric surface. The feel of them against her soft skin sent through him a wave of desire, and he wanted her again. He thought how she never had to try to arouse him, even after all of the years, all of the lovemaking between them. Just a look, a laugh, the sight of her, and he wanted her, even more now than in the beginning. Adversity had bonded them. Passion had strengthened those bonds.

But to please her, that was everything.

"PERFECT. ABSOLUTELY PERFECT," Henri said after reading another communiqué that Diane had written for him to sign. He leaned across the carpeted floor, breathing a sigh of relief for her assistance and drew her lips to his. They had worked through the next night and only now did either of them realize that it was morning, when they could see the sun through the long, uncovered windows near their unruffled bed.

The King's bedchamber at Saint Germain-en-Laye was littered with a spray of documents and state papers. All around them on the red and brown Turkish carpet were books on diplomacy and finance. Many were open to some random page where he had tired of the intricacies and moved on to the next volume. The fragrance of candles burned to a quick filled the room in the early hours of morning.

On the wall above the fireplace was yet another portrait of Diane, one that he had commissioned the previous spring; Diana resplendent, and completely nude. It was a forest scene and the only creature with whom she had shared a canvas was a young deer. Beside his bed was the first sketch he had ever had done of her. It was by the famed artist, Clouet, done a month after the birth of their daughter. He had drawn her in chalk seductively clad in the sheerest lilac-colored silk, her breasts visible, and a curl of hair draped across her shoulder.

"You must let me draw her as I see her, Your Highness, or there is no purpose in it," Clouet had said when Henri grew violent at the voluptuous representation of his love. "To me she is Diana," he had whispered as he began again the rhythmic strokes across the page. "Goddess of the hunt. Divine goddess of the moon. Fascinating . . . tempting . . . and yet, to mere men such as myself, forever . . . unattainable." Since that day, the sketch had gone everywhere with Henri.

When the festivities marking the coronation of the new King were finally at an end, Diane's position was quickly defined. Even before he went to see Montmorency, Henri personally drafted an edict elevating her to Duchesse de Valentinois. In so doing, he restored the duchy that had once belonged to her family, but had been lost many years before for outstanding debts.

In addition to her duties as Head Governess to the royal children, she was also to be present at all meetings of the *conseil des affaires* and the larger *conseil privé.* He leaned on her absolutely, and there was not a soul in France who was allowed to forget it. Despite the return of the once powerful Constable Montmorency and the appointment of all of Henri's childhood friends to major cabinet posts, Diane was considered the voice with the single greatest influence over the King.

Suddenly, the angry gossip against her ceased. Wise ladies of distinction tried to copy her sense of fashion. It was very popular to be blond, and the nobility even discussed the prospect of taking more frequent baths. Palaces, churches and even furniture began to be ornamented with the new royal emblem, the D interlaced with an H. Everywhere the shape of the crescent moon was emblazoned. Women wore them in their hair and had jewelry fashioned in their shape. Astute dignitaries quickly saw the extent of the King's commitment to her. When the Pope in Rome sent a gold rose to the new Queen, he wisely sent Diane an exquisite rope of pearls.

But behind the privacy of their chamber doors, not everything was ideal. The volume of information, foreign correspondence and edicts that were brought to Henri in those first few days were overwhelming. Letters of congratulations had been sent from nearly every ruler in the Christian world and when he could no longer postpone their acknowledgment, he went to Diane, pleading for her assistance. There was so much to assimilate, but he had been given only a matter of weeks to understand that for which his father and elder brother both had been meticulously groomed. In her chamber, surrounded with books and documents, their conversations centered around foreign affairs. They also spoke of the religious situation and the domestic policies which the new Court would support.

At Diane's suggestion, Henri had begun to study his father's policy of taxation. An exorbitant policy that she opposed had left many French citizens threadbare so that they might pay for the King's opulent lifestyle and his quest for Italian soil. Diane softly encouraged Henri in two new courses of action.

First, she suggested that taxation be cut and that what revenues they did acquire be saved. There was a great likelihood that France would once again be forced into war, and both believed that they should be prepared. Second, Diane proposed that the money which was acquired through moderate taxation be reserved for the strengthening of French borders. They also resolved to continue the fight that his father had begun for northern Italy. As a condition of his own marriage, France had been promised Milan, Parma and Pisa. If Henri did not live to see them under French rule, then the shameful alliance that he now endured by his marriage to Catherine, and the loss of Diane as his wife, would be for nothing.

Henri called to one of the pages who flanked the door, requesting quill and ink. Both were quickly produced on a silver tray. He signed the documents with a swirling representation of his name. Then he looked up and handed the pen to Diane.

"Your turn," he said simply.

Like a reflex, Diane reached for the pen and then stopped, her face full of surprise. "But I cannot, *chéri.*"

"Why not? You wrote them. You shall sign them."

Diane looked down at the black ink still wet on the page.

Beside his signature he had placed a dash, indicating the place for her name. She gazed into the fire, of which only the red glow of embers remained.

"To begin with, it would be a major breach of protocol for your mistress to sign, with you, an official state document."

"Oh? About that, I have been studying these things for days now," he said, pointing with a half grin to the spray of books around him, ". . . and I can find nothing that forbids the cosigning of a document by whomever I so choose."

Diane paused, selecting her words carefully. She knew Henri would not be easily put off in this. The Court had now accepted her as Henri's *favourite,* but they would not look so favorably on a paramour who appeared to have ambitions beyond the King's heart.

"It is just that I would prefer to be a more . . . indirect advisor in matters of state. I think it would create far less consternation on the part of the rest of the staff."

"Well, I would not prefer it! You are the lady of my heart and the first lady of France. I cannot, I will not make a move without you! Everyone, whether they are agreeable or not, shall one day come to accept that fact if they intend to stay in good stead with their new King!" As soon as he had said it, his sarcasm softened. Again he proffered her the pen. He lowered his eyes. "Please, *m'amie.* I truly want this, for both of us. I may not be able to make you Queen, but I can see to it that you have all of the power and the glory."

Diane took the quill reluctantly and looked up at him. His dark eyes sparkled full of love. He had never forgotten his promise to marry her and she knew that he would never stop trying to make up for having to break it.

This official document, one of many that would be signed *Henri-Diane,* was only one of a long line of gifts which, since becoming King, Henri had bestowed upon her. Not only had he made her Duchesse de Valentinois, but he had legitimized their daughter. After his coronation, and for the rest of her life, the child was to be known as Diane de France, *légitime.* He had also dispatched

Charles de Guise to Rome, on the child's behalf, to begin marriage negotiations with the grandson of the Pope.

Earlier that month, he had nullified Anne d'Heilly's legal action against Anet, placing it solely back into Diane's hands. But the act of love by the new King for his Diane thought most controversial involved a generous stipend called *La Paulette.*

When she at first refused it, he said it was his way of paying back the money that she had once so generously loaned him in the early days. His advisors had assured him that it was not taken from citizens or taxation. The money came from the purchase of various ecclesiastical and military appointments. It was completely separate from any and all regular funds of the Crown. It was his to give, he said, and he had chosen to give it to her. When he explained that it could be used to finance work at Anet, Diane reluctantly accepted.

"It is one of many crowns that I expect to lay at your feet," he had said. But Diane was not to realize, for nearly two years, the day of Catherine's own coronation, just how seriously Henri had meant what he had said.

30

MONTMORENCY DID NOT LIKE any of the three Guises who were now so well installed at the Court of France. It was poor enough fortune to be required to share his influence with a glorified courtesan but an ambitious trio of sons from Lorraine was simply unacceptable.

Since his return, he found that they had garnered great power. They had been good students of their uncle, the Cardinal de Lorraine. Montmorency now chided himself frequently for not having seen it coming in the years before his exile. Even then, they were planning their ascent. Each step for them had been strategic. Their sister's marriage to the King of Scotland had produced a niece who, by her father's death, was now the Queen. This not only gave them a powerful pawn over which they held control, but the blood tie to royalty elevated their own status. In the preceding months, they had also cleverly worked a marriage for their youngest brother Claude. He was to become the bridegroom of Diane de Poitiers' youngest daughter, Louise, solidifying their standing with both the malleable King and his mistress.

Furthermore, shortly after Henri's coronation, Charles, the Archbishop de Rheims, had been given the honor of going to Rome to negotiate the marriage of the King's natural daughter, Diane, and the Pope's grandson. While he was there, he had also become Cardinal de Guise. Finally, they were doing their best to suggest a marriage between the little Queen of Scots and the French Dauphin, who at the moment was only four years old. Working in a cooperative manner, there was never a time when one of them was not at the King's side. The Cardinal de Lorraine had cultivated his exacting, ambitious nephews and in a slow and steady fashion, they were coming to dominate the entire Court of France.

Montmorency lay back in bed and stared around his bedchamber at Fontainebleau. Things were not as he had remembered them. He had less power and less control over his own wishes. He felt as if he had traded in his battleground with Philippe Chabot, and had received two new fronts in its place. He was not in the least certain if it was the Guises or Madame Diane whom he trusted less.

He gazed out the long windows across from his bed. The sky was miserably gray. The wind howled and hurled a blur of red autumn leaves past the glass. A fresh fire had been stoked in the hearth beside him and he longed to lay back down and burrow beneath the covers like a child. But not today. During the night, the Queen had delivered another daughter and he must go to offer his congratulations. He knew that the King would be disappointed by the appearance of another female child; for it meant a need for more children between them. She had, after all, in fifteen years, managed to produce only one son. The risk of plague or accidental death made another male heir essential.

Montmorency stood while his valet dressed him in a stylish

soft brown leather doublet slashed with a white shirt beneath. His arms were slipped through a full pleated coat of purple velvet. Then he glanced at himself in the mirror as further layers were applied. A gold chain inlaid with rubies running from shoulder to shoulder. Puffed and slashed trunk hose of the same purple fabric as the cape. His toque of brown leather had a narrow stiffened brim and a soft padded crown. An ostrich feather swooped down beside his left ear. Large stoned rings ornamented four of his fingers.

When his costume was finally complete, a small silver chest was brought. Montmorency opened it and took out a gold and ruby rosary. A perfect gift for the Queen, he thought. After he had examined it, he placed it back in the chest and smiled. Yes, perfect. Never mind, he thought, that he had few friends here. He didn't need them. Oh, he knew the gossip. Since his return to power he was called quarrelsome, despotic and self-centered. All of it quite probably was true. But as long as he had one or two highly placed allies, he need not concern himself with his enemies. Feeling prepared, he tucked the silver box under his arm confidently, and left the room to continue his own quest for power.

"Have you seen her? They tell me she is beautiful," asked Catherine.

"Yes. I have just come from the nursery," Henri replied. He tried to stave off the restless feeling that was already overwhelming him after no more than a few moments in her company.

He sat in a large embroidered chair that had been placed for him beside Catherine's bed. She was surrounded by fresh white linen sheets, her head propped by blue and green velvet pillows. At the foot of her bed, her aide, Piero Strozzi, mingled with Catherine's two ladies, never being far from the Queen's reach. One eye was always upon her.

"I am sorry, Henri, that it was not a son this time. But the next one shall be a boy, I am certain of it," Catherine said in a lowered tone of voice.

Henri paled at the thought that there would be need of a next time to bed her. As quickly as he had the thought, he was brought back to the moment by Catherine's hand that she had poised in the air between them. It was several more minutes before he realized that she meant for him to take it. Her fingers were fat and moist around his own. From this confinement she was even fatter still, and there was an odor now that he had never noticed before; a kind of grease smell, like lard rubbed in sweat.

Looking at her swollen and coarse face and the heavy black brows, he wondered how he had ever managed to give her the seed of this child at all, much less of two others. But even as the question arose in his mind, he knew the answer. Diane alone had been responsible for the conception of them all. Each of the times he had meant to make love to her, she had accepted him. But then, when he had surrendered hopelessly to passion's spell, she would pull away. *Go to her,* Diane had whispered. *It is your duty.* And knowing no other release for his ardor, Henri had gone.

"She does not look at all like me, I do not think. She has your coloring, Henri. Actually, she looks rather like your mother, from the portrait your father had commissioned at Blois. I think it would be so perfect if we named her Claude, after your mother."

Henri's eyes were bright, but he did not see her. "Whatever you like," he replied.

"Then I like Claude. I had a boy's name decided upon, which I was going to suggest to you. I quite favor Louis, after the King who reigned before your father. But now that we know it is a girl . . . well I think it shall be wonderful to honor the Queen's memory this way, don't you?"

"What? Oh, Yes."

"Then you approve?"

"Approve of what?"

"Claude; the name Claude for our daughter."

"I told you, whatever you like."

Her tone became more insistent. "What I would like is for you to agree that it is a proper name, and to know that you approve."

"Then I approve."

"Good."

Catherine settled back against the pillows and fingered the white linen sheets that were folded at the point where her belly, only yesterday, had held a child. Henri freed his hand from hers and looked across the room. He could not quite make out the time on the clock on the small table near the foot of the bed, but he was certain that an eternity had passed. When he looked back at the Queen, he could see something was building in her dark smoky eyes.

"You come to me like this only grudgingly and already you want to leave to go to her?"

"Catherine, please, do not begin it all again." He sighed.

"But I have given Your Majesty what you desired; what the kingdom desired. Together we have a son who is heir to the throne, and two daughters more. She is not Queen, I am. Why can you not leave her now?"

Henri sprang from the chair. He loomed over her, his brows fused with anger. "I have three daughters, Madame. You forget Diane de France. And you know that what you ask is impossible."

His words were so simple, so direct, that there was no possibility that she could refute them. But as he reached the foot of the bed, intending to punctuate what he had said with a swift exit, he suddenly remembered the gift which he had brought for her. He turned around and thrust the black silk bundle at her.

"It is a strand of pearls," he said coldly. "I was informed that you admired those that Madame Diane received from His Holiness."

Her eyes were filled with tears as she held up the costly necklace. "Please, Henri. I ask only for a chance. Would you at least consider what I have had to say?"

"There is nothing to consider, Catherine. Nor will there ever be. I am sorry." His duty to his wife thus disposed of, he turned and strode toward the open bedchamber door.

"Then I shall pray for your immortal soul," she called after him.

"You need not pray for my soul, Madame," he replied without turning around. "For it is worth nothing if it means a lifetime without the woman I love."

It was not until he was gone from her sight that she hurled the gift at the open door. The string broke and the floor was washed with small white beads.

"YOUR MAJESTY! What is it?" Montmorency asked, narrowly missing the white spray of pearls across the room. He had rounded the corner to her bedchamber just as the Queen had screeched a profanity at the disappearing King, and tossed the pearls. The moment she saw the Constable, Catherine's thick face softened.

"Oh, my dear friend!" she said in a gentle voice and extended her hand across the bedcovers. "Please forgive me. I have just had a visit from the King. It did not go as I had hoped."

"So I gathered," he replied as he moved toward the heavy poster bed. When he reached her side, he bowed and added, "Your Majesty," acknowledging her in a more reverent tone. The formal part of his salutation past, he stood again and leaned over to kiss her hand. "You look splendid, Madame. Childbirth does agree with you."

"That it does; but it appears to be the only thing that I can do for him that she no longer can."

Montmorency eased into the chair that had been occupied by the King only moments before. Then he handed her the small silver chest, hoping it would create a distraction for her anger.

"A gift for me?"

"Just a small token of my great esteem."

She opened it with the excitement of a child and gazed down at the rosary. "Oh Anne, it is lovely. Thank you."

The curves of his lips straightened, forming one thin bloodless line, as he bristled at the sound of his given name. He allowed no one to address him that way, no one but the Queen. Long ago she had said she liked it, made a habit of it, and that was that.

"Oh, Anne," she cried. "I simply do not know how I am to endure this! I want that woman out of his life, but it seems that I am powerless to do anything about it! I thought for so many years if I simply waited, if I were patient, one day he would grow tired of her. Everyone told me so. But it seems that the older she gets, the greater her hold on him becomes!"

"There are many here who seek to dominate our King, Your Majesty, not the least of whom is his mistress," he managed to whisper before catching the eye of Piero Strozzi who was listening with great interest. "Perhaps, Your Majesty, we could speak more freely in private," he suggested, and then leaned back in his chair, indicating with his posture that he meant to say nothing more in front of an audience.

Catherine waited until the loose pearls were gathered up by two of her ladies before she dismissed them. Strozzi was the last to leave the bedchamber, turning to give the Queen one last opportunity to change her mind; but she did not see him.

"I see this domination of His Majesty in a structural way," he began again once they were alone. "Something not unlike the composition of a house. To carry it further then, each usurper of your rightful power would be a foundation stone. And to topple that house most expediently, one would be well advised to begin with the foundation."

"Go on."

"I shall be blunt, if Your Majesty shall permit it." Catherine nodded her approval and then blew her nose into a lace handkerchief. "The Guises are in favor with the King's mistress. That much is common knowledge, and I need not point to the magnitude of power the Duchesse de Valentinois wields at this Court. Already they have managed to marry their brother, Claude, to her daughter. Your husband saw to it that Charles de Guise was named Cardinal at the tender age of twenty-three. Now they are encouraging His Majesty to bring their niece, Mary, the little Scots Queen, here as a wife to your son. I tell you, the Duchesse and the Guises are a strong power base; very like the foundation of a house. I believe now that if we do not act, they may very well one day control us all!"

"But what can we do?" the Queen asked, now sitting upright in her bed.

"We must begin in stages. As one builds a house, so shall we demolish it. The first stone shall be the Guises."

Catherine had not given up her fantasy of poisoning Diane, but she must admit, this was cleaner. Simpler. Montmorency was an expert in things of which she knew nothing. He did not like Diane or the Guises any more than she did, but the King would never suspect him of any wrongdoing. She knew that it was not wise to be involved in a plan to ruin those whom the King loved, but Catherine was desperate. She had the grave misfortune, along the way, of having fallen in love with her husband. It was far more disheartening since she knew that he did not now, nor would he ever, love her in return. But what her heart and her mind told her were two distinctly different things. The love she bore him was fueled by fantasy; the fantasy that if somehow she could remove the threat, then, just perhaps, she could make him love her.

HENRI HAD LEFT the Queen's apartments half an hour earlier than he had planned. The meeting had angered him; not only because she had insisted on bringing up the issue of Diane, but because when he looked at his wife now, he saw his greatest weakness there, weakness of the flesh. At the age of twenty-nine, Henri's body was hard, and his drive was intense. During the day he spent countless hours riding, fencing and playing *jeu de paume;* but none of these activities ever totally quelled the desire. At night, it would possess him completely until he found release with Diane. As each year passed, the need for her body grew stronger; and she was still a perfect lover. There was no fantasy, no act that she denied him, unless it was time for him to attend to his duties with the Queen. Then she would lock herself away, rewarding him again only after he had fulfilled his obligations to his Crown. She knew him, and she understood his duty better than anyone.

"I wish you to see to the drafting of a proclamation," he said to Antoine de Bourbon, who had waited for him outside the Queen's apartments.

"I wish to bestow a home as a gift for faithful service to the Crown . . . something of that nature. Saint-André can help you

with the wording and all of the legalities. But you are to understand that it must be a formal declaration deeding the property.
There must be no way it can be seen as a gift. It is payment for
service rendered to the Crown. There must be no way that it can
be removed. Is that clear?"

"Indeed, Your Majesty."

"I leave tomorrow to begin toward Italy. Tell Saint-André that
the proclamation is to be delivered as a gift after I have gone so
that no word is leaked of it beforehand." They began to walk
again, proceeding through a large doorway and down a spiral
staircase.

"What is the property, Your Majesty?"

"Chenonceaux."

Bourbon looked up at the King, unable to mask his surprise.
"And the recipient, Sire?"

"Why, Madame Diane, of course," Henri replied with a smile.

DIANE WAS EVEN EARLIER to the council chambers than was the
King. She was sitting at the long table in a carved armchair, her
back to the door. She was dressed in a heavy black-velvet gown
with white collar and cuffs, poring over a volume on foreign affairs. When she heard Henri enter in the company of two of his
secretaries, she stood and curtsied to him.

"Your Majesty," she said with the same respect she always
showed him in public. Henri took her hand. Then, to her surprise,
he kissed her with such abandon that her cheeks burned. She lowered her head to hide their blush.

"Where were you?" he whispered. "When I woke, you were
gone."

"I was with the Queen," Diane cautiously replied.

"I have just come from there. Catherine did not mention you."

"You did not really expect that she would, did you?"

"Perhaps not. But damn her! She could at least make an attempt to live amiably with us. When was it that you saw her?"
Henri waited for her to sit, then sat beside her. Diane lowered her
head again and took a breath.

"It was in the night, *chéri*; while she was in the final stages of her labor. It was a difficult birth, far more difficult than the last two. Her ladies came to me and I am glad they did not wake you. Apparently they still believe me possessed of some kind of imaginary power, because they pleaded with me for a potion to help the Queen. Both Mademoiselles Bonajusti and Cavalcanti were most humble. I know they feared for Her Majesty's life. Fortunately, not long after I arrived, your daughter was born."

He ran his finger along the curve of her cheek and said in a tone just above a whisper, "I shall spend the rest of my life repaying your kindness, you know. Even then, I fear, it shall never be enough."

The chamber doors were opened again and a flurry of activity engulfed the firelit room. Saint-André, Guise, Bourbon, Marck and the Cardinal de Lorraine were issued in and took their seats around the King and Diane. The new Cardinal, Charles de Guise, just returned from Rome, followed them in his new crimson cassock and biretta. Montmorency was the last to make an entrance in a costume of purple velvet, edged in gold. When everyone was settled, Robert de La Marck stood.

"The issue at hand is the Scottish situation," said Diane's son-in-law.

"Your Majesty," said François de Guise, "the problems there have escalated dramatically. The Scottish troops have suffered heavy losses against the English, who are at this very moment attempting to claim our little niece, Queen Mary."

"It is not safe for her there," his brother agreed. "The English know we oppose a marriage between her and the young King of England. That puts her life in immediate danger. Just two months ago, English troops sought to take the child from the Scots with the support of eighteen thousand men."

"Your Majesty, the people in Scotland are pleading with us to intercede," noted the Cardinal de Lorraine to further his nephew's ambitious cause. "They will do as the French will them, to avoid an alliance with England."

"Would your sister agree to allow the child to be raised in

France?" asked the King, rubbing his thumb and forefinger along the line of his beard.

"Our sister's foremost concern is for the child," François replied.

As Diane leaned back in her chair, she watched in silent fascination as the two brothers weaved their intricate plan upon the King. Perhaps it was because she had not wanted to see it, but she had never seen their ambition so apparent as it was today. In her early years at Court, her opinion of them had been colored by gratitude. They had both been kind to her. She could not afford then to see beyond their courtesy. There had been far too many other dragons to slay.

But many things had changed. Their intentions were clear. Since Charles had become Cardinal de Guise, undoubtedly they would seek a Dukedom for François. They already had the marriage of her own daughter Louise to their younger brother Claude. Now they meant for little Mary to marry the Dauphin. If they were to achieve that, there would be no limit to their power. Bringing the little Queen to France was the pièce de résistance in their master plan and yet, like the growth of a cancer, even Madame Diane, with all of her influence, was powerless against the slow, insidious growth of the house of Guise.

31

*Y*OU GAVE HER CHENONCEAUX? How could you, when you promised it to me?"

Catherine had stormed onto the *jeu de paume* court where the King had just positioned himself to receive a serve from Jacques de Saint-André. Henri was dressed all in white, with a wide-brimmed straw hat to shield the sun from his eyes. On the sidelines, a collection of courtiers were brought to a hush at sight of the Queen. She came to a sudden stop at the edge of the court, her hands placed firmly on her wide hips. Henri lowered his racket and faced her.

"Who, Madame, is your informant?"

"My informant?" she repeated, and gave a wounded little laugh. "You dare to ask me such a thing when you promised Chenonceaux to me?"

Henri strutted across the court until they were facing one another, then put his hand on her shoulder.

"I think it would be more appropriate if we discussed this matter privately. Perhaps this evening."

"And why is that? So that you can justify it somehow? So that I will not be able to contest it? So no one will know that you preferred to give a chateau to your courtesan, rather than to your Queen! I wanted that house, Henri, and you knew it!"

He had never seen her like this. The onlookers hung on her every word, convinced that by fortune, they were being made privy to the makings of a great scandal. But just as they were beginning to enjoy the rare ravings of the usually submissive Queen, Montmorency and a collection of guards moved in from the sidelines and began to escort them back toward the chateau. When they had gone, Henri dropped his racket to the ground. He wondered who it was that might have told her. No one had known but Saint-André and Bourbon, and he trusted them both.

"Jacques, do you know about this?"

Saint-André moved from the opposite side of the rope toward the King and Queen. "No, Your Majesty. I am afraid I do not."

"Oh, do not look to blame him!" the Queen raged. "It is fully your doing. Did you not think that I would find out one day in some manner or other? So tell me, perhaps I shall learn from it. What did she do to get you to give it to her instead of to me?"

Now she was wailing. Her swollen face was flushed red, and her words were disjointed. Italian. French. Then back to Italian. He looked over her shoulder at Saint-André. He simply shrugged. Henri tried to calm her anger by telling her that on the same day that he had arranged the deed for Chenonceaux, he had conferred upon her the gift of the Barony of Tour en Auvergne. That domain had once belonged to her grandmother, and he had thought it would please her to have it returned.

"And so you thought you could simply give me anything else to quiet me? Perhaps you have forgotten that Chenonceaux is property of the Crown. It is not yours to give and no deeds or gifts, no matter how you disguise them, will ever alter that fact!" Only then did she take a breath before she added, "I warn you, Henri, tread lightly with me. I am no longer your puppet." In her anger she had gone too far. She saw the rage building in his eyes.

"Do you dare to threaten me, Madame?"

Their eyes were locked. Neither moved. But then, as she stood facing him, Henri began to see the pain behind the anger; the pain that he alone had caused her. His compassion for her startled him.

"Catherine, please, you can have any other place you like. There is a large chateau on a bluff overlooking the valley. It is called Chaumont and it is an exquisite chateau, far grander than Chenonceaux. Please, let me give it to you. I would really like to do that for you."

"I want only Chenonceaux." Her tone once again was cold and resolute. She said the words in Italian because she knew that it would anger him.

"Well, you cannot have it!" he replied in French. "It belongs to Madame now, and no matter what you thought I said, it was always meant for her."

Henri left the *jeu de paume* court before she could protest further. He knew if he stayed to reason with her, she would only begin to weep, or worse, to threaten Diane and neither prospect was he prepared to face without the use of violence against her.

HENRI DID NOT ARRIVE at Saint Germain-en-Laye until after midnight, and although he was tired from the long ride, he was glad to know that he had left Catherine and her tears behind him. He had not planned to leave until morning, but he could not bear to look upon her sad, puffy face another moment. It made him angry. Everything about her made him angry, and the fact that, seven months after the birth of Princess Claude, she again carried his child was like salt in a raw wound.

Surrounded by his entourage, he mounted the steps toward the royal nursery, and began the long walk down the torch-lit corridor. The six-year-old Queen of Scots was now installed here and with Diane, who was returning from Anet the following morning, he had planned formally to greet her.

"Please, Your Majesty, allow me to wake the servants and ready the children if you mean to see them tonight," Montmorency argued.

"That will not be necessary. I only want to look in on them. No sense in rousing the staff for that."

As they rounded the corner, Henri removed his gloves and handed them to Saint-André. He then pulled off his plumed leather toque and ran his fingers through his matted hair. Even this late at night it was still hot, and he could feel the sweat and dust on his face and on his scalp. If Diane had been there, it would have been a wonderful night for a swim in the moat. But he never had much inclination to surrender himself to the water without her beside him. He did, however, long to pull off his shoes and stockings and soak his feet in a basin of cool water. That idea had struck him for the past several hours as he rode toward the castle.

He opened the door to his son's room first. The hinges let out a long, high-pitched squeal. The unexpected sound woke the guard whose duty it was to sleep beside the Dauphin. The young man, still in uniform, sprang from his cot and drew his dagger. In an instant he was poised over the King.

"Easy, my boy! Easy!" Montmorency whispered. He stepped in to illuminate Henri's face.

When the guard recognized him as the King, he lowered his dagger and fell into a deep and reverent bow.

"Well done, Captain. Much thanks," said Henri as he slipped past the bewildered guard. He strode quietly across the room to the small canopied bed in which his son slept. Carefully, he pulled back the gold-fringed bedcurtain and peered inside. The boy resembled an angel, curled on his side; his sandy blond hair tousled, and one small hand curled near his mouth. The King bent down and kissed him. Then he moved away and drew the curtains together again.

He visited each of his children's bedchambers in the same manner; next the baby, Claude, then Elizabeth, and finally Diane. When he opened the last door, it surprised him that there was no guard springing to his feet, but across the room he could see the shadowy figure of a woman. She sat with her back to the door near the fireplace hearth. Henri could not make out her face because it was turned, but he could see that her gown and headdress were black. *Of course it was her,* he thought. *It must be!* She had come early to surprise him, and here he was early as well. His heart sprang up at the prospect of an unexpected night together.

"That will be all, gentlemen. Good night," he said, leaning back out into the hall.

When he looked back into his daughter's chamber, the figure still had not moved. She must not have heard him come in. He closed the door and then rushed across the room.

"When did you arrive? Good God, do you know how I have missed you? Why did you not send word that you would be early . . . I . . ."

As he muttered the words he went down onto his knees before her. It was only then, in the silver light of the moon, that he could see that the woman before him was not Diane.

"HOW IN THE DEVIL did you get in here?" he raged. "Guard!" Henri sprang to his feet and reached for his dagger.

"Your Majesty, sir, if I might explain . . ."

The woman stood before him. He could see clearly now, in the light from the moon, that she did not look at all like Diane. She was not a woman but a girl. Her hair, where it peeked out from beneath her headdress, was not blond but red. It was a curious color, somewhere between the color of wine and the color of rust. Her eyes were small and dark and her lips were full.

"Who are you?"

"Janet Stuart, Your Majesty," she replied and then curtsied properly. "Now if you would be good enough to let me explain . . ."

"Papa! Papa, is that you?"

Henri's daughter, Diane, tore back the bedcurtains and bolted from the bed in the long white, billowing nightgown. She leapt eagerly into her father's arms. Henri held her and kissed her, forgetting the presence of the strange young woman who stood before them.

"I see that you have already met Lady Flemming," Diane said. "I am so glad, Papa. She is simply the nicest lady. She came from Scotland, you know . . . with the little Queen. All week long she has been telling us tales about Scotland, and teaching us new games. Tonight she told me a story and when I asked her, she even stayed with me until I fell asleep. I have trouble falling asleep sometimes, Papa, and she really was so kind." After the long string of words had tumbled from her mouth, his daughter yawned and then began to rub her eyes. Henri looked back at the woman.

"So it is Lady Flemming, is it?"

"At Your Majesty's service," she replied, and lowered her head again.

Her diction was harsh and the accent wholly Scottish. When she raised her head again, she was smiling. It was a crooked smile and with her lips parted, he could see that she had a space between her front teeth. It was the strangest sensation because the moment that she smiled, it changed her entire appearance. She went from possessing the elegance of an aristocrat to the earthy sensuality of a barmaid. Her gown was holly green, not black as he had first thought and it was cut straight across her chest at such a low point that her large breasts swelled beneath a ribbon of white lace. She was not beautiful, but there was a broadly voluptuous quality about her that he had never seen before in a woman.

All of this passed in no more than a few brief moments after he had called for his guards. The room was now filled with them, their swords all poised. Montmorency too was standing with his dagger readied. In one of the smaller doorways, two bewildered nurses stood in white cotton sleeping gowns and caps with their candles in their hands. Diane looked up at him, then at the guards.

"What is the matter, Papa? Has something happened?"

Henri looked at his guards, then back at Lady Flemming as though he was trying to make up his mind.

"It is all right. Everyone may return to bed. There has just been a small misunderstanding."

The nurses muttered something between themselves and one advanced to the little girl to lead her back to bed. But Diane ran the other way, toward Janet Stuart.

"May I kiss you good night, Lady Flemming?"

"I would be honored if you would, Mademoiselle," she replied in French so poorly constructed that Henri put a finger to his lips and lowered his head to keep from chuckling. After she kissed Lady Flemming, and then her father, Diane surrendered to the waiting governess. Then the guards retired. Henri did not see the sneer on Montmorency's lips as he lingered for a moment at the door, turned and then departed.

"I am very sorry, Your Majesty, to have caused such a disturbance."

"It appears that my daughter would have me play the fool in this matter, Lady Flemming, not you," he said, as he warmed his hands by the fire. "I believe that it is I who owe you an apology."

"That is not necessary, Your Majesty."

"Your presence in this room surprised me. I . . . thought that you were someone else."

"May I add, Sire, at the risk of seeming forward, that I wish I had been that someone else you so hoped to see."

Janet Stuart cast a seductive glance at him as she said it, and then just as he might have taken offense, she began to laugh. The base sensuality and the gap-tooth smile reappeared. Though he tried to avert his gaze, he could not help but watch her full apricot breasts heave beneath the constraints of the holly green gown.

MONTMORENCY HAD BEEN the first to reach the little girl's chamber after the King called for his guard. He had been nearby, on the way to his own apartments. He returned to the nursery at the precise moment the woman stood beside the hearth, the shimmering silver moon lighting her face. He had also seen the King's eyes.

He considered what he had witnessed to be the single greatest stroke of fortune since the day the Dauphin had died, naming Henri heir. He believed what he had told Catherine. The Crown was in danger, for it was not a King who ruled France, but rather a triumvirate of power. The Guises were one source, Diane de Poitiers another and himself a third. What he had not told her was that he would not rest until he alone influenced the King. After seeing Henri tonight so captivated, Anne de Montmorency knew that, at last, he had been given just the means to see his dream become reality.

"I shall destroy them all," he muttered, "brick by brick . . . by brick. But not the Guises after all. Now it is Diane de Poitiers who shall be first."

THE NEXT DAY, after Diane arrived at Saint Germain-en-Laye, she and Henri went together to meet the Queen of Scots. Henri was awestruck by what a beautiful child she was. She had her uncle François' long thin frame and his russet hair, which cascaded onto her tiny shoulders in large ringlets. It was held back at the top by a coronet of diamonds and emeralds. She was, however, the image of her mother, Marie, with the same green eyes and little rosebud mouth. Henri understood the moment he received her what a sacrifice it had been for the Dowager Queen Marie de Guise to surrender her little daughter. It was then that he vowed to himself that not only would she be accorded every privilege, she would be treated as his own child.

She came to the grand hall in the company of her own Scottish train. Around the dais where Henri sat beside Diane, François de Guise and his brother Charles stood with Antoine de Bourbon and the King's sister Marguerite. Another group of courtiers stood at the back of the room, including the Venetian and Scottish Ambassadors. Mary walked the length of the grand hall with four young ladies-in-waiting and her Governess, Janet Stuart . . . Lady Flemming.

Henri bristled when he saw her again. He had hoped she would not come. Something unwelcome had stirred in him last night when they met. As he looked at her across the long crimson carpet, that same thing about her now both stirred and repelled him. He did his best to avoid her gaze.

"Your Majesty, it is a great honor." Mary curtsied. She spoke in Scottish and Lady Flemming repeated her words in French.

Henri rose from his throne and took the three steps down the carpeted dais toward her. He then took the little girl into his arms and held her as though she were one of his own children.

"Welcome, my daughter. Welcome indeed. You are the very image of your mother. Do you know that?"

Again Lady Flemming interceded, translating the King's words.

"My Uncle, His Eminence, the Cardinal de Guise, told me so just yesterday, although I confess I do not see the likeness, Your Majesty."

The reply came first in Scottish, then in French. Henri saw the flicker of sadness in her young eyes at the reference to her mother, even before there could be a translation. He quickly sought to change the subject.

"So tell me. Are you finding your accommodations thus far here in France to your liking? I have had you installed with the Princess Elizabeth, as this is a big old place and I thought that at first you might enjoy the benefit of her company."

Mary looked over at Elizabeth, and the two young children smiled at one another. "I thank you, Sir. Your daughter has been most kind."

When there was a break in the conversation, François de Guise stepped forward. "Your Majesty, the Queen of Scots would also have me present the ladies of her train to yourself and Madame, if you would find it agreeable."

The four young ladies-in-waiting and Lady Flemming advanced. The latter, whose gaze was openly seductive, never took her eyes from the King. As he tried desperately not to look at her, Henri only heard enough to know that each of the little servants to the Queen was named Mary. François de Guise attempted a bit of humor at the coincidence, but the King did not smile. Suddenly he wanted to be anywhere but there. Women, especially this many, made him ill at ease. He never had anything to say to them, nor anything in common with them. The exception to that had always been Diane de Poitiers.

"And this, Your Majesty, is Janet Stuart, Lady Flemming. She is the Queen's Governess. And as you can see," said Guise, "she is also the Queen's interpreter."

Janet advanced toward the King and curtsied. The gown she now wore was equally low, and equally seductive as the one she had been wearing the night before. This one was ash-gray. The square bodice was lined with delicate pearls.

"Your Majesty," she said in a deep, smoky voice, and then rose from her curtsy.

"Well, Lady Flemming, please impart to Her Majesty for me that anything she needs or should desire are hers, and that I will look forward to many future meetings, hopefully of a more informal nature."

"As will we both, Your Majesty."

When Mary and her train had left the grand hall, Henri sank back down in his throne. His face was flushed and his heart was racing. He could not recall ever having felt so awkward as he did at this moment. As if Diane could hear what he was thinking, he put a hand over his eyes and waited for several minutes to collect himself before he spoke.

"Guise, do you know the convent at Poissy?"

"Yes, of course, Your Majesty."

"I want the Queen's four attendants sent there for schooling."

"But, Your Majesty, they are the child's only link with her homeland."

"Precisely. They are also her only link with that barbarous and ill-sounding language she now speaks. She is a Queen, Guise, and with the four of them constantly by her side, she has no hope of ever mastering French."

At this proclamation, there was a buzz of gossip set off among the crowd who had gathered at the back of the room.

"And her Governess, the Lady Flemming, Your Majesty? Is she to be relieved of her duty as well?"

The color rushed crimson into his cheeks. He tried to look casually at Diane. It would be for the best, he thought; better to cut the child's ties completely with Scotland. Better for him.

Diane leaned over and whispered to him behind a gold ring. "Perhaps you should reconsider such a move, *chéri*. She is such a small child, who, if you proceed, will be completely alone. And after all, you could demand that the Lady Flemming speak nothing but French in Her Majesty's presence."

It was odd, he thought, that Diane should intervene now. She so rarely did until she was called upon. Henri shifted in his seat, feeling temptation's heavy hand upon his shoulder, and the overwhelming guilt for the sensation.

But there were other thoughts; himself as a child, alone in a Spanish prison, not much older than little Queen Mary. He could see a little boy, as though from a distance, alone in the cold stone cell and cruel guards parading outside his door, parroting his cries for help. Deprived of even his brother's company throughout the ordeal, he had even forgotten how to speak French. Perhaps Diane was right. To deprive the child of her last remaining security, when she was only five years old, was not only selfish, it was cruel. The very same action forced on him had created a wound, and then a scar from which he never would heal. He had been thinking of himself; of last night; of the dark, unsettling feeling that Janet Stuart had unleashed in him.

"Of course you are right, *m'amie*," he said. "No, Guise. Lady Flemming shall not be relieved of her duty. But she is to be instructed that when she is the presence of Her Majesty, she is to speak only French. Oh, and Guise, see to it that they are both fitted with some new French designs. We simply cannot have them dressing like that in a civilized Court."

TWO DAYS AFTER the King had left her at Fontainebleau, Catherine's sitting room was darkened with long sheets of black silk. They had been applied to the windows of her apartments for her consultation. Luc Gauier, the Queen's astrologer, had been there for less than an hour and already the room was filled with thick blue smoke. The aroma of candles, incense and Catherine's pungent musk hung in the still summer air like a poisonous cloud, trapped by the long black drapes.

Gauier sat slumped-shouldered, with his eyes closed at one end of the long table. He wore a long, bright blue coat with flared sleeves and black felt cap. As his head rolled gently from side to side, he made a continuous low humming sound from the back of his throat. On the table before him, on pieces of stained parchment, were various sizes of circles and triangles. On the floor beside his chair, in a small pile of sand, he had fashioned the shape of a pentacle.

Catherine sat pensively across from the astrologer, as beads of sweat dripped from above her full lips. She had been instructed to say nothing. Gauier would speak only when he felt that the stars and the planets were properly aligned.

"There is a danger to the King . . ." he finally said. The words were low and garbled, almost inaudible. Catherine's breath quickened as she leaned toward him, not daring to speak until she was told to do so.

"It will come in a form of combat . . ." Again he paused. Catherine watched his fists, which were placed on top of the table, clench and relax. She wiped the perspiration from her upper lip with a blue embroidered handkerchief. Finally, Gauier opened his eyes and looked down at the shapes fashioned on the parchment. He moved a candle closer and then looked over at the sand on the floor. "It will be a single combat . . . and he may die from this encounter."

She felt a chill as beads of perspiration ran between her breasts beneath the heavy layers of silk and velvet. Then she began to go numb. She felt it first in her hands; then her arms, as it moved upward toward her throat. She was paralyzed with fear. Gauier looked at her directly, the signal that she was now permitted to speak. She licked her dry lips and swallowed, hoping to moisten her throat enough to bring the words from her mind.

"Can it be prevented?"

Once again, Gauier consulted the pentacle in the sand, then

looked at the shapes on the table. "He must engage in no combat in the forty-first year. Then, if he passes through that year, I see that he will live to the age of sixty-nine." Again he looked at the Queen with a glass-eyed stare as though he was completely unmoved by what he had said. Catherine was silent.

"Does Your Majesty wish to know anything further?" he finally asked. His tone was slow and even. He could just as easily have been conversing about Plato as predicting the death of her husband.

"Monsieur Gauier, you must repeat this to the King. You must warn him!"

"His Majesty does not believe. Such a move would be futile."

"But he may believe if you were to tell him about your other prediction long ago concerning him; that you predicted he would become King long before his brother died. If you do that, then perhaps we have a chance to save him!"

"Your Majesty knows that we may not alter what is already written in the stars."

"But you said there was a chance! You can do it. You must! You said combat. Clearly, if he does not do battle, he will survive. Is that not true?"

"The stars say that he *may* survive, Your Majesty. The direction of change in the heavens is not for me to decide."

"Please, Monsieur! I shall pay you whatever you desire, but you must consult with His Majesty. He must be warned! God save us, he is your King! I cannot lose him now, I cannot!"

Gauier glanced around the room. He knew that the King was a great skeptic and he did not relish subjecting his gift of prophecy to such rigorous doubt. Still, she was the Queen and she had seen to a substantial commission for him, along with a very fashionable house in Paris. If he did not do as she asked, there would be no reason for her to retain him. After another moment's reflection, the Queen's astrologer agreed.

*H*ENRI AGREED TO MEET with Catherine after his fencing match in the courtyard, but he went to her apartments reluctantly. He did not believe in astrology, nor did he approve of the prophets who made their living from her by bending the truth to fit her fantasies. Still, he agreed. His reason was simple. She had managed to appeal to him, as she always did, when he was most weak. He felt badly about the slight over Chenonceaux and he saw this concession as a way to make amends. When Catherine explained to him that Gauier had made predictions that he must hear, Henri did not have the heart to refuse her. So now he would go and hear the ominous words of doom, consider himself warned, and thereby satisfy his wife and his guilt.

"So then, where is he?" Henri asked from the door. "He is late and I am very busy."

"He will be here. That I promise you. Would you care for a cup of wine?"

Henri descended the two carpet-covered steps and strode into the Queen's receiving room. Catherine was sitting alone at a small gaming table near a window. She wore purple satin edged in gold, loose around the middle to allow for her latest pregnancy. Around her neck she wore a collar of pearls with a large garnet pendant. Her frizzled black hair poked out from her cap, just above her forehead.

As the King advanced into the incense-laced center of the Queen's rooms, one of her ladies came forward with a tray. In the center were two rare crystal goblets with white wine from Anjou. Henri sat down beside Catherine at the table. This, no doubt, would be used for their consultation with Gauier. To Henri's surprise, there were no candles, no magic wands and no jars of powder or mysterious liquid arranged before them. There was only an ordinary deck of cards and their crystal goblets.

Henri settled into the chair that creaked as he moved, and he felt a small tug at his heart when he looked at her now, so carefully groomed for his visit. Yet, Catherine looked tired and she was heavier than he had ever seen her. He thought how the children that she carried seemed to dominate her body long before the time of their birth. Though her abdomen seemed swollen nearly to capacity, this child, their fourth, was not due for another four months.

"Monsieur Luc Gauier," Lucrezia announced as the astrologer, in his long blue robe, hurried down the steps and into her chamber.

"Your Majesty," he said, bowing before the King and his bene-factress. In one hand he held a book of Egyptian hieroglyphics. In the other was an astrolabe, an instrument for observing the position of the celestial bodies. *The tools of his trade,* thought Henri smugly. Gauier is no different than the Queen's confidant, Ruggieri, nor any of the other mystics who were now so popular at his Court. Again Gauier bowed to the King as he drew nearer to the table.

"Yes, yes. Now do sit down," Henri said impatiently and then emptied his goblet in one swallow. "I understand from the Queen that you have something that you wish me to know."

Gauier cringed at the King's irreverent tone. He was making light of the situation. He fought the urge to take his prophecies and leave the cynical King to the winds of his own fate but the pleading eyes of the Queen forced him into the other chair.

"Very well then," said Gauier and he leaned back, closed his eyes and took a deep breath. "Several days ago, I consulted with the Queen. It was at that time that I came to fear for Your Majesty's safety. During our consultation, I saw that you are in danger. The stars confirmed my prediction."

Henri made no attempt to conceal a snicker. The mystic looked up and stopped.

"Go on," Catherine urged.

Again Gauier took a breath. "I see that there is danger to Your Majesty in combat. The danger shall come to you in a single com-bat, in an enclosed field, and it shall be cast upon you in your forty-first year." Gauier looked up. For a moment, no more, he saw the King's face freeze. His hands rested motionless on top of the table. The arrogant countenance had vanished. Gauier, who took it as a sign, continued. "If Your Majesty should survive it, you would live to be sixty-nine years old. That is, as it is written in the stars," he said, gesturing toward the astrolabe. When he looked back up, the King's countenance had changed again. Now there was a hard pinched expression on his face and his dark brows were fused in a frown. The skeptic had returned.

"That is preposterous and unfounded, Monsieur, and I strongly resent your inflicting yourself on the Queen like this and frightening her with your prophecies of doom!"

"Tell him, Monsieur Gauier, please tell him!"

"Very well, Madame, for you. But only for you. Your Majesty, this is not my only prophecy. I made another prediction in your regard some time ago. I foresaw that you would be King of France after your father." Gauier leaned across the table toward the King and thrust a slip of parchment boldly at him. "Your Majesty shall see that I committed this prophecy to paper in the year 1536, well before your elder brother's tragic demise."

He watched victoriously as Henri lowered his eyes to study the paper. "As Your Majesty can plainly see, the document was not only signed and witnessed by the Queen, but also by Monsieur Strozzi and a number of other senior members of her household."

Henri glanced at Catherine, her bulging black eyes pleading with him to believe the mystic. He looked back down at the paper once again. Gauier could not have known then that his brother François would die. In those years no one ever expected that Henri would one day be King. His body was rigid, his fists clenched on top of the table, but he fought to maintain the countenance of a King. What would Diane think if he now chose to follow the dictates of a soothsayer?

"Monsieur," he finally said, "perhaps what you say is true. But it does not bother me to die at the hand of another, provided he is brave and valiant and that the glory for this life remain mine."

Catherine looked at him; her eyes, as always, were brimming with tears but she could say nothing.

Seeing the grim expression on both of their faces, Henri stood and shook his head. "Now, Monsieur Gauier, if there is nothing else . . ."

When he could see that neither of them meant to reply, he quickly left the room.

AFTER HIS REASON had returned and he was away from Catherine, Henri dismissed the ominous predictions as nothing more than a stroke of fortune. Anyone could have written such a thing in hopes of elevating himself if it did later actually come true. In fact, the King reasoned, Gauier could have registered a number of predictions then produce the appropriate one when and if it was called for. After all, there were plagues. There were wars. It was not inconceivable that his brother could accidentally have died. The mystic, like everyone else, knew that. As he walked alone down the shadowy corridor, Henri convinced himself that the letter had been nothing more than the well-orchestrated plan of a masterful opportunist. The Court was full of them.

As to the prediction that he would one day die in single combat, Henri chose to fall back on the laws of France. The laws of his country had long prohibited a King's participation in a duel. Such a fate was impossible. As he walked, Henri systematically argued away all of the fears that he had first felt in Catherine's chamber. Mystics and prophets were in league with the devil. He had been wrong even to have listened to such an evil man, to have believed for a moment such nonsense. But as he walked, the ominous cloud of doubt surged up again, and he began to remember another time. Another place. It was Cauterets. The tiny inn and an old woman. Though Henri could no longer recall her face, her words had remained with him through the years. She had told Diane with the greatest conviction that she would bear three children when her marriage had given her only two. The daughter they now shared had been that third child.

But her last words had been most mystifying, and Henri had discounted them, believing that they related to her relationship with his father. Until now. *You have the power to lead; to change,* the old woman had said. *One day you will have more power than you can imagine, over a great many lives . . . and it will come to you through your power over one who adores you.* Of course! It was he, not his father, who was that one!

Henri quickened his pace and then broke into a run. Diane was waiting for him in the chapel. Now he was desperate to see her. Together they would pray to God. That alone would wash away the evil feeling of doom that his wife's mystic had hung over him.

HENRI'S CORONATION OATH had been to drive heresy from the realm, and as *Le Roi très Chrétien,* he took the oath with gravity. Where his father had vacillated between sympathy for the Reformers to moves of unbridled harshness, Henri was unswerving in his faith. He was a devout Catholic, as were those in power around him. He believed that it was his duty to rid France of the threat posed by the Reformation that would divide not only the Church, but the country. Yet, despite his single-mindedness, the movement had grown. It was no longer simply the preoccupation of the ruling class, or dinner conversation for idle lords and ladies. The message had filtered down to the ranks of peddlers, cobblers and weavers. Secret meetings late into the night were held in every town of France and they had grown to such proportions that even the government was at a loss to stop them.

Yet he was not so plagued by the growth of the dissenters as he was by the accepted punishment for their heresy: death at the stake by burning. In Diane's safe arms, the wounds of the past had begun to heal and Henri had grown into a gentle man. The notion of taking a man's life in so savage a manner because of his beliefs disturbed him deeply. If he could understand, perhaps he could help to reunite the two factions which were slowly tearing France apart. Late into the night they spoke of it. He told Diane and the Cardinal de Guise that he wanted to speak with one of them; hear their claims. Perhaps with patience, he could come to understand what had driven them away from the Church, and just perhaps he could find a way to make them want to return.

"I want you to bring me a prisoner, Charles," the King had said to Guise. "Someone unafraid to speak with me about his beliefs."

"With all due respect, Your Majesty, that would be most irregular. Those people are the enemy, not only against you, but against God."

"Well, something has got to be done to put an end to this. And after all, if I do not understand the enemy, how can I hope to win the war?"

Charles de Guise recalled the encounter with the King as he wound his way down the dark stone staircase into the bowels of the French prison. Here criminals and heretics waited together for their trials. Some waited for their executions, or simply for death to rescue them from the torment of their own excrement and the rancorous, infected cells.

Charles had little sympathy as he strode past the small black holes from which came the haunting moans and pleading cries of nameless, faceless men. He believed that they had sinned. They had earned their fate. He made the sign of the cross and moved along the dark and narrow pathway. Finally he reached an alcove where the guard kept a table, a lamp and some files on the men whom he guarded.

"No, no. These are all wrong!" he said, tossing the dossiers of several prisoners back onto the table. "I want someone less pronounced. These are all men of letters. If any of these men have their way, they will all but convince the King about their heresy, not dissuade him!" The Cardinal grabbed the stack of files from which the three had been chosen. The guard moved in with a torch so that the Cardinal could read. After a moment he selected one. A smile broadened on his thin face. "This one, yes this one. He will do perfectly."

"But Your Eminence, he is nothing but a simple tailor. He ain't fit for talking to the King!"

"Precisely, Monsieur. Quite precisely. Prepare him for His Majesty, and see that he has a bath. My men will be back in one hour to collect him."

Guise turned around and began to walk back down the corridor which would lead him up to the rue Saint-Antoine and the fresh air of freedom. He lowered his head and quickened his pace until he was forced to stop. A line of prisoners chained together at the wrist were being transported from one place to another. The man who led them was discussing cell assignments with another guard, and the prisoners blocked his path. Charles tried to look away. The odor was vile. The men were filthy and depressing, and he was to have supper with Madame Diane when this disagreeable business was complete. But the men did not move, and he could not pass without brushing his crimson silk gown against their soiled brown rags.

Finally the Cardinal looked up again. It was an involuntary movement. He had not planned to meet the brutal stares of any of them, but the face of one, he was at a loss to avoid. He was two men back in the row of ten, but he was taller than the others and he held his head high, so that it would have been impossible not to see him. The man leered at Charles from behind a grimy brown face and white hair; his yellow teeth flashed a curious smile of recognition. He would have been any other anonymous prisoner had it not been for those eyes. They were familiar. For the instant that they stared at one another, Charles felt certain that he knew the man. But before he could place him, the guard returned, shouted something, and the queue of prisoners was issued down the hall.

The man and Charles's memory of him faded back into the darkness as he climbed from the acrid-smelling pit, back to the world of the living. It was not until much later that evening, in the stylish house of the Duchesse de Valentinois, that the Cardinal would recall the identity of the prisoner with the haunting eyes.

DIANE'S NEW HOUSE in Paris was the sprawling, white stone Hotél d'Etampes on the rue Saint-Antoine. At Henri's urgings, she had bought the grand estate of the former *favourite* for herself so that she could be near the palace and Henri.

Since their fear of poisoning, he had ceased to feel safe at the prospect of having his wife and his mistress housed together for any length of time. Catherine's increasing involvement with alchemy and her association with poison mongers did little to allay his fears. When one of the King's apothecaries informed him that a poison could now be produced, the effect of which was so gradual that it could kill and yet go undetected, he insisted on the move.

L'Hôtel de Graville, as L'Hôtel d'Etampes had been renamed, was a very stately and impressive old manor situated in the most fashionable area of Paris. It was on a long, tree-lined causeway in a strategic position between the royal palace Les Tournelles and L'Hôtel de Guise. Since Diane refused to let Henri purchase it for her, he had it completely furnished in black and white and provided a giant staff of servants to surprise her.

The Duchesse de Valentinois was still known as Madame Diane to her intimates, and the Court she held was a small one. She preferred the company of a few sincere friends to the vast gatherings of the previous reign. It was therefore considered a great achievement to be invited for a meal or an afternoon poetry reading. One's importance to the Crown could be determined not only by position, but now by whether he dined at the palace, or at the L'Hôtel de Graville.

Charles de Guise sat with Diane and the King in her black and white dining hall. He leaned back, lay his head against the velvet-covered chair and watched a long wax taper slowly drip wax onto Madame Diane's hand-embroidered tablecloth. He had drunk more than his usual share of wine this evening, in an effort to stave off the sights and the odors of the Conciergerie. But still his mind was filled with it. Beside him, the King had just pulled Diane onto his lap, and now sat gazing rapturously at her. They were whispering to one another and for the first time in a long while, he hadn't a care what they were saying.

Across from him, Saint-André and Bourbon engaged in a lively debate about Italian and French architecture; that much he could hear. Despite the fact that there were few things in the world Charles de Guise liked so much as the subject of architecture, he did not intervene. His mind was plagued by the identity of the mysterious prisoner he had seen that afternoon. Who could

it have been? Did he really know the man, or had he just been reminded of someone?

After the meal was removed, everyone turned to the two large
double doors stenciled in black with the royal emblem through
which the heretic would now be brought. Henri had not meant
for this interview to be taken as sport. He had hoped only to be
enlightened about the Reformation. To his chagrin, his guests,
nonetheless, were laughing and gossiping amongst themselves as
though some drama were about to be performed. They seemed to
care little that, in this room, the fate of a man's life would soon be
decided.

"Suddenly I wish this were over," he whispered to Diane.
"Though my intentions were constructive, I fear they have been
all but lost on everyone else."

"You can always cancel, *chéri.*"

"No. I have committed myself to hear the man out. I must see
it through."

The prisoner who was presented to the King was a small
insignificant-looking man with a thin, bony face and small blue
eyes. Still in chains, he stumbled through the door between two
guards. What surprised everyone more than his appearance, was
his manner. He was haughty and he possessed the confidence of
an invited guest rather than a condemned man.

The prisoner, who was a tailor from Paris, stood before the
King and Diane. With simple and precise words, he responded to
each question put to him in turn by the various guests. No matter
what he was asked, he responded in the same manner. When he
was questioned about his contempt for the Holy Mass, his reply
became insolent. He never wavered. Finally, it was time for the
King to question him. Henri stood and paced the length of the
room, his hands clasped behind his back.

"So then. Here you are, before the most noble and highly
placed men of France. To my surprise, you reply boldly; even dar-
ingly. Nothing about our questions appears to ruffle you. And so
now you are to be given an opportunity to speak directly to your
King." Henri neared the man. He felt his own impatience. "Tell

me, Monsieur, why is it that when most men would show great humility in your place, you choose to maintain a most ill-advised hauteur?"

The tailor looked with renewed confidence, directly at the King. "My reasons, Your Majesty, are simple. I have been chosen by God Almighty to reveal His true doctrines to you. I never doubted that one day this opportunity would come. Since it is my true destiny, and I know it, I am able to maintain, through anything, the dignity that God has given me."

That God should speak through this man, rather than through the King of France, was too much. Henri threw up his arms and turned back to the ring of his friends who were seated behind him. All of them but Diane had questioned the prisoner.

"I give up. I have nothing further to add. Madame, have you anything to say to this man?"

Before she could reply, the tailor stepped forward, pursed his lips and spit at her. "Madame, you are an evil woman! Be satisfied with having already poisoned France. Do not now mingle your venom and infamy with anything so holy as God's truth, for fear that He may send a plague upon the King and his entire realm!"

Henri whipped around, his face white with rage. He lunged forward, grabbing the man by the collar. "How dare you!" he seethed. "On your knees, swine! Do you hear me? On your knees!" When the man refused, Henri used one powerful hand to the top of his head to force the prisoner down. No one dared to intervene.

"Humble yourself to her! Now!"

"To Diane de Poitiers, never!"

Henri pulled his hair so that the tailor's head was drawn backward with a quick snapping movement. "Madame! She is Madame to you and anyone at all who hopes to live in my presence!"

After another moment, when it was clear that the tailor was not going to comply, Diane stood. She walked across the room away from the exchange. Saint-André put a hand on the King's shoulder.

"Perhaps Your Majesty should let the guards see to his punishment from here."

Henri leered at the man. His fists were still clenched and

poised up near his chest, as though at any moment he might strike again.

"You are fortunate, sir, that I do not kill you myself! Your death is bound to be far less painful at the hands of the executioner than it would have been with me! I can no longer bear the sight of you. Now take him away from here at once! Have him tried immediately. I want nothing further to do with him."

The prisoner, who said nothing in his own defense, was then led from Diane's dining hall. The other guests attempted to occupy themselves with idle conversation as Henri moved to Diane, and a young page stood before her trying to clean the front of her gown with a wet cloth. When she knew that Henri was behind her, she issued the page away.

"I am so sorry," she whispered, still not turning to face him.

"What could you possibly have to be sorry for?"

"For the position in which I seem to have put you with your people."

Henri could not reply. His feelings were a mixture of raging anger at the man who had wounded her, and an overwhelming tenderness; a desire to protect her. He put his hands on her shoulders from behind and whispered to her.

"Let me send them all away so that we may retire. Let me show you how dear you are to me."

"Oh, Henri, I am afraid my company would be dreadful just now."

"That would be impossible. Please, m'amie, let me just be near you."

Diane turned around and faced him with a weak smile. Her eyes were full of a pain that he had almost forgotten. It made him feel more helpless than he had since long before his father's death.

"I thank you for your concern, chéri, but I think just now I would rather be alone. Oh, please do not look so worried. I shall be fine. I promise."

"I leave for Saint Germain-en-Laye at dawn . . ."

"Yes, perhaps that is best."

"But you will be there for Catherine's coronation. You promised me that."

"That I did," she assured him. "And I shall keep my word."

He longed to object. He wanted to say anything at all that would make her stay with him, but that would be selfish. Reluctantly, he took his one remaining hand from her shoulder and let her go. The other guests watched discreetly as the Duchesse de Valentinois crossed the room and left alone.

When she was gone, Henri called Charles de Guise to his side. "Follow her, will you."

"Of course, Your Majesty."

"I think she may need your counsel just now, more than my own. And Charles, whatever you do, please be gentle with her. She is more fragile than a great many of you would have her be."

THE CARDINAL SEARCHED for nearly an hour before he found Diane in her private oratory. She was alone, kneeling in the shadows on her crimson velvet prie-dieu. He knelt beside her and made the sign of the cross. After a moment when she saw him, she stood, genuflected and left the room.

He followed her and they walked out into the garden before either of them spoke. Diane took in the fresh aroma of spring; the new musk roses, to steady her. From the side, Charles could see that her eyes were red and her lips were swollen from crying.

"You mustn't let an old man upset you. His reason and judgment were lost to him long ago when he quit the Church. It is certain that the devil guides him now."

"It is not only the tailor, though his words expressed many of my own feelings."

Diane put her arm through his as they walked down a flight of stone steps into the small vegetable garden behind the kitchens. Charles could see that she was fighting valiantly to suppress her tears.

"There have been other words that have come to me in the form of rumors," she continued. "At first I believed them to be nothing more than envy. But now I no longer know what to believe. I have prayed to God. I ask if I could not better serve His Majesty if I were to take the veil; perhaps surrender myself to a nunnery where I am no longer a temptation to the King or a disgrace to his people. But I get no reply."

Charles was silent. He must think.

Diane de Poitiers was one of the only people he had ever come to respect at the French Court. She was direct and honest. Those qualities had drawn him instantly to her that first time at Chenonceaux when he was no more than a boy. He also knew that she did not consider such a proposition lightly. He felt a great surge of power at this realization; as though the fate of France rested in his own two hands. She was not cruel or calculating. Behind the veneer of cool reserve, she was like every other woman; soft and unsure, and fiercely protective of the man she loved.

In the silent moments that followed, Charles found himself considering the prospect of her absence from Court. The voice of his ambition was nearly deafening. If he chose to encourage it, his own influence and that of his family would surely increase. Then an image of the King sprang to his mind. The image was from that one summer when Diane had been forced by some mysterious illness to stay at Anet. The King had been beside himself. Everyone had seen it. There could be little doubt of his complete dependence on her. Perhaps France would suffer a far worse fate if she were gone. He fingered the heavy cross at the point of his chest and finally looked at her.

"You, Madame, have a mission higher than even a life in service to God can provide. It is a mission that I believe you alone can perform." Diane looked up at him with surprise, though still she did not speak. "These are difficult times for the Church," he continued. "The wolf of heresy is at our door. You know that it presses further each day to overtake us. I have seen you with His Majesty, Madame. I know of his dedication to you. It is my firm belief, as a minister of God, that you alone have the power with the King to hold him firm in his duty."

"That may be true. I know that he trusts me, but at what price?" Diane cast her arms down by her sides and turned her gaze up toward the trees. "Oh, Charles, every day of my life, every time I open my eyes, I commit a sin against God and against the Church.

You know, they have begun to call me His Majesty's courtesan. Once that was a designation I found the most vile in the world. Now I do not know anymore that they are so far from the truth."

He put a comforting hand on her shoulder. "Then how better for you to win your salvation than by holding a great King to his obligation to persecute those who betray God? You alone can do it, Madame. He relies on you for everything."

She turned back to face him, her pleading eyes completely disarming. "But to achieve this end," she said. "I must commit the sin of adultery. For the rest of my life and that of the King I fear that it is too much to ask God to forgive."

Then, he did not know what it was or why, but it came to him. Perhaps it was the thoughts of Chenonceaux, the place where they first had met all those years ago. Perhaps it was the injured look on her face; the one he had seen only one other time; that same evening of their meeting at the little chateau on the river. Whatever had triggered it, he now knew beyond any doubt the identity of the man he had seen that afternoon. The man who had caught his eye in the dim, foul-smelling Paris prison was the Duchesse de Valentinois' former lover, Jacques de Montgommery.

33

CERTAINLY YOU WERE MISTAKEN," said François de Guise, his gaunt face rich with shadows and full of surprise.

"I thought as much in the beginning," Charles finally replied, far more calm than his brother. "I too thought that such a thing was impossible in so civilized an age. And if I had not been met with those eyes myself, perhaps I would not have believed it either. But if you had seen him then, François, as I did, I promise you, there would be no doubt in your mind."

The two brothers stood gazing up at a huge wall tapestry which had recently been installed in the main salon of the Hotel de Guise in Paris. The tapestry told the story of Sisyphus, King of Corinth, who had been condemned to push a heavy boulder up a never-ending hill. Charles had especially liked the story because it reminded him of the struggles that his own family had endured to reach their present level of power.

"But Montgommery was such a fixture here at Court for as long as I can recall," said François. "His position as Captain of the Scots Guard was always secure."

"Secure perhaps in the last regime. Not the current one. You know quite well that King Henri detests him, and why. I suspect His Majesty was simply biding his time, waiting for a legitimate reason to be rid of him, as he was with anyone left over from his father's Court . . . No, dear brother, there is no mistake. The man in that prison is Captain Montgommery. On that, I would stake my life."

François stroked his neat russet-colored beard. "So that is what became of him after he led such a disaster at Lagny-sur-Marne. I had heard that King Henri confiscated his estates and that he was relieved in disgrace for having allowed such unnecessary violence and bloodshed. But I never suspected—"

"He flaunted his affair with the Duchesse de Valentinois to anyone who would listen. And in the most lurid detail. I would imagine that the good Captain is paying for that as much as for any military blunders."

"Actually, now that I think about it, I cannot say that it is much of a loss. There never was a more pompous, a more con-ceited man than he."

"Except perhaps Constable Montmorency." Charles smiled.

"Indeed," the brothers agreed as they strolled across the tiled floor together toward a large green and gold brocade couch.

"Well, you must tell Madame Diane what you know," François finally said. The Cardinal looked at him as they sat down.

"I considered that option. But I cannot see what possible pur-pose it would serve."

"Oh, Charles, really! Do you not recall some years ago, how our uncle taught us the value of the game of chess? Well, I have come to discover that he was absolutely right. Strategy. It is all strategy. When Madame Diane discovers what has become of Montgommery, she will, of course, use all of her resources to free him. And can you imagine, even for a moment, the response by the King, who looks upon her as if her very soul belonged to him?"

"But what if it creates a breach between them?" asked the Cardinal.

"Precisely, dear brother. What if it does? What do you suppose would happen to the will of the King without the woman around who leads him by the nose?"

"I was under the impression that you liked Madame Diane."

"That I do. But I have the good of the family to consider; and on that score, all is fair."

"Need I remind you that her daughter is our brother's wife? That by their marriage, Diane de Poitiers is part of our family? And for that matter, do you realize that this could just as easily work against us as in our favor? I know His Majesty would sooner be rid of his entire Court than lose Madame. If we were caught trying to undermine her—"

"How could we be found guilty in any of this? We would simply be reporting information, and then letting fate take its course. Oh, the deuce, brother, this is delicious! So delicious!"

"You can be very cruel, François." Charles shook his head. "I had forgotten that about you. May I remind you that we owe everything, our entire elevation here, to her favor?"

François sprang from the couch and turned back so that he was looming over his brother. "I am the eldest, Charles. You know it is not in your power to oppose me in this."

"So that is what it has come down to." The Cardinal paused a moment. He looked away as though he were deep in reflection, since he knew how much his very impatient brother disliked it. "Well, I have one final trip to make after the Queen's coronation. It was to have been a trip to Ferrara to finalize the terms of your marriage. But I have been thinking these past few days that perhaps I shall not go after all. Since, as you say, you are the oldest, perhaps you could better negotiate your own alliance."

"My younger brother threatening me?" asked François, his eye-brows arched.

"Oh, such a nasty word. No, not threatening; only reminding you of my own persuasive power. One thing you never did learn from our uncle about the game of chess, dear François, was the patience that it requires to succeed. Trust me on this score with Madame. I have only our best interest at heart in my silence. When the time is right, neither of us shall be disappointed. On that you have my word."

As HENRI STEPPED from his horse he could see his daughters. They were sitting on a large embroidered blanket beneath the shade of a rustling beech tree at the far end of the courtyard. Elizabeth and Diane each had an embroidery hoop before her. Little Mary, the Scots Queen, who had just turned six, was receiving a lesson on the lute. Around them, a ring of courtly lords and ladies sat in attendance. The strains of the simple tune played by Mary whispered on the breeze and made him smile. He was always so glad to see for himself that his children were as well as Humières had written that they were.

The day after the incident with the tailor, Henri had been required to leave Paris for Saint Germain-en-Laye. He was to hear vespers with the townspeople and perform a laying on of hands to those who suffered from scrofula. He had not wanted to leave Diane alone in Paris after what had happened, but he knew that his duty to his people must come before his personal concerns. He tried to put the event out of his mind now as he stood near his horse, gazing at the little girls and their attendants, all of whom were still unaware of his presence. He stepped forward a few paces so that he could conceal himself behind a tall conical-shaped yew.

Diane was now fourteen, and he could see even from a distance that she had grown into a very pretty young woman. She was the only child who had inherited his own ink-black hair and olive skin. Those dark features were in contrast to her bright blue eyes; her mother's eyes. His heart sank at the prospect of surrendering her to such a boldly political marriage as one with the

Pope's grandson. But for all he had done to legitimize her, he could not forget that she was still a bastard child. Such a powerful match for her would assure him that, no matter what became of him, she would always be well provided for. As he had reluctantly come to understand the reason for his own match, one day she would come to understand hers.

He studied each of his daughters from a distance. Pretty Mary, who was almost like a daughter. Petite Elizabeth. Then he noticed that among the children's attendants was Lady Flemming. She stood behind the Queen of Scots, laughing as the child erred on the piece she was playing. Henri looked at her and he was uncertain of what he could possibly have found inviting about her that night in his daughter's room. She laughed too loudly, was too plump and was much too forward for his taste.

"Shall I inform them that Your Majesty has returned, and that you wish an audience with them?" Saint-André whispered to the King. Just as he was about to reply, something caused Diane to look up and see her father across the courtyard.

"Papa!" she cried, casting down her embroidery hoop and taking up her gown so that she could run. Elizabeth, who was now five, followed her half-sister. Henri bent down and took them both into his arms. After several minutes of welcoming kisses and hugs, Queen Mary and her Governess, the Lady Flemming, approached.

"We thought that you were not coming until Thursday!" said Diane. "Monsieur d'Humières told us that you had been delayed. Oh, but what a wonderful surprise!"

Elizabeth sat on her father's knee with her arms around his neck while Diane spoke from the other side. "François, Elizabeth and I have staged a play for you and Madame Diane. But our brother, I am afraid, keeps forgetting his lines, and I am certain he shall not be ready until Saturday at the least to perform it." She began to look around. "Where is Madame Diane? Did she not come with you? Oh, she promised that she would come!"

Lady Flemming and her charge neared them just as the King's eldest daughter had begun her inquiry about the Duchesse de Valentinois.

"I am sorry, *ma mignonne,* no, she has not come with me. Business has kept her in Paris a few days longer than she had intended. But you know that she sends all of you her love."

When Henri stood again, he found himself facing Lady Flemming. She stood before him in a gown he thought more appropriate to a brothel than the environs of the royal nursery. It was sewn of crimson damask, and like the one she had worn the last time he had seen her, this one was cut to the lowest possible point of her bosom that propriety would allow. The velvet yoke around her gown and her hood were of black velvet. The colors against her russet hair were the most boldly inappropriate he had ever seen.

The little Queen and her Governess bowed to the King and Henri did his best to turn his attention toward the younger of the two. He bent down again and took her hand as his own daughters looked on.

"Welcome home, Your Majesty. It is very good to see you again," she said.

The King smiled, pleased at the effort that she had undertaken to speak to him, this time in French.

"You must have worked very hard, my daughter, since we last met," he replied, still smiling. The little girl's face lit up with the joy only a child knows at the approval of a parent.

"She wished to surprise Your Majesty," said Lady Flemming.

"And so she has." Once again Henri stood, and again he was faced with the buxom Scottish beauty. "It appears that you are doing an admirable job with the Queen, Lady Flemming."

"The construction of her words are her own, Your Majesty, but I assure you the sentiments are shared by us both." Then she flashed the same gap-toothed smile that, until that moment, he had forgotten. Before he could reply, she bent down to herd the girls back to their tasks. "Come, ladies. Certainly His Majesty will want to have some time to himself before supper."

She had turned to leave, but then stopped and turned back around. The look was more chaste; almost demure, as though she was another person entirely. "Will Your Majesty be dining with the children tonight, or should you prefer to take your meal alone?"

"No. Of course not," he managed to say without staring. "I shall dine, as always when I am here, in the company of my family."

"Then I shall, with pleasure, prepare the Queen of Scots to attend you."

This time when she turned away, her skirts swirled behind her. Her perfume, a combination of orange and spice, caught the summer breeze around them. The Cardinal de Guise, who had been standing beside the King for the entire exchange, took in an animated breath and sighed.

"Ah! If I were not a man of God, I think that I should be hopelessly in love."

Henri shot him an evil glance. "But you are, thank Heaven, a man of God, and speaking for the Holy Father, we will both thank you kindly to remember that!"

THAT EVENING, the King had supper served in his apartments rather than in the formal dining hall. He sat between his daughter Diane and Mary, the Queen of Scots. The Dauphin, François and Elizabeth, the more precocious of the royal children, were kept apart. They were made to behave properly by Madame and Monsieur d'Humières, who sat at the other end of the table. The King's two youngest children did not attend their father's banquet, Claude being not quite two, and Louis having been ill nearly continuously since his birth the previous autumn.

"I understand, Papa, that I am to be married soon," Diane began as she took another candied plum from the silver tray and then looked directly at her father. Henri was caught off guard, not only by what she had said, but how she had said it.

He had wanted to tell her in his own time and in a much more private manner than this. But gossip at Court was swift, and now it was done. "And what do you think of the idea?" he cautiously asked.

"If you have chosen him for me, Papa, I am certain that he is a good man. I shall not be one to oppose your will."

Despite her decorous words, as Henri looked at her he saw

sadness. He thought how she wore this dutiful exterior with the same grace as her mother.

"Ah, I fear that there is a good deal more behind those pretty eyes of yours than you would have me believe."

Diane looked away, hiding instinctively that part of herself that she knew would betray her. Henri took her chin in his finger and raised it. "Now, what is this, *ma mignonne*? We have no secrets from one another, do we?"

She glanced around the room. Charles and François de Guise were seated too closely. They could not speak privately. Carefully, she daubed the corners of her mouth with an embroidered napkin, then stood and excused herself from the table. She walked alone through an open glass door, and out onto the marble terrace. Henri followed her.

Outside, they stood beside one another for a long time, amid the far off sounds composed by the Court musicians. But soon their strains were lost to the shrill scratching night music of the crickets in the shrubbery beneath them.

"I am in love, Papa," she finally announced.

"In love? With whom?"

"It does not matter his name now, since there is no possibility for me to be with him. He is only a member of your Majesty's Guard, not someone suitable as a husband. Even though I understand and accept that, I cannot help but feel a boundless sense of loss at having to marry a man I do not love."

Henri was stunned. He looked over at his daughter who he believed to be the mirror image of himself. In her he saw the same vulnerability; the same sensitivity. The pain that he felt for her now was an old pain from a long-possessed wound. It was the memory of his own beginning with Diane, and how he had once been forced to give her up to Montgommery and face his own duty.

The memory of Diane and Jacques de Montgommery still haunted him. He had always been the one imperfect facet in what Henri believed to be an otherwise perfect love affair with his goddess. Henri had never recovered from the bitter jealousy of what had passed between the two of them after he had been forced to marry Catherine. That another man could have taken possession of her heart, or her body, which he believed to have been born solely for him, was intolerable. But, that Montgommery had such knowledge of his Diane and then spread it like cheap kitchen gossip, fueled within him a raging jealousy that he would have done anything to avenge . . . Anything.

Henri took a labored breath. "Whoever it is, Diane, I want you to promise me that you will not see him again."

"But, Papa, he is at the very least my friend, as Madame Diane is a friend to you."

"Promise me, child! You will marry the Duke of Castro and that shall be the end of it. Believe me, I do know how you feel, but you must understand that it is your duty to leave him behind and to marry the man who has been chosen for you."

"Just as it was your duty to leave Madame Diane behind so that you could marry the Queen?"

Henri clutched his chest. Her words would have been insolent, but the tone with which she had said them were so sincere, so honest, that he could find no fault with her. The tension between father and daughter slipped away.

"You did want to marry her, didn't you, Papa? But they made you marry Her Majesty instead, because it was your duty."

"Yes, *ma mignonne,* I did want to marry her, very much." Henri took his daughter's hand and turned to face her. "And that I did not will go with me to my grave as the single greatest regret of my life."

Diane turned away. She looked down into the garden at the rustling chestnut trees, and did not speak.

"What is it, Diane? You do not believe me?"

"Perhaps what I wonder is too bold a thing for even me to ask you, Papa."

"Ask me what you like."

As she turned back to face him, her blue eyes sparkled in the moonlight, and for a moment, just a moment, he believed that he was looking at her mother.

"I can understand about the Queen. That is your duty. But if you loved Madame as much as you say, how did you get another woman with me?"

Her words were still sincere. She had never asked him about the story of the alleged Piedmontese peasant whom her real mother had fabricated. Henri's face flushed with color as he led her a few steps to a stone bench. He sat down beside her and rested his elbows on his thighs. How could he explain an infidelity to a woman he worshipped? An infidelity that never happened. Yet he felt that she deserved some kind of reply. He struggled to find one worthy of the daughter whom he adored.

"Sometimes things happen between adults," he began slowly. "We make mistakes; decisions that are not easily explained later, when one is called upon to do so. But you must believe this, *ma mignonne,* whatever I did, whatever Madame did, you are never to doubt the great love that we both have for you. Your knowing that is the most important thing in the world to me."

She kissed his cheek and looked into his eyes. "Do you know what I wish, Papa? More than anything else, I wish that Madame Diane were my mother. Yes, that is my wish. I have always felt it, even when I was very small. She was so kind to me. I know that you probably think me very foolish for having such a wish, but to have been born of a love so rare, like the one you share with Madame . . ." When she looked up, she saw her father's face drawn and his lips parted. "What is it, Papa? Have I said something to displease you? Oh, please tell me you are not cross."

Henri was unable to speak. He felt as if his heart were breaking. All the years of lying, of hiding the truth from her, when all along the child wanted nothing more than to be precisely who she was. He had never longed so much as at this moment to tell her the truth. But he had promised and, no matter what, he would not falter. Not now.

"No. I am fine, truly. It was just, I suppose, sitting here, looking at what a fine young woman you have become, and about to be married, I was just a bit overwhelmed, that is all. Nothing for you to worry about." Again he took her hands and squeezed them gently. "Now, I want to say something serious to you. It is something I want desperately for you to hear because you know, don't you, that you have always been my favorite. Oh, I know that such a sentiment is unfair to the others, but nevertheless, it is true. You were my first child, and that makes the love I bear for you like nothing else in the world. Many years ago, when I was given up in marriage, no one spoke to me like this. No one explained anything, or cared how I felt. It was my role and I was told to take it in stride. I want things to be easier for you, *ma mignonne*. So, you will believe me, I hope, when I say that I do know how you feel to love someone whom you can never marry. It is precisely because I know it so well that I tell you now, my decision on your husband is truly in your best interest. You are of royal blood, Diane. You are the first born child of the King of France, and I wish desperately to see your future secured."

Diane could say nothing else, so instead she leaned over to hug her father and in the shadow of the moonlight, she saw him weeping. It was at that moment that she first began to suspect the truth.

HENRI TOSSED AND TURNED beneath his bedcovers, unable to rid his mind of his daughter's haunting words. *I wish Madame Diane were my mother . . . I wish . . .* How wonderful and yet how strange, he thought that they should both love Diane de Poitiers so deeply. To both want, more than anything, that bond with her when she was despised by so many others. Much of it was envy. They had learned to live with it, but the words of one crazed tailor had made a difference. Like it or not, it was Catherine, not Diane, who was Queen; a fact that stimulated much resentment, not unlike a general preference for an abandoned puppy over a well-bred hunting hound.

He could think of nothing but his Diane. He found as the light of dawn burst through the long casement windows that he was overcome by his physical need of her. A sense of impotence about her refusing to see him at L'Hôtel de Graville had come with him to Saint Germain-en-Laye. But now here, without her, the need returned with the dark fury of a tempest, and this time neither wine nor sleep could quell it. He wanted to be with her; to hold her and convince her that he worshipped her as much now as in the beginning. No words from a witless tailor could change that. He wanted to tell her that she alone was the thing that was right in his life, and that she always would be. There would be no rest . . . no release again until she and all the world knew it. He had only to wait until the tenth of July . . . only a few more days.

ON THE TENTH OF JULY, the morning of Catherine's coronation, Diane sat on a stool in a purple satin shift and white stockings as Clothilde dressed her hair with diamonds and pearls. From the open window beside her, she could see the black and white banners hung from all of the windows, as they flapped in the warm summer breeze. The banners bore what was now the official royal emblem, and they were sprinkled with silver crescents.

Preparations were nearly complete, and everywhere she saw a splendor and extravagance unmatched in France. The official decorations were a triumph of classic style. Philibert de L'Orme, the man who was renovating Anet, and Jean Goujon had worked to create a new elegance to mark the reign of Henri II. Gone from France were the ribald jesters, the mummers and the sort of broad humor that marked the previous reign. Gone were the salamanders and the Italian designs. Their goal was to draw attention to the grand buildings along the route to the Cathedral de Saint-Denis that had been erected specifically for the event. Now on buildings there were crescents and D and H emblems. There was a fountain with a great thundering Jupiter (the symbol of royal omnipotence), and platforms on which allegories from *Le Roman de la rose* would be performed.

Hélène brought out the black velvet bag which contained Diane's gown for the ceremony, but Diane did not see it. Her mind was miles from her dressing table and from the attendants who rushed around her with shoes, petticoats and jewels. This was Catherine's coronation; the day when all of France would acknowledge her as their Queen. Although she had kept silent, it was curious, even to her, why Henri had chosen to afford his wife so great an honor. Diane knew that there had been no outcry; such a move was not called for by the people who had never completely accepted their Italian Queen.

Even though others had begun to whisper that the King kept his aging mistress out of obligation now, not love, Diane had ignored it as envious gossip. She had thought her own relationship with Henri stronger than ever. The only explanation was that the gossip was really the truth. Things must have changed between Henri and Catherine in ways he felt unable to tell her.

Of course that was it. Catherine had given him four children. He had come to accept that he could not divorce her. He had finally realized he could never make Diane his Queen. Once the hurt and the shock of that realization had faded, Diane promised herself that she would attend the procession with the same selfless dignity that she had for the past sixteen years.

"Madame, there appears to be some mistake."

Hélène held the gown up for Diane's approval. Her own lips were parted and her brows were raised with surprise as she waited for Diane to turn around. When Diane made no move, Hélène cleared her throat, and then with a weak uncertain voice said, "I put your gown in this bag myself yesterday and yet now there is another in its place, and this ermine cape is with it."

Diane was finally drawn back from her thoughts. She turned around and looked at the gown as Hélène continued, her eyes still fixed with amazement.

"Madame, I am so sorry, but your gown . . . the one you had chosen to wear, to be honest, Madame, it is nowhere to be found."

Before them in Hélène's arms was an elaborate costume which Diane had never seen before. It was white moiré silk encrusted with jewels. Emeralds, rubies and sapphires were sewn into the embroidered lace bodice, and there was topaz in the large marten fur cuffs. Pearls nearly obscured the fabric of the skirt. Diane's mouth fell open as she reached out to touch the elegant and costly gown.

"A clue to the confusion may be in this, Madame," said Clothilde as she handed her a small sealed slip of parchment. "I only just now received it from the King's messenger."

Diane looked at the gown again and then opened the note. It began with a poem written in Henri's own hand:

Never swore vassal truer faith, my Princess, for a
Prince new-crowned, than my love's pledge, that
shall be found
Steadfast in face of time, and death.

Wear this my love, for yourself, for France, and
for the man who has known, all of his life, but one
God and one love.

The royal cortege wound its way through the street to the Cathedral de Saint-Denis as crowds of Parisians cheered their Sovereign and their Queen. The cobblestones were strewn with white rose petals. People leaned from windows and stood on balconies to catch a glimpse of the procession as they strode solemnly on a path of gold cloth. First, there were heralds dressed in glittering black and white. Musicians followed, playing trumpets, flageolets and bass viols. Bishops and abbots all bore their crosiers as incense puffed from braziers around them. Then came a hundred members of the King's Guard, all riding horses paired in black and white. The aging, white-haired Cardinal de Lorraine, in his flowing red gown, bore a great gold cross.

Behind the King and Queen came the Dauphin, the Queen of Scots, and the other royal children. Then came Diane de Poitiers in her jewel-encrusted gown and ermine cape in a position scandalously close to the royal family. To her surprise, behind her were her own two daughters by Louis de Brézé, who had been instructed by the King to follow her in the ceremony.

Light streamed into the cathedral and a great collection of celestial voices sung in the nave. Catherine sat on one raised dais, Diane sat on another of equal height. But it was not until the cathedral was packed with guests that two Captains advanced upon Diane to remove her cape. As the overgarment fell away, everyone saw that the ceremonial gown worn by the King's mistress was an exact duplicate of the one worn by the Queen.

"I would not have believed it if I had not seen it myself," whispered François de Guise to his brother, Charles, as the King, the last to be seated, sat on the ceremonial dais not beside Catherine, but beside Diane.

"I thought she only wore black," Charles replied in Italian, hoping to make their conversation less conspicuous.

"It would seem that there are some occasions when even she is willing to break from tradition."

"Oh, to know what the Queen is thinking just now," Charles mused.

"Or the Duchesse de Valentinois!"

Charles looked over at his elder brother with an expression of real surprise. "Oh my, but you do not think that his mistress could have known anything about this, do you? Such a supposition would be scandalous, even for her!"

"Of course she knew," snapped François. "Do not be so naive! It was probably her idea. What better coup for the King's courtesan than to outshine the Queen in the very same gown, and on the day of her coronation! His Majesty certainly is not bright enough to have thought up so complex a slight without her assistance. You know as well as I that she positively rules him. Actually, it is little wonder that something like this would have happened."

"Well, I still find it shocking," Charles whispered as the ceremony began.

"But you do know what they say. He always wanted her to be Queen. I know personally that it was going on years ago, even before the Queen arrived in France. Can you imagine, he was no more than a boy when it began between them. Perhaps with this daring display he is finally repaying her for her years of . . . instruction!"

When she could tastefully manage a sideways glance at the

King, Diane found him draped in heavy ermine and beaming with pride. His black eyes sparkled and he continued to fight a smile. She had never been more horrified.

What must they think of me? To have the audacity to wear the very gown that the Queen is wearing for her coronation . . . it is simply too much! He has done this; he has switched the gowns, arranged my place here on the dais, all in an awkward and scandalous tribute!

The ceremony was long and the cathedral was warmed by the month of July, but no one seemed in the least disinterested. Throughout the pews, courtiers and guests whispered sentiments of shock and surprise beneath the echoed tones of the Mass. Those who had been puzzled by the King's intention to honor, so publicly, a Queen whom he did not love, were now enlightened to his purpose.

Catherine sat quietly on her throne as the Latin words were uttered, never daring to look beside her at her husband and his mistress, who had managed once again to garner the attention that had been intended for her.

As the Cardinal de Lorraine completed the Mass, Françoise de La Marck, Diane's eldest daughter, moved from her place and walked up the five gold and crimson steps to the throne. The cavernous cathedral fell to a hush. Due to the weight of the Queen's crown, provisions had been made for it to be removed for a period of time during the elaborate ceremony. Unbeknownst to Diane, the King had insisted that the honor of removing the crown go to her daughter, Françoise.

Catherine, weighed down by layers of silk and jewels, gazed at the daughter of her rival with an impotent resignation. Then, in a move that was so bold, so completely blatant that even the Cardinal de Guise could not stifle a gasp, Françoise de La Marck made the move that the King had personally implored her to do. She carefully lifted the heavily jeweled coronet from the Queen's head, and then solemnly placed it on a crimson velvet cushion that lay directly at her mother's feet.

In the foremost pew, François de Guise leaned toward his brother, Charles, his own thin lips parted in utter disbelief.

"Now will you tell her about Montgommery?" he whispered. "Because if you will not, I promise you, I will!"

A ND DO YOU REALLY BELIEVE that with this plan, eventually we can win back Boulogne?" Henri asked Montmorency.

"The English have only a garrison of five hundred men on the coast at Ambleteuse. We need only win that and then, it is just down the road to Boulogne, and to victory."

Henri leaned back in his velvet-covered chair and stroked the point of his dark beard. The two men sat alone in his private study at Les Tournelles. Long white tapers lit the room and spilled wax onto the desk and the map that was spread between them.

Henri had long made clear his intention of winning back Boulogne, the strategic port city on the French side of the channel. Montmorency had told him that now with the English forces divided between France and Scotland, this would be the optimum time for victory. Besides Boulogne, the English spread into forts at five key points in the region, including Ambleteuse and Blaconet to the north. Hostilities between England and France had reached a fever pitch over the removal of the young Queen of Scots to the safety of France. If the sparring continued, war with England seemed imminent. Montmorency took this opportunity to propose an attack on the strongly garrisoned province of Boulogne, while the English were too highly diversified to defend it.

"Well . . . Boulogne is ours . . ."

"That it is, Your Majesty."

". . . and I do mean to have it. Very well then. Yes, I am in accord with you, Monty. If you have faith that it will work, then I shall support you completely. We shall win back Boulogne or lose this realm trying. And I am going with you."

"Such a move is hardly necessary, Your Majesty."

"But it is necessary. I need to be away from all of this for a while. God, it has been so long, and I need to feel the dirt beneath my nails and the wind at my back. I am as much a warrior as I am a King!"

Montmorency lifted his goblet toward Henri and then smiled. "Then we shall be honored to have Your Majesty lead us all."

THREE DAYS AFTER Henry left for Boulogne, Charles de Guise made his decision to divulge what he had seen in Paris. It was nearly nine o'clock and he stood beside Diane, at whose table he now regularly dined. He stretched his arms over his head, as though he were relaxed and satisfied. But beneath the crimson robes and calm exterior was great trepidation about what he must do to her.

He liked Diane de Poitiers. He always had. Still, if he was going to do it, he must speak now while the King was away. He must set in motion the wheels, so that the most momentum could be gained before His Majesty's return. It was cruel to inflict something so powerful into such an impenetrable bond, but he must think first of his family; he must think of himself.

Over the past few years, Diane had become more cautious with them. Several times she had intervened with the King against them. With her gone from Court, there would be no one to obstruct the brothers' rise to power but one man: Constable Montmorency.

Although greed played a part in their ambition, something far more powerful motivated them. The brothers were aroused by the prospect of further glory for the house of Guise. Theirs was a proud house stemming from their claim to royal blood. They believed themselves descended from the Kings of Naples, Sicily and Jerusalem, and for all of their efforts, fate seemed, of late, to be resting in their corner. By the recent deaths of both their uncle, the Cardinal de Lorraine, and their father, the Duc de Guise, Charles and François had adopted the titles respectively. Such a turn of events had given each of them more power and more influence with which to challenge their last remaining rivals. The house of Guise was now completely in their very ambitious hands.

"Madame," Charles finally said. "I wonder if a walk in the moonlight would serve you as greatly as it would me, after so sumptuous a meal. I am afraid I shall not get a wink of sleep if I do not take a stroll before I retire. I should be ever grateful for your company."

It was not his custom to interrupt a conversation, and Diane looked curiously up at him from between the King's sister and Hélène. "All right, Charles. If you like."

They walked out of the salon and into the garden. The night air was warm and filled with buzzing gnats and fireflies, and a quarter moon shimmered with the intensity of a full one.

Charles took in a deep breath as Diane slid her arm into his. His red robe, neatly pressed, brushed against the black velvet of her gown.

"I wanted to thank you personally for that very generous gift to L'Hôpital de Saint-Gervais. They so desperately need assistance."

"The hospitals in Paris are sorely in need. It is my duty to help as much as I can," she replied as they strolled between the neatly clipped hedges of the formal parterre.

Charles saw that the incident with the tailor had changed Diane. There was a stronger urge than ever before, drawing her away from herself and in the direction of more altruistic concerns. She sought something that would bring distinction to the reign and meaning to her life. Despite the sketches and plans for Anet and Chenonceaux that required her attention, she forced herself to submit to tours of Paris hospitals. In those first few weeks after Henri's departure, by her direct intervention, the Duchesse de Valentinois had managed drastically to decrease the amount of filth and pestilence that she had so shockingly uncovered.

"I think, Madame, that you have begun to make a difference here in the city."

"For the people's sake, I pray that you are right. But then you did not ask me out here to thank me, did you?" she asked as he bent to smell a rose.

"No, you are right, Madame. That is not why I asked you out

here." He clasped his hands before him, as though in prayer, and then turned to face her. All of his movements were precise and considered. He was buying time to phrase the words the least painfully.

"I have struggled for several weeks now with how I might inform you of what I have come to feel you must know. However, it is not with any sense of ease that I do so even now."

"Go on."

"Several weeks ago, when His Majesty assigned me the task of locating an imprisoned heretic with whom he might speak, I confess that I found more than I would have dreamed."

"I should much prefer Your Eminence to spare me your mysterious preambles. Say what it is you mean to say."

"Very well. I went to the Conciergerie, where I knew there was a group of men who had been taken in and tried for crimes against the Church. On that trip, I am sorry to say that I found someone other than the tailor. There was another man imprisoned there; one I recognized, but whom I could not place until just a day or two ago. It had been many years since I had seen him . . . since you and I had seen him together."

A frown changed her elegant face. Her brilliant blue eyes darkened. "I do not enjoy the mystery, Charles. Who was the man and why should you imagine it should be of any importance to me?"

"The man in the Conciergerie, Madame, was Jacques de Montgommery."

She stepped back, stunned by the sound of the name she had not heard for sixteen years. She turned away from him and looked across a rolling lawn to a pond, shimmering in the silver light of the moon. Across the surface, two swans floated silently by.

"Certainly there is some mistake."

"No, Madame. There is no mistake. I thought so myself at first because it had been quite a long time, so I took the liberty of confirming the man's identity with the jailor."

"But why? What had he done to merit imprisonment?"

"That, I do not know. The orders to detain him are vague. They make reference only to disgrace against France, his imprisonment and the subsequent confiscation of his property."

"In spite of what he allowed to occur at Lagny-sur-Marne, he was an honored military commander. How could such a thing happen?" Before the Cardinal could reply, she added, "I must see him!"

"Do you think it wise, Madame? After all, if His Majesty were to discover . . . well, I was young then, but it was no secret how the King felt about the man who was his rival for your affection."

"I must see him, Charles. The King shall be my concern, not yours. You must take me to him at once!"

IT WAS LATE, but a small group of guards flanked Diane and the Cardinal as they galloped through the darkened streets of Paris toward the Conciergerie. Once they arrived, Diane followed him down the narrow, winding stone staircase. It was dark, except for the glow of the torch which the Cardinal held to light their way. The air was old and stale, and it was difficult to breathe without the involuntary reflex of a spasmed cough.

"This is the Duchesse de Valentinois and we have come to see prisoner 5012," Charles announced to the same guard who had given him entry before.

Diane lowered the hood of her cloak so that the guard could see her face. His large eyes widened when he recognized the King's mistress, having been among the fortunate few to see her on the pathway to the Queen's coronation.

"Pardon me for saying so, Madame, but this is no place for a fine lady."

"The prisoner, Monsieur!" the Cardinal interceded.

The guard led them, without further objection, down a dank corridor. There was a stale odor of water and urine. Diane covered her mouth and nose with her cloak until they came before a large iron-studded door. Guise lit the lock while the guard turned the large key that jangled at the end of a ring. When the door was opened, she looked back at Charles.

"I want to see him alone. Please wait for me," she said and took the torch into her own gloved hand. The large iron door swung open with a long, ominous creak and she was issued inside.

Only when the door slammed behind her did she turn around to see the face of the man she had once, long ago, agreed to marry.

Diane looked down upon someone barely recognizable to her now. He was huddled in the corner of the filthy dark cell on a bed of straw, dressed in garments which were neither brown nor gray, but somewhere between a dirty, faded hue of both.

As she held up the torch, she could see that his once elegant waves of blond hair were now thick, matted and entirely white. He wore a rough beard and mustache that obscured his face, all but the eyes; those same shimmering eyes which had revealed themselves to Charles de Guise.

She took a step back as he cast them upon her. The memory of their time together, when she had cared for this man, flooded to the forefront of her mind. As it converged with the sight of what he had now become, her face filled with horror.

"Well, well, well. What is it that brings the good Duchesse de Valentinois out of her tower to see the likes of me?" he muttered in a graveled voice that had not been his when she knew him.

"What has happened? Why, in God's name, are you here?" she asked and moved a few urgent steps closer to him. The jewels around her neck glittered in the torch light. "Oh, never mind why," she continued. "It is not important. I shall have you released at once." She turned back toward the door until his words stopped her.

"It will do you no good. You cannot change the order."

She turned back around. "Then by whose order are you here? I will go to them at once!"

"You cannot intervene."

"I am a very powerful woman now. I can have you freed."

"You shall not like what you discover if you try."

"No matter what you have done, this is no place for someone like you."

Diane looked back down at him. His thin elegant face was withered beneath his beard. His skin was gray from lack of sunlight. She rushed to his side and knelt beside his cot. The yellow straw which covered the floor crushed beneath her heavy gown. The rancid smell of his unwashed flesh and his own excrement overwhelmed her and she forced herself not to cough through sheer determination alone.

Montgommery gazed at her a long time with a new and curious look of contempt. Then he said, "You have done well for yourself, my beauty. Palaces, the Crown Jewels, a coronation even. Highly placed courtesan for nearly sixteen years. Quite a change from the unsure young woman I once knew. Yes, quite well indeed. Even if your rise to power meant the ruin of me." Then he sat up and looked up at her with savage clarity. "I am here by the order of His Majesty, the King of France."

She sat back on her heels as the chill of shock coursed through her. "You cannot mean Henri . . . He could not—"

"That he would, *ma chère*."

"I do not believe you!"

"Believe what you will, but I speak the truth. He has sent me here for the worst sin against the Crown; for having once loved the woman he now loves. He wanted no one to remind him that another man alive had any part of you before he did."

Diane stood, fighting for her balance. "You have not changed, Jacques. You were a filthy liar then and you are even worse, an old pathetic liar now!"

"And what does that make you? You went from being the whore of one King to the courtesan of the next! It would seem that neither of us has much improved."

His words were sharp. In defense, she leveled her palm across his cheek. The smack of flesh echoed in the empty cell. Jacques looked up at her with eyes now a faded dust blue. The door opened. Charles leaned in.

"Madame, are you all right?"

"Please leave us!"

When they had once again closed the heavy door she turned back around.

"I speak the truth," he repeated. "And in your heart you know it. He hated me for ever getting near to your heart. I have made a great many mistakes in my life, Diane, but even for the worst of them, I did not deserve this fate. I had built a new life after you left me. I served the late King with distinction, and the moment his son ascended the throne and found the slightest provocation, it was all taken from me; my house, my property . . . even my honor."

Diane sat back on her heels. "Lagny-sur-Marne was a great loss for France. You were in charge."

"But I bid you, Madame, ask yourself . . . could it possibly have merited this?"

"If I believe what you tell me," she whispered as she moved again toward his cot, "then I surrender all that I have believed for nearly twenty years. I surrender my entire life."

"I am an old man now. My lies have brought me to this place. Perhaps my honesty shall one day set me free. I ask only to die with my son knowing that he has a father whose life was not a complete disgrace."

"A son?"

"Before I met you, many years ago I had a wife who, on the way to her grave, delivered me a son. His name is Gabriel."

"I had no idea that . . . that you were married."

"And I wanted it that way. I kept a great many truths from you, all in the name of my own ambition. After my one disastrous confession to you back then, I saw no reason to tell you anything that might make you think I was less than perfect. That judgment cost me your love."

"Gabriel." She repeated the boy's name as though it was familiar to her.

"He is at Court now; an infantryman in the Scots Guard. There would be no reason for you to have known of him."

"Please, Jacques, let me free you."

"If only you could. The orders that hold me are to be overturned by no one but the King himself. I heard them whispered among the guards when I was first brought here."

"Guard!" she cried out. The heavy studded door swung open once again and a huge bear of a man stood in the doorway holding another candle. "Guard, I want this man released!"

"I am sorry, Madame. That is against my orders."

"Monsieur, do you know who I am?"

"Of course, Madame. You are the Duchesse de Valentinois."

"Then, as you also know, the King is at present in the north. You must know that, in His Majesty's absence, I have the authority to act in his stead. Free this man now on my order and I alone shall answer to the King."

"Please understand, Madame, I have no wish to go against you. It is only that His Majesty was very specific. He said that this prisoner was to be released to no one's custody but his own."

The guard's words were like daggers to her heart, confirming what Jacques de Montgommery had said. She pressed on for his freedom.

"Monsieur, if I am required to write to His Majesty over such a trivial matter as this, when he is busy defending our country, how do you suppose he will react to the jailor who challenged my authority?"

"It is no use, Diane," Montgommery conceded. "He is only doing what he has been commanded by King Henri to do. We cannot fault him for that."

"Well this is far from over," she said. "I will get you out of here, Jacques, one way or another!"

DIANE LEFT HER HOUSE in Paris the morning after she had gone to the Conciergerie. The construction crews and scaffolding had completely taken over at Anet so she could not go there, and she could not bring herself to go to Chenonceaux. Rouen, her family seat, was the farthest point from Paris and from her life with Henri that she knew. If she could have left France, she would have. She wanted to get as far from Jacques de Montgommery and the pain of his words as possible. But before she left, she had seen to it that Gabriel de Montgommery would receive his father's commission as Captain of the Scots Guard. It was the least she could do if what Jacques had said was true.

Her heart ached without ceasing, and finally she surrendered herself to a dull haze that no amount of sleep or wine could conquer. So she swam. Every day she cut through the cool surface of the river, stroke after powerful stroke until she could barely breathe. Only then did she turn onto her back and float on the surface, gasping between her tears for enough air to continue. When she stopped, even for a moment, the thoughts flooded back. There must be some mistake. She refused to believe that after all these years, she did not really know Henri at all. The man she loved was a fair and a gentle man. When the last of the two dogs she had given him had died, he had wept in her arms like a child. How could it be that there was a side of him this heinous that he had kept from her? A side motivated by such unrelenting jealousy that he was moved secretly to imprison a man for nothing more than the crime of having loved her.

She had seen his jealousy before with Montgommery, and earlier with his father, but never once had she considered him capable of such cruelty. Theirs had been an enduring relationship of trust, and if this were true, everything between them was lost.

She came up out of the water and sank naked into the wet sand that ran along the shore. Her chest was heaving from the exertion and beads of water danced on her skin and then faded away in the hot summer sun. The warm wind rushed at her and made her shiver. In a few minutes she was dry. Another letter had come for her that morning and had set off the anger again. Like the others that had come by special messenger from the King, she had instructed Clothilde to burn it unopened. She could not bear to read his poetic words of love or his protestations of fidelity. Hurt, anger and pain all converged on her at once. But one thing she knew without question, Jacques de Montgommery was right; he had not deserved so cruel a fate.

"MADAME, YOU HAVE a visitor," Clothilde, the former pastrycook, announced as she padded, heavy-footed, into the drawing room where Diane sat with a book of verse. She had read the first page again and again without the slightest idea of what it had said. She was sitting motionless in a chair near the window, her skin sticking to her sleeveless white chemise. Her hair was not done into a headdress, but was long around her shoulders. The ends were still wet from her swim.

"I am expecting no one. Tell them to go away."

"Yes, Madame," Clothilde persevered, "but this one . . . well it is the King's daughter, Mademoiselle Diane, and she has come all this way without an escort. Only two guards are waiting for her in the courtyard."

"Diane?" she gasped, springing to her feet and tossing the book to the floor. "Well, of course, show her in!" She wiped a hand across her face. It was wet. She loathed perspiring, but in the middle of August it could not be helped. She pushed back a loose strand of blond hair and straightened her thin chemise. It was the first time in days that she regretted not tending to her toilette.

After a moment, the young girl strode into Diane's drawing room. It took her by surprise how much the child had come to look like Henri. She had that same purposeful gait and strong nose beneath the same tousle of ink-black hair. Diane moved to greet her.

"Well, this is a surprise, *chérie*. Why did you not tell me you were coming? I would have had your room prepared for you." She smiled and extended her arms, but the younger Diane stood stone-faced beneath the arch that led in from the entrance.

"I want to know, Madame, and you must tell me the truth. Are you my real mother?"

Diane's mouth went dry before she felt the blood leave her face. She looked at the child. Someone had told her. It was obvious that she knew. She had always known one day that they would face this, and yet with each passing year, she had come to wish for it less and less.

"Thank you, Clothilde," Diane said to the servant who stood, open-mouthed, behind the King's daughter. "You may leave us now."

Clothilde closed the tall double doors leaving them alone.

"Well then," the child pressed. "Are you?"

"Where did you hear that?"

"Where?" she scoffed. "It matters not where, Madame! Servants gossip. Courtiers whisper things. Did you not suppose I was bound to hear the truth sooner or later?"

"Please, child, come here and sit down."

Diane walked to a long embroidered sofa and indicated the seat beside her, but the child did not follow. Instead, she gripped her forehead and closed her eyes.

"Oh, God . . . God, then you are! I knew it. Just look at you! You cannot even bear to face me!" She covered her face with her hands and began to cry. After a moment she looked up again, her eyes full of tears. "Just tell me one thing. Were you so ashamed of a bastard child? Is that why you did it?"

"Please sit down, *mon coeur*. Let me explain."

"Do not call me that! I am not your heart! I am nothing to you . . . I never was anything to you but an inconvenience!"

"Diane, please."

"God in His Heaven, even your name! How could you have had the audacity to give me your name when you did not even want me?"

"It was—"

"It was horrid of you!"

"It was at your father's insistence."

"And was it his idea as well to save your precious reputation by passing me off in a lie?"

"No!" Diane sprang from the couch. "No, you must never think that. Your father never wanted any of this hidden."

"Then how could you do it? How? All of my life I wanted nothing more than to be your daughter, and now that I am, all I feel for you is contempt!"

"You have that right. But if you are old enough to come here and confront me like an adult, then you are old enough to grant me the courtesy of hearing me out. Please."

Once again she admonished her daughter to sit beside her, but again she refused. Instead, she took a small carved chair near the door. She looked over at her mother, her face filled with contempt. Diane saw the anger behind the tears and took in a deep breath.

"The year that you were conceived, your father was not King. There was a great deal of displeasure over our liaison because it was thought that I was a distraction who would prevent the conception of a rightful heir. It was a very hostile time then, Diane, and there was a great deal of cruelty directed toward me. There was never a time nor a place where I was truly safe. I do not tell you this now to gain your sympathy. I tell you only so that you shall have an accurate basis on which to judge my actions when you come away from here. The final decision, of course, shall be your own.

"Your father was young and he was under a great deal of pressure from the former King to produce an heir with his wife. When I became pregnant before Catherine, he wanted to leave her and legitimize us both."

"Why did he not?"

"You know that I was married before I met your father; that I am older than he, and that I have other children. Even if he had left her, I would never have been considered a suitable wife for him."

"But even if Papa could not marry you, I still do not understand how you could have denied me. You never even told me in private that you were my mother!"

"Diane, you may not believe me right now, but I did it to protect you. One word carelessly uttered by you when you were small, and the danger would have been immense. The King was very angry at both your father and myself for what he considered a flaunting of our relationship before him. My position was tenuous. He wanted me away from Court, and if I had thrown you up as an obstacle to his legitimate grandchildren to try to remain, there was no predicting what would have become of you. At that time, neither I nor your father had the power to protect you."

Diane de France had stopped crying. She studied her mother's face trying to read it for signs of the truth.

"I know it is difficult for you to understand, and you may not agree with the choices we made back then, but your father and I did what we had to do to protect you. For that, my penance has been to live with you near me, never once hearing you call me

maman; never once having you know that there was a bond between us that no one could sever. No matter what you believe, you
must never doubt that the King and I have always loved you."

"That is just what Papa said."

"Then you have spoken to your father about this?"

"No. He was explaining why one day I would have to marry
the Duke of Castro instead of the boy I love. He used his love for
you, and his inability to marry you, as an example of royal duty
that he says I too now must follow."

Diane leaned back in the couch as the color rushed into her
cheeks. "I see," she said in a carefully modulated tone and then
went a step further. "Would you stay and have supper with me?
We could speak further, if you like. I can have the kitchen prepare
your favorite capon pie."

"There is no need to bribe me," she snapped, still not ready
entirely to forgive.

"I am sorry, I did not think that was what I was doing. It was
only my hope that you would stay a while; that perhaps we could . . ."

"Things will be different now between us."

"Yes, I expect they will." Mother and daughter both stood and
drew a tentative step nearer to one another. "But that does not
have to mean that they need to be worse."

"I suppose I understand why you did it. I can accept that it
was a different world than the one I know now. You are not the
only one to have told me of the Duchesse d'Etampes' cruelty toward
you. Since I have no children of my own, I cannot say what I
would have done in your place. But I cannot acknowledge you as
my mother, and you must not ask me to."

"I will accept what you can give, Diane," she gently replied. "I
would settle for you to go on acknowledging me as your special
friend, if that would suit you." She moved a few steps closer to her
daughter. "You may leave if you like. But I would very much like it
if you would stay. No inducements."

"We have much to discuss . . ."

"That we do."

HROUGHOUT THE FALL and winter of 1549, both England and France pressed on toward war, Henri sparing nothing to see Boulogne returned to France. As Montmorency had predicted, Ambleteuse, which had been garrisoned by only 500 men, fell easily to the King's troops.

Ambleteuse was key because this was the harbor through which the English received all of their supplies for Boulogne. Once the port had fallen, and with the advent of winter, the King and the Constable contented themselves with a blockade.

By February, despite the fervor with which both England and France had begun the battle, negotiations commenced. Henri's enthusiasm for the war had been stayed by the death of Pope Paul III and his desire for a new French Pope. The Emperor too was lobbying for his own choice, and Henri knew that whoever was elected, it would mean tension with the Imperial Court and possibly even renewed war. Despite the promise of victory at Boulogne, he was not prepared to go to war with England and the Emperor at the same time. For the moment, he contented himself with the quiet insertion of several of his best commanders in the region.

A truce was finally concluded in March with discussions begun on a possible marriage between England's boy King Edward VI and Henri's eldest daughter, the four-year-old Princess Elizabeth. In April, the Constable's eldest son, François de Montmorency, finally took back Boulogne in the name of the King. Before he returned home, Henri made his triumphal entry into the town that had been lost to France. He then returned to Court in a blaze of triumphant glory. He had won back Boulogne. Julius III, a malleable Pope, had been elected as a compromise candidate, and he was desperate to see Diane. It could not have been more perfect, until he returned home to find that she was gone. In his study at Fontainebleau, in a stack of documents and letters, he discovered the reason.

"She knows! Damn!" he whispered to himself and then tossed the document onto the cold tile floor. It was a formal appeal for the release of prisoner 5012, Jacques de Montgommery, from the Conciergerie. It had been instituted and signed by the Duchesse de Valentinois.

"Where is she?" he raged and then charged at Jacques de Saint-André who stood behind him.

"I am afraid I have no idea, Your Majesty."

"Do not tell me that!" he seethed. "You follow the movements of that lady of hers like a dog in heat!"

Jacques did not reply to the King's ravings, and after a moment, Henri collapsed into a chair at the long conference table near his desk.

"Forgive me, *mon vieux,* I am just so worried. I never expected this, but she knows about Montgommery."

"It is what I feared would happen if Your Majesty insisted on keeping it from her."

"I do not need your reproach, Jacques! The damage is done. Now you must find out where she is for me, and send word that I will come to her at once. If I can only explain why I did it, what my reasons were, then I know that she will forgive me. Dear God, she must!"

"May I offer Your Majesty a suggestion?" The King looked up from his hands. "Your words would carry far more weight, Sire, if they were preceded by the release of the Captain."

"No!" he said, springing from the chair. "He has disgraced his country and he has disgraced Madame Diane. He is where he belongs!"

Jacques said nothing further as he bowed to the King and left the room to attempt to locate Diane.

Henri sat alone before the undraped window, his profile sharp against the light from the moon. He gazed down at his hands; the hands that had loved her, and held her. A fear stirred within him so deeply that his hands, now extended before him, began to tremble.

"If I should lose her . . . ." he whispered, and then shook his head before he could finish the words. But to release the man who, on every battlefield in Europe, had flaunted his affair with the *favourite,* who had explained in detail to everyone who would listen, the passion between them, calling her a common whore dressed as a highly placed courtesan; no, that was a sin he could not forgive.

He knew that she had not heard the gossip. He had managed to keep it from her by threatening her servants and his own. But he had heard it, every harsh and dirty word. She deserved to be avenged. His desire to protect her had only grown more fierce since that first day when she had been confronted by Anne d'Heilly, and his interception had changed their lives.

Diane was more than a mistress. She had made him who he was, and he idolized her. No other man must know his goddess as he did, and so he had taken the first opportunity to silence the man who had tried. He had done it for her. Surely she would understand that. She must.

HENRI LEFT FONTAINEBLEAU at first light, two day after his triumphant return from Boulogne. He was as fearful as a boy again, and as urgent with the need to see Diane. He went on horseback rather than by barge because he knew it would be more swift. She had returned to Chenonceaux from Rouen. That was a good sign.

He rode through the countryside oblivious to the speed, or the sweating of his black Turkish stallion. Saint-André and the royal guardsmen strained to keep pace with him. He pushed the mighty animal ever harder through the gloomy forests and past the russet vineyards that crossed the rolling countryside. When they reached the end of the long column of plane trees that lined the pathway to the chateau, he could see her in the terraced garden. The black of her gown was set off against the facade of pale yellow stone.

Between each neatly laid square, were perfect walks covered

with flesh-colored gravel. Diane stood amid her new garden, collecting white roses. Henri left his horse near the stables and let Jacques lead it to the equerry. He nervously touched his toque, then pulled off his gloves a finger at a time. His heart was pounding with such dread that he thought for a moment it might suddenly stop. He moved a few paces nearer until Diane looked up and saw him. She did not run to him as she might once have done, nor did she call out his name. Instead, she walked slowly toward him still clutching the collection of roses.

"Hello, Henri," she said, but made no move to embrace him. She had not spoken to him with such reserve since that night on the terrace, after he had married Catherine.

"I have missed you," he managed to say as he leaned over to kiss her cheek. "*M'amie*, we must talk."

"Yes."

She began to walk out to the end of the garden on a winding gravel path toward the chateau. He followed a pace behind her, his gloves clutched like a death grip in his hands.

"How did you discover it?" he asked as they finally came into the drawing room.

"What does it matter?" she replied as she closed the doors behind them. "It is only important that I know, and the knowledge that you could have done such a cruel thing has tortured me every day since I discovered it. Please tell me, Henri, how could you have done it? Please make me understand."

Her tone of voice, which had been flat, was now alive and imploring. Her brilliant blue eyes were pleading for a reply. The pain was too great. He turned away.

"I shall not defend my actions, Madame. I can tell you only that I did it, as I have done everything else in my life, for love of you." He stood rigid before her, one hand still gripping his gloves, the other on the dagger at his side.

"For me? How can you stand there and say such a thing? You know that Jacques did not deserve this!"

"You do not know that!"

"For the love of God, Henri, the man has lost three years of his life already to some ancient grudge. Please, I beg you, sign the paper to free him before it is too late!"

There was a greater distance between them now than all the miles to Boulogne. He knew even if he signed the release now, it would do little to close the gap that he had wrought between them. He could not make her understand.

"I cannot. Please trust me. I do not know who has counseled you in my absence, but believe me, Montgommery has earned his fate."

"No one has counseled me, Henri. I went to see him myself. Jacques is no threat to you! He is an old and feeble man, reduced from the life of a gentleman and condemned to a stench-filled hole in the bowels of Paris!"

Henri's eyes narrowed. His face began to patch red and white with anger. He lunged at her. "You saw him?! How dare you go to your old lover when you knew that I was gone? Pitiful bastard haunts me still! I shall kill him! I swear I shall!"

"Henri, please, listen to yourself! You do not need this anger! I do not love him!" Diane grasped his arms above the elbows and tried to make him listen. "I have never loved any man so much as you! You are my life. You are everything to me!"

Like a raging giant, he softened with her gentle words; words for which he had waited in fear that he would never hear again. His dark eyes grew large, his brows arched into a pleading pyramid. Now that she could see the remorse in him, she opened her arms and he fell into her embrace.

"I shall free him. Bring me the paper and I shall sign it. I shall do whatever you wish, only, I must not lose you. Without you there would be no purpose in any of it for me. You know that." He kissed her with the greedy possession of a hungry animal and then buried her in the force of his solid arms. No one saw this side of the King, for no one elicited it but her.

"It is the right thing to do," Diane whispered as she broke free of his grasp. "But no matter what you do, I made a decision of my own before you returned. I may as well tell you now." She walked away from him and advanced to the fireplace hearth where a raging fire burned. There, she surrendered the bunch of musk roses that she had been holding since he first came into the garden. He followed her.

"I must return to Rouen. Louise is with child and I want to be there for her."

"But I do not understand. I agreed to do as you asked."

"And I thank you."

"Please, m'amie, do not do this! I have been away for so long!"

She turned back around, her face full of conviction. She ran a finger along the line of his jaw. "Yes, and the wound from this, from all of this, has had all that time to deepen."

"So you must let me make it up to you! I can . . . I will!"

"Only time can heal the betrayal I feel."

"Betrayal?"

"Yes . . ." she whispered.

"Listen to me! An absence between us cannot solve this. No! Absolutely not. I forbid it. I shall not let you go!"

"Please, do not force this, chéri. Can you not understand how deeply I was hurt by such a deception between us?"

"And you must know that I am sorry for the pain it has caused you . . . the desperation I feel! I would do anything . . . anything to change it!"

"Then give me time . . . please. Oh, Henri . . . I have gone on blindly for so many years thinking, with all that we have been through, that the one thing that would never come between us was ourselves. And yet, here we are."

He lunged at her again, pulling her to his chest and then kissing her again until he nearly choked her with his strength. "But, I love you . . ."

"I know," she replied, touching his cheek. "And I love you."

MONTMORENCY'S STAR ROSE to its zenith following the capture of Boulogne. It had been on his advice that the King had sought the attack, and now the Constable reaped the benefits of a conquering hero. But the pedestal on which he placed himself beside the King was not large enough for three, and he had waited patiently for just the opportunity to unseat the Duchesse de Valentinois.

Catherine too had waited for such an opportunity to expel her. She no longer had any pride when it came to the fight for Henri's affection. For seventeen years she had closed her eyes to the angry pawing of a man who did not wish to be with her. For seventeen years she had been his wife and carried his children, but never his heart. When Montmorency whispered to her that night at supper that he might have a plan, the Queen was ready to listen. He said that with the arrival of little Mary Stuart in France, and the mysterious disappearance from Court of Diane de Poitiers, he had finally found the required circumstance, and she wanted more than anything to believe him.

Montmorency stayed in the Queen's apartment that evening after the conversation circle had finally disbanded. When they were alone she could no longer contain her curiosity. Surrounded by layers of voluminous magenta silk, her black frizzy hair crowned with a spiral of rubies, she sat on a sofa looking up at him.

"Well, what is it? What is your plan?"

Montmorency poured himself another silver goblet of sweet wine and sat down beside her. "What I have to say may not be easy for Your Majesty to hear, but you have only to say the word and I shall speak no further of it."

"No, no. Please go on."

"Tonight at supper," Montmorency began, "I was reminded of the King's attraction to Queen Mary's Governess, Lady Flemming. Though the King tried to avert his eyes, it was the same look I had seen them exchange some time ago. Your Majesty, to be quite plain about it, I believe the woman has caught the King's fancy."

There was the sound of heavy petticoats rustling beneath her as Catherine stiffened. Then a hardened look washed over her heavily featured face. "So, you would propose to swap one whore for another."

"At least initially yes, Your Majesty. It is my belief that she is beautiful enough to sway the King, but not wise enough to keep him."

"Thereby eventually ridding him of both the new and the old."

"Precisely. But meanwhile, Madame Diane, upon her return to Court, would of course stumble upon the news of her lover's infidelity. I am quite certain that since they began with one another, there has been no other between them, which of course would make this discovery all the more disagreeable."

Catherine stood, tugged at the stiff magenta collar around her throat and began to stroll around the room with a stalking kind of intent. "So you believe his indiscretion would be unforgivable to her?"

"I am certain of it. Then, once they are both gotten rid of, Your Majesty can take her rightful and much-deserved place beside the King."

"And of course, you would take yours." There was another pause between them as she considered further. "Should I agree to this scheme, Monsieur, how would you propose to accomplish it?"

"My plan is far-fetched, I will grant you that, but I believe it to be a risk worth taking. His Majesty's demeanor has completely changed since his return from the north. He is vulnerable, and if you will permit me, I believe that he is lonely. As you undoubtedly know, Madame Diane is mysteriously absent. Tomorrow night, if you should agree, it should not prove too difficult a task to ply the King with wine. It must be a quantity considerably more sizable than that to which he is accustomed. When the time is right, His Majesty shall be privy to a performance arranged in his honor. It will feature a dance of nymphs, seductively clad, who will dance around him."

"Of whom you, no doubt, intend for the Lady Flemming to be one."

Montmorency waited on the couch for the Queen to stop pacing and to look back at him. "Will Your Majesty agree to it then?"

"How can you be certain that the Lady will participate?"

"If you will pardon me, for being blunt, an opportunity to bed with the young and handsome King of France is not likely to be rejected by anyone with half an eye or an ounce of ambition."

"Ah, yes. Of course you are right," she conceded as she touched

a line from her cheek to her chin. "Very well. But be advised of
one very important thing, Monsieur Montmorency. If this fails, it
is your head that shall roll, not mine."

HENRI SPENT SEVERAL DAYS at Saint Germain-en-Laye after his
return from Chenonceaux. There, he vacillated between the solitude of the chapel and violent exercise. The latter was the only
way in which he felt able, even for just a while, to stave off his pain
at the loss of Diane. Had he not forced himself to believe that
their estrangement was temporary, he was certain he would have
gone completely mad.

There had been many separations between them over the
years but this was the first time she had ever openly and intentionally sought distance from him. At the source of his pain was
the belief that he had acted to honor her. By committing Montgommery to prison, he had tried to protect her. Yet rather than
trusting him, she had chosen to believe the words of another man.

But this anxiety he felt now was not only for Diane. Her turning away symbolized a lifetime of rejection. Memories of his father and brothers were juxtaposed daily with the echo of her
words, the worst of which was "betrayal." She had opened up something in him; something weak and unsure, and raw. She needed
time to heal, she had said; time to heal from a wound that he had
inflicted. There could be, he thought, no worse pain than this; no
worse torture than the loss of his Diane.

The pain of her absence was made worse by the fact that everything around him now reminded him of her. The shrines he had
built to feel surrounded by her during their separations now haunted
him. The sketches and the oil paintings of her looked down on him
from almost every room; his wardrobe, his staff's uniforms, all
were of black and white. The crescent moons, and their emblem,
were now incorporated into nearly every ceiling and every fixture
of the chateau. The signs had been carved into furniture, sewn
into bedlinens and painted on doors. For all of his efforts now, he
could not escape the memory of her. Everywhere he turned he
was reminded of her . . . and of the betrayal. Eager to forget his

melancholy heart, even for a little while, Henri agreed to attend a banquet given in his honor by Montmorency.

Plates of roasted meats and bowls of fruit shared the table with large vessels of Bordeaux and imported mead. Catherine watched silently as Henri and Montmorency laughed and joked. Much of that was due to the Constable's preparation, more than to the King's attitude. Each time Henri took more than two sips of wine, a steward silently advanced and filled his chalice. His movements were full of such dexterity that the King barely noticed.

When the meal was complete and the two men sat back in their chairs, Montmorency held his hands above his head and firmly clapped them. The musicians, who were arranged behind a screen, changed from their melodic strains to a more exotic theme. Many of the candles were then extinguished and the room filled with the heavy aroma of smoke.

Henri sat back in his chair not quite able, for the effects of the wine, to keep from swaying.

"What? Have you arranged some entertainment, Monty?"

"I had hoped to please Your Majesty by arranging a small performance for you. The plays of Homer, and from them a small scene that I think you shall enjoy."

Henri leaned forward and slapped Montmorency across the back. "Splendid!"

After a moment, four barefoot maidens danced into the room on their toes. They began to swirl around the room in layers of rose-colored silk, cinched at the waist in gold. Before each of their faces was a veil. To highlight their eyes, they had been heavily made up with dark kohl. Three of the dancers were short and plump; Italian girls from Catherine's train. Janet Stuart's flame-red hair and voluptuous form were a bold contrast to the others. It would have been impossible not to notice her.

Catherine watched her husband gaze glassy-eyed at Lady Flemming, who was expertly attempting to seduce him before all of their friends. It took her a great effort to stifle her rage. It was one thing, she thought, to know that her husband had been unfaithful; it was quite another thing to watch it. But then this was not the first time she had seen such a seduction. She remembered the tiny hole she had once cut in the floor of her apartments, and what she had seen in Madame Diane's bedchamber below. She had lain prostrate watching them make love below her, hoping to understand what it was that had so totally captivated her husband. But that invasion of Diane's bedchamber from above had not brought her the satisfaction she had hoped. The same pain she felt watching Diane in her husband's arms, she felt now.

She forced the images and the memories from her mind and kept silent. As she sat fanning her face with a priceless Chinese fan, Catherine studied Lady Flemming. Until Montmorency had spoken her name, she had barely noticed the woman; certainly never considered her a viable challenge to the *favourite*. She actually thought, once she had taken time to examine her, that she was rather ordinary looking. Her beauty was earthy and pagan. She was the complete antithesis of Diane de Poitiers. But then perhaps at the moment, that would be in her favor. And in truth, this was a small price to pay if, once and for all, she could be free of the one woman who had ruined her life.

As the dance continued, Lady Flemming whirled around the King, smelling of ambergris and brushing his body with the sheers of rose-colored silk. Montmorency, who had watched intently since her arrival, paced himself with the deftness of a master. When he knew that the timing was right, he leaned toward the King.

"She is breathtaking, isn't she?"

"Who do you mean?" Henri asked, unable to take his eyes from the dance.

"Why, Lady Flemming, of course."

The sound of her name caused Henri to look at his friend, and then back at the sensual beauty who had so captivated him.

"Little Mary's nurse?" he asked, trying to disguise the fact that he had known her identity all along.

"The very same. When she learned today that I was preparing a little entertainment for Your Majesty, she asked if she might participate."

Henri shifted in his seat and took another swallow from the

ever-full jeweled goblet. Then he looked out again at the dancers. Montmorency watched the King. The music was exotic, the wine was strong and the perfume intoxicating. Henri was completely transfixed, and the Constable knew it.

Finally, he leaned toward the King and spoke behind his hand so that no one else would hear. "I hope that Your Majesty will forgive my boldness, but you are King of all France. You are not like other men. Your Majesty is virile; your appetites are boundless. Your indiscretions are . . . expected." Henri slowly turned his head. His eyes were glazed and his face was flushed.

"What are you driving at, Monty?"

"Just that . . . well, should your love for certain people give way to a more temporary need for gratification . . . such a move would certainly be understood."

"Are you suggesting, my dear Constable, while Madame is away that I bed Lady Flemming?"

"Of course not, Your Majesty. Such an inference would be inappropriate." He paced himself; waited a moment, then added, "What I am saying is that Madame Diane, of course, possesses you exclusively. That is plain for all the world to see. So that a momentary transgression of the flesh, for one so supreme as yourself, would in no way be viewed as a challenge to your heart."

"I will be faithful to her, Monty!" Henri snapped and slammed down his goblet.

"Of course, Your Majesty, I have overstepped myself. Forgive me," he said as he watched Lady Flemming glide from the room and the King's eyes follow after her.

Henry took another long drink of the wine, then set the goblet down. When he looked at the Constable again, his eyes were half closed and he had begun to perspire.

"Very well, Montmorency," he finally muttered resignedly. "Arrange it."

HENRI SAT UP and swung his feet over the edge of the bed. He opened the bedcurtains and gazed into the golden light of the fire.

The rest of the room was dark. It was still the middle of the night but already his head was throbbing. He buried his head in his hands and let out a heavy sigh. He did not need to turn around to know that she was still there with him.

"Dear God, what have I done?" he murmured as he looked down at his own naked body, still bathed in glistening sweat.

He had waited until she had begun to doze, hoping to sneak quietly away. But he must have done something to rouse her. All at once she was behind him, her hands on his shoulders, and she was kissing his neck. He could feel the press of her full breasts against his back; smell the heavy scent of her perfume. When he did not respond, she pulled away.

"What is it, Your Majesty? You're not going to be sick again, are you?"

Henri moaned and lowered his face again into his hands. When they had first arrived in his bedchamber, before he had touched her, the wine had taken its toll and he had been violently ill. But the retching had done nothing to dissuade her and she had, after a time, finally had her way.

"Was it all that bad between us?" she asked in the same thickly accented Scottish that had once made him cringe.

"No. No, it was not. I suppose that is precisely the problem." The muffled words came from between his fingers. Lady Flemming ran her own fingers through his thick hair at the back of his head, pressing her breasts deeper into him. He arched his back, responding to her touch. It felt good to have a woman want him again, and yet, what he had done was forbidden. He had betrayed Diane yet again.

"I have never done this before," he said. When she did not reply he added, ". . . been unfaithful."

"What about your *favourite*?"

Henri took his hands from his face and forced himself to look at her. "It is from her that I have never strayed. No matter where I was or how long we were apart, there has never been, in all those years . . . another woman."

"Well, there is always a first time for everything!" she chuckled and ran the tips of her fingers down his broad back and along the contours of his arms.

It had been different with her than it had ever been with Diane; with her he was always caring. There was a deep tenderness between them. This had been more furious; nearly violent. That dark need, buried deep inside him since his youth, had finally overpowered him. There had been nothing else but his own need, and in it, there had been no choice. He had not cared about this woman; her pleasure or her pain. He moaned again as her hands made their way down to the thick of moist black hair between his legs. Her pink tongue caressed the place behind his ear.

"Please do not . . . I beg you," he whispered helplessly, as she wrapped her slender fingers around his penis and began to move them in a slow even rhythm. "Please," he said again. "I love her, I love Diane."

"Yes, Your Majesty, I know. But you are lonely and alone . . . and she is not here with you now . . . I am."

HENRI'S INDISCRETION with Janet Stuart did not end with his sobriety the following morning. In Diane's absence they seemed quite peculiarly thrown together at every turn, ever increasing the ease and the temptation to fall again from grace. When he rode, she rode with his party. When he dined, he found that she had been invited and was seated next to him. All the while, Henri was completely unaware of the plot against him that had been instigated by his wife and his own best friend.

For her part, Lady Flemming played it like a champion. When they were together she was loud and demanding, making it impossible for those close to the King to remain unaware of what had passed between them. When they were alone, she seduced him shamelessly with the bawdy expertise of a common street whore. But after a fortnight of submission in his bed and hers, trapped between his loneliness and her unrelenting advances, the emptiness returned. The longing for the only woman who could ever truly make him happy descended upon him with a vengeance. It filled him with overwhelming guilt. Then despair. He began to make attempts to avoid her; first subtle, and then more blatant. But as his desire to avoid her increased, her determination to capture him became obsessive. He panicked. He wrote feverish and impassioned letters to Diane, begging her to return to him. When she wrote that she was not yet ready, he pleaded with her to let him come there. But it was to no avail.

"Mother Mary, what am I doing? I must be mad!" Henri rolled over off of Janet Stuart's fleshy wet body, his chest still heaving.

"I think it is called fornicating, Your Majesty," she replied with a devilish, throaty laugh. She lay her head back on the pillows, her mouth wide with a satisfied smile and her red hair fanned out like the petals of a flower.

"I am horrid, absolutely horrid . . . and this! This is unforgivable!"

"I didn't see you complaining an hour ago."

"An hour ago I was drunk!"

"Your Majesty's been drunk every time and yet that hasn't stopped you from calling me to your bed, that I can see!"

Henri raised himself up and tossed a red silk robe across his shoulders, shooting his large muscular arms into the sleeves. He ran his fingers nervously through his matted black hair. His face tightened as he began to pace.

"Oh, what a fool I've been. What a selfish fool! If she leaves me over this, there will be no point in anything . . ."

"Well thank you, indeed!" said Janet, not bothering any longer to use her broken French. "Take what you want from me because you are a King. Well, I am not a whore, Your Majesty, no matter what you think of me!"

Henri turned slowly back around. He could barely look at her for what they had just done together. He went back to her and sat beside her on the bed. Her simplicity at times had reminded him of a child's. It had drawn him. But he no longer found it attractive, and he was at a loss to believe that he ever had.

"If I have offended you, I am sorry; truly I am. You must know that was never my intention."

"No? Then what, precisely, was your intention?" she asked, sitting up and not bothering to cover herself.

"If I only knew," he whispered.

Henri looked at her now, knowing that he had committed with Janet Stuart a far worse sin than betrayal. He had cut away at the foundation of the only relationship in his life that had been built entirely on trust, love and loyalty. He had meant what he had said; without Diane there would be no purpose in any of it. Yet, the moment she was away, he had taken refuge with another woman in his bed. This could not go on. The torrid desire had passed with the novelty. He needed Diane with him, now and always. If she was not ready to return to Court or to him, then he would go to her and bring her back.

"So then, I suppose you are about to tell me that we are through; that you are going back to the Duchesse de Valentinois," she said, bringing him back from the depths of his own despair with her ruddy peasant voice.

"I never left her, really. Not in my heart."

"I will not make it easy for you, you know."

"Very well, then. How much do you want?"

At the sound of his question she laughed. "I do not want your money."

"Then what is it you want from me?"

Janet Stuart touched her own milk-white breasts at the nipples and then lay back on the bedcovers. "Oh, poor dear Henri," she said with a triumphant laugh, "what I want from you, I am afraid I've already got!"

DIANE KNEW WHY Henri was coming to Anet. Secrets were not easily kept in so dynamic a society as the French Court. Hélène had reluctantly told her of the affair several weeks ago, after she had overheard two of the chambermaids speaking in whispers in the corridor.

At first, after she had seen Montgommery, Diane had been overwhelmed with anger, then with disappointment. She had needed to leave. But after his prompt release from the Conciergerie and her own reflection, she began to feel more tolerant. She knew that, in his heart, Henri believed he had done it out of love for her. She had finally decided to return to him, when she had heard about the affair with Lady Flemming.

Diane was wise enough to know that this changed everything. Henri would not have jumped blindly into bed with another woman. He must have come to care for her. In spite of everything that they had built together and everything she stood to lose, she could not go rushing back and remind him of his promises. Such a liaison, if she had half a hope of conquering it, must run its course. If it did not end, she must accept the outcome with the grace and dignity she had always tried to show. After all, she reminded herself that she was now fifty years old. Henri was only thirty-four. She had had him to herself far longer than she could have hoped. If it had not been the Scottish woman, one day it would have been someone else.

She did not blame him. He had become her lover at so young an age, and she knew, in only a way one lover can know another, that before this he had never strayed. Loneliness and curiosity; they were easy enough to understand. She could accept that. But if she and Henri had a future together, it would be because he still wanted her there. She would not use guilt or the past to keep him. She stood in the courtyard approving the newly installed stained-glass windows. They were a masterpiece; the work of the renowned artisan Jean Cousin, glistening black and white in the light from the sun.

Though still not complete, Anet had already been transformed from a barren old keep into a shining Renaissance palace. At Henri's command, it had been fashioned in the classical tradition, not in the tired Italian mode. All of the feudal walls had eventually been surrendered, and in their place, the most opulent palace in all of Europe had begun to emerge. All of Henri's dreams, the sketches that he had shown to Diane three years earlier, were becoming a reality before her eyes. Even during their estrangement, the King had closely supervised all the plans and designs. Much to Catherine's chagrin, he had continued to show the work there far more attention than that which was taking place at his own palaces of Saint Germain-en-Laye or Fontainebleau. He had always seen Anet as the greatest contribution of his reign.

A host of young French talent had been given an opportunity for fame under the King's patronage and Anet would be their path to distinction. Philibert de L'Orme, to whom the overall architecture had been entrusted, worked the new Anet in white Normandy stone. To this he added black silex, so that even the very structure would honor the colors she favored.

He incorporated ample use of Doric columns from antiquity, and a vast open colonnade that ran the length of the three-sided building. This open area faced one of three grand courtyards. The final wing was a massive entrance. Above the gateway was a clock and below it a representation in bronze of Actaeon, a hunter who turned into a stag and was killed by his own hounds. Although it appeared immovable, at the stroke of each hour, the hounds leapt forward and the stag turned to run.

Fabulous fountains and bas-reliefs worked in black and white marble ornamented the grounds. Exquisite chimney pieces, fashioned by Benvenuto Cellini during his stay in France, now found their place at Anet. Everywhere was the royal emblem. It had been emblazoned on the tops of the columns, and worked into the pavement. It was prominent in the doors, the ceilings and already had been woven into the carpets that lined the still-bare rooms of the sprawling chateau.

The goddess Diana was depicted everywhere. But nowhere was it more magnificently displayed than in the west courtyard where there stood a huge fountain by Jean Goujon. Commissioned by the King, it was called *Diane Chasseresse,* depicting the goddess, lying nude, with her dogs Sirius and Procyon, one arm draped around the neck of a stag and holding a bow in the other.

The chateau was vast and although bare and unfinished, Diane had already begun collecting furnishings to make it a home. In Henri's absence, Catherine had once again begun making overtures for Chenonceaux. She grumbled that, as property of the

Crown, the chateau was rightfully hers before it could belong to the Duchesse de Valentinois. Diane wanted to know that there was one home, above all the others, which could never be taken from her. Anet was to be that place.

After she approved the magnificent windows that had been installed along the first floor, she retired. She strolled alone, back into the old part of the house in which she would live until her new wing was complete. She walked down a long covered hallway lined with huge tapestries, each of which recorded episodes in the life of the goddess Diana. Henri would be pleased, she thought.

She cast a glance through one of the long windows down into the courtyard at the workmen below. She and Henri had come a long way toward his dream. Nowhere in France was there such splendor; perhaps nowhere in the world, yet there would be little meaning in it all, if he left her now for Lady Flemming. When she turned the corner that housed her apartments, she was taken up by thoughts of the past, and the future. She was looking down, her hands joined like a temple. She did not see Henri sitting alone beside the fire.

"They have done a remarkable job," he began, his voice tentative and unsure. Diane turned swiftly and saw him sitting there, his legs covered by black silk stockings and crossed at the knee, his muscular body caped in ermine and black velvet. Even at a distance she could see that he had changed. His face was drawn, and for the first time, just the way the sun came through the window behind him, she could see tiny flecks of gray in his dark hair and beard. She moved a few steps closer.

"The entrance is magnificent. So much better than I expected," he said. "I arrived just on the hour to see the clock work. I tell you I thought it had come to life! I knew we were right to trust that craftsman."

Now he was standing and swaying back and forth like an unsure adolescent. "I know that you asked me to wait until you felt ready . . ." he stammered. "But I had to come. We must talk."

Diane moved to a small carved table near the fire that held

several silver and crystal decanters of wine. She selected a silver one with a long thin neck that was filled with white wine from Anjou.

"About Lady Flemming," she said as she poured the wine in two goblets. Her back was turned so that she could not see the expression on his face, but she knew by his silence that he was fighting for the words. Carefully she picked up both goblets and turned to face him.

"Yes, about her," he finally replied, not surprised that she knew.

As she drew nearer and handed him the wine, she could see that his eyes were not only red from lack of sleep, but there were new tiny lines at the corners and along the sides of his mouth. She knew by the tangy smell of sweat and horseflesh that he had not bothered to bathe. She knew that he must have come directly from Paris, if not all the way from Saint Germain-en-Laye.

Diane sat on the edge of a small chair covered in black and white pourpoint. Henri took the goblet that she had offered him and, in the silence, emptied it in one swallow. Then he sat down again. It was awkward. She thought it curious how after so many years of intense intimacy, that they should behave like strangers now with one another. Diane sipped her wine. She knew that how she handled the next few moments would determine the rest of her life.

"And do you love her?"

They were her words. They had come from her mouth, and yet she scarcely knew how she had managed to say them for the pain that gripped her when she had.

"Love her? Great God, no, I do not love her!" Henri lunged from his chair and, in one long dancelike movement, came to rest on his knees at her feet. "My love has always, always belonged to you! Just look around you! You must know that by now!"

Diane could feel herself breathe an audible sigh of relief; her chest expand and contract beneath the tight black velvet bodice. She still had him. She still had her life.

Henri reached up and softly pressed his lips to hers for a single chaste kiss. Then he broke away. "I adore you," he whispered. "That will never change. No matter what you come to think of me."

Diane smiled. "I love you desperately," she said in reply. Then she grew more stoic. "I understand and I accept what has happened, now that I know how you feel."

Instead of her words giving the comfort that she had intended, he seemed to become more troubled. He looked at her a moment more, his dark brows arching over tired eyes, before he stood and left her side. He walked toward the fire and braced his hands upon the mantel that bore their crest. Then he lowered his head.

"She is with child."

Diane's heart stopped. She felt the blood drain from her face. Then, like a volcano, it rushed back into her cheeks, burning red with hot, violent pain. She could not catch her breath. Her mouth went dry. She was glad he could not see her because she knew it would have been impossible to hide the look on her face. She had felt so prepared when he arrived and yet . . . she had not expected this. To be asked to deal with a permanent reminder of his infidelity. Catherine's children she understood, encouraged, because he did not make love to the Queen; he filled her with heirs. Until now, her womb had borne the only fruit of the King's passion: their daughter Diane.

She continued on, trying desperately to catch her breath and yet not show it. Tiny beads of perspiration crept onto her temples but she kept absolutely still. Finally he turned to her.

"Did you hear what I said?"

"I did."

"Oh, *ma bien-aimée*. How can I begin to tell you how truly sorry I am?" He moved toward her as he spoke, shaking his head from side to side. "For the hurt and the disappointment I see in your eyes just now I shall never, never be able to forgive myself. You are the only thing in my world. The only thing! And if I lost you for a dalliance; for a foolish mistake like that . . ."

Finally she gained the strength to look at him. Here was the man with whom she had built a life; by whom she had a child. This man who had displayed his love for her, and had honored her in ways too numerous to count. In that moment of silence between them, a myriad of thoughts raced through her mind. Diane had already forgiven him for the affair. She tried to tell herself that the child did not matter, but it did. She began to consider how it would feel if she raged at him. She wanted to, desperately. She tried to imagine herself screaming and beating his breast for the wrong he had done her, punishing him with her words and her actions. To her complete surprise, she could not see it. What she could see was a man who had worshipped her for twenty years, here before her, and full of regret. She would not reproach him now.

"Well then . . ." Diane said finally. "How shall we handle it?"

Henri looked at her with a disbelief he could not mask. Everything would be all right. The world and the love of his life had been returned to him. He lunged at her again, burying her in his arms and a waterfall of ardent kisses.

"God, how I love you."

An untethered desire rose up in him, and his powerful body rippled with tension. He ran his tongue up her neck and behind her ear. He whispered all of the things she only half believed she would ever hear again. He drew her hand down his doublet, past the buckles and jewels. Then he stopped and looked at her, his eyes sparkling with fire.

It had been such a long, long time.

"COME IN, CHILD. Sit beside me," said Henri, as he patted the empty cushion next to him. He had sent for his eldest daughter as soon as the funeral for his son was over, and they had returned to Les Tournelles.

Diane de France walked slowly into her father's private drawing room. She was gowned in purple velvet with a long gold chain at her waist. Her dark hair was drawn back with a ring of pearls. Her hands were clasped before her, holding a small gold rosary. Although he could see that she had been crying, she walked into his room with grace and dignity. Louis, the King's fourth child, a boy of barely two, and the young girl's favorite, had just that morning been laid to rest.

"Please," he coaxed, when she did not readily sit down beside him. Finally she acquiesced and slid onto the edge of the cushion.

"Ma mignonne," he began as he took her hand. "I know how difficult today has been for you. I know how much you loved your little brother. But death is not an end. It is the beginning of eternal life in the heavenly kingdom. You must remember that. Louis was fortunate to have been called home so soon before the rest of us. I think there is comfort in that."

"Not for me!" she snapped and looked up at him with a flash of her mother's brilliant eyes. "He was special. He was my special one, and now there is no one left to me!"

"Chère Diane, you mustn't say that. You have all of your brothers and sisters. There is little Claude, who adores you, and now baby Charles is here to take Louis' place. If not in your heart at least in your care."

He knew the moment the words left his lips that it had been the wrong thing to say. He had only meant to comfort her. Instead, her eyes narrowed and she glared at him.

"How can you say that to me, Papa? How can you even think it? And I hate that name! Diane! Why did you do it, Papa? Why did you give me her name?"

His heart ached for her. So many things; such confusion that she had been faced with these past months, and he unable to right it with her.

She sprang to her feet and faced him. Her hands were in front of her, held in a pleading gesture. "My entire world seems as if it has crumbled right here in my hands! Everything I believed . . . everyone I loved . . . gone! And on top of it all, to have been given her name!"

"Madame told me that the two of you had begun to make peace."

"This is between you and I, Papa. It does not concern her! Even if she and I were making a start of things, that does not take away the pain of what you have done! To be forced to go through life with the name of the woman who gave me away! How could you do such a thing to me? She told me that you insisted; that she would have named me anything but that."

"Insisted?" he repeated, taking great care this time with the words he spoke. "Yes, that I did. My child, I have never in my life loved another woman but your mother. I loved her the very first moment I saw her, and all of the good that is inside of me, everything that you love, all of it is because of her."

"What has this to do with me?" she raged, turning away. Henri bolted from the couch and turned her back around, forcing her to face him.

"It has everything to do with you! Madame Diane stayed with me through the most gruesome assaults to herself, selflessly nurturing me and helping me to become a King! She loaned me money when I was young and I had none of my own because the King was angry with me. She encouraged me and loved me when everyone else believed that I was lost. You are the product of a union so special and so rare, Diane, that you could have been given no other name but hers." He paused a moment and then added, "I wonder, did she tell you that she nearly died giving you life?"

Diane's eye widened.

"She was told she was too old to have a child; that there would be complications. But she wanted more than anything to give you life once you were inside of her, even if the price meant that once you were born, she must give you up." He watched her face soften. "You did not know your grandfather, the former King, well but he had once fancied your mother for himself. His mistress made her life miserable for all of those years, because of it."

"But to have given me up!"

"She never gave you up. Your mother has been by your side since the day you were born. Can you really tell me there was ever a time that you can recall when she was not there for you? Was there ever a time that she did not read to you, or teach you, or hold you on her knee? Madame has been a mother to you in every way but one, and that gift, the gift of motherhood, she selfishly denied herself to protect your life."

"I had no idea that the King and the Duchesse d'Etampes together—"

"Well they did. They did everything they could to make her leave Court, and leave me. The details are unimportant now, but no matter what they did to her, no matter how bad things were, she would never forsake me. I owe her my life, Diane, and perhaps it is time you know that so do you. Your name means love, *ma chère mignonne.* Wear it with a knowledge and pride that the people who gave you life loved each other against all of those odds."

Tears streamed down her porcelain face. Henri then took her in his arms and held her as she cried. "She told me only that times were different; that it was not safe. I had no idea."

"I am sure you did not know, but you are grown up now, and some things that we must face in this world are not easy."

"How will she ever forgive me? I have been so cruel. Even after she told me, even after she explained, I wanted to believe that her motives had been selfish . . . I was so wrong to doubt her."

"Tell her," said Henri, and as his daughter turned around she saw her mother standing behind them in the shadows near the door.

"Oh, Madame!" she cried. "I am so sorry! Please, can you ever forgive me?" Diane opened her arms and her daughter rushed into them. The girl clung to her until she thought both of their lives might be extinguished by her desperate grasp. Diane ran her hand down her daughter's long dark curls and then looked across at Henri to see tears in his eyes.

"There, there, *mon ange* . . . it is all forgotten," she whispered. "I was wrong, too, not to have told you, but I wanted you to be safe. I wanted desperately for my child . . . our beautiful child, to live the life that she deserved, and that you have. Now you are Diane de France, *légitime,* and I would not, for any pain of my own, have taken that away from you."

Henri moved toward them and encircled them both. "Nothing in this world could ever be more perfect than it is just now," he whispered, ". . . nothing."

DESPITE HENRI'S REASSURANCE and his open devotion to her, the months since her return to Court had not been easy for Diane. She now shared her much-coveted stage with the very pregnant Lady Flemming. But if the situation was uncomfortable for Diane, it was nearly unbearable for Catherine. She was beside herself with the dilemma that she and the Constable had created.

While the King was at Anet with Diane the previous spring, Lady Flemming had taken over a wing at Fontainebleau, hired her own staff and began running up huge expenses. As she began to show signs of her pregnancy, she even gained the confidence to be rude to the Queen. She spoke only her shrill-sounding Scottish, as she now felt entitled to forgo the more difficult yet compulsory French. She only repeated one phrase in the country's native tongue across the echoing corridors of Fontainebleau, and that she did with frightening regularity.

"I have done all that I can, and God be thanked. I am pregnant by the King, for which I count myself both honored and happy!"

Embarrassed by the entire ordeal, Henri dealt with it by avoiding Lady Flemming completely. He refused to discuss the worsening situation, even with Diane. He preferred to pretend that the problem did not exist. He felt he had no choice. Since the product of his brief affair would be partially royal, the child would not be allowed to leave France. Therefore, the royal household seemed hopelessly saddled with the boorish and brazen lady who took every opportunity accorded her to remind Diane of her lover's infidelity.

As the King attended to issues of state, Lady Flemming produced a son. Strong and healthy, his fiery red hair would be forever a reminder to Henri of his indiscretion. Still, he was of royal blood. The boy was his son. Holding the infant moments after his birth, with Diane beside him in a room filled with dignitaries and

Cardinals to welcome the child, he proclaimed the boy his natural son. Lady Flemming had insisted he be named Henri d'Angoulême.

Diane left the woman's apartments after the proclamation, as much to be away from Henri as from Lady Flemming. Glistening with the sweat of labor, the Scottish woman had looked up at Diane with a victorious grin as evil as that of Anne d'Heilly. She had a son named after the King, and it was no secret that she meant to stay at Court. The situation was clearly out of hand. Diane knew she now must act to protect what she had worked for nearly eighteen years to build. There was only one way they could be rid of the usurper; she and Catherine must put aside their grievances long enough to unite.

CATHERINE SOBBED VIOLENTLY at the news that the King had given his bastard son his own name over one of his legitimate children. She did not even seem to care that it was her rival who had delivered the news. The royal brood mare, who was herself eight months pregnant, had begun this sixth confinement with difficulty. She had taken to her bed, at the insistence of her doctors, to prevent a miscarriage. Now, after hearing the news of this newest slight against her, she lay on her side, rocking back and forth between her sobs.

"I know, Your Majesty, that there is no great love between us," Diane began again after she had spoken those first shocking words. "But the King will not intervene against the child's mother; and if we are to change things, I believe you and I must do something."

"What are you talking about? The damage is done!" she wailed and refused all of Lucrezia's, her lady-in-waiting, attempts to comfort her from the other side of the heavy poster bed.

"Perhaps that is true," Diane replied as she loomed above the Queen. "But we face far worse, you and I, if she stays."

Something in the words of her rival, this time, made her stop crying and look up. "But, what are we to do? God help us all, she is the child's mother!"

It was all that she could manage to say. Then, as if seeing the gravity of the situation for the first time, she began to sob more violently. Diane paced the room while Catherine's ladies-in-waiting dotted her brow with chervil-scented water. Her apothecaries tended to her with a gray powder swirled into water, which was then given to her to drink.

As she watched Catherine, Diane realized what she had meant by "the damage is done." It had meant more than the birth of another illegitimate child. She could not believe that she had not thought of it before.

"Mother Mary! You arranged this!"

The Queen ceased her tears almost immediately and looked up again at her husband's mistress. "Leave us," she said to her ladies and to the apothecary.

"How could you do it to Henri?" Diane asked when they were alone.

Catherine paused and then gazed directly at her competitor, the tears now dry. "I wanted to be rid of you," she said simply. "Anne said he knew a way."

Diane stared at her in disbelief. "Anne de Montmorency? Oh! The King's most trusted confidant and friend is nothing more than a common panderer? Dear God! . . . and you . . ."

Catherine's dark, tear-filled eyes cleared. "I am his Queen . . . nothing less."

"News of this will kill the King."

"Then you must not tell him."

"I have no secrets from him." After a moment she softened. "Your Majesty, it will do us no good to be at odds with one another in this. You must try, for once, to put aside your feelings, for Henri's sake."

The two women stared at one another. Catherine considered her rival's words.

"Look, Your Majesty, I am older than she is. You have far more chance of fighting an old mistress than a new one. And at least, when we are in public, I make every effort to accord you the honor that you are due, which certainly cannot be said of the Lady Flemming."

"And if I do not agree to help you?"

"Then the King will be made aware of your plan to unseat me."

"And if I agree?"

"Then the good Constable shall take the fall, and we shall oust Lady Flemming from France."

They were both silent as Catherine considered her options. Diane leaned across the finely woven bedcover toward the Queen. "I know that you do not like me, Your Majesty, and I can understand that, but at least we have come to know what to expect from one another."

Catherine put her own fleshy hand on top of Diane's. "You are right. I do not like you, but I have an even greater dislike of the alternative."

HENRI WAS SUMMONED to the Queen's apartments but he did not arrive there for over an hour. Diane and Catherine had been informed that His Majesty had gone riding in the woods with Saint-André following his son's birth. When he finally arrived, his hair was windblown and his face was flushed. He looked at Diane and then at the Queen as he removed his gloves.

"What is it? Is there something wrong with the child?" he asked impatiently as Saint-André removed his cape. Diane stood beside Catherine's bed. The Queen was propped up by a large spray of pillows and both of them were facing him.

"Well?"

Catherine's eyes welled with tears again and she began to sob into her hands. "Oh, Henri, I do beg you . . ." she began but she could not continue.

Diane walked slowly toward him. "I am afraid, *chéri,* that you and I have been victims of a rather intricate plot."

"What sort of plot?"

"To oust me, and replace me with Lady Flemming."

"Who?!" he raged and his eyes darkened with anger. Diane knew the implications of what she was about to say, but she had no choice if she wished to be rid of her competition before he found a way to be rid of her.

"Montmorency."

"That is not possible!"

"The Queen, who knew of his plan, confessed it to me today."

Henri grew pale and began to search for a chair. Saint-André brought one from a place near the door. When it was before him he changed his mind and advanced toward the Queen's bed.

"Catherine, is this true?"

The Queen, now sobbing uncontrollably, could only nod.

"I cannot believe . . ."

"It would seem that he and Lady Flemming conspired to seduce you in my absence and then saw to it that she was constantly available to you after that."

The King pondered the idea for several moments, in silent disbelief.

"The point of this, however, is one on which the Queen and I are firm. There must be an end to it. Lady Flemming is dangerous and she must leave France."

Catherine managed to raise her head to watch the King's response to this particular declaration. He looked at his mistress and then at his wife.

"But, m'amie, how can I ask such a thing of her, considering the circumstances?"

"You would be better served to ask how you could afford to have her remain here with the Queen and with me."

"What of the child?"

"He shall stay here, of course," Catherine gathered the courage to reply, "along with your other children, and he shall be raised with every honor as your son."

The implication was clear. A natural child of the King did not need his mother to remain at Court. Janet Stuart could be provided for, and then returned to Scotland. Diane was right, the risk of having her remain was too great. Henri had come close to losing her and he could take no more chances. Inwardly, he breathed a small sigh of relief that his wife and his mistress had banded together. By this uncommon alliance, they had not only eased the tension between them, but they had rid him of a predicament that he had not known how to handle.

"Very well," he finally said, looking at one and then the other. "She shall be returned to Scotland as soon as she is able to travel."

MONTMORENCY STOOD ALONE before the King's throne, his hands clasped loosely behind his back. Henri sat leaning on his elbow and gazing across the crimson carpet at the man he had most admired in the world. Until yesterday. A frown darted across his brow when he thought of the deception wrought upon him and Diane. Montmorency saw it and knew precisely why he had been summoned.

"I shall not ask you to deny it, because I could not bear to hear you, of all people, lie to me," Henri said in a chilling tone that the Constable had not heard since François I had so cruelly relieved him of his duty.

Montmorency moved a step forward. His face was dark and solemn. "Whatever you may think of me, I have always loved you. You have been like a son to me. That, you must believe."

"I do believe it, Monty. That is what makes so great a betrayal as this unconscionable."

The Constable felt the same blinding fear he had with the former King the moment before he had heard that his services at Court were no longer needed. "Good Christ, I've not betrayed you! I have acted only in your best interest! In the best interest of France!"

Henri sprung to his feet. "In my best interest? Madame Diane is in my best interest! She is my life! You knew that full well and yet still you sought to destroy her!"

"Please, Henri . . . Your Majesty." He moved nearer. "I do not know what the Queen has told you but—"

"The truth, Monty. Catherine has told me the truth."

"She was desperate. She pleaded with me to help her. I felt I had no choice but to—"

Henri held up a hand to silence him. "Because you have long been a friend to me, this time I shall extend to you a warning. But listen well, my friend, for you shall not be granted the same reprieve the next time. If I ever have reason to believe that you have done anything . . . and I do mean anything, to endanger Madame or my relationship with her, you need never show your face anywhere at this Court again. Now, do we understand one another?"

Montmorency smiled gratefully and then bent in a reverent bow. "Perfectly, Your Majesty."

LADY FLEMMING LEFT the French Court five days later. At half past midnight, she kissed the tiny child good-bye, knowing that she would never see him again. Then she boarded the King's barge on the first leg of her journey home.

The compensation she took with her eased the pain of her loss and ensured that she would make a good marriage once she returned to Scotland. She had wanted the King but she was enough of a realist to know when she had lost. What they had said was true. Diane de Poitiers was too formidable a rival for anyone. Truthfully, the child she had borne the King had meant little more to her than a bargaining chit for her financial security. The monetary compensation for her sacrifice being satisfactory, she gladly, and without conflict, left France.

CATHERINE FELT CERTAIN that this was the best time of her life and that her patience had finally been rewarded. She was long since free of the burden of having been barren, and she had managed to remain Queen of France. Lady Flemming had returned to Scotland and Diane de Poitiers had just turned fifty-one. But most encouraging, in a very public announcement at Parliament, her husband had bestowed upon her the honor of Regent.

In a dispute with the Emperor over German territory, Henri had decided to aid his German neighbors against France's greatest foe. He was determined to lead his men in battle, but in his absence, someone would be required to exercise power. It mattered not that each cannon, gunpowder holder and firearm bore the royal emblem and the image of the crescent moon as a tribute to Diane de Poitiers. A Regent must be someone of royal blood. As Queen of France, at last Catherine had found a place in Henri's life that his mistress could not fill.

A confidence was borne of her newfound strength, and, in Henri's absence, she was convinced that Diane should be the first to feel the force of it. Though she no longer spoke of it to the King, she had never forgiven her for what she believed was the outright theft of Chenonceaux. The years had only sharpened Catherine's desire to possess the little chateau on the river. Though she said that her reasons were many, there was only one with any great importance. She wanted it because it belonged to Diane.

As the days of summer progressed, she plunged headlong into her new duties as Regent. She read and studied with an enthusiasm that she had not felt since she was a young girl in Italy. Through her own henchmen, she also began the search for a loophole through which she might rightfully take possession of Chenonceaux. She was Queen, she reasoned. It was property of the Crown, and no matter what she must do or pay, she meant to take it away from that whore. But, as if by some strange intervention, the fates she monitored and worshipped so closely through her mystics began slowly to turn against her.

After several weeks of study, Catherine discovered that provisions that she personally had allocated for the troops had mysteriously disappeared. Along with the rations had gone the horses and carts intended to deliver them. Enraged at the negative light that such a misdeed would cast upon her, she sent a letter to her friend Montmorency. She ordered that from then on provisions should be transported in the charge of those who would be held responsible for them. It was these acts of piracy alone that could tear the Queen from her infant son. She quickly cut a path to Châlons, which was the base of supplies for the army. There she hoped to uncover the offender herself.

Feeling weak, she stopped at Joinville, the main seat of the Guise family, and a halfway point on the road to Châlons. She did not know, as her train entered the courtyard, that the Cardinal Charles was currently in residence with his good friend and ally, Diane de Poitiers, just back from her holiday at Anet. It was there at Joinville, in the chateau overlooking the flowering banks of the Marne, that the Queen of France fell critically ill.

☞

"GOD HELP US, I have no idea what it is!" declared the royal physician as he hovered over the Queen. He was examining the pustules and red patches on her face and hands with the same unrestrained amazement as if she were already dead.

Diane stood between Charles de Guise and another of Montmorency's nephews, Odet, Cardinal de Châtillon. They looked down on Catherine, whose eyes were covered with an opaque film as she muttered incoherently between moans of pain.

"I doubt if it is the plague," the physician continued. "But as to a firm judgment, I confess I am vexed."

The senior physician to the King, Amboise Paré, had been summoned from his battlefield hospital, but he would not arrive for at least two days. In the meanwhile, Philippe Regnier was charged with her care and could do little more than cover her with washes of rose water and see that she was as comfortable as possible.

"I am certain it is the plague, and I for one am not prepared to die, Her Majesty's service or not!" whispered Lucrezia Alamanni to Marie La Maure. The two ladies-in-waiting to the Queen stood pensively in the corner near the door, as the physician completed his examination. Both women covered their faces with cloths dipped in mint, rosemary and lavender. The mixture was believed to be useful against the plague.

"Nearly everyone else has left her train already. Surely she cannot begrudge us more than the others if we return to Fontainebleau; that is if she survives."

"Whatever it is, she certainly cannot last much longer," agreed Marie. "Just look at her face! She is barely recognizable beneath those oozing sores. Her tongue has swollen so much that she cannot speak. I heard gossip this morning that in Paris they are saying she is dead already."

"It is the purples. I know it is, and they spread like fire through the forest in summer!" Lucrezia ranted. "I am afraid for my family. I cannot stay with her, no matter what the Crown does to me!"

"I wonder who His Majesty will marry when the Queen is gone. I always thought it would be her," Marie said, pointing her chin discreetly in Diane's direction. "But she is getting so old now, and after His Majesty's affair, it is clear he finally has a taste beyond the well-aged fare that he once found so desirable."

After the physician had completed his examination, Diane left the Queen's bedside and swept across the bedchamber to the door where the two servants still stood.

"Madame Alamanni, Mademoiselle La Maure," she said, "the Queen can have no use for you now. If your change in attitude is apparent to me, then it will surely be apparent to her and we cannot risk upsetting her further. Perhaps it would be better for all concerned if you both would retire to Fontainebleau."

"But who will serve Her Majesty?" asked Marie.

"For now, that will be my concern."

"You?" Lucrezia bit her lip.

"I am certain that you both will be summoned again when Her Majesty has recovered."

"Do you not mean *if* she recovers, Madame?" said Marie La Maure. "I have never seen a plague so vile as hers."

"Her recovery is in God's hands, whatever her malady. I trust in the coming days that you shall pray for the return of Her Majesty's good health, as will I."

The Cardinal de Châtillon, who was among the Queen's most intimate friends, was a small man with receding hair and a neat lint-blond beard. He wore the same red robe and heavy gold cross as Charles de Guise, now Cardinal de Lorraine.

After the physician had left, he looked across the room from beside Her Majesty's bed and saw the two ladies with the cloths held before their faces. He advanced in freshly polished dark leather slippers, and stood behind Diane.

"Well then, are we to lose two more of the Queen's faithful?" he asked, his voice curbed with irritation and fatigue from lack of sleep. Diane looked over her shoulder.

"I think, Your Eminence, it is better that they go. The Queen cannot hope to benefit from their fear. Charles," she said, turning toward Guise. "There is no one else. May I count on you to escort them back to Fontainebleau?"

His relief was almost too apparent. "Of course, Madame," he replied as he lowered his head.

"But they have both been with her for years. If even they are not willing to stay, who do you expect to attend Her Majesty in their absence?" asked Châtillon. "Her entire household and Guise's staff have already abandoned us and returned to Fontainebleau."

Diane looked again at the two women, their eyes laced with fear and their faces punctuated by an overwhelming desire to be dismissed.

"I shall stay with Her Majesty," said Diane. "Your Eminence shall have to look to your own heart to know what is right for you."

"It is God's gift," said the Cardinal, "that at least she has not developed the swelling in the pits of her arms. Then we would know that it is the plague. There is comfort in that. If you should like, Madame, out of a sincere and respectful affection for Her Majesty, I too shall stay."

After the final two ladies-in-waiting were dismissed from service, Diane returned to the Queen's side. The dark bed with the heavy velvet curtains hid the Queen's disfigured mass within its folds. She had fallen asleep again and Diane whispered a Hail Mary. The contorted expression of pain and fear on her thick, blemished face had been difficult to bear. It softened a little as she slept.

Diane was not so detached from Catherine as the years and the manipulations might have led her to become. Despite their differences and the man who divided them, they had shared a household, the love of seven children and their lives for nineteen years. Ironically, Catherine's Italian faction, who had filled her head with gossip and kept the hostile fires burning between them, had all run in fear. In the likely hour of her death, Catherine had been abandoned. Of all those who supported her, flattered her and protected her, only her greatest rival remained.

Madame M'amie,

I shall not write a long letter, for I have given the bearer all the news, nor have I the leisure, being now about to make the passage of the river Sarre. I beg leave to tell you that my army is in excellent condition and of fine spirit. I am confident that if we are opposed at the crossing, Our Lord will aid me by His grace, as he has done from the beginning.

I will write nothing else to you, for Monsieur Avanson, who brings you this letter, will give you my messages. Meanwhile, I entreat you will remember him who has never known but one God and one love, and be assured that you will never have cause for shame to have granted me the name of servitor that I beg you to keep for me forever.

Diane neatly folded the letter and lay her head back against the soft crimson velvet of the carved oak chair. She was exhausted. She had not slept nor eaten for three days.

Hélène took the letter from her mistress's limp hand and set it on the small table beside her.

"He does not know about the Queen," said Diane. "It would seem his men have found a reason to keep it from him."

"Please, Madame, you simply cannot go on this way. I beg you. Let me have something made for you to eat and pour you a bath."

"Her Majesty is still alive, and while that is the case, I must continue with her."

"But the Cardinal de Châtillon is with her now, and even he has begged you to get some rest. You can be no good to her like this."

Hélène's words had a ring of truth and Diane cast her tired eyes upon her friend. "I wished that she would die," she whispered, and looked away. "I swear that I did not mean to wish it. I tried to push the thought from my mind, but when she first fell ill, before we knew the extent of it, I found myself thinking how many years it had been and how much simpler my life would be without her anger and her remonstrations against me. It was only a passing thought; no more than a moment, but now I feel somehow, that perhaps I am responsible."

"Madame, that is . . ."

"You must get word to him, Hélène. He has a right to be told. Send a message through Saint-André. Tell him that the Queen is near death. Tell him that he must come at once."

Hélène knew that Diane was rambling. The lack of sleep and the hunger had rendered her words, at times, incoherent. She put a hand to her mistress's forehead to check for signs of fever. She made the sign of the cross when she was met with cool skin. She did not need to coax further. As she looked up again, Diane, who had spent much of the past three days on her feet between the wash basin and the Queen's side, gave in to the cushioning support of the soft velvet chair. Hélène brought a bedcover from the foot of the bed, covered her with it, and stood protectively by for a moment until she was certain that Diane had fallen asleep.

When Diane's eyelids began to flutter and the sculpted muscles of her face relaxed, Hélène walked to the small writing desk at the opposite end of the room. She drew a sheet of parchment from the drawer, dipped a quill into the ink and addressed the letter to Jacques de Saint-André on the battlefield at Metz.

METZ FELL WILLINGLY into the protective hands of the preliminary French troops. The way had been paved through the region several days earlier by possession of Toul. The fact that the Emperor refused to believe the German princes had turned against him until the French troops were nearly at his border had been the final blow.

Henri sat at Châlons, the Queen's unmet destination, in the middle of reviewing his infantry, when Saint-André brought him the news that Catherine was desperately ill.

In his tent, a huge black and white pavilion sixty feet high, Henri collapsed onto his cot and surrendered his head to his hands. Around him was a table covered over with maps, a compass, an empty flagon of wine and two silver goblets. At the entrance, two guards stood sentry. On the wall, held to the tent by a leather thong, was a small painting of Diane done the previous year at Chenonceaux. There were guns, two daggers and his pearl-handled sword. They lay along with the bright blue embroidered pillow, a gift from his daughter, Elizabeth. His silver prie-dieu had been assembled for morning prayer, and some recent sketches in a folio of his children were tossed open across the cot. On the small tortoise-top table beside his cot was the first sketch of Diane done by Clouet, just after the birth of their daughter.

"Hélène says that Madame Diane and the Cardinal de Châtillon are the only two who would stay. The others were all afraid that the attack was dangerous, and that it would spread," said Saint-André. "Word, Your Majesty, I am afraid, is that the Queen may already be dead."

"Is it the plague?" he asked as he ran his fingers through the coarse tufts of his dark hair.

"Monsieur Regnier did not think so, Sire. But to be certain, Madame Diane has had Monsieur Paré recalled from the front to make a final determination. Sire, if it is contagious, as Mademoiselle Gallet says that they believe it is, then I cannot advise you to go."

"Diane is there!" he snapped. "She is risking her own life to nurse the Queen. How could I possibly stay away? I want you and Marck to accompany me," he said boldly, and then he softened. "That is, if you should consent to go."

"My place, as always, is with my King, Your Majesty."

François de Guise ordered the King's trunks packed and his swiftest stallion readied for the ride to Joinville where the Queen lay dying. He did not love Catherine, nor would he ever, but she had given him six children whom he adored. Now, as the years of youthful idealism had passed, he could almost not recall a time when she was not his wife. He had, over the years of their marriage, developed a fondness for the stout Italian woman who tried so desperately to please him.

But the real motivation which drove Henri to leave his tour was the threat to Diane's life, so near to disease. He marveled that, despite everything, she alone had chosen to stay beside the Queen, the woman who openly despised her. His love . . . his goddess . . . his Diana. It could not . . . no, it must not be the plague.

❧

THE PURPLES WERE an epidemic strain of measles. The telltale sign was red patches, some of which formed small blisters and could spread over the entire body. In its extreme form, the tongue became swollen and so grossly distorted that, if untreated, the victim could choke to death.

Ambroise Paré, the Royal Physician, made the conclusive diagnosis the day after the message was dispatched to Saint-André. Diane took a fresh cloth from Hélène and tirelessly applied yet another to the Queen's forehead. Catherine whimpered an inaudible reply at the feel of cool liquid on her burning skin, and then closed her eyes again.

"Will she live?" Diane whispered.

At the end of the Queen's bed, the Cardinal de Châtillon gave some sort of directive to Hélène and she turned to leave the room.

"I cannot say with certainty, Madame. The tongue will have to be bled before we know if she has a chance. If there is going to be a change, it should happen tonight."

Diane sat back down in the small carved chair beside the bed and cast her eyes away in an expressionless stare. Her gown, which had gone unchanged since before the letter had been sent to the King, was crumpled, and it smelled of the aromatic potions which were used to help Her Majesty sleep. She no longer wore a headdress. Her chignon was loose; long strands of blond hair hung in limp ribbons around her face and down the nape of her neck. The room was dark and it had the foreboding smell of death.

Paré looked at her again in disbelief. Had he not seen it himself, he would never have believed it. The mighty Duchesse de Valentinois nursing her great rival, the Queen of France!

"You really should get some rest, Madame. At the very least, take some time to refresh yourself. I am told that His Majesty draws very near."

Diane looked up at him with tired eyes. "No, Monsieur. But I thank you for your concern. I said I would stay with her and I mean to stay."

When Henri came through the double doors to the Queen's bedchamber later that afternoon, Diane was hunched over the bed, her head in her arms. She had finally fallen asleep. Paré rose and bowed to the King. He watched His Majesty's startled face when he saw her so disheveled and asleep near the Queen.

"We all tried to convince her to rest, Your Majesty, but she would not leave the Queen's side."

Henri drew near and ran his gloved hand gently across the back of her head. To have done this, for him . . . for France. He bent down and kissed the top of her head, and then slowly drew back the bedcurtains. Paré watched, with singular fascination, His Majesty shrink from the sight of his wife. She was still covered with dark red blotches and small blisters so that the features of her face were nearly unrecognizable. He lowered the drape again and looked back at his physician.

"What is her condition?"

"Her tongue has been bled, Your Majesty, and the swelling has begun to go down already. It is a good sign. I will know more by nightfall."

Satisfied for the moment that the Queen was not going to die, Henri instructed the physician to inform him immediately of any change. Then, he bent down and, as carefully as if she were a child, took Diane into his muscular arms, and carried her from the Queen's apartments.

THE NEXT MORNING when Diane woke, Henri was already gone. She had a vague recollection of him carrying her to bed and a vague image, as though she had watched it through a filmy piece of silk, that he had made love to her. Only the memory of his voice was clear.

"I do not deserve you . . ." he had whispered over and over, his face wet with grateful tears. "There is no way to repay such kindness."

As her mind slowly rose back to consciousness, she tried to sit up, but her head and limbs were heavy. She looked across the room to the small crystal clock on the table. Eight o'clock. She looked toward the windows. They had been covered with a heavy cloth to create the illusion of darkness. Still, there was enough of a space between the strips of heavy velvet to know that it was morning.

Again she tried to lift her head from the pillows. With some effort she managed to balance herself on her elbows. Her beleaguered body and heavy eyes were drawing her back to sleep, but she fought it.

She called out for Hélène but no one came. After another moment Diane swung her feet to the side of the bed and looked down at them. She was bare, and once freed of the heavy bedcovers she began to shiver. She could not recall the last time she had eaten. Had she had anything since the Queen had arrived at Joinville? That had been four days ago. Or was it five?

Across from her bed, a long mirror framed in gold was fastened to the wall. She looked at herself, and for the first time she saw the dark circles beneath her crimson eyes, and the lines, now more pronounced, near her mouth. She ran a hand across her face as though she might wipe away the image. *The Queen! I must see the Queen! How long have I been asleep? If the Queen has died in the night . . .*

She tossed a fur-lined wrap over her shoulders and called out again to Hélène. This time the door opened and a long shaft of light pierced the darkness.

"Where have you been? I have been calling and yet you did not answer."

"The King gave me the strictest instructions not to wake you."

"But I must return to the Queen! I must change her dressings! Quickly . . . get me a gown!"

She bolted from the bed ignoring her throbbing legs and head. Hélène drew near and looked at her mistress with calming eyes. "The crisis has past, Madame. The swelling has gone down and some of the blisters have begun to scab. Monsieur Paré says the Queen will live. The King is with her now."

Diane looked at her, disbelief clouding her tired eyes. "It is true," Hélène said. "I have just come from her room. His Majesty said that if you are well enough, he shall meet you in the gardens for breakfast. I am to summon him when you are dressed."

It was over. The crisis had passed. Diane sank back onto the edge of the bed, and for the first time since the Queen was stricken, she realized what had really passed between them. She had not considered her own health or the advantage of Catherine's death. She had merely acted by an instinct that fifty years of living had woven into the fabric of who she was. No matter what the consequences, she could no more have turned her back on the desperately ill Queen than she could have ignored one of her own children. She was glad to have done it. No matter what the future held for the three of them.

WHEN CATHERINE OPENED HER EYES, Henri was by her side.

"You are looking much better," he whispered.

She studied him as though the image before her now was just another manifestation of the violent fever. While under its spell, she had seen all manner of twisted, contorted shapes and figures.

"It was very kind of you to come, Henri," she replied, her dry throat cracking from the strain of her first words. Henri reached over to the table beside the bed, took the goblet of water and helped her drink from it. When she had enough, she lay her head back on the pillow, never breaking her astonished gaze from him.

"Why have you come?"

"You are mother to my children, and you are my wife. I am not so much without a heart as you may think," he replied. "Are you in need of anything?"

There was something she wanted to ask, but she was not at all certain that she could bear to hear the reply that she knew in her heart he would give her. Catherine closed her eyes for a moment, trying to gain her strength. When she opened them again she looked at him directly.

"Who was it that attended me after Lucrezia and Marie left for Fontainebleau?"

Henri waited a moment, filled with an awkward mixture of thoughts. Once, long ago, he would have uttered Diane's name without thinking; with bitter hauteur designed to hurt her. But through their years together, things had changed. He no longer despised his wife. He no longer felt the need to wound her with the reality of his love for someone else.

"I am told that Cardinal de Châtillon has remained by your side from the very first."

Catherine looked at him, knowing what he had omitted. The concern in his eyes nearly brought her to tears. It was the first bit of tenderness between them.

"I would like to see the Duchesse de Valentinois," she said. "Would you arrange it?"

"Are you certain?"

"Yes, very. But first I must rest. I am very tired. Leave me now, please. And have her brought to me after noontide. I shall be ready to face her then."

As THE CHURCH BELL struck half past twelve, Diane walked alone into the Queen's bedchamber. In her absence, it had been filled once again with concerned nobles and ladies-in-waiting brought back from Fontainebleau. Catherine was propped up in her bed against a spray of claret-red pillows, the color of which drew attention to the fading blotches on her heavily jowled face and neck. Her dark hair was long around her shoulders, spilling over onto her white nightgown.

When Catherine saw her, she dismissed everyone and waited until the room was clear. Diane paused at the foot of the bed. All four curtains, which had warmed and hidden the Queen, were now tied back against the dark carved posts. A window was open and a gentle breeze had begun to clear the stale air.

"Please, Madame . . . sit down," the Queen said, motioning to the chair beside her bed. "You have spent a great deal of time in that chair these last few days."

"Not really so much, Your Majesty."

"Your modesty is more difficult to bear than I had anticipated," she said, averting her eyes. "Let me speak before my courage abandons me."

"Very well."

"I know that it was you. You stayed with me when the others

were afraid. Though I could not say it then, even in the worst of it, I knew that you were there. You were kind to me, Madame. I would not have expected that."

"Perhaps I would not have expected it of myself, before you were taken ill," she whispered.

There was another long silence during which Catherine seemed to be searching for words. "I owe you my life, Madame. But you know I shall never be able to give you what you want. I shall never give up the fight to win him from you."

"Nor I the fight to keep him," Diane replied.

The two women gazed at one another, a soft kindred spirit borne between them in spite of their fierce rivalry.

"You know I am not at liberty to like you, Madame. I can find nowhere in the annals of history that a Queen condescended to befriend her husband's . . . mistress. I can certainly not find that kind of strength inside myself to set such a precedent; no matter what kindness you have shown me."

Diane nodded softly.

". . . but I do commend your vigilance, and I thank you sincerely for your bravery."

Diane saw the difficulty with which Catherine's words had been delivered and she smiled a tired smile. "And I suppose, never has a mistress found the strength to befriend the wife of the man whom she loves. I cannot help but understand Your Majesty's position."

"Do you suppose . . . that just perhaps, if we had met under different circumstances, Madame, that we might one day have become friends?"

"It is not likely we shall ever know the answer to that, Your Majesty," Diane said. "But had things been different, I know I should have liked that very much."

IN THE SPRING OF THE FOLLOWING YEAR, Henri found a new contentment in life. There had been a victory for France and Germany over the Emperor at Metz, and the taking back of Calais seemed possible as well. He had made peace with his old demons. The trials between them, now over, had only served to strengthen the bond between him and Diane. After his return from the battlefield, together they celebrated the marriage of their daughter Diane de France to Orazio Farnese, Duke of Castro.

After twenty years, Henri had also managed to find a comfortable balance between his mistress and his wife. His royal coffers were full. The French people, long since eased from the burden of François I's heavy taxation, were happy. And the victory at Metz had set him free of the long-standing anger he felt for having been imprisoned by the Emperor.

He believed that building was the symbol of this new life and now that work was finally complete at Anet, he had turned his attentions toward several other projects. At Chenonceaux Diane was having a bridge built from the back of the chateau that would span the river. It would provide a way for them to easily ride together on the richer side of the forest. He had approved plans for the old ballroom at Fontainebleau to be redesigned in her honor, with frescoes and magnificent paintings all in the theme of the goddess Diana. There would also be a wing at the newly renovated Louvre to honor the love of his life.

"I have a surprise for you tonight," Henri teased as he helped her fasten a rope of pearls around her throat.

"I wish you wouldn't, Henri. You spoil me." She laughed.

He ran his hands slowly down her shoulders and then kissed the milk-white skin of her neck. "There is nothing I live for more than to do precisely that. Besides, it was something I promised you a long time ago, and now it seems the perfect time to present them."

"Them?" she repeated with another little laugh. She turned

around and saw the startled look on his face. His lips were parted. His graying temples and beard shimmered in the candlelit room.

"You look absolutely magnificent," he declared as his eyes swept over the length of her gown.

And so she did. Despite all of the jewels that through the years he had bestowed upon her, she still preferred a plain black ball gown and a simple strand of pearls. Tonight she wore black silk from Navarre with a wing collar stiff behind her neck and edged in fine white lace. Around her waist was a white satin cord entwined with a silver chain. As always, she wore two rings that he had given her; one which marked the fallen prospect of their marriage so many years ago, and another that reaffirmed his love for her.

Henri had arranged for a small supper to be held in the library. To this private affair, only the King and Diane's most intimate circle of friends had been invited. Hélène, Princess Marguerite, Saint-André and his wife, Guise and Anne d'Este, the Cardinal de Lorraine, and the Dauphin and Mary Queen of Scots.

Henri and Diane proceeded together down the elegant hall paneled in warm walnut wood. It was draped in tapestries from Bayeux, and dotted with urns in the classical tradition. He had chosen to have the supper there because it was a comfortable room which held many of Diane's most prized possessions. On the floors, in the wainscoting and in the marble and stone was their emblem. It had been emblazoned amid two mottos: *Donec totum impleat orbum* and *Sola vivit in illo* (alone she lived in him).

There were books, all bound in red Moroccan leather and set in long walnut cases. Some of the most rare volumes of the world were there, and several of those had been reworked in a black and white tooled binding. They too had been stamped with the official emblem. Around their friends were the works of Dante and Petrarch, a copy of *The Songs of the Troubadours* and several beautiful translations of Latin poems. Most conspicuous among them was the volume of Oppian's *The Chase* that Henri's father had given her on her first day back at Court, nearly eighteen years before. It was here in a place of prominence, so that she would never forget the price she paid for what she now had.

The aroma of Henri's favorite hors d'oeuvres swirled around the room. There were Perigordian truffles, Roquefort cheeses, cakes made of pine nuts, marzipan biscuits, figs and the best Bordeaux wine. The sounds of laughter from their guests, who were already seated, warmed the richly paneled room. As they passed through the opened doors together, everyone bowed and fell silent.

"Please go on! Enjoy yourselves!" Henri motioned, and squeezed Diane's hand.

The Dauphin and Queen Mary came up to them before they even had a chance to call for a goblet of wine. François could not hide the anxious look on his face and his father could not help but smile at the young man his son had become.

He had been a frail child and was still slight for his age. Only in the past two years had he begun to show any real signs of surviving to manhood. Mary was his complete opposite. Dynamic and bright, they made a balance. She was fiercely protective of him and did her best to mask his weaknesses. It was obvious to everyone that they adored one another. Henri was pleased that they did. Their marriage, when it was time, would be far easier to command and to bear than his daughter Diane's had been. François approached his father now with an intensity of purpose that Henri recalled of himself at that same age.

"Good evening, Your Majesty," he said and bowed before his father. Then he turned to Diane. ". . . and Madame."

Diane smiled down at the boy whom she had raised, charmed by this new intensity. "And good evening to you, Your Highness. Are you enjoying yourself?"

"Oh, very much! Mary . . . the Queen and I were riding most of the afternoon. It really is so beautiful here . . . so free."

Then, as though he had come from the shadows, François de Guise and his wife appeared behind the royal children and hovered around them like doting parents.

"Do they not make a charming couple, Your Majesty?" asked François, his bony face fighting a smile.

"It would seem that two children could not be more well matched," echoed Anne de Guise.

Diane watched Mary blush and lowered her head at her uncle's blatant attempt as intermediary on her behalf.

"Careful, François my old friend, your ambition is showing," laughed the King as he patted Mary's head. He then excused himself and swept farther into the room, still clutching the hand of the Duchesse de Valentinois.

"Great Zeus!" Guise raged as he tore the little girl from the Dauphin's side and marched her across the room by the shoulder. "How long will he make me wait? The Constable is likely to move in with a choice of his own if I do not have the King's assurances before long. Mary, have you been doing your part to endear yourself to His Majesty and the boy? Oh, of course you haven't! If you had, I would have your future secured by now. He is considering someone else for the Dauphin. I know it! He must be. That can be the only reason for this delay."

Guise had good reason for concern. There was far more at stake with the prospect of a marriage between his niece and the first son of the King than the future of Scotland. There was the future of his family and his own position in France to consider. Montmorency had protested vehemently against such a match, seeing the power and position it would bring to the Guises, and he had taken every opportunity to persuade the King against it.

Several extravagant courses were lain before the guests who finally made their way to the long oak table beside the fire. Carnations and roses in an elegant silver bowl served as the centerpiece. The linen beneath it was perfumed. As they settled in to dine, a group of musicians began to play the King's favorite music.

Great plates of roasted turtledove, pheasant and quail were followed in a procession by sweet cup custard, sugared capons and wine from every region of France. It was not until after the King's guests had eaten enough, were proffered perfumed toothpicks and sat comfortably amid the fragrant smoke spewed from a large silver vessel to aromatize the room, did Henri stand. He held up a goblet and waited for his guests to quiet. As he did, a line of servants laid before each guest a goblet made of rare crystal and etched with gold. Each was filled with a thick anise brandy.

"My friends," he began, "tonight we celebrate Anet."

Applause broke out around the room, and Henry began to smile. "Anet is truly the crowning achievement of my reign. Now, after six years, it is finally complete. This palace, full of beautiful art, classical sculpture and every modern luxury known, is a tribute to one woman without whose trust, support and love I would surely not be King."

Again there was applause before Henri continued.

"These goblets, which you now hold, were made to commemorate this evening, and this woman. Small and gentle, they are fashioned in the exact shape of the most elegant breasts in all of France."

The startled rumble of whispered voices rose like a wave amid more applause. Henri leaned over to kiss Diane's cheek, and the surprise on her face was missed by no one.

It had been a whim, a passing comment between the two of them in a private moment long ago, she thought. And now, like everything else he had promised, Henri had made even this thing . . . this minor thing between them, into reality. She was completely overcome.

"Now please, join me in a toast, everyone, to my goddess, the woman of my heart . . . to Madame Diane!"

"To Madame Diane!"

"COME, LET'S TAKE A WALK. I want to see you in the moonlight and have you all to myself for a while," Henri whispered to Diane as the rest of their guests sat nibbling at the silver trays of candied fruit, and listening to a selection played on the harp and flute.

They walked down the long hall from the library and outside into the crisp night air. Henri held her hand as they descended the stone stairway that had been fashioned into the shape of a crescent. Each of them was still holding their near-empty goblets of brandy. They walked beneath the gallery, both of them gazing out at the brilliant night sky full of stars. The rest of their guests, those not invited to his small party, would be at dinner in the grand dining hall for at least another hour. So for a time, Henri had the peace and quiet with Diane that he craved.

They strolled past the staircase where the gardens were enclosed on three sides by a long open gallery supported by pillars. The gardens themselves were a masterpiece, cut into formal squares accented with two large marble fountains at the intersections of the paths. They were composed of hedges cut down into the shape of their two monograms.

"Do you know what we need here?" he asked wistfully, feeling the effects of the wine and the fatigue of the day's exercise. Diane looked at him. "We need a lake! And a private island in the center!"

"Oh, indeed!" She laughed as they came to the point where there was a small pavilion. It was composed of an open temple of columns and a dome covered by crescent moons.

"I am quite serious about this, *m'amie*. Anet has everything else: baths, stables, fountains, a moat. But I want to be able to see you in the moonlight. Yes, right here!" he declared, motioning to a knoll before them as the ideas danced in his head. "We can take water from the river, which is very near, and then at night when everyone else is sleeping . . ."

"But, Henri, the cost."

"That shall be the least of our worries. I am swimming in loans from the war, and just waiting to give my very restless men something to do, now that there is no one for them to fight. I can think of nothing better. Oh yes, it is perfect. And I will make an island in the center where the two of us alone shall go. It will be our private place where no one else shall be permitted. Oh, tell me that you like the idea, please!"

He was pleading in that wide-eyed, childlike way that seemed impossible to refuse. Diane gave in to a smile, and then leaned over to kiss his cheek.

"I think it is a charming idea," she finally conceded. "Only if we can afford it."

"Will you please cease your worries about money. You forget I am the King!" he said and then laughed at the sound of it. "The only thing that gives me real joy in this world, is pleasing you. That is the only reason I shall do it, you know; if it pleases you."

He turned back toward the knoll. "Oh, yes. This is splendid! I shall set Philibert de L'Orme to work on it at once!"

Diane said nothing further, but she knew that he did not have as much money as he professed. Their daughter's wedding the previous month to the Pope's nephew had depleted the royal coffers substantially. Henri had insisted that the event be equally grand as any he would accord to any of his other children. That point had never been open for discussion; not even with Diane.

"Do you suppose she is happy?" he asked, certain she would know what he meant.

"I think she did her duty to her King and to her country. I know our daughter finds great comfort in that."

"So you think I did the wrong thing by marrying her to Farnese?" he asked with a keen smile, knowing the tone of her voice better than she did.

"The Duke of Castro is a highly decorated officer who showed great valor at Metz. His family is also very powerful. I think he is a good match for the eldest child of a King."

"Judicious reply," he smiled. They walked a few paces further. "She wanted to marry someone else, you know."

"She knew that it was not possible, *chéri,* as you always knew it would not be possible to marry me."

Again he smiled. "Your instinct does you credit. You always did know just the right thing to say to me."

He stopped again and turned to her. "But perhaps, *m'amie,* without knowing it, I have committed she whom I love most dearly to this same life of purgatory that I endure for my love of you."

"Diane is a wise child. She sees in your eyes what loving me has cost you; what price we all pay for it, even the Queen. She will learn by our mistake."

Henri put his arm around her as they strolled in the shimmering glow of the spring moon, and their bodies cast shadows on the rolling lawn. He tried desperately to think of something else, but his mind was full of the past; old decisions, old regrets.

"I wonder what would have become of me if you had married

Montgommery," he said, as he led their way up another flight of stone stairs.

"I suspect the history that is yet to be written of us both would have been much kinder."

"What do you suppose they shall write of my reign when I am gone?"

Diane stopped and turned toward him on the steps. The full face of the moon reflected on her tireless eyes as they shimmered.

"They shall say that you were a kind and a good King. But perhaps they shall add that you were far more ruled by your mysterious passion for an old widow, much as an ordinary man, not a Sovereign should have been."

"Yes, I hope they shall say that. I should like it if they did. As I grow older, as I see so clearly my own mortality now, those things, history, seem somehow more important to me. Along with that is the memory of you. I should like history to remember you as I know you; for your kind and good heart, your beauty and your grace. But Anet, Chenonceaux, the paintings and sculptures of you, shall certainly speak for themselves if I cannot."

"Talk of mortality in so young a man?" she asked with a smile.

"It is just that it could happen anytime, and the older I get the more aware of it I become. An accident. An unexpected illness, like the fatal ones to which both of my brothers succumbed. I just need to see my things in order. I want you to know, and the world to know, what you have meant to me."

"What is it, Henri? What has upset you like this? Have you been listening to Catherine's orations again about that man from Provence whom they claim is a prophet?"

Even though they had never spoken of it, he knew that she meant Michel Nostradamus. His name was in all polite conversation at Court, and his almanacs had so captivated the Queen that she was rarely without them or the opportunity to quote from them. Out of deference to Diane and her staunch opposition to mysticism, Henri had remained silent. He had also refused to read the profusion of available literature. But more each day, he felt himself drawn toward the possibility. Perhaps, just perhaps, they really could truly predict the future. At the root of it was the afternoon he had spent with Catherine and Luc Gauier. He had never forgotten the prophecy of the Queen's mystic.

There is danger to you in single combat, on an enclosed field . . .

"If anything should happen to me, unexpectedly you know, I want you to know that I would change nothing about my life, about our life together. It is very important, no matter what people whisper about us as the years pass, that you know I adore you more now than ever."

"Well, I have heard just about enough!" she declared, poising her hands on her hips. "If anyone shall be called home to God in the near future, it surely shall be me."

"*Jésu!* Do not say such a thing! Do not even think it!"

"But it is true, Henri, and we both know it. My time shall come long before yours, and it is I who should say that I regret nothing in my life."

He paused a moment. Finally, the stricken expression on his face changed to a little half smile. "Nothing? Not even those early years under the wrath of my father's mistress, and the fear of his own recriminations?"

"Nothing. Not even that. Because they were years filled with you and that would have been worth enduring anything."

Henri reached out and touched a strand of hair near her face. "God, I shall be sad when we are gone. Never again to touch this beautiful face, or to see your smile."

He sounded so melancholy. They had spent a lifetime together and she could no longer recall what life had been like without him. She broke the tense silence by taking the last bit of anise brandy into her mouth and holding it there until it began to burn. Then she kissed him. Lips on his, she trickled liquid fire down his throat. He opened his eyes in astonished delight.

"How you always manage to enchant me," he whispered. "Diane de Poitiers, you are an amazing woman."

Then she held up the empty crystal goblet to the light of the moon to examine it. A smile broke across her own lips as she looked back at him.

"The exact shape, hmm?"

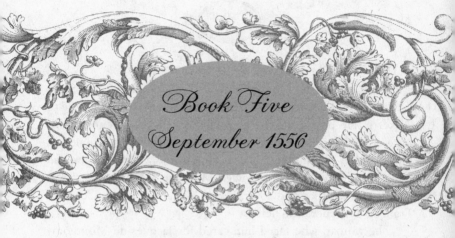

Book Five
September 1556

The young lion will overcome
the older one
on the field of combat
he will pierce his eyes through a
golden cage.
Two wounds made one, then he dies
a cruel death.

—NOSTRADAMUS

38

*H*OW IS HE TODAY?"

Gabriel de Montgommery, the Captain of the Scots Guard, asked the question still half out of breath from the ride to Auxerre. He pulled off the heavy leather gloves and tossed his cape across a simple straw chair, barely looking at her. Tall and blond and in the full bloom of youth, Gabriel was handsome and bore the countenance of privilege. What he did not possess was the easy grace that had so endeared his father to the Court of François I a generation before.

The woman who faced him cared for Jacques de Montgommery now that he was out of prison. She was a former lady's maid to Anne d'Heilly named Caroline d'Estillac, a woman Diane de Poitiers had once pleaded with him to marry. But Gabriel knew only that she was a tired-looking spinster with white straw hair and tragic blue eyes whom his father had known in some capacity at the Court of the previous King.

"He is not well, I am afraid," she whispered through pale lips. "When he coughs now it is full of blood, and both of his legs are swollen. When he speaks, he rambles on as though it was another time and another place." She lowered her head. "I pray God will soon be merciful with him."

Gabriel removed his toque and lowered his own head to pass through the doorway into the small, musty enclosure that served as living area and bedroom. The furnishings were simple. In the center of the room was a scarred oak trestle table. Against one wall was a cupboard full of crockery. A fire blazed from the soot-stained hearth. Beside it was a cot in which Jacques lay. It took longer than it had in the past for father to recognize son. Gabriel knelt by his father's side and took his hand.

"I have brought something for you, Papa. I've given them to Caroline. There are all your favorites: sweetmeats, and jams and some fresh apricots from Fontainebleau."

"I do not want them!" he growled with his last ounce of breath. "I do not want anything from him! Take them away."

"But you must eat something, or you shall never get strong again."

"I am not going to get strong again, Gabriel. I am going to die."

"You mustn't say such things. Of course you shall recover. I am making a good wage now in your old position as Captain, and soon I shall be able to buy us a house; a proper house, with servants and your own apartments, and even a garden if you like."

"It is foolish for you to wish such things, Gabriel. I will die right here. I am ready to die now. It does not frighten me and it should not frighten you. I am so tired of the pain, of the disgrace. I am ready to rest."

Gabriel's eyes filled with tears as he looked at the shell of the man. Justice. It all came down to that. Once great, the Montgommerys were a family in disgrace. All of their money and their estates had been confiscated with his father's arrest. Although his life was eventually returned to him, it was only at a point so weak and frail that he was nearly at death's door. But things would not go unavenged. Having been made Captain of the Scots Guard, Gabriel was now in a position of just enough power to do something about it. Without benefit of knowing it, Gabriel de Montgommery had become his father's son; tall, elegant and ruthless. He would not forget. He had only one purpose and one motive now.

"The King did this to you," he whispered through his tears. "And that woman too."

"They played their parts."

"I shall avenge you, Father. I swear it! Your life has been snuffed out so senselessly, and by God in his Heaven, I do promise you, His Majesty shall pay for it!"

Jacques patted his son's hand with his last remaining bit of strength. "You are a good boy, Gabriel. You always were. You shall do as you must, I know that. But take care when you do, for one thing I have learned in this life is that no matter how long it takes, vengeance turned outward always returns home to rest."

"Never mind the words of wisdom, Papa. They are lost on me. Nothing matters now so much as seeing you avenged!"

A STRANGE COMBINATION of curiosity and fear captivated Henri as he lay Nostradamus's book on the night table. He had finally read it. He glanced over at Diane, glad that she was asleep. The dedication of *Centuries* to the King of France had served its purpose. It had so taken the rest of the Court, everyone having read it, that the King himself, late at night in his bed, had finally surrendered to his own curiosity.

It appeared that Nostradamus's cryptic quatrains were predicting doom for France, and possibly even his own demise. Henri recalled the passage that was thought to pertain to himself . . .

> *The young lion will overcome the older one*
> *On the field of combat in single battle*
> *He will pierce his eyes through a golden cage*
> *Two wounds made one, then he dies a cruel death.*

His instinct was to cast it aside as rubbish, work of the devil, and to throw himself on his prie-dieu to beg forgiveness simply for having read it. The future was the arena of God, not man. But since the day he had sat across the table from the Queen's mystic, something inside Henri had changed. The staunch objection had gradually turned to reasonable skepticism; then to sincere interest. He loathed to admit it, but Catherine's passion for the dark realm of mysticism had influenced him. Now this work, which echoed Gauier's warning, turned his skin to ice.

He had heard the whispers about the forewarning quatrain. As with Gauier's admonition, it too predicted his death in combat. But as he now lay in Diane's canopied black oak bed in the dark of night, his concerns were of things greater than his own mortality. If the man was truly a prophet, and if he could see the future as he claimed, it opened up a wealth of avenues to a King with the fate of an entire country on his shoulders. Religion. The Emperor's son, Philip II. The return of Milan and Calais to France.

Henri reached across the covers and brushed a hand along her velvet cheek. He listened to her breathe then kissed the nape of her neck where her hair fell away. Diane did not stir. Her sweet face was reassuring to him. He still had not decided how he would tell her that he was going to meet with the prophet. He knew that she would not approve. But something so great in him had been moved by this man's writings that he would not rest until he had pursued it as far as he could.

A WHITE-HAIRED MAN was pushed past the throngs of people by two royal guards, and ushered into the audience chamber. Henri's first view of the great prophet, Michel Nostradamus, was a surprising one. He was short and inconsequential-looking, with opalescent eyes and the frailty of age etched deep on his face. Henri had not expected the great man of vision to be so old, nor so average in appearance. With a flip of his jeweled hand, the room was cleared by two other guardsmen, and the great double doors were sealed. The two men were alone. Nostradamus had been granted a private audience.

"Welcome!" Henri said as he stood on the dais of his throne, hands on hips, suppressing a look of surprise. He advanced alone and let the old man, clad in a four-pointed hat and the austere black physicians' robes, bow to him.

"As you can see, your visit to Paris has caused quite a stir," said Henri, referring to the maze of people who had gathered within the palace walls and around the great iron gates facing the rue Saint-Antoine.

"I have grown accustomed to their stares because I understand them," Nostradamus replied with a resonating tone of dignity that Henri immediately admired. "It is a privilege, at any price, to be given such an audience with Your Majesty."

"Pretty words," Henri said with a weak smile, "but you shall entertain Us far more fully with the substance of your insights than with their dressing."

"Then Your Majesty does not oppose such things as running in opposition to God?"

Henri sank back in his throne and indicated the chair that faced his own. When he snapped his fingers, two stewards advanced from a false-fronted door at the end of the room. One bore a silver tray with a crystal wine decanter, the other a similar tray with two rare crystal goblets. He wished to give himself time to consider the prophet's question. They first handed the King a goblet, and then one was offered to Nostradamus. Henri waited to speak until they were once again alone.

"What We believe, Monsieur Nostradamus, is that it is God's grace that has apparently granted you this gift of sight," the King finally said, speaking formally. "God shall determine Our fate, and that of Our family. Although you have written a great deal presumably about Us, We do not bring you here now to speak of those writings."

The old man could not contain his surprise. He had considered this invitation to the Court of France a victory. He had prepared to speak to the King, a known skeptic, of his personal future.

"Our greater concern, Monsieur Nostradamus, is for France. If your skills have not been exaggerated, you must tell Us how We shall fare against Spain and the new ruler, the Emperor's son, Philip. We should like to know how Our causes might best be advanced."

Nostradamus faced him squarely; his eyes hardly seemed to blink. "France shall one day know a greater power and glory than Spain, that is true," he said, "but Your Majesty must know that the glory of which I speak shall not be achieved without great cost in both lives and money."

"Glory is rarely achieved without the payment of a handsome price, Monsieur. Speak to Us of Calais. Shall We take it back under French rule from the clutches of the Queen of England?"

"Once again Your Majesty shall soon count Calais as part of France."

"Splendid!" Henri smiled. "I knew it. And Our victory in Italy over the Emperor's son shall cap Our power!"

"I am afraid not, Your Majesty. The victory of which I spoke against Spain shall belong to a future King of France. Not to you."

Henri's dark brows lowered over black marble eyes. "Then that is a prophecy that we must change, Monsieur Nostradamus."

"Respectfully, Your Majesty, I do not believe it will be in your power to do so. Almighty God has decided, in his infinite wisdom, to allow me to see the future . . . not to change it."

"So then you would have Us stand aside and make no attempt to regain French land, since the word of one man, namely your-self, says it will not be so? If We did that, Monsieur; if We did nothing, not only would We be called a coward, but We would merely be fulfilling your prophecies rather than the destiny of France."

"I believe that the outcome shall be the same whatever Your Majesty decides to do. But as King, you have a choice to spare the innocent lives of many Frenchmen by choosing not to act."

"So you would counsel Us to cease activity in Italy?"

"I would say that you should know great sorrow and loss if you do not."

Henri sprung from his throne. The meeting was over.

"We thank you, Monsieur," he said, extending his hand. "And now, We are told that the Queen is most anxious to meet with you. Then, the royal guards shall see you safely conducted to L'Hotel de Sens. Perhaps, before you return to Provence, we shall meet again. This has been most enlightening."

"I shall pray to God that it has been," the prophet replied as he lowered his head, then added, "I am always at Your Majesty's service."

Nostradamus made no further attempt to warn the King of the overwhelming premonition of doom that he sensed as they sat alone together. There would have been no point, because the fu-ture, black and menacing, also whispered that there was nothing anyone could have done to prevent it if he had.

❧

"HIS MAJESTY APPROACHES, and he wishes an audience with you!" Lucrezia announced to the Queen with excitement.

Catherine looked up from her embroidery stand near the fire. She was certain that she could not possibly have heard correctly. "Henri wishes to see me at this hour of the day?" she whispered in disbelief.

"Yes, Your Majesty. He sent Monsieur de Saint-André ahead to announce himself to you."

It seemed impossible for Catherine to comprehend as she struggled to bring her hulking body to her feet. Lucrezia whisked away the embroidery material while Marie daubed her with fresh Italian musk.

"My jewels! Quickly, my jewels!" she cried. "The ones I had made for my presentation to parliament! Lucrezia, my hair. Oh dear, what of my hair?"

"Very pretty, Your Majesty."

"And my gown? Is it all right?"

The jewels were fastened at her neck and more musk was applied to her wrists and throat. The room was blue with it. Catherine stood in the center of her receiving room, swaying back and forth like an adolescent girl. As Henri came toward her, everyone in the Queen's apartments bowed or curtsied. He kissed her cheek with a sensitivity that overwhelmed her.

"Leave us please for a few moments. We have private business with the Queen," he said and waited until they had all gone. Then he led her slowly to a forest green velvet couch in the center of the room. They sat down beside one another as awkwardly as two children newly betrothed.

"May I have something brought for us?" she asked. "It will take only a moment."

The smile that passed across Henri's lips was strained. "Thank you no, Madame. I cannot stay."

He turned to face her and took the small fleshy fingers of one of her hands in his own. It was warm and moist and he felt a churning in the pit of his stomach, but he suppressed it. "I have had a great deal of time to think of late, and I find that I have been remiss. I have not told you that I owe you a great deal of thanks."

"Thanks? For what?"

"It is no secret to you that I had reservations when I was required to name you Regent in my absence. I was, however, informed soon afterward by my staff that your performance in that capacity was exceptional." He took a difficult breath. "Catherine . . . no matter what has passed between us over the years, you did not hesitate to come to my aid when it mattered. This country and I owe you a debt of gratitude that cannot be easily repaid."

Catherine was completely overwhelmed. It was the first time she could recall that Henri had ever thanked her for anything, and one of the few times in twenty-four years as his wife that his overtures toward her had been genuine. Then he handed her a small chest of painted oak, studded in silver. She looked up at him, her brown eyes brimming with tears.

"What is it, Henri? What did Monsieur Nostradamus tell you yesterday?"

"Can a man not, when he feels so inclined, honor his wife? Well go on, open it!"

Catherine pushed back the lid and let out a gasp. Inside, on a bed of red velvet, was a national medal fashioned by Clouet. On one side was her image and on the other was the face of the King. Tears rolled down her full painted cheeks, staining them. She looked back at him, unable to speak.

"You deserve this recognition, Catherine. I truly hope that it pleases you."

She looked back down at the medal as though it might have disappeared as Henri offered her a handkerchief and waited for her to dry her eyes. She knew about all the medals he had struck in honor of Diane de Poitiers over the years. It had been another recognition of which she had been deprived by her husband's obsession. But now, in this rare private moment between them, she could think of nothing but forgiving him everything.

"I know that these years have been difficult for you and that I have often been less than kind."

"You need say nothing more, Henri."

"But I want to." His tone was gentle. His words were honest. She fingered the medal. "You have been a good wife and you have tried your best to please me. We have rejoiced with the births of ten beautiful children, and together we have suffered the loss of three of them . . . Oh, mine was a miserable youth, Catherine. I was tormented by so many things, and I know I gave you cause for nothing but to despise me. Still, you never did. I just want to say now, for everything, I thank you . . . truly, thank you, and I hope that finally now there can be peace between us."

He was gone before Catherine had stopped crying.

She was still sitting on the embroidered couch when Lucrezia and the Cardinal de Châtillon returned. To say that she had been stunned by his coming, much less by his words, was as grave an understatement as she thought there might be. He actually cared for her. He had said as much. It did not even matter that he was leaving her now to go to his mistress. Diane was finally inconsequential. Catherine was Queen. When he had really needed something, he had turned to her, not to Diane, and she had not disappointed him. Her entire life and her future had changed in that one exacting moment between them. She had guessed there was hope before today; now she knew. It was she who would match his step, she who would stand beside him and she with whom he would share history, at last.

39

"CALAIS HAS BEEN TAKEN in the name of the King of France!"

Henri's secretary, Florimond Robertet, stormed into the grand gallery at Anet, past a sea of startled faces who stopped their laughing and dancing and turned to listen. The King was

hosting a New Year's feast in honor of the Duchesse de Valentinois and the room was packed to capacity with the most highly
placed French and Italian ambassadors and nobles. The room was
dressed with holly and ivy, and the fireplace hearth overflowed
with traditional New Year's gifts. There were long white-sheeted
tables full of nougat, pastries, jams and special holiday hypocras.
Everywhere was the scent of pine. Henri was on the dance floor
with his daughter, Elizabeth, and Diane was being led through a
Galliard by the Dauphin, François. No one moved as Robertet spoke.

"Praise be to God!" Henri finally declared with a resounding
holler and thrust his fist into the air. Then he pulled his daughter
to his chest and kissed her. Everyone followed the King, hugging
and kissing those who had the good fortune to be nearest. Diane
embraced the Dauphin and he rejoiced with the others. But to
this simple boy, even at the age of fifteen, the gravity of the implications of the victory for France, to whom Calais had been lost
almost 200 years before, was still hopelessly lost.

Across the floor near a banquet table, an overwhelmed Cardinal de Lorraine hoisted a heavy silver goblet studded with jewels
and then emptied it with one swallow. *He has done it,* thought
Charles. *My brother has taken Calais! A victory of this magnitude was needed
to raise us in favor and François did not disappoint me.*

Beside him, Anne d'Este, his brother's wife, wept with joy,
knowing the implications for the entire family of her husband's
victory. After order was restored to the crowd and everyone began
to lift their goblets in a cheer for France, the Dauphin requested
another dance with Diane. She curtsied respectfully and then
obliged him.

"You dance very well, Madame," he said as he awkwardly tried
to keep the beat to the music. "Is it true that you taught the King
to dance?"

"I did, many years ago, when he was just your age, as a matter
of fact."

"I think His Majesty owes a great many things to you."

"Your Highness is very kind to think so, even if it is untrue."

"No. I am certain it is true. I only pray one day to be as happy in my marriage to the Queen of Scots as the King of France is with you."

François was a sensitive and thoughtful boy, and perhaps next to her own daughter by the King, she loved him best of all the remaining seven royal children. They had formed an early attachment to one another because he had been the first. The feeling had always been mutual. He quite plainly adored her. Even with the bevy of nurses and tutors to confuse him, for the first two years of his life, he had persisted in calling Diane *maman*. Their conversation now, as they danced the Galliard, was stopped by François' velvet slippered foot on top of her toes. Diane grimaced beneath the sudden missed beat.

"Oh, please forgive me, Madame. Are you all right?"

"Yes, of course. It is nothing at all. But careful now or you shall lose the beat," she said, directing him back to their dance. "Listen to the music. Catch it again. There you go!"

The boy looked down at his feet and his movements became more labored. "I am afraid I am a dreadful dancer Madame. The only person whose feet I do not manage to injure is the Queen of Scots."

"Your Highness is very fond of her," Diane observed.

"I adore her. She is the kindest, most gentle girl . . . We knew from the first that we should always be together. I pray that one day His Majesty shall agree to our marriage, but he has put it off for so long I sometimes fear as much as Mary that he may desire us otherwise matched."

Diane knew that she was being used as a conduit to the King by this awkward segue, and could not help but be charmed by the boy's conviction. Like the Dauphin, she too believed them ideally matched. Their attraction and devotion to one another had been instant and had been sustained these past ten years since the Queen of Scots had come to live in France. But Diane also understood and agreed with Henri's reserve in the matter. There was more at stake than a young boy's *coup de coeur*. Such a match would bring unparalleled power to the house of Guise and give it an unsurpassed influence with the Crown.

Once there had been no question in either of their minds that such a match would be desirable. Both François de Guise and his brother, the Cardinal de Lorraine, had always supported her. But time and the power that they now possessed had changed the brothers; had deepened their desire for ultimate control. After Henri had named François as Lieutenant-General, the ingratiating veneer that they had always exhibited at Court, and especially to her, had slowly fallen away. In its place were arrogance, entitlement and deceit.

The Cardinal, who had given up his table years ago to dine with the Duchesse de Valentinois, now returned to his own chateaux in Paris and Joinville. He regularly responded to requests for his company with polite excuses. Neither Charles nor François attended Diane with the frequency they once had, or felt the need for civility toward her as a primary concern. Their younger brother, Claude, her son-in-law, was the one family exception.

If it were possible for them to be more disliked at Court than Montmorency, the Guises now were. But despite the pervasiveness of his doubts against them, the King of France was an honorable man who made a promise and kept it. Diane knew without needing to ask that this victory in Calais, thanks to the leadership of François de Guise, would finally be paid for with the marriage of the Dauphin of France to their niece, the Queen of Scots.

"THE KINGDOM HASN'T THE MONEY for such a marriage and I haven't the inclination, but what else can I do?" Henri asked.

Before dawn, while everyone else slept, Diane and Henri bathed alone together among the water lilies, in the new lake he had built for them at Anet. "Guise is owed the marriage of his niece for his victory in Calais, and I know very well I must agree to it."

Diane brushed the wet hair from his eyes under the moonlight. "But you do not trust him with so much power."

"Not anymore."

"You have as good as promised him the match."

"Yes, and I fear I shall be forced to make good on my word."

Diane stepped naked from the water and wrapped herself in a large blue blanket. Henri followed her and they sat on the stone bench listening to the birds and watching the early-morning mist rise from the lake. She looked for a long time at the perfectly still surface on the water before she spoke.

"The Guises were once our friends . . ."

He looked at her, then mouthed the words of Tacitus with a disparaging sigh, "But lust of power burns more fiercely than all the passions combined."

IN THE AUTUMN OF 1558, the death of England's Queen Mary changed the political playing field yet again. Suddenly now, Philip II, the Emperor's son and Mary's husband, was a widower. If a marital alliance could be made between France and Spain, there might well be a true peace at last. Like his father before him, Henri was finally tired of the battles and tired of the death. He had won back Calais but he had paid a heavy price.

Henri had grown to manhood wanting to possess Italy because his father, and the King before him, had wanted Italy. It had been his duty to fight the Emperor and his heir. But now he had begun to think of how many had died for the cause, how much money had been spent and how many sacrifices had been made over nothing more than patches of land. Henri was tired now as his father before him had been tired. He wanted there to be an end to it. He wanted to enjoy his life and the family God had given him in peace.

Thirteen months after François de Guise's brilliant victory and the marriage of Mary Queen of Scots to the Dauphin, the

King of France stunned his advisors by agreeing to two treaty weddings. His sister, Marguerite, would marry the Duke of Savoy and his eldest daughter, Elizabeth, would become the bride of his greatest rival, Philip II. It was a marriage of Spain to France. An end to all of the fighting. At last.

WHEN THE TREATY of Cateau-Cambresis was ratified in April, Henri, Diane and the entire Court turned their attention to the upcoming treaty weddings. It was to be a double union, first uniting King Philip II of Spain, by proxy, with Henri's fourteen-year-old daughter, Elizabeth, and the King's spinster sister, Marguerite de Valois, with Emmanuel-Philibert, Duke of Savoy. Henri, who still touted jousting as the ultimate chivalric spectacle, commanded a full round of tournaments to commence upon the arrival of the throngs of Spanish nobles and courtiers who came to Paris for the wedding.

A newly renovated Paris shone proudly beneath the pageantry and celebration. Brightly colored banners that also sported the royal emblem hung from paned windows. Roofs and windows of houses near the jousting field were rented out at great prices. In the shadow of the Bastille, scaffolding was erected all around Les Tournelles where the joust would be held.

This great renewal of the French capital that the Spanish and other dignitaries now saw was due to the influence of one woman, and everyone was made to know it. Diane de Poitiers had not forgotten the foul rancorous odors of the sewers of Paris, all of them teaming with disease. Nor could she erase from her mind the tenement houses and barefoot children who wandered through the city streets when she had first returned to Court twenty-six years ago. Her work to reform the city hospitals had expanded into reform of the city itself. Residents followed the lead of their King and his mistress, who had begun reconstruction of the Louvre Palace. The old thatch-roof houses in Saint-Honoré were being replaced by stately mansions, many of them exhibiting the *favourite*'s designs. New pride in the city was clear.

"You have done it, Madame!" they cheered as she rode her handsome black stallion through the rue de Saint-Antoine beside the King.

"God save Diane de Poitiers!"

FIRST THERE WAS BLOOD washed across her mind like paint on canvas; red liquid oozing through her unconsciousness. Flash. A thunderbolt of lightning, and then the screams. Wrenching wails of agony. Twisted contorted faces, moaning, pleading . . . praying.

Then she woke.

Catherine bolted erect in her bed, her chest heaving with terror. Her heart was pounding with such ferocity that she could not breathe. She gasped, then screamed again.

"Your Majesty! What is it?" Lucrezia darted into the room in her nightclothes. One look at the stricken face of the Queen and she knew.

"Did you have the dream again?"

"Oh . . . yes . . . yes, and it was so real! It was real! I know it. His Majesty is in danger." Catherine grabbed the shoulders of her lady-in-waiting as she sat down on the side of the bed. Marie, who had come in behind her, poured her a goblet of wine from a decanter on the night table, then helped her drink it. In the preceding weeks, this had become a nightly ritual for the women of Catherine's train.

"Now, Your Majesty, you know it was just a dream. The physician warned you about eating so late in the evening," Lucrezia carefully chided.

"But I did not eat anything! Oh, do you not see, the King is in grave danger, I know it! Gauier was right. I feel it. Monsieur Nostradamus even confirmed it. Oh, dear God, there must be something I can do!"

"But, Madame, the war is over. There can be no more danger for him. He is safely installed at L'Hôtel de Graville."

The two women looked at one another. "Would you like me to send for him?" Marie asked.

"No! No, that shall not be necessary," she replied and then

took in a deep breath to clear her mind. She wiped a hand across her brow and felt the perspiration. "Oh, Lucrezia, it was so real!"

Both of her ladies-in-waiting watched the Queen's fear transform into an unbearable look of remorse as her heavy eyebrows parted. "I know there is danger to him. I feel it to the very core of my soul and yet, it seems that there is not one thing I can do to save him."

She sank back against her pillows, spent by the ordeal.

"If Your Majesty will not let me send for the King, then you must go to him at first light," Marie said. "I fear you shall have no peace from these nightmares until you do what you can."

"It is the joust," Catherine murmured, not having heard Marie's words. "He was not meant to die in battle after all, but in a battle of a different kind." She closed her eyes. "The young lion . . ." she began to whisper, "will overcome the older one, on the field of combat in single battle . . . then he dies a cruel death."

"His Majesty must be warned," said Lucrezia.

"I am his Queen, I must warn him! He cannot . . . he must not die, now that he is finally nearly mine!"

Catherine bolted from her bed. "What is the time?"

"Just past four, Your Majesty. Not yet dawn."

"I must go now! I must warn him now before it is too late. His Majesty is scheduled to joust today. He must not. I know it! Send Madelena at once to dress me, and send word to the equerry that I shall need a horse readied by the half hour."

"Your Majesty, are you certain that you want to go to him now?" Lucrezia asked, lowering her eyes. "It is quite likely that you shall not find him alone if you do."

"That does not matter. Do you not see, either of you? Nothing matters anymore if he dies! Please, Lucrezia, just do as I ask. I shall face what I must when I arrive at L'Hôtel de Graville."

DIANE SLEPT FITFULLY. She could not seem to find a comfortable position beneath the heavy bedding. She was surprised that all of her tossing and turning had not awakened Henri. She finally opened her eyes again, surrendering to the insomnia, and looked over at him. His face was peaceful. Soft. It reminded her of him when he was a boy. When they had first met. She watched the gentle fluttering of his lashes, the unguarded parting of his lips.

"Beloved," she whispered, and ran a finger across his bearded chin.

What would my life have been without you? If I had not written to you from Chenonceaux, would I have been alone as Montgommery once thought? Lonely? Plagued by regret?

Her thoughts took her to the day just past. The wedding of Henri's daughter, Elizabeth. They had attended together with the pride of parents as the young woman had taken her vows. Their own daughter was also well married. After Diane de France's first husband had been lost at the battle of Hesdin, she was now wisely and strategically married to Anne de Montmorency's eldest son, François.

Their children were given to good marriages. Finally, there was peace in France. Henri and Diane had everything they could possibly have wanted. She touched her own chest where the Crown Jewels still lay. He had insisted she wear them to the wedding despite her own reservations. So she had cast off her pearls, putting in their place the gift that had marked the beginning of their reign as King and unofficial Queen.

She gazed down at a large ruby set in gold that lay between her breasts. He had made love to her like this, with the same passion as when he had first given them to her. *Wear them for me,* he had bid her. *Wear them for me tonight when we are alone.*

She rolled onto her back and gazed up at the canopy. Twenty-six majestic shining years. Even now she marveled at the idea that he had told her all those years ago, *I have known but one God and one love.* He had kept his word, though even she had never expected it to last this long.

"Forgive me, Your Majesty, but you cannot go in there! You cannot . . ."

Jacques de Saint-André's insistent voice pierced the calm darkness as Catherine swept past him and into the bedchamber of the Duchesse de Valentinois.

"It is all right, Jacques," Diane said as he stood open-mouthed beside the door. Henri, now roused by the commotion, sat up in bed, his eyes squinting from the beam of light at the door. He lit the candle beside the bed. The early-morning sun was just beginning to come up and filter pink through the long paned windows.

"Great Zeus, Catherine! Have you any idea what time it is?" he asked, holding the candle near the clock. When she did not reply he looked up and was met by her waxen, tear-stained face. Diane sat up and wrapped herself in a robe, but not before Catherine could be spared the sight of the Crown Jewels still glittering around her rival's throat.

"Well, what is it that has troubled you to come all this way over here in the middle of the night?" he asked, rubbing his eyes again.

She rushed at him as Diane moved away from the bed. "Oh, Henri, I beg you not to joust today. Please do not!"

"What are you saying?"

"The prophecy from the *Centuries*! This is what he meant!"

"Nostradamus? Catherine, that is absurd. The threat of that was laid to rest long ago when I returned from Calais. Besides, his words say that harm shall come in *combat*. I face no such action in the lists. What has brought this about?"

"I have been having the most awful dreams."

He tried not to laugh at her for all the pain in her eyes, but he could not contain himself. He rose from the bed, wrapped himself in a robe and stood before her. Her trembling had moved him, and he draped an arm around her.

"Here, come here and sit down. May I have some wine brought for you?"

Diane stood near the fire saying nothing. Saint-André remained motionless by the door.

"No. I want nothing but to hear you say you shall not joust." Long streaming tears flowed down onto her round face as she pleaded.

"Catherine, that is foolishness. I am a knight, a gentleman. I must . . . I want to joust. It is a matter of honor now that I have committed myself to it. What would my people think of me if I withdrew now? They would say that their King was a coward; that he was weak. No, I must joust and I shall not have you going on like this and frightening yourself or Madame." Then he softened again. "I shall be fine. You shall see. Really. There is nothing for you to worry about. The danger is past. It was over in Calais. I promise you."

AFTER SHE HAD BATHED in cold water, Diane returned to her bedchamber. Henri was standing in the center of the room being fitted in new armor by two of his grooms. Saint-André stood beside the King on one side, Montmorency on the other. Outside were the sound of townspeople shuffling past L'Hôtel de Graville on their way to Les Tournelles for the day of jousts.

"I think you have never looked so handsome," Diane said, pausing to look at him as she leaned against the door. Henri smiled at her. The armor had been especially made for this event. It was wrought of silver, tooled in black and completely covered with their emblem. Her crescent. His letter H with the crescent above it. The ultimate symbol. The goddess of the moon who still, and forever, ruled him.

"Then you like it," he said. "It was to be a surprise, but you've ruined that."

"It is exquisite."

"It is Spanish silver."

"Now that is a surprise." She smiled.

"Yes, well, I thought it time to put the last of my demons to rest."

Once he had her approval, Henri stood still as his grooms stripped off the layers of silver and he stood before them in plain black shirt and stockings. His feet were bare. Montmorency and Saint-André both gave the armor to the grooms who would see it safely transported to the field, then left the room with them.

"Do you think she could be right?" Diane asked once they were alone.

Henri looked up with an expression that said he had not heard her correctly. "You were listening."

"It is only a very few steps from the fireplace to our bed, *chéri*. I could not help but hear."

Henri went to her, took her in his arms and began softly to laugh. "Can this be? My own beautiful Diane falling victim to the words of a man skirting the bounds of heresy?"

"Do not make light of it, Henri, please. There is more than one voice of doubt at Court that has been silenced by this man's words. They say Monsieur Nostradamus is rarely wrong."

"He is vague, *m'amie*. He molds the prophecy to the event, just like that fortune-teller in Cauterets, do you remember?"

"She predicted I would have a third child and that I would come to have great power."

"If you had read Nostradamus's work, what I tell you would be imminently clear. He also predicted doom in combat, and you can see very well that France is at peace. We are celebrating a wedding. Does it look to you as if there is any danger of combat in Paris?"

"That is a matter of semantics. I don't know, perhaps the Queen is right. Perhaps it would be better if you did not joust today."

"Not you too! How can you ask that of me, *m'amie,* when I have had the armor made especially to honor you? I want to ride for that honor, as I did all those years ago, when I was just a boy. It is the very same field in which I shall ride today. It is an anniversary of sorts, do you not think? I was a child then; no more than ten, but you found something worthwhile in me even then. You alone made me a King. I want to wear your scarf on my lance, so that all the world shall know that our love is stronger, more impenetrable than ever. How can you deny me that?"

She looked at the winsome expression on his face; the one so capable of seducing her to whatever end he desired.

"Well, can you?" he asked again.

"I suppose there is nothing I can say . . ."

THE DAY WAS HOT, and all of Paris sweltered in the heat of the tightly packed courtyard of Les Tournelles. The jousting had lasted all day with matches between François de Guise and Charles de Brissac and François de Montmorency and Admiral Coligny. The royal heralds called out each new contest with the accompanying fanfare of trumpets. Finally, as the afternoon sun began to pale, it came time for the King to joust. His match had been saved until the last to arouse the crowds.

The Queen sat in one tribune looped in blue silk and stamped with gold fleurs-de-lys. Beside her were the Dauphin, Queen Mary, the Duc de Savoy and her astrologer, Gauier. Diane had her own tribune beside the Queen. Hers was draped in black with small white crescents and the royal emblem in the center worked in diamonds. She was flanked by her daughter, Diane de France, the Cardinal de Lorraine and the Princess Marguerite. Other galleries had been assembled for the King's distinguished guests and members of the Court, who now sat soaked with sweat in the unrelenting late-afternoon sun.

As the sunset stained the western sky, the heralds finally called out the King's entrance from his pavilion. Everyone rose to their feet. Trumpets blared as Henri's horse cantered proudly into the lists. This was the third day of tournaments and the crowd had waited patiently for their Sovereign. Now, at the prospect of the magnificent spectacle which lay before them, there exploded a frenzy of adulation. The crowds tossed flowers toward him from the stands as His Majesty rode Compère, a magnificent Spanish stallion belonging to the Duke of Savoy.

Henri sat proudly in his saddle in his new suit of armor, gleaming against the sunset. His helmet was plumed with feathers of black and white. A black banner bearing their emblem ran across his breastplate. He waved to the crowd and the diamonds on the black trappings of his horse shimmered in the sunlight.

The two riders met in the center of the field and then converged on Diane's tribune. It was not until they had both reached her, their visors open, that Diane and those around her tribune heard the announcement. His Majesty's opponent would be the new Captain of the Scots Guard, Gabriel de Montgommery, Jacques' son!

The face of the warrior before her now had once long ago belonged to Jacques de Montgommery. Diane was so surprised by the young man's uncanny resemblance to his father that she held a hand over her mouth. He was tall and thin, as his father once had been, with the same honey-colored hair and soft, almost feminine features. Gazing at him took her back to a young man who had wagered her a coin that he knew the will of the King better than she. It brought her forward to the memory of a weary, aging nobleman held captive in the bowels of a Paris prison.

Diane's heart stopped as both men saluted her. She could not speak. Her lips, parted by fear, formed a tiny breathless gasp. Seeing the son of her former lover, his eyes tinged with what she knew was hate, filled her with fear. Was this to be revenge by the son for what had happened to the father? She longed to call out to stop the match, but Henri was too invested in the romance of the pageantry that he had created to honor her. He waved to the crowds and they cheered even more wildly.

"I ride for the love of you!" he declared to Diane but loudly enough for all to hear.

As the crowds cheered and hung over the barrier, their daughter tossed him a white rose, Diane's favorite flower. It was yet another symbol of her parents' great love. He held it up to the crowds in one silver gauntleted hand. Henri led his horse a few steps closer to the stands so that he could take the black silk scarf that he would sport on the end of his lance.

Diane looked at him, his beautiful dark eyes crinkled into a smile. He was happy. He was doing what he loved best in the world. She could insist and he might comply, but she could not ask him to do that. Reluctantly, she surrendered the scarf. First he kissed it, then placed it on the tip of his lance. The deafening applause rose to a crescendo.

Damn Catherine for frightening me like this! I can think of nothing but those vile prophecies. I have only to make it a little while longer and it shall all be over.

Henri looked at her again. Once the scarf was secured, he put his hand over his heart and smiled at her. Then he closed his visor and galloped onto the field.

She leaned uneasily into her seat between her daughter and the Cardinal de Lorraine.

"It shall soon be over," she whispered and clutched her pearl rosary. "Pray God."

THE LANCES WERE LEVELED and the two horses lunged at one another in a swirl of dust. Shadows of the two mighty steeds lengthened across the vast yard. The crowds fell silent as no man managed to fell the other. Montgommery was a worthy opponent, not so easily unseated as the King had hoped. The two men circled the field to the sound of thunderous clambering hooves and returned to their places.

Henri readied himself again. He was hot and tired. He could feel the sweat run down his chest beneath his armor. It was not so easy as it had been in his youth. But he must do this. He must do it for Diane. Henri dug his jeweled spurs into the horse. He gripped the jeweled pommel. Again they charged. Two silhouettes approached one another on the steadily darkening field. Again the cheers and shouts of the crowd rose up. Suddenly he felt his body jerk backward with a powerful force; his neck snapped forward and then back, but there was no pain. It had been a sharp blow to his breastplate. He held tight to the pommel. He began to reel in his saddle, but he held fast as they passed one another. As he recovered, the crowd roared their praise.

"Thank God," Diane muttered as she clutched her rosary, knowing that now it was finally over.

Henri rode to the end of the field where Montmorency sat in the judges' box. He raised his visor. "Have a fresh lance brought for me," he said. "I shall have one more go at the little bastard before the day is through."

"But Your Majesty, the rules are clear. This marks the end of the match."

"The deuce it does! I am King and I say we shall go once more!"

He was becoming obstinate, but Montmorency had been on such tenuous ground lately that he dare not push the King too hard. He left the judges' box and walked down beside his mount.

"Your Majesty knows full well you are not yourself today," he whispered, looking up at Henri.

"But how shall it look to everyone if I do not win? I have dedicated this match to Madame Diane."

Before Montmorency could reply, Henri turned his horse away and trotted back out onto the field.

"A new lance, Monty!" he shouted without lowering his visor and trotted back to his place on the field.

"Good Lord, what is he doing?" Catherine muttered.

"It would appear that His Majesty wishes to go another round," replied the Duke of Savoy.

"He cannot! He must not. He is tired. Can no one see that? He must be made to stop!"

"And who would have the courage to insist that he did?"

"You shall do it!" she said, turning to her eldest son. "François, call your father. Remind him of my dream. Beg him not to run again!"

The pallid young Dauphin stood beside his mother.

"Do it, boy! Do it now! There is no time to spare!"

DIANE SHIFTED IN HER SEAT as another lance was brought for the King. Even though the sun had nearly set, the air was still warm and thick with flies. She opened her fan and began to wave it before her face, trying desperately not to think of the prophecy or of Gabriel de Montgommery. But there was one coincidence even she could not ignore. She had heard the verse.

The young lion will overcome the older one. The words of the prophecy echoed back at her . . . On the young man's shield, God help them all, was the face of a lion.

"Soon," she muttered. "It shall be over soon." Tonight she would scold him for being so obstinate and for insisting on another round when it was so warm and so late.

The two men, poised in opposition, readied their horses again. Their lances were lowered. Henri had refused to receive a message from the Queen through his son. He could not afford to break his concentration, not when he was feeling like this. He was dizzy and he had not managed to steady himself completely after Montgommery's blow. He began to falter again, and he leaned more heavily on the pommel of his saddle. The Queen sprang to her feet and the crowds were hushed. Montmorency and François de Guise stood and began to move toward the field but the King waved them away. Then the two horses charged full speed at one another. Dust blew in a great cloud around them.

Diane felt her heart stop. She sat motionless, not even breathing as both men shattered their long lances against one another nearly at the same moment. Henri's fell from his arm, as it should. Montgommery's did not. Instead, the splintered end of the long wooden weapon, which had broken against the King's breastplate, flew upward. It caught on Henri's unlatched visor, which he had lowered but forgotten to fasten, and large jagged splinters of wood plunged full force into Henri's right eye.

Diane leaned against the Cardinal and watched in horror with the rest of the Court. Blood sprayed from his visor as he faltered on the still-charging horse. He then grasped the braided mane and began to fall.

"Oh, dear God, no . . . Henri, no . . ."

She could not move. She could not breathe. The sense of alarm spread through her before the comprehension. Then, all around was white, blinding light. No sound.

Guise and Montmorency rushed forward, both jumping across the barrier catching the King as he fell. They helped him to the ground. A great flood of frenzied onlookers rushed onto the field. The hushed cries and the incredulous moans echoed through the pewter sky for their beloved Sovereign. The Dauphin fainted into the hands of his new wife, the Queen of Scots. Catherine cried out and gripped the arms of her chair as Henri was lain in the dusty yard.

"The prophecy!" she wailed. "The prophecy!"

When she saw that he lay motionless on the ground, Diane rose from her chair and began to scale the railing of her tribune trying to get to him. Halfway over the wall, her foot caught in the black velvet banner. Tears streamed down her cheek as the Cardinal de Lorraine rushed from his seat, his own face stricken with horror, and helped her from an instinct born of twenty years of service. He held her hand as he jumped down onto the field, not knowing how to stop her. The shocked crowd surged around her and she was swallowed up in the sobs and cries; their shoving arms and legs all clambering toward the King. As she struggled, she felt her gown tear. Someone stepped on her train. Her headdress was being pulled from behind. An elbow plunged into her ribs. As though pulled by the strong current of a great wave, she felt herself steadily consumed.

"Please, let me pass!" she cried, but her voice was lost to all of the other sounds of terror. *This cannot be! It cannot!* Tears filled her eyes and streaked down her face so quickly that she could barely see.

"Let me pass, I command you!"

Her heart crashed against her rib cage and she began to strike out at the people around her with the aimless fury of a madwoman. A scream clawed in her throat and she cried out to everyone, and to no one.

Then, before her on horseback, she saw that a royal guard was trying to clear a path through which they might carry the King from the field. She could see him struggling to part the frenzied crowd.

"You there! Guard!" she shrieked. "Help me get to the King! It is I, the Duchesse de Valentinois!"

But her words were in vain. The guard never looked at her; never acknowledged her cries as anything more than one of the collective grieving howls of the other anonymous masses who swirled around him. Then the crowds surged again, pushing her farther and farther from the path. The harder she struggled to advance, the farther away she was pulled. She was crying now, blinded by her tears, but finally, through the sobbing and the whispers of horror, she saw Henri's lifeless body, pulled from his armor and soaked in blood, pass before her.

"Oh . . . oh, dear God in Heaven, let me by . . . I beg you, please! You must let me by. Do none of you know who I am?"

❦

"OH, JACQUES, THANK God you've come!" Hélène cried as she ran to the door of L'Hôtel de Graville and gave in to Saint-André's open arms. "Is it over?" she whispered into the safety of his dearest friend's heavy blue doublet.

"No. But they say it shall be soon."

"Oh . . . God save us!"

"It has been nine days. The wound has begun to abscess."

She led him into the receiving room to a small couch covered over in black leather and studded with silver. He then lent her his handkerchief and she daubed at her eyes, but it did no good to stop the tears.

"How is Madame?" he finally asked.

"Her life is over. How can she be?"

"Oh, this is just so hideous. If I could only do something . . . anything at all! But we are so helpless!"

"Can you get her in to see the King?"

Hélène's tear-filled eyes were hopeful. Jacques could not bear the sight of them. They had become dear friends in twenty-six years' service to each of their masters. Both of them had lived a lifetime through the love of Henri and Diane. He lowered his head, unable to reply.

"It is just so unfair!" she cried. "He is still so young. They are so much in love."

She fell back into his arms and began to sob again. "Now everything will change," he said quietly as she cried. "Her old friend, the Cardinal de Lorraine, has already had her apartments taken over in his name at Saint Germain-en-Laye and Fontainebleau."

"I should expect no less from him, barbarous hypocrite!"

"Shh! *Mon amie,* be careful how you speak. He, with his brother, shall control the country for the boy King now."

"There is no need for worry. There is no one here with her but myself. They have all gone; all of them running to the Queen; and His Majesty is not even dead! Oh, is there any hope at all that he may live through this?"

"None."

Jacques said the word and the pain of it tore at his heart. Until that moment he had not allowed himself to consider what would surely come to pass before another day had ended.

"He has always been so good to us," he whispered. "He is my friend. I cannot imagine him gone. What will life be like without him for me . . . for Madame . . . for all of us?" He turned to Hélène. "She must go away. It will not be safe for her here when he is gone. She does know that, doesn't she?"

"Madame waits only for word that the King is dead."

"Will you go with her?"

"I must. My place is with her."

"Yes." He lowered his head again.

"And what will you do?"

"I must stay. As Marshal, I can see that the will of our great King is not forgotten. I must do that for him; for both he and Madame."

In his arms she wept openly, unable to control the tempest of sorrow. The intensity between them was broken by the sight of Diane, who stood silently in the arched doorway. Her face was drawn and her eyes were glazed. Jacques and Hélène both rose to their feet when they saw her.

"Is he . . . dead?"

"No, Madame. Not yet," Jacques whispered in reply.

"Then it was good of you to come. His Majesty shall be told of your faith when he recovers, and you shall not go unrewarded," she managed in a voice rough and strained from screaming.

"Madame," he began and then moved toward her, feeling a surge of emotion. He had been, he recalled, her very first friend at Court. Now he would be her last. "I am sorry that I do not come here bearing you good news. They say it is nearly over for him. He has endured a great deal of pain and now is only occasionally conscious."

He did not tell her the rest of the truth, that through the nine days of half-conscious, drug-induced rambling, he had cried out her name, pleading for her to be brought to him and that the Queen had forbid it.

Hélène helped Diane into a chair near the fireplace hearth.

"It pains me to say this, but Her Majesty . . . Queen Catherine, forced me to bring a letter from the Dauphin, who they are now calling the King. She insisted that it be me who bore it to you."

Reluctantly Jacques unfolded the royal communiqué. He looked over at Hélène for support, but she was crying again.

"Please read it," Diane said as she gazed out of the open window beside the fire.

> *Due to your evil influence with the King, my father, you merit severe punishment. But, in my royal clemency, I do not wish to take away further from you than that which, in his death, has already been taken. Nevertheless, you must restore all the jewels that the King, my father, has given you. You must also restore the rightful property of the Crown known as Chenonceaux.*

"The spineless little bastard! How could he?" Hélène cried. "He always loved you so!"

"You must not blame François. He is a simple boy. He does as he is told by his far more powerful mother. The King always feared he would not outgrow her domination."

Losing Chenonceaux was far more painful than she would ever let them know. After everything it had meant to her and Henri, everything he had done to see it secured, she still would lose it to Catherine. But like her grief, that too was a private matter.

"Well, then. So that is it," she said with a note of finality but still no hint of tears. She would not, could not give in to them. She was still the Duchesse de Valentinois, and Henri was still King. She must remember that, until the very end.

"He loved you very much, Jacques," she quietly said. "He knew that you were a good and honorable man. He would be pleased to know that you had not forsaken him."

THAT AFTERNOON, the heavy doors to L'Hôtel de Graville closed behind her, and she rode slowly through the streets of Paris for what she knew would be the last time. Past the Church of Saint-Paul where she had so often gone to pray, past L'Hopital de Saint-

Gervais, now gleaming white with fresh paint. Finally, past the lists on the rue Saint-Antoine.

The horror of the history there was now frozen in her mind, as she looked across the road behind the heavy iron gates now locked to everyone. There in the distance was the grand facade of Les Tournelles behind which Henri, her love and her life, lay dying. She pulled the reins of her horse.

"Stop here," she said to Hélène and Clothilde.

"Oh, but we mustn't," Hélène objected. "It cannot be safe here now."

Diane looked at her with the same vacant gaze she had had that morning, but her voice was full of pain. "Hélène, I must at least try to see him. Perhaps someone shall have half a heart."

Diane stepped down from her white stallion, *Amour*. He had been a gift from Henri just last New Year. She could have ridden no other. She walked alone toward the gates while Clothilde and Hélène held her horse steady across the road from the palace. Four guards, newly uniformed in crimson and gold, stood at attention at the large iron gates. Behind them another string of guards lined the inner courtyard. All traces of black and white now were gone.

"I wish to see the King."

"No one sees the King," the guard replied.

Diane pulled back the hood of her black satin cape to expose her face.

"You do not understand. I am the Duchesse de Valentinois. His Majesty shall certainly see me if he is told that I am here. I know that there is not much time left."

"It is you who do not understand, Madame," the guard replied without looking at her. "My orders are to admit no one, especially the Duchesse de Valentinois, if she has the courage to come here."

The words stung, and yet at the same time, she could have expected nothing else. She took a small step backward.

"Of course," she replied and moved to leave. As she did, she turned back around and faced, once again, the stone-faced guard.

"Perhaps then you could tell me, Captain, does France have a new King?"

"You shall know it along with the rest of France, Madame. I can tell you nothing more."

Diane walked the few paces across the busy street and mounted her white horse again, this time with far greater effort.

"Where shall we go?" Hélène asked as they turned their horses from the palace and headed down the cobbled street.

"Home, Hélène, to Chenonceaux. One last time."

THEY HELD A VIGIL over the dying King, but tentative and expectant, they appeared more like vultures than concerned friends. Catherine sat at his side while the Cardinal de Lorraine, his brother François de Guise, and Anne de Montmorency stood behind her looking down at the King much of the time. The room was dark. Timeless. It was full of the scent of medicine and herbs. Death was near.

At the foot of the bed, a host of physicians, apothecaries and mystics worked feverishly to find anything that might spare his life. Everything had been tried. A potion of rosewater and vinegar to revive him, barley gruel for the fever. Surgery was performed to extract the splinters that they could see, and then he was purged with a mixture of rhubarb and camomile. Over the nine days that had passed between periods of lucid conversations and fitful hallucinations, Henri was also repeatedly bled and purged. But now the grotesque distortions to his face indicated that an abscess had formed. In their desire to combat this turn of events, Catherine ordered the extreme.

"Then take them all and kill them!" she said. "Do what you must, but we must save the King!"

André Vesalius, the noted Imperial Physician to Philip II, who had come directly from Brussels and arrived three days after the accident, stood beside the Queen with the King's surgeon. The notion was to take four prisoners already condemned to death and kill them. If they could re-enact the accident on their skulls, perhaps they would find where the rest of the splinters had gone, and how to retrieve them.

"It is a gamble, Your Majesty," Vesalius warned. "We have never encountered anything even close to this sort of injury before."

"Then you must try it," she replied, coming to her feet. "You have no choice. There is no chance that his life shall be spared without it."

"I fear that is true," he conceded.

"Then do it! Kill as many as you need! I shall authorize it."

Catherine sat back down and looked over at Henri, to whose moans and tortured cries she had grown numb over the past nine days. She knew that the pain must be unbearable and yet she was helpless to stop it. The death of four prisoners was the only way. She took his hand once again and rubbed her thumb over the warm but lifeless flesh. *So much wasted time,* she thought. *So many regrets. But now you are finally mine. I finally have you away from her . . . away from her spell, and in the shade of my love, you shall grow strong again. You shall recover and we shall have the life which she has denied us for so long.*

In the days since the accident, before the abscess, they had talked together of many things; their son's ascension, and of Marguerite's marriage to the Duke of Savoy. He had insisted on the treaty wedding taking place in spite of his absence. He had given Catherine instructions, now that she would rule France with her young son. But his last request had been the most difficult to hear, and since she had not left his side, there was no way to be spared.

"I want to see her, Catherine," he muttered again, his face swollen and covered with blood-soaked dressings.

"Hush. You must rest now."

He tried to smile but the act was full of effort. "I shall have plenty of time for that soon enough. Please, Catherine, do not begrudge me this one thing in my final hour. I beg you, I must see Diane before my last rites. You know that once my final confession is heard . . . I cannot see her."

Catherine did not reply.

"Please," he repeated, his voice growing fainter. "I shall ask nothing else of you but to see her one last time."

Catherine pushed the sound of his pleading earlier that day from her mind once again. Diane's name had begun to haunt her. But it was not the first time. He had been asking for her and calling out her name since a few hours after the accident. She could not help now but be a little glad that he was no longer well enough to plead with her. She squeezed his hand after Vesalius and the physician adjourned to the end of the bed. Then she lifted it to her fleshy lips and kissed it.

"*M'amie?*" he muttered almost incoherently. Catherine shivered. That phrase. It was what he called Diane in their private hours. She knew because, God help her, she had heard it when she gazed at them through the hole in her apartment floor so long ago. She pushed away a fit of anger and the feelings of betrayal. There was no time for that now. She had lost so many years waiting. *Odiate et expiate;* Hate and wait. But she would not bring Diane de Poitiers back here. Not now.

Now Henri belonged to her.

"Yes, *chéri,* it is I," she replied in a softer voice than her own, and then swallowed hard. "You knew I could not stay away."

"Oh, yes. I knew it." He tried to smile but the bandages now covered nearly all of his face. "I knew you would find a way to come to me . . ."

There was a long silence and Catherine began to fear that he had recognized her voice.

"I am sorry, but I do not think . . . I shall make it through this one, *m'amie.* I held on to see you again, but I am so very tired now . . . so tired."

"Does it hurt too desperately?" she asked, clutching his hand in her own and trying her best to imitate the voice of the Duchesse de Valentinois.

"Only when I think of being without you."

"Please, try not to speak. You shall only tire yourself more."

"I must tell you this. Please. Oh, Diane . . . my own Diane. You always knew . . . didn't you? No matter what obstacle we faced . . . you always knew what was in my heart."

"Yes, *chéri*," she replied and brought his hand to her heavy cheek. Then she kissed it again.

"Please . . . let me hear the words from your lips, as you have heard them from mine. All of my life . . ." he began and then stopped, waiting for her to finish the phrase.

The pain of it was unbearable, but Catherine struggled to compose herself as the tears spilled down her face and she sobbed quietly. She knew what he wanted to hear; the words meant for only one other person to whisper. But she had heard them too, and now for this one precious moment, he was hers.

"I have known . . ." she finally said with steeled determination, "but one God . . . and one love."

"*Oui, mon coeur*," he whispered. "*Un vrai amour.*"

Then, content that he had said adieu to the goddess with whom he had shared his life, he quietly turned his head, and let go of life.

"I T SHOULD HAVE BEEN ME TO DIE," she whispered . . . "it should have been me."

Diane's eyes were heavy. She closed them for a moment, wishing she could close them forever. She wanted to be alone with her pain and the Queen's guards had given her a last few moments. Like a wounded animal, she had limped lifelessly back to the security of their home at Chenonceaux, and now she wanted nothing more than to try to heal herself here. But they had followed her, and now Catherine de Medici was finally taking it away.

She walked slowly from the alcove into their bedchamber. In the stillness of the afternoon her senses heightened. She noticed each article and every inch of the room, seizing it as she had never done. Time reverted back to the last time they had been here together. On the night table lay his favorite volume of *Amadis de Gaul,* his page marked by a scarlet ribbon. Beside it was an enamel by Limosin, and his silver hairbrush. On a tall table across the room was the official state medal encased in purple velvet depicting the two of them together on horseback. Behind it on the wall was the tapestry he had brought back from Calais on his final campaign. It was a blend of blue, green and ruby red silk depicting the labors of Hercules. It was so full of him and his spirit. It had hung there for nearly two years, and until today she had simply overlooked it as just another example of his extravagant devotion to her.

She stood gazing at the tapestry, tears running down her face. The Queen had mandated that nothing be removed from Chenonceaux. Diane had already surrendered her house in Paris, all of the furnishings, tapestries, artwork, and most of the gifts from the King. Her apartments at Saint Germain-en-Laye and Fontainebleau, full of twenty-six years of acquisitions and of memories, had now been taken over by Charles de Guise. Even before Henri had been entombed, Catherine had prepared her revenge. Gifts, even personal ones, were now property of the state. She could take with her what she could carry, and nothing more. Making her choose was revenge in itself.

The clock struck six. A blue glass vase on a table near the window filtered the dusty afternoon sunlight. It cast a kaleidoscope of colors against the wall. It had been a birthday present to her from the Sultan Suleiman. Beside it was a tooled leather jewel casket, a gift from the Pope. In it lay the Crown Jewels. Like all of the jewelry Henri had given her, these too would remain.

Slowly, and with a movement full of great effort, she approached the table. She could almost see his face the night he had given them to her. *I promised you one day that I would lay the world at your feet,* he had said. *These,* ma bien-aimée, *are only the beginning.*

She opened the case and the jewels glittered in the sunlight from the nearby window. Diamonds. Rubies. Emeralds. A fortune lay before her, and yet none of it meant anything to her now. But what came next would be far more difficult. She took in a deep breath and let it out. The pain was dark; black and demonic.

She wiped away her tears and then held up both of her hands. They trembled with age and with grief. She looked at them through cascading tears and then gently slid from her left hand the first ring he had given her. It was a ruby and diamond ring with which he had asked her to be his wife when they both still believed there had been half a chance. Another he had given her as a renewal of their love.

Finally, and as painfully as if she were parting with a piece of herself, she slid the last ring from her hand. It was a large damascened initial H that he had sent her after Catherine's illness at Joinville. The Queen had been specific about its return.

She sank slowly into a chair before the fire. It was a tall chair of dark Italian leather, worn by the shape of his body. He had loved it so much that sitting in it now was almost like feeling him there with her. She closed her eyes and rocked back and forth, the sobs tearing her throat and racking her body. For twelve years they had lovingly transformed this chateau into a grand palace full of the symbol of their love. From the ceiling beams to the embroidered slipcovers, Chenonceaux symbolized them; their tastes and their life together. Yet, despite everything Henri had done to secure it for her, now Catherine was taking even that away.

The score was even.

Finally, in a move she had been avoiding all day, she forced herself to look above the mantel at his final portrait. He had chosen to be painted next to his horse, in his black and silver armor. It was an image so proud and full of life that she could barely bring herself to look at it. His life had been snuffed out so early, so senselessly. He had barely a chance to be a great King.

The tears that she had fought for nine days continued to flow like rain from her dim blue eyes. She closed them again, straining to recall his voice; needing to recall the contours of his body that time had worn into the dark leather chair. Then she surrendered her face to her hands. He was really gone and there was nothing left for her now. The pain stabbed at her heart and she recoiled from it, rocking back and forth in his large leather-covered chair.

"It should have been me to die first, *chéri*," she whispered again through her tears, "for it would have been far easier to watch you lose your love for me, than to watch you lose your life, as I have done."

Epilogue
1561

Alas, my God, how deeply I regret
The time I wasted in my youth,
For now how many times I have been spurred
On, in having Diane for my only mistress.

—HENRI II

42

*G*RAND-MÈRE, it is the Queen of Scots!"
Diane's granddaughter rushed from the large window that faced out onto the stone courtyard. Diane sat in a large velvet chair by the fire surrounded by her daughters, Diane de France, Louise, her son-in-law, Claude de Guise and two scruffy gray lap dogs. She had been so taken up by the passage that she was reading as her children played cards that she had not heard the horses outside or the activity in her own foyer.

"That is foolish, child," she scoffed with indifference. "Her Majesty would have no reason to come to Anet after all of this time."

"But it is true, just the same!" The little girl rushed at her, her face gleaming with excitement and the ringlets of blond hair flowing behind her. "I remember Her Majesty's red hair, and she is all dressed in white, the mourning attire for King François. I know it is she!"

Before Diane could respond, Hélène tapped on the door and came into the library. The two lap dogs scampered one after the other yelping at Hélène, who quickly closed the doors behind herself. Diane saw that her maid's face was flushed.

"Forgive me, Madame," she said, "but Queen Mary waits in the foyer and prays that you will see her."

Diane lay down Henri's favorite volume of Ronsard's poetry and stood. She did not look back at her granddaughter. "Why of course, Hélène. Please show Her Majesty in."

The early death of her husband had aged Mary Stuart. She had been Queen of France for only sixteen months before a mysterious ear infection had claimed her young husband. In spite of her grief, she was still breathtakingly beautiful, with the same milk-white skin and hair the color of fire, but gone now was the shy innocence which had so endeared her to Henri. Diane had not seen her since the afternoon when they had sat across from one another in the painted tribune at Les Tournelles, the day Henri had been fatally wounded.

"Your Majesty," said Diane as she and everyone else sank into proper bows and curtsies. Mary stood before them in a gown of white Spanish lace, the high neck bordered with pearls and the long cuff edged with white satin. Her hair was pulled away from her face and her head was covered with a jeweled headdress and a long white veil.

"Please, please, not for me. Not here," she said and rushed into Diane's arms.

"Dear one," whispered Diane as they embraced. "It is good to see you again."

"Not half so good as it is to see you, Madame."

Mary kissed Diane's cheeks and then gazed at her, so overwhelmed that she was unable to speak for several moments.

"I am leaving France," she finally said with a tone so full of emotion that Diane knew it had taken all of her strength to do it.

"You can come to no agreement with Catherine, then?"

Across the room Diane and Henri's daughter watched her former playmate as she struggled to reply.

"She wants no accord with me, Madame. She wants the title of dowager to herself."

"Ah, yes," Diane said with an ironic smile, knowing as no one else could the far-reaching effects of Catherine's bitterness. "Will you marry Don Carlos, then?"

"I shall return to Scotland. I am needed there. Much is transpiring with England. But I shall return to my homeland as the widow of the King of France, not as another man's wife." There was a pause and then she added, "It is rumored that Queen Catherine wants Philip's son, Don Carlos, for her own daughter, Marguerite, and his stalling with regard to our negotiations makes me believe it is true."

Diane led Mary to the two chairs by the fire in which she and Louise had been sitting. The only sound was the rustling of taffeta as the newly widowed Queen adjusted her skirts. Louise, Claude de Guise and Diane de France stood in the corner of the room near the door, all of them moved to silence. As Diane looked at the young girl whom she had raised from childhood, she knew then that Mary had come to say good-bye.

"How I loved this place in my youth," said Mary as she lay her head against the back of the chair and took a slow sip of wine from the silver goblet Hélène had poured for her. Diane followed her eyes above the fireplace hearth to the profile portrait of Henri done the year she had been brought to Court. Around it on the mantel lay a sprinkling of spring flowers: daisies, bluebells and roses. "You know that Anet is the closest thing to a home I have ever had, Madame. I shall miss it terribly."

Diane knew that returning to the cold and unforgiving shores of Scotland had not been the first choice of this delicate girl. But now with the proposal of marriage to Don Carlos seemingly collapsed, there was nothing left for her in France. Catherine had long been jealous of her younger, more beautiful daughter-in-law. She had also despised her for having been so close to Diane, and for having had so great an influence on the young King. She understood that François' death was now a reason to be rid of her at last.

"How is it for you now? I mean, does the loss become easier to bear?" She looked over at Diane with tear-filled eyes.

"The loss shall be with you forever," Diane said. "With the dawn of every day, with every breath you take, there are thoughts of the past and a kind of void; like living and not living. But yes . . . for you, *mon coeur*, with time, it shall get easier."

The fire between them cracked and popped, and for another moment there was no other sound.

"I understand that the marriage of your granddaughter, Diane, to the nephew of the King of Navarre shall proceed next month as planned," Mary said, struggling to wipe away the continual flow of tears.

"Yes, Antoine de Bourbon was a good friend. He has graciously agreed to proceed."

"Such a thing shows that your years at Court meant a great deal more than just an alliance with His Majesty. I am glad for you, Madame, that all was not lost when King Henri died."

Diane looked at her, her thin lips parted and her proud cheekbones as elegant as the day they had first met.

"Oh, but it was. All of it for me was lost forever at Les Tournelles."

"I tried desperately to come sooner," Mary said, squeezing her hand. "You must know that. But the Queen forbid my doing so, and my husband agreed with her. I loved him with all my heart and soul, but you know that he never was strong enough to contradict her."

Diane managed a half smile. "I understand," she said quietly.

"But now everything has changed, and I could not leave France without first seeing you."

"I am honored that you should feel that way about your old Governess."

"So many things have changed at Court since you left, Madame. It is a different world. Now Charles is King and my uncles have more power than they did before. They virtually run the country for Queen Catherine."

Diane looked at her, knowing by the tone in her voice that there was something else. "What is it, Mary? Do not spare me what you have truly come to say."

As she looked at the young girl, Diane could see that her eyes were tinged with sadness.

"Queen Catherine now wears your rings."

Diane took a controlled breath. "Such news does not surprise me."

"But they are your beautiful rings, Madame!" she said, springing from her chair, ". . . from the King!"

"The Queen wears them. They are hers." She looked up at Mary whose brilliant green eyes still filled with tears.

"Oh, do not weep for me, child. I need only my memories to

remind me of what was true. Even my rings shall not bring her the same peace."

Claude de Guise advanced and offered his handkerchief to Mary. She took it from him, touched his shoulder and then dried her eyes. She took a deep breath and looked once again at the portrait over the mantel.

"He loved you very much, Madame. It is not difficult to understand why."

"Doubtless you are alone in your conviction, but you are very kind to say so."

"I only speak the truth. Oh, I owe you that and so much more. You treated me as if I were your own daughter. You helped make my life here bearable. My allegiance has always been to you. I know that is why she detests me so."

"Tell me, then, the fate of young Captain Montgommery."

It was the first time she had been able to bring herself to inquire about the man who had single-handedly altered not only her life, but the course of history.

Mary looked at her, trembling and unsure, but when she looked at Madame Diane she knew that she must continue. So much had been kept from her. She had a right to know this. "Before his death, King Henri sought to pardon him, Madame."

"And was His Majesty's wish fulfilled?"

Mary lowered her head. "The King's opponent fled from Court after the tourney. I take no pleasure in telling you that they say he is a Protestant, Madame, and that now . . . well now, he rides for their cause with a banner displaying a splintered lance."

The two women looked at one another, their shared loss open and raw. After a moment, Mary held out her hand. In it was a small purple pouch that she offered to Diane.

"But I come for something more than to bear you news, Madame. I believe this is the most difficult thing that I shall ever do," the young Queen began with an uneven voice. "Before he died, King Henri put the contents of this pouch in my hand. He did not speak, for the others around us, but the way he looked at me, I knew he meant for you to have it. I believe, Madame, that he knew I would see it safely back to you. I am only sorry that it has taken so long."

For the past year and a half, Diane had lived her life without thinking. Without feeling. The immeasurably long days passed into endless nights. Today became yesterday, like all of the other yesterdays. Winter, spring and summer all passed; autumn had come and gone. Through them all she had watched her own life with a detachment, as though she too had died. It had helped her bear the overwhelming pain of those first months without him. Now, hearing Henri's name again from the lips of someone who had adored him, was an opening up of the old wound. She fought a wellspring of tears and struggled to find the strength to loosen the black velvet strings. What she saw stripped her of the protective cloak behind which she had protected herself since Henri's death. She gasped a little wounded sound as the small ivory crescent and gold chain fell into the palm of her hand.

A flood of tears cascaded down her cheeks as the images rushed back at her. The emblem around his neck. His dark glittering eyes above it. The confident smile on his face the day of the joust. She faltered as she searched with her trembling hand for the chair behind her. She strained every muscle in her body to fight the tears, but such an attempt was useless. In their cruel separation he had still found a way to reach her. Even now, long after his death, he was still pledging his love to her. Mary was right. He had chosen her as messenger because he knew that she would not forsake him. She held the crescent to her chest now and felt the tears wash down her face. Across the room Louise de Brézé quietly wiped her own tears as her husband squeezed her other hand. They all knew what the pendant had meant.

"Oh, Madame, please, I had hoped to bring you peace . . . if I have upset you . . ." Mary began but her words fell away.

Diane eased herself back into the chair by the fire and looked at the crescent through a new stream of tears. She held it up to the light, tracing its outline with trembling fingers.

"No, child, you have given me a great gift in this. I thank you," she whispered and when she could steady her hands enough to do it, finally she slipped the delicate gold chain over her head. She held it for a moment to her breast. Then she stood and Mary came to her. The two women embraced one final time.

DIANE WENT OUTSIDE alone after the Queen's train had left Anet. They would go first to Calais where a ship would then take her from the only life she could recall, to the harsh land of Scotland that now she would rule. Diane felt a bittersweet sensation at the loss. Mary would have been a grand Queen for France had she been given a real chance to rule with François. But now Scotland, and perhaps one day England, would benefit from this second loss to France.

The cool, colorless evening air stung her face and she felt the salty residue of tears on her cheeks. Mary had risked a great deal taking the crescent and she knew she would never be able to repay her. Nor could Mary ever know what it meant to her. In some small way, the girl had given Henri back to her.

As she walked across the lawn, she found herself heading in the direction of the lake, the lake Henri had constructed for her. Though the evening air was brisk, she slipped off her velvet slippers and felt the wet grass beneath her feet. *Life. Beautiful, fragile life,* she thought.

She remembered the morning after his coronation when he had shown her the preliminary sketches for Anet. He had been so full of the future then. *I want Anet to be a tribute to you, and to our love, so that one day, when we are both gone, people will look at it and know that he who was King for a time lived his life in devotion only to her.*

She looked back up the hillside toward the grand chateau of black and white stone, with each of its gables stamped with their crest. He had kept his word. History would not forget them.

As the path turned, she looked down onto the lake. Two swans, one black, one white, glided across the smooth surface of the water. She watched the shadows on the water as the crickets began their sharp evening music. Then there were voices; the sound of children's laughter. Two of her daughter's children played near the shore with their Governess. They did not see her. She stopped behind a tree hoping to savor the moment; to watch them. So very, very young. So untarnished by life. Somehow she began to feel lighter looking at them. The pain ebbed. Mary had wished her peace. She would get it from them. Then she felt it; as gently as the first time he had touched her; Henri's hand on her shoulder. She did not move to turn around, for there would have been no comfort to her in reality. Instead she closed her eyes; believing.

"How I miss you, my beloved," she whispered. *"Comme je te manque . . . comme je t'adore."*

As she stood behind the tree watching her grandchildren, a gentle mist began to fall and the leaves rustled on the trees around her. Then, as subtly as it had come, the sensation of Henri was gone. She waited a moment, afraid to move, hoping that it would return. But her movements made no difference. She was once again alone. Suddenly she began to shiver but she could not bring herself to leave, not just yet. She looked up through the tangle of branches to the gray monochrome of sky and, in it, the quarter moon; *your moon,* Henri called it.

Buoyed by a new sense of peace, she smiled. *It really has been a magnificent life,* she thought. Finally there were no regrets; no bitterness. Yes, now Catherine de Medici did rule France as Dowager for yet another son, but Diane alone had known the one thing that her rival had wanted most: Henri's love. Her life had been so enriched by him. What had been between them for twenty-six years had defied all the odds.

Diane would take what they had shared to her grave as a treasure greater than all the riches of France. For the first time since Henri died, the pain began to pass through her. As she looked again at the moon, and then the stars, she knew from a place deep in her soul that her time was nearing its end. Soon the hand of God would shine down upon her and, in all of His radiant glory, He would pull her toward eternity. There at last, in the Kingdom of Heaven, she and Henri would be together forever. When she could, she turned slowly, and began to walk alone, back up the flagstone path. As she stepped into the silver glow of the quarter moon, she caught herself smiling.

AUTHOR'S NOTE

WHILE THIS IS a work of fiction, great care was taken to recount the historical events as they occurred. There were, however, two incidents that were added for the sake of continuity. First, there is no historical proof that Henri II ordered an imprisonment of Jacques de Montgommery or that a relationship of any consequence existed between the Captain of the Scots Guard and Diane de Poitiers. It is true, however, that shortly after Henri II became King, Montgommery's distinguished military career came to an abrupt end. He lost his estates and was disgraced. It is also true that it was his son, Gabriel, who later killed the King in what various chroniclers of the day concluded to have been an intentional act. (To support the theory that it was not an accident, after the death of Henri II, Gabriel Montgommery rode defiantly throughout France with a broken lance as his crest.)

Second, there is no concrete proof that Diane de France, Henri II's natural child, was the daughter of Diane de Poitiers. The notion, however, is based on pervasive rumor and gossip at the Valois Court. The child was indeed raised with the other royal children and did bear the name of the woman with whom he shared his life. Thus, while fictional in nature, the suppositions I have made in these two instances were rooted in some degree of historical possibility.

—DH

A Reader's Group Guide

Courtesan

By Diane Haeger

About the Book

Courtesan is a story of courtly love and true romance, of legendary devotion and devastating loss. Amid the intrigues of the French Court, Prince Henri and Diane de Poitiers give in to their attraction, changing both their lives forever. Despite Henri's political marriage to Catherine de Medici, he forever seeks ways to communicate to France that it is Diane who is his "true queen." It is Diane who enjoys unrivaled power, thanks to the generosity and devotion of her lover. But it is Diane who risks losing all by linking her life to Henri.

The questions below are designed to help guide your discussion of the book.

Questions for Discussion

1. Though Henri seems unswervingly confident in his relationship with Diane, Diane herself admits to herself at the end of his life that she is amazed that his affections have lasted so long. How would you explain how his devotion to Diane remained so strong?

2. What kind of a ruler do you think Henri is for France? What are his leading motivations and interests?

3. What motivations cause Diane to remain with Catherine through her illness? Is this a purely selfless act?

4. After Catherine's illness, she suggests that the two women could have been friends in different circumstances. Do you think this is true? Why or why not?

5. In what ways did François and Anne's romance differ from Henri and Diane's affair? Which do you think was better suited to Court life?

6. Discuss Henri's feelings for Catherine. Could his marriage have been a happy one if Diane had not been in the picture? Why or why not?

7. In her early years at Court, what does Diane see in Jacques de Montgommery? Is she sincerely taken in by his offers of friendship, or is she just desperate for an ally?

8. When Diane returns to Court, general rules of behavior and sexual license in particular seem much looser than during her previous visits. What factors do you think are responsible for this shift? What—or who—gives the Court its character? Do you think this licentious mood continues under Henri's reign?

9. What do you think of Anne de Montmorency's fatherly feelings toward Henri? Does Monty genuinely care for Henri? What do you think he would have wanted for Henri's life and reign?

10. Why are Henri and Diane so enchanted by Cauterets? Compare the way their romance develops at Court with the way they bond away from it—whether at Cauterets, Chenonceaux, or Anet.

11. Why does Catherine allow Henri to continue his relationship with Diane? Did she have any choice in the matter?

12. Discuss Henri and Anne's encounters with Protestantism in the book. Between the burnt parish church in Cauterets and the Protestant prisoner brought to Diane's house in Paris, do they seem to be getting an accurate picture of the Protestant movement? Do you think they understand why the movement is popular and powerful?

13. Do you think there is anything to the rumors that Diane secured her husband's pardon by sharing sexual favors with King François? Why or why not?

14. Discuss the role of the supernatural in the book. More than one fortune-teller's forecast is borne out in the course of the story, including the predictions of Diane's third child and the timing and cause of Henri's death. What does the author seem to be saying about intuition and fate?

❧

ABOUT THE AUTHOR

DIANE HAEGER is the author of four previous historical novels, including *The Ruby Ring* and *My Dearest Cecilia*. She lives in California with her husband and family.

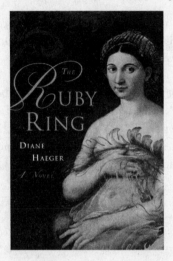